I0643206

# The Dance Between

Christopher Katalinas

Published by Christopher Katalinas, 2023.

This is a work of fiction. Similarities to real people, places, or events are entirely coincidental.

THE DANCE BETWEEN

**First edition. September 1, 2023.**

Copyright © 2023 Christopher Katalinas.

ISBN: 979-8988360919

Written by Christopher Katalinas.

For my mother, whose keen mind set me on this path nineteen years ago.For my father, who sees the shine in everything.For my sister, whose strength is greater than my own.

For all my family, friends, and the ones I've yet to meet.

For who I was, am, and who I've yet to be.

# Epigraph

*"I wish I could show you when you are lonely or in darkness the astonishing light of your own being."*
   *– Hafiz*

# The Part You Skip

Nobody reads this part of a book. *I* don't read this part of a book. Thus, I absolve you, dear reader, of any feelings of shame you may feel in skipping this, and wish you a speedy journey to the first page of *The Dance Between's* first chapter!

But who knows? Maybe you'll enjoy sticking around.

I have been a voracious reader of fantasy and sci-fi my whole life. Like Anton Ego from Ratatouille, I don't just like this genre, I *love* it. I wasn't the kid who made friends on the playground—I was the one who sat aside and read Eoin Colfer and Cornelia Funke until my teachers and parents became concerned. But even after I set my reading down—sometimes for years at a time—this love persisted.

We are capable of such wonderful poetry through the creation of worlds steeped in magic and magic-like technology, elevating real-world commentary to such beautiful, dreamlike heights that everything else around us simply melts away for a while. Difficult or abstract concepts become decipherable through the eyes of allegory. The struggles, hopes, and perceptions of the author are revealed on every page. And though I may never read the About the Author sections either, I feel as though I come to know how they dream, if only a little bit. There's magic here, and in more ways than one.

Thus, it is with no surprise that at the ages of fourteen, eighteen, and twenty-one I tried writing three respective novels of my very own (none of which were *The Dance Between*) only to toss them each out through sheer displeasure over my writing quality. But on the fourth go between the ages of twenty-three and twenty-eight? Well, here we are.

*The Dance Between* came about all because I happened to hear the right song at the right time and place of my life (Serity by Vallis Alps.)

It washed over me, and with it came the story of a lost boy and girl who lived in a castle on a hill. I had first intended for it to be a webcomic, but I'm not a comic artist, and frankly I couldn't stop writing until it became a book... or two. It's rather long, isn't it?

Oddly enough this happened because the Pandemic not only afforded me time to write, but time to learn *how* to write. Several self-study books and online courses later, again, here we are. Somehow this story survived my ire.

Though I will largely avoid discussing the allegory put into this novel, I would like to discuss the inspiration behind it. For most of my life I've suffered from derealization, which is defined as "the symptom in which the subject feels as though the world around them is unreal, and that they are detached from it." Admittedly this is a self-diagnosis, but that is honestly the default feeling that I struggle with on a regular basis. Through this novel I've done my best to convey what it is like, and it is my hope that you, the reader, can experience that sensation of detachment. It isn't a particularly awful feeling, but one of contradictions; content but restless, happy but sad, loved but lonely. It's like living a waking dream. So, if you're looking for epic fantasy, reader, you will not find it here.

But on that dramatic note, let's take a moment to discuss you. In all likelihood, you, the person reading The Part That Everyone Skips, are someone who has been a part of my life in some capacity (else, why would you be reading this?) Which means that in some shape or form you've made me smile.

Maybe you're my parents who have given me so much, and have sacrificed so much of yourselves and your time to make a wonderful life for my sister and I. Perhaps you're my younger sister, who annoyed me all the time in our youth—times I look back on with love and appreciation over how you've grown. Perhaps you're another family member whom I cherish; someone who has become as much a part of me as I to you. Or maybe you're a friend who's laughed with me, who's seen me through my darkest moments, and who chooses to walk by my side no matter how deep the night gets. Someone who picked me of all people to be your friend.

Or maybe you really are one of the strangers who bought my story, the very prospect of which fills me with euphoria. Such a simple action on your behalf, my friend, means more to me than you know. Which may sound dramatic, but consider this: you didn't *just* invest your money in this book hoping that you'd enjoy it, but have also willingly chosen to invest your time in reading it! That's a double-investment! And there's no greater compliment a complete stranger could ever give me!

In addition to all this gratitude I would like to sincerely thank the wonderful Claire Ashgrove for her impeccable copy-editing (if there are any mistakes it's because I went back and changed things), Sylvia Landis for her beta-read, Jack Baker for his concept art, JC Pouzols and Lena Yang for their work on my story's cover art, Brandon Sanderson for his free writing lectures online, and my friends Patrick, Anna, and Kayli for their feedback and support during this story's earliest stages.

Finally, it is with such joy that I wish you, reader, whoever you may be, a wonderful journey. Thank you for your interest in my world. May you enjoy reading this labor of love as much as I enjoyed making it.

Sincerely,

Chris

PS: This is a work of fiction. Names, characters, places, and incidents are products of the author's imagination or are used fictitiously. Any resemblance to actual events, locales, or persons, living or dead, is entirely coincidental.

Part 1:
# Overture

# Chapter 1

*May my song pierce your slumber, my lady of silver, bearer of such lonely fate. May you hear and remember my sorrows and joys, for the night is short, and the hour is late.*

A grand, imposing castle stood before a wide courtyard, staring down at squads of drilling soldiers clad in green as they hurled lightning down the field to strike the mountainside. A spire rose from the ground at every corner of the structure, each with a pointed top and faded-blue tiles. They guarded its body like silent sentinels, with their eyes turned out to face the world, and all the dangers it might bring. Smaller, flat-topped towers trailed away from the walls to a lower shelf of rock, as though the castle had moved and left pieces of itself behind.

Within the castle's bulk stood a tower taller than any other—the leader of the sentinels. The wind, borne of snowy mountaintops and eager to race down their slopes, buffeted its side, lending the monolith a voice to groan. It was a thing of contradictions: whimsical, but sober. Regal, but crude. Beautiful, but terrible. One had to know its purpose to understand.

Inset into the castle's walls were magnificent windows of stained glass and shimmering metal. They glowed orange in the setting sun's light, enhancing the structure's facade and elevating its countenance. But even with such jewelry, it remained the face of an old, grumpy giant, sitting on its plateau and glaring down at the rest of the world, as if to say, 'stay away!' The rest of the world must have heard because it was the only building to call the peak its home. All the other, smaller,

1

less-imposing buildings contented themselves with the forests far below, hidden beneath the canopy and wrapping around the mountain's base, fleeing the behemoth's stony gaze.

But the castle, its windows, its sentinels, and its tall, cynical tower were not the only observers of its strange, magical denizens. Above the gardens, shaded by all manner of dense foliage, was an outcrop of rock fondly named the Overlook. It was a place that begged not to be seen, to remain hidden; to stay a secret known only to the few lucky enough to find it and quiet enough to keep it. For what makes a secret a special, precious thing, is its silence.

It was here where two figures lounged on ragged blankets, stolen from the castle's soldiers at great risk to themselves. They were the secret's only acolytes, and they devoted all their hearts and minds to keeping it that way. Nobody knew silence as well as they.

"What about that one?" asked the first.

"I call her, 'Lady Boil.'"

"She doesn't look that pimply to me. Far from it."

"She gets angry a lot," the second figure explained. "And when she does her face gets red enough to boil water. Then she starts slapping people."

The first speaker shook her head. "I don't know if I'd call her that then. Maybe something like, 'Lady Doom' instead, on account of how she hands out doom to everyone around her."

"That's dumb."

"Don't be jealous. It doesn't suit you."

The shadows across the grounds grew longer as the sun sank behind the mountain's ridge. A kind breeze blew over the cliffside as the evening bells rang out, banishing the day's heat. The flowers in the courtyard garden, normally vibrant enough to make any painter weep, had been robbed of their colors and replaced with a pervasive shade of gold. It was with great hope that the boy, the second of the two speakers, wished that he might walk among them one day.

Both he and his friend had their spyglasses to their faces, spying on the soldiers as they went about their business. The boy had collectively named them all Fablings, on account of the fantastical features each of them sported, with no two ever being exactly alike. They could have only been born from a story.

"I'll call her what I want," he said, brushing his ratty brown-blond hair back from his face. It had never felt the bristles of a comb, and only rarely the edge of a knife. "My name sounds much better than 'lady doom.'"

His companion—the elder of the two by several years—sighed, and readjusted the blanket over her head. "I'm not arguing with you. Go ahead and be flowery."

The iron helm of a knight peeked out from beneath her covering, made for a head two sizes bigger than hers, sweeping along her skull to hide all her hair and most of her cheeks. Where once the metal had been lavishly emblazoned with silver celestial embossments, now it was scratched and worn. Its visor slumped over her forehead in a perpetual fight to shade the green in her irises. But it always lost.

She moved her glass, training it on someone new. "What about that one by the flyers? What about him?"

The boy followed her path, moving his glass from the lady near the geisthound kennels to fix it on a short soldier with leaves growing out of his shirt. "The one with the bark-looking skin?"

"No, the one with half a wing."

The boy moved his spyglass again to peer at a sorry-looking figure with a pair of lace wings on his back. One of them was broken. "Raindrop," he said.

The corner of the girl's mouth tightened in a practiced manner, waiting for an explanation that never came. Finally, she said, "Well? Why is he called that?"

"He always looks ready to fall to the ground, like a raindrop," the boy said, following their target as he shuffled from one side of the courtyard to the other. He had a stack of papers in his arms, which he clutched tighter as he weaved between a squad of soldiers.

The girl laughed. "You've got a funny way of seeing people."

"What do you mean?"

"Nothing."

"What would you call him then?"

"Pariah. Or maybe Lost Cause."

She added a bite to her words that was both nonchalant and unnecessary. It made the boy pause. "Lily—"

"No, he doesn't look like a Lily. I would know. How about, 'Forsaken?' Cause it looks like the gods—oooo, that must've hurt."

Lily laughed as a bigger, burlier figure with four arms shoved Raindrop, causing the latter to stumble, fall, and drop his papers in every direction. The breeze quickly picked up the sheets and carried them away, proving to be not as kind to Raindrop as it had been to his observers. "Or Fallen, cause, y'know, that must've hurt. But you were right, he *was* ready to fall," she said.

The boy sighed, watching as Raindrop flicked his hands and caught the wind in his grip before it could slip away entirely, reeling the floating papers back within reach. He tried mimicking the gesture, waving his hand in the hopes he could summon the wind himself one day. "Why are you so mean today?"

"You think I'm mean? I'm like this every day."

The boy put down his spyglass and turned a hazel eye on her. On his other he wore an eyepatch with a large scar poking out from beneath. The grisly wound traveled along his face from the top of his left brow and swooped down his cheek, exiting at the jawbone. Another scar, just barely visible at the hollow of his throat, peeked out from the collar of his shirt in the shape of a star exploding in all directions, seared into his skin. "Lily, what's going on?"

"I told you," Lily said absently, still looking through her spyglass. "Nothing."

The boy watched her a moment longer. When she stayed quiet, he scowled. "Fine."

Lily shook her head, keeping her eyes on the courtyard below. "Don't get dramatic."

"I tell you everything, Lily."

"Sometimes I wish you wouldn't," she muttered.

The boy's expression fell. At his sullen silence, Lily put her glass down and turned to him, revealing a cherubic face. "Having a tantrum?"

The boy crossed his arms. "You can try to hide it, but I know when you're upset."

"I'm not upset."

"You're never like this without a reason."

She shrugged. "Maybe I just don't like him."

"You've never met him."

"But you said it yourself, I'm a heartless little girl who doesn't tell you everything."

The boy huffed indignantly. "I never said that!"

"Yeah, well, it's what you meant."

He stared at her in disbelief for several breaths before grunting and standing up. He was done with this back-and-forth. Gods only knew how often they'd gone through it before.

"Sevi." She sighed. "Stop."

"I'm going to get food," Sevi said, turning away.

Lily watched for a moment, allowing him to walk a distance away, before finally throwing up her hands. "Gods. *Fine.*"

Sevi stopped, turning to face her expectantly. His clothing—threadbare and torn—hung loosely on a lean frame that was hollowed out from years of hunger. Lily was in no better shape, but he could pride himself in the extra head of height he had on her. She, however, could boast of retaining her shadow. His own had been absent for quite some time.

"I hate it when you do this," Lily grumbled. "I wasn't going to tell you, just because I *knew* this would put you into one of your sulking *moods*, but hey, you went there yourself." She crossed her arms.

Sevi scoffed. "You know, I don't have—"

"I heard something coming from the mines last night."

His protest died on his lips as quickly as it formed.

"They weren't the kind of echoes you'd hear from Outside, or the kitchen," Lily continued. "It sounded... not like an animal, but not like the normal cavern sounds. More like scratching, or hammering, as if something had struck a wall."

A shiver washed through Sevi. He clutched a hand to his chest, touching the scar beneath his shirt. His lungs fluttered, and his heartbeat spiked.

Seeming to have expected this, Lily immediately raised her hands in a placating gesture. "See, I knew you would... ugh. Relax. I checked it out. We're still sealed up tight. Whoever or whatever it was must've just gotten lost in the mines, if they ever existed at all. Maybe it was a large rock falling. Maybe it caused a cascade somewhere. Echoes are weird in the Cut."

Sevi nodded and closed his eyes, forcing his breathing to settle. He didn't say anything for a moment. When he opened them, it was just in time to catch Lily scooping up a pebble. She chucked it at his face with frightening accuracy, bouncing it off his nose.

"Get me something, too, while you're at it." She settled back down with her spyglass.

"What?"

"Food. Get. Me. Food," she said slowly, enunciating each word. "I've been lying on my belly all day. I could use something to eat."

Sevi inhaled and let his breath go, bit by bit, until the tightness in his chest loosened. "Food. Right. Yeah."

"Do you have your iron?"

Sevi patted at his clothing until he felt the familiar handle of a small, needly knife, wrapped with cloth in his pants pocket. "Yes."

"Whistle, too?"

Sevi reached into another pocket and brought out a well-used signal whistle carved from bone. He blew two chirps into it.

Lily nodded in approval. "Will you be stopping by the garden?"

"Only if I can't get enough food from the kitchens. I have enough effizinum to last another couple nights."

"You're all set, then. And it's alright, Sev," she added, throwing him a smile. "Relax yourself, or you might break."

Sevi shot her another scowl. He grabbed some rope and a dirty pack, slinging them over his shoulder before stepping away. Leaving Lily to her surveyance, he set his mind to the daunting task of finding them a meal.

# Chapter 2

*There once was a castle on the mountaintop high, a jewel for the whole world to see. Within its walls lived a girl and a boy, an unlikely family.*

Near the Overlook lay a tunnel that cut into the heart of the mountain—one of many others. Soft, fading light filtered in from the ceiling and walls, seeping in from thin crevices in the rock.

Sevi took a moment to adapt his sight. He flipped up the eyepatch that covered his scarred, perfectly functioning eye, and shifted it over to his useless, unadjusted eye. He had discovered in his first months living in the Cut that having a cloth over one eye would keep it continually adjusted to the dark, as annoying as it was to wear.

He moved deeper into the tunnel, and the further he went, the more vibrant it became. Exotic vines and moss thickened along the walls, glowing with colorful bioluminescence bright enough to show the edges of the path. Light motes twinkled and floated about dreamily on a gentle draft, and shimmer lizards, bright even in the dark with their purple and green hides, skittered away as his footsteps approached.

They had never gotten used to his presence. He would've fed them in hopes of gaining their trust, but Lily had chided him for wasting food the first time he'd tried, and he'd given up. Sometimes he wished she would be a little less practical.

She had taught him everything on how to survive the Cut. He had no doubt she would've been fine on her own—perhaps even happier. But their partnership allowed room to split tasks, such as spying on the castle's soldiers while he gathered food, or so she said. He privately believed she just hated kitchen duty and wanted to keep lounging in the sun.

But they were partners, now and forever, and he would play his part.

The path took him to a rough section of wall containing the outline of a crudely bricked-up tunnel. He took a moment to place his hand on it, looking at it from floor to ceiling for any noticeable gaps before finally giving it a pat. He muttered, "Still sealed tight."

A sound in the Cut was always amplified. What Lily heard could've been anything. That's what he told himself, at least, in order to tear his gaze away. It was enough to let him move on but not before he'd conducted his regular ritual.

He called out, "Shy? I'm here. Are you out there?"

No answer. One more failed attempt. Sevi was used to it, but it never stopped disappointing him. He missed Shy's quiet, nonsensical company, and scavenging for food would have been easier with them around. He'd keep calling. Maybe one day they would come out of the dark.

He wound his way deeper into the mountain, walking down a slope until he hit the lip of a subterranean escarpment. A peg had been hammered into a stone next to the drop, holding a well-used rope that trailed over the side. Sevi hooked the crook of his arm around it and easily slid off the rock, carefully rappelling down to the floor a couple stories below.

At its base, the tunnels split off into two separate directions. He took the left, downward-sloping tunnel at an easy pace, until the exotic plants and rocky walls slowly gave way to chiseled stone. He stopped and moved his eyepatch back to his light-adjusted eye, placed one hand on the wall for guidance, and walked forward.

The light inside the tunnel grew brighter, and the plants and floating motes faded away as he crossed over the threshold into the open air. The path had set him on a narrow cliff hugging the castle's outer walls, hidden by light brush and overlooking a vast swath of unsettled forest far below.

A sky, awash with the dying light of day, stretched out before him, full of big, fluffy clouds passing over a glistening river in the distance. Strong gusts of wind carrying the smell of mountain water buffeted his body, eager to knock him from his perch should his attention slip for even a moment.

He breathed in deeply and pressed on, reaching a gap in the cliff that dipped down to a lower level, where he attached a rope to the trunk of a nearby tree that had found purchase in the stone. Securing it, he rappelled down another level and moved a short distance to where a patch of leaves rested. He reached into them, took hold of the wicker frame they were attached to, and moved it aside, revealing a crack in the stone big enough to get through. He entered quickly, then moved the covering back into place.

In darkness once more, Sevi moved his patch and hopped off a narrow ledge, striding into a small, snug room. Two tunnels branched off left and right. The same exotic plants from the caves lined the walls, but less in quantity and thinner. They would disappear entirely the deeper into the castle he went. He often wondered why that was—why shouldn't they grow just as thickly here as they did in the mountain? But the plants had nothing to say to him, no matter how often he'd asked.

Taking the tunnel to the right, Sevi walked a short distance before being alerted by a familiar collection of muffled sounds humming through the walls. He placed a hand on the inner stone of the tunnel and walked more slowly. *They've lit the logs. Good.*

The tunnel narrowed as he reached the end, forcing him to squeeze uncomfortably into the bigger room beyond. It was half-full of items gathered over years of hoarding from different places in the castle. Two makeshift beds made of raggedly stitched cloth lay in the corners, each stuffed with straw.

It was also not unoccupied.

Curled up in a corner, snug in its small, cracked alcove, lay a drake made out of fire. But only when awake. For the moment, it slept soundly, steamy wisps of smoke curling up from its apathetic form, smoldering as dark as charcoal in its slumber. It looked almost endearing in this state, with a wide, flat head and big eyes, but at any moment it could spring awake, and its stony skin would crack with flames, turning it from a lump of coal into a blazing inferno.

It terrified Sevi. Lily had wanted to kill it, citing all the many reasons why having a sentient ball of fire in their tunnels was a bad thing. Some part of him wanted to let her, to never see its terrible flames again, but... it was all alone. All it wanted was a home, and it never once tried to hurt them. How could he kill something that only wished to live?

They eventually compromised and chose to run it off instead. But it always came back. Seeing it in their bedroom had become a regular, unwelcome occurrence, constantly threatening to burn up their belongings. But it never did, thus Lily never tried to kill it again, and they all settled into an annoying game of chase that had lasted years.

Not seeking to risk its ire alone, Sevi carefully tiptoed around it, making sure that the pail of water left in the corner had been kept full. Nodding with satisfaction, he checked one last item before moving on. Shifting aside a wooden crate, he ensured that a certain special box underneath hadn't been discovered by the drake.

It looked pristine. He set the crate back down, adding whatever meager camouflage he could to dress it up as unappealingly as possible, then moved to the other side of the room where yet another tunnel waited for him.

After another short walk, he got down onto his knees, slid his hand along the wall, and gripped the edge of a cracked stone with the tips of his fingers. He gingerly wiggled it from its place as quietly as he could. When it was free, he moved his patch to put his daylight eye to the revealed hole and peered into the room beyond.

His sight was obscured by the top of a table pushed against the wall, but he could see the boots of people moving about. Some of them walked barefoot with feet that looked far more suited for animals than people.

He settled in and waited for his moment.

It was not possible to pick out any specific conversation from the clamor of the kitchens, but he could gauge how busy they were by the number of curses and annoyed shouts as the crew prepared dinner for the castle garrison. It was in moments like these, where he had nothing to do but wait, that Sevi let his mind drift.

He tried matching faces to feet. Was that Quickscale with the bare purple, scaly toes? Sevi wondered if he'd ever gotten the strings on his lute replaced. Was that Sandflower, with the pristine red-leather boots, so different from the others? Had she ever found her missing bracelet? He'd keep an eye out, in case it had fallen anywhere near the floor. Maybe if he found it, he could find a way to put it where she'd see it.

But over time the number of boots began to dwindle as the cooks ended their shifts, having successfully fed the soldiers for another day. Eventually they all left, save for one, who had settled heavily into a chair with little intent of leaving it anytime soon. His characteristic snores soon rattled into the air with gusto—so full of personality that Sevi had taken to calling him Rumbles.

"Now, Shy?" Sevi asked the air. After a moment without an answer, he nodded to himself, and placed the spystone back. He missed Shy more than ever whenever he had to leave the Cut.

He reached over and pulled at a larger stone with an inset handle just to the right, slowly shifting it out of the way until he'd revealed a hole big enough to crawl through. Leaving his pack behind, he got on all fours and carefully worked himself through, listening attentively for any changes in the remaining cook's breathing. When he was satisfied that all was well, he quietly pulled himself out from under the table entirely without so much as a scuff of shoes.

He popped up just to the side of the sleeping cook's chair. He hadn't moved a muscle. Old, stout, short Rumbles, with the characteristically pointed ears that marked him as a Fabling, was always charged with cleaning the kitchen at the end of the day. But he never did, and he always got yelled at for it. At least until Sevi started helping him some couple of months ago.

It had become the perfect relationship. Sevi got all the food that Rumbles failed to toss, while Rumbles appeared to be doing his job. The old man seemed just as content with it as Sevi was and never seemed to bother looking into it, so long as he got his sleep.

Sevi smiled at the old man. A small cloud of butterflies had a habit of forming around him whenever he dreamed, appearing from thin air as Sevi watched and landing all along the cook's body. They flashed their bright, blue wings at him as he stepped away. "I hope your dreams are lovely," Sevi whispered.

Today was a particularly lucky day. Rumbles hadn't touched his broom yet, and the room was completely littered with a myriad of food scraps, all haphazardly strewn about the counters. A fireplace, inset into the same wall where the firedrake rested, still had tiny flames flickering in its half-doused coals.

Sevi carefully looked around for any signs of the other cooks before getting to work. He focused on whatever larger scraps he could find, stuffing them into every pocket, navigating the kitchen as thoroughly and discreetly as possible while timing the cook's snores to muffle the sounds of his scrounging. He avoided most of the fuller looking foods—he'd learned long ago that when the big, tasty things went missing, the Fablings started looking.

When his pockets were overflowing, he turned back toward the wall, ready to exit, until he noticed something he couldn't ignore. Sitting on top of the sleeping cook's knee was a half-eaten pot pie, glistening with a warm golden-brown crust and stuffed with a filling that smelled divine from across the room. Rumbles had fallen asleep before he could finish it.

It was Sevi's favorite meal. He was lucky to get his hands on one once or twice a year.

Sevi knew he shouldn't. He really, really shouldn't. Lily had always warned him not to take chances and to favor certainty more than possibility. But the growling of his stomach was too incessant and the potential reward too great. He could practically taste the first bite already, bursting with a rare, rich, savory flavor that he only experienced in memory.

He wiped fresh saliva from his lips and carefully approached the cook, eyeing his face for any signs of wakefulness, placing the outsides of his feet down first and rolling onto the rest in order to limit his noise as much as possible. He reached out with each hand, touching his fingertips to the pie's sides, ready to lift it off his leg as lightly as a sparrow lifted from its perch.

Voices appeared down the hallway. Sevi jerked his hands back, grazing the pie with enough force to shake it precariously on the cook's leg. The man's face twitched.

A door opened somewhere, followed shortly by approaching footsteps.

Sevi panicked and immediately dove under the table toward his tunnels, but stopped himself from going through altogether. Those footsteps were too close. There'd be no time to place the stone back, not without anyone hearing it, and if he moved too fast back into the Cut, he could give himself away. Terrified, he bunched himself back as much as he could manage, pulling his thin, iron knife out just as the kitchen door swung open.

"... and... close... be back in time for the Turning," the first person said, their voice becoming discernable as they entered the room. They sounded male.

"I'm not so sure," the second person said, also male. "We've—wait a minute... By the Amber. Heh. Look at this. Hey, Cirrus, wake up. Is it true? Have you *actually* been cleaning the place? There are significantly less pieces of garbage around than I was expecting."

The cook snorted. "Eh? What? Clean?"

The second man said, "Yes, the place looks half cleared. Were you so hungry that you ate it all, or have you found someone who's actually lower than you to subjugate? I refuse to believe that after all this time you've only just now started doing your job."

"Errm..."

"He's never cleaned without command. Maybe he opened the door and let all the birds come in for a bite," said the first voice.

"Get to work. You can sleep when it's done," said the second voice.

"Mrrg." Rumbles lumbered up from his chair.

Sevi watched him pick his meal up, eyeing the pie, somehow managing to feel mournful amid his fear. The cook placed it on the counter as he grabbed a broom and began sweeping up.

The first speaker started up again. "Raine, all I'm saying is that we can put in our leave. If nothing happens then we can at least enjoy the festival."

Raine. Somewhere in the back of Sevi's mind he connected the name to the person. It belonged to one of the castle's officers. Staring up through the table, Sevi envisioned a man with a long face, dark hair, and eyes as sharp as his ears. Sevi had always called him Rockman given his unshakable demeanor, which would make the first speaker Thistlebee—a name given on account of how he always hovered around Rockman, like a honeybee to a flower, and the spiky, thistle-like hair he had sprouting from his head.

"Except everyone is doing the same thing," Rockman said. "Getting approval will be a nightmare. If you wanted to go you should've asked the Matron two weeks ago, instead of trying to suck up to me."

"They hadn't made it to the castle two weeks ago," Thistlebee said, an edge creeping into his voice.

"They haven't made it *now*," Rockman insisted.

"Do you really believe that?"

"Of course."

A bumping sound close to Sevi halted their conversation.

Sevi's breath caught in his throat. He jerked his head toward the noise and nearly bit through his tongue. There was a long, pregnant pause.

"What was that?" Thistlebee said curiously.

Sevi put a hand over his mouth, trembling violently. His grip tightened on the iron in his other hand as he desperately tried to ready the courage to cut at any arms that might reach for him. It was all he could do not to bolt.

The two pairs of boots began scuffing about, meandering over toward the source of the noise. One stopped by the table beside the fireplace, situated right next to Sevi's own, and their owner began to bend down on their knees.

"I bet it's Cirrus' custodian," Thistlebee said.

Sevi felt his heart stop.

"What do you—*moon above!*"

Thistlebee darted up off the floor as a scaly, wriggling creature flashing incandescent colors streaked out from under the counter and skittered away, scrabbling around the room with quick, lateral dashes and a flurry of claws.

"Get it!" Rockman yelled.

"Is that the thing you passed your job to, Cirrus? Do you need to be replaced again?"

"What?" Rumbles grumbled.

"Shut up and get it!" Rockman yelled again. "I've always wanted to try one!"

The three Fablings, after more scuffing and sliding on the paved floor, chased the creature all over the kitchen before it found its chance and darted under the kitchen door. In the commotion, Rumbles' half-eaten pie was knocked to the floor, splattering on impact as it landed upside-down.

The cook cried out, "Oh just great!"

"Get it! *Get it!*" Rockman demanded fervently.

All three dashed out of the room, chasing the creature down the hall, leaving Sevi alone. Over fifty breaths passed before the knots in his chest loosened. He took another few just to stop shaking.

He looked behind himself at the tunnel, then back out at the kitchen. There lay the pie. Ruined, maybe... or maybe it tasted just fine.

He flashed one last glance at the door before darting out, snatching the pie off the floor, and scurrying back into the Cut. Shaking with nerves, Sevi looked down at the messy remains of the treasure. He smiled with relief as he gingerly put it to the side, then hurriedly pushed the entry-stone back where it belonged.

With the wall resealed, he slumped against the stone and yanked his eyepatch off his head, taking a moment to gather himself. Close. That had been too close.

"Lily is getting the floor scraps this time, Shy," he said to no one. "And if she doesn't like it then she can get the next batch herself."

Putting the pie into his pack and slinging it over his shoulder, he turned and tiptoed back around the sleeping firedrake and out of the castle, putting distance between himself and the kitchens. He thanked the gods that shadows couldn't speak, imagining the stern critique they would've given his sloppy performance as he fled into his tunnels.

# Chapter 3

*The boy was a mouse who kept his head down, seen only by lizard and stone. Each morning he went out to look for himself, each evening he came back alone.*

It was nighttime when Sevi returned. The walk gave him too much time to stew over his near discovery, and he had come to the conclusion that he had been a complete and utter idiot.

He would've been in a cell at that very moment if the lizard had been any less skittish, or perhaps thrown to the geisthounds as their next meal. Aside from dying painfully, the scariest part of that would be how the creatures turned transparent whenever they got excited. He would be torn apart by things he couldn't even see.

Still, it was hard to feel too upset when he had a hearty meal in his pack. Lily would be elated with the treat, and she didn't need to know about all the unpleasantness.

He stopped at the mouth of the Overlook and set his pack down, bringing out the prize of his expedition. He drew his whistle from his pocket before stepping out, bringing it to his lips and blowing the soft, trilling notes of a mountain jay's call. When Lily's answering notes failed to arrive, he repeated the pattern.

Still nothing.

Frowning, he slowly crept forward, throwing a cautious glance around the cliff for the dull dome of his friend's helmet. She wasn't where he'd left her.

He called out as loud as he dared. "Lily? Are you there?"

Silence.

He moved his gaze from side to side, scanning the dark for any flashes of metal, but the swaying and shifting of the surrounding leaves looked just as bright in the moonlight. Any one of their shimmers could have been her. Perhaps she had moved back into the Cut?

*Or has she gotten captured?* he thought nervously. He was beginning to panic when the familiar, lilting sound of an answering mountain jay called out behind him, playful and sonorous. He turned on his heel to face the other way just as a figure swung down at him from a branch and jerked their upside-down face into his.

"Is that a pie?" Lily exclaimed.

Sevi jumped and smacked the pie directly into her face.

They both froze. An oppressive silence filled the cliffside, broken only by the sound of pie pieces gathering in the rim of Lily's visor and dripping to the ground. The moment stretched on. And on. And on. Until Sevi finally took a step back, clutching at his shirt.

"Sevi," Lily said slowly, muffled.

Sevi gulped. "Yeah?"

"There's pie in my face."

He clenched his shirt. "Yeah."

"Would you kindly get it off?"

"Yeah."

"So I can climb down and thank you for it?"

Sevi quietly gripped the rim of what remained of the pie and peeled it slowly from her face, but the more of her expression he revealed, the more he wanted to put it back on. She looked ready to smack him, but she plucked her lips methodically after several breaths and brightened. "Well, at least it tastes good."

She flicked her hand at him, and he took a step back. When he was a decent distance away, she swung her body and unhooked her legs from the branch in one fluid motion, dropping down with practiced ease onto the rocks.

"You're not mad?" Sevi asked.

"I might've been, if the cook had used anything other than lamb," she said, wiping her face and licking her fingers.

"Really?"

"No, not really." She gave him a frigid look. "You ruined our meal and messed up my face."

Sevi looked down, clutching at what remained of the pie. There was so little of it left, now—a mediocre prize for his efforts. "I'm sorry. You... you shouldn't have snuck up on me like that! Why didn't you answer my whistle?"

"I was keeping an eye out for any raised alarm. You were taking too long, and I got to thinking, 'gee, I guess today is the day that Sevi got caught.' When you finally showed I figured a prank might serve you right for being so slow. But I think we can both see how bad of an idea that was."

She wiped her hand across her face and flicked it, contemptuously splattering the ground with filling. A lump grew in Sevi's throat—she didn't know how close she was to the truth. He kept his eyes fixed on the remains in his hands, unable to defend himself.

Lily's expression softened after a while. "How much is left?"

Half-eaten and splattered twice, there might've been barely enough for a quarter of a meal each. "With the other scraps I could get, probably enough for both of us?"

"Oh joy."

Sevi screwed up his face. To blazes with not telling her, she should *know* how hard he tried to get a decent meal for once. "I went through a lot for this, Lily. I was almost caught by *three* Fablings. If a shimmer lizard hadn't caught their attention, I'd be in the *tower* right now!"

"Really?" she said flatly. "Sure you weren't being a coward and freaking out, like usual?"

"Yes, really!"

She paused, but the look on her face filled him with worry. She settled her gaze on the pie as if she could divine its past, saying slowly, "How, exactly, did three Fablings almost catch you?"

Suddenly nervous, Sevi gulped. "A lizard in the kitchen made a noise while I was outside of the Cut. It bolted before they could find me."

Lily frowned. "Why were you outside of the Cut when there were three people in the room?"

18

"They weren't there at first," he said, omitting any mention of the first sleeping cook. She would've yelled at him for leaving the Cut with *anybody* in the room, regardless of their heavy sleeping habits.

"Mm," she hummed, thinking. "And what, exactly, did you go through just to get that?"

Sevi looked down at his hands, then back up at her. He opened his mouth, but paused, realizing too late how he'd implicated himself. "I—it was burnt... they threw it away," he attempted, his stomach sinking at his stutter.

She stared at him.

His heart thumped loudly in his ears.

"I imagine it was pretty tasty looking before it was thrown in my face," she said, smiling tightly. "Did those cooks come looking for it?"

"Lily—"

"Shut up, Sevi." Lily shook her head. "Remind me again. What's our first rule?"

Sevi dropped his head to stare at the ground. "I just wanted to have something nice," he mumbled bleakly. "And to surprise you."

"And do you think it's nice enough to risk us being captured and killed for it, stupid boy?" Lily asked, folding her arms across her chest with a glare. "Because I don't. Next time you can surprise me by using your brain for once."

Sevi didn't say anything, choosing only to glare back at her, fighting sudden tears. All he'd wanted was to share a nice meal with her. But she was right, as usual. He shouldn't have done it. And he knew he shouldn't have done it, too, which was the worst part.

"*No risks*, Sevi," Lily enunciated. She stepped up before him, maintaining her hard look, completely indifferent to his glare. "If one of us gets caught, we all get caught. You try risking yourself for something as silly as a pie again, and I'll throw you down the mountain. Do you hear me?"

Sevi reached up and wiped his eyes. It was moments like these, under the fierce scrutiny of his friend's judgment, that his mind was torn in several ways at once. Part of him wanted to yell at her for her caution, citing the squalor they lived in and the lack of joy that came with a life of survival. Part of him wanted to run into the tunnels and away from her anger, never to suffer under it again. And yet another part wanted nothing more than to shrivel up and trudge along behind her, dutifully following her lead, as long as she'd stop yelling. It was this last part that normally won, and this time was no different.

*Sorry, Rumbles.* He sagged his shoulders. "Fine, Lily," he mumbled. "I won't do it again."

"Good boy." Lily nodded, stepping away. "Now. Gimme my scraps and whatever's left of my share of the pie. Might as well make something of it." She sat down at her usual spot, pulling out a well-used cloth to wipe down her face and the rim of her helmet. "I'll have my revenge later."

Sevi wiped his face again and gathered the rest of the food. He laid out an assortment of meat scraps, vegetables, and several small, overripe purple fruits that Lily liked. Her eyes widened at the sight of them, though she tried to hide it. She was good at that. But he'd known her for too long, and he tried not to smile as he gave her each one. It was a meager apology, but one she accepted.

They moved beneath the branches of their favorite lounging tree before digging in with their hands, avoiding each other's gazes and falling into a strained silence. Wind blew softly through the leaves overhead, and torchlight flickered to life among the castle grounds far below as the night shift took their posts.

It felt good to eat. It rounded out the edges of Sevi's emotions, dulling the sting of his shame. And blessedly, the taste of the pie had not been dampened from its abuse. It was just as good as he had hoped, and he savored every bite, drawing out the flavor for as long as possible.

With bellies as full as they could have hoped, he and Lily lounged back against the trunk of their tree and enjoyed the nighttime ambiance of the mountainside, until whatever leftover tension between them had eased away on its own. Sevi always enjoyed these kinds of silences with her. They felt secure, somehow, as though any spoken word was meaningless fluff in the face of their quiet.

He peered at Lily from the corner of his eye. She sat still with her hands in her lap, enjoying the breeze with her eyes closed as it blew through her helmet, making a faint whistling sound.

A thought occurred to him. He looked out across the courtyard, watching the guards patrolling the castle walls. "Why don't they ever see you?"

She took a moment to reply, as if being summoned from a great distance away. "Who?"

"The guards down there. We can see their torches; why can't they see your helmet in the moonlight?"

"I'm sitting under a copse of trees in the mountains at night. It's hardly the same as standing up and waving a torch over my head."

"I can see metal glinting off of them," Sevi persisted.

"Then maybe they should find some trees to hide under," she threw back. "Besides. Shiny isn't something that I would call this helmet anymore."

"I think it's dangerous to be sitting up like that on a full moon."

Lily angled her head toward him and cracked an eye open. "Are you serious?"

Sevi nodded, raising his eyebrows.

"Is this payback for me yelling at you?"

"You're the one always telling me to be careful, Lil."

She stared at him for several breaths, but he didn't back down. Groaning with more drama than was necessary, Lily shifted and slumped down onto her blanket, then rolled with a dramatic huff until she lay face up with her fingers laced over her belly. "Happy?"

"You could just take it off," Sevi said for what might have been the five-hundredth time since he'd known her.

She snorted. "This or nothing, Sev."

Sevi dropped the issue. He didn't know why he bothered anymore—the mountain was less stubborn than her, especially when it came to her helmet. "Speaking of torches, the firedrake is in our room again."

"No way. Incredible. My surprise is bottomless." Lily didn't even look up. "Did it touch my stuff?"

"No."

"Did it touch *your* stuff? I don't want you mooning over your silver when it melts."

"No, Lily, it didn't touch anything."

"Hrm." Lily muttered under her breath. "We should kill the thing already. This is ridiculous."

He smiled faintly and turned back to face the castle, focusing on the sky. The stars were out, coating the heavens in pinpricks of light, forming a magnificent backdrop behind the castle's noble-looking spires. A full moon was rising, and he noticed, maybe for the first time ever, how the stars only began after a certain distance away from its hazy blue ring.

That was funny. It was such a minor thing, and so obvious, yet he had only noticed it now. He gently cocked his head to the side, allowing a new puzzlement to work its way through him. "How bright do the stars shine?" he said softly. Maybe the shadows knew.

"What?" Lily said.

Sevi looked at her sheepishly. He hadn't meant for her to hear. "The stars... We can see them with a full moon, and they're so tiny. But only a certain distance away, see? So how bright does something have to be to shine like that? As bright as a torch? As bright as the moon? And how far away from the moon do they need to be?"

Lily didn't answer. In fact, she had gone very still. He turned to face her, wondering if she had fallen asleep, only to find her helplessly laughing into the crook of her arm.

"Shh! Lily!" Sevi dropped to the rocks, going completely prone. Voices carried in the mountains, and she was just a little too loud.

"I'm sorry, I'm s-sorry!" She chuckled, wrestling with her laughter. Her head shook so much that her visor fell.

Sevi leveled a hard glare at her, but she turned on her side, looking away from him. "How is this being careful? What? What's so funny?"

"Tembra take me," she said through blessedly subsiding giggles. She lifted her visor back up. "Leave it to you to ask the silliest questions."

Sevi flushed. "It's not silly." He said it so quietly that he might as well have been talking to himself.

Lily, grinning, flicked a look in his direction, then turned back to the sky. "No, it's not. I guess I'm just reminded of something."

"Reminded of what?"

She shook her head. "It's nothing. But when you find the answer to that question, Sevi, you let me know. I'm interested in finding out."

Sevi maintained his glare, but she ignored it, settling in to watch the stars. Eventually, he copied her, rolling onto his back and looking up.

They lapsed into another silence. Sevi wasn't so sure how he felt about this one. It felt awkward... or maybe that was just him. A spot of light drifted by Lily, who casually raised her hand beneath it, holding it on her finger. Sevi turned his head at her motion and squinted, then frowned. It was one of the floating motes from the Cut.

He shook his head. "It takes me ages to catch one of those things, and one just lands on you."

She shrugged.

"Are they bugs?"

"Of course they are," Lily replied, shifting her hand to look at the mote from a new angle. "What else would they be?"

They both watched it for several breaths before it rose from her hand, carried off by a swift wind to join the thousands of other lights hanging in the sky. Soon they could no longer distinguish it from the stars.

"Hey, Lily?"

"Mm?"

"Would you tell a story?"

She regarded him with one raised eyebrow. "I suppose. What kind of story?"

"Anything."

"Anything. Hmm." She stared up at the moon and clicked her tongue. "Have I told you the story of the three sisters?"

Sevi wracked his brain for several breaths. It was hard to remember; she'd told him countless stories over the years. "I don't think you have."

"We do have a full moon tonight," she said softly. An oddly pensive look crossed her face. "It's as good a story to tell as any."

Sevi turned to face her entirely.

"Don't interrupt me this time, understand?"

"I won't." She looked at him with open skepticism. He sighed and drew his finger across his heart. "Promise."

Satisfied, she began her tale.

"It is said, once upon a time, that the moon and her sisters were born into darkness. The only light they could see was a light in the distance. Far, far away from them, in a place they could never reach. So they learned how to make their own light and shared the secret among themselves, so that they could see each other, and know that they weren't alone.

"But even with that light, and even with their sisters, they each wanted a friend. Someone they could confide in other than each other. Someone that would give them a love they didn't already know. Thus, they each created their ideal companion from the light of their own bodies.

"The youngest sister made a shining friend with beautiful wings, so that they could fly beside them through the night sky and play with her whenever she wanted. The middle sister made a perceptive friend with a beautiful voice that could sing any song, tell any story, and be heard from even the deepest abyss, so if they ever got separated, she could find them again. The eldest sister made a tender friend of beautiful form, so that she would finally know a lover, who might lift her heart to places she had never known before."

Sevi's perception narrowed just as it always did whenever Lily told her stories. She kept her talent hidden behind a layer of stoicism, but she was a born storyteller; a weaver at her loom, binding threads into beautiful tapestries. This time was no different, and gradually, the world around him fell away, replaced entirely by the world she made. Bursting with curiosity, he had to bite his tongue to avoid bombarding her with questions, unwilling to risk her ire for a second time.

"But one day," Lily continued, "after more turns of Eonin's wheel than anyone could count, the sisters reached that distant light and found it to be warm. So very, incredibly warm, not like the cold light that the three had made at all. And in this light, they found two creatures much like themselves, locked in an endless, touchless embrace, overlooking a creation built between them, where both the shapeless and the shapeful were made into one.

"Overjoyed, the sisters sped through the night toward this creation, eager to feel such warmth, eager to know something other than the touch of oblivion. They wanted to join Iaela, the world we know and love, and brought the light they had woven together as a gift they hoped to share.

"But its parents—Sorvathos the Father, and Avinaea the Mother—wouldn't let them fall from the sky to join it. And worse, the light that had sustained them through the dark, so beautiful and uplifting to themselves, was not seen as such to Iaela. So there, the sisters hovered, having come so far in search of anything other than night, and unwilling to brave it once more with salvation hanging before them.

"They begged. They pleaded. They cried. They wove their light into such fantastical shapes to excite and astound. They tried gathering bunches of themselves and throwing it out so far that the entire sky was filled with an array of bright, glittering diamonds, so that Iaela would not know the dark as they did. They tried singing the songs and telling the stories they'd made, filling the heavens with music and wonder. They tried teaching Iaela and its children how to use such light for themselves, so that they, too, might make wonder. But all was meaningless. All was to no avail.

"And their companions, who had only ever known the love of their creators, grew jealous at the fixation of their makers. The lover tried seducing the Father, and when he fell for her charms and opened his embrace to her, they tried to kill him. So the Father struck the lover down, and the eldest sister too.

"The one with the beautiful voice tried apologizing to the Mother, and in repentance, sung the Mother a story so beautiful that all who heard it wept. And when the Mother slowly fell asleep, they tried to kill her. But the Father, attentive after his failure, saw all, and brought his vengeance down upon the singer, and the middle sister, too.

"Then the one who could soar across the skies with wings of light, so small, so delicate, so pure and without malice, spread their feathers wide and stood before Iaela so that such wrath would not touch the youngest sister. They were not as beautiful as the lover, nor as charming as the singer, yet in their eyes they held all the splendor of the cosmos. When the Mother and Father saw this they stayed their hands, and invited this strange companion to treat with them on Iaela.

"And when they descended... they stayed.

"The youngest sister was left alone in the sky without her sisters, and without her dearest friend. Angry and distraught, it is said that she cried for one hundred years, staining the world with her tears and cursing her companion and all their progeny to die if they so much as touched a single drop of her misery. And there she remains in the sky to this day, too afraid to brave the night for a new land, waiting for the chance to finally fall from the heavens. The end."

The world came back with the sound of wind rushing through bushes, filling the silence made by Lily's final word. She fixed her gaze on the moon, as if at any moment it would split into three.

"That was beautiful," Sevi said softly.

Lily smiled wryly. "But?"

"It was sad."

"Not all stories are happy ones," she said. "And you did ask for any kind of story."

Sevi turned onto his back to stare up at the moon with her. "We have plenty of sad stories between us without adding more."

Lily snorted. "I'll keep it to myself next time."

Sevi glanced at her. Her wistfulness had disappeared. "I liked it, Lily. Thank you. As always."

"Mm," she mumbled. Then she jabbed a finger up at the sky. "What do you call those?"

Sevi looked to where she pointed but saw nothing. "I think they're called stars, Lily."

"Not what I mean, dummy. Have you named them?"

"The stars? No. Why?"

"You've named every Fabling in the castle but never thought to name the constellations?" she asked, humored.

Sevi shrugged. "Fablings have more life about them."

Lily shook her head. "My my, a game we haven't played yet." She resettled her arms back behind her helmet, getting comfortable. "Go ahead and start. Those ones right there. What would you call them?"

"Hm." Sevi scrutinized the smattering of dots she indicated, coming up with a picture in his mind. "Nightling bolts. See how they line up into three jagged streaks, like lightning bursting from the clouds, ready to strike the ground?"

Lily nodded after a moment. "I could see that."

"What would you call them?"

"The three soldiers. Marching across the sky to some far-off battle that no one cares about." She pointed at another cluster. "What about those ones?"

"Those curl more smoothly," Sevi replied. "It's like they're swimming around the other stars, like the night is their lake and the surrounding stars are a bunch of boats in their way, trying to capture them. It looks like a large sea serpent."

"Sea serpent it is." Lily pointed again. "What about those?"

"Those two?" Sevi took longer to answer. There was less to work with, but they were very bright; far brighter than their neighbors. He went with the first thing that came to mind. "They look like dancers to me."

Lily paused. "How so?"

"Well, they're off to the side, apart from everyone else, but they're shining bright enough that, if you squint, it looks like their light is touching. Like two people holding hands and spinning across the sky."

Lily chuckled. "Hiding away from everyone you mean."

Sevi shrugged. "Maybe. I guess so."

"I'm going to call that one Sevi, and that one Lily. Lily is much brighter and more beautiful than Sevi, but she lets Sevi hang around."

"Shut up, Lily."

"Like a pet."

Sevi scrunched up a small handful of rocks and tossed them at her, making her laugh.

"Just don't ask me to dance with you," she said.

"I doubt you even can."

"Better than you could, I'll bet."

Sevi grimaced, ignoring her smirk. They both turned their gaze to different patterns of stars in the sky, privately coming up with names that they'd later share and argue over when they were good and ready to. The trees rustled and swayed around them, scratching their leaves together in a soft lullaby, joined by the voices of hundreds of chirping bugs. With so much noise, it wasn't much of a silence at all. Not when the world around them had so much to say.

Big, fluffy clouds outlined in blue light moved lazily through the sky, casting spots of the land into deeper shadow as they drifted across the moon. The rest of the world might have been still with sleep, robbed of the vigor that only daylight could bestow, but the heavens never tired. Always moving. Always changing. In its steady, hypnotic motion, Sevi found his energy stolen from him, taken by the breeze and given to the clouds to help push themselves along to faraway lands. Maybe his parents were there, just beyond the horizon, waiting for him to come home.

He sighed irritably. It was a useless thought, entirely unwelcome among his musings and one he'd tried to stop wondering over. His parents were dead, along with everyone else who used to live in the castle. He closed his eyes and surrendered to his creeping drowsiness. "Lily?"

"Mm?"

"Will it rain tonight?"

"I don't think so."

Sevi reached into one of his pockets and pulled out a small drawstring bag. Dipping his fingers into it, he scraped up what little bit of powder remained on his fingertips and dropped it on his tongue. When it congealed into a paste, he smeared it along the roof of his mouth. "Want to sleep out here?"

There was a smile in Lily's voice when she spoke. "You read my mind." With one of his own, Sevi took a long breath and happily succumbed to the medicine, letting it pull him down into a deep, dreamless slumber.

# Chapter 4

*The girl was a flower, a friend, his best in the world, with a wit just as sharp as her thorns. Her head was held high with the helm of a knight, but her heart was as low as the floor.*

———⟡———

"**S**EVI."

Sevi jerked awake to someone shaking him. Jolting into a sitting position, he would have rammed his skull against Lily's helmet if she hadn't yanked her head back in time.

"What, what is it?" he stammered, furiously wiping the sleep from his eyes.

"*Hurry, you idiot!*" She took a hold of his shirt and practically dragged him backward.

He flipped onto all fours and scrambled in the direction she pulled him, all but jumping under the thicker branches of the Overlook's trees. He whipped his head around, searching for the danger. "What's happening?" he whispered nervously.

Lily had her face up to the sky with an unreadable expression, scanning the clouds through the leaves. Sevi only then realized that the birdsong along the mountain had gone quiet, replaced with a dull, distant rumbling.

"Do *not* move out from under these branches until it passes, whatever you do," Lily said.

"Until what—"

A fearsome roar smothered his question as a massive, flying creature swooped into the sky over the rim of the mountains, streaking above their heads in a blazing trail of gold. It hung suspended in the air like a schooner launching from a cresting wave and tossed into the clouds, then its nose tipped ever so slightly toward the ground, and it fell, plummeting down the side of the mountain with a flash of shimmering wings.

The sharp, rattling sound of creaking wood under great strain accompanied the roar of its fiery breath, leaving a wind in its wake hot enough to feel from a hundred meters away. It moved with slow, purposeful motion, swaying in the wind at a pace faster than any creature Sevi had ever known.

He watched it with wide, terrified eyes. It was a dragon, coming to lay waste to the castle and all its occupants, bellowing out its molten breath in challenge to the soldiers who guarded it. The creature turned as it neared one of the turrets, granting a view of its full figure.

It wasn't a dragon. It was a ship. A giant, flying frigate, strung up by a cloud and pushed by an angry fire streaming from its back. Golden floral motifs curled down its sides from bow to stern, catching in the sunlight and gleaming as brilliantly as scales. Two wings made of the same cloth as the balloon's canvas spread to either side of it, shuddering in the air before collapsing altogether, bunching tightly inward on themselves and then disappearing into slots in the hull.

Fear and awe twisted together inside of Sevi's belly, but the longer he watched, the more his amazement won out. A ship. A *flying* ship!

The vessel changed course, veering over the castle grounds directly toward a tower that jutted up from a level below the plateau, connected to the main courtyard by a bridge. At its pace, it looked ready to crash into the stone, until the fires at its stern dimmed and extinguished completely. It veered off to the side, turning effortlessly around the battlement and losing speed in the process.

Its fires flared sporadically, giving its movements some control against the wind until it had expertly slowed to a near stop beside the tower, drifting at a speed that kept it stationary, and giving time for the tiny figures on its deck to get to work. They scurried about, hurriedly throwing ropes out to equally tiny people on the tower's parapets, who then quickly tied them down, anchoring the ship completely.

Lily sighed. "Alright, they've made tether. We should be fine." She stretched, walking out of the deep shade of the trees and into a gentle patch of morning sun, but not before throwing a blanket over her helmet. She picked a spot to sit and settled down, lounging as easily as ever.

Sevi, meanwhile, could barely contain himself. "What. Is. *That?*"

"Skysailer," Lily said. "Galeskipper. Windfish. I call them airships myself. Easier to say."

"You've seen one before?" Sevi asked with equal amounts of surprise and detachment. Lily knew everything. Why wouldn't she know about airships, too?

"A long time ago. I didn't think..." She trailed off, staring at the ship. "We're lucky I was awake. Otherwise, they would've gotten a good look at us, completely bare and lying on our asses."

"I need my spyglass!"

"Me too."

They laid down on their bellies and pulled out their glasses. Carefully ensuring that any reflective bits had been properly shielded from the sun before peering through, they watched as the soldiers around and aboard the aircraft stabilized the gangplank. Then they arranged themselves in orderly rows, standing at attention as an even more elaborately uniformed man with jet-black hair appeared from belowdecks. He passed each person without a glance, stepping onto the landing with slow, precise steps and a straight, proud back.

But more interesting than he was the bound, disheveled-looking man that trailed behind. He had a head covered by a burlap sack, and his wrists were fused together, presumably bound. Several large-looking soldiers flanked him, leading him by a rope, yet he stood taller than each.

"Their uniforms are green, but they're different from the ones in the castle," Sevi said. "Who are they?"

"Nobody good, if I were to guess," Lily replied absently.

The presumed leader of the group paused to speak to a familiar woman, who crisply saluted him.

"What did you call that lady again?" Lily asked Sevi.

"Owl."

31

"Because?"

"Have you ever seen how she frightens others? How she can make a dozen people freeze up and start talking with the same voice? She's scary. And quiet about it."

"And this has nothing to do with how pinched her face is? All scrunched like an owl?"

"Maybe a little bit."

"Aha!"

"What?"

"Heh. Nothing."

The group trailing the leader waited attentively until he had finished speaking. The one soldier pulling the prisoner gave the rope a tug and laughed silently through Sevi's scope as he fell to the ground. The other guards joined in, with one even aiming a kick at the fallen man's ribs. Their leader never turned, moving ahead with an air of indifference.

The ramparts cleared in his wake. All he passed were pulled from their duties, captured by the gravity of his presence.

Lily put down her spyglass. "Well. This'll be a fun week."

Sevi followed suit. "What do you think they'll do to him?"

"Whatever they'd like, I'm sure."

The size of Sevi's smile nearly split his face completely. "I need to get down to the castle!" He started to stand, positively buzzing with excitement. Something *new* was happening!

Lily shot her hand out and grabbed his wrist. "Oh no, you don't."

Sevi froze mid-motion and flicked his gaze to her in surprise. She looked serious—more so than usual. Her grip was bordering on painful. He tried to shake her off. "Let me go, Lily. I'm just going down to watch."

"No, you're not. You're going to stay away from the castle until that thing leaves," she said, jabbing a finger at the airship for emphasis.

Sevi tilted his head at her. "Why?"

"Was I the only one that saw that huge godsdamned military march? This isn't normal, Sevi. We don't know what's going on."

He jerked his hand, breaking her hold. "The whole castle is military, Lily."

"Full of the usual, bumbling, lazy idiots we've named and love. And now they're all at attention with—from what I can tell—a top-level prisoner, led by someone who clearly has more power than Owl. What if any of these newcomers are able to hear you moving through the walls? Or see through stone?"

She shook her head. "I don't need you going down there, banging on the walls of the Cut as you please and giving us away just to play pretend again. Not until the airship leaves or until things die down and I have the chance to scout."

Sevi's face flushed red. "You don't know that any of them can do any of those things, and they've never caught me before."

"I can think of a few times they got close. Like *yesterday*."

"Because of a *lizard!*" he said loudly. "I haven't come *close* to being caught in three *summers!* I'm twice as quiet as you!"

"And half as smart, so you even out," she said with a critical quirk of her eyebrow, the kind that dared him to say otherwise. The kind that said, 'you know I'm right.'

He hated that look. That familiar jumble of feelings quickly grew inside him again, filling him from his head to his belly and tearing him in separate directions. This time, the anger won.

He abruptly turned and walked away from her.

"Sevi," Lily's voice softened. "Don't go. Do you want to put us in danger again?"

"No, but I want this," he said, voice shaking as he slung his pack over his shoulder. "I need to go. This is one of the few things that I have."

"No, you don't," Lily said sternly. "They have a prisoner, Sevi. Do you know what they're going to do to him? You've seen the tower. I know you know."

He didn't say anything.

"What's down there is ugly," she continued, "and an ugly world isn't for you."

Sevi looked back at that, meeting Lily's stare. She lifted her chin. "Not now. Not tomorrow. Maybe never. It's not worth it. You don't *need* it. So, I'm *begging* you, *don't go*. It's too dangerous."

Sevi gritted his teeth. "You're not my mother." He readjusted his pack with more strength than necessary before striding toward the Cut.

"Sevi! *Sevi!*" Lily called after him. But she didn't follow, and he didn't look back.

# Chapter 5

*One day a dragon flew into the keep, as grand and as gold as the sun! A warrior lay caged in its ivory teeth, outmatched, outwitted, outdone.*

Sevi was angry, hurt, embarrassed, and every other kind of frustrated emotion that he could feel. He was stuck away from civilization, feeding off of scraps, terrified of being discovered, and wondering each day, "Maybe this is when they'll find me." One of his few joys was going into the castle and watching its occupants from its many cracks and spyholes.

He'd pretend he was there with the soldiers, mimicking their movements like he was the one who had just spilled the wine, or that he was Owl giving the orders, or stealing more bread for his pet mountain goat until it was fat enough to eat. In his world away from the world, he had to do all that he could to keep himself from losing his mind. He needed something to ground him. Something to distract him. Something to look forward to. If he didn't, he'd fall apart.

Lily knew that. And she had tried to stop him.

He wouldn't have been half as safe without her. He knew that. She was also normally right. He *knew* that. But she always made it out like she could see *everything* that was going to happen. She had taught him all he knew, so couldn't she trust him to be careful? Or had all that gone up in smoke over one blazing shimmer lizard?

Silence was his life, whether he liked it or not. He knew how to live it, and he'd try to get *something* out of it however he could.

Stupid life. Stupid Lily.

Lost in thought, he realized he'd forgotten to adjust his eyepatch. Righting it, he straightened his back and set off again with a purpose, mumbling to himself all the way to the tunnels nearest the kitchens. Once there, he took a left instead of a right, heading away from all the savory smells of the other corridor and toward where his boring world became interesting.

A few large rats with bluish fur and large eyes burst from around the corner, chirping at him and startling him out of his reverie. He stumbled back, unable to stifle instinctive thoughts of, "Oh Gods Lily was right, I'm caught." Growling, he aimed a half-hearted kick at the pests, glaring at their mangey rears before continuing on his way.

His path led him on all sorts of twists, turns, and narrow corridors that he had to squeeze through. The Cut always traveled around the outer walls of the castle, but its inner workings were a maze. Some tunnels were wide enough for him and Lily to stand side by side. Some were so thin that he had to suck in his belly and walk sideways. Some had sudden ends, some only appeared to end, and some had walls thin enough that it was possible for those on the other side to hear him if he wasn't careful. This, however, meant that Sevi could just as easily hear through them himself.

Such a wall ran along a corridor near the throne room, where all the soldiers mustered whenever something important was happening. Many of them took the opportunity to gossip before being forced to stand at attention, and sure enough, a fresh babble of voices rose just on the other side of the stone. Sevi held his breath, watched his step, and gently pressed his ear to the brick where pieces of mortar had fallen away.

"... you... here... send us home?"

Sevi concentrated on the sound of the first voice, using it as a focus to sharpen his hearing.

"Hard to say... there's been reports of... ment... in... est. If anything, we'll... more recruits."

"Must be serious enough to send a Skyfarer to us."

Sevi jerked his head a little in surprise at the third voice. The speaker must have been leaning against the wall just beyond his ear.

"I just... see home. We've buried... tunnel. Haven't found... in. So, what's the..."

"You think... all don't want... home? The point is... keeping... long enough to protect ourselves."

"It's only been four years. You can suck it up, Eldhart."

"Don't sulk. Moon above, I forget how freshly turned you are. We'll see the tree again soon."

Someone said something garbled. Sevi couldn't make it out.

"Yes, that's Nightshade. Just... and don't draw attention to..."

"Why would... be here, though?"

"Like I said. Must be serious. Let's hope I'm wrong."

"... go in?"

"Yeah... hate this..."

The speakers moved away. Sevi kept his ear to the wall in the hopes that others would replace them. The Fablings had made references to things like, "the tree," "amber," "turned," and so on since forever. Clearly every soldier knew what those things were, and to Sevi's detriment, had all mutually decided not to exposit further. Not even Lily could understand it. It left him with a pit of curiosity in his chest that he had learned to ignore but had never fully gone away.

With no other noise beyond the wall but the faint stamping of boots, Sevi moved his head back and carefully tiptoed down the Cut alongside the marching soldiers, acting as though he were one of them. When his path ended at the wall that encapsulated the throne room, he took a left, heading for a piece of it that was particularly dear to him.

He had taken a long, long time working on the stone here, hammering it gently to get a nice, inconspicuous crevice in the wall, and then gently working it out. It had taken him a few tries, but he had finally picked a spot with the right vantage point behind the thrones, allowing him to look over the assembled masses like a king. The corridor was pinched where the windows were set, making the space a little cramped, but he could handle the discomfort. The reward was worth it by far.

Setting down his pack, Sevi slowly and carefully worked the rock loose as quietly as possible, until he was welcomed by the glorious view of the throne room. Every soldier in the castle had assembled, standing at attention toward his wall. He breathed out at the sight.

Today, they were *his* army, and he was their king.

To his dismay, the captain of the airship had taken position at the head of the assembly and was already addressing them. He could only see the man's back from his narrow vantage point, standing rigidly with his hands clasped comfortably behind him. A sword hung at his hip, and his jacket fell down to just a handspan above the floor. Sevi quickly set to work copying him, straightening his own body like a proper leader of a proper army.

"And today, we find ourselves with one of those despicable creatures whom we've toiled against for so long, brought to heel by *my* hand!"

"Very good, Captain Redwood," came a chorus of replies, all in unison.

"If I didn't know better, I would think that I'm accomplishing your job for you, Regal Company. Am I correct in that assumption?"

Sevi did his best to mouth along to the speech, half a breath behind every word.

"Yes, Captain Redwood," the assembly said, again altogether, as though speaking with one voice.

"And why is that?"

"You are a fine leader and soldier, Captain Redwood. Better than any one of us."

Again, in unison. Sevi paused. Owl could make her soldiers act as she wanted, affecting perhaps five or six people at a time at most. This... this was the entire blazing *castle*.

A shiver went up his spine.

But then the man started speaking again. He had very expressive hands. Sevi shook himself free of his worries, choosing to be drawn instead to the energetic motions the captain used to command the stage. He was really laying it on though, and Sevi couldn't help but giggle.

"That's *right*," Captain Redwood said imperiously.

Sevi tried to match the way the captain stuck his nose up in the air, scrunching his face up to what he imagined was a haughty expression.

"It is widely known how far Regal Company has fallen since its inception, and I would hope that, if *nothing* else, you lowly derelicts remain aware of that fact at all times.

"But fear not—a time may come... oh yes, a time will come... very, very soon, where you all might prove yourselves once more, and throw off this shameful stain in which you've all seen fit to wallow in. But you may start by taking care of our new guest. So why don't we say hello?"

The soldiers broke into a cacophony of hooting and hollering, becoming vastly more animated all at once. A Fabling roughly pushed the captive from the airship next to Captain Redwood and threw the man's head covering off.

Though Sevi couldn't see his face, he noticed that the man lacked pointed ears. It made sense—every other prisoner in the castle was human. He wore a blue coat, and though it wasn't as decorated as Captain Redwood's, it was enough to make him look important. Oddly, despite his circumstances, his posture seemed to resemble the captain's. Unbent. Tall. Proud.

Sevi wondered what he had to be proud about. He switched his own demeanor from matching the captain to the prisoner instead, stilling the emphatic motions of Redwood and becoming more... contemplative. He wondered what it was like to stand there, helpless before a jeering, hostile crowd with hands tied together. The very thought made him queasy.

"Yes, our lovely new guest will enjoy the finest treatment," the captain continued. But he wound his hand back as he spoke and slapped it across the prisoner's face. "The best bed," *slap*, "the tastiest food," *slap*, "and *anything* he could want!" *Slap, slap, slap.* "Why, our guest here has achieved a great victory! He, a loyal lesion—pardon, 'legion' soldier, has finally reclaimed his dear, dear castle!"

The crowd howled with laughter, going for a good while before cutting off abruptly, as if all the air had been sucked out of the room. Sevi's shiver spread from his spine to his chest.

"Lieutenant, make sure that our guest is so very, very comfortable. Place him in our finest cell in our finest tower. I want him to look out on the land and know, deep in his heart"—he tutted—"it's not his."

*Oh, very exciting.* Sevi tried to push his unease away in order to truly capture the coyness in Redwood's mannerisms. *This is just like a story.*

"Now, to more important matters. Obviously, you all have heard the rumors that—"

The prisoner casually turned his head and spit on Captain Redwood's shoe, cutting the captain off mid-sentence.

Silence. A long, long silence. All the soldiers remained still without gasps, outrage, ridicule, or insults. But there was tension in the room, exaggerated by the way the assembly turned their heads as one to stare at the man in blue.

Sevi held his breath. He pressed his eyes to the slot in the wall, gluing his forehead to the stone in anticipation. An eternity passed before Captain Redwood sighed, nonchalantly drew his sword, and stabbed the prisoner through the shoulder so deep that it burst out his back.

No words. No contemptuous disregard. Just sheer, apathetic violence. The horror of it made Sevi gasp in shock.

It must've been too loud.

Aside from the prisoner's gasp of pain, it was the only sound anyone made at all. The captain's head turned from staring daggers at the prisoner to the wall shielding Sevi, his expression swiftly morphing from annoyed to confused, as though his anger was but a passing thought.

He scanned the wall from top to bottom, giving Sevi a good look at his face. It was smooth and pale, with maroon streaks patching his skin from his long ears to his neck, and his shiny black hair was smoothed back from his forehead to tightly hug his scalp. When his face passed into shadow his eyes glinted with a golden light, hidden just beneath the black of his pupils.

He withdrew his sword from the prisoner's body just as casually as he had pushed it in. The man slumped to the ground, hitting the floor with a moan. No one rushed to catch him. Then Redwood stepped around the thrones, maintaining his curious expression. He cocked his head to the side while he brought out a pocket cloth and wiped the blade of its running blood, regarding the wall with far more curiosity than Sevi was comfortable with.

Sevi's heart leapt into his throat. He scrambled for the stone piece on the floor, blindly searching for wherever he'd set it. The walls seemed to close in around him as though to suffocate him, screaming, *'You shouldn't have come, you shouldn't have come!'*

He didn't know if he made it in time, but he found the spystone and got it back in its place with frenetic, shaking fingers. He set his back to the same wall and clutched for his knife, breathing heavily and listening desperately for any sound of a raised alarm. All he heard was the sound of his heartbeat.

"Matron," Captain Redwood finally said, muffled through the stone. There was a pause as someone, presumably, responded. "Save for the guards, everyone is in attendance?"

Another pause.

"Mm. Did you...? You did? That's what I thought. Do you have some—ah. Wait... Well. It's gone now. How... Hm."

Redwood stopped talking for a dozen breaths. "Perhaps it's a rat or two. Have the grounds cleaned of vermin and check your stores for anything missing. I would not be surprised if your cretinous regiment has been lax with its rations. Anyway. I believe punishment is in order."

Captain Redwood started up again a distance away. An eternity seemed to pass before Sevi felt safe enough to breathe again.

Then a hand clamped over his mouth.

He screamed into it and grabbed at its fingers, jumping high enough to nearly collide with the ceiling. Its grip only tightened, pulling him violently to face a direction. Staring back at him from the dark were two large, green, familiar eyes, set on the very angry face of a very angry girl.

"Move," Lily growled through clenched teeth. She grabbed Sevi's wrist, pulling him away from the wall, and forced him into the deeper darkness of the Cut.

# Chapter 6

*The boy had to see! He scurried to watch, the girl warned him sharply to stay. Blind to the havoc the dragon could wreak, he soon gave his small self away.*

---

"**I**'m twice as quiet as you!" Lily mocked.

Sevi stayed quiet, focusing on only putting hand and foot in front of the other as he and Lily squeezed, crawled, and climbed their way out of the castle. The further away they got, the more vocal Lily became.

"They've never caught me before, except that time when I tried making an entrance into the barracks to get a fresh pillow. Or the time when I tried getting flowers from the courtyard. Or the time when I just couldn't help laughing at the play in the throne room. Or when they almost caught me in the kitchen *yesterday*, and now twice in as many days. Gods, I sure am quiet. More like twice as likely to get caught!'"

"Please... those were years ago, before I knew what to do. I said I was sorry," Sevi mumbled.

"I'm going to go right up to the damned wall and push my mouth to the stone and outright scream into a room full of bloodthirsty soldiers, and they'll never hear a thing!"

"That wall was made of stone and almost a handspan thick, Lily! How was I supposed to know that hundreds of people wouldn't make a sound?"

"You couldn't, which is why you never should've gone, *like I told you.*"

"So what, I'm supposed to—"

"You're *supposed* to be *quiet!*" Lily yelled, jerking her head around to glare at him.

Sevi flinched.

"Almost caught twice in two days, Sevi, and you've only gotten through by the scrape of your nails. Shut. *Up.*"

Sevi trailed behind her in silence. His anger had withered into a pitiful thing, and any excuse he came up with was just as wretched. Once again, Lily's warnings had proven right.

The way back to the Overlook dragged on for far longer than any of his previous treks. The colorful plants and vines, normally so bright and welcoming, did little to better his mood. If anything, they only worsened it. Why should they be happy, content to just hang there and be pretty, while he should suffer through his mistake?

His chance to leave Lily only came when they made it to the base of the sheer wall leading up, where the tunnels split. He stopped a distance away while Lily grabbed the rope. She didn't turn around.

"I'll be in the garden," he said.

"I don't care." She hauled her way up the rope with an angry energy, only stopping once to wipe her face before disappearing over the ledge, and never once looking back at him.

Sevi watched her vanish, heavy with emotion. She very clearly wanted to be alone. The least he could do was oblige her.

He started up the trail leading away from the Overlook's escarpment, lugging his feet heavily through the gravel. He felt as though his head had parted from his body, trying to distance itself from the painful emotions churning around in his gut. Terror in thinking that he'd irrevocably betrayed her trust this time, hurt over her words and his own self-loathing, shame for being the one to put them both at risk, more terror that he would not be able to return to the castle's Cut for some time. It was all in such a tangle, worse than ever before.

The path was a lengthy one, curling around and around the mountain higher than even the Overlook. Sometimes it branched in a confusing web, but he knew the main tunnel well enough. He'd worn a faint trail into it over the years.

And at its end, high in the sky away from the castle (and Lily) lay his secret garden. Their other source of food, and his one other escape. It could never compare to the majesty of the castle's own vibrant field, but it was his, and he cared for it deeply.

The cave couldn't have been more than a dozen armspans across. In the middle of it was a humble patch of dirt, stark against the stone. In it was every kind of plant that Sevi could get his hands on, be it from off the mountain or grown from the seeds harvested in his regular kitchen raids. A small window in the ceiling, a story or so off the ground, rested at an angle to the sky, allowing light and rain in. He had hammered crude wooden footholds made of branches into the wall below it a couple years ago, allowing him to climb out whenever he needed some fresh air beyond the castle's sight.

The garden's silence was different from the others, as were its voices. More personal. More curated. At the Overlook, the world spoke to him with a vast, old, soothing voice, and wrapped him in a comfortable quiet that could lull him to sleep. The sounds of the castle, meanwhile, were muted and mysterious, as the Cut's only nature was darkness and solitude. It was loath to part with any secret no matter how small, and it demanded his compliance if he wanted to continue living there.

But here? Here he grew his own voices and harvested his own silence. Here, he moved every rock, planted every sprout, and gathered every fruit. Here, he told his garden how to be, and when he spoke, the garden listened. But what made their relationship special was that when the garden spoke, he listened right back. And the garden thanked him for it.

He took stock of who was currently speaking the loudest. Some of the plants were flowering, some had bright lights glowing from within, some seemed to sway in hypnotic ways of their own accord, and some were just beginning to bear fruit and vegetables. Picking out several issues and tasks that needed his attention, he wasted no time in getting to work, all too eager to lose himself in a song of color and life.

Two buckets lay beneath several dripping stalactites, and over the course of a day had grown full with water. He took them, but disturbed a small chorus of bubbletoads upon moving them, who swelled up into big, yellow balls at the disturbance, warning him to stay away.

He smiled softly at them. They weren't an unusual sight, attracted by the moisture of the buckets, and Sevi found himself fond of their grumpy expressions, especially when they bloated. "I'm only borrowing these," he promised. "I'll give them back."

Stepping away, he carefully began watering the garden, giving each plant the care and attention it needed. Some were pruned of dying leaves, some were trimmed, some were ready for harvesting, and some needed replanting altogether. But sometimes he'd come across a stalk that had just decided to die, without any reason or warning. He'd made a lot of mistakes lately. Maybe those were his fault, too.

The day stretched on, passing without notice as he slowly lost himself in his work. Sometimes a guilty thought worked its way into his brain, like *"all your fault," "put Lily in danger,"* and *"what is wrong with you."* Sometimes they would ricochet in his skull without remorse, only dulled by putting his attention elsewhere.

In many ways his garden was a perfect distraction. It always offered work to be done. Always had something to care for. Except it didn't. Not really.

A garden could only be worked for so long every day before caring became smothering, and when he reached that point, there wasn't anything left to help him drown out the noise. In the end, his feelings, proving unstaunchable, came as cruelly and suddenly as the first frost of every winter, reducing the worth of his garden to useless, withered husks.

He sat there in the dirt, looking dismally at a batch of flowers he'd replanted closer to the light. What was even the point of all this work when summer would end one day? His small, copper trowel dipped in his grip. Tears welled in his eyes, no longer suppressible.

Sevi scrubbed at his face, furious with his own weakness. Loathing it. *Despising* it. *"All your fault, Sevi. It's all your fault."*

He deeply missed Shy's company. Shy never said anything. They never accused him of anything, wanted anything of him, or expected anything from him. They only existed, watched, and listened when he needed them to, with their big eyes and the funny way they blinked. They used to be with him all the time. What had he done to make them run away?

"Shy... are you there? I could really use you right now," he said, looking down at the dirt and waving his hand about in the light as if it could summon his friend. But it didn't. He was alone.

Focusing on the bright, red petals of the flowers before him, he tried to lose himself in the way the sunlight diffused in their crisp, green leaves, or how delightful their nectar smelled. Their beauty made for a wonderful excuse not to think, replacing all his ugly thoughts. He ran his gaze upward to face the sky, watching the clouds through the gap in the rock.

He felt a sudden, desperate need to get a better look. Maybe the sky could reach down and pull his thoughts right out of him. Heaving himself from the dirt, he patted himself down and walked over to the rungs, placing his hand on the closest one and pulling himself up. One by one. One by one. *All your fault. All your fault.*

Then his head left the protection of the mountain, and he was greeted with the full force of the valley's scenery. The boughs of the forest below bent and swayed, their branches curling down all at once whenever a gale brushed over them. Red specks marking village rooftops poked up from the trees in a huddle a distance away, where the town at the base of the mountain wrapped around and disappeared from view, blocked by a mountain wall. The sound of a waterfall nearby as it fell into a basin filled his ears, carried by the rushing wind. The river it fed could just barely be seen among the shifting trees, sparkling like a cluster of diamonds.

Sevi breathed in deeply and closed his eyes, slowly spreading his arms out wide, letting the wind flow through his tattered clothing. He felt like he was flying. When he opened his eyes, he saw himself on the deck of a great wooden airship, high above the clouds. Higher than the tallest mountain. Propelled by a blazing fire into a vast azure sky.

He stood proud, like a captain before an army, like a prisoner who refused to bow, letting it carry him far, far away from an indifferent world of stone to a land of free eternity.

Then he blinked, and he was back in the cave. Shallow tears drizzled down his face, growing smaller as exhaustion took him. He wiped each one away and leaned forward against the sun-warm rock with a sigh, staring out.

His thoughts drifted back to Lily. How could he apologize? How could he prove to her that she could trust him again?

*By never messing up again*, he thought, flicking a loose pebble away from the window. *By being perfect from now on. By doing exactly what she tells me.*

Something fluttered next to his ear, startling him from his thoughts. He jerked his head, and the fluttering moved off a distance. Then it looped around to the other ear and he snapped around to face it.

"AH!" He yanked his head back as he came nose to nose with a tiny, green woman, hovering on a pair of translucent wings. The creature mimicked his motion, flapping back a safe distance away.

"Ah." Sevi breathed, placing one hand on his chest. "Oh, Alyda."

Taking another moment to be extra certain he had calmed, the little green fairy girl caught the hem of her flower-petal skirt and curtsied in midair, dipping her bald head down in a nod. She fixed her big, crystalline eyes on his face and gave him her widest, most dazzling smile, then chimed out a single musical note, as if to say, "*At your service.*"

"Please stop scaring me like that."

Alyda shrugged her tiny shoulders and smirked unrepentantly, then waved her hand, signing, "*Maybe when it stops being funny.*"

"Please. I'm not in the mood," Sevi mumbled. He put his chin on his arms and stared back out through the window, returning to his brooding.

Alyda flew around, keeping herself in his line of sight, and settled on the lip of stone in front of him with a questioning quirk of her head. Her wings flicked idly behind her, much like a butterfly at rest, but her face was solemn and knowing. She'd seen him like this many times before.

She chimed a few more notes and crossed her arms in such a way that said, "*Do you really want to be left alone?*"

"I don't know if I want to talk about it," he said.

Alyda raised and dropped her shoulders in an exaggerated sigh. She beckoned her hand at him in a 'come here' gesture. "*You're going to eventually, so let's do this now.*"

Sevi blinked and snorted a chuckle. She knew how to read him. Perhaps it came naturally to her, being unable to speak and having solely expressed herself through body language. Or maybe it simply came with years of familiarity.

"Alright. Let me get down from here. Are you hungry? I'm sure there's some fruit ready to eat."

Sevi climbed back down the wall with Alyda riding on his shoulder, casting a faint, emerald aura around her body, outlining her in the half-light of the cave. Walking around the garden, Sevi cut a small wild strawberry off its vine and offered it to her, which she took all too happily.

The pair sat down in their favorite spot for conversation—a large, mostly flat rock they used as a small table, with a smaller rock for Sevi to sit on. On the other side was a plant with broad leaves that Alyda could perch on comfortably. Her body was so slender and light that it would barely bend.

She settled down, nibbling on the strawberry in her arms, but taking great care not to get her dress dirty. When she had gotten comfortable, Sevi asked, "So... how are you, Alyda?"

Alyda shrugged, nodding her head from side to side. "*So-so. Just living.*"

Sevi smiled softly. "I see. It's... it's good to see you. I'm sorry that you've caught me—"

Alyda flicked her wrist and flapped her wings in a short, rapid burst, waving him off.

"Right, yeah. You're used to it, aren't you?"

She shrugged, wiping her mouth with the back of her hand.

"I had a fight with Lily. It wasn't our normal arguing. I... I really messed up."

The fairy flicked her long ears gently against her skull at that, watching him more seriously as she took another bite.

"I went to the castle. I... I just wanted to see. They've got some... they captured someone important. Important enough for someone dangerous to come to the garrison. They stabbed him. I gasped. I've never... I've never seen that. All the blood. I... they... they heard me. They almost *found* me."

Alyda set down her strawberry, looking worried.

"They heard me. I was so close to—" Sevi stopped to wipe his face, heaving in a shuddering breath as he fought fresh tears. "And then, Lily was there. She got me away."

Sevi slumped forward on the table with his head in his hands, going quiet. He felt empty again, save for the same thoughts swirling around in his head. *All your fault. How to apologize. What to do now.*

"I've been getting worse, I think," he said. "I used to be more careful. I used to be terrified of just the *thought* of leaving the tunnels. But now? I'm thinking of it almost every day. I'm taking more chances... and that almost ruined everything."

Horrible visions flashed through his mind of the soldiers getting their hands on him, or worse, Lily and Alyda. The barest thought of one of them wrapping their hand around Alyda's little neck was enough to make his stomach churn, adding to his guilt.

Alyda lifted from her perch and settled neatly on his head with her legs tucked beneath her. Sevi felt the touch of her tiny hand as it gently held his forehead, tapping him comfortingly. *"There there, little boy, there there."*

Sevi smiled ruefully. Even a creature as small as her pitied him. But it helped, as always. "Thank you, Aly. That's very nice."

She responded with another flicker of wings. He felt her body shift, and her small hands clutched at locks of his hair just before her upside-down face popped into view right between his eyes. He pulled his head back in surprise.

She gave him a knowing look.

"What is it?"

Alyda shook his locks in her hands, then beat her wings once in a snappy, pointed burst.

"You want me to stop crying," Sevi said flatly.

She nodded, and for good measure, reached down with a precarious tottering of her body to swipe at a tear running down his cheek.

Sevi laughed a little at that, reaching up to her with a flat palm. "Please don't hurt yourself."

The fairy gracefully stepped onto his hand in one smooth motion, a fluid skip more than a step, and turned on her heel to face him, idly opening and closing her wings with a patronized look. She fixed it sternly on him and placed one tiny fist on her hip, then shook her index finger at his face, dipping her head to the side. When she opened her mouth a small, lilting chime rang out, but it was less like the music of her previous notes, and more like glass shaking against glass.

She broke into a fit of coughing that shook her entire body, forcing her to cover her mouth with the crook of her arm. Sevi lifted a hand in concern, but she quickly waved it off, shaking her head. When the fit passed, she turned back to him, a little embarrassed but otherwise composed, then crossed her arms and stamped her foot in his palm.

He shook his head. "You've lost me, Aly."

She raised an eyebrow, then pointed at him. After a moment, she pointed to her own heart, tapping her chest, then firmly pointed to the room's exit with a rigid finality, flaring her wings out for good measure.

Sevi's heart sank. "You think I should go back to Lily."

Alyda nodded curtly and stamped her foot again. She lifted her hand and made the sign of a person walking across it with the other, then pointed at him, and then out of the cave again. *"Yes, little boy, get to it."*

"What, now? So soon? Can't I... she doesn't—"

Alyda's twinkling voice rang out, louder, and emphasized with her smacking her closed fist into her open palm. *"Don't make me beat you up!"*

"I'm bigger than you," Sevi mumbled.

Alyda scoffed, grabbing her sides to really show off the humor in that statement.

"Fine. Whatever you say, fairy godmother."

Alyda rolled her eyes but broke into a smile before lifting off from his hand, keeping eye-level with him.

"What are you doing now?" He folded his hands behind his back, trying to put off his departure for as long as possible. "Going back out again?"

The fairy shook her head and reached into her dress' only pocket, hauling out several big seeds that filled her arms and bringing a new smile to Sevi's face. "These aren't more poison ivy seeds, are they?"

Alyda made an affronted gesture that bordered on rude.

*So much sass in a creature so small,* Sevi thought, grinning. "Find a good place for them... and wish me luck."

Alyda nodded, smiling at him, and tilted her head with her chin jutting out. *"Get going."*

"I will, I will... and thanks, Alyda. As always."

She dipped her head in a nod and spun about in the air, fluttering away until the leaves of their garden swallowed her glow entirely. Sevi took one heaving sigh before fixing on the long, dark tunnel ahead. Composing himself, he gathered his things, righted his eyepatch, and headed for the Overlook.

# Chapter 7

*Thorns burst from the flower, prickling into his hide, he fled to where no one could find. Where a petal grew soft, where a world could not reach, where a light had known only to shine.*

———— ⊸❦⊷ ————

"What about you, Shy? You're the only one that hasn't said anything."

Sevi grunted as he lifted himself up the rope to the Overlook, sore from all the garden work. His own voice echoed back at him. It had been that way through the walk, but he had needed someone to talk to.

"Why do I even bother? Maybe I should give up on you," he said, trying to goad a response. Which failed. Again.

He reached the top and took a moment to catch his breath. He had no idea if Lily was still too angry to talk, but he had to try. She was his best friend, and he wasn't going to lose her. Even if it meant giving up his trips to the castle.

Trudging the final stretch to the cliffside, he took out his signal whistle and blew the mournful notes that sounded his arrival. There was no reply. That didn't bode well. Steeling himself, he crossed the cave's threshold, ready as he could be to face his friend.

"L-Lily," he called, shaky despite his best efforts. He looked to her usual spot and found it empty. Wrinkling his brow, he peered up into the trees. She couldn't have been in the mood to play another joke.

Sure enough, the branches were clear, as were the largest rocks, and all the bushes. That was odd. Why would she climb up here only to climb back down? He craned his neck up along the mountainside. Maybe she felt like exploring a higher perch. She'd never do that, though; that would have exposed her too much.

Yet, he hadn't passed her in the tunnels, and the door to the mines was still sealed. Had one of the flying soldiers finally passed close enough to notice her? Had her helmet given her away at long last?

The thought worried him. He leaned against a tree and stared off toward the castle, trying to squash the nervousness in his chest. The grounds were still largely devoid of their usual retinue of soldiers, save for those manning the walls. They didn't *look* like they had captured an intruder. No, she had to have descended the mountain again.

His gaze drifted to the airship, taken by it despite his concern. It really was beautiful. And yet, in a sense, it had become his jailor, forcing him into the mountain for as long as it floated there. A needle of irritation prodded at him, which turned into hate the longer he stared.

"What are you even doing here?" He sneered. "You couldn't take your stupid prisoner *anywhere* else?"

Sevi sat on the ground and contemptuously turned his gaze back to the castle, running it along the tallest tower. The man in blue would be there by now. It had been fairly empty of late, so he wouldn't have much company, which was probably for the best. Sometimes, when he was in the Cut, Sevi would catch the faint sound of a scream coming from it. It wasn't a pleasant thing to be surprised with in a dark, cramped tunnel, let alone being forced to listen to it all day from the confines of a jail cell.

He wondered how the man was faring. Was his back still unbent? Was he still standing proudly behind his bars? Or had the fearsome Captain Redwood taken his sword and sliced him until he no longer could?

Sevi was struck by a sudden thought that made him freeze. Something Lily had said moments before he'd left for the throne room. *I don't need you going down there,* she had said. *Not until...*

"No," he murmured.

*Not until the airship leaves, or I have the chance to scout around.*

He jerked forward, staring hard at the tower. The thought wouldn't leave his head. Lily had to have gone to the castle, and where would be the first place she'd go if she ever thought they were in danger?

*Where she could keep watch.*

"She wouldn't," he muttered, then louder, "Not this time. After *yelling* at me!"

He curled his fingers into bone-white fists, then turned on his heels and bolted back into the tunnels. He knew where to find her.

S evi scrambled through the Cut as quickly as he could, only stopping when he hit the castle walls and forcing his steps to slow with great effort. As much as he wanted to keep running, he had to be careful. No more noisy mistakes.

The tunnels felt more oppressive than usual, as though the walls were actively hindering him from reaching the tower. Perhaps they now held him in contempt for nearly betraying their secrets. He made sure to keep his curses under his breath so the Cut wouldn't hear.

He rarely ever went up this way anymore, and had to focus on the path more than usual. Where once he would climb the tower for the view, or watch the prisoners in their cells, now he avoided the area altogether. As callous as it was, the prisoners were depressing to watch, not to mention uninteresting. They were locked in their cells with nothing to do and looked more like Lily and himself than the Fablings, missing quills for hair and without any extra limbs at all. Who would want to watch someone like that?

It wasn't that he looked down on them though—he empathized with their situation, he really did. He knew what it was like to be locked within stone walls with no way out. But being confronted with their misery on a semi-regular basis, and with no way to help them, did little but sadden him.

He stopped at the vertical shaft that would bring him up. Wind whistled from above, blowing across his face, bringing the scent of unwashed bodies and decay along with it. Wrinkling his nose, Sevi steeled himself and reached up for a handhold in the rock, forcing himself to climb.

It didn't take long for him to resent the fact that there was even a tunnel here at all as his arms began to scream for mercy. *Who in deep Abeya puts a tunnel in a prison tower?*

Stopping on each floor offered some reprieve between climbs, but none held any sign of Lily. His body gave out on him by the time he made it to the highest level, and he collapsed onto the ground with an exhausted groan.

After the blood ringing in his ears subsided, he gradually realized that, unlike the other floors, this one had voices. His heart leapt, and he pushed off the floor with a groan. The ceiling here was low, forcing him to move forward in a half-crouch towards the source of the noise. He carefully poked his head around a corner.

And there was Lily. Her back was to him with her face pressed to the wall, peering into the cell beyond.

Sevi gathered his breath. He still didn't know what to say to her. Here he was, at the castle, disobeying her wishes, and only just now realizing how it lessened some of the weight of his apology. It would have been better if he'd waited for her at the Overlook. But what was she *doing* here, undermining the very caution she preached? While he sat wrestling with this indecision, Lily beat him to the first word.

"Leave," she said.

Sevi's breath caught in his throat. That one word was like a slap across the face. She had a right to still be angry with him; he couldn't argue that. But *he* had a right to know what she was doing here. Why had she left without telling him? What if something had happened to her? He never would've known.

"What are you doing here?" he asked.

"*Sightseeing,*" she said exasperatedly, still not looking at him. "Now, go away. I don't need you putting us in danger for a second time today."

His cheeks flushed. "What happened to keeping our heads down? Why do you get to come stick your face against a castle wall, but I can't?"

"I think we both know the answer to that."

Sevi clenched his teeth. He felt the shyness, always present, instinctively pull him away—urging him to just crawl back down the shaft where it was dark and safe. But something made him push. "You tried to keep me away," he said. "What happened to them being able to see through stone? What... what makes you so special?"

She turned from the wall with a dangerous look in her eye that made him regret his choice of words. "You don't want me to answer that," she growled.

"I... I think I do." He swallowed, attempting to glare back. "After h-how you yelled at me? You owe me that."

Lily slowly crossed her arms, letting him squirm under her glare for several long moments. Finally, she took a deep, weary breath. "Fine, I'll tell you," she said, icy and patronizing. She uncrossed her arms and placed one hand over the peephole, muffling the sounds beyond and any that she'd make. "Want to know why I left you behind? It's because you're a *child*."

Sevi's anger sprung at once to the forefront of his being with more lucidity than ever. He only narrowly remembered to keep his voice down before it exploded out of him. "*You're barely seventeen!*"

"I may as well be fifty compared to you," Lily said, eyes tight and eyebrows heavy. "Every moment that either of us are in this castle is a moment we might be discovered. Every move we make, every action, is one we must weigh carefully. You don't. You *never* have. It's been up to me to keep both of our hides safe, which I've done rather efficiently for *years*. Why should I take *you* seriously when you don't take *anything* seriously, not even our safety?

"I warned you," she continued, prodding a finger at him, "explicitly, not to come down here until I made sure we were secure, and you didn't listen. So, tell me, Sevi, after all your recent selfishness, why, in all Iaela, should I owe you a single godsdamned *thing?*"

Blood pumped in Sevi's ears. Lily watched him with a raised eyebrow. "Well?"

Something in him snapped. Yet his anger, so pervasive in every corner of his body, all drained away. He adopted a dispassionate stare, similar to the very ones she'd given him over so many years, and he leveled his head at her with an eyebrow raised in a perfect mirror of her own. Coldly, and very slowly, he said, "Remind me why I'm here, Lily."

Lily paused, showing faint cracks in her wintery mask. The uncertainty, no matter how faint, looked strange on her. "What?"

"Why am I here?" Sevi repeated, trying his best not to talk as patronizingly to her as she had to him.

"You're not supposed to be, which is why I want you to *leave*. Did you lose yourself again?" Lily scrunched her face at him. She looked as though he'd asked her what a rock was when they lived inside a mountain.

"No. Tell me, right now, why I'm living in these blazing *tunnels*."

She searched his face. "We've already had this conversation. It's safe here. No matter how hard you try to make it otherwise."

Sevi clenched his finger in the dust. "Safe from *what?* From the Fablings? Why would they care about *us?* I was a servant, and you were a gutter rat, right? We're nobodies. Yet year after year you make us stay here, with nothing but the cold, rocks and rats. All I have in this world is you, Alyda, and Shy, and you're the only one who talks. Yet all you ever tell me is, 'don't go out there, Sev, it's not safe out there, Sev,' as though it were any safer in here. So why am I here, Lily? What are we hiding from? And why should I listen to anything *you* say when you never actually say *anything?*"

Lily gaped at him, leaving Sevi to stare her down. He raised an eyebrow and crossed his arms in an imitation of her, trying to hide how badly he was shaking. "Well?"

She kept quiet, but her expression changed. It was still flat, but less harsh. More... vulnerable, somehow. He had taken the splinters in her face and deepened them, but not to the point where he could see beyond. She wouldn't let her facade slip entirely.

"I'm n-not moving," he pushed, "until you either tell me why I'm stuck like this, or what you're doing here." He wiped tears from his eyes, fixing her with a pleading look. He didn't want to fight anymore. He'd come here to make amends, not to make new arguments.

She kept staring at him. The silence that stretched between them was greater than any other, full of frustration, confusion, and things unsaid. Slowly, the ice in her face regrew until he gave up trying to read her altogether, leaving her to answer when she was ready.

"I..." Lily began slowly, shrugging one shoulder. "I don't know. I don't know, Sevi. I don't know why the two of us survived, but we did. We're here, and there's nowhere else to go. You *know* this, just as you know how dangerous Outside is. Just look at all the people they've filled this tower with. They don't look like *them*," she said, waving her hand aimlessly at the castle. "They look like us. If they catch us, they'll lock us up in here along with the rest, and we have no way of knowing how many Fablings there are out there. All of Elkra could be overrun, for all we know."

She paused, patting the stone brick of the inner wall for emphasis. "So, it's better to fight the enemy we know rather than the one we don't. *That's* why I'm here, alright? To keep you safe. Both of us. I'm doing what I have to, and I need you to trust that it's what's best. But I can't do that with you around making me worry. So please, Sev. *Please.* Go back. We can talk about this later."

Her softened toned made Sevi pause with no small amount of surprise. *Did she really just say 'please?'*

"What's best, Lily?" he asked, lowering his voice to match hers. "Please, give me something. Just... just let me know what's going on. I promise I won't get in your way. I'll stay quiet and do whatever you say. If this is my home, too, then let me help you protect it. We're partners, now and forever, right?"

Lily drew in a deep breath and let out a ragged sigh. "Stupid boy. Using my own words against me," she grumbled, kneading her brow in her hand. She turned to look at the spyhole, then back at Sevi, calculating something privately. Another silence passed where they regarded each other, but it felt less angry—perhaps even hopeful. Like the whole Cut was holding its breath in anticipation of her answer.

She rolled her eyes. "Fine. Fine! I'll let you keep watch with me."

It took a moment for Sevi to process her words. His body drooped, and he breathed out a slow breath. "Thank you, Lily."

"Never thought I'd see the day." She leveled a finger at him, fixing him with a serious expression. "Say that I know best."

He blinked. "You know best."

"Say that you're going to do what I say, when I say it."

"I'm going to do what you say, when you say it," he said without hesitation.

"Good. You can bet the Father that I'll hold you to your word, and if you even *think* about breaking it, then I'm going to throw your ass off the mountain and laugh every time you bounce."

She turned back to the peephole. Sevi could still feel his heart pumping as he edged closer to her, like a hammer beating through his chest. Emotions swirled around inside of him in a maelstrom, but they didn't pull him apart—they coalesced into the stunning realization that he'd actually stood up to her. And he'd *won*, or at least come to a compromise. And that meant more to him than anything else in the world, even more than whatever was happening on the other side of the wall.

# Chapter 8

*Bolstered in her grace, seeking peace with the girl, yet she dared the danger without fear! In their biting, their scratching, their harsh words of hurt, the warrior swayed in his bier.*

―――――――◦◦◦◦――――――――

"Look through here, and be quiet," Lily said, shifting aside. "You'll see the castle's new guest."

Pushing his eye to the wall, Sevi peered into the other room, only to stiffen in shock. The prisoner no longer stood proud and unbeaten but was sitting tied to a chair. His clothes were ripped and bloody, and his breathing was so labored that Sevi could hear it across the cell.

A hand slid across Sevi's mouth. Bringing his head back in surprise, he fixed Lily with an annoyed look. She pulled back after several breaths. "Just in case."

Turning back to the room, Sevi noticed that there were two soldiers lounging at its periphery. Neither was Captain Redwood. In fact, Sevi wasn't certain he'd ever seen them before. He couldn't recall their names, given or otherwise, and their uniforms, while green, looked to be more leathery than the normal garb of the castle soldiers.

"How long will it last?" the first one asked after a while. He was slender and had red hair that seemed to fade into feathers at the tips.

"Until he next takes a shit, then it's open season," said the second. He was bulky, with tight skin that seemed to fight to keep his muscles on his body, and when he moved, he left a wisp of smoke behind.

"I'm going to have him pull his nails off, one by one," the feathery one said with sadistic joy.

"I'd like to do something with needles. Haven't decided what though," the second one said, matching his comrade's tone.

Sevi pulled away, sickened, and whispered to Lily, "What's this all about?"

"Interrogation," she replied, leaning against the wall and lowering her voice to a soft whisper. "They're going to torture him."

Sevi glanced back at the wall. "It looks like they've already done that."

"No, they beat the crap out of him until he passed out. First for spitting on their prissy leader, then probably for daring to bleed on his uniform."

He grimaced. "Ah."

"Mm. Our hosts haven't been gentle."

"Why are you watching something like this?"

Lily bit her bottom lip in thought. He could almost see the wheels turning inside her head. "There's something odd about him. I watched him for a bit when I went down to save your skin. He's not just a criminal, he's a prize. And he..." She trailed off.

"He what?"

"He almost looked like he wants to be here."

Sevi furrowed his brow. The man had looked dignified in defeat, but eager for it?

"I know it's a silly thought," Lily said, "but he didn't look... I don't know, broken?" She scrunched her eyebrows together, as though trying to understand her own thoughts.

Sevi shrugged. "Maybe he's just proud."

She shook her head. "No, I saw his face. He almost looked like he was trying not to laugh. Who laughs in front of a mob of enemies? And when you think about it, if he's somebody important, why was he brought in alone? He absolutely would've had guards."

"Maybe they killed them?"

"No, no," she said absently. "Why deprive yourself of more prisoners to interrogate?"

Sevi hesitantly turned back to study the prisoner. He was older, with skin tanned by the sun, graying hair, and a beard. His strange military uniform sat tightly on his chest, as if just beneath it lay a slab of muscle that could rival that of the bulky guard's. The rope around his chest and limbs only enhanced the effect, spilling the excess of his form over the bonds.

He had slumped forward in his chair as far as the ropes would allow. What was visible of his face was mottled purple and red from a heavy-handed beating, and the shoulder of his jacket was stained red where Captain Redwood's sword had run him through, soaked up only by some haphazard bandages.

Sevi bit his lip. "Who is he, Lily? Where does he come from? Is... is the castle at war with someone?"

"That's what I was hoping to find out." Lily sighed.

The guards' conversation petered out when they both agreed that it was time for food, as there would be "plenty of time for fun with the prisoner afterward," as the first one put it. They left, shutting the door with an ominous *clang* that echoed along the tower's inner stairwell, leaving the prisoner entirely alone.

"Did I just hear them leave?" Lily asked, putting the ear of her helmet to the wall.

"Yes, they just walked out."

"Move aside."

Sevi stepped away, allowing Lily back in. He watched her face as she peered through, trying to gauge her thoughts from her expression. As the moments silently stretched on without any change, he eased himself into a seat against the stone and turned one ear against the wall, listening for anything interesting.

Enough time passed that the gravity of the situation lost its weight. Bored, Sevi scooped up small clumps of tiny pebbles and chucked them against the far wall, trying to get them as close as possible. He gave up after a while and finally asked, "What are we waiting for?"

Lily's shoulders jolted as though she had been dragged from a daydream. "I have a hunch," she said simply.

"About what?"

She paused, still staring through the wall. "I think he's... wait... ah." A smile curled on her face, giving her the smug 'I was right' look Sevi was so familiar with. "There he goes. What a lovely actor."

Sevi moved closer. "What? What's happening? What do you mean?"

"Our bloody friend is awake and breaking free of his rope," she said, still grinning. "I can't believe it. He probably faked the damage from his wounds early on. He's certainly old enough for a trick like that to work, but still, he must be built like a brick. Patient, too, to wait this long."

Sevi shot an amazed look at her. "And he's cutting himself loose? How did he get the knife?"

"I wouldn't call it a knife, but the clever bastard just threw up a metal tube. I'm guessing something sharp is inside."

"A metal tube?" If Sevi's eyes could have grown any wider, they would've eaten his forehead.

Lily nodded, giggling softly to herself. "Small enough to swallow and big enough to keep from coming out the other end, at least for a bit." She pulled away from the hole, waving Sevi over to take a look while she tried to regain her composure.

Sevi put his eye back to the peephole. The prisoner was still in his chair, but his chest had been drenched in vomit. On his lap was indeed a metal tube, which he was gingerly moving to his hand with gentle, practiced rocks of his body. When it had rolled down his thigh to his knees, he stretched out his bound hand and grabbed it, breaking into a grin that shone through his ruined face the moment it slipped into his fingers. He pressed his thumb into its top half until it popped off altogether, revealing a small knife. With a determined grunt, he reversed his grip on its handle and began slowly and methodically sawing at the rope around his wrist.

"He's cutting through!" Sevi exclaimed.

"I told you," Lily said, moving off to the side. "And for the last time, keep your voice down."

The man made agonizingly slow progress, managing only one strained motion per breath. But eventually, after many patient, purposeful cuts, the rope broke, and he moved swiftly to the others without pause, cutting each in almost no time at all. "Yes..." He exhaled loudly, standing up from the chair. "Aah, done with the easy part."

He muttered to himself, loud enough to echo around the cell. He groaned and stretched, clearly wracked with pain, but his back was straight with the same sturdy determination Sevi had seen in the throne room.

"Dumb goblin bastards." The prisoner placed a palm on the wall and started walking around the outskirts of the room, dragging his fingers along the stone. He seemed resolved to touch every single brick in the cell. "Where... this one... no... no..."

"Um, Lily." A cold trickle of fear ran down Sevi's spine as a sneaking suspicion washed over him. "He's free. And he's doing something."

"Is he?" Lily said apathetically, shifting rocks around behind him.

"Yes, I think he's—"

"Ha!" the man exclaimed, just on the other side of their wall.

Sevi jolted away from the peephole, starting as individual bricks were inexplicably pulled forward and away from him. Each one made a loud *thunk* that reverberated through the tunnel, as if some hidden mechanism was being locked into place.

Sevi shuffled backward, wide-eyed, until his back hit the opposite wall.

One by one, more and more bricks followed the first, and still Lily did nothing, leaving him to stare in horror alone. *Ka-thunk. Ka-thunk. Ka-thunk. Ka-thunk-brrrrrr.*

Sevi dug his fingers into the stone as the cell wall shifted completely, throwing up a cloud of dust and spilling light into the Cut. It slowly swung inward toward him, then stopped. The prisoner grunted and heaved his weight against it, refusing to let it rest, and it creeped forward once more.

"Yes, yes, I knew it! I knew it," the man said, over and over, until the narrow opening had grown wide enough for him to squeeze through. He ducked his head and crouched down onto all fours, tightly bending his enormous body to fit into the newly revealed passage with another round of muttering. "Why did they make it so sm—"

The man stopped mid-sentence, staring in shock at Sevi's shoes.

His gaze moved up, running along Sevi's leg and torso with gut-wrenching slowness, until he finally met his eyes. They were a startling blue—bluer than any icicle or flower Sevi had ever seen—and were so clear that he could almost see the man's thoughts beneath, working through some severe calculation.

Sevi's heart was ready to burst out of his chest. He broke into a cold sweat that quickly soaked his clothes. A torturous silence passed between them, more terrifying than nearly being caught by the cooks to be turned into stew. More than even Captain Redwood.

He'd always had a wall between him and the Outside, but the Cut had betrayed him. It had opened willingly for an *Outsider*.

*He knew. He knew about the Cut!*

"Who're *you?*" the prisoner demanded.

Then Lily slammed a rock across his head.

It connected with his skull with a heavy *thump*, sending him into the dust. He barely uttered a grunt before going limp and flopping to the stone.

Sevi frantically flicked his gaze from him to Lily and back. Lily regarded the would-be escapee for a long, long moment, then sighed and tossed the rock away. She turned to face Sevi and crossed her arms. "Want to help me with this?"

The floor stretched between them, growing as long as the mountain was tall, until Sevi observed Lily across a great distance. His chest bounced rapidly with panicked breaths until his sight went black around the edges, yet she was as impassive and serious as ever, regarding him through a mask once more.

He couldn't breathe. Couldn't think. Couldn't be. The walls seemed to squeeze at him, crushing inward, pressing any air from his lungs. What just happened? What *just* happened? *What did she just do?*

"Well?" Lily prompted.

The floor snapped back to its proper size, bringing him back to reality. His mouth, hanging open, had gone dry. He croaked, "W-what?"

"We need to get him back in his chair."

"What?"

"Help. Me. Put. Him. In. The. Room."

65

Sevi stared down at the prisoner's lifeless form. *Put him back in the room?*

"Those guards will be back soon, Sevi," Lily continued urgently. "We need to put him back and get this door closed before they arrive."

"But... they'll hurt him."

Lily rolled her eyes. "Yeeeess," she said slowly, "but they won't find the Cut, or more importantly, us."

"But—"

"Sev." Lily placed her hands on his shoulders. "This man knew about the Cut. He let himself get captured and came to our tunnels for a *reason*. Letting him go could spell disaster for us, so we need to cover ourselves and make sure that whatever he was planning *doesn't* happen."

Sevi closed his eyes and dragged in long, deep breaths, desperate for air, completely unable to order his thoughts. His insides were tearing him up again, with fear driving him to bolt. It became so much to bear that his head left his body altogether, floating up to the low-hanging ceiling where it couldn't experience what the rest of him felt.

"Come on, Sev," Lily said softly. "You promised."

He reached forward and took Lily's wrists, searching for a body to anchor him lest he float away completely. He was breaking. He couldn't let that happen.

Visions of hands pulling him out from under a kitchen table and throwing him onto a chopping block filled his mind, followed by an imposing man with glowing yellow eyes and a terrible smile. His recent failures. His lack of judgment. All coming to haunt him in this terrible moment. And beneath them, the flickers of a fire.

Lily was right. Lily was always right. She had always done what was best to keep them safe, *always*, while he always seemed to make a mess of things. What did he know, in the end? What could he possibly do other than follow her? What argument could he make after fiercely demanding to stay?

He never should have come.

"Al-alright." He managed a strained, weak smile. "Alright, Lily... y-you know best." He finally opened his eyes, watching her through a watery film of tears.

Lily stared at him intently, looking deeply into his eyes. Her mask broke, showing the expression beneath for a few fleeting breaths. It wasn't stern, but neither was it compassionate, and it retreated all too quickly. With a nod, she crawled back to the prisoner. "Get his other leg," she ordered.

Sevi hesitated for several moments before moving, taking one leg while Lily took the other. They both heaved together, straining under the large man's weight, only able to drag him by the barest of margins with every tug. Lily had said it best: the man was built like a brick.

Though he tried to fight it, Sevi couldn't help but be overcome by guilt. They were resigning this man to torture and death. He had been so brave, so clever, and so close to freedom. If only Lily hadn't been so perceptive.

The sound of a conversation intruded on his thoughts, echoing up the stairwell, and accompanied by the ominous sound of approaching footsteps. Sevi and Lily both froze, snapping their heads toward the cell door as the voices crept closer, and closer.

Lily recovered first. "His arms, get his arms!"

She frantically ran to the other side of the prisoner, pulling at him with a renewed sense of urgency. They had only managed to drag the man halfway out of the tunnel. His body, strewn across its threshold, prevented any chance of closing it. When the cell door opened, the way into the Cut would be laid bare for all to see, and two more chairs would be added to the room.

Sevi stood for an eternity before this realization successfully worked its way into his addled brain. Seeing this, the Fablings wouldn't think they were trying to put the prisoner back, but that they were helping him *escape!*

He dropped the man's leg and hurried to his arms, heaving him back into the Cut. The weight hadn't changed, but now he was aided by the strength that came with raw terror.

"*Move!*" Lily commanded in a furious whisper, pulling in desperation until the man's boots finally cleared the edge of the hidden door's frame. Lily immediately dropped his arm and scurried over to the open wall, throwing her weight against the door. Sevi joined her after only a moment's hesitation, praying that Mother Avinaea and Father Sorvathos were watching over them both as they pushed it back into place.

Stone hit stone, and the false bricks *thunked* back into their slots one after another, locking far too loudly. Not three breaths after, the cell door opened on squeaky hinges, and the two guards returned. Sevi and Lily both froze, pressing their ears to the stone and staring at each other with wide, scared eyes.

The first guard called out, "Ooooh wakey wakeyyy—"

His voice stopped short.

Silence from the wall. Tense. Anxious. The kind that had recently become too familiar.

"There's no one here," the second man said.

"I can see that."

More silence.

"Did he escape?"

"Must've."

Silence again.

"Captain Redwood won't like this."

Yet another, but this one stretched far, far longer than the others. Then the cell erupted with shouting.

"WHERE'D HE GO?"

"I DON'T KNOW! I DON'T KNOW!"

"SEARCH THE PLACE!"

"SEARCH WHERE? *THERE'S NOTHING HERE!*"

"CHECK THE WALLS! CHECK THE FUCKING CORNERS!"

"MAYBE HE'S INVISIBLE!"

"MAYBE!"

Sevi's eyes flicked nervously to the peephole, then up at Lily. She shook her head at him, mouthing *no* with a very heavy brow, looking ready to pounce on him if he dared as much as a glance.

He'd promised to do whatever she said, but the fear inside him was too great. If they found the false wall, they'd have to start running. He needed to risk it.

He dove forward and peered into the room. The guards were frantically looking over every pebble, brick, and speck of dust that littered the floor with anguished expressions. They took hold of and tugged at the window's iron bars, and all but danced around in the middle of the room with flailing arms as if they could pull their missing prisoner out of thin air.

Lily curled her fingers in his hair and tugged, yanking his head away from the hole. She gave him an unkind glare and emphatically put a finger to her lips.

Then someone new spoke, and her eyes went wide.

"Hello, gentlemen," Captain Redwood said in a smooth, dispassionate voice.

"Captain Redwood!" The two guards echoed in unison, ceasing their scuffle.

"Gentlemen... where is our honored guest?"

"I... we—"

"Because, to me, it looks like he's not in bed." Captain Redwood spoke coolly, but there was a layer of cruelty beneath his words. Patient. Hungry.

"He... he's—"

"He, he, he's not here. Is that it? Is that what you're trying to say?"

The guards were silent.

"Well?"

"Yes. Yes, sir."

"That's what I thought."

What followed were the most violent and miserable screams of pain that Sevi had heard in his entire life. The ground reverberated faintly as each man fell to the floor, one after the other, crying out sharply with loud, anguished wails that echoed far too well in the tight confines of the cell.

Sevi's gaze shifted back to the peephole, but once more, Lily put her hand out and covered his mouth, forcing his head up. She looked pale and more frightened than he'd ever seen her, with eyes as wide as saucers. Her jaw clenched tighter and tighter the longer the men's screaming continued, until she looked certain to break her teeth.

Their cries weakened over time, dulling into pitiful whimpers before cutting off all at once. For a dozen breaths, nothing moved. No one spoke. It was a silence Sevi had never experienced, and it was far, far too horrible.

"Hmph." The captain drew something steely from a scabbard. There was the sound of wet meat being cut, then another long pause. Time seemed to slow. Dizziness swept over Sevi, wrapping around him and stealing his strength.

"Matron?" Redwood said.

A voice came from further away. "Yes, sir?"

"Put the guard on high alert and clean up this filth."

"Yes, sir."

The captain's footsteps stomped away, the cell door slammed shut, and Sevi fell to the ground and wept.

# Chapter 9

*Meant as his tomb, and now his salvation, from its lid he leapt out with a yell! The girl, unforgiving, once more bared her thorns, and down the old warrior fell.*

S evi curled himself into a ball with his hands clasped to his ears, trying and failing to staunch the haunting, painful wails that lingered. Lily paced back and forth, muttering under her breath and kicking at any impudent rock that dared to get in her way. "Blackest night," she cursed. "Stupid. Stupid. *Stupid!*"

Sevi looked away, unable to keep himself from wondering if somehow this had been all his fault again. He never should have come here. He should've left when he had the chance.

"That's enough, Sevi," Lily called, but she may as well have been on the other side of the mountains. Her voice sounded so incredibly far away.

Lily marched over and smacked him behind the head. "Get. Up," she hissed through her teeth.

Sevi looked up at her but didn't stand. The barest amount of comprehension crossed his mind as he stared into her eyes, fiery and filled with determination. *Brave Lily*, he thought. *Always in control.*

"For all Gods' sake, *get. Up*. You're leaving."

"Leaving," Sevi echoed hollowly.

"Yes. Out of here, right now," she ordered, pointing toward the duct. He tried to do as she said, pushing his wobbling arms against the ground, and managed to lift himself from his fetal position. But his legs shook too violently once he got his knees beneath him, and he only fell back down with a small, choked gasp.

"I can't," he mumbled, slumping back against the wall and bringing his knees to his chest.

Lily gritted her teeth but said nothing. She crossed her arms and walked back and forth as best as she could. She was short, but even she had to hunch over in the tunnel. It would've looked comical in any other situation.

But then she stopped. The anger drained from her face all at once, replaced by her stony, emotionless mask. It surprised Sevi enough to break him from his despondency. He stared at her through watery eyes, searching for the cause, and only putting it together when she bent down to grab a large rock slab with both hands. She hoisted it up to her chest and turned to the prisoner with a dangerous look in her eye.

A part of Sevi split from the rest of himself in a way he'd never felt before, slipping into his limbs and forcing him from the floor. He bolted up from his seat before he even knew what he was doing, scrambling through the dust as much as his shaky, uncertain self would allow, and forced himself between Lily and the prisoner.

He stood before her, hunched over and jutting his chin out in a weak attempt to look resolute.

Lily regarded him frigidly. "Out of the way, Sevi."

"N-no," Sevi stuttered, trembling.

"*Move.*" Lily clenched her jaw, and for a moment, he was frightened that she might hit him with the rock instead.

"*No*," Sevi repeated, fiercely rubbing his eyes, "No m-more."

The screams of Redwood's guards continued to keen in his mind. He could only envision what had happened to them, and his unbridled imagination held no end of grisly thoughts. He couldn't allow Lily to become like Redwood. He couldn't let her kill a helpless man. She wasn't a monster like him.

"If I don't do this," Lily said, taking a purposeful step toward him, "he will threaten our home. He'll threaten us. He'll kill us in our sleep or reveal us to the Outside."

"I d-don't care." Sevi kept his chin set, unmoving. "No more, Lily. This... this is too much. You're not a killer. *We're* not killers."

"I'll be whatever I have to be to keep us safe. And since you're finally up, why don't you, at long last, get out of here while I take care of this."

"No. I'm not—"

"What I say, when I say it," she said. "You *promised*."

Sevi snapped his jaw shut and closed his eyes, but he didn't move. "I didn't promise to help you kill anyone. I just... I just wanted to *help* you."

"You can help me by leaving." She tried to get past him again, but he stopped her once more. Her scowl deepened a frightening amount.

"No. There's... there's another way," he said.

Lily snorted derisively. "Please. What else could we do, oh trembling one?"

"W-we get him out. Out of the Cut. Before he wakes up."

Lily actually laughed at that, belting out a short bark that sounded half-crazed around the edges. "Do you remember the combination of bricks this guy pulled from the wall? Because I don't."

"We don't put him back in the room. We—"

"*Excuse* me?"

"We don't put him back. We bring him to the mines."

Her jaw dropped in disbelief. "I think I have cotton in my ears."

"Lily—"

"*Don't.*"

The walls sang with the force behind the one word, echoing it over and over again in layers until it softly tapered out. She clamped her mouth shut. "Don't '*Lily*' me," she said, quieter. "Together we're not even half this man's weight, and we'd have to carry him down the tower, through the tunnels, over the cliff's chasm, up the rope of the escarpment, and then, finally, we'd have to unseal the tunnel to the mines, then reseal it, and all before he wakes up."

Her gaze could've bored a hole through a mountain. Sevi was quiet for a long, long moment, maintaining the standoff with her. He couldn't yell back; his anger had deserted him. He couldn't flee; that would mean abandoning the prisoner. He had to try to reason with her.

"I... h-have rope. Still only lightly worn. We could... we could tie it around him and l-lower him down the chute. Then we could d-drag him, at least to the cliff. I don't... don't know how we'll get him up the ledge... maybe tie him to the tree and pull him up. The escarpment... Also a problem. But the soldiers don't go into the mines, and the geisthounds can't smell us underground. He'll be safe there. Safer. We don't have to tell him about the poison in the mountain."

"Or we could just crush his head and be done with it."

"Lily! *Stop!*" Sevi nearly screamed. He balled his fists and pushed all the emotions swirling around his belly into his eyes, hitting her with the full force of his passion. "You are *not* going to kill this man! *You are not a monster!*"

Lily reeled her head back in surprise. Her mouth dropped open, moving wordlessly up and down as though her voice had gotten lost in her throat. When it found its way out after several breaths of silence, it wasn't hers.

"Or, jus' an idea, he could walk the whole bloody way on his own damn legs, thank you."

Lily and Sevi quickly spun about. The prisoner was shaking his head and groaning, fully awake, albeit in obvious pain given the strain on his face. "Godsdamn it, my head hurts," he grumbled, wearily getting up on all fours and lolling his head to look at them both. "Can't tell if it's the beatin' that done it, or you two starlings yammerin' like old lovers."

Lily grabbed a fistful of Sevi's shirt and yanked him back, forcing herself between him and the man. "You stay away," she said, brandishing her rock as if to throw it at his head, "or I *will* kill you."

"I have no doubt about that, little lass," he groaned. A muttering stream of complaints about his many aches and bruises fell from his lips with every stretch. "So I s'pose it's good that we want the same thing."

"Your skull caved in like crushed fruit?"

"Me out o' these tunnels, and out o' yer hair," the man chuckled, unperturbed by her threats or her rock. "And after that little show in me old cell—"

"When did you wake up?" Lily demanded.

The man shrugged. "About midway of me former guards gettin' the stick. But as I were sayin, after that little show and your... tasteful greetin,' I need to get a move on. However..." He eyed them thoughtfully. "I'll reckon you rats know all this castle's dirty secrets. The mines, was it?"

Sevi reached out and put a hand on Lily's shoulder. She darted a look back at him, trying to hide her emotions, but her mask had enough cracks to see the heat of her anger beneath. The situation had spiraled completely out of her control—a first in however long he'd known her.

He stared at her for several breaths, then looked to the prisoner, who watched him with a surprisingly patient expression. It was the second time he'd ever met a stranger's eyes. He felt himself shy away, but the man made no move to attack.

The prisoner's movements were sluggish, his breathing heavy, and blood ran down his face from where Lily had struck him. Though he was large, a fact only emphasized by the narrow tunnel, there was a deep weariness in his face, no matter how hard he seemed to try to hide it. He looked barely alive as it was.

"Lily," Sevi whispered, "I want him gone, but I won't kill him."

"You won't have to," she said darkly, glaring at the man from the corner of her eye.

"And if you try," Sevi continued, squeezing her shoulder, "I'll..."

"You'll what?" Lily muttered.

He met her eyes but couldn't bring himself to answer. He would never try to hurt her, but he wouldn't hurt this man either. It was unthinkable, even when confronted by Lily's cold logic. And the man didn't appear to be outright hostile—wary, maybe, but his cordial demeanor was entirely different from what Sevi might have expected from someone who had taken a full day's worth of beatings. Maybe they could work together.

"Tick tock, missy," the man said. "I'll be on me way soon, and I may make a little more noise than needed if I happen ta get lost. Which I'm certain is more likely to happen than not, considerin' this fresh bump on me head."

He said it in a lilting tone, but the insinuated threat was clear as day, and Sevi's hopes of compromise waned as Lily stiffened beneath his touch.

She eyed Sevi once more. His heart thumped painfully, as though it would rather flee his body than suffer her stare. He shook his head and clenched her shoulder in a silent plea. She slumped, and with a tired groan, she very pointedly dropped the rock with a *crack*.

Sevi let out a breath he hadn't realized he'd been holding. Lily swatted his hand off and crossed her arms. The man nodded approvingly. "Good. I think it'd be best if we all just get along, eh? I'll even pay ya as a show o' me goodwill. Got somethin' ya want?"

"You knew about these tunnels," Lily said, bulling past his offer. "Why don't you just make your way yourself?"

"Aye, suppose I could. But I only had a partial map, and me memories aren't so good anymore."

She tilted her head. "A map?"

"To help me get out," he said gruffly.

"Did you come here on purpose?"

He barked a laugh. "Does it look like I did?"

Lily said nothing.

"Will ya help me or not, kid?"

She shook her head and turned back to Sevi. "Get in front and lead the way."

"Me?" Sevi flicked his gaze between her and the prisoner.

"This was your idea," Lily said tersely, arching her eyebrow. "*You* do the work."

The prisoner chuckled. "An' if I try anythin' the missy clubs me from behind again?"

"That's right, *chum*," Lily said, mimicking his accent. "What was it you said?" She reached up her sleeve and yanked out a small rusty blade, holding it loosely at her side. The man's eyes flicked down to it. She grinned a wicked smile. "You'll get the *stick*."

# Chapter 10

*Hushed by his presence, scared for their home, they sought the warrior's sleep. But the dragon came stomping with intention most dire, thus the company of two were made three.*

Sevi led the way down the tower with one eye always looking up. Partly to check that the prisoner wasn't trying anything, and partly to check that Lily hadn't stabbed him when he wasn't looking. One of these things, Sevi felt, was more likely to happen than the others.

Their progress was slow going. The prisoner not only had to fight his injuries, but also the tightness of the tunnels. Sevi had never considered it before, but after watching the man struggle to squeeze himself through the various corners and chokepoints, he realized that an adult would naturally have a much worse time navigating the Cut than he would himself. It was a comforting thought.

Getting down the tower itself was as much of a task as expected. The soldier seemed constantly in danger of losing his grip in the chute, cursing and yelping in surprise whenever his foot or hand gave out. Sevi winced over all the noise, in competition with the loud thumping of his heart. He wondered how exactly they were supposed to get up the rope to the Overlook if the man seemed so intent on alerting every blazing person in the castle on the way.

He wasn't sure what would be worse: getting caught, or Lily saying "I told you so." But he couldn't give the man too much grief—Sevi knew just how frustrating a body's treachery could be. The prisoner was right to hate it.

The man *was* above him though. And if his grip failed, he'd fall right on top of Sevi's head and squash him flat. He hurried along down the chute, putting some distance between himself and the others until he finally hit the bottom and stepped aside, watching as the two gradually caught up with him.

"Quick one, aren't you, lad?" The prisoner huffed, stepping down.

Sevi shrugged, watching Lily touch down shortly after and covertly draw her knife.

"Yeah... So. What be yer names?" the man continued. Sevi shuffled awkwardly. The man stretched himself out as best as he could with a sigh, watching him expectantly.

Sevi hadn't expected any sort of conversation. And strangely, the man's tone and expression continued to be entirely at odds with their circumstances—jovial, unbothered, even oblivious. As though he were taking a stroll through a garden among friends rather than stealing away within a secret network of tunnels, surrounded by enemies, and beaten to a pulp.

"Se—" Sevi started to respond, but a flash of Lily's eyes behind the prisoner made him stop.

"'Seh?' C'mon, lad, you can do it." The man chuckled.

"What do you care?" Lily interjected. "We won't know each other long enough for it to matter."

"Aye, but it's downright awkward with you lot. You must be the grimmest kids I've ever met. And what's with the helmet?"

"Awkward?" Lily laughed cheerlessly. She quickly clapped a hand over her mouth. "You're funny. You remind me of one of the clowns the garrison brought up last summer. What was his name again... Blumpo? Blambo? Blumpkin! That was it! I'm going to call you Blumpkin from now on."

The man quirked an eyebrow. "Aye, I suppose that's one o' me better defining features. Wanna hear a joke?"

"No. Get moving, Blumpkin."

"What do you get—"

"I don't care."

He continued anyway. "—when you cross a fairy with a sword?"

"I still don't care."

"A fairy's tail. Get it? Cause you kill—"

Sevi stifled a laugh. Not at the awful joke, but the situation. It was about as absurd as a fever dream.

The man brightened. "See? The lad likes it."

"We can't all have refined tastes, Blumpkin."

"The name's Digby, actually."

"No, it isn't."

"Yes, it is."

"Not anymore, Blumpkin. Now move."

Digby chuckled but settled into silence as they walked. Sevi wondered again at the man. Where was he getting all his enthusiasm?

They eventually arrived at the cliff exit. Digby exhaled a sigh as the tunnel opened up and allowed his hulking form more space. Lily never took her eyes off him, maintaining a cold, hard glare, and fiddling with her knife more than Sevi was comfortable with. He tried not to worry as he turned away, shifting the brush to the cliffside.

Then the tunnels erupted with a loud, whistling roar, making him jump back.

All three of them turned to stare down the passage leading toward the kitchen. It was alight with a flickering orange glow, and thrashing sounds echoed from what could only be his and Lily's room.

*Blazes.* Just what he needed right now.

"What is that?" Digby asked. "Should I be worried?"

"It's the firedrake," Sevi said. "It must've woken up."

"Firedrake? What?" Digby scrunched his face.

"Yes... I'll go calm it down," Sevi said, taking a step forward.

"Leave it be," Lily said, stopping him.

"It could burn up our room!"

"Yeah, well, don't you think we have bigger problems right now? Like. A *lot* bigger. Particularly around the middle."

Digby grunted. "Har har."

Sevi didn't say anything, keeping his attention on the drake's crackling roars. "I can't afford to lose that blanket, Lily. I'll never get through the winter."

Lily groaned, grabbing her helmet with both hands and pulling it down tightly on her skull. She spoke in a slow, patronizing tone. "This kind man here would like to leave. What kind of hosts would we be if we didn't show him the door?"

"But—"

"If your blanket burns, I'll get you a new one—that's to say if this is *actually* about your blanket. We can come back when we're done with him, *alright?*" She shot him a not-so-subtle look that screamed, '*I told you so.*'

Sevi looked between her and the tunnel as another plume of fire billowed up, trailing smoke up along the ceiling and venting through the exit. Sevi took a deep breath. Letting the firedrake rampage itself to sleep was the smart thing to do. Lily was right, there were bigger things to worry about, and the drake was such a scary thing when it was awake. Best to leave it be.

The reasoning almost worked.

"I need to go, Lily."

"SEVI."

"I'll be right back!"

Sevi sprinted down the tunnel before she could say anything else, careening toward the firelight. The air grew hotter and dryer the closer he got, lightly toasting his skin as he entered the bedroom and fell through a wall of boiling heat.

The firedrake was fully awake and very unhappy. It growled deep enough to shake its whole body, reverberating with hot air as it circled in place, snapping at nothing with hungry, restless bites. Flames licked out from wherever it stepped, filling the room with sparks and smoke until it got too painful to breathe.

Covering his mouth, Sevi stood on tiptoe and pulled a loose stone out of the outside wall, trying to get as much of the fetid air out as he could.

The firedrake whipped its serpentine head around to face him and roared out a dull, crackling hiss. Sevi jumped and flattened himself against the stone, at once imagining the drake's molten maw sinking into his bare skin, crunching bone and burning marrow with every bite.

Taking a deep, shaky breath, he inched along the outskirts of the room toward his treasure, taking slow, measured movements while sweating profusely. He couldn't allow himself to look away from the salamander, fearing the moment he did would be the moment it attacked, but the deeper he stared into its eyes, the more sluggish he became, until he finally stopped completely.

Something came over him. A numb feeling that coursed through his brain and down his body, making his breath catch. The flames coiling out of the salamander moved hypnotically, curling and uncurling in a deadly, beautiful dance that demanded his attention. Wafting across the room to wrap around him, the flames tugged at something inside his belly, threatening to pull him inside-out, if he only allowed them to.

The firedrake coiled its back and sprung its front legs forward in a terrifying roar of challenge, and its hold on him broke with a jolt. Sevi snapped to attention and jerked away, abandoning all caution as he dove for his treasure, shoving a pile of rubble aside to get to his hidden box.

Fishing it out, he opened it and swiftly extracted the long silver necklace inside. Its thick, gleaming star pendant swung for a moment, glinting in the salamander's light before he shoved it into his pocket and tossed its empty container aside.

The firedrake kept its stance and hissed at Sevi like a kettle. In his panic, Sevi had half a mind to throw the pail of water on the creature and be done with it, just as Lily had always wanted.

But even now, he couldn't do it. With a grunt of frustration, he instead took the pail and dumped the water in a semicircle around the drake's alcove and out toward their beds, fireproofing the room as best as he could. There was nothing else he could think to do.

The firedrake immediately coiled back, hissing as a single claw touched the deadly liquid, sending up a cloud of steam. It glared hatefully at Sevi, but it made no move to attack.

"That's the best I can do, Shy," Sevi mumbled. He pointed a finger at the drake while he backed away. "You better not b-burn up our stuff!"

The drake hissed even louder, the flames around it brightened, and Sevi bolted from the room before he got burned.

When he got back to the tunnel, he found Digby, for his part, looking very relaxed, having taken the time to lounge on the ground with a restful expression. Lily, meanwhile, was the exact opposite, standing with her arms crossed tautly across her chest a safe distance away. She stared daggers at Sevi when he emerged, covered in soot.

"Um... I—"

"Get moving," Lily snapped, cutting him off.

Digby grunted, slowly getting to his feet. "Get it all sorted, lad? That was quick as a dragonfly."

"Yes... everything's fine." Sevi sighed, wiping his face.

"Hardly." Lily scoffed. "Now get moving. I'm tired of all this excitement."

"A firedrake, was it?" Digby continued.

"Yes." Sevi fell uncertainly back into place at the head of their column.

Digby looked down the tunnel where the lizard's light still flickered. "Never seen one o' them before."

Sevi shrugged his shoulders noncommittally, not knowing what to say. Maybe they didn't have firedrakes in the Outside, but he had them in the Cut. He stepped out of the hole and turned around to help the man. Digby was in even worse shape after his climb down the tower, and he struggled with getting out.

"Hrrm. Well. 'Sevi' and 'Lily,' was it?" Digby said, taking Sevi's hand in his. Sevi tried to pull him out, but the man stayed put, only smiling at him from the dark of the tunnel. "Nice to meet you both." Digby pumped his hand in a shake.

Sevi's mouth fell gently open. Lily's helmet shook behind Digby, catching the distant light of the firedrake, and a tired groan sighed out from underneath it.

Sevi gritted his teeth and stifled the urge to throw himself off the cliff before Lily got the chance.

The way up the cliff ledge was, as everyone suspected, an issue. Digby could only manage to pull himself up a single handspan every dozen breaths or so, and Sevi couldn't lift his weight from the top no matter how hard he pulled. Lily lazed about below, watching with mild, cynical amusement.

Sevi's nerves frayed with anxiety every moment he was out in the open. He could hear the sound of soldiers moving frantically around just on the other side of the wall, searching for their lost prisoner throughout the castle grounds.

Then the sound of braying geisthounds rose above the din, and he gulped, praying that the wind would not favor them. The hounds could jump as high as two stories if motivated. If they caught their scent the cliffside's castle wall would be a trifle for them to scale, and there would be nowhere to hide.

After a palm-sweatingly exorbitant amount of time, Digby managed to crawl over the ledge, and after a period of rest that took even longer, they got him on his feet and lumbering into the mountain tunnels.

Upon moving far enough away from the entrance, Sevi brought out a makeshift torch for Digby's sake and lit it, shying away from the flame. The man had trouble moving in the dim subterranean light and seemed perpetually distracted by the plants. He jumped in surprise when they curled away from the light of the fire.

Shaking his head, Digby turned toward the torchlight, then froze. "What in Iaela," he muttered, staring at the ground.

Sevi followed his gaze. "What is it?"

"Where's your shadow?"

Digby held out his arm, demonstrating how it blocked the light, while no part of Sevi did. Sevi blinked. He'd gotten so used to not having one that he'd stopped considering it an oddity. "Oh. Um. They ran away."

Digby looked incredulously at him. "Come again?"

Sevi shrugged. "I'm looking for them."

"Stop talking, start walking," Lily grumbled, taking the torch from Sevi and ending their conversation.

Digby gave Sevi an odd look that he felt on the back of his head when he turned around. He did his best to ignore it.

Upon reaching the Overlook's escarpment, Digby stopped and stared hopelessly up the sheer rock wall, leaning heavily against the side of the cave. "By Vikellin. I can see why the lass has her doubts," he said, sounding concerned for the first time.

"What, you don't think you can manage it, Blumpkin?" Lily gibed.

"Maybe with a full brew of coffee and a body that wasn't held together by aught but its skin. Me arm has gone limp after all this squirreling around, and the wound on my shoulder has ripped open." He peered underneath his bloodstained coat and winced visibly at what he saw.

Lily watched him, then turned on Sevi. "Alright, little hero, this was your idea. What now?"

Sevi opened his mouth to say, "I'm not sure," when a thought struck him. Something Digby had said gave him an idea. The longer he thought about it, the more it invigorated him. "Coffee, you said?"

Digby raised his eyebrows at Sevi. "Aye, but that was more banter than anythin'."

"I... may have something," Sevi said slowly.

"Oh Gods, not again." Lily groaned.

"It's alright, Lily." Sevi smiled, looking toward the garden tunnel. "You'll like it this time."

Lily turned to follow his gaze. He watched her face, reading all the familiar ways it shifted while she pieced together his plan in her usual quick-witted way. She hummed. "I see. Be fast, then."

Sevi turned toward the tunnel. Digby asked, "What's happening?"

"Shut up and lie down, Blumpkin. He'll be a while," Lily said.

Sevi spared one last glance at the two before moving away at a light jog. When the torchlight had disappeared altogether, and the full light of the mountain's plants came into focus, he adjusted his eyepatch and squared his shoulders, jogging through the mountain as quickly as he could. He had a plant that could get Digby up the cliff.

A fair while later he came skidding to a halt in the garden's chamber, cursing how long it took to climb so high. Golden light filtered in from above, basking the room in the evening's fading glow. Sevi doubled over, gasping for air, and called out between breaths. "Ah. Alyda! Are you here?"

It took several moments, but a plant finally rustled, and the small fairy girl emerged with a yawn from beneath the blanket of a large leaf. She turned groggily and stared at Sevi with a weary, twinkling chime, rubbing her eyes and looking cross.

"Hey, Alyda, I'm sorry. It's an emergency," Sevi panted.

Alyda's ears perked up at that. She stood on shaky legs and lifted off from the leaf, flying to him and stopping a comfortable distance away. She stretched out her limbs with a crack of joints, then crossed her arms expectantly for several breaths before flicking her hands. "*This better be important.*"

"I need that plant with the blue leaves and purple petals. You replanted it somewhere, right?"

Alyda quirked her head to the side and traced a shape in the air with her finger.

"No, not the one with heart petals, the thinner ones that look like bristles."

Alyda thought for a moment, then noticeably brightened in both expression and light. She waved at him and took off in the opposite direction, darting into the plants.

Sevi followed closely around the outside, doing his best to avoid stepping on his garden until he had to. He found her close to the center, heaving a large leaf aside in her little arms, and letting out a grateful chime when Sevi helped. Beneath it was the exact flower he was looking for, with healthy purple nettles and a vibrant blue stem.

"Yes! Perfect! Is this the only one?"

Alyda chimed uncertainly, pointing to the rest of the garden and then making an 'x' with her arms. "*It's the only one I know about.*"

"Ah, hmm." Sevi hesitated. "Are the seeds ready to be harvested?"

Alyda hovered up to the flower's mouth and pushed her hand into the center of it, sinking her arm in down to her shoulder and rummaging around. After a dozen or so breaths, she withdrew with a frown and shook her head. Empty.

If he wanted to help Digby, Sevi would have to uproot the only flower.

Sevi felt his enthusiasm fade. "I, um." He sighed. There really wasn't a choice. "When you go out again, would you please look for another one?"

Alyda nodded firmly, entwining her fingers and cracking her knuckles. "*Count on it.*"

Sevi steeled himself. "I'm sorry. You're going to help someone," he whispered to the plant. Pinching the flower's stem at the base, he carefully pulled it from the ground with a sickening snap of roots. He winced as it came free, cradling it in his open palms. He hoped it would be enough, otherwise he would've killed it for nothing.

"I've got to go again. Wish me luck. I'm... well, I'm not sure if this will work." He laughed nervously, looking from the plant to his friend.

Alyda gestured for him to elaborate.

"There's a stranger in our tunnels," he said, making her eyes widen in surprise. "He's badly hurt, and we need to get him up to the mines. Do you remember what this did to Lily?"

Alyda paused, then broke into a smirk as she signed, "*I remember all too well.*"

"I'm going to give it to him and hope that it's enough. Thanks for your help. I'll be back to tell you how it went."

She nodded and gave him a firm, shooing wave. "*I expect you to. Now, get out of here.*"

He returned a weak smile and quickly reached to her with a hand, which she leaned into and hugged, before retreating off a distance and shooing him away once more.

He turned around and left, unsure of his plan, but eager to try.

When he got back to the others, he was surprised to see not just Digby lounging about but Lily as well. She had even slipped her visor down to shade her eyes from the torch, which she had passed off to Digby.

"Ah. The lad's back," Digby mumbled, almost sounding disappointed. He propped himself up with a strained groan. "Thank the gods. The lass isn't much of a talker. Find another firedrake out there?"

Lily tipped her visor up with a finger and tilted her head to look at Sevi but made no move to get up. "What'd you bring?"

Sevi, still catching his breath, presented the flower to them. "This... um. This should help. I think."

Digby squinted and moved the torch in Sevi's direction. "Is that a weed?"

"It's a flower. I call it a Violet Crown."

"How is a weed going to help?"

Lily laughed. Digby looked at her, confused. Sevi swallowed a lump in his throat. "Um... it makes you feel awake, and... it does something that makes you forget how tired you are. Kind of like coffee. When you grind its leaves and roots... and the flower petals can help with headaches. But um..."

Digby stared at him in disbelief. "All o' that in one silly little weed?"

"Flower," Sevi mumbled.

"Sevi ground one up for my breakfast once, looking for a new herb," Lily said, standing up. "I don't think I slept that night."

"That *night?*" Digby repeated incredulously.

"Well, no. Maybe it was an hour. Time got all... narrow? You get what I mean. I'll say this though" —she chuckled— "when the effects wore off, I dropped like a stone."

Digby shook his head. "And where did you come by this, lad?"

Sevi didn't say anything, only offering another noncommittal shrug. He looked at Lily as she walked over, nodding to herself. "I think this could work," she said, taking the flower from him. "We grind this up, feed it to him, he rattles so hard his shirt falls off, and we get him up this rock and out of our lives. Everyone wins."

Digby grunted, leaning forward. "Aye, out of your lives, but I'd prefer the shirt stays on, thank you."

Lily snorted. "So would we all."

"Alright then, glad we're in agreement. Give it here, lass."

"In a moment, just wait there." Lily tore off the roots and handed the stem back to Sevi. "Grind up the leaves; I'll do the roots."

Sevi nodded and did as he was asked. On a thought, he ground up the flower's purple petals as well—Digby looked like he could use all the help he could get. Gathering everything up and chucking the barren stem away, Sevi and Lily both brought the plant powder to Digby and lightly settled it in his cupped palms.

Sevi said, "This will take a little while. Um..."

"And when it hits, you'll want to run the length of the castle and back," Lily continued for him. "But you can't let yourself. Even though you'll be feeling fine, your body is still injured. I don't need you falling to pieces before we get you out—not after all this work." She cocked her head. "Well, actually—"

"Aye, aye, no need for that," Digby waved her away, looking doubtful. "Well, here we go." With a tip of his head, he threw back everything at once, grimacing the moment it hit his tongue, but he managed to swallow it all in one go. "Oooh, *gods of sun and harvest,* that's *bitter!*"

Lily laughed. "But you cleaned your plate."

Digby hacked up a series of gross-sounding coughs. "Do either of ya have any water?"

"You're being dramatic," Lily said.

"No, I really don' think I am." He coughed again, rubbing his tongue with the back of his sleeve. "But fine. Alright. What now?"

"Now you wait here." Lily took Sevi by the arm and turned him away from Digby, lowering her voice. "Can you watch him for me?"

Sevi lowered his voice to match hers, but his eyebrows flew up at the suggestion. "Why?"

"I'm going to go on ahead. Something isn't sitting right with me," she muttered. "Blumpkin has to be a scout. For who, I don't know, but the Fablings really didn't like him—even more than the other humans they've locked up in the tower. And none of them ever had a uniform like his. Maybe some of his friends are waiting for him nearby, ready to rescue him."

Sevi felt a chill climb up his spine at the thought of more strangers in their tunnels. "What are you going to do?"

Lily grimaced and shook her head. "I'm going topside. Going to take a peek around with my spyglass, see if anything or anyone stands out." She trailed off, reaching up to tiredly wipe her face. She left her hand on her mouth, observing him from over her fingers. "But I don't like leaving you alone with him," she said softly.

Sevi glanced over at Digby. He had been watching them the entire time with his hands folded in his lap. He gave Sevi a polite smile and a little wave. Sevi eyed him, biting his lip. "Go on, Lily," he said after some deliberation. "Digby has been beaten half to death, and he doesn't know the Cut like I do. If he tries anything, or if we get into trouble, I'll call you with my whistle."

Lily said nothing for a while, regarding him with a heavy brow. "Sevi, a lot has happened today. Are you sure?"

"Yes... Yes, I think so." Sensing an opportunity, Sevi turned his mouth up in a sudden smirk. "Are you going soft on me, Flowergirl?"

Lily paused, then punched him in the arm. "Shut up."

"Worry over me like that, and I'll start to think you actually like me." He grinned, rubbing his shoulder.

"In the same way somebody still likes their puppy after it peed all over the floor." She shook her head, but she bore a wide smile full of teeth; the kind Sevi rarely got to see on her.

Sevi chuckled, lapsing into a comfortable silence with her.

"Ahem." Digby coughed. "Are you two done conspirin'?"

Lily didn't look over, saying softly to Sevi, "Try to stay focused while I'm gone, alright? No more close calls. No getting friendly with him. And yell if he tries anything." She gave him an encouraging pat, then walked over to the escarpment, grabbing a hold of the rope.

"I'm going up," she called. "The tunnel to the mine is blocked. I'm going to start unsealing it. Sevi will stay here with you and make sure the poison works."

Digby straightened his back. "Poison?"

Lily flashed a dangerous grin at him, saying nothing more as she hauled herself up. Her helmet caught the torchlight just as she disappeared over the edge.

"She was kiddin', right, lad?" Digby asked Sevi cautiously.

"Oh yes, yes of course, I would, I could never, I don't even h-have poisonous plants!" Sevi stuttered, frantically trying to assure him. "At least that I know of!"

"That you know of?" Digby repeated.

"I didn't poison you," Sevi amended.

Digby stared at him, but nodded, leaning back against the stone with a tired huff. "Aye... alright... Well. The lass has got a wicked tongue, hasn't she?"

"You have no idea."

They shared a look. Digby broke into a slow grin. Sevi felt himself doing the same, until they both chuckled.

"Aye, I suppose you would have it worse," Digby said.

Sevi didn't reply, looking up at the lip of the escarpment as his smile faded.

"How'd you meet her?"

Sevi stayed silent. *No getting friendly with the prisoner.*

Digby watched him, and when he continued to say nothing, he waved a dismissive hand. "Aye, well, you two make the pair. Can't believe you're both mad enough to be scrambling around in here."

Sevi shrugged, unsure of what to say. It wasn't any more dangerous than Outside.

"Do ya ever leave?"

"No," Sevi said, averting his eyes. *As much as I'd like to.*

Digby furrowed his brow. "Why?"

"It's not safe." *Stop talking to me.*

Digby's expression turned skeptical. "It'd be a lot safer than here, lad."

"No," Sevi said again. "Not when—not with *them* around."

"Them? Who? The goblins?"

"The soldiers."

"Yeah, the goblins." Digby smiled oddly at him. "What if they disappeared? Would you come out then?"

Sevi had no reply. He'd never thought of that ever being a possibility before. The Fablings were a fact of life—they ruled the castle, and he scurried around in its walls. That's how it had always been, and how it would always be.

"Ya know," Digby said, softening his voice. "Since you've been saving me life an' all, I wouldn't mind it if you and yer friend were to come back with me, even if the lass doesn't care fer me. I'd make sure you were looked after. No more hiding in the walls like little mice. You'd be right where ya both belong, with yer own kind, and they'd be all too happy ta do fer you what ya done fer me."

Sevi's eyes widened. He'd wanted to leave these tunnels for years, and here was a man saying he could help him do just that? He wrapped his arms around himself. *Can it really be that simple? Did the Father deliver this man to be our protector? To lead us to the Outside?*

*He'll threaten us.*

Lily's voice intruded on his musing, unbidden, bringing an entire deluge of frightful thoughts with it. He didn't know this man. He didn't know why he was here, or why he'd been arrested, or where he was going once he left. He could be a real criminal, or maybe he wanted to get revenge on Lily for almost killing him, out where he had friends and could be in control.

Anxiety welled again, cutting down the burgeoning hope sprouting in Sevi's chest. Everything that had gone wrong lately had happened because he'd stopped listening to Lily, and here was a stranger waving everything he'd ever wanted in his face. It was far too good to be true. If Lily didn't trust him, then neither would he.

But Digby persisted. "You'd have food, and a warm place to sleep."

Sevi put his hands over his ears. He needed to gather himself, and his mind was too full of words to make room for Digby's. *Lies. Awful. Unsafe.* The tunnels were his home, and they were beautiful, and anything outside of them was dangerous.

He fell inward on himself. He didn't want to hear anything else the man had to say, tempting him with freedom and security. They were lies. There was something wrong. He was a stranger. An intruder. He couldn't be trusted, no matter how much Sevi wanted to.

"Alright, alright, *easy*, lad," Digby called, voice hitching with concern.

Sevi looked at the man. He had his hand raised in a placating gesture, and from the look on his face, Sevi must have seemed ready to split in two.

Sevi got his breath to still, then crouched down and wrapped his arms around his legs. "This is my home," he said. "I... I don't want to leave... I think."

An awkward silence stretched between them. Sevi didn't look up. It felt odd—he hadn't had an awkward silence with a stranger since the first time he'd met Lily. He'd forgotten what it felt like.

"Gods, if I'm a tragedy with kids," Digby muttered. "Lad, chin up, alright? If ya feel like stayin', then stay. I'll not be the one to push ya out of here. I think you're absolutely *mad* ta do it, but I'm in no shape ta fight ya, and... well there it is, innit?"

Wiping his face, Sevi tentatively looked back up at Digby, who appeared all sorts of flustered. He took a long while before saying anything. "Alright."

"Alright." Digby clapped his hands together, looking relieved. "Promise me one thing though, if I could ask anythin' of ya."

Sevi wiped his face again. "Maybe."

"If things ever get messy around here, run away. Don't stay in the castle. Understand?"

Sevi frowned. "No. Why? Is something going to happen?"

"I—" Digby grimaced. "I can't say anythin' else."

Sevi squinted suspiciously. "What do you mean?"

Digby dragged in a long breath and sighed. This time he was the one to avert his eyes. "I've gabbed too much. I can't discuss it if yer not comin' with me."

Sevi's hand crept down to his pocket where his signal whistle rested. The more Digby talked, the more he felt inclined to call for Lily.

"Let's talk about somethin' else," the soldier said, abruptly changing the topic. "This medicine is takin' its sweet time."

Sevi said nothing.

Digby shifted awkwardly. "So, how long ya been here?"

"A while," Sevi said shortly.

Digby didn't look pleased at the answer. "Don't go turnin' into the lass on me. I'm sorry I can't say more, I've got a lot on me shoulders. Ask me somethin' else, anythin' at all, and I'll answer it. Fair?"

Sevi paused. A dozen questions churned in his head, whispering to him in Lily's voice. Smart questions, like, who was he really? Where did he come from? Did he have other people nearby? Where would he be taking them if they left the tunnels? But the question that came out of his mouth wasn't any of those.

"You... you came in on the airship," he said slowly.

Digby raised his eyebrows. "Aye. I didn't get any special treatment, but you're not wrong."

"But... what was it like? To fly?"

Digby chuckled. "I was bound, gagged, and stuffed under the deck, lad."

Sevi's face fell. "Oh."

Digby paused. "But, if I were more of a poet, I'd say it were a lot like a boat at sea."

"The sea?" Sevi had only ever heard about the sea from Lily's stories.

"Aye. Felt like the rocking of waves, except we was floatin' in the air. Tilting one way, then another, and held up by naught but a giant pillow." He shook his head, getting lost in the memory. "Weren't a pleasant feeling, if I'm bein' honest, stuck still in the dark and listening to that giant wooden tub creak about, with that awful roar of its fires that pushed us along. I was always wonderin' when we'd fall from the sky... but maybe if I were on deck with the wind in me face... Aye, I could like that."

Sevi could see it as if he were there. Every word the man spoke painted a picture for him, and the longing inside of him grew, becoming something greater than when he'd stood in his window to the sky. To *fly*. How incredible would that be!

"But who in their right mind puts fire on a wooden boat, especially one that flies?" Digby continued, grinning. "Right? The whole ship is high up in the air and hanging by ro-HAAAAAA!"

Digby's eyes bugged out and he jolted to his feet, throwing the torch to the side. Sevi jumped straight into the air, going tense. "What!?"

"THERE'S A FUCKING DEMON IN ME CHEST!"

Digby was practically hopping, all fatigue gone in a flash. He sprung forward and back, walked around madly without direction, then leaned down on his knees and sucked in a deep breath. "My GODS what a hit! By the gods of sun and sky, I could wrestle a *bear!*"

Sevi was speechless... but only for a moment. He tossed his head back and positively *howled* with laughter. He clutched at his sides, bending forward and laughing until his chest hurt and tears ran down his face. Gods. The man was crazy, and *Gods*, it felt so good to *laugh!*

"Alright. Alright, alright. let me at that rope. Let me at it! C'mon, lad!" Digby huffed and did a small jump, shaking out his body and darting a crazed expression at Sevi. He marched right up to the rope and grabbed a hold with his good arm, wrapped his thighs tightly against it, and started inchworming himself up a handspan at a time. He tried reaching overhead with his bad arm in his excitement, but Sevi had the wherewithal to call out.

"Don't use that arm," he warned, retrieving the torch before grabbing the rope himself. "You might not feel it, but it's still hurt, just like Lily said!"

"Wuzzat, lad? I can't hear you; there's too much roaring in me ears!" Digby called back.

"No, *don't*. Oh, blazes."

Sevi watched helplessly as the battered soldier went up and up, crawling his way to the rocky ledge in his renewed fervor, and finally throwing himself onto the outcrop. He heaved air into his lungs so loudly that Sevi could hear it from below.

Hampered by the torch, Sevi stepped onto the lip with far less gusto, walking around Digby's legs and raising the light above his prone body. "Ahh. Hah. That weed is godsdamn brilliant, lad!" Digby panted, grinning like a fool at the ceiling.

Sevi grinned, caught in the man's good humor. "Well... I'm happy it worked. We should move, though; Lily is waiting for us."

"Right! Let's!" Digby pushed off the ground and stumbled ahead. Sevi watched him, shaking his head at the realization that, against Lily's wishes, he was beginning to like the old man.

# Chapter 11

*Through the great Cut of Elkra the mouse led the way, with warrior and flower behind. But no journey of man, nor those for a mouse, are without their fires to mind.*

———————

When they found Lily, she was up against the sealed tunnel, sluggishly picking rock out of its threshold while cursing up a storm. Sevi and Digby approached, with the latter hopping about from foot to foot, looking like he desperately wanted to run about the place, but was holding it in with an effort. Sevi glanced at him and had to stifle another laugh. His pupils had swallowed the blue in his eyes.

"So, it worked. Good." Lily grunted, hefting another rock out. "Help me with this. Just work on the top half. Rather than unsealing the whole thing we might be able to get by just by making enough room for Blumpkin to squeeze through."

"It's Digby. Digby Digby Digby," the old man grumbled somewhat frantically, rushing forward. He took hold of a rock and began shifting them at twice the speed Lily was moving. Lily, finding herself shoved out of the way, got to her feet and stepped back to stand beside Sevi, watching the man with mild surprise.

"Maybe we shouldn't have given him all of it," Sevi mumbled out of the side of his mouth.

Lily clicked her tongue. The corner of her lips turned up. "I don't know. This night has been a giant pain in my ass, but I'm kind of enjoying this."

"He's not supposed to be moving like this," Sevi persisted.

"Try telling him that." Lily jerked a thumb at Digby, already elbow-deep in the pile of stones.

Digby ignored them entirely, too focused on his task. His upper body soon disappeared as he reached further into the hollowed-out tunnel, singing a lilting song that echoed oddly in the tight space.

"So... anything?" Sevi asked Lily.

She frowned. "Not a thing. And somehow that worries me even more."

"He mentioned something to me below. He made it sound like something might happen to the castle, and that we should be ready to run if it does."

"He didn't say what?"

Sevi shook his head. "He tried convincing me to leave with him, though."

Lily turned a dark glare at the back of the soldier's head and regarded the knife in her hand, but before she or Sevi could do anything, Digby pulled himself from the hole and turned around to face them.

"Hey." He slowly put his back against the wall, looking unsteady on his feet. He was covered with streaks of reddish dust from head to toe. "I think that weed is finally runnin' through me," he slurred. "I don't suppose one of you could get the rest?"

Lily took an unexpected step back and dropped her hand. Her expression caught Sevi's attention, changing from a scowl to worry, until her face was as white as a freshly laundered sheet. He took a step toward her, reaching out in concern. "Lily? What is it?"

She shot a glance at him and shook her head, then wound her hand back and smacked him across his shoulders. "Your turn," she said loudly.

Sevi stumbled, looking from her to the soldier. Digby nodded at him. "Thanks, lad. Will just be a moment, I'm sure."

Sevi turned back to Lily, darting his eyes from her face to her knife. "Please don't," he said softly.

She grimaced at him but said nothing. Sighing, he turned around to face Digby, handing the torch off to the man before approaching the threshold. He had carved a hole big enough for Sevi to fit his slight frame into, and then some.

Tucking his eyepatch behind his ear, Sevi pushed himself into the tunnel down to his shins. He touched the rock ahead, grabbing hold and carefully prying the first rock out of the mortar with slow, firm shakes. The cement was crumbly and badly mixed, barely holding the pile together, and came apart easily under his grasp. It might've explained how Digby was able to make such good progress.

He tugged and passed each piece back far enough to kick them out the rest of the way. Dust and debris had him coughing with every new stone, making for slow, annoying work, forcing him to pause every few breaths just to wipe his face.

Irritated and eager to be done, Sevi eventually resorted to hacking at the mortar with another stone to loosen the cement, coughing harder as more and more dust enveloped him, until he had to cover his mouth and nose with his shirt. Someone called something to him from out of the tunnel. Sevi called back. "What?" They called out again, but it didn't make a difference. Sevi chose to ignore it, renewing his digging.

Someone tapped his boot. Sevi tilted his face to look back. "Alright, one moment!" He heaved out the latest stone with a grunt. The surrounding rock immediately crumbled. Stone after stone smacked his face and head, threatening to bury him under the mountain's collective weight. He clenched, and a terrified scream ripped from his throat, only to have his lungs immediately filled with coarse, dusty air.

A powerful tug on his ankles yanked him out of the tunnel down to his waist. Another tug ejected him out entirely. Sevi scrabbled and flailed as he came flying back, landing on the ground in a grimy, convulsing heap.

"Easy, easy. Ya alright?" Digby said, getting on his knees off to Sevi's side and wiping the dust from his face with his sleeve. "You're alright, c'mon."

Sevi looked around for Lily and spotted her where he'd left her, midway from standing up from the ground. Her face was one of mild concern—a lot, for her—but she immediately relaxed on seeing nothing was wrong with him. She completed the motion and stood up entirely, leaning back against the cave wall, and nodded to him.

He eased, trying to nod back as he coughed out a lungful of dust. "Than—ack. Thank you, Digby," he sputtered.

"Anytime," Digby said. "What in Iaela happened in there?"

"Rocks." Sevi coughed. "Rocks came loose. Fell all over me."

"Came loose, eh?" Digby stood and turned to the tunnel. He held up the torch and reached forward with his free hand, standing like that for several moments. When he turned back, he had a beaming smile stretched across his face. "The lad's done it! There's a breeze comin' through!"

"Now, now, I'm pretty sure we all 'done it,' Blumpkin," Lily said. "But more importantly, now you can leave."

"I—what, no shake goodbye?" Digby offered his hand in her direction. She responded by scooping up a handful of pebbles and plinking one right off his forehead from clear across the room.

"Nope. This was the deal. Get you out of here, then never see your dumb face again." She tossed another rock off his chest. "So, get out of here. Pretty please."

Digby raised his eyebrows, shaking his head. "Yer a steely one lass. Ya know that?"

"One of me many definin' features," she said, mocking his way of speaking again. She tossed another stone at him.

He deflected it with a swat, and chuckled. "Alright. Suppose I owe ya that much." He turned his gaze down to look at Sevi again, nodding a little. He walked over to him and stretched out his hand. "Thanks fer everythin,' lad. An' fer not killin' me." He tossed a conspiratorial wink at Lily. She tossed another rock at him.

Sevi looked from the hand in front of his nose to Digby's face, full of wrinkles, cuts, and bruises, yet smiling like it had been nothing short of a wonderful day. At that moment, Sevi felt an unexpectedly deep admiration for the man. Through all the hardship, he'd somehow found something to smile about.

Sevi clasped the old soldier's hand and let Digby hoist him to his feet, standing awkwardly while Digby regarded him with a strange look.

"What is it?" Sevi asked.

"Eh. Look, I know you're in no mind ta leave with me, but if I ever see the two of you again, I'll be sure to repay the service ya done me today. And that's a promise, ya understand?"

Sevi smiled. "I—"

"You can repay us immediately by never seeing us again," Lily called, crossing her arms. "Now go."

Sevi fell silent, flicking his gaze between her and Digby. Digby eyed Lily for a moment, then Sevi, and when neither spoke, he nodded slowly. "Alright. If that's what ya want, I suppose. Just remember what I said, lad." Digby straightened himself. "Now how do I get out of this place?"

"We don't know much about the mines," Lily said, "but there used to be a cave entrance into them near the castle gardens. So maybe start with going in any other direction."

"Easy enough to remember," Digby said.

"Are you leaving or what?"

"Aye, Captain Lily," the man said with a salute.

Lily narrowed her eyes.

"Goodbye, Digby. I'm also happy we didn't kill you," Sevi said. A lump of guilt swelled in his throat, and he found himself saying, "Um... the mines are full of poison. So be careful."

"Thanks, lad. I'm aware," Digby said. "Look after yourselves. And each other."

With that, the soldier turned from them, putting the torch ahead of him before squeezing into the tunnel, muttering until he fell out the other side. Righting himself, he spared one final glance at them, standing with only the upper part of his body in frame. He nodded once more in solemn parting before stepping out of sight, disappearing into the mines and out of their lives forever.

Sevi and Lily stood in silence. With the torch gone, the bioluminescence of the plants gradually bloomed back into view, illuminating the rock with their ghostly, colorful light. He looked at Lily. "Um... That was—"

"You need to bathe," Lily said, walking away. "Don't come to the Overlook until you've found a cave pool to dip in. And dusted your clothes," she added over her shoulder, stepping off into the darkness.

Sevi watched her back as she faded from view, then glanced at the hollowed-out tunnel one last time. It had been a long, exhausting, *dangerous* day. But they had somehow gotten through. A bath, no matter how cold, was everything he needed.

# Chapter 12

*With a salve most potent and powerfully brisk, the warrior charged out with a cry! Stone split before him, deepest night shied away, and he bade his dear saviors goodbye.*

———— ෴ ————

S evi gently curled his finger around a rainbow sprout, momentarily forgetting his work. It shimmered with the same vibrant hues as its parents on the walls, fresh with new life.

*Welcome to the world, little one. Were you here to see what happened yesterday?*

Going to bed after a particularly memorable event and waking up the next morning, only to go about business as usual, felt unreal—as though yesterday were a dream. All those near misses with the Fablings. Seeing a flying ship. Rescuing Digby. But he only had to look at the very tunnel he was resealing to know the truth, as immutable as the mountain around him.

He wiped his brow and left the newborn plant alone, then picked up another rock and pushed it back where it came from. How had Digby made this look so easy? *By being a giant, hulking soldier hopped up on Violet Crown,* Sevi supposed.

He'd spent an hour on the work already, refilling the tunnel stone by stone. His arms and legs were burning, and he'd covered himself in a fine mist of muddy-red dust, making last night's bath worthless. And to top it off, Lily was nowhere to be found. But maybe that was a good thing. He'd gone against her wishes more times than he could count—another fact as plain as stone. Perhaps they'd need more time apart.

But among all his mistakes, saving Digby had been right. That much he knew.

After another circuit of piling rocks in, Sevi sat back against the wall and closed his eyes, listening to the wind flow through the cave from the mouth up ahead, swaying the Cut's vines with a rustling of leaves. He listened to the stalactites dripping tiny drops of water from the ceiling in a delicate rhythm that, when joined with their siblings, created a song. He listened to his own breath, filling his chest and flowing out in a slow, steady rhythm, adding to the melody.

The mountain's Cut had a silence all its own—secret, secluded, yet as beautiful as that of the world outside. It was slow, patient, and until recently, unchanging.

Several long moments of stillness passed before he opened his eyes and looked up at the mostly filled tunnel. He wondered what was on the other side. What was Digby doing today? Did he find the way out, or had he lost himself in the mountain?

Thoughts of his offer to take him from the Cut circled again in Sevi's mind. He couldn't help but wonder over what could've happened if he had said yes. Perhaps there were bigger, more impressive caverns to explore deeper in the mines where the poison didn't reach. Maybe there were cave people surrounded by veins of gold and silver.

He shook his head. It didn't matter what he thought or how he felt. There was nothing left to do but get back to his life.

He picked up another rock, heaving it into the hole. Then another. Then another. *Clack, clack, crick, clack*, until he had drowned out his bothersome mind with the sounds.

But then he closed his hand over a vacant space where a stone should have been. He looked around with confusion and found that no other rocks remained. He huffed in relief, then turned his back and sunk against the very wall he'd just filled. Grunting softly, he laid his head back against the cool stone, closing his eyes to savor a well-earned rest. He'd take another bath in a bit, in case some of the poison had gotten on him. Then he'd go in search of a meal.

Only a moment had passed, but when Sevi opened his eyes, he knew it had been more. He jerked awake as the coarse cawing of a lost raven sounded loudly through the tunnels, intruding on the stillness that had lulled him asleep. A flicker of black flew by, stark against the glowing plants along the opposite wall.

"Shy?" Sevi called drowsily, wiping his eyes clear as he turned his gaze to track it. "Lily?"

The bird cawed again, laughing as it melded into the cave's darkness on a path toward the Overlook. Sevi winced at its grating voice. *Stupid bird.*

He swatted a branch of leaves away from his face and was rewarded with a jumble of music as berries fell into his lap, irritating him further. He wondered at how much time had passed, dreading the possibility that he had missed the castle's mealtime. *At least it wasn't long enough to dream,* he thought, reaching up to scratch his head.

He paused. *Music?*

Pushing his drowsiness aside, he turned his head and came face-to-face with a branch full of glowing chromatic leaves, pulsing along the edges in a variety of dancing colors. Sevi squinted at it. It hadn't been there before. Had he slept long enough for plants to grow around him?

Reaching a tentative hand forward, he pushed his finger onto its blade then let go, and a single musical note chimed out as the leaf flicked back up into place, rippling with sudden color at the disturbance. It sounded softer than a bell but louder than a breeze flowing over the ears. Sevi ran his gaze along the plant, following its branches, then gasped. "Mother below. Father above."

It wasn't just one bush. A full, glistening garden of color, filled with flowers and plants he'd only ever dreamed of, had sprouted out of the cavern floor. Trunks and stems of every size spiraled up into the air as though the cave had just politely parted itself and let them in, happy to host such refined company. Some of the plants bore the same swollen, delicious-looking berries that now sat in his lap, ripe and probably bursting with sweetness. He was tempted to take a handful and throw them in his mouth, but he'd learned long ago never to eat a suspicious berry without proper examination.

In the back of his mind Sevi wondered if he was dreaming, finding this weird even for a place like the Cut. A small, pleasant smile grew along his face as he stood, looking around with childlike fascination. It being out of the ordinary made it no less incredible. Was this simply how some tunnel plants grew? All at once when no one was watching?

He brushed his hand along the leaves of the closest bush, trailing his fingers over its smooth, verdurous leaves. He strode carefully through the shrubbery, letting his hand slip from leaf to leaf and wondering just how far this newfound garden extended. Wherever his hand went, a soft, lilting jumble of notes chimed out, as delicate and lovely as Alyda's voice. It didn't quite make a song, but maybe he could turn it into one if he found the right notes.

Overcome by a whim, he sprung through a dense thicket of the plants, startling a chorus of noises from its denizens that echoed through the corridor, and whirling all the glowing mote-bugs up into the air in a zephyr of dancing lights. Bubble frogs leaped from their hiding places, bloating up in alarm with angry croaks and rolling away as bright, yellow spheres, adding their bumbling, bouncing hops to the performance.

Sevi laughed, spreading his arms to either side of him, quickly getting lost in a sea of color and sound. The Cut had come to life in a whole new way, and it was *radiant*.

He was so caught up in it that, in his haste, he missed a root completely and fell, ending his short-lived romp. His head hit the stone and bounced, making him gasp and clutch at his skull. When it stopped ringing, he let out a laugh and spread his arms flat across the floor, smiling up at the new life around him. If Lily were there, she might've gotten irritated and demanded that he quiet down. But she wasn't, so he just laughed louder.

It felt good. Better than good, it felt wonderful. He laughed until it hurt, and only subsided when he couldn't breathe, grinning like a fool at all the glow-bugs swaying around in the air above.

Something new caught his attention out of the corner of his eye; a peculiar shape, different from the other plants. He tilted his head for a better look, eager for more discovery, only to freeze.

Poking out from underneath a bush, clutching at nothing with sick, pallid fingers, was a human hand, covered in dark, viscous blood.

At first Sevi thought it was a trick of the light. That the blood pooling beneath it was merely a deep shadow, and its gnarled forearm just another branch among many. He blinked and furiously wiped at his face, trying to clear the stain of its ugly shape from his mind. But no. It remained. And it wasn't until his heart began to thump through his chest that his brain caught up with his eyes.

He slapped his hand on the ground and scrambled backward as his joy broke violently into pieces. His palm struck something wet, splattering his face in an unknown liquid and stopping him in his tracks. Lifting up his hand with wide eyes, he was met with the grisly sight of rotten ichor running slickly down his fingers.

He screamed and scrambled to his feet, running down the tunnel through a field of plants whose music now sounded like mocking laughter, discordant and terrible.

The walls screamed back at him, filling the Cut with his horror. Rocks and dust kicked up with every step, stinging his ankles. The confines of the tunnels rocked and shifted, squeezing in around him, eager to lock him in the darkness with the body and whatever had killed them.

He rounded a corner and struck something with such momentum that he went tumbling to the ground, pulling whatever he hit along with him. The floor slipped away as he started to roll, spinning head over feet down the slope until something strong hooked into his shirt and tugged him back hard.

He clawed at the gravel with scratched, bloody fingers, going rigid with tension, until he came to a halt. When his heart finally stopped pumping in his ears and his vision cleared, he saw that his ankles now dangled over the steep drop of the tunnel's escarpment. If he had slid but a bit further...

Yelping, Sevi scrambled back, flinging his arms out for any sort of purchase and smacking something soft.

"*OW!*" Lily barked, bringing her hand down hard across his head. "*Knock it off!*"

Stunned, Sevi stopped long enough for Lily to push him off her, but she kept a hold of his shirt and dragged him back further from the edge.

"How many times am I going to save your ass this week?" she grumbled, dropping him none too gently and standing straight.

She took a moment to inspect herself, then jumped and hurriedly dusted herself off, even taking out a flask from her belt and pouring water all over her hands and arms. She furiously rubbed herself clean, looking at him with gritted teeth. "What in every god's name is *wrong* with you, Sevi?"

"Lily. LIL—"

"Stop shouting!"

"There... there's a body. A body!" Sevi panted, pointing back the way he came with wide, manic eyes. Lily raised her eyebrow. "I was s-sleeping. After finishing with the tunnel. I woke up, and there were these bushes all around me—"

"Bushes?"

"Yes!"

Lily shook her head, still dabbing at her arms and clothes. "Gods, this better not stain. Explain. What happened?"

"It was under a bush, covered in blood." Sevi quieted, and he looked off distantly across the cavern. Something else scratched at his brain next to the image of the hand, dancing around the edges of his focus, but unable to join the rest of his thoughts. "Blood everywhere... so much..."

Lily regarded him silently. After a moment, she blew a huff of air out of her nose and reached up to rub her eyes. "Alright. Let's go take a look."

Sevi, staring dysphorically at the floor, gradually came to attention. "Look?"

"Yeah, if there's more people in our caves then we need to know." Lily motioned her head back toward the tunnel and walked ahead. "Especially if they're killers. But I really hope you're wrong, Sevi."

Sevi followed close behind with his arms wrapped around himself. "I-I know what I saw." Lily merely shrugged.

The two set off the way Sevi had come, silent and watchful. Sevi couldn't stop twitching, feeling unbearably nervous. The idea that a killer was waiting behind every shadow and rocky outcrop had him jumping at the smallest sound. The drippings of the stalactites weren't a song, they were the killer's footsteps as they got nearer. The wind wasn't a breath, it was a moan of pain from the killer's latest victim. He clutched at his head. All that blood. All that *blood*.

"Sevi. Sevi, hey," Lily was saying, making him look up. They'd made it back to the cavern without him realizing. "Are these the plants?" she asked with a curious tone, indicating the cavern's new flora. She'd put on her invisible mask, flattening her face and stilling her body, looking ready to defend them both and their home if it came to it. Sevi nodded, shaking a little. Lily wordlessly drew her small knife from her sleeve, holding it in front of herself. She whispered to him, "Do you have a knife?"

"It's in my pack. I didn't think I would need one."

"Then pick up a rock and stay behind me," she said lowly, fixing her gaze on the room ahead. Sevi did as he was told, grabbing a well-shaped stone and taking position behind her. Lily stepped forward cautiously. "First we look around. Then show me the body."

They paced around the room from beginning to end. Each moment stretched on for an eternity as Sevi's senses sharpened with hyperawareness, whipping around at the smallest provocation.

Lily took extra care around the tunnel Sevi had refilled until she seemed convinced that there weren't any gaps that someone might've squeezed through. When the last plant was brushed aside, Lily sighed and put away her knife. "Where's the body?"

Still holding onto his rock, Sevi retraced his steps as best as he could, but could only narrow it down to the general area he'd seen it. They both took an end and searched with tentative, wary steps, moving toward each other and looking under every bush down to its roots. Sevi's knees shook every time he bent low enough to peer into the underbrush, scared that he'd come face to face with a bloodless corpse at any moment.

Then something horribly familiar caught his gaze, and he froze in place. "Lily," he whispered weakly as he stepped away from a puddle of blood. His handprints were dimly visible on the stone. "Here!"

Lily joined him and looked down. She knelt and placed two fingers into the blood before lifting them to her nose, smelling it. She followed the puddle to the bush it came from with her eyes, as did Sevi.

There lay the hand. A deep nausea welled up inside of him. He was about to turn away when Lily brushed past him and grabbed a hold of the hand's wrist, yanking its arm out all at once.

Sevi yelped.

Lily turned and thrust a branch toward him. Sevi froze, staring at it in confusion. He wiped at his face, thinking the dark was playing tricks on him, but no. It was gnarled, it was dark, it was hand-like, but it was very much just a piece of wood.

Sevi shook his head, uncomprehending.

"The body?" Lily asked softly.

"I... I..."

"Turn around," she prompted.

"I—"

"Please turn around, Sevi."

He shook his head again, unable to tear his gaze away from the lifeless piece of wood. Losing her patience, Lily took his arm and turned him around herself, studying the back of him. "Did you know that your back was covered in berry pulp?"

"What?"

"It's not blood, Sev," she said, raising her fingers up to his face. "Smell."

Sevi, after a pause, moved his face forward and inhaled. "It's... sweet," he said at last.

"Mhm." Lily wiped her hand on her pants.

"No body?" Sevi asked slowly.

"No body."

Realization finally dawned on him. No body. And nobody. No killer.

He let out a sound. It began as a puff of air, then grew into a chuckle. Then his belly jumped, and he exploded into a fit of hysterical laughter. He slumped against the cave wall, catching jagged bits of rock in his clothing as he slid down to the floor with tears running down his face.

Lily watched him uncertainly as he cackled to the ceiling with his head thrown back, a jumble of warring emotions skittering around inside of him like angry spiders. His laughter slowly subsided, but his tears stayed behind. Sevi stared up at his friend as he choked out raw, shuddering sobs, then slowly crossed his arms around his knees and collapsed his head against them, expelling a slew of nervous energy in a rush all at once, until there was nothing left but bone-deep exhaustion.

*Gods... Not again. Please.*

After a long, long while of him crying into his arms, Lily placed a gentle hand on his shoulder. "Sevi," she said hesitantly. "You've had a hard couple days. Let's get you to the bedroom, alright?"

Sevi laughed, bitterly this time. "With the firedrake?"

"I'll chase it out."

"It'll just come back. It always does."

"Well... let's try anyway."

Sevi dragged his arm across his face, saying nothing.

"Alright," Lily said, gently scooping her arm under his, helping him to his feet. He didn't resist. She wrinkled her nose at him. "You need another bath, you know."

Sevi managed another emotionless chuckle, letting her pull him forward. "Yeah."

"Do you have enough powder to sleep?"

"I think so..."

"Good."

"Lily."

"Mm?"

"Thank you."

Her cool façade cracked unexpectedly as she turned to eye him, conveying some internal conflict through the furrow of her brow. But as the moment stretched on, she turned away, and merely tightened her grip on him. "You're welcome."

# Chapter 13

*Is that where it started—where the embers first stoked? Such has been my tired question to plead. Could the imminent pain have been easily lost if not for but the slightest of seeds?*

L ily went ahead of Sevi and scared the firedrake out of their room. He listened to the sounds of their struggle, wincing at how loud some of the crashes were. He hoped their belongings would survive the fight, if they hadn't already burned.

The light in the room blazed brightly, and the scuff of claw striking stone grew closer. He pressed himself hard against the wall as the firedrake streaked past him with an angry, serpentine hiss, blazing a trail of cinders behind itself and bolting out through the cliff-side entrance. Lily was right behind it, chasing it with a fresh bucket of water and tossing its contents in the creature's wake as an added threat to never return. But it would. It always did.

They then both blocked up its alcove with whatever junk they had lying around for good measure, and Sevi was finally able to drag himself into the sorry sack of hay that he called a bed. If Lily hadn't reminded him to take his powder, he would have been unconscious the moment he hit the burlap.

He must've gotten his dosage wrong, though, as he slept for the rest of the day and throughout the night. But when he awoke the next morning, Lily was there, just as he knew she'd be, sitting right next to him with a bowl of fruit and scraps of—

"Is that *bacon?*"

"The very same," she said, popping a tiny piece into her mouth.

He propped himself up on his elbows. "You scavenged?"

"Hey, I scavenge!"

Sevi gave her a blank stare.

"Sometimes."

Sevi continued to stare.

"Would you shut up and eat already? I went to a lot of effort for this."

"Did you though?"

She scowled. "I guess you don't want your share."

"No, I do! Give it here."

"Say please."

"Please."

"In the way I like it, since you had to be rude."

Sevi flattened his voice to a deadpan. "Would you please give me a share of your most prosperous bounty, oh Lily, Queen of the Cut, most benevolent bestower of meals?"

"You forgot, 'most selfless, beautiful, and gracious savior.'"

"Can I please just have some food?"

The corner of Lily's mouth turned up in a smirk. "I suppose the Queen can be merciful."

She divided their meal evenly and handed him his portion in a cracked wooden bowl. His stomach growled loudly at the smell. Lily liked her purple fruit, but they would never compare to *bacon*.

He put as much gratitude as he could muster in the nod he gave her. She wasn't partial to grand emotional gestures, and she didn't like him fawning over her in any way. But she had her own way of showing that she cared. He could see it, and she knew that he knew, which was enough.

When they finished eating, Lily set down her bowl and clapped him on the shoulder. "So. Between... everything, these past several days have been awful, right?" Sevi nodded slowly. "The nice thing is that we can always change that. So let me ask you this—are you ready, Sevi?" She gave him a small, duplicitous grin.

He felt a prickle at the nape of his neck. "For what?"

"To get back to our lives."

Sevi almost made a wry face. He had made his decision to remain in the Cut where it was safe, ready to follow Lily wherever she went. Yet the realization that he would be returning to the same routine felt... odd. It was familiar. It was stable. But a dream was hard to kill, and there were no airships in the Cut.

Lily didn't have to know that, though. He took a deep breath and sighed. "I'd like that... But why do I feel like you have something planned?"

"Because I do. I had my ears to the walls while you were sleeping," she said, standing up and stretching her limbs. "That captain has left his flock of pretty little idiots to go into town, looking for his escaped convict."

Sevi's mind flashed back to the horrid screeching of the guards at the hands of Captain Redwood, and he felt a pang of worry for Digby. If he had suffered before he'd escaped, he'd suffer twice as much if he was caught again.

"More importantly," she continued, offering her hand out to Sevi, "he's taken a fair bit of soldiers with him."

Sevi took it without question, looking up at her. "What are you getting at?"

She pulled him to his feet. "Let's take a walk. See what we can get up to. Maybe there's some mischief to be done."

Sevi's eyebrows shot up. "But you said—"

"Not to go around banging on all the walls with that thick skull of yours while the whole damn castle was at attention. But there's hardly anyone around, so I doubt they'll hear us. Even with your fat head."

"Says the girl in the rusty helmet?"

"My helmet is *not* rusty." She paused, then grinned. "I pull it off though."

Sevi bubbled out a sudden laugh, and Lily joined in. It was nice to feel a bit of familiarity with her again. The guilt of the past couple days had sat heavy and stagnant in his chest, permeated with visions of her scowl. The sound of her joy put him at ease. "Does this mean you've forgiven me? For yesterday?"

She frowned and went silent. "This and that are two separate things."

His hope died as swiftly as it had sprouted. "What do you mean?"

"You're... You know. You're seeing things again," she said, shifting awkwardly.

He closed his eyes and lowered his head, clutching at his shirt. Saying it made it real. "Oh."

"Yeah." She cleared her throat. "We've got to get that under control."

"I see," he said, looking back up at her. "What do you have in mind?"

She stepped forward and patted his shoulder. "Grab your things and follow me."

They took their packs and set off into the Cut. Lily led the way, taking him on a winding trail to the opposite side of the castle. Though she didn't say where they were going, the route they took was telling. "Lily, are we—"

"Shh. You'll spoil the surprise."

"I already know the surprise," he said with a soft smile.

After a little further, she stopped and started shifting around against the wall, blocking his line of sight with her body. "Let me see. I know I marked it... Ah!" she said triumphantly, coming across a decent sized brick with an 'X' chiseled across its face. She waved at it and stepped aside. "After you."

He took hold of the stone and pried it loose, letting a vast swath of warm daylight into their tunnels. As he'd suspected, outside was a paved flagstone bridge that stretched across the sky. It traversed a gap in the plateau to the top of a lower tower, tied to which swayed the airship, glistening in the sun against a sea of clouds.

"Ta-da," Lily said, leaning against the wall opposite the hole. "Now you can moon over it as long as you want."

Sevi didn't need her permission. He ran his gaze over the airship from bow to stern, soaking in the sight of the miraculous boat that defied the pull of Mother Avinaea's embrace. His shoulders pushed forward, pressing into the wall to help him get as good of a view as he could manage. Each of its features was more intriguing than the last, from its decorated hull to its golden prow.

The large metal tubes at its back lay still, empty of their fire, tucked somewhere deep within their gaping black maws. The gilded, reddish wood of its hull flowed luxuriously down its sides, shining in the light, and cut so precisely that it could have been carved from a single log. Green flags bearing a tree fluttered in the breeze, whipping about above the heads of several guards who walked along the deck, utterly oblivious to the marvel of engineering at their feet.

Sevi found himself in awe all over again. *How can something so heavy-looking fly, let alone carry people?*

"Wow," he breathed. "It's more beautiful up close."

"Mm." Lily hummed.

"How does it fly?"

"Magic."

"Where did all its fire come from?"

"Gathered from the sun itself."

Sevi shot her a look. "Is that true?"

"As true as me," she said, adding a wink.

He looked back at the ship. *Gathered from the sun.* What a wondrous feat that would be. Surely such a thing could *only* be magical. "You said Redwood left to chase after Digby. Why didn't he take this? I bet you could see everything from up there."

"You've looked down from the mountain before. Do you think you could easily spot Blumpkin's face in a forest from the Overlook, even with a spyglass? No, they'll send it out if they pick up his trail, then use it to keep eyes on him."

Sevi nodded to her point, slumping back against the wall beside her. He lifted his face, enjoying the warmth of the sun on his skin, staring out the hole into the world beyond. "So. What was this about mischief?"

"I thought you'd never ask." She smiled, pulling her bag into her lap. Lifting the flap, she reached in and rummaged around.

Sevi crossed his arms and shrugged his shoulders. His thoughts flashed briefly to the vision of the dismembered limb. One taste of the Outside, and he'd started slipping back into places he had never wanted to revisit. "Lily," he began, "I understand why you're doing this, and I appreciate it. The airship was thoughtful of you, but I think I'd rather sleep. I don't want to be awake if I'm... you know."

Lily stopped moving. "You would go back to sleep rather than explore?"

He blushed. "I—"

"You?" There was a ghost of a smile on her lips.

"I'm just not sure about this. We don't take risks. Our first rule, like you said."

Lily was overcome by an odd look that wiped her smile away before it could form completely. "Sevi. Something is coming, isn't it? Blumpkin said it himself. We don't know what, or why. But we need to be ready." She looked seriously at him. "I need you by my side, alert and clear when it does, not drugged and asleep. Ignoring the visions worked last time, and since this is the only way I know how to help you, I'm willing to risk a little danger if that's what it takes."

She turned back to her bag. "We'll still be careful. It'll be fine as long as we don't make a scene. Too much of a scene, anyway. No capers. No leaving the Cut. No rescuing sad little Blumpkins. And if things get dangerous, we leave the moment they do. You just promise to tell me if you start feeling off again, alright?"

Sevi studied her. Her shoulders were tense, and she didn't meet his eye, focused entirely on the contents of her knapsack. "Why don't you just leave me?"

She stopped again to stare at him in open surprise. "What a dumb question."

"I mean it, Lil," he said, unable to keep the malaise from his voice. "All I've ever done is make living here hard for you. Why are you making such an effort for me? Why not push me out or go off on your own once and for all?"

"In order: one, I can take it; two, we're friends; and three, do I really need to make you say the words again?" She reached out with a closed fist. "Hold this." He opened his palm. She placed a pebble in it, asking him, "Do you know what this is?"

"It's a r—wait. Is this a *firesnap seed*?" he exclaimed, holding it up.

"The very same," she said, lifting her other hand from the bag to reveal a small box full of them.

"Did you steal these from my garden?"

"Maybe."

"And Alyda let you!"

"Maybe."

"*Why?*"

She grinned and flicked one at him with her thumb. He caught it with a flinch.

"Mischief, silly boy."

# Chapter 14

*Had the boy not been so curious of heart, nor clever with petal and plum, perhaps the two would have lived happily after, no misery, nor crying to come.*

Three soldiers sat in a row on a stone bench in the castle courtyard, all in various states of nonchalance. Where just recently there was a whole battalion performing drills and standing at attention with perfect discipline, now there were only stragglers and layabouts content to loiter. Sevi wondered if Owl had joined the captain in his hunt for Digby—she would've wasted no time in swooping in, claws at the ready to punish the trio below him otherwise.

The tree just on the other side of the wall made an ideal spot to relax. Its branches were wide and made for cool cover from the glaring sun above in an otherwise mostly shelterless courtyard. A fountain, fed by crisp, chilling water from one of many mountain streams, babbled just next to it, offering easy refreshment. And to complete the ensemble, the bench was wide enough to sit a group of people, making conversation easy. It was too tempting of a space for any slacking soldier to ignore.

And also, the perfect place to spy.

The nice thing about a castle with a tunnel behind every wall was that Sevi and Lily could get into the courtyard itself through the battlements that ran around its perimeter. This section of the wall ran along a natural outcrop, boosting it up a full head of height from the yard below. Coupled with the natural shield of branches from the tree, Lily, who had carved out the spyhole herself, had deemed it the perfect place to throw things at the soldiers while they went about their drills.

"Think they found him?" the shortest said. He had green hair that grew out of his head like small, skinny vines, and was pulled back in a tail. His leg swung idly to and fro as he whittled at a twig, too short to touch the ground.

"Hrm," grumbled the tall one, skinny as a sapling and just as pointy looking. Their head was oddly shaped, seemingly running into their neck without the separation of a jawline, and there was no obvious indication whether they were a lady or a man. They were so skinny that they had to repeatedly fix the jacket on their shoulders, or it would have fallen off.

"Why didn't we just take the ship out?" whined the corpulent one with her head tilted back, looking up at the sky. Her ears were extra long, running along the sides of her head like sharpened knives and decorated with a manner of sparkling glass earrings. "We could spot the little bloodstained Slagger from miles away and sic the geisthounds on him."

"Hrrm," the thin one replied.

"Suppose we could," said the short one. "Why didn't we?"

The woman craned her neck and looked around, radiating suspicion through her posture. It was a long moment before she answered. "If I were to guess, something has got Redwood scared," she whispered, leaning closer to the green one as if the tall one wasn't even there. "Scared enough to stay here and miss the Turning. By all accounts, we shouldn't even be here."

"Hrrm."

The short one spit, not looking at her, focusing instead on his whittling. "How do you figure, Holly?"

Holly glared at him. His whittling began to slow, and his body tightened, until he was positively trembling. A hiss of pain rolled from his lips. Sighing, he set the twig down. "Sap and stone, fine. Would you please tell me more about your theory, Senior Airman Hollyglos?"

"Hrrm."

"That's better," Holly said with a smile in her voice. She settled back against the wall, smiling up at the sky with her hands on her belly. "I'm so glad you asked, Airman Twig. I have some thoughts."

Lily pressed the side of her helmet against Sevi's head, effectively pushing his face away from the spyhole and replacing it with her own. "So, who're these three?"

Sevi rubbed his cheek. "I'm not sure. I don't think I've ever seen them."

"They must've come in with the red-dick guy."

"Redwood?"

"I know what I said. We'll have to name them, then. What do you think?"

"Well... the big lady called the small one Twig, and he called her Holly. Hollyglass? Glowse?"

"Not sure if the tall one even has a mouth," Lily muttered. She pulled out some firesnap seeds, humming as she gave half to Sevi. "What would you call them if you didn't know their names?"

"Hmm. I think... the small one would be Stump, because his green hair looks like moss growing on a log. The tall one with the pointy shoulders and ears would be Willowbarb, cause they sound like a willow tree creaking in the wind. And the big one I'd call Pear. She's kind of shaped like one, isn't she?"

Lily snorted. "I like that one."

Her smirk didn't sit well with him. "Maybe I won't, actually."

"That's alright. I will."

"Hmm."

"Easy there, Willowbarb."

Sevi narrowed his eyes. "You're oddly cheerful all of a sudden."

"It's been a long few days," she said, flicking a seed into the air and catching it with her other hand. "I'm looking forward to what happens next."

"So those nasty little hunters are just waiting, you understand?" Hollyglos went on outside, fanning her face with one meaty, four-fingered hand. "They want us to poke our noses out and tear our balloon to shreds with their nasty little birds. Do you know how much work it takes to make one? How many lightblossoms must be woven?"

Twig shook his head, sounding more and more fatigued with every word Hollyglos said. "No, Senior Airman Hollyglos. How much does it take?"

"Hrrm."

"Enough to break my poor back if we need to make another," she grumbled, leaning back and closing her eyes with a dramatic sigh. "And damn Finch and Ashern to the deepest spires of the Underroot for losing that damn Slagger."

"Hrr-RRRM!"

"What!? What's wrong with you, you walking tree trunk?"

Lily nailed the tall one right in the back of the head, popping the firesnap hard enough against their skull to make it burst and immediately combust, burning brightly for more than a breath before the juices in the seed burnt all the fuel its shell could provide.

Enthralled, she covered her mouth to hide the snickers that had her belly bouncing. She waved Sevi away, silently urging him to clear from the peephole while Willowbarb hopped about, darting their sharp head around at every angle in confusion.

"What, are you dancing for us, Acantha?" Hollyglos said with a scowl in her voice.

"She's not terrible," came the somewhat less bored voice of Stump.

Lily peeked down out of the peephole, lifting her helmet up gently from her forehead to get a better look. Her grin was so wide it stretched out from the confines of her hand. She waved at Sevi again, this time beckoning him to come quickly. He hesitated before joining her, getting a good look at the chaos she had caused. He gulped. "I'm not so sure about—"

"Oh hush," she said. "Do you trust me?"

"Of course, but—"

"I know best, right?"

"Yes, but—"

"Then trust me when I say that I know this is best for you." She smirked, taking and filling his hand with all her firesnaps. She lifted it up to eye level and stared at him intently from the other side. "Throw!"

Startled, Sevi's first instinct was to wind his fist back and chuck every single firesnap seed through the hole at once, raining them down on the unsuspecting trio of soldiers like a clutch of fiery hailstones.

Lily's jaw dropped. "I meant throw *one at a time!*" She shoved him away from the hole again, but this time he shoved back, until they compromised and each had an eye looking out.

"Would you sit down already? Why is she—HOLY LAILYN ABOVE!" Stump yelled.

"OW. OW! What did you do? *What did you two shitheels do!*" Hollyglos demanded, jumping up from her seat with more speed than her bulk suggested.

"Hrrrrm! *Hrrrrm!*"

"It's the tree! Get away from the tree!" Stump continued to shout.

"My *ass* it was the tree!" Hollyglos roared. "It was YOU! I don't know what you did, but I'm certain you did it!"

"HRRRRRRM!"

"And she agrees with me!"

"No, she *doesn't!*"

"Stand *still*, you little shit, so I can—NO! GET *BACK* HERE!"

Lily trembled against the side of Sevi's head. Sevi backed away, clutching at the hem of his shirt. "I... Lily, I—"

"You beautiful creature."

Sevi gaped. Lily backed away from the peephole with a red face, putting the spystone gently back into place. With it sealed, she turned to face him, took a deep breath, then threw her head back and laughed. Loud, unrestrained, cackling laughter.

It rolled out of her in one giddy, unbroken song until she doubled over, slumped against the wall with tears streaming down her cheeks. It was enough to catch, and suddenly everything felt so absurd. Gods, why had he *done* that? He bent over and bellowed along with her, twining their laughter into one, filling the impassive walls of the Cut with their guffaws. Sevi slumped opposite her, fighting to get himself under control.

"Y-you... *wonderful* moron!" Lily said breathlessly, wiping her eyes. "I should really tell you off for something like that, but *Gods,* that was so *funny!*"

Sevi shook his head, giggling in sporadic, hiccupping fits. "Did you see Princess trying to chase Stump around?"

"Princess? What happened to Pear?"

"I didn't like the way you laughed at it! It was mean!"

"Pear, Princess, whatever! She was moving so quickly I thought her legs would snap! But she... Gods, she moved so *fast!*"

And then they were laughing all over again, making faces at each other and mimicking how silly the three soldiers had looked, wishing that they each had more seeds to throw.

"Come on," Lily chuckled, tapping his arm. "We can't stop now."

They left the area before their noise could draw the attention of the geisthounds, snaking their way toward the barracks. It was a smaller building attached to the exterior of the castle just to the side of the yard, and though the tunnels didn't extend into it, they were able to peer in through the castle itself.

They'd carved this spyhole out close to the ground, making it less likely for anyone to notice. But still, near so many soldiers, separated by only a handspan of stone, they felt it best if they quieted to a whisper. The room was cast in a dim blue light, shuttered to keep the bothersome sun out as best as possible, and the air was filled with the subtle and not-so-subtle sounds of sleeping, shifting bodies.

Sevi moved away, crouching next to Lily while she took a turn surveying the room. "We're not throwing more firesnaps on them, are we?"

"No, too risky. We're going to wait instead."

Sevi tilted his head in confusion. "Wait for what?"

"I'll know it when I see it." She shrugged.

"You don't have a plan?"

"Sometimes you have to let the plan find you."

As insightful as that sounded, it was immediately undermined a short while later when Lily leaned against the wall and tilted her helmet's visor over her eyes. "Alright, they're just a room full of sleepers. You take the first watch, and let me know when something interesting happens."

Sevi rolled his eyes. Her watch hadn't lasted two hundred breaths. "Alright, but why don't we just go somewhere else?"

"Because I have a headache, and I need a nap."

"So do I," he said pointedly.

"I was up late keeping an eye on things while you were out, Sev. And getting food. And making sure Alyda was alright. I'm beat. Can you at least let me shut my eyes for a bit?"

"That's... fair."

"Just give me a few dozen breaths," Lily said, settling herself against the wall. "Wake me if you need me."

Sevi settled himself on the ground and looked through the gap in the wall, watching the soldiers and listening to their snores. After the first fifty breaths, Lily joined them, snoring noisily herself. After two hundred breaths without any activity, Sevi's interest in the room waned considerably. After four hundred, he was ready to join Lily.

He was just beginning to slip into sleep when a group of soldiers opened the barracks door. Streams of light lanced across the room, breaching its dull gloom. A chorus of half-conscious groans erupted, sending faces of every shape and size burying into their pillows.

"Wakey, wakey!" cried the lead soldier, striding in with a confident swagger. He was stripped down to his waist with a towel over his shoulder, fresh from the shower cabinets and barely dry. He went down the line of upright feet, smacking ankle after ankle. "Shift change, get up, you lazy rats! This is your *nice* awakening. If you want to feel the *mean* one, I dare you to keep the lieutenant waiting!"

"You heard 'im!" said a lady, also stripped to her waist with a cloth wrapped tightly around her chest. She copied everything the man was doing, but a little louder. "Any weight that falls on him is gonna fall on me, so get outta here! Hey, that's *my* bed!"

She took one straw mattress and flipped it up with both hands, tumbling its occupant out with a confused cry. This went on for some time, with more and more half-naked soldiers filing in while the sleeping ones, after lethargically donning their uniforms, listlessly filed out.

Sevi felt his body still. Something felt off. Something about the way the soldiers moved, and the way the light caught on their bodies. He'd peered into the Outside so many times over so many years and had never felt an ounce of shame over it, but watching this display felt wrong, somehow. It conveyed a sense of intimacy that he'd never really felt before, making him feel like an intruder. And why did the Cut suddenly feel so hot?

"What's that noise?"

Sevi jolted away from the hole, quickly averting his eyes. Lily was looking at him curiously with a single thumb pushing up her visor. "Wh-what?"

He cursed his stutter. What did he have to be embarrassed over? Lily maintained her expression. "What did you do," she said, more as a statement than a question.

"Nothing!"

"Out of the way," she grumbled, pushing him aside.

A dozen breaths crept by. Lily's expression changed from one of mild interest, to confusion, to revelation, and finally to the curling smirk she only wore when something happened at his expense. She turned her gaze on him and gently placed her chin in her hand, propped up by a single elbow. "My, my, Sevi. Growing up, are we?"

Sevi blanked. "Huh?"

"I mean, I can't say I blame you. That lady with the blond hair and the butterfly wings, stripped down to her waist and everything? That would make any young man blush."

"What!?"

"You called her Big Eyes, right? Are you sure it was her eyes you were looking at?"

"I—what's that even mean?"

"Of course, that muscley man with the dark hair is a fine creature, too," she added, turning her eye back to the barracks with a scandalous grin. "A creature like that could also make a young man blush."

Ironically, Sevi did. Which made him scowl. She was flustering him, and he didn't know how or why. He hadn't done anything! His hands curled into fists at his sides. "What are you talking about?"

She chuckled. "We'll talk when you're older. I think I've found our mischief."

Sevi's head burned hot enough for smoke to pour from his ears. He couldn't summon a response, so he just looked at her. Lily tilted her head toward the room. "They're closing up the windows again, getting ready to get some sleep. But the one closest to our wall here," she said, breaking off to pat the stone, "is doing a bit of reading by candlelight, first."

"So?"

"They've left the candle on the ground next to our little peephole. Along with their book."

Sevi stared at her. "You don't mean—"

"I do." Lily grinned, taking out a rag from one of her pockets which she then curled around her hands at both ends. Before he could object, she whipped the piece of cloth in a frenzy, fanning a gust of wind through the spyhole. She kept at it until someone shouted.

When Lily moved back to the wall, a bright, orange light now danced across her face, reflecting off the teeth in her smile. More shouts of alarm followed the first, and she had to cover her mouth with her hand, waving Sevi over to take a look at her handiwork.

Sevi looked through the wall in time to see a man dancing about, using his own covers to desperately beat at the book he'd so carelessly left near an open flame. The atmosphere of the room, previously full of tired, weary people ready for bed, had now filled with a chorus of jeers and laughter.

"What's wrong, Dew? Fleas in your bed?"

"Honestly, it's not *that* cold in here."

The jumping man was a spectacle to be sure, but the fire held Sevi's gaze the most. No matter how funny the display, he always drifted back to it, and when it flared up during the brief moment the whirling blanket stoked its flames, something inside him rattled loose. Just as it had with the firedrake.

He really, really didn't like it.

Lily touched his scalp from behind, and the feeling disappeared. Sevi shook his head, turning to face her. "So, what do you think?" she asked.

Sevi didn't answer until the fire went out, blinking as though waking from a dream. The strange feeling inside of him extinguished along with it, and all the laughter he should have been having at the man's expense rose up inside of him at once.

He pushed off from the wall, shaking Lily's hand off and placing his own over his mouth. He turned and crawled away as quietly and carefully as he could, deeper into the castle where the stone was thicker. When he made it far enough, he doubled over and laughed until the walls were singing with the sound.

Lily clapped a hand on his shoulder. "What can I say? I'm an artist at work!"

# Chapter 15

*The boy had a history most horrid, severe, distressing, dreadful, and aching.*
*Lost in a veil draped over his eyes; a fog that was close to its breaking.*

---

"We could try it tonight. He still isn't back yet. Neither of them are," Honeydew said softly, but not soft enough. She was by far one of the prettier soldiers, with swirling skin patterns ranging from gold to pink in a flawless gradient, but her uniform never seemed to fit her properly. Not because it was too big or small, or because she had small spines along her back poking from her coat, but something else. Something that Sevi could never put his finger on.

"You know we wouldn't get far," Copperhead replied, clutching one of Honeydew's hands in both of hers. Her dull, reddish braids were pulled back with a metal band, laying down her back and glowing in the light of early evening. Though Sevi could never tell if it was actually metal or if it just looked like it was, he had always wondered how she could walk around without breaking her neck—there was just so much hair.

"We could... I could break into the cellar and steal however much amber we need. You know how little the Matron thinks of me. She'd never expect it."

"Love, even if you did, and even if I could get us a pair of horses, and even if we rode as fast as a cresting wind from the boundaries of Matron's and Redwood's control, what then? There is a lot of country between us and home, and no one is going to help us."

"We could... I could hide among the other soldiers leaving for the Turning. Then we could both go home. And there will be so much chaos there with all the freshly joined humans—we could disappear in it all."

"You know that won't work either."

There was a delicate, awkward pause beyond the wall, so uncomfortable that Sevi could feel it radiating through the stone. Lily broke it with a sound of disgust. "Sorvathos save me from this. Would these two just kiss already?" she grumbled, pulling her helmet down in irritation.

Sevi took another peek. "They are."

"Fantastic! Let's not be voyeurs. That would be wrong," Lily said, standing up.

"Just... please. Don't go back. Promise me that you'll stay with me," Honeydew continued, sounding like she was on the verge of tears. "I'm scared, Zinnia. This isn't what I expected."

"I promise, Lav," Copperhead said. "I'll retract my request tomorrow. I'm not going anywhere."

"Gods above and below, let's just get out of here," Lily implored.

Sevi chuckled, sneaking one last look at the Fabling lovers. He caught sight of a flower growing between their clasped hands before he slid the spystone back in its place, muffling their conversation. Their tones could still be heard ever so slightly through the wall, making Lily squirm every breath that she was subjected to it. She kept pulling her helmet down until they had moved a significant distance away.

"That. Was. Terrible," she groaned. "You'd think that after several years they would have found *anything* else to talk about, but noooo, just, 'let us run away, my love! This place isn't meant for us! Also, every moment we talk is one I'm not sucking your face, so how about a little more of that and a little less of this?' *Ugh*. I wish you hadn't thrown away all our firesnaps."

Sevi didn't mind it himself. Though he rarely understood half of what they ever talked about, they were always cute to listen to. "So, what now?"

"Now? It's almost dinner, and I need to replace some of the food I lost watching *that*."

"Should we stop by the kitchens?"

"Let's," she said, then tilted her head to the side in thought. "Certain bits aside, it's been a nice day. How about we climb the Sunset Tower? It'll be a good way to end it."

The thought appealed to Sevi. "Think there's enough time to grab Aly? We haven't had dinner together in a while."

"If you think you can get her out of the garden. And you'll have to run, that's a long trek."

He shrugged. "Then I'll run."

"Alright. Go get her, and I'll see if I can get us any scraps. Let's meet at the top of the tower. And grab something ripe in case I come up empty."

Parting ways at the cliffside, they each went about their tasks. Sevi jogged as quickly as he dared all the way to the garden, where he found Alyda laying out several juicy berries for a dinner of her own. It took a little convincing, but she eventually relented, storing one of the berries inside her pocket before flying up to perch on his shoulder. Upon her suggestion, they gathered several ripe ferofruits and longroots to take with them.

The sun sat low on the horizon by the time Sevi and Alyda climbed the Sunset Tower. Lily was already waiting for them. She had been unable to get any food from the kitchens and sat in a grumpy mood until Sevi handed her what he'd gathered. Pulling out a large stone from the outer wall, they each leaned against the wall opposite and munched away on their meager supper, watching the sun slowly creep down to touch the mountain range.

Wind whistled through the open gap, less of a spyhole and more of a blatant window. A passing flying Fabling might have discovered it, but it was very, very unlikely to be picked out against the rest of the castle's bulwark. As far as Sevi was concerned, the scenery outweighed the risk.

Alyda let out a tiny belch and waved at Sevi for his canteen. He lifted it to her and waited patiently for her to have her fill. It didn't take long. "This was nice," he said, taking a swig himself. "Thank you, Lily. I... I think this helped."

"Mmhm. It's what I do. Sier Lily the Benevolent."

"And thank you for joining us, Aly," he added.

Alyda flicked her wings and shot him a look. "*You're welcome. Thanks for remembering to include me.*"

Sevi settled his hands in his lap, staring pensively out across the sky. But with nothing else to do, his thoughts turned once more to Digby and his warning. This very well could be the last nice day he'd have in a while... or ever. And the longer he thought it over, the more the thought soured in his head. What were they doing? Why were they playing when doom could come crashing down upon their heads at any moment?

"Whatcha thinkin' about?" Lily said, breaking him from his thoughts.

"Nothing."

"Yes, you are. You've got that 'I'm worried but don't want to talk about it' look."

Sevi huffed. Why did he even bother?

"I thought you told me everything?" Lily persisted.

"I do, I just... don't feel like talking."

"Why not?"

He clenched his jaw, all too familiar with how this would end. She would annoy him to the end of time until he finally cracked. Better to put an end to the game than waste all his energy. "Do you think Digby made it out?"

Lily frowned. "If he had been caught, that captain would've returned with him by now. But I guess, in a best-case scenario, he died from his wounds somewhere in the mountains." She grinned darkly. "Are you worried about him?"

"A little."

"You shouldn't," she said, shaking her head. "He's gone. What's done is done."

Sevi turned a skeptical gaze on her. "We were exposed, Lily. Someone out there knows about us now."

Lily shrugged. "I know that, but what can we do about it? There's nowhere else for us to go, not with all the Fablings out there. We could try getting out through the mines if we had to run, but we'd have to risk the poison, and we don't know those tunnels. Not to mention what could be waiting for us if we got out the other side.

"No. We know the castle, we know the Cut, and we know each other. We can't say the same for—" She broke off, waving her hand across the world. "All *that*. So, let's focus on what we do know, and prepare for what we don't... after we've enjoyed ourselves."

She winked at him. As usual, Sevi felt himself get swept up in her confidence. Digby's intrusion had shaken but not toppled her. She was Lily, in control and ready to lead. And he was ready to follow.

He smiled at her and turned his gaze back to the sunset. A cool, evening wind blew in, making Alyda shiver. With a flutter of wings, she lifted up from her spot and settled herself in the crook of Sevi's arm where it was warmer.

"What if we'd gone?" Sevi said, staring at the world. What lay just on the other side of that rocky wall? Where did the sun go when it set?

Lily placed her hand on his shoulder. "We didn't know him. He used us to escape this place. We have no idea what he would've done to us the moment his fate was out of our hands."

Sevi thought back on the old man's crinkly, smiling face. He had been nothing but friendly, even after Lily had clobbered him over the head. Could that really have been nothing but a lie? "I guess you're right. It doesn't matter either way."

"No, it doesn't." Lily turned to face the sun along with him. A flock of birds drifted lazily across its face, circling around the mountain air currents in a graceful dance. "There you go again, bringing my mood down."

"Sorry."

She shrugged. Alyda coughed gently, covering her mouth with a hand to muffle the awful, grating chimes that came out. Sevi offered her the canteen again. "Hey, Lily?"

"Mm?"

"How about a story?"

"Now?"

He nodded. Alyda poked her head up from his side and leaned against his leg, flicking her ears with interest.

"Both of you..." She clicked her tongue and hummed to herself in thought. "Sure. Why not? Have I told the tale of Sier Califf and the Coven?"

"Thrice," Sevi said.

"Lujenne and the Bumblebee?"

Alyda chimed and waved her hand dismissively. *"Boring. Next."*

"Little gremlin." Lily grimaced. "How about the Sunchaser?"

Sevi and Alyda shared a look, then each nodded at Lily.

"Alright then. This story comes from a place far, far away, where there are no mountains nor trees. Only plains, full of tall grass and seas of sand, filled by people known as the Salakiri."

Sevi turned his body completely around to face her, and Alyda resettled herself on his leg, tucking her dress comfortably beneath her knees. Lily went on. "The sun wasn't always as we know it to be now. It was slow, and lazy, and disregarded the destruction its heat caused the Salakiri living below. The—"

Sevi interjected, "I thought Sorvathos was the sun? He wouldn't do something like that."

"The Salakiri don't believe in the Father."

"How come? He's right there!"

"How should I know?" Lily grumbled. "Do you want to hear the story or not?"

Sevi shrugged apologetically. Lily kept her scowl on him for several breaths before resuming. "His sister, the moon, tried to reason with him. While his light was harsh, hers was cool and soothing, and could heal the wounds left by his heat. Whenever he passed overhead, she would be there to follow in his wake, shedding her light across the world to heal its burns. But she could only do so much, and whenever her power waned, she had to disappear from the sky to where sun, and stars, and clouds go to sleep. When she was rested, she returned, ready to heal once more.

"But her brother never rested like she did, and slowly, he made wounds in Iaela that even she could not heal. Realizing that she needed help, she turned to the people below.

"Of the Salakiri, there was a prince named Badim. He was not taller, nor stronger, nor smarter than many, but none could ride a horse like he could, and he was revered among his armies for it. It was said that within him lived the very spirit of the wind, as not only did every horse he touch become tame the moment his fingers brushed its hide, but they could run clear across Iaela without so much as a drop of water, faster than even their quickest sandlungs."

"What's a sandlung?"

"Some kind of lizard, I think. Now shush. So, one night, when her brother had passed over the horizon, instead of taking a day to rest, the moon vanished from the sky and came to Badim in the form of a horse. From the moment he touched her, he knew what she was, and what she'd come to ask of him. He agreed without complaint. The sun had killed so many of his people, and if he could put an end to its oppression, he would. So, he kissed his wife and child goodbye and rode off with her into the night."

"What—"

Her glare silenced Sevi before he could continue. "When the sun returned the next morning, both his sister and Badim were waiting for him. He ignored them as usual, focused only on his slow, scorched path, drunk on his radiance. When he was directly overhead, Badim wrapped his arms around the mare's neck and filled her with all the power of a typhoon. And with a magnificent cry the two leapt into the sky, bringing a storm with them unlike anything the world had seen before.

"Upon reaching the sun, they began to circle it, catching it in a net of howling, shrieking gusts so fierce and cold that it threatened to snuff his light out for good. For the first time in his life, the sun knew true fear. He ran, bursting from the gale and streaking across the sky faster than ever before, never in one place long enough to burn the land as he once did.

"Thus, the moon brought Badim with her up into the heavens, to pursue her brother if he ever slowed again, and named him the Sunchaser, Champion of the Winds. And there he remains, ready to ride with a storm at his back whenever called. The end."

Sevi let out a breath. Alyda quivered on his knee, turning to look back at him with a wide, toothy smile—one that he reflected. "That was good," he said.

Lily shrugged, but it was smug.

"How do you know so many stories?"

"I just picked 'em up."

"Where?"

"Does it matter?"

Sevi tilted his head. "I guess not."

Lily nodded and crossed her arms. "So. Feeling better?"

"Oh, yes."

"Were you still seeing things today?"

"No."

"And you still have your medicine?"

"I'll need another batch soon."

"Then make some soon."

"I will."

"I mean it, Sev. Don't put it off again. If I have to wake up to your screaming one more—"

"You'll throw me off the mountain. I will, *Sier* Lily," Sevi said, cutting her off. "So, you can stop mothering me."

"Wanna see what mothers do when their boys don't behave?" Lily said, cracking her knuckles. He stared skeptically at her. She raised a closed fist in response.

The last meager slivers of the sun poked up over the rim of the mountains, wavering slightly, reaching for the rest of the sky in one last attempt to prevent it from being swallowed by another night. Sevi imagined he was on an airship streaking after it, chasing it across the heavens like Badim.

He closed his eyes and summoned the vision of himself standing on its deck, face into the wind with his two best friends at his sides. Lily could be the captain. She'd probably demand it, actually. Alyda could be the lookout, but did flying ships even need lookouts? Maybe the chef, then. He wouldn't need any title himself; he'd just be happy to fly.

The sun disappeared, and the castle was abruptly swallowed in shade. Sevi opened his eyes at the change, and Lily let out a deep, satisfied breath, as though the view had filled up what empty space remained in her belly. Alyda coughed and wrapped her arms around herself, shivering more violently without the sun's warmth.

# THE DANCE BETWEEN

"Let's head down," Lily said. "It's a shame. A day isn't very long, is it?"

# Chapter 16

*How quiet the sun, tasting death every day. How peaceful a soothing wind goes. How few were the days in the grace of such warmth. How sudden the storm is to blow.*

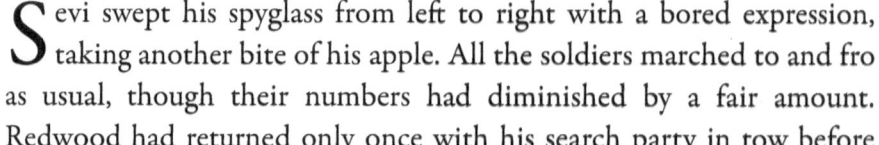

S evi swept his spyglass from left to right with a bored expression, taking another bite of his apple. All the soldiers marched to and fro as usual, though their numbers had diminished by a fair amount. Redwood had returned only once with his search party in tow before setting off again, and that had been two days ago. His fervor to catch Digby was rather astonishing.

Lily let out a snore on his right. He sighed and put his spyglass down. Just another normal day.

After their escapades, Lily had made certain that they were prepared for anything coming their way. Raids on the kitchen were increased as much as they dared. Whatever could be harvested from Sevi and Alyda's garden was to be collected and dried. They maintained a vigil on the castle night and day, keeping watch for anything unusual that could be construed as dangerous.

Lily had wanted to move all their belongings from the bedroom to the mountain, but the potential noise made in getting everything up the cliff had proven too great a risk. So, they kept it as it was and left some stores behind in case they were forced from the cliff to the castle.

Sevi settled his chin on his arm and tried not to wish for something to happen. It was maddening to wait for a tragedy to start when he knew it was coming. It was like watching an approaching thunderstorm—knowing the rain and lightning will close in eventually but having to sit there in the sun before it swallowed everything.

He took another bite of his fruit and munched on it sullenly, staring at the castle and all its watchful towers—they would surely make better sentinels than he ever could. No doubt the Fablings would raise the alarm far before he spotted anything, so why was he wasting the energy?

He reached into his pocket and pulled out his treasure, looping the chain around his hand and holding it as high up to the light as he dared, watching its bulky silver star swing gently in the breeze. He'd kept it by his side ever since the incident with the firedrake and had been loath to part from it under the threat of impending doom. He allowed its gentle silver shimmers to hypnotize him, drawing him into its delicate embossments until he no longer focused on his worries.

Lily shifted in her sleep, pulling his attention away. He stared at her, running his gaze over the engravings on her helm to the large one at its front, so similar to the one in his hand. He held the pendant up so that his star aligned with hers. "Sevi and Lily," he said softly. "Two stars alone in the night."

Lily grunted, making him jump. He tightened his body instinctively, preparing himself for a gibe, but relaxed when she stilled. "Oh, thank the gods," he murmured, rubbing his face.

Turning back to the castle, he held the star up in his fingers, regarding it against the backdrop of the surrounding lands. "Have you seen what's out there?" he asked it softly. "Did you used to travel in the pocket of a merchant from land to land? How did you come to me?"

The pendant sparkled silently.

"You've never made for very good company. What do you think, Shy? Do you think that maybe a knight from one of Lily's stories used to wear this?"

Shy didn't answer, either.

Sevi stared forlornly down at his absent shadow. "I guess you'll have to do," Sevi said, taking the necklace and putting it over his head. "I'm sorry that you can't go back in your box. I know you're too precious to wear. But this is for the best. I think something is going to happen. We can't go back down as much as we did, and if the firedrake comes back..."

He shuddered. Such a horrible thing. He pictured the little salamander's flames in his mind, but the moment he did, he couldn't think of anything else. It filled up the empty spaces in his head, overflowing until it leaked from his eyes like tiny burning tears licking at the edges of his vision.

He thought it was a trick of the light and tried blinking them away, but no. They stayed, manifesting behind his eyelids as mere flickers, and then bursting into focus as a true, burning blaze.

He leapt up from the ground, losing his grip on the apple in his haste, and the fire disappeared.

Sweat poured from his skin as he drew a shaky breath.

*No...*

Lily stirred, turning on her side again. The simple act anchored him, breaking his trance. The pounding in his ears gradually subsided, but a weight seemed to settle on his shoulders, dragging him down to the ground. He winced and realized that he'd closed his fist in a death grip around his pendant, digging his flesh into the points of the star.

Drawing in a shaky breath and letting it out through his teeth, he forced his fingers to relax and closed his eyes. *All is fine,* he said to himself, then repeated it several more times. *You're not crazy. All is fine.*

Except it wasn't. It was like the salamander had crawled inside his head and set it alight. But it was gone, right? Lily had chased it away.

*But it always comes back.*

He looked at Lily. They hadn't raided the kitchen that day. What if the salamander had returned? It would destroy their supplies.

*It's gone. But what if it's not?*

What would she do? Should he wake her up?

No. If this turned out to be another one of his episodes, then he didn't want her to know. He needed to be better, so that she could count on him when it mattered, and that meant holding himself together as tightly as he could. He needed to know that the salamander was gone. No firedrake meant no fire.

Taking a twig, he wrote, '*firedrake, will be back*' in the dirt. Glancing once more at his friend, he nodded to himself before picking up his pack and turning to leave. He could handle this foolish task on his own.

The new plants around the resealed wall were still there. The berries and fruit on their leaves had shriveled up and died not long after they'd grown, littering the ground with dry husks. Sevi kept a wide berth from them, stepping as far out of their way as he could, and averted his gaze from the mine's bricked tunnel altogether.

He spent the rest of the walk in quiet contemplation, making plans on what he would do if the worst had come to pass. He could probably manage stealing a blanket from the soldiers' bunk room somehow; they stole each others' stuff so often that they'd never assume a boy living in the walls was behind it.

Of course, that would require unsealing a bigger brick, which was horrifyingly dangerous. And then there were their bed sacks. There was no way he could be quiet about stealing one of those, as all the hay was kept near the stables. He'd have to go back to sleeping on a pile of rags or risk going Outside altogether.

But his fears were unfounded. He saw no sign of the firedrake when he made it to his room, though it had left quite a bit of heavy charring where it had thrashed about in its fight with Lily.

Some of the clothing Sevi had left too close to its heat would probably have to be repurposed into something else, but everything else was there—the new stores of dried food he'd stored away, the small boxes of stolen utensils, the weird glass tool people used to read, and everything else he and Lily had gathered over the years.

He'd been worrying over nothing, just like he'd suspected. The room was fine. There was no fire. All was fire.

Fire.

His room disappeared.

He was in a field, a garden, and everything was on fire. Bodies sprawled all around, and Gods, some of them still twitched. A great roaring of a hundred voices filled his ears, and metal struck metal as human knights fought human peasants, cut down one after another before his very eyes and squirting blood all over the precious plants. One was rushing toward him.

Fire washed through everything until even the beautiful flowers were consumed and killed, chasing after the charging peasant as though he brought Torment itself with him, burning the dying men, filling the air with their screams of pain until their throats burnt to ash. A sword came swinging down and—

Sevi threw himself backward and slammed into the wall, knocking over piles of belongings with a crash. His clothes were drenched with sweat. He'd brought his knees to his chest and stretched out his arms, fending off a blow that hadn't come.

He closed his eyes, hopelessly heaving in breaths that couldn't fill him, and clutched at his pendant beneath his shirt.

*Why?*

His whole body shook. He stared at his hands. Then he clutched at his hair and pulled it angrily by the root.

*WHY?*

He began to sob, holding his head, desperately trying to keep it on his shoulders lest his insanity spin it from his neck. Everything had been better. He had been *better* for *years!* But no. It was all a dream. There was no getting better. He was crazy, and there was no fixing it.

He'd lasted a while. He'd convinced himself that it had gone away, but he'd slipped. Now the visions were back, and worse than ever before.

It was too much. Sleep. He needed to sleep. If he couldn't see, if he couldn't feel, then he couldn't see and feel what wasn't real. That could help. It would. Then *he* could help and be exactly what Lily and Alyda needed.

He dug into his pocket for his effizine powder and yanked the pouch out, undoing the drawstrings with trembling fingers. He turned it over in his palm.

Empty.

Lily's phantom voice whispered to him from the past. *Don't put it off again.*

He pushed off from the floor, wobbling on shaky legs out of the bedroom. He needed to get to his garden before he burned from the inside out.

# Chapter 17

*A flower can only be so resplendent. Beauty only distracts for so long.*
*Slumbering fires were suddenly blazing, crackling their vindictive songs.*

S evi fought to move his legs with every step, clutching his pounding head with one hand while pulling himself along the wall with the other. Not far. Just a little bit more. Maybe if he said it enough times the garden would appear before him, and he could finally rest.

He went over the recipe again and again in his head. *Grind raw effezine roots into powder. Mix with loranum pollen. Add a handful of water. Stir into a paste. Apply to the roof of the mouth or above the upper lip. Let the fumes do the rest.*

He ignored everything else, focusing on the familiarity of the recipe and not the fires that licked at the back of his mind, flashing into focus every time he blinked.

"Shy. Please. I know you're here. Hide me from this. Take me away, anywhere but here... please."

Sevi twitched at every sound. His skin crawled like a thousand bugs wriggled along his body, scratching him with their tiny legs. The fire in his head had sunk into his very blood and was pushing at his skin, trying to get out. He hurried even faster, gasping with frantic breaths until his vision went dim around the edges.

"Did you ever learn to talk? Say something. Please..."

"We're lost."

Sevi stopped dead in his tracks. "Sh-Shy?" He couldn't see his shadow in the dark, but that didn't mean they weren't there.

"We're not lost."

"You took the wrong tunnel."

"*We* took the wrong tunnel."

"I thought you said we weren't a republic."

"We are when the fingers are pointing at me. Now hush, that's an order."

Sevi's blood ran cold. That wasn't Shy. He took a step back, staring ahead in confusion. Had Digby returned? Had he brought people with him?

"Let's go back and take the path that loops down."

"Hang on, let me just snip one of these mellomarks. They're good luck."

"Can you believe this? Do you think one of those kids made this?"

"Had to be. Keep an eye out for them, but focus on your task."

"Aye."

"Are we sure this will work?"

"No."

"Lovely."

"Yeah. Let's go."

Sevi's breath caught as several sets of footsteps came walking his way. He scrambled behind a tall stalagmite, scrunching himself up into a ball, but he couldn't get himself behind it entirely. He covered his mouth with his hand as the footsteps got nearer and nearer, not trusting himself to breathe, praying to whichever gods were listening that he wouldn't be seen.

"Sh-Shy. If you're there. Hide me. Save me. *Please.*"

A torch poked around the bend, followed by the invaders. Sevi watched wide-eyed as the fire reflected menacingly off the slick cavern walls, growing brighter by the second. It had come for him after all.

The vines along the ceiling curled up and dimmed at the offensive light as it passed. Sevi ducked his head down against his chest and squeezed his eyes shut. If he couldn't see it, it'd disappear. But the flames were there when he closed his eyes, too.

The first stranger walked by his hiding place, crunching gravel underfoot, but said nothing.

The second one sneezed as they went by, echoing loudly. Sevi dug his nails into his arm and cheek, biting back a terrified cry.

"Cover your mouth," a masculine voice said, moving slower than the others.

An eternity went by before they passed, and the torchlight faded. Sevi risked a peek around the rock, staring after the men as they went. He caught a flash of green on their clothing as they disappeared into the dark. The same green as the castle's soldiers.

It was a long, long time before Sevi left his hiding place, waiting far longer than was needed for the echoes of their footsteps to fade.

*The soldiers from the castle have found us.*

He needed his medicine now more than ever. He needed to face them beside his friends with a clear head. But... his garden. *They had been in his garden!*

He ran the rest of the way and burst into the room in a frenzy, running straight for his patch of plants. "Alyda. Alyda!" He cried her name in a desperate hush, scared of risking a yell lest the strangers come back. He fell to his knees, brushing plants aside left and right, looking for his friend's familiar glow and praying to the Mother that she was alright.

A soft chime, tentative and scared, rang out from under the broad leaves of a thettleback bush. He rushed to the plant and very carefully peeled its branches back. Alyda valiantly held a sharpened stick at him with a terrified expression from underneath.

It melted as soon as she saw him. She dropped her weapon and zipped herself out in a sharp flap of wings, running into his face and wrapping her small arms around his cheeks. She squeezed him in a trembling hug, pressing her head against the side of his nose.

Sevi felt a half-manic laugh burst from the back of his throat as he fell backward, cupping her in both hands. "Oh, thank the gods. You're alright. They're gone now." He tried his best to sound certain, to be brave for the little fairy. But he couldn't believe his own words.

Alyda squeezed his face once more before letting go, pushing back to hover in the air. She flung her hands about, gesticulating wildly with a cacophony of chimes until she fell into another one of her coughing fits.

"I don't know. I..." Sevi clutched at his head. He just. Wanted. To. Sleep. But Alyda kept going, filling his burning head with her grating music. "Alyda. Stop. Stop."

She stopped.

"Listen. Can... can you go get Lily? She... she was at the Overlook. She'll know what to do."

Alyda slowly crossed her arms, giving him a critical look, and made a sign with her hands. "*And leave you here alone?*"

"Please, Aly," he pleaded. "I can't do this. Not on my own. I'm... My head is burning again."

Alyda's wings slowed, and he lifted a hand to support her, letting her drop into his palm at face level. She looked at him worriedly, stepping forward to place a hand on his forehead as if to check his temperature.

"We have to make sure she knows. You can get there far more quickly and quietly than I can."

The look on her face lingered but became increasingly skeptical. She repeated, "*And leave you here alone?*"

But he didn't budge. Eventually, she shook her head and let out a weary breath. She hovered off his hand, reached out to touch his head with both hands, and lay a gentle kiss on his skin.

"Thanks, Aly," he whispered. "Don't worry, I'm going to hide here. I'll be here when you get back."

Alyda patted his head once, resting her hand on him for a long moment in a silent offering of comfort. She pulled back a short distance, idling in front of him with concern carved into every facet of her tiny face, but nodded.

*Bless her. She's far braver than something so small has any right to be.*
"Go," Sevi said, smiling, reaching out to her with the tips of his fingers and shooing her away.

Huffing, his friend snapped her wings in a crisp salute, hopped up and down in the air with a quick burst of energy, then zipped up and out through the skylight in a green streak, losing her glow in the bright light of day.

Sevi harvested the effezine the moment she was gone.

# Chapter 18

*Quick was the forest to whither in anguish, lithe was the knife at its work. A garden of sleep cannot shelter nor shield, when nightmares crawl out of the dirt.*

As past experience had shown, a medicinal sleep, when administered incorrectly, came with tremendously vivid dreams and nightmares. But when done right, it came with nothing at all. It was a testament to Sevi's knowledge of botany that, despite his trembling hands, he only slightly ruined the dosage.

It didn't matter. When not taking the medicine meant horrible visions, and taking the wrong dosage meant horrible dreams, then he was only doomed if he didn't try. And the fires were growing, reaching for him everywhere he looked, stretching out of the corners of his sight into his waking eyes. He had no time for precision. He needed to escape.

The moment the paste had congealed, he spread it all along the roof of his mouth, then covered himself with leaves and curled in the dirt. A numbness crept up his body, beginning in his fingertips and toes and slithering up his limbs. Darkness clouded his visions of fire, smothering them with their inky black, until he could see nothing at all. He met it like an old friend, and it took him all too readily.

The dream that swept over him was fuzzy at first, as though viewed through a murky puddle of water. He sat in a chair, facing a group of featureless people wearing long, strange, colorful regalia. Some of them hung suspended in midair with wings of lace, flapping in slow motion.

Fingers stroked through his hair, and when he looked up a blond woman without a face looked back. As jarring as she was, she didn't feel scary. She felt safe. He leaned against her, hugging her with arms smaller than they should've been, and buried his face against her side.

She delicately extracted his hands and lifted him into the air in front of her. Her body glowed with a dim light. He smiled at her. Warm. Happy. Content. And he could tell she was smiling back.

She dropped him abruptly. He fell for one heart-stopping moment, pulled down through the air harder and quicker than normal.

He landed in a pile of leaves. Each frond and stem shook against his body, trying to crawl into his mouth and ears. He waved his hands about, batting them away, and came tumbling out along the ground, rolling to a rest at the foot of a massive tree with branches that stretched to cover the sky. Ethereal light filtered down between its slowly swaying limbs.

Sevi slowly looked around. To the left, the leaves shimmered yellow. To the right, they faded into the blue of the sky. Something blinked into existence out of the corner of his eye, and when he turned back, another person was lying down beside him. Their whole body was fuzzy, with not even their clothing discernible through the charcoal fog that shrouded them.

They were splayed out along the ground just like Sevi, comfortably gazing up at the tree without a care. Feeling no malice, Sevi turned his head to look back at the sky, trying to make it out through the many light beams and leaves.

His limbs moved slowly, as though he were wading through mud, but he managed to bring himself up from the ground. He was in the castle garden, strolling through its plants like he'd always dreamed of doing. Flowers swayed to his left and right on an unfelt wind, and in the distance, dancing at the edges of his perception, were a pair of voices.

He moved toward them and found their owners hiding on the other side of a large bush—one tall, one small, but both indescribable. A spyglass twice as big as the one he carried had been propped up on a stand and pointed at the sky. Their voices, so tantalizingly familiar, might be discernable if he only took a single step closer.

But the fire had chased him into his dreams.

The ground shook, cracking in large spiking spider webs that sprouted in a wide circle around him, until rock and soil split. Flames burst through the garden's open wounds with a ravenous hunger, roaring up into the sky in giant pillars of hate. The smaller sparks that crackled out of them fell lazily to the ground, where they feasted upon every blade of grass and dry twig until they grew into orange snakes that slithered along the rock, racing toward him.

He turned and ran, calling for the person under the tree, but found only an imprint in the ground where they had lain.

Tripping over an exposed root, Sevi fell. He clawed his way backward under the tree, seeking its protection. Alone and helpless, he pressed himself into the trunk and waved his hand at the fire as if he could ward it off, shielding his face from its harmful glow.

The trunk thrummed against his back. Something hammered at it from inside, getting closer, and stronger, and faster.

Roots lifted themselves from the soil, forming black, sinister silhouettes against the malicious inferno before him. Their sharp, wriggling fingers hung frozen, then slowly turned toward him as if sensing his presence, carefully closing the distance between them and spreading to allow no room for escape.

They stilled, then tore through the air on a path to his heart.

The ground gave way. The sharp fingers of each tendril passed just over Sevi's head as he was pulled down into the dark, cold underworld, bellowing out a scream from frozen lips that no one could hear.

The nightmare, relentless, only chased him into the waking world. The cavern walls shook as he awoke, and a deep, reverberating rumble bounced around the narrow tunnels, beating oppressively against his eardrums. Sevi sluggishly covered them with his hands, suffering under the aftereffects of the medicine.

The air outside whistled as something rushed through it, growing louder, and louder, until something massive struck and shook the ground, rattling the cave and causing small stalactites to break from their perches.

The brilliant creatures of the Cut had fled. Some of the plants in his garden curled inward on themselves, terrified. Muffled screams rose in a building murmur, and smoke streamed past the ceiling's skylight, barely visible in the faint glow of the moon.

What was happening?

"Al-y-da!" he called. His tongue was slow and stupid in his numb face. "Lil-y!"

They were nowhere in the cave. He scrunched his fingers in the dirt and dust, fighting against the drug. *Need to get up. Need to find them. Need help.*

He clawed his way up the nearest wall on unsteady legs, putting as much of his weight on the stone as he could. "Lily," he called again. The screams outside were his only answer.

Another, more violent *boom* shook the cavern, throwing him off balance. He flailed his arms wildly, stumbled forward and smashed his cheek against the wall, tearing a grisly gash open to his cheekbone. He reeled back, blood dripping down his face. But the pain gave him something to focus on, driving away some of the fog.

He kept one hand on the wound and placed the other on the wall. He couldn't stay there. He needed to get out.

Sevi walked from his garden, placing one shaky foot in front of the other, growing stronger with each step as the effizine gradually wore off. *Are those people still here?* He couldn't summon his faculties well enough to be scared. *The Overlook... Lily was at the Overlook.*

With no better heading, he walked the long way to the escarpment where the tunnels branched. The noises of the outside world grew louder and more terrifying the closer he got, until they were almost deafening, echoing loudly and sporadically through the Cut.

He grabbed hold of the rope and tried to hoist himself up, but his strength gave out quickly, and he sagged to the ground, clutching uselessly at the worn fibers.

Sevi's chest vibrated raggedly with exertion. Meters of rope might as well have been a mile, and it was with sudden clarity that he realized how

Digby must have felt. But he had to make the climb. Lily could still be up there. What if she was trapped? What if she was hurt or captured?

He needed to find her. She'd know what to do. And if she was captured, he'd go with her. He'd never leave her behind. It's what she would do for him.

Gritting his teeth, he steeled his resolve. Clenching his ankles around the rope, he began worming his way up. He rested frequently, fighting off his dizziness, pushing past his desire to surrender to the fall. He almost didn't comprehend it when he had reached the top, grasping for a rope that wasn't there and finding emptiness instead.

Sevi flung himself over the lip of the rock, drawing in deep, shaky breaths. His arms were dead weight, and his head was throbbing with a headache that had gone from painful to splitting. The harsh stone beneath him felt inviting and warm—more comfortable than trudging through a dark, shaking cavern to gods-knew-what.

*Lily is probably fine. Still sleeping where I left her. The shaking will stop. Everything will be fine if I just close my eyes again and wake up.*

Lily's voice cut through his own. *We're partners. Now and forever.*

The words rang through his head over and over again, refusing to be ignored. He pulled himself up to a sitting position with tremendous effort, clutching at his head as though it would keep his skull together. But it was melting through the gaps in his fingers.

"Help me, Sh-Shy," He breathed, his voice catching as a fresh stab of pain jabbed through him. "I know you're still here. You h-have to be. Please."

A piece of darkness before him wavered. Sevi wiped his watery eyes and stretched out his hand, clutching at air. There was a long, hopeless silence—one that he hadn't felt since his first nights in the Cut, full of solitude and despair.

No one was there to hear him. No one was there to save him. Only darkness and hard, unfeeling stone.

Until he was lifted to his feet.

As if Mother Avinaea had heard his pleas herself, an unseen force wrapped around his wrists and pulled. Sevi stumbled, falling hard against the wall of the cave once more.

A faint smile appeared on his lips once his surprise wore off. "I knew it," he mumbled. "Thank you."

There was just enough light filtering in from all the cracks and holes in the ceiling for him to just barely make out the rest of the tunnel. He forced himself to keep moving, walking through the strange berry bushes next to the mine's entrance. Their glow had gone out, and they now lay withered and dead.

But not just them. All the plants were dead, from the vines that stretched from the ceiling to the sparkling moss that covered the ground. And the mine he'd spent so long resealing had been reopened in its entirety.

A dark, sinister hole bored through the rock that stood gloomy and eternal, silently mocking all his efforts to keep Outside from getting in. It gaped at him with a black maw, breathing out a poisonous wind, eager to pull him from his home the moment he let his guard down.

He wouldn't let it get the chance. He hurried along, putting it behind him on a slow march up the final incline to the Overlook. The light increased the closer he got to the exit, broken by erratic flashes and crashes violent enough to rival any thunderstorm. Sevi reached reflexively to adjust his eyepatch as he left the tunnels, but it was gone.

"Lily?" he called. "Alyda?"

No response. He reached for his signal whistle with shaking hands and blew out a sputtering chirp. A loud, piercing whistle screeched through the air in answer just before another heavy *boom* shook the mountain, deafening him and sending him tumbling to the ground. He cried out, calling his friends' names, unable to hear even his own voice.

A hazy orange glow rose from beneath the cliff. Wisps of flickering embers blew up into the air, rising into the darkening sky. Fear gripped at Sevi's heart. It was the fire—it had to be. It was still chasing him. But now it had taken his friends.

He pushed himself forward with ringing ears, crawling to the Overlook's edge and peering beyond its foliage.

Everything... everything was on fire.

Sevi jolted in fear.

*"I said don't move!"*

Sevi didn't listen.

The face of the left soldier wrinkled in confusion, then realization. "Wait! WAIT!"

The weapon flared. Something punched Sevi in the chest. Pain lanced through his body, flinging him backward over the edge of the cliff and into open air.

The last thing he saw were the branches of the Overlook's trees, swaying beneath a sky devoid of stars as the smoke from the fires climbed to eat them, too.

Then darkness claimed him, and he saw no more.

# Part 2:
# Movement

# Chapter 19

*The walls of their cradle burned down with a whimper, from Outside, a snake slithered in. Her bitter tale racing swift to its ending. His only just set to begin.*

---

First there was nothing. Then there was pain.

Sevi awakened with a flail of his arms, instinctively trying to ward off the next rock that would come rushing up to crush him. He regretted it immediately.

Pain tore through him the moment he twitched, paying for every motion a hundredfold with a fresh blossom of agony that burst from his chest. His brain fuzzed, threatening to pull him back down into unconsciousness unless he stilled.

His chest rose and fell with panic and agony both old and new. It wasn't until he'd settled that he realized his head wasn't lying on jagged rock at the bottom of a cliff, but on something... indescribably soft. It made him pause, at odds with his latest memory. He tentatively pressed his cheek against it, and it sank without resistance.

*It's a pillow.* A real, honest pillow, stuffed with real feathers, and smelling of... of soap. Flowers. Something clean. And now that he focused, he realized his whole body was lying on something nearly as soft, too. A real, honest mattress.

*Is this real?*

He cracked open his eyes and was met with darkness. Nothing, everywhere he looked.

Panicked, he shook his head in frantic jerks as if he could jostle the dark out of his head. *Gods. I'm blind!*

Something snorted next to him—a deep, rolling sound that came from something bigger than himself.

Sevi stopped.

The creature—or person, Sevi hoped—creaked as they shifted, as if made of wood, and let out a long, drowsy yawn. It moved closer, grunting while cracking its limbs. Sevi flinched away with a sharp intake of breath.

It stopped. A warmth crept up Sevi's side as the creature leaned over him, close enough for Sevi to feel its breath on his face.

"Hey." It spoke with a melodic, male-sounding tenor, rumbling out in a way that sounded wonderfully human.

*A person. An Outsider. A Fabling?* Sevi desperately tried to pretend he was dead.

"Hey. Kid," the man said louder.

*Go away. Go away. Go away.*

The man grabbed Sevi's shoulder and shook him gently. Sevi gasped at the fresh pain that crackled through him at his touch.

"You're awake," the man said with a smile in his voice. "Oh, thank the Mother, you're awake!"

Sevi, trembling, shied away from his grip as best as he could, scrunching his face with discomfort and silently praying the man would stop touching him.

"Sorry!" The man withdrew his hand. "Ah, sorry. I'm just. I'm just glad you're—I can't believe it. Hey! Lea! The kid's awake!"

The man practically shouted with excitement. A chorus of angry curses rose up all around Sevi, making him cringe and dig his nails into the mattress as his anxiety threatened to overwhelm him completely. It wasn't just one person. There were many. Outsiders on all sides.

He wanted to throw up.

"Shut the fuck up, corporal," snapped an irritated voice.

The first speaker, the corporal, didn't say anything else. Sevi's bed shook with his footsteps as he marched across the floorboards at a fast pace.

Sevi tried to huddle under the thin sheet draped across him, making himself as small as possible. This was it. He'd been found and brought to the Outside. He'd survived the fall off the Overlook only to die at the hands of the Fablings. Maybe they'd torture him like they'd tortured Digby. Maybe they'd throw him into a cold cell in the tower and leave him to rot. Maybe they'd eat him.

He raised a weak hand to his face as tears began to well. His fingers brushed against fabric, and he froze. Exploring higher, he found a band wound tightly across his eyes all the way to the top of his head. He was wearing a bandage!

Running his hands down his chest, he realized most of his body had been wrapped. He scrabbled at the linen strips, wincing as they grazed against a myriad of scabs and scrapes that crisscrossed his face. "Shy. Please. Help me get this off."

His sheet was yanked from him before he could tear the bandage away, blowing air down his body. Sevi cringed, trying—and failing—to curl up any further. It hurt too much.

"Please. Please don't hurt me," he begged. He tried lifting an arm to ward the strangers away but only managed to flop the limb awkwardly.

Someone chuckled. "I don't think I've ever been so insulted in my life," they said, sounding distinctly feminine.

There was an answering laugh. "You do have some meaty hands, Lea. Sometimes I wonder if your job is to finish the goblins' work for them."

"Why would I finish you off, Reynam, when I can take these meaty hands and push that spike deeper into your shoulder. Slowly. It's more enjoyable to watch."

"Mmm. 'Finishing off.' 'Slowly pushing in.' Is there something you want to tell me, Lea?"

"Yes. Could you please breathe in another direction?"

Her voice changed toward the end of the sentence, growing louder as she moved in closer, tickling Sevi's face with long strands of loose hair. She lay her hands softly on his shoulder but didn't press in like the man named Reynam had. A cold metal band, however, touched him from where her wrist lay, making him shiver.

"Be still, child," she said, softening her tone. He still flinched. She went on, "I know it hurts, but I need to unwrap your bandages and check the wounds on your head. We don't want them getting infected, right?"

There was something in her voice. Something that evoked calm when she spoke, like the promise of a cool breeze on a hot day. He couldn't understand it, but his body did. It unwound itself, loosening his anxious muscles ever so gently, until he had the barest semblance of calm. He wasn't at ease by any stretch, but he stopped trying to squirm away.

"Good boy," the lady murmured. Her hand lifted from his shoulder and touched his head, joined by her other as she slowly unclipped and unwound the wrappings covering his scalp. "Lean forward a little for me—that's it."

Tilting his head until his chin touched his chest, he felt his heart thumping through his jawbone, fluttering like a glowmoth. It wasn't until the last wrapping came off, revealing the room around him, that he exhaled a breath he hadn't realized he'd been holding.

He could *see!*

Sevi blinked rapidly while his eyes adjusted to the sudden light, bringing the hazy silhouettes of his surroundings sluggishly into focus. It was daytime, and he... he was in the castle's barracks. People. Outside people. *Human* people, lay in every bunk, with some even resting on blankets spread across the floor. All had some kind of injury—some were worse than others.

Sevi took in the two figures around him. One of them was a man, standing near the foot of his bed with a grin on his face and an arm in a sling. His smile had such levity to it that it pulled the gaze away from his heavily swollen eye, bruised blue. *He must be Reynam.*

Sevi froze. He recognized him. He was one of the soldiers from the Overlook. He had tried to stop the one who'd attacked him.

Reynam stood with an unbothered, confident posture that Sevi had seen on the more important Fablings of the castle. He wore a soldier's uniform rakishly and unkempt, but in a dark charcoal gray as opposed to the deep green of a Fabling. His hair was silky black and hung down to his shoulders, almost melding into his coat, and his skin was a smooth, natural tan. He nodded at Sevi, catching his stare, but didn't say or do anything other than smile his little grin.

Sevi couldn't see the lady with her fussing over his head, but she smelled nice. Like a garden. And coffee.

His gaze wandered while she prodded at him, touching her fingers to his bare, shaved scalp, observing wounds he could only feel. Unsure of what to do, he took the opportunity to eye the walls of the room, trying to inconspicuously find where the one that led into the Cut was. But everything looked different on the Outside, and he couldn't look in every direction with the lady clutching at his head.

The soldier must've seen Sevi's apprehension. "Don't worry, kid, you're quite literally in good hands. Good, big, meaty hands."

One of Lea's hands left Sevi's head. Reynam's eyes flicked up to watch it, and his grin broadened at whatever he saw. Lea said, "If you're not going to be helpful, corporal, then leave. I'm working."

"I'm always being helpful, Doctor," Reynam replied. "Here, I've got something for the kid." He reached with his good arm for the pocket under his slinged one, grimacing with difficulty. "You know, in hindsight, I should have asked Tarlow to put it in the other pocket. He probably did it to annoy me. Almost... there!"

With a flourish, the man pulled out a silver pendant on a shining metal chain.

Sevi's necklace.

Sevi stared covetously at it. The sight of it in someone else's hands sickened him. He instinctively tried reaching for it, desperate to take it back.

"Stop moving," Lea reprimanded above, pouring a soft cream on his head that stung where it touched.

Sevi let his arm drop, but his eyes never left his necklace. He wanted it back with an intensity that surprised him.

"This, right here, is one amazing necklace kid," Reynam said, walking over to Sevi's side. "Able to stop a bullet? Incredible. Wish I had been wearing one when I got spiked. Cassik here probably wishes he'd had one for his face after the beating it took, but on the bright side, he might have a good future as a shovel ahead of him."

"What beating?" the man on Sevi's left said crisply.

"I digress though," Reynam continued, smiling again. He brought the pendant closer to Sevi, offering it to him face-up in his palm. "This is good jewelry. A pure silver face and etchings so skillfully carved that it would make any jeweler worth their iron cry. And worth who knows how many glaras." The man ran his thumb along its edge. "I've only ever seen one other like it."

Sevi peered closer at the pendant's face. Its normally gleaming metal had been tarnished with black residue, as if burned. But the worst offense was the small metal ball that had embedded itself in the middle, denting it inward and mushrooming outward until it had lodged itself in completely.

Sevi tried reaching for it again, but Reynam gently pulled it away. "Where did you get it?" Reynam asked softly. His voice changed. He stared at Sevi oddly, no longer looking relaxed. His grin was still there, but it didn't look real, as though it had disappeared and left a ghost behind. Sevi shied away from him again, suddenly afraid.

"Reynam," Lea cautioned. Her voice had changed, too, becoming hard like whenever Lily scolded him.

*Oh, Gods. Lily. Alyda. Where are they?*

Reynam glanced up at Lea, then back down at Sevi. He shrugged, rolling whatever had come over him off his shoulders, and placed the necklace in Sevi's lap. "I tried to polish it for you as best as I could, but..." He wiggled the fingers of his injured hand. "And I wanted to get that bullet out, but then I thought, with luck like that, why not carry it around with you?"

Sevi tentatively reached for the pendant, worried Reynam would change his mind and move it away from him again. Straining to lift his arm, he managed to get his hand over it and pull it weakly to his chest. He closed his eyes, holding onto the one familiar piece of his life that he could touch.

Lea started wrapping his head back up but blessedly left his eyes uncovered. "I think I must be going crazy," she said. "You're being nice to something without breasts for once."

There was a smattering of chuckles from the surrounding soldiers. Reynam scowled, but it was fleeting. "It's the least I can do for the hero of the resistance," he said, leaning forward and gently nudging Sevi's shoulder again, making him wince. "Especially after we'd almost shot him. I'd heard about you, you know—we had orders from the Daring Digby himself, just before he keeled over, to look out for the shadowless boy and the helmeted girl. From what I heard of your friend, I might've let Solen take a crack at *her*, but not you, kid. That's a joke, for the record. But speaking of, from the looks of it, you have a shadow just like the rest of us, don't you?"

Sevi's eyes widened. Reynam paused to lift Sevi's arm. Sevi let him, staring at the shadow he cast across the bed.

"Old codger was probably seeing things," Reynam chuckled, letting go of his arm. "Anyway. Thank the gods for thick silver pendants. And cliff trees, am I right? Kid? Hey, you alright?"

No. He wasn't.

Waking up in the Outside. Finding humans in place of Fablings. Lily and Alyda missing. Shy connected with him once more. It was all too much too quickly, and when Reynam had called him the hero of the resistance, something else clicked into place.

Digby had wanted to be captured. He'd come to the castle for a reason.

He had been looking for something. That something was the entrance to the mines.

He had warned that the Fablings would disappear forever. Because these soldiers had planned to travel through the mines from somewhere else and annihilate them all.

And they had. All thanks to Sevi.

Tears welled and spilled down his cheeks as the realization punched him in the chest harder than any bullet. All those people with lives he'd watched over for years, who he'd given names to, who were the only living souls he'd ever known outside of Lily, Alyda, and Shy. All gone. All dead. All because of him. It wracked his body with an anguish he'd never known, wrapping him in a tight grip and squeezing him until he couldn't breathe.

"Reynam!" Lea dropped her hands from Sevi's head.

"What?"

"*Thank you*, corporal, for all the help," Lea said flatly. She finally walked into Sevi's view, stalking toward Reynam like a mother cave rat protecting her young. She was about the same age as Reynam, though shorter and portly, with long, shiny black hair and honey-tan skin gathered in a band midway down her back. She made up for the height difference with an aura of silent, directed control, keeping her back straight and proud.

The surrounding beds went silent at the tone of her voice. "Go see Mel for that salve," she ordered.

Reynam, looking confused, said, "I didn't—"

"Go, Reynam. Please."

Reynam's gaze flicked between her and Sevi. Sevi avoided his eyes, looking sullenly down at his lap. Reynam stood there for several breaths before sighing and straightening. "Feel better, kid," he said, then muttered a stoic, "Doctor" to Lea. He spared another glance at Sevi before annoyedly turning and walking away.

Lea breathed a long, irritated sigh. "That man," she said, shaking her head. She turned to face Sevi, who was trying to wipe his face with the back of his arm. She had eyes the color of walnut, which softened as she looked at him.

"He means well," she said, bringing the chair over to Sevi's side and sitting down. She leaned forward and delicately dabbed at the corner of his eyes with her sleeve, avoiding his wounds as best as she could. "Most days he'd come in, ask how you were doing, then sit right here."

She finished wiping his face and settled against the edge of his mattress, giving him a small smile. Her gaze flicked down to the necklace in Sevi's fingers. "His way of apologizing for what happened. He just doesn't know when to stop talking."

The soldiers on the left and right of them grunted or laughed in affirmation. The one on the right, a lady, piped in, "Yeah. It'll be nice to have a little peace from him. He likes to flirt with the lady officers when he's not prodding at Cassik. It's gotten pretty annoying."

"Sad that you're not one of them, Loma?" the one to the left, Cassik, said.

"Psh. I think I'd rather kiss a horse. You might be projecting, Cassik."

There was a fresh round of chuckles, until Lea silenced them all with a sharp whistle. "That's enough, kids." A small number of them apologized before turning away from her, moving their attention to anything but her stare. "Here's the point," Lea said to Sevi. "The bullet aside, no one here is going to hurt you. Just the opposite, my whole job is to fix you. So, stay in bed, try not to move, and listen to what I say. Those cracked ribs have a long way to go." She raised her eyebrows expectantly, looking at Sevi for confirmation.

Sevi said nothing. He wanted nothing more than to jump out the window, run into the mountain, and disappear forever. Or maybe just jump off it. It's what a filthy murderer like him deserved. But Lea held his gaze with such intensity that he could only nod.

She nodded in return. "Good." She stood up and righted her robe. "Get some sleep. We'll be by with food and, hopefully, new bandages by sundown." She turned to walk away.

"W-wait," Sevi croaked.

The doctor stopped mid-stride and looked at him expectantly.

"Lily."

"Is that the girl Reynam mentioned?"

Sevi nodded.

"No little girls have gone on my table. But I'll ask around." With another nod, the doctor left him and moved on to the next bed.

Sevi huddled under the covers, doing his best to muffle his tears. The Fablings were gone. He was finally out of the Cut and surrounded by people—humans, just like him. It was exactly what he'd always hoped for.

He'd never felt more alone.

# Chapter 20

*Once there was a mouse who'd made a castle his home, until a fire had burned it all down. Once there was a flower who protected her ward, but where was that poor flower now?*

------ ✦ ------

Sevi saw the faceless lady in his dreams again that night. She was in a new outfit, shining in blue and gold finery, and led him by the hand through the stony tunnels of the Cut. This time, he struggled in her grip, fighting a hopeless battle against every step she took. She no longer felt safe, nor kind. It was all a lie. She was taking him Outside, where the death and fire were. She wanted him to see it. She wanted to force him from his home.

He couldn't go. He wouldn't.

But it was hopeless. They crossed the threshold, and when the light from the waiting blaze sprung up and rolled over their bodies as sudden as a mountain storm, he burst from his dream with a heaving, panicked lurch.

The resulting pain made him cringe with agony, clutching at his ribs and chest. His bandages clung uncomfortably to his skin, drenched in sweat, and a cut on his chest had reopened, staining the wrapping red.

He looked tiredly around the bunkroom, trying to ignore the pain. The room was illuminated by the ghostly half-glow of the moon, peeking through the shuttered windows in thin beams of light. It was peaceful. Yet the blood roaring in his ears, and the collective sounds of dozens of drowsing soldiers made him doubt that sleep would come again soon.

Sevi laid his head back against the pillow and closed his eyes. It didn't take a single breath for the guilt to find him again. *I murdered hundreds of people. And two of them might have been my best friends.*

Fresh tears slid down his face. *All your fault. All your fault.*

"Hmm," a soft, undulating voice rumbled.

Sevi snapped his eyes open. He wiped his face, looking toward the sound. It was close. "H-hello?"

None of the soldiers stirred except to roll in their sleep or let out a snore. He stared at Cassik, then Loma. Neither moved.

"Hmm," the voice said again, and his bed gently shook.

He dug his fingers into his mattress. Ghosts. Freshly made from the battle, seeking revenge for their untimely deaths. There was no other explanation.

He fearfully looked across the room, scanning for any grisly phantasms floating above the floor. But as the moments passed, and the monsters in his mind failed to appear, his death grip on his bed loosened. He let out a breath and eased back into his mattress.

But then his gaze settled on a patch of the room that was darker than most. It could've been the outline of a person, but it was slightly translucent—easily missed unless looking right at it. And then the patch moved.

Toward him.

*Oh, my Gods. It really is a ghost.*

Sevi tried to speak, bringing his bedsheet up as if it could offer any kind of protection. "P-please don't hurt me. I didn't mean to do it!"

The ghost didn't listen. It moved closer, stepping into the light, standing judgingly before him halfway down his bed. Two pale, dim, glowing white orbs appeared where its head would have been. Each one blinked at him asynchronously, one after the other, floating delicately in a swirling cloak of ink. Sevi gasped and dropped the sheet.

It wasn't a ghost. It was a shadow.

"Shy!" Sevi wheezed, opening his arms. The shadow moved closer but stopped before it reached him. The two orbs hovering in its formless head angled down at the floorboards and blinked, one after the other.

"Can't you move?" Sevi asked, trying to lean toward his friend.

The orbs looked up at him. Sevi peered closer. Small wisping trails of shadow were falling gently from the creature's body, dissipating in the soft blue light of the moon.

"Shy. You're losing all your dark." Sevi lifted his hand as a strand of darkness detached itself from the creature and floated near, disappearing entirely at his touch. "Is this why I haven't seen you in so long? How did this happen?"

"Hmm." Shy hummed harmonically. More of their body poured from their chest, fading away like smoke.

"I've been better, too." Sevi inclined his head toward the rest of his body, offering a weak smile. The shadow blinked in response. "Where have you been? And you can hum now? When did that happen?"

Shy remained silent.

"Have... have you seen Lily? Or Alyda?"

Shy shook along their edges but didn't conclusively respond. Pushing down his disappointment, Sevi tentatively tried lifting his hand toward the shadow, spreading his fingers out. His chest tightened with emotion. "It's *really* good to see you. You saved me, didn't you? Back in the Cut? You helped me up."

Shockingly, and at the cost of much of its body, a tendril from the shadow split off in the vague shape of an arm and rose in the air, mirroring Sevi's motion.

Sevi stared, wide-eyed. "When did you learn to do that?"

Cassik snorted and began to turn. Sevi jerked his head toward him, and Shy whipped their tendril arm back, losing even more of their body in the process.

"No!" Sevi whispered despondently. "Don't go!"

With every breath, Shy lost more of themselves. A fresh wave of fear washed through Sevi, and he stretched his arm out again. "Shy, listen, find Lily! Find Alyda! Tell them where I am! Tell them I'm alright!"

The vanishing shadow seemed to push itself toward Sevi in a futile last attempt to get to him before their body fell away, leaving two glowing orbs hanging suspended in the moonlight before they, too, faded and disappeared.

Sevi froze with his hand still out, reaching for the place the shadow had just been as though he could grab the night by the edges and gather his friend's darkness together again.

"Hey, kid."

Sevi tore his gaze away and dropped his arm, wincing as it hit the mattress. Cassik eyed him from beneath squinted eyelids weighed down by sleep. He muttered, "You alright?"

Sevi gulped, looking from him to the floorboards. "Y-yes."

"Night terrors?" The man yawned matter-of-factly.

"Yes," Sevi mumbled again.

"You get used to them. Just... try to be... a little... quieter..." His voice trailed off, and before Sevi could blink, he was snoring again.

Sevi watched the soldier until his panic subsided. When he could breathe normally, he slid under his sheet, morosely dropping his head onto the pillow. He kept his eyes open for a while, hoping that Shy had only disappeared to avoid being found, and would reappear soon. But they didn't.

"Find Lily, Shy," he whispered to the dark, surrendering to exhaustion. He held his arm out to a moonbeam before sleep could take him completely. A shadow formed across his bed, exactly where it always should have been.

# Chapter 21

*The boy was alone, a wound at his heart, saved by a star from the sky. With shadows for friends, and people for foe, and all of his life gone awry.*

---

Outside life was far different from what Sevi had imagined it to be. The soldiers seemed to be making no effort to eat him or run him through with swords. On the contrary, they seemed to treat him with geniality—if not affection in some cases—patting him on the foot as they walked by and greeting him with a smile.

The doctor, Lea, would periodically go through the barracks-turned-clinic to check on how he and the other patients were doing, treating him with the same professional disinterest that she gave everyone else. Then she would retreat to a desk that had been moved to the front of the room, where she would direct the other workers as needed while chugging her coffee. Sometimes she would bring him a kind of hard, sweet treat called 'candy,' which made him only crave more when it was gone.

Sevi couldn't bring himself to smile back at them, though he knew he should treat the Outsiders with as much courtesy as they showed him. They were human, and most likely the rightful owners of the castle, which technically made him their guest in several ways. But he knew nothing about them save for their animosity toward the Fablings, making it hard not to see them as dangerous. And after years of isolation in the Cut, he had a hard time rationalizing any feelings of kinship towards them just because they all had rounded ears.

It was wonderful to be reunited with his shadow, though. Shy refused to take form again no matter how often he called their name, but it was no small comfort to have them with him again, mirroring his actions in the light like any proper shadow should. It felt like he was whole again.

As one week turned into two, and two into four, his feelings of solitude only deepened. Doctor Lea never found anything regarding a young girl in a knight's helm running around, nor did he hear anything about a little green fairy. Not knowing what had happened to them was somehow worse than learning they had died. If he knew—as miserable as he would be—he could cry for them, instead of living every day with an anxiety that ate him from the belly out.

Compounding his worry was the monotony. The first week lying in bed with no hope of escaping had him in a state of constant fear, mixed with intermittent depression over his part in the invasion. Doctor Lea and her aides regulated the times he could get out of bed very strictly, limiting when he could limp over to the water closet to thrice a day. He never tried to leave the barracks and doubted he was even allowed. By the end of the second week, his fear had faded, but the routine held.

He'd tried giving names to the other people in the room, just as he had the Fablings, but they all looked so... normal. It was much harder to come up with something he could remember when nobody had extra limbs or feathers for hair.

Sometimes Reynam would come in to get his wound looked at by Doctor Lea, then he would walk by Sevi's bunk and talk at him rather than to him. Sevi didn't quite enjoy listening to his stories. He only ever talked about all the people he'd met, loved, or gambled with, and he'd always work some sly question in about Sevi and his necklace. Not to mention the fact that he was still one of the men who had shot him. But he regularly got distracted whenever a female officer happened to walk by and would cut the conversation blessedly short.

The only thing that ever changed were the people. Some would get better and leave. Some would get covered in a sheet and carried out. Though some, like Cassik and Loma, were just as badly hurt as Sevi and went nowhere, much to his delight. Though they couldn't approach Lily's skill, listening to their adventures almost made everything bearable.

It had taken weeks for him to feel comfortable around them. Most days he was too tired and in too much pain to stay awake longer than a few hours, and he could only feel so at ease with complete strangers after years of isolation. But as the three of them slowly healed, they started talking.

Much like Reynam, they had tried asking Sevi personal questions that he either didn't want to or couldn't answer. But after his silence failed to break, they satisfied themselves with talking to each other, using him as their captive audience. Unlike Reynam's boring, bragging tales, however, theirs involved wondrous events of where they'd been and who they'd fought. And they never ran out of things to talk about.

"Do you remember that time when that one greenblood almost launched me onto the next continent?" Loma began, scratching her severely burned shoulder through its bandage. Doctor Lea had given up warning her about that.

She had short-cropped hair she never bothered to comb, and her body was lean with toned muscle. Her family came from a place called the Spirithorn River, which separated the countries of Elkra and Áilé, and she frequently griped she hadn't inherited any Áiléan height from her dad. He was apparently infirm, but had a fighter's spirit despite his circumstances, and bemoaned the fact he couldn't join the army when the call went out. So, she had joined in his stead.

"You mean besides their latest attempt?" Cassik grimaced, adjusting the bandages over his wounded leg. A falling stone had partially crushed it. He'd been warned he might never walk on it again, but he held on to hope.

He had a glossy black beard that tightly hugged his face, and shoulder-length black hair that was swept up in a knot. His family had relocated to Elkra two generations ago from the country of Salakir—a country that Sevi was delighted to find actually existed—in order to avoid the war with the Arathean Empire, eventually settling on the Tiburan border. He had stayed to defend their home rather than relocate his family when the Fablings invaded.

"Obviously," Loma said. "I barely left the ground this time around."

"What's a greenblood?" Sevi asked her.

"The blaggards we just kicked out of this castle," Loma answered triumphantly. "You know, the Fae."

A hollow pang of guilt drummed at Sevi's chest. "Oh. I call them Fablings."

"'Called,' you mean." Loma snickered.

"So, what happened?" Sevi asked, hurrying her back to the main subject.

"Right. There we were," she said, lowering her voice to enhance the drama. "Out on patrol in the Ettleveil Woods, making our way back to camp. A full moon hung in the sky, which only made things worse. The brush was dense, and the trees stood like walls, fencing us in with their thick trunks and tight spacing. We had only just stopped for a breather at the latest path marker when the goblin came flying in low on a pair of dragonfly wings. Empyrean scar owls were hot on its tail, and it was already crackling with an evil blue magic, ready to massacre the whole platoon. It must've been a lost scout and figured if it was going to go out, it'd take some of us with it. I can respect that in hindsight."

"Only because you didn't die," Cassik interjected.

"Right. If it had killed me, I wouldn't be around respecting much of anything, least of all Cassik. But I'm still here, and I'm still not respecting Cassik." She winked conspiratorially at Sevi, drawing a laugh from him.

"What did you do?" Sevi asked.

"I wish I could say I did anything, but I was still green around the ears at the time. Greener than a gobber's blood... so I froze," she grumbled, looking annoyed. "Reynam was the one who shot it down."

"Reynam?" Sevi said.

"Unfortunately," Cassik said. "The reason why he can get away with acting like such a shi—" He broke off mid-word and glanced at Sevi, then over at Loma.

"Pigheaded, boorish lout?" she offered.

"That," Cassik said. "It's because, *frankly*, he's the best shot in the army. Even invented a small spyglass to attach to his rifle. Most of us are sporting one now."

Sevi blinked in surprise. That explained the man's unending wealth of confidence. "I... would not have guessed."

"Most wouldn't." Cassik snorted.

"So, what did he do?"

"Like I said, he shot it down." Loma shrugged. "Popped it right in the chest from thirty meters. But he used a regular old bullet, so it didn't burn up, and it had built up a lot of speed at that point. So, when it fell, it fell toward us. Here's the thing about greenblood magic, kid," Loma said seriously, leaning in. "It doesn't just go away when they die. Once it's going, it's going, so that thing was a flying bomb coming at us at the speed of a sprinting horse."

Sevi's eyes widened. "What happened?"

"It hit the ground a few meters away from us, exploded, and sent us all flying into the trees!" She laughed merrily, seemingly delighted by the memory of her near-death experience. "Some bruises, maybe a sprain or two, but no one died. I'll tell you though, one of those branches went right up—"

"*Loma*," Cassik warned.

"Well, all I'll say is that I couldn't sit down for a week!"

"I still say that's nothing compared to getting turned to stone," Cassik boasted.

"Oh, *here* we go. You did *not* get turned to stone, you got hexed and froze for a couple days, you big baby," Loma said.

"I was there, you charred cow. I *know* what it was."

"Liar."

"Heifer."

"Um." Sevi raised a hand, and to his surprise, they quieted, both turning to him with open expressions. "Can you do any of those things?"

"Do what?" Cassik asked.

"Like... turn someone to stone? Or make lightning? I've seen the Fab... the Fae, cast magic before, but never humans. Can adults do it, too?"

Cassik shook his head. "I'm afraid that's a greenblood skill alone. But we do have the Runics. I'm surprised you don't know that—they're in so many plays."

"Who are they?"

"They're rune makers. Whenever they carve their language into something, it becomes enchanted. But they're very rare, and very peculiar. When the fighting broke out, the goblins targeted them and their order specifically among all others, and they quickly went into hiding. Nowadays, anything carved by a Runic is either fake or ridiculously expensive."

Sevi leaned forward, eyes wide. "Could I become a Runic?"

Cassik smiled sympathetically at him. "I'm afraid—"

"Shut it, Cassik," Loma chimed in. "Anything's possible, kid. Not everyone can be a Runic, but you'll never know until you get the chance, right?"

Sevi smiled at the thought.

She nodded affirmatively. "Now how about that time we actually met a Runic? Do you remember that, Cass?"

"How could I forget? He just appeared in the middle of camp one morning and never said a word. Kept staring at me funny, too," Cassik grumbled.

But then, Doctor Lea discharged them both. Loma's arm and torso had recuperated from most of her burns well enough to satisfy the staff, so she left with a bottle of salve and a smile, promising she'd come by to visit when she could. Cassik's treatment changed shortly afterward from rest to exercise in order to improve the muscle and blood flow that had atrophied in his leg. If he was lucky, it wouldn't go lame. He left on a pair of crutches, eager to find a mattress that wasn't "filled with gravel," as he put it.

With their beds empty, nothing to occupy his time, and no end to his imprisonment in sight, Sevi's waking mind swiftly sunk into his darkest thoughts and stayed there. All he could think about, day in and day out, was the destruction he'd caused. He'd only wanted to help Digby, but he'd let an entire army into his tunnels so it could go to war. Because of that, he might have only succeeded in getting his best friends, probably the old soldier himself, and every living Fabling, killed. How was he supposed to live with that?

Sleep provided no comfort, plaguing him with nightmares full of fire and death that got progressively worse on each successive night. They always started with a fire and ended with a man pointing a rifle at him. When enough room had opened up in the barracks, some of the patients nearest him asked to be moved away so they wouldn't be disturbed by his screaming. Doctor Lea had given him what sleeping medicine she could spare, but there wasn't much, and it never worked as well as his effizine. Its scarcity forced him into withdrawal, adding to his suffering.

When he got well enough to walk without assistance, he chose to lay in bed. When the staff came by with food, he let it go untouched. When Reynam, Loma, or any of the soldiers passed by, he pretended he was asleep. He had stopped coming up with names for people after a dozen or so of them had been carried out under a sheet.

Doctor Lea told him almost every day that he was getting better. He didn't feel better. He felt much, much worse. All he wanted was to go back into the Cut; to look for his friends and to escape this suddenly confusing world. But the Cut as he knew it was gone.

Then one day, something changed. He woke to find an unfamiliar man sitting in the chair next to his bed, reading a book. He was well-kempt, wearing a grander uniform than any of the other soldiers, with gold trim to compliment a long, dark blue coat as opposed to the commonly worn charcoal. His skin was remarkably unblemished and a dark shade of ebony—a stark contrast to the cream and caramel hues of the other soldiers. His hair was dark and shaved short, hugging his skull with the barest of lengths, and an intricate gold earring in the guise of a serpent traveled along the rim of his ear to end at the lobe.

The way he sat in his chair was immediately familiar to Sevi, like one of the Fabling leaders at the head of a table while their underlings read their reports. Legs crossed at the knees. Back straight. Chin up. Quiet. Dignified. In control. Yet he looked completely at ease, with the ghost of a smile haunting the corner of his mouth, ready to come to life at a moment's notice.

Any soldiers walking by reacted noticeably different to him than they did each other. All would pause, lift their hand up to their far shoulder, and bow their head before moving on. All except Doctor Lea who, always busy, never seemed to register he was even there. The man returned each gesture with one of his own but seemed more interested in his book.

The infirmary was oddly quiet. Whatever undischarged soldiers left on the far side of the room spoke in whispers. The ones closest to Sevi's bed didn't speak at all.

The man broke into a grin, chuckling to himself as he turned a page. His eyes wandered at the break in his attention, catching Sevi's gaze before he could pretend to sleep. The man's grin widened, and he gently closed his book with one hand.

"Good afternoon," he said in a light accent. He set the book on the ground and twined his fingers together in his lap, smiling at Sevi like an old friend. "I was beginning to worry that you'd sleep the day away, *risho*."

Sevi stared morosely at the man. Whatever his purpose, he just wanted him to go away.

"It's rude to stare. At least, I'm told it is. So, you shouldn't." He adopted a humored look. "It's strange. I'm sure this is common knowledge here, yet everyone does it anyway. I've come to believe that they really love how I look. Do you love how I look?"

The man straightened his uniform as if to show it off. Sevi scrunched his face in confusion despite every attempt to keep his dour mood.

"No? *Kinna*. Shame. I am beautiful." The man lowered his hand. "Why then stare and be silent?"

He gave Sevi a respectable amount of time to answer. Sevi refused to.

"This is no way to introduce yourself," he said, dropping his joviality. "Where I come from, introductions are the most important part of meeting someone. If you fail the first time, you must work for a dozen chances more to get it right. Surely you do not want to go through that?"

Sevi clenched his jaw and tightened his hands into fists.

"Ah, I see what the problem is," the man continued, smiling again. "You need help. That is fair. I have yet to introduce myself, so use this chance to learn. And unlike you, I will not waste my opportunity." The man raised his chin. "I am Captain Caldwin River Ta'Runa, previously known as Sandro Adhal Ta'Runa, and Alai Royash Ta'Runa before that, and Orro Tawme Ta'Runa before that. I have been a son, a student, a sailor, a merchant, a glassmaker, a husband, a fisherman, a husband again, a traveler, a castaway, and now a soldier for the Embers of Korina, and a husband for a third time. *Ik Earuna kah'eshaa.* You may call me Captain Caldwin River or Captain River." He nodded to Sevi when he'd finished. "Now you."

Sevi refused to budge. Lily had once told him to be mindful of Digby, and whenever he broke one of her rules, disaster always followed. This was no different. Who was to say that this Captain River wasn't here because he'd heard from Cassik and Loma that Sevi had spoken with them? And now he wanted something from him. Just like Reynam. Just like Digby.

Captain River sighed. "Fine. Then we sit here, and I stare at you until you speak." And he did just that. Straightening his posture and leaning against the back of hid chair, he settled in and fixed his gaze on Sevi.

Sevi was skeptical, but the moment dragged on, and an awkward silence fell between them. The nearest soldiers, clearly pretending not to listen in, eventually failed to hide their stares. The captain didn't even seem to blink. Sevi tried turning on his side, but he could feel a dozen pairs of eyes boring into his back along with the captain's. Eventually, he couldn't take it anymore.

"Sevi," he relented, grumbling through gritted teeth.

There was a pregnant pause. Sevi wondered if he'd been heard. "*Sevi?*" Captain River said at last, his voice laced with shock.

The captain's tone got Sevi to turn back. Captain River's eyebrows were nearly touching his hairline, and his eyelids were peeled back in complete surprise.

"What?" Sevi asked.

"That's *it?* That's an *awful* introduction! Your name is much too short. And you only have *one!*"

Anger quickly quashed Sevi's curiosity. He channeled his memory of Lily and fixed the hardest glare he could summon on the man, wishing it would reduce him to ash. Captain River shook his head, oblivious to Sevi's fury. "We will work on this," he said. "You have much to learn."

"Why are you here, *Captain River?*" Sevi asked icily.

Captain River's smile returned. "To meet the hero of the resistance. The boy who opened the mountain's doorway. You have been here for so long that I felt it was time to speak."

Resenting the reminder of his part in the battle, Sevi turned away again, presenting his back to the man. He didn't need this conversation, or whatever *this* really was.

"Trying to sleep? Again? But surely you are hungry?" Captain River bent and picked up a tray containing a bowl of soup and a piece of candy. "I hear from Doctor Lea that you have stopped eating. Are you ill? I would be surprised. She said that you have been healing quite well, such is the gift of youth. Though I am certain she was being modest. Her knowledge of medicine is without equal among our peers; you are truly fortunate to have her as your doctor."

Sevi kept quiet. He was done talking.

"*Kinna*. Lieutenant Digby will be unhappy to hear that the boy who saved his life survived getting shot off a cliff, only to lie down and starve himself." The captain sighed dramatically and began unwrapping the candy from its paper.

Sevi sat back up, staring at the captain. "Digby?"

"*Kha*. He was very worried about you." Captain River popped the sweet into his mouth and rolled it around. "Cut up, bashed on the head, very thirsty, walked through a whole mountain, half alive, and when he got to camp, the only thing we could hear from his mutterings was the word, 'children.'"

He shook his head. "When he woke, we heard more. We thought he had dreamed you; some strange spirit of the mind to help him through his torture. But here you are. Though I am sad to see you have a shadow. I would have liked to have not seen one."

Sevi, for the first time in weeks, was filled with raw emotion. He choked down a rising sob, refusing to let it out. "Reynam said... Is... is he...?"

"The old man is alive," Captain River said with a smile. "And he still worries for you. He is not yet well to make the journey up the mountain and remains behind in our camp at its base. You will see him again in time."

Sevi closed his eyes, losing his hold on his tears. He hadn't gotten *everyone* killed.

"Now," the captain said, picking up the tray on his lap and standing. "Lea tells me that you can walk. When you have eaten and are strong, I would like to take you around the castle you helped us to free and ask of you a few questions." He smiled, placing the tray of soup across Sevi's thighs. "You have my word upon Earuna that no harm will come to you. And should a question come up that you do not like, then you need not answer."

Sevi wiped his face with the back of his arm. "I—"

The captain spoke over him. "And if you would truly rather stay in your bed..." Leaning down, he picked up the book he'd been reading, dusted the cover off, and placed it on Sevi's lap as well. "Then you may have this to pass the time."

Sevi wiped away his tears and stared down at the book and the soup. "I—"

He was interrupted a second time by the sudden appearance of a man with skin as dark as the captain's, who stepped beside Captain River with a salute. Noticing Sevi's gaze, the captain turned to the newcomer with an expectant eyebrow raised. "Yes, Tahno?"

"Message, sir." Both Tahno's accent and earring matched Captain River's.

The captain glanced apologetically at Sevi. "Very well."

Tahno produced a paper from his pocket, which the captain plucked from his fingers and opened. His expression remained unchanged until he had finished reading. "Ah, I am called elsewhere," he said forlornly. "I hope that you will decide to join me, *risho*. Keep in mind. If you join me, the more you talk, the more I will talk." He smiled. "I hope you will like the book."

The captain turned on his heel and walked away with the messenger before Sevi could say anything, leaving him alone with his new book and a cold bowl of soup.

# Chapter 22

*His tears would not bring back what he had lost, nor lessen the depth of his gloom. Pushed in life's flow, how the water ran white, towards an end we were forced to resume.*

---

Sevi wrestled with Captain River's offer for several days. Accepting it might give him the chance to escape into the Cut, but would that be wise? The army knew about the tunnels, and his friends were missing. He knew of no Outside place to hide, had no one to rely on, and had no plan. At least here he was fed.

A piece of him was still waiting for the blade over his head to fall. He could happily daydream when there was a wall between him and the world, but years of fear and hunger had conditioned him to avoid hope in practice.

But after four days, he made up his mind. He would go with the captain. He imagined if Lily were here, she'd urge him to walk the grounds to get as much information as he could, then use that information to come up with something he could use. Maybe it would give him the chance to leave a message in the Cut, in case his friends were still there.

He had tried searching the walls of the barracks for its spystone, but there were too many eyes on him, and he was quickly caught every time he tried. The bunk closest to where he believed it to be, distinguished by smoke stains on its mattress, was occupied, and Doctor Lea and her aides were far too considerate to be unobservant. He had used his nightmares as an excuse, claiming he was sleepwalking, but he could only say that so many times before they strapped him to the bed. Sevi wouldn't give up, though. He wasn't Lily. He couldn't plan like her. But he would try.

Gods... He missed her. Her and Alyda. He prayed to Sorvathos every day that He had kept them safe, and that Avinaea was providing them both with whatever She could give.

Captain River arrived promptly after breakfast the day after Sevi sent for him. Sevi had felt well enough to eat and was reading the captain's book when he came stepping up with a benevolent smile. Another soldier followed him, stopping a careful distance away with a rifle propped against his shoulder, watching all that went on in the room with a careful eye.

Sevi marked his page and pushed away his disappointment. He'd been enjoying its story about a queen cursed to live upside-down, always in danger of falling into the sky, and afraid of anything blue as consequence. The Cut didn't extend into the castle's library, and books like this had been a hard thing to come by. He'd learned to treasure them, which is what made it so difficult to tear out some of its pages.

"Good morning, *risho*," the captain said, clicking the heels of his well-polished boots together. The overly chipper salute made some of the infirmary's residents smile.

Sevi closed the book without a word. He had resolved to limit his speech with Captain River as much as possible. If the Embers of Korina had healed him only to gain some kind of information from him, then he would do whatever he could to prolong his stay. He wouldn't answer a single question, no matter how many times he was asked. At least, that's what he told himself. Digby's treatment at the hands of Redwood remained a vivid memory.

Captain River's smile widened as he got up. "It pleases me to see you reading the book. The sea is not kind to paper, and I regretfully had to limit my readings when I sailed. Have you enjoyed it?"

Sevi gave him a shrug. The captain didn't seem to mind. "It is a lovely day for a walk. But stay close, my guard is very restless." He gave Sevi another pleasant smile and gestured for him to follow, turning toward the main door.

Sevi patted his pocket for peace of mind, then his chest for luck, before stepping away from the bed he'd called his home for months. *It's time to be like Lily.*

Doctor Lea stopped in her ministrations to watch him go, quirking the corner of her mouth up and waving at him before returning to her patient. He eyeballed the guard as he went by, trying to summon up the courage he imagined Lily would have, but when the guard met his gaze with a cold, unyielding stare he felt himself crumble like an old leaf. He hurried after the captain and didn't look back.

Captain River opened the door, and Sevi beheld a perspective of the castle he'd never experienced. The first thing he noticed was that there were many, many more soldiers outside of the infirmary than there ever were inside of it, all going about whatever task compelled them, or just loitering around the outskirts. He took an unconscious step backward, reflexively shying away from the crowd of Outsiders. *Is the man who shot me out here?*

But the captain prevented his retreat, ushering him forward encouragingly. Gulping, Sevi steeled himself and took a step. He couldn't give up just yet.

A covered stone pathway wrapped around the outside of the courtyard. Thinly carved columns detailed with various flowering etchings held up its roof—a vestige of beauty in a landscape reduced by war. Tiny holes carved up the walkway without any noticeable pattern, accompanied by gouges, caved-in portions of ceiling, and a gratuitous number of soot marks from where the fire had raged its deadly path.

Beyond the walkway lay the gardens, or what remained of them. Craters indicating great impacts pocketed the field in no apparent order. The kennels, once so full of braying, ghostly dogs, had been reduced to a pile of rubble. Brown tents had been pitched in an orderly section off to the side where land had been more preserved.

But the greatest difference of all was the long, wide trench gouged into the ground from where the keel of the airship had dragged, before finally smashing through the outer wall, narrowly missing he and Lily's spying tree. It was missing its balloon and had fallen to rest on its side, laying across the ground like the carcass of a mighty beast.

Sevi clutched at his shirt. It hurt to see such a wondrous thing reduced from the marvel of his memory to the pathetic creature before him. *How could something so formidable be brought down?*

A flurry of soldiers scrambled around its base, calling out to one another. Some lobbed ropes over the lip of its angled deck, then fed the other ends into half a dozen wooden devices. Others filled in holes bearing half-buried logs, set in an orderly line that ran parallel to the ship.

Sevi stopped to watch and nearly collided with a passing soldier. The soldier opened her mouth to protest, but when she saw Captain River, she turned it into a salute and moved on. Captain River, patting at different pockets on his jacket, nodded distractedly to her and managed a quick salute in return.

"Where is it?" he muttered, glancing at Sevi. "Would you have any iron on you?"

Sevi looked at him quizzically.

"Forgive me. I know it is here somewhere, I just have to... Here, take this, I will find it later." He waved for Sevi to step closer and slid something off his wrist. "Put it on," he said, holding his hand out.

Sevi opened his palm and was given an uninteresting, unremarkable, split metal bracelet.

"Never take that off while you remain in the army," the captain said gravely. "And when you must, keep it safe."

Sevi stared at it, but complied, wrapping the band around his wrist. He assumed it was to mark him as human. A Fae would have burned at its touch.

"Good. Now let us walk!" Captain River said elatedly, proceeding to clasp his hands behind his back and stand completely still.

Sevi's face had scrunched up so often by now that it was starting to hurt. He watched the captain as soldiers flowed around them, all nodding to River while completely ignoring Sevi. A trio of children, two boys and a girl, followed them, chasing after a ball and giggling as they stepped in time with the throng.

Sevi looked around uncertainly, searching for some cue he had missed. "Um..."

"Yes?" River asked.

"Are... we walking?"

"Yes." He didn't budge.

"Well. Where are we going?"

"Where would you like to go?"

Sevi's face actually did hurt now. "Me?"

"You," Captain River replied matter-of-factly. "This is your walk."

Of all the different scenarios Sevi had played out in his mind regarding this excursion, *this* wasn't one of them. For his plan to work he needed an opportunity to get away from his captors, or at the very least be shielded from their view for moments at a time. But if *they* were following *him* around then he'd never get the chance.

He stood awkwardly still until his sore, healing legs twitched in protest, demanding relief. Suddenly unsure of everything, Sevi darted his gaze around the courtyard, expecting a trick. Were they waiting for him to run? Was this some kind of twisted game where they'd chase him down and kill him, like a hunt? Had they actually healed him only to torture him?

*Stop*, Sevi shouted in his mind, closing his eyes and silencing his paranoia. He took deep breaths, shutting off everything around him, and focused only on his breathing. When he reopened them, River hadn't moved, standing just as expectantly as ever.

Sevi gulped. *Maybe this isn't a trick.* He looked around the courtyard again, trying to come to a decision. Where could he go that would give him his opportunity?

He could ask to see the throne room. All the most important Fablings gathered there in the daytime, working at desks while Owl sat on one of the thrones. Surely the human soldiers would be no different, and the room was certainly big enough to hide behind a column or two.

Maybe he could walk up one of the towers to see all the grounds at once and slip around the curve of the staircase to one of the walls. Or maybe he could just ask to walk back into the Cut outright and look for any sign of Lily. But what if...

He was struck by a thought. *What if she doesn't want to be found?*

His gaze went back to the airship and all the soldiers scrambling around its base. *What if I went somewhere that I could be found, instead?*

"I'd... like to walk to that," he said, pointing at the airship and trying to sound casual.

Captain River followed Sevi's finger and smiled. "Ah, a fine choice. I will admit I had hoped you would want to go near, as today we wake the sleeping dragon. Within a fortnight, perhaps two, we may give it back its wings."

River let out a sigh, looking at the airship with unconcealed longing. "I have been on a dinghy, frigate, *korikia, shala'runi,* and every ship in between," he said wistfully, "but never one like that. It was a great shame to crash it." He stared a moment longer before clearing his throat. "Well. Let us walk." He went ahead.

Sevi hesitated, glancing at the guard behind him. He had his stare fixed squarely on Sevi, meeting his gaze with professional dispassion.

A shred of hope died in Sevi's chest.

He followed the captain, taking the opportunity to look around the remnants of the gardens and the castle's mighty walls. In a sense, it was much like how it had always been: full of soldiers that marched, drilled, guarded, lounged, or otherwise busied themselves in some fashion. Most of the garden's plants had been trampled, burnt, or completely destroyed, much to his dismay. But small buds poked out of the ground in pockets, bright green with new growth. Not everything had been killed.

Curiously, on the far side of the garden where the plateau ended at the mountain, another large group of soldiers had gathered to passionately attack the rock with shovels and pickaxes. The metal on each tool glinted in the light as they were raised and brought down, clinking distantly across the courtyard. A flag had been hoisted along the battlements near them.

Sevi froze. Its emblem looked just like the star on his necklace.

"Where are you from, *risho*?"

Startled from his thoughts, Sevi turned at the sound of River's voice. The captain had stopped ahead to look back at him, waiting for him to catch up. Sevi opened his mouth automatically to reply, but closed it at the last moment.

*Be quiet. Be smart. Be like Lily.*

"What... what do you want with me?" Sevi asked instead, trying to bull over River's questions with his own.

The captain raised his eyebrows. "A question for a question, an answer for an answer."

That was not the reaction Sevi had been hoping for.

"Come, it is not a hard question. The more you talk, the more I talk. Surely there are things you wish to know?" Captain River said.

Sevi shuffled his feet. *Yes.* There were *many* things he wanted to know, like *why their flag had his necklace on it.* But he'd sworn not to answer anything, no matter how tempting it was. So, he crossed his arms and stared at the ground instead.

"Hmm," the captain hummed. "Another one. Where are your parents? They must worry for you."

Sevi clenched his jaw, looking at anything other than the captain.

"How about your life? How long have you lived here? The Fae were, I am sure, very scary. Did you see them do anything strange? Anything horrible?"

Sevi flattened his face, trying to wear one of Lily's masks, and looked without emotion at Captain River, daring him to see through it.

"Do you have a favorite color?"

His mask cracked.

That same blazing smile reappeared on Captain River's face. "Surely that one is not so hard to answer?" River asked innocently, needling Sevi further.

Sevi's facade broke entirely with a scowl. River's smile widened. The man seemed to get under his skin as easily as cracking an egg, and he knew it. When Lily wanted to get something out of him, she did it swiftly and cleverly. But River was being slow, persistent, and clearly enjoyed the effort. That irritated Sevi far more than anything.

"Well. Plenty of the day is left to think over your answers. There are, of course, many colors to choose from." Captain River turned from him to continue toward the airship, leaving Sevi to glare daggers into his back.

As they approached, Captain River slowed and stopped a distance away, placing his hands behind his back and watching the men while they worked. Sevi stepped up next to him, keeping a distance between them. A large worker broke off from the group and moved toward them, wiping the sweat from his brow and raising a salute to the captain. "Captain," the man said simply.

"Lieutenant," the captain replied. "I see that the winches have arrived."

"Aye sir," the lieutenant said. "But Ilondia t'werent known for its shipbuilding, and it still isn't, no matter how they like to pretend. I've seen toothpicks bigger'n these."

"I see. What are we doing in light of this?"

"We'll give the rope another angle. We're stakin' the lines down with some big iron moorings to lessen the stress, so if she starts to fall we'll have a little warnin.' Gerna proposed we be ready with beams to prop her up as she lifts."

"Will we be?" the captain inquired.

"Absolutely not, sir," the lieutenant said. "If she lays back down, she'll snap anythin' under it, wood and bone alike."

Captain River nodded slowly. "Sensible. Any other issues?"

"The soil is a wee bit damp, and it may give under too much weight. But the brace-holes are deep, and we've mixed in a little limestone from the mountain to make 'crete," he said, nodding toward where the other workers were mining. "Only more we can do is let the sun bake the topsoil a wee bit longer. But there's no knowin' when another storm will blow through, and I'd rather have her up and sinking into mud than havin' me men pullin' in the rain. Crazy mountain weather, never liked it," he grumbled.

"Will we be using the cloud kegs?" Captain River asked.

"The replacement balloon isn't ready yet. We need more materials."

"Why do we not wait?"

"Because Lady Grommand won't stop breathin' down me neck about it."

"I see," Captain River said, quietly mulling something over. "Admirable work, Altha. I see no reason to delay. Please report if there is more you need."

"Friends with any giants?"

The captain chuckled. "Yes, but the old man is still recovering."

"Pity." With a nod, Lieutenant Altha turned away, returning to his work.

Sevi hadn't forgotten his mission, but he didn't need to fake his fascination. Captain River, blessedly, said nothing, ostensibly as content to watch in silence as he was. Soon enough a call went up among the men and women to stand clear. On cue, a number of the workers retreated a safe distance away, spreading out in a circle that ringed around the ship. The closest kept a distance from Captain River and Sevi, darting glances at them while whispering to themselves.

Another batch of people approached the winches. Two soldiers each took the wheel-crank while two more held down the base of each machine for extra support, adding their body weight to that of the stone counterweights in place. When all had announced their readiness, Lieutenant Altha took his place behind them in the middle of the line and raised his hand to the sky.

"Ready! TURN!" he shouted.

A chorus of grunts erupted from the soldiers as they strained against the monumental weight of the fallen behemoth. The lines went taut, creaking and crackling in protest at the sudden pressure, but the ship didn't budge.

"TURN!" Altha shouted again

Again the soldiers turned their wheels. The hull moaned.

"TURN!"

The ship groaned again, and it slowly lifted the barest of handspans off the ground.

Muffled cheers went up from down the line, and the soldiers hanging back applauded, yelling their encouragement. The workers turned their wheels again, and again, and again, and with each revolution of the cranks, they pulled the ship a little more upright. Several more turns had it sitting nearly diagonal to the ground.

Sevi watched with wordless anticipation, expecting the hull to go crashing back to the soil in a heap of broken wood at any moment, but it never did. All the courtyard's sounds faded as every eye turned to watch the ship rise.

With one final crank, the ship stood upright, falling toward the working soldiers and catching on the logs with a creaking moan, exactly as planned. A cheer went up from everyone, and those that had hung back surged forward.

Lieutenant Altha shouted, "TIE HER DOWN!"

But as he yelled, so did Captain River.

"GET CLEAR!" River bellowed, springing forward to grab two soldiers by the collars.

The line nearest to River and Sevi snapped.

The frayed rope whipped back toward its winch and slammed into it with all the force of a battering ram, faster than anyone could blink. A cloud of dust and debris erupted from the dirt, engulfing those nearest that machine.

A shocked silence fell upon the gathering. Sevi stood stunned. It had happened too quickly to comprehend. Clutching at his chest, he watched the blue of River's uniform disappear into the haze, running toward the danger without hesitation, followed moments later by the soldiers in waiting.

Acidic bile rose in his throat as unbidden memories of the invasion flashed into his mind, blurring his vision. Distantly, he registered the outline of his guard chasing after the captain, adding his own uniform to the mob. Then the screams of pain howled out over the crowd, and everyone rushed around at once, jostling Sevi as they went.

Sevi threw up his arms to shield himself, swallowing down the urge to retch as he tried to back away. Person after person ran by. So many uniforms. So many bearded faces. Any one of them could have belonged to the man that had shot him, and he was far too exposed. He needed to get away.

He pushed himself out of the crowd, stumbling toward one of the logs and leaning against it. People ran across the courtyard, some with their rifles as though ready to shoot the airship in retaliation. Off to the side, that same trio of children he'd seen pass by earlier watched him with concerned expressions, leaving their toy forgotten on the ground. No one else so much as spared a glance. He'd been left alone.

Without wasting another breath Sevi half stumbled, half scurried away from the mob, hurrying toward the other side of the now right-side-up ship and his true destination.

The spying tree had a rope around it, placed there on stakes shortly after Sevi and Lily's prank to ward off anyone seeking to make use of its bench. Somehow it had survived the fires. Sevi jumped over it with a wobble, but kept his footing. His heart pumped faster; he anticipated the horrific moment someone would notice his escape and shoot him again.

Finding purchase in the bark, he kicked his feet off the trunk and stone, hoisting himself up branch by branch. Lining his sight up with that of the bench below, he found the area he thought contained the spystone and hammered his hands against the wall, testing it until the heel of his palm struck something loose and sunk in.

His heart soared. Reeling his hand back and harnessing all his nervous energy, he slammed his palm forward again and shoved the brick into the Cut until it popped out. Then he reached into his pocket, pulled out one of the papers he'd torn from Captain River's book, and hurled it inside after the dislodged stone.

"BOY!"

Sevi jerked his head, flicking his eyes to the soldier below. His guard. He tensed in preparation for the bullet, but the man hadn't leveled his rifle at him. He had it slung over his shoulder and stood with his hands on his hips, looking completely incensed.

Sevi didn't move. Not because he was afraid of being shot, but because he was now terrified of what might happen if he climbed down. The guard turned to look behind him and lifted a hand to his mouth. "Over here, sir!"

The blue of Captain River's coat appeared from around the other side of the ship, significantly dirtier than before. The captain approached slowly and solemnly, shoulders hunched and hands at his sides.

When he approached the tree, he stopped rigidly just outside its fence and placed his hands behind his back, tilting his head up to look at Sevi with a frown. When Sevi didn't move, he lifted his hand up and flicked his fingers in a wordless command.

Sevi flushed. Hiding his face from the captain's inscrutable gaze, he hesitantly reached for the branches, climbing down with the finality of a man heading to the gallows. He mistimed a step and slipped off the last branch, tumbling harshly into the grass and mud to rest at River's feet.

Captain River said nothing. Sevi's gaze drifted upward from River's boots, noticing the fresh dark stains on his jacket before meeting the man's eyes. He didn't look angry. He looked disappointed. As though Sevi had failed some unspoken test.

"He was doing something to the wall. He dropped this, sir," the guard said to River, handing over one of the papers Sevi had ripped from River's book.

River remained silent while he studied it. Sevi slowly climbed to his feet, looking down and wretchedly clutching at the hem of his dirtied shirt, dripping with mud and wishing the ground would swallow him.

Captain River's hand slowly came into view. With a gentle touch, he took something from Sevi's chest and lifted it in his palm. His necklace. It had fallen from his shirt along with the papers.

Sevi flicked his gaze from the star to River's face. Moments passed. The captain gazed at the damaged pendant with a deeply furrowed brow. "Our walk," he said at last, sliding the pendant into Sevi's collar, "is over."

# Chapter 23

*Lost on his own, seeking his friends, in joy or in tears, he'd pursue. Where to search? How to chase? How to act on his own? The world was more than he ever knew!*

"Hey, kid. Heard you managed to upset Captain River. Congratulations, I've been trying to do that for years." Reynam gave Sevi's foot a friendly pat as he sat next to the bed, fishing out a pipe and stuffing it full of foul-smelling leaves.

Sevi glanced up at the soldier from his book with a frown. It had been two days since the accident at the airship, and Captain River had not come back to visit, leaving him plenty of time to worry over how he was to be disciplined. The injured had been placed several beds away from his own, adding fresh cries of pain to an infirmary bereft of them for months. It brought back upsetting memories of his first nights waking up here, surrounded by the dying.

"What's the trick to it?" Reynam continued, pulling a thin twig from a box of similarly thin twigs. "I've already tried high-pitched funny voices, so that can't be it. Is it the way you never stop talking?" Reynam struck the twig against the box and a fire sprung from its tip.

Sevi flinched away from the flame. Reynam froze mid-motion with his brow raised. "Or maybe it's how you are just the pinnacle of stoicism. No reactions. Unfeeling. Truly unshakable is what you are."

He brought the flame to the bowl of the pipe, lighting the leaves inside before setting the stem to his lips. Extinguishing the twig with a flick of his hand, he leaned back and dragged in the smoke with a look of satisfaction.

"And you're the pinnacle of paying attention, Reynam," Doctor Lea said, walking by out of nowhere and plucking the pipe from his lips. Wasting no time in emptying its contents on the ground, she stamped out the embers and fixed the corporal with a dispassionate stare. "Only ever needing to be told once rather than a dozen times how much I hate the smell of pipeleaves in my clinic."

Reynam watched her feet with annoyance, but when he turned his face up his irritation had been replaced with a smile. "Why should I deprive myself of eleven more chances to talk with you, Lea?"

"Want me to throw him out?" she asked Sevi, pointedly ignoring the man.

Sevi looked between them. Reynam widened his eyes at Sevi and lowered his head, shaking it slowly like a begging geisthound pup. Sevi regarded him for several heartbeats. He disliked the man's company, but he hadn't done anything to warrant being thrown out altogether. Sighing, he looked at Doctor Lea and shook his head.

The doctor huffed. Reynam's expression went from soliciting to triumphant, turning a wide smile on Lea that only seemed to irritate her further. She spared a cool look for him then, but his joy stood fast beneath it. "When he starts to bother you, let me know. Throwing him out can be a pleasure," she said.

"Know what else would give you pleasure?" Reynam said.

Doctor Lea stilled. Sevi shrunk in his bed. He'd been in the clinic long enough to know what the look on her face meant, having last seen it when one of her aides spilled a silver vial on her. She had torn into the poor man so thoroughly that it was a surprise to find him still standing by the end. Sevi had privately named her Stonefoot after the small, deadly felines that frequented the mountain, always going still before striking with daunting precision.

Lea lowered her voice, speaking slowly and softly. "Think very carefully over your next choice of words, corporal."

Reynam spread his arms and said jubilantly, "Getting out of this clinic for once! Gods, Lea, I think I've only ever seen you in here or at the mess hall. When was the last time you took a break? Or shopped for spices? I know how much you like to cook, and there's a town right *there!*"

Lea balked. "I'm needed here," she said flatly.

"You're needed out *there,* too!"

Lea turned the corner of her mouth up, forming a critical smile. Undaunted, Reynam fished around in his breast pocket and pulled out a small steely coin—a glara, as he called it—and held it up to the light. "How about this," he said. "Crowns, you come out with me for one day and have some fun for a change. Suns, I leave your clinic and don't come back for a week."

Doctor Lea considered the coin for several breaths. "Corporal?"

"Yeah?"

"Smoke in here again, and I'll snuff your pipe out with your clothes."

"Understood, Doctor." He shook his head, placing the coin back into his pocket with a grin. "Mark my words, I'll get you to have fun one of these days."

Lea grimaced as though the very thought left a sour taste in her mouth before tossing his pipe into his lap and moving to a bed where a regal, bearded man sat in blue finery. Reynam watched her go with an oddly glum half-smile. "Always a pleasure." Sighing, he turned back to Sevi.

Sevi stared at him.

"What?" Reynam said. Sevi shrugged, dropping his gaze to the book. Reynam took his pipe and put it back into his pocket, huffing through his nose. "You still have that necklace, kid?"

Sevi tiredly breathed out. Again, with the necklace. He nodded, not looking up from the page.

"Are you going to tell me where you got it today?"

Sevi shook his head.

"Kid. I have been visiting you for months now, and I had to get your name from *Lea.* You think I like sitting around sick people for hours, suffering under her lectures?" He scooted his chair closer to Sevi's bed. "You have to give me *something.*"

Sevi fixed him with a look. He had done his best to avoid conversation with the corporal, hoping that the less interesting he appeared, the more likely that Reynam would leave him alone. It hadn't worked, and he was tired of these exchanges. "You shot me," he said simply.

Reynam leapt on the comment as though ready for it. "No, *I* didn't. That was Solen. *I* tried to *stop* him from shooting you. Remember?"

Sevi frowned. "What's so special about my necklace?"

Reynam clenched his jaw, and his expression went flat. "I need to know. It's important."

"Why?"

The corporal made an exasperated sound and crossed his arms, turning his head to glare off into space. He clenched his jaw as he worked over a private thought. "I told you. There aren't many necklaces like that. The only other one I've come across is... unavailable to me. And I think..." He made another exasperated noise. "Look, do *not* repeat what I'm about to tell you, understand?"

Sevi shifted uncertainly on his pillow, nodding tentatively. The man looked more serious than he had ever seen. Reynam leaned in and dropped his voice. "That necklace has a very startling resemblance to one my father once made," he said slowly. "One in a set of two. He sold them just before he died."

Sevi reached for his chest, instinctively clutching at the star around his neck. Reynam's gaze followed his hand. "There's no way in Nightfall that I'm claiming the first one," he said with a rueful smile, "and this one..."

He clenched his jaw again. "I thought about taking it from you while you were out. I'm not proud of it, but I did." He rubbed his eyes. "But it didn't seem right to steal from the kid that saved Digby, especially after the blasted thing saved your life—who knows what kind of bad luck *that* would bring down on me. I had to talk with you first." He chuckled ruefully. "I may be an asshole, but I'm an asshole with standards."

Sevi tightened his grip. "You can't have it," he said with a tremor. He thought he smelled burning, as if the flames from his dreams were sparking up under his bed.

Reynam looked back up, covering his mouth with his hand. "Is there any use in offering to buy it off you?" Sevi vigorously shook his head. "I thought so. How about this." A smile returned to his face. He reached back into his pocket and retrieved his coin, raising it up so Sevi could see it. The side facing him had a sun embossed on it. "Crowns, you come out for some fun in lieu of Lea, and answer a few questions I have about where you got that necklace. You have my word that I won't try to take it from you, for whatever that's worth. Suns, I leave the clinic for a week."

Sevi's face hardened, and he shook his head again. He was *not* answering any questions. Not to Captain River, and certainly not to Reynam.

"Driving a hard bargain, eh kid?" Reynam half-smiled. "Fine. What is it you want?"

Sevi was so, so tired of this. What exactly did these people expect from him? He was just a boy, who happened to help their cause by *mistake*, who happened to have a shiny necklace, who happened to be nothing special. Why did they care about him at all? *Think like Lily*, he reminded himself. "I want to go back into my tunnels," he said.

Reynam frowned. "I'm not—"

A groan of pain several beds over cut him off. It was time for Doctor Lea and her staff to change bandages. Sevi winced at the sounds. Reynam glanced at the commotion, absently rolling the coin over his fingers. "Hm. Alright."

Sevi's heart leapt. "Alright?"

"Sure, kid. Crowns you give me answers. Suns you get to go back into the tunnels for a day."

Sevi squinted at the man. "Just like that?"

"Just like that." Reynam smiled. "I'll work it out with Lea and the captain. You have my word."

Sevi took a deep breath. Clenching the bedsheet, he nodded reluctantly. "Alright. Deal."

"Deal," Reynam said, smiling wider. Placing the coin on his thumb, he flicked it up into the air over Sevi's bed. Sevi watched it climb, unable to breathe as it caught the light at its apex and tumbled swiftly back down to the bedsheet.

It landed with the Sun facing up.

"Yes!" Sevi breathed.

"NO!" Reynam exclaimed louder than him.

"Please keep it down!" Doctor Lea called from across the room.

Sevi flinched, turning to the man with sudden nervousness. "Does this mean I can go?"

"No!" Reynam said again, equally shocked and annoyed. "I mean... that didn't count!"

"What? Why not!"

"That was the wrong coin! We needed to flip my *lucky* coin!" Reynam fished around in the same pocket he'd pulled the coin from. "You have that necklace that saved your life and all, it's only fair that I get a bit of luck myself." He pulled out a second coin that looked like the first, but with an engraved crown facing out. "This was the one I meant to use!"

"But we already flipped! I won!"

"But I didn't get to use my *lucky* coin," Reynam said, waving the coin around.

"I'm *not* flipping again! I *won!*"

"*Kid.* I *can't* let you go."

Sevi stared at him. "So that was a *lie?*"

Reynam's mouth snapped shut. He looked away from Sevi and angrily pulled the first coin off the bed, putting them both back into separate pockets. "I'm sorry, kid. I just... I *can't*. I don't have the power."

"Why not?"

"Because Captain River wants you to stay right here."

Sevi flung his arms out. "*Why?* What does anyone want with me? And where would I *go?* The tunnels are right here in the castle, and you people are everywhere!"

"Sorry, kid. Orders are orders." Reynam shook his head. "Would you please, *please,* just tell me where you *got the damn necklace!*"

Sevi crossed his arms and looked away, fuming. He glared holes into his bedsheet for several long, angry heartbeats, then opened his mouth to call for Doctor Lea, completely resolved to take her up on her offer to throw the corporal out. He was *done.* This was *total—*

His gaze caught the corner of his necklace, poking out of the collar of his shirt. He froze. An idea slowly grabbed hold of him. *Think like Lily.*

But this idea was going to hurt.

"I..." He licked his lips, taking one last moment to mull it over. "I have a deal for you," he began, looking warily at Reynam. "I'll answer some of your questions."

Reynam regarded him with surprise. "Really?"

"Yes. If—"

"There's the 'if.'" Reynam sighed. "And I bet I know what it'll be."

"If you let me into the tunnels," Sevi continued.

"There it is."

"And to make sure I come back..." Sevi slowly lifted the necklace over his head, placing the star in his palm. "I will give you this to hold, but *only* until I return."

Reynam didn't say anything. When Sevi looked up, he found him staring covetously at the pendant, all traces of humor gone. "Even after telling you that I nearly stole it from you?"

Sevi nodded slowly. "Yes."

"Even though I just tried to con you?"

"'Con me?'"

"Lied to you."

"Oh. Yes."

"And even though, if you get caught, they'll whip you for running off?" Reynam eyed him meaningfully. "Or worse?"

Sevi's throat went dry and he clutched the star more tightly. He hadn't considered that. *Be brave like Lily. Be brave like Lily.* He closed his eyes and repeated the words over and over again, trying to find his courage. All he found were flashes of Digby's beaten and bloodied face in the dark of his eyelids. Phantom pains sprouted along his chest in memory of the bullet that sent him tumbling down the mountain.

But he hadn't gotten shot in the garden after throwing his message into the Cut. Could his luck hold? Was he willing to risk pain like that again? Was he willing to risk giving his one treasure to a liar?

"Yes," he said aloud.

Reynam grinned. "Then I'll see what I can do."

# Chapter 24

*Through the Embers he stumbled, alive but unwell, a wolf sought a leg in his loathing. Brave for a mouse, he grabbed the loose threads of a fox in a dress of wolf's clothing.*

S everal days later, Captain River returned, greeting Sevi with his usual good humor. "Hello again, *risho*. Have you started growing into your bed?"

Sevi looked warily at the captain, silently clenching the spine of his book. This moment had taken longer to arrive than he'd expected. He had hoped to finish the story first; the queen had just come into possession of a pair of metal shoes that weighed her down enough to float.

The captain stood at the foot of the bed with his hands behind his back. His uniform had been cleaned so thoroughly that it was hard to believe that blood had ever stained it. Or maybe he just had a spare.

"Have you been well this week?" Captain River inquired. Sevi remained silent. "Still so quiet. Privates Novar and Tammavin had said you were talkative. Cassik and Loma," he clarified at Sevi's expression, moving to his side. His smile slowly faded. "I have taken time to give you some thought."

Sevi tensed. Taking a breath, he put the book aside.

"I have realized that your... distrust? Fear? Either are good words." He nodded. "Your fear of our army might not be unfounded." He fixed Sevi with a gentle, pitying expression, all traces of banality gone. "How long have you been living here, Sevi? One year? Two? More?"

Sevi swallowed and looked away.

"A long time," River said softly. "Made longer by the loneliness... the fear of being caught by those creatures. The darkness." He shook his head. "I have seen your tunnels. That is no place for a child to live. But I have heard of your garden as well, and you have done a remarkable job, *risho*, considering your circumstances."

"You had no right," Sevi sputtered before he could stop himself. He clamped his mouth shut the moment the last word fell out. How dare he. How *dare* he, or *any* of these soldiers invade his home, *especially* his garden!

River raised his hands placatingly. "If I have offended—which I now think I have—it was not my intent. I am sorry."

Sevi hung his head. Dozens of emotions threatened to overwhelm him—emotions he had been keeping at bay through fear, anxiety, and bitterness. Anger at having his home as he knew it taken from him. Shame over his part in it. Fear that he'd never see his only friends again. Anxiety over what was going to happen to him. He clenched and unclenched his bedsheet, fighting every urge to bolt from the room.

Captain River kept talking. "And after living like that, this happens," he said, gesturing slowly at everything. "We march into your house, and one of our soldiers almost kills you. I confess, when I heard that your necklace bore our emblem, I had thought you were one of us. But then I saw it. And the more I learn, the more confusing this becomes." River shook his head. "Who are you, *risho*? Will you tell me?"

Sevi furled and unfurled his fingers. He couldn't breathe, let alone answer. River waited, staying quiet while he gathered himself. When Sevi felt some semblance of stability, he shook his head, and whispered, "I can't."

More silence. Sevi didn't open his eyes.

"I see," Captain River said softly. "Then we will continue not knowing what to do with you, until you decide to speak."

"Why?" Sevi asked, shaking his head. "What do you want from me? I have nothing. I *am* nothing. I'm not Fae. I'm a tunnel rat. And not a very smart one. Why do you, or Reynam, or anyone care?"

Captain River sighed. "Answers for answers, *risho*."

*Don't believe him,* Lily's phantom voice whispered.

Sevi closed his eyes and gripped his sheet so tightly his fingers might've pushed through it. He couldn't decide. The Embers of Korina had fed him. Clothed him. Healed him. But they wanted something from him. Just as Digby had used him and smiled while he'd done it. "I don't know," he said hoarsely. "I don't know if I can trust you."

"You've spent months in our care. Why do you still not trust us?" River asked.

Sevi wiped his nose. "L-like you said... I've been living here a long time."

"That... is fair, I suppose. I do not mind it if you stay in this bed for longer while you decide. However," the captain added, lifting his voice ever so slightly, "perhaps you will allow me to make up?"

Sevi opened his eyes at that, furrowing his brow at River. The captain's smile had returned. "Will you allow me to apologize?"

"What do you mean?"

"I, Captain Caldwin River Ta'Runa, hereby extend an offer to you, Sevi of small name, to dine with the officers of the Embers of Korina as an apology for our mistreatment. And as thanks for your efforts in rescuing our dear Lieutenant Digby Asgaillin, who would like to thank you personally once he arrives."

Sevi started. River smiled. "Dinner is tonight. I can find nicer clothes for you, should you decide to join. Will you?"

Sevi leaned back against his pillow. After the incident at the airship, he'd expected to be thrown into the tower. But dinner? "I... I'm not sure."

"I promise that the food will be nothing like the soup you have eaten these past several months," River added. "And, just as always, you need not speak, should you not wish it."

Sevi opened his mouth to answer when something caught his ear. A soft, muffled chime. His head flicked instinctively in its direction, pulling his attention away from River entirely.

He knew that sound.

"*Risho?*"

Sevi jumped a little, and hurriedly stammered out, "Ah... M-may I think about it?"

Captain River grimaced. "You may, but do not take long. I cannot promise that tomorrow's dinner will be so enjoyable. I will send a messenger in one hour. You will have an answer for me then, yes?"

Sevi vigorously nodded his head.

"Good." A look of worry crossed the captain's face. "Are you well? You look pale."

"I'm fine! Just... just not sure of being around more people."

The captain's face cleared, and he chuckled. "The only things the officers will bite are their turkey legs. Yet another reason to join us. Have you had turkey?"

Sevi shook his head, bouncing his foot impatiently under the sheet.

"Very tasty creature. I wish they were sea birds. Ah, well. Do think over my offer, *risho*. It would hurt my feelings if you declined." With his hands behind his back, the captain turned in a stately manner and walked away.

Sevi waited until he had left the clinic before swinging himself out of bed. One of Doctor Lea's assistants walked by carrying a bowl of water, casting a curious glance at him as he stood up. Sevi smiled awkwardly at her, nodding as she moved on.

As casually as he could manage, he walked over to the window next to Cassik's former bed and pretended to admire the view outside. It was on the side of the building perpendicular to the courtyard, off the main path enough that foot traffic was light.

"Alyda?" Sevi whispered hopefully. Then a little louder. "Alyda? Is that you?"

No response. The pane rattled softly in the wind, struck by a rolling mountain breeze that carried a bundle of leaves. Several stuck to the glass, startling him. "Alyda!" Sevi said pleadingly to the glass again. Had he imagined her chime?

One of the leaves stuck out an arm. Sevi almost jerked back, stopping himself at the last moment as a tiny, bald head poked out with it.

"Oh, my *Gods*," Sevi breathed, digging his nails into the window's inset. "Alyda. You're *alive!*"

The fairy girl's face lit up like a tiny sun as she broke into a smile. She lifted one small hand and placed it on the window. He did the same, mirroring her. Her expression gradually marred as small tears rolled down her cheeks, looking both happy and distressed. Chiming sobs resonated softly through the glass, just barely loud enough for Sevi to hear. He couldn't blame her. He was doing the same.

"You're alive," he said again softly, sniffling. "Thank the Gods. Thank them all!"

They tarried in the moment, each staring at the other. Alyda withdrew her hand first, wiping it across her eyes before fishing for something behind the leaf. She pulled out a petal. A *lily* petal.

"Lily," Sevi breathed, choking on another sob. "She's alive. You're both *alive*."

A weight on his shoulders finally fell free, lifting him from the ground like the upside-down queen. He wiped at his face. "Alyda, where is she? Where are you both hiding? Can you come get me?"

Alyda dropped the petal, letting the wind carry it off. Leaning in, she blew her breath across the pane of glass, fogging it up. But the exertion seemed to irritate her, adding a dark, strangled blue to her cheeks, and she had to break off as a coughing fit wracked her body.

She disappeared behind the leaf for far longer than Sevi would have liked. When her head reappeared, she tried it again, pointedly ignoring the concerned look he gave her. In the fog, she drew the outline of a fire. Sevi's breath caught in his throat at the implication. But then the fairy drew another shape: a pie. "I see. I see!" he exclaimed. "I understand! I'll... I'll find you! I'll be there! Tonight!"

"Child?"

Sevi whipped around. Doctor Lea stood a short distance away, watching him with concern, along with several others. He put his back up against the window, trying to shield Alyda with his head. "Y-yes?"

The doctor looked at him curiously. Gradually, horrifyingly, her eyes drifted to the window.

"What? What is it?" Sevi tried again.

It didn't slow her. Doctor Lea strode forward purposefully, nudging him aside and peering out the window with a critical eye.

Sevi's breath caught in his throat. He immediately looked to the leaf that shielded Alyda. Her silhouette had disappeared. "C-can I help you, Doctor Lea?"

Lea didn't say anything, looking through the glass with a curious expression. She turned to look down at him, maintaining her look of bewilderment, and raised her hand to his forehead. "Do you have a fever?"

"Um... no?"

"Do you feel alright then? You've been talking to yourself rather vigorously back here," she said, flipping her hand over and trying the other side.

Sevi shook his head, gently tossing her hand off. "N-no. I'm fine."

"Are you sure? Do you need more water?"

"No, I... Actually. I do need something," he said slowly. "Could you please get a message to Corporal Reynam for me?"

# Chapter 25

*On the end called, and on, the mouse ran. There came a familiar light. Revealing the path to his family ahead if he ran with the fox through the night.*

———— ✦ ————

Sevi felt silly as he spread his arms and allowed Doctor Lea to help him with the dress coat. He had waved off the silly-looking pants that seemed too poofy at the thighs and too tight at the calves. But he couldn't be spared from the scratchy, white, longsleeve shirt, the tight, clinching, gray waistcoat, and the blue frock coat that was so big on him that Lea rolled up the sleeves.

"Smile, kid. It's not like you're heading to the magistrate," Reynam said from the side, lounging in an empty infirmary bed with a smirk on his face. "But then again..."

"Hush," Doctor Lea said absently, patting the coat where it bunched until it fell free. She stood back and looked him over with a critical eye. "Are you certain you won't wear the pants?"

Sevi grimaced. "Very. Why can't I wear my regular clothes?"

"Officers and their guests are required to dress up when they gather for leisure," Doctor Lea said.

"And they're chronically illiterate, having no idea what 'leisure' means no matter how often you try to teach them," Reynam added.

"Sounds like someone I know," Doctor Lea said quietly, giving Sevi a private smirk.

He smiled uneasily at her in return, lifting his arms one more time, observing how loosely the sleeves hung. He did his best not to look miserable.

"Don't fret," Doctor Lea said, placing a hand on his cheek. "It's only dinner. You'll be back here before you know it."

"More like Torment," Reynam said. "He's going to be in there with Saller, and that woman—"

Lea cut him off. "You're not helping." The soldier raised his hands in apology and lapsed back into silence, for however long it would last. Lea turned back to Sevi. "It'll be stuffy. There will be a level of decorum around the table, which you couldn't possibly know. So just stick with Captain River and do what he does, and you'll be fine, alright?"

Sevi nodded and took a deep breath. "Alright... I'm ready."

Doctor Lea turned to Reynam. "Look after him, corporal."

"Don't worry, Lea. The kid and I are good buddies now, he'll be safe with me." Reynam tossed a sly wink at Sevi that made him clench his teeth. He then swung his legs out of bed and grabbed hold of his rifle, standing at attention with a click of his heels to give Sevi a crisp salute. "This way, sir. If you please, sir."

Sevi scowled but marched forward, doing his best to lift his head up high. *I've survived worse than this. Surely, I can survive dinner. Right?*

Doctor Lea waved goodbye as Reynam followed, lifting his feet high and swinging his arms in a comical march until they were out the door. The corporal then fell in next to Sevi, taking the lead. "Our deal?"

"What about it?" Sevi asked.

"Is it still on?"

"Of course, it is."

"Then give me the necklace."

Sevi lifted his hand to his chest without thinking, then dropped it almost immediately. "After the dinner."

"What if I want it now?" Reynam asked, glancing at Sevi from the corner of his eye.

"You can't always get what you want, corporal." Sevi slowly wrinkled his brow, piecing together what had just come out of his mouth moments before Reynam burst into a laugh.

"You've been around Lea too much! She's rubbed off on you." He chuckled, clapping Sevi on the shoulder. "I like you, kid. You're smarter than you look. But keep this in mind: if you're somehow trying to play me, don't."

His voice dropped really low on the last word, and he dug his figners into Sevi, adding force to the warning. Sevi tried not to tremble, focusing on the path ahead instead. A cold, slithering feeling crawled up his neck.

He turned his head, catching Reynam in an attempt to lift the necklace out of Sevi's shirt. Reynam didn't even look away. He smiled very pointedly, gave the chain a gentle tug, then dropped it with a flourish of his hand. Sevi clamped a hand over his chest, pausing mid-step to force Reynam to walk ahead of him entirely. The soldier laughed.

Their path took them toward the throne room. Its two large double doors had been thrown wide open. It filled Sevi with a sense of wonder as he entered not as a scavenger, but as a guest, looking around the expansive ceilings as though they were brand new.

Voices echoed distantly and dissonantly across its vaulted arches, like a group of shadows had gathered above to gossip over what went on below. The walls had been stripped of any tapestries and replaced by worn, tattered flags bearing the army's mark. Soldiers stood in clusters, deep in conversation. Some argued over charts and papers laid out over tables.

But not all wore the same uniforms. While most had been outfitted in heavy cotton jackets, others were draped in long leather coats, as though in preparation for a horseback ride. And even more curiously, some of them had large raptors on their shoulders, all wearing hoods that shielded their eyes. A few of their number sat at tables coating a thin, silvery substance on pairs of metal talons that looked to fit over the claws of their birds.

One of the creatures, perched on the shoulder of a grizzled looking man, cocked its head at Sevi and shifted its feet as he neared. It spread its wings wide and started flapping as he passed, causing the man to pause in his conversation in order to calm it.

Sevi hurried his pace, looking back. "Who are they?"

Reynam apathetically followed his gaze. "Empyreans. Fairy killers."

"Why do they have those birds?"

"The best way to hunt something that flies is with something else that flies." Reynam turned away as if that was explanation enough.

They dipped down a side corridor toward the kitchens, and the smell of fresh cooking hit Sevi like a punch to the belly. A dozen different tantalizing scents drifted through the air, calling him to come slake the hunger he'd been carrying for years.

He realized with a start that, tonight, his food would be *fresh*. No scrounging. No scraps. No danger of being caught. And no more soup. He almost ran the rest of the hallway, overtaking Reynam in his eagerness.

Two figures stood near the end, flanking a door to the side. One was a soldier in full dress, resting his rifle against the wall and looking incredibly bored. The second, more impressive-looking figure was clad from head to toe in a set of dull, slate armor without a breadth of skin to be seen, standing vigil with their faceplate down and a sword clutched in their gauntlets. Beyond them both at the very end of the hallway were the doorways leading to the cellar and the kitchen.

"Ho, Horny," Reynam called.

The sleepy-looking man slowly turned his head to face Reynam with a frown. "It's Hornki."

"That's what I said. How's the watch? Slay any rats?"

The man's gaze flicked down to Reynam's shoes and back up, sizing up the corporal like a piece of meat. "Not yet."

"Shame. They're everywhere, and we're all out of cats," Reynam continued smoothly. "If you'd like to go apply for the position, I hear that Captain Vykka is taking applications in the mess. You might even get a fish to chew on."

Hornki clenched his hands. "What do you want, corporal?"

"Oh, I'm just here to drop off our beloved tunnel rat. But he's not for eating, so you'll have to get dinner elsewhere." Reynam stepped aside and raised his arm, presenting Sevi with false deference.

Hornki's beady gaze regarded Sevi coolly. Sevi gulped and stood up straight, keeping his arms stiffly at his sides. "H-hello," he stuttered.

"Come now, Hornki," Reynam said. "Would you be a good sport and go meow at River? He asked for the kid specifically."

Hornki's gaze slid back to Reynam. A vein pulsed at his temple. "Show me your iron."

"Really, Hor—"

"*Show* me. *Sir*," the soldier growled, reaching for the knife at his belt.

Sevi jolted and took a large step back, while Reynam, for his part, ignored it entirely. "No need to hiss." He tutted, then rolled back his sleeve to show a metal band wrapped around his forearm.

Hornki reached out and touched it, then scowled. Reynam wiggled his eyebrows. The guard turned his glare on Sevi. "Now the kid."

Sevi gulped and mimicked Reynam. He still had the iron band that River had given him, and he thanked the stars above that he had remembered to put it on.

The sight of it did nothing to disperse Hornki's foul mood—if anything it made it worse. Without a word, he opened the door a crack and swiftly disappeared through the gap, leaving Reynam and Sevi in the hall with the silent knight. Sevi eyed the weapon in the knight's hands. It looked sharp enough to cleave him and Reynam in two at once.

"Ah, that was fun. It's always the grouchy ones who give the best reactions," Reynam said, turning Sevi's attention away. "I hope you appreciate this, kid. I'm giving up a party for this."

"Why do you do that?" Sevi asked.

Reynam leaned against the wall where Hornki had been standing, tilting his head against the stone. "Do what?"

"Make fun of everyone. It's mean."

"Who says I'm making fun of anyone? Maybe this is how I show my affection."

"By insulting them?"

He smirked. "Oh, yes. You never really know a person's character until you've harassed them a dozen times. I'll bet you twenty glara that I can get one more cat joke in on Horny."

Sevi opened his mouth just as the door opened back up, spilling light, laughter, and music into the hallway. A smiling, freshly groomed

Captain River wearing a fancy dress coat stepped out, trailed by a dissonantly gloomy-looking Hornki.

"Ah, *risho!* I am truly happy to see you here," the captain said, taking Sevi's hand and pumping it in a genteel shake. "And not a moment too soon. We are expecting one, maybe two more of us to join, which gives us time to introduce you. Have you worked on your introduction?"

Sevi's mouth failed him in the sudden light and noise. Captain River released his hand to hold his shoulder. "That is alright. As I have said, we will work on it! Please, come in, come in." He stepped aside and spread his free arm in welcome.

"Pardon me, Captain, may I have a word before you go?" Reynam asked, far more respectfully than when he spoke to Hornki. Or Sevi. Or most people, really. Sevi tried not to look surprised.

"Yes, Corporal Reynam?" Captain River asked.

"I told Doctor Lea that I'd watch over the kid, in case anything should happen. He's been... *off*, lately, shall we say." Reynam turned a pitying gaze on Sevi for just a breath before looking back at the captain. "I was wondering if I might take Corporal Hornki's position for the evening, if that would be alright with you, sir."

Captain River looked surprised. "My. How—what is a good word—*unusual*. I would have thought that you would prefer to go to your own party tonight."

"Yeah, well, what can I say? I have an unfortunate weakness for doctors, sir."

"Ah. I have heard that you have been visiting our *risho* suspiciously often, haven't you?" Captain River smiled and turned to Sevi. "Would you like your friend to stay, young man?"

If Sevi could've glared at Reynam without arousing suspicion, he would've, and somehow, he could tell that Reynam knew that. Which only made him want to glare *more*. Sevi gripped his knuckles, but stiffly dipped his chin once in affirmation. Reynam smiled.

"Wonderful. Corporal Hornki, you're relieved of duty," Captain River announced. "Please go enjoy your evening."

"*Reeer, fft fft!* Git!"

"Corporal?" Captain River prompted.

Reynam waved apologetically. "Sorry, sir, I thought I saw a cat."

"Ah... well. Please do not go chasing after it."

"Wouldn't dream of it, sir."

Reynam shot Sevi a sly wink just before he and River stepped through the door. The knight moved for the first time, turning to watch them go, until the door closed with a heavy *thunk*, sealing Sevi in a room filled with the leaders of the force that had destroyed his home.

# Chapter 26

*Forces untold moving hushful and calm, sparing no toil to enthrall. What becomes of an enchanter at the river's end? What shadow waits at the waterfall?*

Sevi gulped and stepped away from the door with his hand on his chest, observing the room in increments. He'd seen it from the Cut before. It had elaborate sconces along the walls, and a long, mahogany table in the middle with enough chairs to seat everyone at the party and more. The great chandelier in the center of the ceiling had been lit, casting a magnificent glow.

At the very head of the table, closest to the kitchen door, was a chair more elaborately decorated than the others, with faded golden suns etched into its wood. Owl, the former Matron of the castle, used to sit there alone whenever she ate. She was gone now, and the normally spacious room was more crowded than ever.

At least two dozen men and women were scattered about. Some wore long, crisp blue coats exactly like Captain River's. Some had eschewed their uniforms in favor of well-cut, luxurious clothing that hung loosely on their arms and thighs. One man hung apart from the group in a dark, slate, leather duster, swirling a goblet in his hand and watching the room with boredom.

Bust most importantly, nobody looked like Solen—the man who had shot Sevi.

"Let me introduce you to my *isi'kaa*," River said, intruding on Sevi's observations. He walked ahead, paving a way through the crowd for Sevi

211

to follow. Some people turned to watch as they went, giving Sevi curious looks. He avoided their eyes, focusing only on his feet.

*Coward,* Lily's voice whispered.

He straightened himself and looked ahead. *Be like her.*

The captain led Sevi to a pair of men. The taller one wore a military uniform, while the other had on a well-fitting doublet. As River approached, the one in uniform turned to greet him with a smile, then leaned in to give him a kiss on the cheek—a gesture River returned. The two spoke privately for a moment before River waved Sevi forward.

"This is the boy I have told you about," the captain said, smiling at Sevi.

The man stepped forward. He was well-groomed, with short, black hair, a trimmed beard, green eyes, and skin tanned by the sun. The way his clothes fell suggested a fit figure, with his sleeves wrapping tightly around his forearms. He stuck a hand out to Sevi and gave him a warm smile full of teeth. "Ah, the tunnel mouse. Hero to our cause. Caldwin has told me all about you."

Sevi reluctantly placed his sweaty palm into the man's firm grip, wincing at how tightly he squeezed. "It's n-nice to meet you, Isseeka," Sevi mumbled.

The man stopped shaking and glanced at River with a wry grin. The two shared a chuckle. "My name is Lorr, actually. *Isi'kaa* is what my husband calls me."

"Oh... sorry," Sevi said.

Lorr waved dismissively. "No offense taken."

"Give him your full name," River prompted.

From the way that Lorr rolled his eyes and emotionlessly recited, "Captain Lorr Ferdino Gallan, assistant financial officer," Sevi got the impression that Captain River asked him to do that a lot. River made a disappointed sound, which Captain Lorr pointedly ignored.

River turned to the second man and beckoned at him, but he waved him off. "You can introduce me if you'd like, River. I like how you do it."

"This, *risho,* is Innavin Targa, former farmer, current playwright, and husband of Lieutenant Ryaliss Targa," Captain River said. Innavin greeted Sevi with a polite bow of his head. His face was completely shaven, and his blond, shoulder-length hair had been slicked back and nestled behind his ears. "He comes only for the food," River added.

Innavin grinned. "That's not true. Sometimes it's only to embarrass my wife."

"And... hm. Where is my aide?" River asked, looking around.

"Tahno stepped out," Lorr supplied. "He claimed to have had too much to drink."

"Which means he's back in the library," Innavin added.

Captain River sighed. "*Kinna*. I had hoped to introduce him to our *risho*. You two would like each other—he's the one who recommended that book. But when you do meet, kindly do not tell him that you tore out its pages. He would be most upset about that." Captain River nodded to Sevi with a knowing smile. "But now it is your turn."

Sevi sighed. "I'm Sevi... just Sevi."

Lorr pursed his lips and glanced at Innavin, who took a sip of his drink to cover his laughter. Captain River frowned. "*Risho*. Somehow, you have managed to do even worse the second time."

Sevi rolled his eyes and shrugged helplessly. "That's all I've got!"

River's frown deepened. "You have more. You could say, 'I am Sevi of the tunnels,' or 'gardentender Sevi,' or 'Sevi, savior of Digby Asgaillin.' See? It is already better!"

Lorr shook his head. "Don't listen to him, Sevi. I think it was fine the way it was. Gods know my name would be just as short if Caldwin wasn't here to remind me that I had two more." He chuckled. "Why don't we get you something to drink?"

"He's still just a boy, Lorr," Innavin interjected.

Lorr waved Innavin off and stepped away, working around a group of people toward a side table where several pitchers had been set out. Innavin shook his head. "If he brings you anything that tastes funny, spit it out over his clothes," he told Sevi. "He enjoys wine more than he should and wants everyone else to as well."

"One of his more persistent habits," River agreed.

Sevi watched Lorr, unable to help his curiosity. As far as he could remember, he'd only ever drank water. The thought of having something more made his stomach growl with excitement.

"It's good to see that you've healed up nicely," Innavin continued after taking another drink. "I can barely see it."

"See what?" Sevi asked.

"The scar." The man trailed his finger down the side of his face. "I imagine that you cracked your head open pretty badly after tumbling over the cliff."

Sevi's hand flew to his eye, suddenly self-conscious. "Oh... no. I've always had this."

"Oh. Well, not to worry, everyone loves a scar. It adds character to your body. It's how I met my wife if you can believe it."

"Ah, here it is," River sighed, shaking his head. "Maybe I'll go help my *isi'kaa* gather the drinks."

"Quiet, River," Innavin said. "You're no one to complain."

River laughed. "A fair point."

"Thank you." Innavin turned back to Sevi. "Have you ever seen someone get struck by lightning, Sevi?"

Sevi raised his eyebrows and shook his head.

"Not many people have! I didn't think it was even possible myself. It always seems to want to hit trees." Innavin downed the rest of his goblet in one swig, then placed the empty cup on the main table. "I was a younger lad, out working in the fields of my father's farm with my brothers, when the heavens themselves split open and brought their fury down upon me!"

He unbuttoned his doublet, widening a hole large enough to grab the collar of his undershirt. "But I must be made of flesh stronger than the breath of the storm goddess Noruva herself, for she could not pierce me! Behold!"

With a flourish, he tugged his collar down and revealed a long, swirling, dull-red scar that traveled up from his chest, which then branched off into other, smaller tendrils, culminating in a mesmerizing web-like pattern. Sevi had never seen anything like it. It looked as though a spider had dug into his body and made its web in his veins.

"I never knew what hit me!" Innavin continued. "One moment I had my plow in hand, the next my brother was punching me in the chest, beating the very air into my lungs until I—"

"Oh, great, Vin lasted maybe half an hour before taking his shirt off," Lorr said, returning with two goblets in addition to his own. He handed one to River, who raised it and clinked it to Lorr's.

"I was in the middle of a story, Lorr." Innavin frowned, letting go of his collar.

"One we've heard far too often." Lorr reached over with the other goblet and handed it to Sevi with a smile. "Here you are, lad. The strongest stuff we have."

"Ah ah ah, wait a murmur." Innavin swooped in and plucked the goblet from Sevi's grasp. He waved it around under his nose.

"For all Gods' sake, Targa, it was a joke," Lorr grumbled.

"The last time you handed me a goblet it took a slap across the face from Rya to wake me up. And that was two days after I drank it." Innavin took a sip, licked his lips, and looked off into the distance. He nodded after a moment. "Good. No poison here, my lord," he said, handing it back to Sevi.

Sevi took it uncertainly, as if it had suddenly sprouted wings and eyestalks. All this over a drink? He hesitantly brought the cup to his lips under the eyes of the three men, taking a tentative sip with a tip of his hand.

And Gods. It was *delicious*.

A burst of fruity flavors and sugar washed over his tongue, trickling pleasantly down his throat and leaving an aftertaste that lingered with a vaguely minty sensation. He closed his eyes, begging the flavors to never leave, and immediately brought the goblet back up to his lips when they did. He upended the rest of it in one drought, too eager to have more and too impatient to pace himself, holding his breath until he had drained the cup of every drop.

River laughed. "Slowly, there is more."

"You really think I'd hand this kid a cup of viscyth, Innavin? He can't be more than twelve, maybe thirteen winters old," Lorr said.

"It didn't hurt to check." Innavin shrugged.

Sevi wiped the back of his hand across his mouth, staring wide-eyed at Lorr. "What is this?"

"Plumaberry juice. I skipped the spirits altogether. No offense, lad, but you don't look like you've even tasted ale yet."

"Can I have more?"

"Of course! The table's right there."

The table he indicated still had far too many people around it. Sevi made no move toward it.

*Coward*, Lily's voice whispered again.

"Shut up," Sevi mumbled.

"What?" Lorr said.

"Um... maybe later," Sevi said louder.

"Suit yourself." Lorr shrugged, taking a sip of his own drink.

"May I please get back to my story?" Innavin asked.

Lorr sighed. "If you must."

"Wonderful. Where was I? Right, so, there I was, lying on my back with my brother pounding on my chest, thinking that would be my last miserable sight of the world, when—"

A low cheer went up from the other side of the room before Innavin could continue, cutting him off. He groaned irritably as people all around turned to see but became elated when he turned himself.

One by one, everyone broke out into smiles and joined with cheers of their own, until the whole room was brought into the celebration. Sevi tried to see what they were so excited for but was pushed around as people moved closer to its source, including Lorr and Innavin. His gaze flicked wildly about as he was squeezed from all sides by the passing bodies. A hand found his shoulder and tugged him back, pulling him into empty space. Sevi looked up at Captain River's smiling face as he patted his shoulder reassuringly.

"The old man is here," the captain said, gesturing to the front of the room. Sevi followed River's hand. The man he indicated was hard to miss—he stood several heads taller than almost everyone else.

Lieutenant Digby had returned.

# Chapter 27

*The current was subtle, the roar was too distant; from the waters, out stretched a hand. An old warrior joined the mouse on his journey while a viper approached from the land.*

---

At first, Sevi found himself smiling along with everyone as the old soldier hobbled forward on a cane, shaking hands and laughing with everyone that ran to greet him. He hadn't untangled his feelings toward the lieutenant yet—Digby hadn't been overtly deceptive, but he'd used Sevi as a means to kill. It was a hard thing to forgive. But Sevi couldn't deny it was good to see him alive.

The man looked exhausted as he came further into view, with purple bags hanging under his eyes and ruddy cheeks Sevi could see from a distance. Each of his steps was heavily supported by his cane, which he relied on with obvious discomfort. On one of his steps, an overly eager party guest knocked it with their foot and sent him stumbling. Sevi moved forward, impulsively wanting to go to his aid, but then his eyes fell upon the woman escorting him.

She was nearly as tall as Digby and caught his arm without issue. Her dark, raven hair was held up in an intricately woven braid and gathered tightly behind her head, as neat and organized as the rest of her. She wore a long, blue coat just like all the other officers, but had it tailored to fit her athletic form, with a charcoal vest beneath it as an accent to the white breaches she wore. Two sword sheaths swung at her hips, one long, one short, and around her neck gleamed a dull iron band.

Her skin was pale, almost hauntingly so, made only more unnerving by the complete lack of compassion on her face amid all the joy. She did not smile once as she guided Digby by the arm, easing him into a chair at the table.

But more terrifying than her was the faceless woman behind her, flowing in her wake as smoothly as a shadow. She had pulled her hair back and swathed herself in a black party gown from neck to toe, as if she'd been plucked from Sevi's mind and invited to the event herself.

Sevi broke into a cold sweat and stumbled back, staring wide-eyed as the woman's blank face turned leisurely in his direction, picking him out from all the other faces in the room.

"Careful," River said, grabbing Sevi by the shoulders before he could fall backward. Sevi snapped his head up to look at the captain, trembling. River dropped his good humor immediately. "Are you well?"

"That woman. Do you see her, too?" Sevi asked.

"Which woman? The commander?" River nodded to the raven-haired lady.

Sevi looked again. The commander had left Digby's side and had taken position at the head of the table, but the faceless woman at her shoulder was gone.

"Who is she?" Sevi whispered, looking around the room in case the phantom had slipped into the crowd. *I can't... I can't be this bad. Not yet.*

"She is Commander—" River started, but as a hush fell over the gathering, he brought a finger to his lips and mouthed the word, "later."

Lorr extracted himself from the fray and rejoined them, sliding his arm companionably behind River's back to stand facing the commander together. The room fell silent without so much as a stern look, as all turned expectantly toward her.

One person handed her a goblet. She did not drink from it, nor did she speak. Instead, she pulled a small, silver circle on a chain out of her coat pocket and flicked the lid on its face open, staring down at it with such a cold intensity that it froze everyone in the room, binding them all in her spell.

A gentle ticking could be heard above the low pitch of everyone's breathing. *Tick. Tick. Tick.* Sevi clutched at his head as an ache sprouted between his eyes. *I... I know that sound,* he thought.

"The hour has come," The commander said. "The hour of the Treachery." She snapped the lid shut with a *click*. She spoke soft and low—not how a leader should speak at *all*. Her dark eyes slid purposefully over the crowd, regarding every single person in the room with equal gravity, as though she could see everything about them. All that they were, had been, and would become, while giving nothing of herself in return. It reminded Sevi of the flat expression Lily had perfected, keeping all her emotions inside whenever she'd needed to. But while Lily had a mask, this woman had *armor*.

She seemed to pause when her gaze landed on him. He took a step back, gripping at River tightly, looking for anything to shield himself from her. But then she moved on, and he was released. Captain River patted his shoulder, and he stepped away out of embarrassment.

"I apologize for the delay in hosting this celebration," the commander continued. "It did not seem right to have it without our lieutenant. But now that he has recovered, I believe it is in our best interest that we make up for lost time."

She stopped and took a deep breath. "Time... How many years has it been since I last walked these halls? I no longer remember. What should have been years of joy spent with family, years of love, of growing old together in peace, were stolen from us and became years of bloodshed, sacrifice, and heartache instead.

"But tonight, as I stand here with you all on the very stone where it began, I am reminded of the strength, bravery, and resolve that each and every one of you have exhibited over the years. For one night, I do not see the carnage that has haunted my dreams. For one night, I do not see the horror brought to bear upon us by the Faen scourge. Instead, I see you, my friends, and the spirits of all those men and women who fell upon this long, bloody road in the hopes of seeing our home again."

She tilted her goblet, spilling her drink onto the floor. As one, the other officers did the same. "Our dead are with us tonight," she said. "So tonight, let us live for them."

She raised her cup. Everyone else did the same, standing together in solidarity. Sevi, having not filled his own when he'd had the chance, stood awkwardly glancing at the beverage table. He lowered his head out of respect for the moment and hoped that would be enough.

When everyone had taken a drink, the commander continued. "Incidentally, our enemy, it seems, has finally understood that we will not cease in our efforts to reclaim what rightfully belongs to us. Their airships have lessened over our skies, harried all the way to their borders by our Empyrean falconers. Their spies are being found and executed more efficiently than ever, due in no small part to our Silver Initiative. And their commanders are being tracked, hunted, and eliminated, like the evil tyrants they are. Soon, *they* will be the ones to know what it is like to be preyed upon, as we wrench every last stolen pebble and blade of grass from their thieving hands and put them back where they *belong.*"

This roused a round of applause from everyone, and even then, the commander did not smile. She brought her free hand up for silence, and when things quieted, she motioned with the goblet to the congregation at large. "One final point before we eat," she proclaimed. "Tonight, I raise my cup to you all, and I ask that when you return to your companies, you do the same for your soldiers. We could not have made it this far without your leadership. *I* could not have made it this far. Because of you, and all the men and women under you, this war may be coming to an end."

The room shook with a cheer so thunderous that it put the previous one to shame, sweeping over all in the room until every person was fiercely laughing, weeping, or embracing. The officers and their guests went around shaking hands and loudly congratulating one another, rocking back and forth in place with every hug as though their excitement could only be expressed through motion.

The commander brought her goblet to her lips and took another drink, then drew out the chair at the head of the table, taking her seat next to Digby without another word.

"Captain River?" Sevi began, turning toward the captain, only to widen his eyes in surprise at how passionately he and Lorr were kissing. Sevi averted his gaze, choosing to stare at the ground instead. Unable to take part in the festivity, he backed up slowly until he stood at the edge of the room and out of everyone's way, clutching at the hem of his waistcoat.

Looking upon the room, it was hard not to feel like a brick in the wall. People were lining up to refill their drinks, all with broad, beaming smiles on their faces, and both Captain River and his friends had been swept up in the sudden cheer. It was the perfect opportunity to slip back into the hallway, where Reynam was waiting for him.

But was it the right time? What if Captain River came searching for him? He supposed that he could look around the room for the entrystone into the Cut while everyone was busy—maybe he could find it if he aligned the perspective from his memory.

He'd only taken a single tentative step when a glance back at the commander made him stop. She had not moved from her chair and was speaking with Digby, but a gripping fear took hold of Sevi's heart and squeezed.

He would not try it. Not while she was around. *She... she would know.*

Something moved in front of him, and he jolted in alarm. A little girl stood before him, gripping a silver bowl to her chest and staring with wide, hazel eyes. Her hair was combed back and flowed loosely along her shoulders, and a smattering of freckles dotted the bridge of her nose and cheekbones. Sevi met her stare with confusion. She didn't move.

"Um... hi," he said. She said nothing. Sevi awkwardly looked around. "Um... are your parents nearby?"

The girl shook her head, pulling her locks out of place.

"Oh." Sevi paused awkwardly. "Well... I'm going to go now. I—" He stopped, squinting at her. "Wait. I've seen you before, haven't I? Are you the girl from the gardens?"

She smiled softly and gave him a timid nod. His heart went out to her. She had seen the accident, too. "Where are the other two?" Sevi looked around again. There were a lot of big, moving bodies, any one of which could easily step on a girl so small. "You shouldn't be here alone, right?" She nodded and clutched the silver bowl tighter to her chest. Sevi's gaze drifted down to it and froze.

That wasn't a bowl. That was *Lily's helmet.*

He stared at it for almost ten breaths just to be certain his eyes weren't playing tricks on him. When he was sure, he took a deep breath and stepped toward the girl. "*Where did you get that?*"

The little girl's eyes widened. She took a scared step back, then opened her mouth.

"*Risho!*" Sevi spun around. Captain River approached, flushed and smiling. "What are you doing over here?" When Sevi turned back to the girl, it was just in time to see her disappearing into the crowd behind a dozen legs. "Come, say hi to the old man," Captain River said, placing a hand on Sevi's shoulder. "He is eager to see you!"

"Wait, *no*," Sevi said loudly. Something was *wrong*.

"What is it?" Captain River asked, stopping.

Sevi clenched at the hem of his waistcoat again, staring feverishly around the room, but it was no use. "Captain River," he said, turning to bore his gaze into the man. "Have you found Lily?"

Captain River blinked. "I am sorry?"

"*Have you found her?*"

Captain River gave him a measured look, then slowly shook his head. "That is something that I would have quickly told you. Why do you ask?"

Sevi took a deep breath and closed his eyes. Lily's voice whispered softly to him once again. *Have you been taking your medicine?*

No. He hadn't. Not for two months, and he'd been having the nightmares to prove it. He thought of the faceless lady, and the more he thought about it, the more it made sense. *First her, now this. What's more likely? That Lily has lost her helmet, the one thing she'd never go without, or that I'm seeing things that aren't there? That I'm...*

He breathed in a long breath and let it out through his teeth. *That I'm crazy again?*

Captain River lightly shook him. "Sevi?"

"I'm fine," Sevi lied, trying to keep the tremor from his voice.

"Are you certain? Shall we step out?"

*No,* Sevi thought hurriedly, *I need to leave alone.* "I'm *fine*," he said again, giving Captain River as confident a smile as he could muster. He'd seen plenty of confident smiles before. People wore them all the time. "Please, let's go see Digby."

Captain River tilted his head, running his gaze along Sevi's face with a furrowed brow. Sevi maintained his smile. "Very well," he said at last. "Please. This way."

The table was steadily filling up as people finished refilling their goblets and took their seats. Sevi's gaze drifted once more to the woman at its head as they approached, drawn to the commander despite his hesitation. "Captain River, who is the commander?"

"She is Commander Tiersa Grommand, founder of this army, and former Promina of Queen Korina. She has been our leader for many years," he replied. "She looks frightening, yes? I thought so, too, when I first met her. She is not so bad. Although, it would not hurt to be very respectful to her, should she speak to you."

River patted his back and said nothing more. Sevi gulped, standing up straight as Digby and Tiersa both turned to face them.

"Lad!" Digby exclaimed, spreading his arms. His cheeks were red, and he smelled like plumaberry juice, but stronger. Sevi made no move towards the offered embrace, but his reserve did nothing to tarnish the lieutenant's good humor. "So, you took me offer after all! It's good to see ya out of those tunnels, boy! And... I'll be damned." His eyes widened. "Did ya find yer shadow?"

Sevi looked down at his feet and shuffled in place. "Um... more like it found me."

Digby shook his head. "Great. Now no one will believe me. Is the lass here with ya?" Sevi reached for his necklace and clenched at his shirt, gently shaking his head. Digby's smile fell, and his face softened with sympathy. "Ah. I see. I'm sorry. Is she...?"

"We did not find any children on the battlefield," River filled in. "It is possible that his friend fled when the fighting started. We are still looking for her."

"Ah, good!" Digby exclaimed, his smile returning. "Don't worry, lad, we'll find yer sharp-tongued friend. She was too smart to find herself in the middle of that mess, mark me on it. Now pull up a seat! How've ya been farin' here? The food's not great, but it be better lately."

"Um..." Sevi swallowed again, making no move to sit, and looked nervously between Digby and Commander Tiersa. She had reclined in her high-backed chair, disinterestedly swishing the contents of her goblet around. "I've... I've been fine. The food's been fine."

"I heard that some gobshite took a shot at you and sent ya over a cliff," Digby said, his mood darkening. He looked up at River. "Was that right?"

"Yes," River confirmed.

"Have they been punished, sir?"

"He has."

"Good." Digby nodded. "I'm glad he was a lousy shot. Still, I'm sure the tumble down wasn't fun, eh, lad?"

Sevi's grip on his waistcoat tightened in memory of rock after rock rushing up into him, crushing the breath from his lungs. The fibers in the fabric of his shirt started to snap.

River grimaced and cleared his throat. Digby's smile faltered again. "What? What is it?"

Captain River looked at Sevi with a silent question on his face, but when Sevi continued to say nothing, River answered for him. "It did, indeed, not look fun. The boy was in bed nearly as long as you, Lieutenant."

Digby grimaced and muttered a curse under his breath, looking apologetically at Sevi. "Ya remember when I said I was a tragedy with kids? That hasn't changed. I ferget that talkin' about old wounds should be a pastime left fer gray dogs like me. Ya don't need any of that faff. Not tonight, eh?" He tilted his head, giving him a rueful smile. "Please, sit down, join me fer dinner. It should be out at any moment."

"Has the boy been tested yet?" Commander Tiersa said.

All joviality on the officers' faces disappeared as River and Digby both turned toward their commander. She had not looked up from her cup. Sevi paled.

"My lady." River bowed his head. "He wears my personal iron, and he is unharmed."

"All who enter the army must be tested, Captain. The last thing we need is a greenblood in our ranks," Commander Grommand replied, still swishing her drink.

"Doctor Lea would not have allowed him to go untested," River persisted.

"Do you know that for a fact?"

"She has assured me that—"

"Do either of you have a vial?" the commander interrupted.

"No, my lady, I would not bring one to a celebration," River said.

"I'm empty, too, Commander," Digby said.

Captain River cleared his throat. "Lady Ti—"

"Bring the boy to me," the commander ordered, setting her goblet down and reaching for her belt.

River and Digby traded a furtive glance. Digby frowned, and merely shrugged. River sighed, and nudged Sevi's shoulder once more. "Yes, Commander. Come here, *risho*," he said aloud, but leaned down to whisper in Sevi's ear. "I am sorry. Be respectful."

Sevi's chest strained as though he had been hit by another bullet. His feet felt like two cobblestone blocks, slowing him down so drastically that River had to press into his back to move him forward. Commander Tiersa stared at him as she brought out a glass vial filled with a silver liquid and topped with a flip-lid. She reached up to her hair and pulled out a black hairpin.

River stopped Sevi a step away from her chair. He stood before her, frozen. Tiersa's lips moved, but Sevi didn't hear her. His heart was beating too loudly. Raising an eyebrow, she looked past him at River. The captain sighed and reached down to scoop Sevi's hand up in his own, palm-side up. Tiersa swiftly jabbed her pin into Sevi's index finger, drawing blood in one smooth motion. The pain pierced his mental fog and brought his gaze down to stare at the ruby bead forming on his fingertip.

Thumbing the vial open, Tiersa turned his finger over its open mouth and shook it gently, dislodging the drop of blood into the liquid. She then raised it up to the light and swirled it around.

Sevi's empty stomach churned and knotted in on itself, banishing any hunger beneath the weight of his terror. Time slowed as Commander Tiersa patiently waited for something to happen, staring at the glass. And waited. And waited.

The vial remained unchanged. Blowing air from her nose, she nodded and carefully placed both the pin and vial back. Picking up her goblet, she sat back in her chair and beckoned her other hand at River.

River took Sevi by the shoulders and steered him away, swapping places with him so that he stood next to the commander in his stead. He leaned forward and whispered something into Tiersa's ear. She exchanged a word with him, then flicked her hand dismissively.

With a nod, Captain River stood back up and marched Sevi down the table, far away from Digby and the commander. Sevi didn't pay attention to where they were going, all he cared about was going away from *her*.

"I am sorry," River said again. He moved to Sevi's front and placed his hands on Sevi's biceps, staring at him with concern. "Are you well?"

Sevi shook his head furiously. No. He was definitely *not* well. There was too much noise, and not enough silence. Too many things that made him doubt his own sanity. Too many loud, strange people, and all they ever did was stare at him, or poke their dumb noses in his business, or poke their awful needles into his fingers. Hang dinner. Hang this whole *place*. This wasn't the castle he knew anymore, and he wanted *out*.

"I would like to go back to my bed now. Please," Sevi whispered, not meeting River's eyes.

"You have not had dinner yet."

"I'm not hungry," Sevi mumbled.

Captain River stared at him for several breaths before nodding. "I will save a leg of turkey and send it to you." He smiled reassuringly. "You did well tonight, *risho*. Let us have Reynam escort you to your bed. I will come see you tomorrow, if my duties allow it."

Silently turning on his heel, Sevi walked toward the door without River's direction. He didn't look back to see if the captain followed. He no longer cared.

# Chapter 28

*Darkness became her, ice watched her with envy, her fangs pierced the toughest of hide. Though the mouse fled such venom, though the dawn came to break, such fates could only coincide.*

---

"**B**ack so soon? I know officers are stuffy—no offense, sir—but it's hardly been an hour," Reynam said to River and Sevi as they stepped out.

"Sevi is not feeling well. Please escort him back to the infirmary," Captain River said.

Reynam gave a lazy salute. "Can do, sir."

River nodded to the soldier before turning back to Sevi. "As I said. You did well tonight. I hope you have a good evening." River turned his hand palm-up and placed the side of it to his chest, then swept it fluidly out toward Sevi. "*Liko kasii imi shavi laowa.*"

Sevi's mind had detached from his body again. All he could do was stare blankly at Captain River's strange gesture. River didn't seem to mind, though. The captain gave him one last small smile before stepping back through the door, closing it behind him.

Reynam gave Sevi an odd look. "What was that about?"

Sevi didn't answer, looking around the hallway instead while his body reassembled itself. The knight was gone. No one else was around. And the party would be getting its food soon, leaving the kitchens empty. On top of all that, he had his shadow back.

Sevi closed his eyes and took a deep, exhausted breath. As much as he would prefer crawling into bed and sleeping off the night, he was in the perfect position to move. Swallowing his fear, he grabbed the chain of his necklace and pulled it out of his shirt, staring at its solid silver star with its caved-in face one last time before holding it out to Reynam. "I'm trusting you."

Reynam looked from Sevi to the necklace and back. "A regrettably bad decision," he said, taking it from him.

Sevi's heart lurched as he parted with its familiar weight. "I'm not answering your questions if I don't get it back."

"Who's to say I don't just keep the necklace?"

Sevi gritted his teeth and tried not to cry in frustration. *Be like Lily,* he reminded himself again. Taking a deep, irritated breath, he summoned all the atrocious emotions he'd felt that night and drew upon them for strength. "Then... then I won't come back. What else is there for me here?"

Reynam quirked an eyebrow at him.

"Y-you don't know a thing about the tunnels here, but I know *everything,*" he lied. Digby's trick with the wall proved otherwise, but Reynam didn't know that. "And... I also know that, even if I'm found, *you* will get punished for it, too, and everyone will know about how the clever Corporal Reynam couldn't even manage a *child.*"

"So, you're saying I should beat you over the head now, then drag your unconscious body back to Lea?" Reynam asked nonchalantly.

Sevi gulped. His brain churned for ideas in a panic, and eventually sputtered out inspiration. "I'm saying... others know that necklace is mine. Doctor Lea, *and* Captain River. And when I wake up, I will tell them about how you took it from me."

Reynam flashed a smile. "Oh, those bruises on him, sir? The lad tried to escape. I tried to calm him, but he turned his fists on me. Necklace? No, sir, I didn't pick up any necklace, sir, maybe it fell off him during the struggle, sir."

Sevi lost control of his voice. "You're *Corporal Reynam.* You're mean to *everyone,* while Captain Lorr called me 'the hero of the cause' tonight. They... they'll find out. They'll *punish* you. And all because you didn't follow our deal!"

Sevi's voice grew to a high, frantic pitch toward the end, cracking on the last word. *Why can't this man just do what we agreed!*

Reynam lapsed into silence, but his grin did not waver, and as the moments passed, it only grew wider, and wider, until the soldier finally threw his head back and *laughed.*

Sevi stared dumbfounded at the corporal as he bent over with his hands on his knees, his body convulsing with the strength of his laughter until the empty corridor sang with his guffaws. He was so loud that the door opened, and a woman stuck her head out. "*What* is going *on* out here, Corporal?" she demanded.

"I—heh—I'm sorry, Captain. I just heard a funny joke, is all. You know how boring it gets on duty, especially all alone outside of a party, and I'll take whatever distraction I can get." He waved his hand as if shooing the question away, then stood up straight and saluted. His chest still stuttered with restrained laughter. "Nothing to report out here, ma'am. All is well."

The captain turned her attention from him to Sevi, considering something. A noise went up from inside, and she turned her head to see. The intoxicating aroma of freshly cooked meat filled the air, making Sevi's stomach growl in response. It smelled *wonderful.*

"Keep it down. Don't make me come out here again," the lady grumbled. She closed the door before she could get a response.

"Yes, ma'am," Reynam said to the empty air, dropping the salute. He put both of his hands along with Sevi's necklace into his pants pockets. "I'm sorry, kid. I couldn't help myself." He turned back to him. "Really. Whatever you think of me, know this: you've impressed me. You come across as this frail, fearful little mouse, but that's not all there is to you, is it?"

He gave Sevi a grin full of teeth, then shook his head and jerked his chin forward. "Get out of here. But come back before the party ends. You have one hour."

Reynam turned his back to Sevi and took his position beside the door with arms crossed. When Sevi, still staring in shock, didn't move, he shooed him with a hand. "Go on. You have my word that I'll uphold our deal, for whatever that's worth to you. So get out of here before I drag the cat back over."

Sevi opened his mouth, grasping for something to say, but shook his head. He decided that whatever the man was playing at, it could wait. What little time he had couldn't be wasted on this, not when Lily and Alyda were so close.

He turned away, but not before giving Reynam a wary glare. Striding quickly to the kitchen door at the end of the corridor, he placed his ear to the wood. Faint noises of someone moving around could be heard, but they quieted at the sound of another door opening somewhere in the room. Noise from the party filtered in for just a moment before shutting off abruptly. The cooks were still bringing the feast to the officers.

He glanced back down the hallway to make sure that no one was watching. Reynam was very pointedly not looking in his direction. Satisfied, he turned the knob as gingerly as possible and cracked open the door, taking a peek before committing on entering. It was empty, as he thought, but as past experience had so recently taught him, that could change at any moment.

Opening the door just enough to work his body in, he slipped into the room without a sound. He smiled down at his shadow. "We're in the kitchens, Shy," he whispered.

The shadow didn't move. Sevi kept talking to it as he crept toward the table hiding the Cut's entrystone. "I've always wanted to take you here," he murmured, keeping his eye on the dining room door. "This would've been so much easier with you here. Where have you been all these years?"

His path took him past the empty chair where Rumbles used to sit and sleep, and he had to suppress the melancholy that welled up. A burst of laughter came from the other room, making him jump. When he turned his gaze landed on something further down the table—a sight so beautiful it made him pause. A huge, roasted bird, lying on the counter on a silver platter, with fresh steam rising off its crisped, honey-brown skin, framed by the crackling flames of the fireplace. It must've been fresh off the spit. And the smell... Gods, the *smell*. It wafted to him beckoningly, enticing him to come closer, if only for a taste.

Sevi's hunger came rushing back at once. His stomach, robbed of this feast, now demanded it all with a vengeance. And so what if he stole a morsel? Just a bite, just to see how it tasted. Surely the officers couldn't eat *all* of such a big meal!

*Our rule, Sevi,* Lily's phantom whispered.

Sevi's heart sank. He'd been here before, coaxed into a false sense of security moments before disaster. He wasn't about to let it happen again, not with Lily and Alyda waiting for him. With a sigh, he gave the platter one last look of longing before crouching low and dipping beneath the table toward the entrystone.

And came face-to-face with a man.

Sevi yelped, hitting his head on the tabletop and stumbling out from underneath. The man, lying on his side with eyes closed and one hand under his head, stirred. He yawned, stretching with a groan and lifting his free hand up to rub his face. Scrambling backward, Sevi pressed his back into the wood of the island. "Who's that?" the man grumbled, blinking rapidly and squinting.

Sevi bolted from the floor, hurrying around the island.

"Hey... *hey!*" the man called after him. The table shuddered as he bumped his head against it and let out a curse.

Sevi called to his shadow, "Shy. *Shy.* Please, wake up!"

"Get back here!"

The man's boots scraped on the floor as he stood, turning Sevi's blood to ice. "Shy!" Sevi whispered more incessantly. "Save me!"

There was a tug on his feet, and Shy rose from the floor, flickering darkly against the firelight as they took a form of their own. Their thick, inky body and dim white orbs pooled upward into the air until it reached a shallow height, looking much darker than when Sevi had last seen them.

The shadow blinked their orbs at him and reeled inward on themselves with a wriggle. Then they sprung, spreading their gelatinous body in all directions and wrapping themselves around Sevi like a blanket, chilling him wherever they touched.

Sevi remembered to take a deep breath before being enveloped completely. He watched through the shadow's translucent body as a pair of legs appeared from around the counter.

"I said—" The man stopped, staring at Sevi in bewilderment. Sevi's heart sank, suddenly fearful that Shy hadn't recovered enough dark.

The door to the dining room opened. "Yeah, there's one left," a new voice said. Sevi turned to see another chef walking in, pausing at the sight of the man. "Hal? You alright?"

"He—" Hal muttered, rubbing his eyes with his hand. "I swear—the door didn't—Did you see a boy run past you?"

"What? A boy?" The lady cocked her head. "What are you talking about?"

"He was... He was right here. I'd bet my last coppen on it."

Humored, the lady ran her eyes over Sevi, glossing past him as if he weren't there. "Sure you weren't still dreaming?"

"I—" Hal blinked, rubbing his eyes again. "I guess."

"Well. Since you're up. Help me take the last of this out, then go find your tent before you get yelled at again."

Hal shook his head. "Right. Yeah." He stepped forward. His path took him dangerously close, so Sevi gently lifted himself up on all fours and inched himself away as quietly as possible, praying for each chef to hurry up. His lungs were beginning to hurt.

"Haunted by ghosts now?" Hal muttered, picking up the roasted bird's platter and walking into the dining room.

The lady held the door open for him. When he'd cleared it, she cast one last faintly curious look around the kitchen before closing it shut.

Sevi flailed his arms. With a rush of wind, Shy's inky body withdrew, snapping back into itself inside of Sevi's shadow. They blinked asynchronously at him while he dragged in blessed, beautiful lungfuls of air, greedily inhaling his fill and swearing never to take it for granted again.

Sevi stared at Shy, then at the door, then back at Shy. "That... was *far*... too close, Shy. *Why* did you take so *long?*" Shy made no reply. "We are going to talk about this *later*."

Wiggling at their edges, Shy's orbs went out, and they sank noiselessly back into Sevi's shadow until the two were completely indistinguishable again. Gritting his teeth, Sevi shuffled beneath the table and tried not to curse his friend. Touching his hands to the entrystone and pushing, he turned his thoughts to reuniting with Lily and Alyda. Just a bit further, and they'd all be together again.

Except the stone didn't budge.

Panic swept through him anew. He pushed harder, but it refused to move. "Lily. Lily!" he whispered frantically, darting a quick look around before pounding on the stone. "Alyda! Are either of you there? It's me! I'm here!"

Silence. Possibly the worst silence Sevi had experienced since Captain Redwood. They had to be here. They *had* to be.

A scratching sound came from behind the wall. Sevi stopped pounding. Rock ground against rock, and a small hole opened up, big enough to fit the bald head of one tiny, green fairy.

Alyda twinkled loudly with delight at the sight of him, chiming out several harmonious notes until she was loudly shushed from behind her. She cast an irritated glance back, but it was fleeting. Sevi beamed at her, and a powerful mixture of joy and relief swiftly overcame his fear. He reached a finger out to her, but she flicked her gaze about the room and quickly disappeared back into the Cut.

The hole resealed itself. With a soft grinding sound and the rush of air, the entrystone began to move, gradually pulling backward into the Cut before being pushed off to the side. The soft call of a mountain jay came from within, and an open hand appeared from the dark, reaching for his.

Sevi clasped it without hesitation, and with a strong tug, was pulled back into the pathways of his old home. "*Lily—*"

He was thrown backward before he could finish. All the air in his lungs rushed out of him as someone grappled him into the fiercest hug of his life, squeezing him so hard that he couldn't have escaped if he tried.

"You stupid, *stupid* boy," Lily whispered.

# Chapter 29

*The shore offered respite, as brief as could be. Within its stone weathered a flower. He held onto her. She held onto him. And they whispered their joy through the hour.*

———— ❦ ————

Sevi wrapped his arms around his friend and held her close, burying his face against the side of her beat-up helmet. Its ugly dome had never looked so beautiful—and it was on her head, right where it should be.

They latched onto each other for far longer than they should have, each trembling quietly. A small weight pressed in against Sevi's cheek as Alyda chimed out her twinkling voice, shaky with tears of her own. Distantly, some part of him recognized how incredible it was to see Lily crying—*actually* crying—but he shushed it before it could say something that ruined the moment.

Lily recovered first. Sniffing, she wiped her eyes and sat up, dusting herself off. "Alright, enough with the dribble. Help me with the stone, this thing weighs a ton."

Sevi laughed, tears still running down his face. "I missed you too, Lily."

Alyda lifted from his cheek and hovered next to his shoulder as he got up. Together, he and Lily hoisted the entrystone and slid it back into the wall, smothering the light and noise from Outside entirely. Lily propped a wooden plank behind it, ensuring no one else could come in.

With Alyda's light to guide them, the trio moved toward the bedroom. "That man under the table lies there every day," Lily grumbled. "Thank the gods we left supplies here. How did you get him to move?"

"You'll never believe it, but *Shy* helped me," Sevi said excitedly.

"The shadow's back?" Lily stopped to look at him in surprise.

"That's right!"

Sevi grinned as she furrowed her brow. Lily moved around his side to see behind him, where Alyda's light had the shadow pointing. "Well. Where is it?"

Sevi blinked and looked down at his feet. To his horror, he found himself shadowless once more. "No. *Shy!*" Sevi called out desperately. "I'm *sorry!* I'm sorry for yelling at you! Please come back!"

His voice echoed back at him. Nothing moved in the darkness. Sevi hung his head. He'd found two friends and lost one again in the process.

"Hey," Lily said, taking his arm. "Come on. Let's get to the bedroom."

"But—"

"It's probably for the best. That shadow isn't natural."

"They're my friend, Lily."

Lily shrugged. "Well, maybe it's having a little fun, being back in the Cut? There's a lot of darkness around for it to play in."

He stared off into the tunnel, hoping to find a patch of shadow darker than the rest.

"I got your letter," Lily continued, walking ahead of him again. "That was some show you put on in the gardens."

Sevi took a deep breath and followed her. "You were watching?"

"No, I've mostly been hiding here since the battle. But I asked Alyda to keep an eye on the courtyard. I figured that if you were still... around, you'd make it to a garden somehow. She told me all about what happened, and brought back your smelly, crumpled-up note. Did you write with broth or something?"

Sevi shrugged. "It was all I had. Has the firedrake returned?"

"No, thank the gods. I've got enough to deal with as it is. If we're lucky the battle killed it or ran it off. Maybe it thought all the explosions were from a fire *dragon* and got scared."

Stepping into the bedroom, Sevi took a look around. Three things became immediately apparent. First, all their junk had been shoved up against the tunnel that led to the Overlook, forming a makeshift, flimsy-looking barricade. Second, despite her protests about Hal the floor-sleeper, Lily had wasted no time in stealing every bit of food from the kitchen that she could. An assortment of jars, packages, fruits, and vegetables had been shoved into a corner to form a small heap that crept a fair way up the wall.

Third, despite years of longing to leave, he realized just how much he'd missed their bedroom in the time he'd been away, and a rush of memories flooded him all at once. Alyda performing new tricks of flight, creating shapes in the air with the afterimage of her glow. Lily teaching him how to properly spy, and wait, and listen to the Fablings for the right time to scavenge. The three of them huddling with each other, enjoying the heat of the kitchens during the winters, when the mountain wind made things icy and unbearable.

It was dark. Musty. Cramped. Lonely. But it was all he'd known. It was their secret, and that made it special.

Lily, oblivious to his nostalgia, unceremoniously slumped into her sleeping sack with a tired sigh and wiped her face. "We," she said, tilting her head toward him, "have a lot to talk about."

Sevi nodded, dragging his bed next to hers. Alyda settled between them, casting her green light across them both. "Yes. We do," he said. "There's a lot going on Outside, and I can't stay for long."

"Really?"

Sevi nodded. "I only have an hour."

"Why's that? Actually, make that part of your explanation." Lily leaned forward. "Where should we start?"

Sevi shook his head, staring at his feet. There was so much he wanted to know, and he wanted to ask it all at once. "I thought you were dead for so long, Lily," he said softly. He reached over and scooted a small, shoddily sewn cushion toward Alyda—her own sleeping sack, for the rare times when she joined them here. She chimed once in thanks, moving it under her. He looked at Lily. "Where were you when the fighting started?"

"I wanted to ask you the same thing," Lily replied. "The note you left implied you were checking on the firedrake, but you never came back. I didn't really care at the time; I'd assumed that you'd gone to pee or went up to the garden or something. So, I waited. And waited. Until Alyda came darting up to me in broad daylight, jingling louder than a ringing bell, and that's when I knew something was wrong."

Her face became strained. "I tried to get to you, Sevi," she said softly, not looking at him. "I tried everything I could. But when I went down the mountain, the mines had been unsealed. People were coming out, armed to the teeth. I... I couldn't get through."

She wiped her face. "I ran back to the Overlook with Alyda. I climbed up the cliff into the trees... and I hid. Godsdamnit, I hid." She hammered her fist against the floor.

"It's alright, Lily," Sevi said gently.

"It's not," Lily bitterly refuted. "I had to send Alyda back out for you, and Gods bless her brave little spirit, she went." Alyda fluttered her wings and chimed at the praise, looking proudly at Lily. "But when she came back," Lily said, her voice changing, "she signed that you were sleeping in your garden, and that she couldn't wake you up. She found this."

She picked something up from the floor. Sevi's stomach dropped before the shriveled effizine plant husk even hit the light.

"I was in those trees for hours, worrying about your stupid hide every second, asking myself, 'what if they caught you' and 'what if they hurt you?' I was there long enough to watch the fighting start. Long enough to watch you walk out, half-drugged and stupid, only to get *shot* and *thrown over a cliff*. I thought you *died*."

She tossed the stem angrily at him, rage leaking into her every word. "I told you I needed you alert and clear, not drugged and asleep. Why then, Sevi, in all fucking Iaela, did you *dose* yourself, with people in our fucking *tunnels?*"

Sevi flinched as the dead plant struck his shin, looking away in shame. He had held onto the hope that she wouldn't find out about that. If he lied to her, she would see right through him. She always could. And that didn't seem right—not after being reunited. He swallowed and clenched his shirt, saying quietly, "Do you remember when I saw that arm in the bushes?"

Lily fixed him with a critical stare. "Yeah. I think I remember. You nearly sprained my wrist."

"The visions haven't stopped." Sevi's eyes welled again. "They've... they've gotten worse, actually." He trembled as the words came out, forcing the truth from his lips before they got stuck in his throat. "My dreams have... I'm seeing them when I'm awake now. And when I made the effizine paste, I was... I was going crazy."

It all came tumbling out. "I was so *scared*, Lily. I was losing my *mind*. I saw things. Horrible things. I think... I don't know *what* I think anymore." He clutched his head, tangling his fingers in his hair. "When the fire came after me again, all I wanted was to get away from it, but it was everywhere I looked. I saw those soldiers in the Cut, and I knew we were in danger, but all I could think about was ending it. The fire. The smoke. The bodies. And then I woke up and it all became *real*."

Sevi buried his face in his arms. His body heaved, wracked by his cries. He heard the flutter of wings. Alyda settled on his knee with a sad chime, patting him reassuringly. Sevi stayed like that for some time, falling deeper into a maelstrom of guilt and fear, until a hand wrapped around his ankle and squeezed.

"Sevi," Lily said quietly. He wiped his face before looking up, preparing himself for the disappointment that was surely on her face. But all he saw was sadness. She asked him gently, "Do you remember the day we met?"

A laugh bubbled unexpectedly out of his throat. Like all memories he'd actively tried to forget, that particular one had only latched on, sucking on his mind like a blood-drunk tick. "Yeah... I remember."

"Do you remember how you were? Covered in blood, half-burned, and rambling like a madman?"

"Yes. Please don't remind me," he murmured, staring forlornly at his feet. *Blood. Fear. A girl with a torch.*

"Are you afraid that you're going back to that? Or that I and Alyda will leave if you do?"

Sevi fell into a glassy stupor. She had voiced his worst fear—that they would leave him and disappear back into the darkness of the Cut from whence Lily first came.

Lily took his hand in hers and squeezed it tightly, denying him the chance to sink deeper into himself. He looked at her with mild surprise. "Sevi. You got through that," she said. "It didn't beat you. If you're thinking that you're going crazy again, then tell me, and I'll *help* you. I didn't leave you then. I'm not leaving you now. And I'm... you..."

She stumbled uncharacteristically over her words, pulling even more of Sevi's attention away from himself. Her face had twisted oddly, with her jaw clenched and her eyebrows knit tightly together. Her hand tightened around his own. "I am so, *so* angry over what you did. That you just ran away. But I'm so thankful that you're still alive. And that's the only time you'll ever hear me say that." She raised her index finger and waved it around in his face. "Once. *Once.* If you have *any* more near-death experiences, then so help me Gods, you'll wish the bullet got you, because I will throw your sorry ass over the mountain for a *second* time."

She leveled a look at him, lowering her chin against her chest and meeting his eyes with all the seriousness in the world. But as the silence stretched on, Sevi smiled. And then she smiled. Their smiles grew into chuckles, then laughter, shaking them so hard that Alyda had to take off from Sevi's knee. She hovered between them, looking at the two like she couldn't decide if she was the only sane person in the room, which only made them laugh harder.

Then they were hugging again.

Lily extracted herself. "So." She sniffed, wiping her nose. "What happened to you? Is the Outside everything you thought it'd be?"

"No, not at all. But I suppose it hasn't been terrible." Alyda settled back down on his knee, smoothing out the wrinkles on her flower dress, looking just as keen as Lily to hear his story. Sevi cleared his throat, then told them everything.

Lily snorted when he'd finished. "So Blumpkin made it. Why am I not surprised? I'm sure those soldiers would've treated me very differently."

Sevi chuckled. "Maybe."

"And they have a flag with your necklace on it? What do you think that's about?"

"I'm not sure, but they seem very interested in figuring it out." Sevi sighed. "I'd rather they quit asking. As if I'd know anything useful."

"Mm." Lily hummed, looking off in thought. She leaned back onto her hands and let her legs go limp, staring off into the near distance with another vacant expression. Something was churning around in her head, and when Lily got like that, Sevi found it best to just leave her be. Eventually, she turned to him and said, "Sevi, considering everything, you have done shockingly well."

Sevi looked at her with surprise. "I have?"

"The Embers love you. And their leaders—some of them at least—are clearly sticking their necks out for you, despite your repeated efforts to stymie their questions. And you put that asshole Reynam down when he tried to flex his weight on you. Sevi, I don't think I've ever been more proud of you."

Sevi felt himself blush. "Um... Thank you. You know, through everything, I was always asking myself what you would do if you were in my place."

"A fair thing to ask yourself. I'm pretty much perfect." Lily grinned a cocky smile. Sevi laughed. Alyda coughed, and not in one of her fits. "Hush up, you little bean sprout," Lily grumbled at her.

Her praise warmed Sevi deep in his chest. In a strange way, though the circumstances were far different than what he'd imagined, he had managed to impress her. Then a thought came to him that dampened his mood considerably. "Lily... you were right."

"I normally am," she said. "But about what?"

"We shouldn't have helped Digby." Sevi wrapped his arms around his knees. "None of this would've happened. We... I got everyone in the castle... they're all..." The tears threatened to come up again. The only thing that stopped them was Lily's harsh laugh.

"Don't think so highly of yourself," she said. "You forget, I saw the whole thing."

"What do you mean?"

"Those soldiers didn't just come out of our tunnels. They came out of our mines, along the road to town, up the slagging *cliffside*, and, I *swear* to you, jumped off of the mountain peaks! Those ones had massive sheets tied around their bodies with cord, and it floated them all the way down."

After two months of guilt, Sevi refused to accept off-hand that he had played no part in the slaughter. "But maybe less would have died. Maybe the Cut would still be a secret."

"Maybe, maybe not," Lily said. "That's a matter left only to fate to decide. Not silly little boys like you."

"But—"

"Sevi," Lily stopped him. "Did you take a sword and go charging out of the Cut? Did you shoot anyone? Did you plan the invasion? No. You saved an old man and fell off a cliff. So, here's another first for you: I was *wrong*."

She squeezed his shin. "There was no stopping them. What happened here happened because *they* wanted it to, not us. Not you. After seeing it all, there's no doubt in my mind that they would've come no matter what. So don't think about it," she finished, patting his leg.

He couldn't just drop the issue after turning it around in his head for so long, even after her impassioned speech... but she helped. He nodded, trying to force himself to believe her. "That's incredible, though. Floating people without wings? Is that how the airship was taken down? By the floaters?"

"Partly." Lily scrunched her face in an odd smirk. "Birds helped."

Sevi thought back to the falconers in the throne room. "Birds?"

"Birds," Lily affirmed. "I don't know how they controlled them, maybe signal whistles or lights or something. But there was so much noise that I don't know how a whistle of all things could be heard through it all." She shook her head. "When the airship slowed to make a pass at the castle grounds, a cloud of raptors flew down from the mountains and swarmed everything on deck, including the balloon. Nothing survived. Not that I could see at least."

She closed her eyes at the memory as if she could see it behind her eyelids. "Then a lucky floater managed to land on the ship and take the wheel, only to immediately crash it into the ground." She chuckled. "I don't know what they were thinking. You can't just drive one of those things like a boat."

Sevi shook his head in disbelief, finding it too fantastical to take in. It was like something from a stage play. "How do you know so much about those airships?"

He regretted asking the moment it came out. She smirked, but her eyes hardened, as they always did whenever he asked her details from her life. "I think a better question right now would be how much time do you have left before you need to get back?"

Sevi's stomach dropped. *Oh no.* He bolted up from the floor, sending Alyda tumbling into the air with a ring of indignation. "BLAZES," he swore. "*I need to get—*" He sputtered as Alyda flew by, chucking a fistful of something from her pocket at his face in retribution.

Lily chuckled. "Yes, you do."

Words poured frantically from Sevi's mouth. "What do we do now, Lily? What's the plan? I don't think I can hold off their questions forever—I promised Reynam answers just so I could get here, but after that, what then? What if Captain River decides to just throw me out eventually and I have to leave you here and—"

"Sevi, Sev, stop," Lily shushed him, standing and taking his shoulders. "Listen. Do whatever you can to remain in their good graces—whatever you can think of. Here, they like you. They feed you, clothe you, and shelter you. If you're thrown outside of the castle, you won't get that treatment, and I won't be able to help. Blackest night, I might never find you again if I can't get out of these walls."

"What if... what if you came with me and we left together? I'm sure they'd let you go if I asked."

"Remember when I tried to kill Blumpkin?"

Sevi said nothing at that.

"Exactly. They'd hang me over the walls by my thumbs. So, here's what you'll do. If you're afraid that they'll throw you out because you won't answer their questions, then answer them. There's nothing you can say that will harm you or me, just don't tell them where I'm hiding. And don't mention anything about Alyda, considering how they feel about Fae."

Alyda hovered next to Lily's shoulder, bobbing her head vigorously in agreement.

"In the meantime, I'll come up with a plan, while you keep your eyes and ears open for anything we can use. Alyda can take messages back and forth in an emergency, but I don't want her going out in the open if we can help it. So, find the Cut's spystone in the barracks—I'll open it up from my side, and with luck, no one will notice. Oh, and speaking of whistles, I'm guessing you dropped yours."

She rummaged around in her pockets, then held her closed fist out toward Sevi. He opened his hand, and she dropped a whistle carved out of bone with a lily flower etched into its sides onto his palm.

Lily continued. "A few patrols came through in the week after the battle, sweeping for hideaways, but lately they've left the tunnels alone to focus on the Outside. Kind of impractical to guard anything in here when you can just guard its entrances. So, if you're ever in trouble, find the Cut, blow this whistle, and I'll come find you. Or Alyda will. Alright?"

Sevi nodded solemnly, staring at the instrument. "I... I don't want to go back out there, Lily," he whispered, closing his fingers over the precious gift. "The way things work. The people. It's not like anything we've seen."

"I don't blame you," Lily said, patting his arm. "But I know you can do it."

Sevi choked down a sudden sob and moved forward to embrace her one last time. Alyda joined in on Sevi's shoulder, none of them wanting to let go of the others.

Lily grunted and drew back. "Get out of here. We'll see you soon, alright?"

"Alright," Sevi sniffed, reluctantly pulling away. "Bye, Alyda. Bye, Lily."

"Only bye for now, silly boy."

Forcing a smile he didn't feel, Sevi turned reluctantly from his friends and left, dragging his heart away from where it belonged.

# Chapter 30

*In a light they held dear, with words bitter and loving, in a land both eternal and not. They called for the sun to allow the night's stay, but in time, time itself starts to rot.*

---

The metal can flew off of its perch with a loud, ringing *pop*. It caught the sun as it sailed through the air, carried by the strong mountain breeze to land a distance away, only to be joined quickly after by a sibling as the second can in the line of nine fell victim to Reynam's rifle.

Reynam cranked the gun's lever, expelling a hollow, brass shell and rapidly switching to the third target, then the fourth and fifth. Smoke wisped out of the weapon, curling and fading in the air as the sound of his last shot faded, bouncing distantly off the mountainside.

Sevi hesitantly lowered his hands from his ears, watching with consternation. Reynam moved his face away from his rifle's scope and grinned. "Damn, I'm good," he said, more to himself than Sevi.

It was the morning after the party. When Sevi had returned, Reynam had merely nodded and escorted him back to the barracks without a word. He hadn't asked Sevi his questions, nor had he given back his necklace. When asked why, Reynam replied, "I never said when I would. Gotta learn to spot the finer details, kid. You got a freebie with the coin, but now I'm not pulling any punches."

Sevi had glowered in response and immediately turned to go find Doctor Lea, but Reynam had stopped him, promising he'd ask his questions in the morning if Sevi would just do one thing for him. As it turned out, that one thing was this, and Reynam had hurried him out of the clinic so fast that Sevi hadn't had time for breakfast. It hadn't helped his mood.

However, true to Lily's prediction, Shy had returned in the night, and Sevi had made sure to spend time whispering his apologies to them while Reynam set up the range, promising that he'd never yell at them again.

"Why are we here again?" Sevi asked loudly. He hadn't quite been able to cover his ears in time for the first shot.

"What, afraid of sunlight?" Reynam set the butt of his rifle on the ground while he brought his pipe out to light, taking a deep puff of the pungent smoke.

Sevi's nose wrinkled at the smell. He could see why Doctor Lea didn't like it. Reynam spoke out of the corner of his mouth, "Remember when I said that you'd take Lea's place and come out for some fun? Well, this is what I meant. At least, it's the closest thing to fun until the next party. Which reminds me, next time you want to run off, make sure it's when I've got latrine duty."

"*Sssh!*" Sevi shushed frantically, whipping his head around for anyone listening. Reynam grinned and puffed his pipe. Sevi fixed him with a glare. "This isn't fun, and I didn't agree to this."

"You haven't even tried it yet," Reynam countered. "C'mon, come over here."

Sevi's stomach dropped as he eyed the deceptively dangerous metal stick in Reynam's hands. He didn't like the rifles. He didn't like their noise, their smell, or how easy it was to shoot someone down from twenty meters away as efficiently as Reynam could. "I don't think I want to."

"But if you just sit there then you won't be able to play the game," Reynam said. "You're a kid, and kids like games, don't they?"

Sevi scowled. "We already played a game. You lied to try to win."

"Careful, you're starting to look like Lea." Reynam laughed. "You'll like this one much more, trust me."

"Why's that?"

"Because it's one we can't cheat in." Reynam picked the rifle from the ground and quickly pulled the lever, ejecting the hollow shell from his last shot. "Here's how it'll work. You take this rifle, you point it at those cans, and for each one you hit, you get to ignore one of my questions if you want. I have four questions for you, and there's four rounds left in the gun. At the end, I give you back the necklace, as promised. So..." He offered the rifle. "Shall we? It's a pretty fair deal if I say so myself."

Sevi eyed the weapon again, running his gaze from the stock to the barrel. Memory of having three of those metal tubes pointed at him flashed through his mind, and he slowly closed his arms across his chest. "I don't... I don't want to touch that thing."

Reynam blinked in surprise. "Are you really passing up an opportunity to get squarely out of our deal with all the coin?"

Sevi looked away and swallowed. "I said I don't want to touch it. It almost killed me."

"But you're the one holding it this time."

Sevi shook his head. "I'd rather you just ask your questions and give me back my necklace."

Reynam frowned. "That's hardly fun."

"Fun? You've been bothering me for *weeks* and—"

"How about this," Reynam said loudly, talking over him. "Since you drive such a hard bargain. For every target that I *miss*, you get to ignore a question."

Sevi gaped at him. Reynam watched him expectantly over a long puff of his pipe. "Or I *guess* I could just ask you the questions, if you really want, since I'm more likely to sprout wings and fly than I am to miss any of those cans."

*Then why play the game!* Sevi shook his head. "You're *crazy*."

Reynam barked out a laugh, almost dropping his pipe. "Kid, I take that as a compliment. Now then."

With a kick of his boot, Reynam flicked the rifle up into his arms and pressed the butt of it into his shoulder in one smooth motion. He took aim, and with a firm squeeze of the trigger, popped the sixth can in the row as easily as breathing. He hadn't even taken the pipe from his mouth. "That's one," Reynam said.

Sevi darkly considered tracking Digby down and asking him how much getting a blade through the shoulder hurt, because somehow, he believed it would be less than this. "Fine. What's your first question?"

"The same one I've been asking you for months," Reynam said. "*Where*. Did you *get*. The *necklace*."

Sevi gave him an ambiguous look. "You're not going to like the answer."

"Try me." Reynam set his rifle down with the barrel pointing up.

"Fine." Sevi shrugged. "I don't know."

Reynam paused, then chuckled. "You're right, I don't like that at all. Try again, and this time tell the truth."

"I am. I have no idea where I got that necklace. When I woke up, it was around my neck, and I had these scars on my chest and eye." Sevi pulled the collar of his shirt down, bearing the scar that matched the contours of the necklace's star.

Reynam looked critically at the wound, opening and closing his mouth. It took him a long time to get his words out, and when he did, they tottered on the edge of anger. "You mean to tell me that you have *amnesia?*"

Sevi opened his mouth, then curled his lips in a smirk that could match one of Reynam's. "Is that one of your questions?"

Spitting his pipe out of his mouth in a fit of rage, Reynam brought his rifle back up and shot the seventh can off its perch without more than a glance. "What's the *first* thing you remember?" he spat.

Sevi's smile disappeared. Reynam hadn't set the rifle down this time. Gulping, he stuttered, "I-I was in the tunnels. In the dark. Three, maybe four summers ago. Hungry. My clothes were all torn up. Lily found me. I d-don't remember anything before that, I swear."

The tension in Reynam's shoulders slowly eased away. He lowered the rifle and crossed his arms over his chest, looking down the range with his chin angled toward his collar. "How do you even know your own name?"

"I don't know. I don't know! I just do." Sevi shrugged hopelessly. "I was a servant in the castle along with my parents b-before the Fae invaded, I think, and got stuck in the tunnels. Lily was the one who found me. I wouldn't know anything if not for her. I swear, that's all I remember!"

"Servant?" Reynam frowned. "Does the name Enstrova mean anything to you?"

Sevi sighed, crumbling under sudden exhaustion. He put his head into his hands, rubbing his eyes with the heels of his palms. "No... Are we still playing the game?"

A shot rang out. Sevi didn't need to look up to know that the eighth can now had a bullet-sized hole through the middle of it. Silence fell. When he raised his head, he found Reynam still clutching his rifle to his shoulder, staring into its eyeglass with a hardened expression. "What about Argennium?" he asked. "Does that mean anything to you?"

*"Reynam!"*

Sevi flicked his head around. Marching up the path from the castle was Doctor Lea, holding onto a sunhat against the wind. It would've looked charming if not for the anger staining her face. When she saw Sevi she softened, but her expression came rushing back the moment Reynam spoke. "Not now, Lea, I'm winning a game," Reynam called.

"I don't care if you're winning the war *yourself*," she yelled, drawing more attention than Reynam's bullets. "*Nobody* takes my patients out of my ward without permission! Not even you!"

Sevi shot a look at Reynam. A faint smile crossed the corporal's face as he mouthed the word, "oops."

"Sevi, come here," Doctor Lea waved.

"Don't go anywhere, kid, we're not done yet." Reynam lowered the rifle into the crook of his arm before turning to face the doctor. "Lea, listen. This has been a very disappointing morning so far. I am so, *so* sorry that I took your perfectly healthy baby boy out of his crib, but I *promise* that I'll bring him back with all ten fingers and toes after this. So can you please, *just* this once, cut me a little slack?"

"If you wanted slack, you should've been a fisherman instead of a corporal," Lea said, marching up to him with her chin up in challenge. "My infirmary. *My* rules."

A gust of wind blew Lea's coat open, robbing her rebuttal of some dignity. Sevi caught a sparkle of amber glass in the lining before she hurriedly closed it, crossing her arms across her chest with a flustered glare. Reynam met her gaze with a bemused smile. "Mm. And if you wanted to protect your head from the sun, you shouldn't have worn a hat with a hole in it."

He yanked the hat from her head before she could react, and with flawless execution, threw it out over the range, raised his rifle, and shot the final bullet straight through its crown. He pulled the lever of his rifle, ejecting the final shell from its chamber as the now ruined headwear floated gracefully in the breeze to land primly in the dirt a distance away.

Reynam sneered. "My range. *My* rules. And rule number one, as it just so happens, is *no sunhats.*"

"You—" Doctor Lea gaped in shock. "You—"

"Ah, that felt good!" Reynam laughed loudly. "Look at that, kid! I *missed* a *can!* Guess you don't have to answer anymore!"

Lea stared at the remains of her hat, balling her fingers into fists so intensely that her arms shook. Her face contorted with rage, ready to unleash it with a vengeance, but it evaporated in a flash when her gaze landed on something in the grass.

Reynam stopped laughing, watching her change in demeanor with suspicion. Staring at him with a look so calculating that it cleaned the smile from his face entirely, the doctor pointedly stepped forward and slammed her foot down on his pipe, snapping its stem cleanly in two. Now it was his turn to gape. "You should really clear *your* range of its trash, *corporal,*" Doctor Lea said.

Something snapped between them. They stepped forward and started shouting at each other, pointing back and forth between the hat, the pipe, Sevi, one another, and pretty much everything in view. Then they started yelling at each other in an entirely different *language,* both looking so impassioned that Sevi believed either of them could burst at any moment, and he slowly backed away.

A hand fell upon his shoulder. "The doctor lass moves fast," Digby said breathily, furrowing his brow at the scene before him. "Ah, godsdamnit. They're at it again. Oi, lovers! I'm takin' the lad with me for a bit!" The two continued arguing without pause, deaf to all voices but their own. Shaking his head, Digby turned to Sevi. "Would ya step away with me fer a bit?"

Sevi glanced at Reynam and Doctor Lea just in time to see one of the doctor's hands catch Reynam on the jaw during one of her many charged gestures. Sevi flinched. It might've been an accident, but he didn't want to be there to see whatever happened next. "Yes please."

Digby nodded, nudging Sevi away. When Reynam's voice rose higher, Digby moved Sevi faster, hobbling on his cane. "She knew what had happened the second she found ya out of bed," Digby told him, gesturing back to Doctor Lea. "These fights between her and the corporal are nothin' new."

"I've seen," Sevi replied, blushing on their behalf as an increasing number of people around the courtyard stopped and stared at the pair. "Why are you here?"

"Well." Digby coughed, looking uncomfortable. "Ya seemed a wee bit pale las' night. Cap'n River is busy today and wanted me to check in on ya. Are ya alright?"

Sevi stiffened in memory of the commander and his visions. As though reading his mind, Digby said, "Try not to think too poorly of the commander, if ya can. She has us all at heart in whatever she does."

Sevi didn't answer.

"I wasn't much on me words myself. The drink had gotten me far before I'd even set foot in the room. So fer that at least, I wanted ta apologize." He patted Sevi's shoulder. "Fergiven?"

Sevi shrugged, avoiding eye contact. "Yes," he said flatly.

Digby nodded. "I'm glad. But while I'm here, I also wanted ta give ya thanks." He extended his hand. "Fer savin' me life back in the tunnels. I needed ta tell ya that personally, man to man."

Sevi stared at the hand. Even after Lily's speech about inevitability, even after how glad he was to find that the old man had survived, he had still been the harbinger of all his troubles. Was he looking for something else from him? Like Captain River and Reynam?

He studied the way the man held himself, trying to spy any of the gestures he himself made whenever he tried lying to Lily. Were his muscles tense? Was he shifting his feet, or looking away? But when he met the man's gaze, searching for any sign of a lie, he couldn't find a single thing. "You're welcome," Sevi said awkwardly, placing his hand in the man's large palm.

Digby shook it once and lapsed into silence. "So... yeah." He coughed.

"Yeah..." Sevi echoed.

Sevi got the impression that the officer was just as uncomfortable as he was. Digby's gaze wandered, as if searching for someone or something. Sevi did the same, shuffling his feet.

"Well..." Digby's focus fell on something over Sevi's head, and he slowly brightened. "Have ya seen the ship yet?"

Sevi nodded. "A few days ago. The rope snapped."

"The rope..." Digby's eyes widened. "You were there durin' the incident."

Sevi nodded again. "Captain River wanted to ask me questions. We went for a walk."

"Curse me fer a Fae-bitten fool." Digby rubbed his eyes. "I'd fergotten. The captain already told me this. I really need ta lay off the wine; I'm too old to drink like I'm not."

Sevi shrugged. He wanted to drop the subject.

"Well," Digby huffed. "How about we go crack 'er open?"

Sevi blinked. "I'm sorry?"

"By way of thanks, fer the aforementioned lifesaving. I remember you askin' about it. They have her all tethered down now, and maybe you'd like to climb up on 'er deck and get a proper view, since yer last excursion was cut so short. Can even sneak a look below deck if you'd like."

"Go *inside* the airship?" Sevi repeated.

"Aye," Digby said, crinkling his face with a smile. "Might make up fer the tragedy ya had ta endure on the last attempt."

Sevi turned his head to look across the yard, watching the soldiers hard at work repairing the airship's hull, adding the sound of their hammers to that of the miners chipping away at the mountain. They had put up more logs on the opposite side of the ship to keep it upright and had removed most of the ropes from the winches. "Won't we be in the way?"

"One of the perks of havin' marks on yer shoulder, lad, is that you're never in the way." Digby chuckled. "So, I suppose it'll be less of a sneak, and more of an escapade."

"What about...?" Sevi gestured at Digby's cane.

"Bah. I barely feel it anymore." Digby waved Sevi off. "It's more me bones now than anythin'. Don't worry about me."

Sevi turned back to the ship, playing through the memory of the snapping rope. *What else could go wrong? What if the logs fail, and the ship goes crashing down with us inside?*

It was a scary thought. But even through all the turmoil, his desire to stand on its decks had endured. It flared up brightly inside of him, overwhelming his fear completely. Smiling softly, Sevi looked at Digby and gave him a shallow nod.

"Aye?" Digby asked.

"Aye," Sevi said.

Digby tapped his cane. "Let's get to it, then."

They walked shoulder to shoulder, approaching the side of the ship together. Digby called up one of the workers and spoke with him briefly. The soldier then led them to a rope ladder that had been thrown over the ship's railing, cut so long that its bottom half had to be rolled up. "After you," Digby said with a gesture to Sevi.

Sevi took hold of the ladder and stared up at the looming wooden hull, almost two stories tall, and gulped. "Is it safe?"

"Course it is." Digby smacked the ship with the head of his cane. "Don't worry. If you fall, we'll catch ya."

The gesture didn't fill Sevi with confidence. He tested the first rung with his foot, feeling out how the ladder gave beneath him and gingerly adding more weight. It swung a little bit with nothing to support it, shifting him off balance. Grabbing its sides to keep from falling, he resettled himself, gritted his teeth, and reached up with his other foot for the second rung. It didn't snap.

*Of course, it didn't snap*, Sevi chided himself. *You weigh half of anyone here!* Gritting his teeth, he repeated the process, placing one foot over the other. He felt the rope stabilize when he was halfway up, and when he looked down, he saw that Digby had taken hold of the bottom rungs for him. The old soldier touched two fingers to his forehead in a friendly salute.

Sevi nodded his thanks and hauled himself up the rest of the way with much less difficulty. Stepping down on stable wood, he tested his footing for two steps despite himself. No one else appeared to be on deck. Then something clattered loudly next to him, making him jump and spin. Digby's cane rattled off the deck, bouncing twice before going still.

Staring back over the side of the ship, he watched Digby grab hold of the ladder and gingerly begin the same climb. He called out to Sevi when he was halfway up. "This brings back memories, eh, lad?" It took Sevi a moment to understand, but when it dawned on him, he couldn't help but smile. Digby called again, "Got any more of them weeds on ya?"

"Flower! And no!" Sevi called back.

"Shame. Could use one right now!" But for all his grumbling and lumbering, he was making decent time, aided by his naturally long reach. Sevi picked up his cane and handed it to him when he made it to the top. "Thanks, lad," Digby wheezed, sucking in a deep breath. "Hah, I'm gettin' old."

Sevi chuckled.

"Somethin' funny?" Digby turned a critical eye on him. His tone was accusing, but his smile countered it.

"No," Sevi said, smiling back.

Digby grinned wider. "Too right. Well, take a gander."

Turning his head, Sevi observed the ship properly for the first time. Its wood was covered in a myriad of scars, and it had a post at every corner that would have acted as support for the balloon. To the stern was the wheel, placed a step higher than the deck, allowing the helmsman the best view of all that went on. Two mechanisms with a series of levers flanked it on either side, as well as a large metal block with glass panels, standing out amid the surrounding wood.

Behind the controls lay a narrow door leading into a single small cabin, and sticking up into the air just off the deck behind that was the rudder, bent with damage. Lining the deck's frame to the port and starboard were a series of metal rungs threaded with cable, running all the way to the ship's snapped prow.

And beyond that... beyond that was the world.

Far below, Sevi could see the edges of the town nestled against the mountain, poking up between the trees and framed by the great, sparkling river in the distance. Small sloops with unfurled sails moved sluggishly through its current, lethargically coming or going to who knew where. Further still, fading into the distance, the mountain range stretched on to lands that Sevi had only dreamed of, where large, white clouds descended to touch the horizon.

With a breath, Sevi entered a world of his own. He stepped forward, tentatively spreading his hands in the light of the sun, closing his eyes as the wind whipped through his hair. The hull shook beneath his feet, as if the vessel were impatient to return to the sky where it belonged, carrying Sevi with it on a grand adventure to parts unknown.

It was like he was in his sky window again, yet so much better. Sevi's eyes watered, but whether it was from the wind or not, he could not say. Here he was. On the airship, out of the Cut, with the world at his feet. He had pictured a moment like this so many times, but never in a lifetime did he think he could ever experience it.

When Sevi looked out across the land, no longer constrained by the stony borders of the Overlook, a wave of dissonance washed over him. His life was no longer bound by the Cut and its tunnels, yet a whole world lay beyond the castle still. He'd heard the Fablings regularly discuss 'going home,' and there were always a few who left for a time, only to come back months later. But where was home for them? Did those left behind ever look out from these very walls and wish to be somewhere else? Somewhere as fantastical as the places of his daydreams?

For years, he had sat and watched over events he'd never been able to experience, be it a full, warm meal or simply walking through a garden without fear for his life. The gardens might have been trampled, and his warm meals might have been soup, but he was alive, and he no longer went hungry.

His life was different. Unpredictable. Uncontrollable. Scary. Just as all the lands beyond the walls of the castle were destined to be, full of people equally unknowable and frightening. Sevi was part of it all now, absent the safety of a stone wall to hide behind whether he liked it or not.

"You alright, lad?" Digby asked.

The moment faded at the soldier's voice. Sevi dropped his hands and wiped his nose, needing to clear his throat before he could speak. "I'm fine."

Digby strode up next to him, leaning on his cane and watching Sevi with a thoughtful expression. He gingerly placed a hand on his shoulder. "Don't worry. It'll be alright. We'll find the lass."

Sevi looked up at him. "What?"

"Lily, right? She was a tough girl. Is. *Is* a tough girl." Digby shook his head, grimacing. "She has a level head on her shoulders—even I could tell that much, so I'm sure she'll be back. Mark me for it."

Sevi searched Digby's face. He had shown enthusiasm at the idea that Lily was still alive during the party, too. "Why are you so eager to find her?"

Digby's face wrinkled at the question. "Pardon?"

"What will you do to her?"

"*Do* to her?" Digby cocked his head. "What're ya gettin' at, lad?"

"She tried to kill you."

Digby snorted. "An' don't I remember it. But she only did it to protect ya, as I recall." At Sevi's blank look, he said, "Do ya remember, back in the tunnels, how she put herself between you an' me the moment she heard me voice? Nobody does that unless they care an awful lot about someone."

Sevi blushed.

Digby laughed. "Anyway, we'll find her. But in the meantime, how about we see what's below?"

Sevi didn't follow Digby immediately, needing a moment to sort through his thoughts. If Digby had forgiven her, did that mean that Lily could come out of hiding? They'd have to discuss it as soon as possible. Maybe Shy could help him get to her—if the creature ever decided to form itself again.

Gathering his wits, he walked to the steps leading down to the lower deck. It was dark, and the rhythmic pounding of hammers could be heard reverberating from further below where the workers beat against the hull. Digby had to hunch in order to fit himself under the low-hanging ceiling. "Even the greenbloods. They couldn't have made it a head taller? I miss Áilé," he grumbled.

Sevi squinted, trying to make out the fuzzy shapes belowdecks, wishing that he'd still had his eyepatch. When his eyes finally adjusted, he saw a dozen or so hammocks in varying states of disrepair hung loosely from the ceiling. A series of pipes ran down from just below where the helm would be, hugging the ceiling and walls before disappearing into a lower deck. Some ran to the bow of the ship, stacked neatly on top of each other and shining dully in the dim light.

The edges of the floor were littered with piles of debris, brushed lazily out of the way and forgotten. And far off toward the front of the room, gathered in a massive bundle, appeared to be the tattered remains of a gargantuan canvas.

Digby walked up to the mass and prodded it with his cane. "This thing is blockin' the steps dow—" He broke off, leaning in against the cloth. "Huh. Come, look at this."

Sevi stepped carefully across the floor to stand next to him. Digby glanced over. "Watch this." He hooked some of the fabric with the tip of his cane and pushed it into a beam of light filtering through the floorboards. The moment the canvas hit the stream, it lit up like a reflecting pool, shimmering and glistening as though water glided just beneath its surface. When Digby prodded it again, it rippled, spreading out in all directions from where the force originated.

"What is this?" Sevi asked, squatting down and poking at it himself, quickly fascinated by its patterns and shapes. "Why is it doing that?"

"Haven't the foggiest."

Sevi stood up and looked over the fabric again. This must've been what was left of the balloon. "It's certainly pretty," he said. The fabric shimmered everywhere the light touched. When he'd seen the ship fly overhead, he'd assumed that the light dancing off it had merely been reflections from the sun.

"Mm. It'll be a sight once we get 'er back up," Digby mused.

Sevi had to nod again. The very thought thrilled him. *Perhaps if Lily, Alyda, and I haven't escaped by the time it's done, they'll let me ride on it.*

"How about a souvenir?" Digby asked. Sevi looked at him questioningly just as he turned his back to shift debris about with his cane. "I'm sure all o' the important bits have been picked clean, so I don't mind taking a scrap or two meself." He bent down low with a strained grunt and picked out a crude wooden carving of a bird, showing it to Sevi. "I won't say a word, if you'll do me the same kindness, agreed?"

Digby winked, pocketing the carving. Sevi pursed his lips, unsure how he felt about that. He reminded himself that he had been stealing the Fae's garbage for years, and they were all dead now. Taking something from the ship wasn't likely to land him in any trouble.

He half-heartedly walked around the cabin, nudging through refuse with his foot. But the absurdity of the situation wouldn't leave him. It only grabbed a tighter hold, and with it came the realization of where exactly he was.

Two months ago, he had been a tunnel rat, running through the walls of the castle and living off of scraps to survive. His life hadn't been comfortable, but he lived it well. Now, he didn't know anything anymore. Now he was on a grounded airship, rummaging through the belongings of the dead with one of the very soldiers that had killed them. The thought clung to him like a grimy film, making him feel dirty and wretched.

Sevi swept his gaze across all the empty hammocks—beds that would never see their owners again. Just like the beds in the barracks. Lady Boil. Owl. Raindrop. Rumbles. Fae that would never again know the comfort of a moonlit night. Fae that might have hurt him, had they ever caught him. Or maybe, one day, they could have been friends.

But now he'd never know.

He ended his sweep at the back of Digby's head. All the fondness he held for the soldier vanished, and the guilt he'd felt for months filled the hollow spaces left behind. A question spilled out of him before he could quell it. "Why did you do it?"

"Eh? What lad?" Digby turned around.

"W-why?" Sevi gulped, shoving the tremor in his voice down. He didn't want to ask it. He didn't want to fight. Lily had told him to ingratiate himself to the Embers, but before he knew what he was doing, his anger shoved past his trepidation and his voice began to rise. "Why did you do it? Why did you *kill* them?" He looked Digby dead in the eye, possessed by a sudden righteousness. "They had *lives*. Lives I *watched*. They weren't always nice to each other, but neither are *you* all. And now they're gone."

He wrapped his arms around himself. "Honeydew. Copperhead... Even Rockman and Thistlebee. They just wanted to go home. They were *scared*. And I... I *helped* you. I just wanted to *help* you. And that makes me... I... *I didn't ask for this!*"

Clutching at the sudden headache battering his skull, Sevi pressed himself back against the curved wall of the cabin, sliding down it to sit in an anguished heap on the floor amid the rest of the trash. Self-loathing had returned with a vengeance, threatening to choke the air out of his lungs one more time as his vision slowly turned black, strained by the rush of blood pumping through his body.

He didn't know how long he sat like that. If Digby said something, he didn't hear it; he was far too upset to focus on anything other than dragging in the next breath. When he finally looked up, tear-stricken, he found the old soldier sitting across from him in a hammock with both hands on the head of his cane, staring silently at him. Sevi closed his arms around his knees and leaned his head forward. "I'm sorry," he croaked, barely more than a whisper.

The only sound between them was the thrumming of hammers, as loud and frequent as Sevi's heartbeat. It was a curious silence, both quiet and loud at the same time—full of slow regard, yet just beyond a thin width of wood, the world beat on without hesitation.

Eventually, Digby reached over and deliberately unbuttoned his left sleeve, rolling the cuff up his forearm. He held it out toward Sevi. "It's dark in 'ere, but can you see this?"

Sevi lifted his head and wiped his eyes. Squinting through the darkness, he could just make out a woven band tied around Digby's wrist. Sniffling, he nodded.

"Me wife made me this. I made her one in return, when we were married some odd couple dozen years ago." Digby pulled his arm back, turning his wrist around in thought. "She wore green that day. It went so well with her hair. She had lovely, beautiful red hair. And when she came out wearin' that dress, I thought... I thought, by Gods, I could be struck dead by Tembra and lost under Abeya's twilight sky for all time, right then and there, and the littlest memory of her from that moment would be enough to warm me forever."

He looked up at the ceiling with a faint smile on his lips, adrift in his memories. "Her name was Annilia," he said softly. "She was the love of me life. An' four years ago, the Fae took her from me."

The lieutenant took a moment to wipe his eye with a thumb before continuing. "We were never blessed with little ones like you. In a way, that made me happy. I never did think I'd be a good da. But as long as I had her with me, it was enough. More than enough. About damn everything I wanted in life was her. And now she's gone. But ol' Digby is still here, and not without trying."

He rolled his cane in his fingers. "We lived near their forests, right on the edges of the map. O' course, it weren't always the case. We used to live right down below," he said, cocking his head to the side. "Right at the bottom o' the mountain. I was a builder for this castle, right here." He thumped the tip of his cane on the floorboards. "She a maid for the king what wanted it built. But when the last stone was put in, she says to me, 'Dig, why don't we go see the stoneoaks? The ones so big that the Fae make houses of 'em? I want to see their leaves, do you think they're made of crystal, like all the stories? Let's leave this place! The king is such a grabby, senile ol' coot anyhow.'"

Digby chuckled. "So that was it. We left. We lived on the border for so many years, laughing, dancing, and loving under that crystal canopy. That king an' queen we served died and new ones came in, but we weren't there to be ordered about by 'em. Our lives were our own, to be lived as we wanted... They were the best years of me life."

His expression darkened. "But then the Night of Treachery came. Those Fae... they made us go *mad*. That new king an' queen got cut to pieces by their own people, an' me village... Me village, so happy to trade with them goblins on their borders, got the ax first; turned on and butchered like pigs. I only survived cause I had left fer the town over to purchase a new horse that day. The smoke was high enough to see from there. But understand, I tried going back to get her. Father help me, I tried to protect her. I tried so *hard*."

Digby tightened his grip on his cane. He looked at Sevi with his jaw set and his eyebrows sitting stormily over his eyes. "Me retribution is me own, and nothin' to do with you, lad. Yer not the killer here. I am. I wanted to tell you and the lass what was comin' so badly, but ya refused to come wit' me, and if either of ya got caught by the greenbloods they would've learned of the attack. But the fact remains that I still came into yer house and used you to set it alight just like them Fae did to mine, and if they did anythin' ta hurt yer friend cause o' me, then I'll let Tembra take me soul to Torment and be glad about it. I'll make right with ya one day, and you can mark me on that above all else."

He stood up from the hammock and made his way over to Sevi, offering him his hand. Tentatively, Sevi took it, and was pulled to his feet. Digby shifted his cane and clasped his palm with both of his, lowered himself to one knee, and looked directly into his eyes. "But if I may ask one thing of ya, I ask that you know this. I had a life once, too. An' because of those greenbloods, I'll never get her back."

# Chapter 31

*Which is the brightest of stars in the sky? The streaks that fall down till they're dead? Or are they the ones that can never stop burning; the ones that hang over your head?*

The light of day was blinding when they emerged from belowdecks, solemn and reticent. Digby waited for Sevi at the ladder, leaning heavily on his cane and looking grim.

Sevi avoided his eyes. Digby's story weighed heavily on his mind, leaving him without a grasp on how to behave. Thoughts and feelings churned in his belly in a familiar turmoil, compounding his discomfort, and gradually turning into pure aversion. He just wanted to go back into the Cut where there was peace, or barring that, his bed in the infirmary. Hopefully Reynam, Captain River, and everyone else in the whole blazing army would leave him alone for half a measly breath.

Digby gripped him by the arm, stopping him before the ladder. "Lad." Sevi turned but wouldn't look up. He heard him sigh. "Let's not leave with such a bad cloud o'er our heads. Let's get you yer souvenir, yeah?"

He let go of Sevi and walked away. Sevi briefly glanced up. Instead of going back belowdecks like he'd expected, the man had stepped up to the cabin behind the helm to stare at its door.

Digby looked back at him with a frown. "There's no handle. No hinges, either." He placed his hands on the wood, heaving at it. When it didn't budge, he probed its edges with his fingers, seeking purchase, while growing increasingly irritated. "How the dusk do you manage it?

The captain had said he'd taken care of this. Do I... is there a hidden latch?" He finally shook his head and backed away. "Hang this." Leaning on his cane, he reeled his foot back and stomped the door as hard as he could.

The door didn't like that.

Vines of light burst across the door's wooden face the moment his boot connected, flaring with light and blasting the soldier back like a ragdoll. Digby slammed bodily against the wheel of the ship, slumping into its spokes and getting tangled in the surrounding metal levers, before sliding to the deck with a *thump*.

Sevi jumped with alarm and rushed to his side, looking down at his limp figure in horror. "Help," he whispered, then yelled, "HELP!"

The hammering along the ship slowed, then stopped. Shouts rang out in their place. A voice called, "HOOO, UP THERE! DO YOU NEED ASSISTANCE?"

Sevi opened his mouth, but a powerful grip wrapped around his wrist, pulling his attention back to Digby. Digby coughed, sharply shaking his head and blinking rapidly. "Belay that. Help me up."

Sevi took him by the arm and tried to hoist him up, but he couldn't support his weight, leaving Digby to do most of the work anyway. Getting shakily to his feet, Digby leaned against the helm and hoarsely shouted, "BELAY THAT! ALL IS WELL!"

There was a moment of silence. Someone yelled, "ARE YOU CERTAIN?"

"AYE! BUT I MUST ASK YA TA NOT MIND THE FOLLOWIN' SOUNDS! I'M ABOUT TA DISCHARGE ME GUN!"

Another voice from below called, "TROUBLE?"

"NAY!" Digby brushed his coat aside, mumbling, "Just pissed off."

He reached for a holster on his hip and pulled out what looked to be a smaller, handheld version of a rifle, with a protruding cylinder caught in its middle. Sevi hastily brought his hands up to his ears just as Digby thumbed back a lever on its head, grabbed its grip with two hands, and fired a round at the door. The vines of light wavered. He fired again, and again, and on the third shot, the bands flickered and dissipated altogether.

Sevi stared in shock. Digby scowled. "Godsdamned Fae *bullshit*. I *just* had me leg fixed." He leaned against the helm, pocketing the weapon back in its carrier. He shrugged a little sheepishly upon noticing Sevi's expression. "Sorry, lad, lost me head. River warned me that he'd run into some spellcraft when they'd first run through the ship, but I thought it had been taken care of. Probably shouldn't have shot it. Bet I'll be chewed out for that, later."

Sevi turned his gaze back to the door and its three new bullet holes. "Was that magic?"

"Aye. Doesn't much like iron. Haven't the faintest idea why."

Sevi nodded. He and Lily had carried iron knives with them at all times through the castle for that very reason. It was why his garden had a copper trowel, and why Alyda avoided sitting on Lily's shoulder. By Lily's account, not only would the metal burn a Fae wherever it touched, but it would dispel any hexes they tried to cast. He'd never seen it work in practice, until now.

"How did it *do* that? I thought only Fae could cast magic," Sevi said. Recalling his conversation with Cassik and Loma, he asked, "Do the Fae have Runics, too?"

"Oh, aye, they've got everythin.' Lightnin' spewin out of their hands. Flyin' ships. Godsdamned doors that can hit back. If it weren't for iron and quicksilver, they'd've reduced this country to ash by now."

Sevi approached the door's threshold. He carefully reached out, grazing its surface with the tips of his fingers. "Careful, lad, there could be more. Take a step back," Digby ordered. But at Sevi's gentle touch, the door changed. Cracks appeared wherever he put his hand, spreading out in thin, snaking webs, before crumbling like sand in an hourglass to land in a dusty heap at his feet. Bit by bit the way forward cleared, revealing the room behind until nothing of the door remained but sand and sawdust.

Digby, watching the wood dissolve, shook his head. "How in Iaela did the captain open this the first time? Did the door grow *back* or somethin'?" He grimaced as he pushed off from the wheel, keeping his weight off his freshly injured leg. Limping to the threshold, he stuck his head inside, peering cautiously around. "Let me go in first. If this thing re-grew itself, then who knows what else did."

Light filtered in from small portholes, casting the room in an ethereal half-gloom. Motes of dust floated in and out of the beams, aggravated by Digby's steps. The cabin was otherwise dark, cramped, and cluttered, but whether that was the result of the crash or the product of a reckless search, Sevi didn't know. A small, thin bed had been bolted to the floor—the lone survivor of the mess. Everything else had been jostled, spilled, or broken, from the bunk chest to a small writing desk.

Sevi stayed rigidly in the doorway. "Digby, I don't need anything. Let's just go."

"Hang on. What's this?" Digby reached down and lifted up a small black box with a grunt, dusting it off. "This looks fancy. Why was this left 'ere? Please tell me this has—oh. Good." He undid a small latch and flicked it open. His face went blank when he looked inside.

"What is it?" Sevi asked.

Digby reached in and pulled out what looked to be a large, black, fruit pit. "A seed." He frowned, turning it around in the light. He glanced at Sevi and shrugged. "Want this? Maybe you can grow more weeds out of it."

Sevi eyed the pit from across the room. He didn't need long to decide. A seed from the Fae was too good to pass up. "*Yes.* Can I... can I grow it in my garden?"

Digby shrugged. "I don't see why not. I'll ask the cap'n."

"Oy! Everythin' alright up here!"

Both Sevi and Digby turned toward the door. Digby put the pit back into the box and handed it to Sevi. "Who's there?" he called.

"Corporal Nivi Auschane! Who am I talkin' to?"

Gesturing toward the door, Digby nudged Sevi to turn around, and they both maneuvered to the exit. A woman had poked her head up from the ladder, staring guardedly at Digby and Sevi from across the deck. She had a rifle strung across her back.

Digby waved at her. "Lieutenant Asgaillin. We're alright! Just finishin' up! Let's go, lad," he said to Sevi. Glancing at the cabin's dark, open doorway one last time, Sevi followed him back across the deck.

"Sorry ta disturb ya, sir," the soldier said, making room for them to climb back down the ladder with her. "We heard the shots an' thought ya could've been fightin' off a loose prisoner."

"Loose prisoner?" Digby asked, dropping his cane to the ground below before climbing down the ladder himself.

"Aye, sir. Several were freshly caught from town." The woman jumped the last few rungs, landing on the ground with a *huff*.

"Ah. I'd heard of the raid. Was Nightshade with 'em?"

"No, sir. Got through again."

"No surprises, unfortunately," Digby said, stepping off the ladder and retrieving his cane.

"One that they did catch has been stirrin' up a ruckus, though," Nivi said. "Slipped his ropes twice, so they clapped him in irons. Thought he might've slipped those, too, after his skin peeled off."

"Thank you, corporal." Digby nodded. "Anyone come lookin' fer me while I was up there?"

"No, sir."

"Alright. That'll be all then."

The woman nodded, placing her hand to her far shoulder and bowing gently at the waist before returning to her work with the other carpenters. Digby said, "Well, lad, why don't we get ya back to the barracks fer some lunch? I'm sure that our lovers have stopped squawkin' at each other by now."

Sevi nodded absently, falling into step behind Digby. A question formed slowly in his mind. "Digby?"

"Mm?"

"That woman said that you all bound one of the Fae in iron."

"Aye."

"And that his skin was falling off..."

Digby tightened his mouth, shifting his gaze to look ahead.

"Are you... are you torturing him?" Sevi asked.

Digby took a long, deep breath and exhaled loudly through his nose. "It's not my call. I have no love for the greenbloods, but were it up to me, I'd just dust 'em. No point in torture. Eventually the wretch will say anythin' ta make it stop. The goblins sure enjoy handing it out, though," he grumbled darkly.

Sevi felt sick to his stomach. "Dust them?"

"Aye. Iron and steel make up the backbone of the army, but we owe all our success to something else." He reached for his belt and undid a clasp on a pouch. When he withdrew his hand, he was holding a vial just like the one that Commander Grommand had used on Sevi's blood the night before. He shook the glass, swirling its shimmering silver contents around in the sunlight. "Seen this before?"

"Only last night."

Digby smiled ironically, keeping the vial up for several breaths longer before tucking it back away. "Quicksilver. Deadly enough to us humans—being around this stuff too long will drive ya mad, if not outright kill ya. But get any amount of this into a Fae's body and... well. Sparin' ya the gristle, they burn up in a blink and crumble to dust."

Realization washed over Sevi. "So when the commander took my blood—"

"She was testin' if ya were under the influence of a Fae," Digby finished for him. "Quicksilver makes a white spark when touched by faeblood. But the goblins like to play with their food sometimes. Sometimes they turn humans inta thralls."

Sevi shook his head. Not even Lily had known about that. "What are thralls?"

"Mindless slaves," Digby said, stopping as a squad of soldiers walked past in formation. "See, we have ourselves a magic liquid that burns 'em up. But they have their own, pumping through their veins at all times, that can turn any man, woman, or child into their loyal dogs. One sip of their blood an' you're at their feet. S'why ya should never eat or drink anythin' they give ya. Unless, of course, ya have some iron in your belly." Digby frowned. "I'm surprised ya haven't heard any of this before."

Sevi sighed. Reynam already knew, so why not Digby? "I don't remember any of my life before several years ago."

"Sorry?" Digby stopped in his tracks. When Sevi nodded, he raised his eyebrows. "An' here I thought it was just that ya were livin' in a cave."

Sevi shrugged. "That hasn't helped, I'm sure."

"How did it happen?" Sevi gave him a blank look. "Ah. Right. Well now you know. An' anyway, here we are."

Following Digby's gesture, Sevi discovered with some surprise that they had already made it back to the infirmary. He reached for the handle but paused before going in. "Digby, if I was under the influence of the Fae, how would the commander have known?"

"The quicksilver would've turned green at yer blood."

"And if it had?"

Digby grimaced. "It didn't. So, no use talkin' about it. Now go and get some lunch in ya. An' please give Lea me regards. I'll be seeing her about me freshly bruised leg soon."

# Chapter 32

*Just beyond the edge of his sight the enchanter and shade beckoned sweetly. "Come hither, come forward, come join me my love. Shall we whisper sweet nothings discreetly?"*

---

Sevi laid in his new, smoke-stained bed against the inner wall of the barracks several days after his visit to the ship with Digby, shielding his latest reading material from view with his pillow. He ran his fingers gently over the wrinkled paper, as if touching the flourishing script would help him understand it any better.

*Have plan to escape. Meet me when able.*

Sevi read the words over again for good measure. He didn't know how to feel about leaving the one piece of familiarity he'd ever had to go into the unknown. It was exhilarating. It was intimidating. It was *terrifying*. Absolutely terrifying.

In his dreams he was always safe. He could control the journey, destination, and outcome. But what little he'd experienced of life in the Outside had been... different. Not like his daydreams at all. Could he really do it? Could he really leave this place behind?

He anxiously curled his fingers. *As long as I'm with Lily and Alyda.*

"Sevi?"

Flinching at his name, Sevi hid the note under his pillow before turning on his side. Doctor Lea stood at the foot of his bed holding a plate full of freshly cooked vegetables and a hot cup of coffee. She tilted her head at him. "Are you alright?"

"Y-*ahem*. Yes, I'm fine," he said, sitting up, further obscuring his pillow with his body.

"Is the new bed any better?"

Sevi jerked his chin in a quick nod. "Yes, it's much warmer here, away from the outer wall."

"Are you sure you don't want another bunk?" she said, eyeing the smoke stains.

"It's fine. I've slept on worse." Sevi smiled shakily.

"If you're sure." The doctor lapsed into silence, but lingered at the edge of the bed, looking as though she had more to say.

"Are you alright, doctor?" Sevi asked.

Her lips turned up in a faint smirk. "Yes, Doctor Sevi, except for the pain in my butt. But he's banned from the clinic at the moment."

Sevi chuckled. She joined him. When they subsided, she took a seat on the edge of his mattress, placing her cup aside and her plate in her lap. "I do have to ask you something."

"What is it?"

"Have you considered what you're going to do?"

Sevi furrowed his brow, wondering for an instant if she was somehow referring to Lily's letter. She continued, "It's been several months now, and you no longer need my ministration. Have you decided what you're going to do?"

He stopped himself from glancing back at his pillow. "I... what do you mean?"

Doctor Lea sighed. "I'm sorry to say that you may be leaving my infirmary sometime soon."

Sevi's heart stopped. "Wh-what do you mean?"

"From what I understand," Lea said slowly, "you have nowhere to go, else you would have been in a greater hurry to leave this place. But after what you did for Digby, everyone was willing to allow you to stay for as long as you wanted. That still holds true." She leveled a meaningful look at him. "Additionally, the lieutenant has mentioned that you have amnesia."

Sevi gave her a measured nod. "Yes. Are y-you going to throw me out for that?"

Lea chuckled. "Of course not. But that isn't something medicine can fix. And the world outside this castle will be very unforgiving for a child like you." She placed a tender hand over his, staring compassionately at him. "Ask if you can stay with us. We will get you a space to call your own. Maybe Captain River or Lieutenant Digby can be persuaded to take you on as a squire."

He stared fearfully at her. "Why are you telling me this, doctor? What's going on?"

She pursed her lips and tightened her grip on his hand. "Captain River's aide came in this morning. You are to be dressed in your formal wear and brought before the commander after dinner."

Sevi's stopped heart started beating again, louder than any gunshot. "No," he whispered, closing his eyes. He pulled his hand away from the doctor's and folded it over his chest, feeling the bullet's sting as though it were fresh.

"Sevi, listen to me," Lea said, placing her hand on his arm. "Nothing is going to happen. The commander is tough, but she isn't cruel. You've done nothing to warrant her ire. And if worse comes to worst, tell her that I asked you to be my assistant. I could always use another pair of hands, and from what I understand, you have a garden in these mountains. That means you must have some knowledge of botany, yes?"

This time he reached for her hand himself, desperately trying not to cry, seeking something to keep him tethered to the moment. She took it and clasped it in both of hers, leaning toward him to offer comfort. When the plate in her lap tottered, threatening to fall, she drew back with a jolt and grabbed it, freezing in place as though expecting it to jump from her hands.

She smiled in embarrassment, which drew a choked laugh out of Sevi. "It's probably cold by now anyway," she said, standing up from the bed. "I'm going to go eat this. You take the time to prepare yourself for this evening. And, again, don't worry. You'll be fine."

The doctor's confident smile was meant to encourage him as she turned away, but the faceless woman that appeared from behind her back prevented that.

**❝** *He's* not supposed to be here, Caldwin," Doctor Lea said sternly.

"I know you missed me, Lea. No need to pretend. Speaking of missing things, where did your hat go? You normally keep it on your desk, don't you?" Reynam said.

"And where's your pipe, corporal? You normally keep it shoved up your ass, don't you? That would explain why it always smelled like—"

"*Silence*, please," Captain River ordered. "The corporal is accompanying me tonight, Doctor Lea. He will be out of your infirmary shortly. Where is Sevi? I see that his bed is empty."

Doctor Lea spent a few breaths glaring at Reynam before answering. "He asked to move to the inner wall where it's warmer. He's over there."

"Ah. I see him. Hello, *risho*," Captain River said to Sevi as he approached. Reynam and Digby trailed behind him. "Why do you choose this bed? It appears to be stained."

"Hey, kid," Reynam said.

"Lad." Digby nodded.

"I see that you have gotten properly dressed," Captain River continued. "This is good. Are you ready to meet the commander?"

Sevi stood up stiffly, straightening the ill-fitting uniform until it hung right. Of course, he wasn't ready. He wanted nothing more than to have the commander forget his existence. Or, barring that, crawl back into bed and pretend to be too sick to go.

*Stay in their good graces. Remember what Doctor Lea said. And be like Lily.* "I—I am," he stuttered.

"We'll be there, too. Right behind ya," Digby said.

"And we should probably get moving. Let us not keep the commander waiting," River said, moving off ahead of them with purpose. Digby nodded once to Sevi before following. Reynam, meanwhile, stayed behind and brought his hand out of his pocket...

... holding Sevi's necklace.

"A deal is a deal," he said, holding it out to him by its chain. "I would've given it to you sooner, but you know." He jerked his head in Doctor Lea's general direction. As Sevi reached for it, Reynam moved it further away. He settled into a pointed silence, staring steadily at Sevi from behind his black locks for several heartbeats. "Let me lay my cards down. You've tempted me with this twice. Don't do it again unless you intend to give it to me, got it?"

He deposited the jewelry unceremoniously into Sevi's palm. Sevi closed his fingers over the familiar weight of the star, then put it around his neck without a word. He certainly wouldn't.

"Sevi!" Captain River called.

"Let's get going," Reynam said, draping his arm around Sevi's shoulder and steering him forward. "Can't keep Her Majesty waiting."

The company was silent as they walked through the castle, moving from the first level to the second. Sevi listed the names of each room as they passed, sketching a mental map out in an attempt to divine their destination. *Throne Room. Lonely Stairwell. Eastern Hallway. Little Bedroom? Many Beds Bedroom? Chamberpot Room? Um...*

As usual, things in the Outside looked different, and it was hard to keep it in his head. But he got a sneaking suspicion as they marched, which was only confirmed when they rounded a corner to find a pair of ornate double doors at the end of a hall.

*Big Bedroom.*

Owl used to sleep in there. Sevi would peek in every now and again, but nothing interesting ever seemed to happen. There was one time when he'd encountered her wrestling with a winged man on the bed, but it was dark, and the sheets had obscured the view. He'd never seen it happen again, so eventually he just stopped going, finding more joy in the livelier sections of the castle.

Leading the company, Captain River stopped outside the doors and knocked, then stepped back and straightened his jacket. The other soldiers did the same. When the doors opened, a woman with blond hair in a uniform even more impressive than Captain River's stood there, meeting the group with an expectant expression. Her uniform was a spotless white draped with golden accents, rather than blue or charcoal, and her body glittered like a tiny sun whenever she moved.

"Promina. We have come as ordered," Captain River said formally, sweeping his hand up to the opposite shoulder and bowing. As one, Digby and Reynam did the same. Sevi gave a jerky bow at the waist, doing his best to copy them.

The lady nodded and stepped aside. "She's waiting for you."

Captain River declined his head respectfully, moving past her into the room beyond, followed less quickly by Digby on his cane, and Reynam with Sevi. To Sevi's surprise, the room was not the Big Bedroom. It was smaller, with a table in the middle of two cozy-looking armchairs that sat opposite from each other.

The walls were adorned with ornate paintings and elaborate sconces of trailing vines, leaves, and other floral motifs. A small fireplace was set into the wall, unlit. Across from the doors they entered was an identical pair, which Sevi suspected must be the true entrance into the Big Bedroom.

Standing before them at the table, unavailing herself of either armchair, was Commander Tiersa Grommand in full uniform, reading through a stack of papers. She still wore her swords.

Captain River snapped his bootheels together in a crisp salute before giving her the same bow he'd given the lady named Promina, albeit more deeply. "Commander Grommand," he said with a deep level of ritualistic formality. "We have come as ordered."

The commander didn't immediately look up from her paper. She scanned the document for several breaths before she finally set it down and brought out that same strange ticking silver disk from her pocket, clicking open its lid. She stared at it for several breaths before putting it away, moving her dark gaze over the four of them. She then nodded once to Promina, who stepped out of the room and closed the door behind her.

"Let's get to it then," Commander Tiersa said flatly. She held her hands behind her back and squared her shoulders, looking at Captain River without a hint of cheer. "We are here to discuss the rogue element in my army and its fate. As I believe it to be a rather minor issue, I have not elected to waste the Regent Council's time with it. Captain Caldwin River, however, believes there is more to it. Present your case, Captain."

Captain River flicked his head once in a quick bow of recognition and took a step forward. "Madam Commander. Many questions have been raised over our young Sevi of the Tunnels and his origins. He comes from the mountain itself, with no home, in the company of an unknown girl we have yet to find. As you have discovered yourself, my lady, he is not Fae, nor is he controlled by one. And, recently, it has been discovered that he has no memory of himself beyond several years ago. Both my officer and my corporal will support this claim, having heard this from him themselves."

Sevi glanced at Reynam and Digby. Neither looked at him.

"Three omens have shown themselves in his time among us that I believe to be a sign of his ancestry. I do not think he is any simple wandering boy. The first was the book I gave him, which he has been caught reading many times by myself and others. Homeless boys in this country do not read. Homeless boys in this country do not know *how* to read. Only children of great houses learn the skill."

Sevi watched the back of Captain River's head. What was he talking about? Had the captain been *testing* him?

"Being able to read is hardly as special as it once was," the commander said, nonplussed.

"Allow me to continue. The second omen is the necklace he wears. It is identical to the one the commander herself wears, which I would humbly request that she produce now."

Commander Tiersa blinked very slowly. When Captain River did not continue, she reached up to her neck and slowly pulled at a thin, silver chain just beneath the iron collar she wore. The metal slithered smoothly over her skin, until she gave it a gentle tug and extracted the entire pendant from underneath her shirt.

Sevi recognized it immediately.

"Sevi?" Captain River said softly.

Sevi jumped, blinking rapidly as he tore his eyes from the shining, silver star glistening in the torchlight against the Commander's breast.

He took a step back, feeling suddenly very cold. *What is happening. What is happening?*

"*Risho*," Captain River prompted, moving toward him. He placed his hands on Sevi's shoulders, forcing him to look into his eyes. "Please. Be strong. Let us see the necklace."

With shaking hands, Sevi reached into his shirt and numbly pulled out the necklace that Reynam had only just returned. Captain River nodded his head appreciatively, taking the necklace out of Sevi's palms with a quick pluck of his fingers. Standing up straight, he draped the necklace's chain over his hand and held the star up to the light as he reapproached the commander.

Commander Tiersa in turn held her own star up. Except for the bullet lodged starkly in the middle of Sevi's, they were a perfect match. She gave the captain a skeptical look. "Jewelry isn't hard to fake, River. I assume this is why Enstrova is here?"

"Yes, my lady," Captain River confirmed. "Corporal?"

Reynam glanced at Sevi, smiling faintly. "Commander. I've had the opportunity to study the necklace at length." Reaching into his breast pocket, he pulled out the head of a small spyglass attached to a string. "It's real, my lady. I'd know my father's handiwork anywhere."

The commander studied Reynam's face for a long time, then brought her attention back to Sevi's necklace. For the first time since he'd seen her, Commander Grommand's face slowly morphed into an expression other than disinterest: open, confounded anger.

She leveled a venomous look at Sevi, moving her hand slowly to the hilt of her left blade. "*Where did you get this,*" she hissed. Sevi clutched at his chest.

"The boy does not know," Captain River interjected, moving himself between her and Sevi. "Which brings us to the third omen. His memory. Commander Tiersa, when did the Night of Treachery occur?"

Silence. Sevi could not see the commander's expression from behind River, but the captain's body posture had changed significantly. It was charged. Rigid. Expectant. Both Digby and Reynam looked just as still, as if they, too, understood.

Commander Tiersa said softly, "Four winters ago."

"Around when our *risho* lost his identity, according to Corporal Enstrova," Captain River said.

It was so quiet that a needle could be dropped, and all would hear it land.

"And... a fourth omen," Captain River said softer. "His name is Sevi."

"There are many Sevis now." Commander Tiersa's voice had weakened greatly, soaked with uncharacteristic disbelief.

"At his age?" Captain River asked just as lowly. "At this castle? Wearing that necklace?"

More silence, until River was forcefully moved aside by the commander, leaving Sevi to take the full brunt of the commander's focus. She approached him purposefully, looking him up and down with a critical gaze from his feet to his scarred eye. Everyone studied her in turn—no one more than Sevi. "Do you know me?" she murmured to him.

Sevi gulped. He could only shake his head under the weight of her stare. She regarded him for several more heartbeats before abruptly straightening. "I am taking this boy into my chambers."

Captain River started. "My lady?"

"I will test him," she said, never breaking eye contact with Sevi. She didn't even blink. "If he is who you say he is, then this will reveal it beyond a doubt. If not, you will remove him from my army, my castle, and my sight, forever."

"My lady—"

"*Shut it, River,*" she barked, making Sevi jump. "You brought him to me with this ridiculous theory, knowing exactly how I would feel. You have no further room to argue."

Reluctantly, Captain River bowed at the waist and backed off, casting a pitying look at Sevi.

"Come with me, boy," Commander Tiersa commanded, turning and marching away from him. Sevi didn't move.

He couldn't. He only stood there, clutching his shirt.

"*Now!*"

Sevi jumped. Fearful tears sprung to the corners of his eyes, and with a wretched hiccup, he unsteadily moved toward her and the second set of doors. Before he reached her, Captain River moved forward and gingerly hung Sevi's necklace back around his head. He touched his shoulder, offering him silent encouragement, then solemnly withdrew.

Commander Tiersa opened one of the doors, looking expectantly at Sevi. He moved through with leaden footfalls, taking in the Big Bedroom. It was exactly the way he remembered it, full of excessively large furniture from the bed wide enough to fit three, to the window and its seat that nearly took up a full wall. A sizable desk with a complimenting mirror, a sofa, a bathtub, and a fireplace accompanied these furnishings.

When he was far enough in, the commander closed the door with a loud, angry *thump*, sealing them in alone together. Sevi tried to speak, to tell the commander what Doctor Lea had told him to say, to explain how he wasn't a bad person and that he only ever wanted to grow plants and that he'd been promised he wouldn't be thrown out for having amnesia. Anything and everything he could think of to try to stop her from booting him out the gates. Because whatever this test was, he wasn't going to succeed. He'd be cast out, all alone. And he would never see Lily or Alyda again.

But Commander Tiersa ignored him. She marched to the fireplace where a crackling fire burned, striding with heavy stomps, looking for all the world as though the marble edifice had personally slighted her, and she planned to run her swords right through it. "Come here," she ordered again, stopping before the hearth and flicking her fingers at him.

Fresh tears rolled down Sevi's cheeks. "Please. Not the fire."

She frowned at him. "I'm not sticking you into it if that's what you're thinking."

"Then wh-what—"

"*Come.*" She gritted her teeth in a sneer. "My patience wears thin."

Sevi trudged haltingly toward her, vibrating with barely contained anxiety. *Be like Lily. Be like Lily. Be like Lily.*

*I can't.*

*I must.*

*If you're ever in trouble, I'll come find you,* Lily's voice whispered. Sevi quickly reached into his pocket for Lily's whistle and squeezed it, praying for his friend's strength as he approached. He stopped before the commander, looking down into the floorboards, unwilling to meet her stare.

She grabbed him by the wrist. He jerked back. "Please. *Please* no. You *said!*" But her grip was as iron as the collar on her neck. She brought his hand up to the underside of the hearth's mantle stone. Sparks snapped hungrily at his fingertips, splaying three flickering shadows across the fireplace's threshold. Dimly, distantly, he realized the stone had a star carved into it. A very familiar star.

She pressed his hand into the mantle. They both froze. She fixed her eyes on the stone. He fixed his on her face.

Then the stone moved.

She gasped and stepped back, letting him go. He floundered, moving rapidly away from the hearth the moment he was freed. The fire that blazed within darkened into an oily shade of black, sparkling with tiny white pinpricks of light like a piece of the night sky had been plucked from the heavens and set alight. It burst from the hearth, licking hungrily up the wall like a starving creature let loose, seeking fuel to burn.

Sevi panicked. *No. Nonono. It's back. It's back!*

He tripped over his legs and hit the floor hard, crawling backward on his hands and feet in terror until his spine hit the footboard of the bed, watching as the black flame grew. The stone melted wherever it touched, dissolving like smoke that quickly wisped away and vanished. When the fire had reached the ceiling, its whipping, sinister tendrils suddenly froze. Then, faster than a turtle closing its shell, each of its embers streaked back into the hearth, retreating into the bulk of the fire's blaze before swirling around in a whirling vortex that snuffed itself out entirely, pitching the room into gloom.

The fire hadn't left a single scorch mark, but it had consumed the hearth down to the tiniest pebble, leaving a gaping hole where it once stood. Beyond it, Sevi could make out a room; one that he had never seen from the Cut before.

"It's true," Commander Tiersa murmured.

Sevi looked to the commander. Her tall, imposing figure had remained a mere handspan away from the flames, fearless and unmoving.

She slowly turned around to face him. Her expression was obscured in the half-light, but tears sparkled starkly on her alabaster cheeks.

"Isevidel," she whispered.

# Chapter 33

*"Such creatures you've found on your journey thus far! Will they watch as you wake with a kiss? Or perhaps a fire most comfortably hot? You could be so much warmer than this!"*

What happened next was more unexpected to Sevi than Captain River's revelations, more unbelievable than a fire eating a stone wall, and even more astonishing than seeing Commander Tiersa cry.

Commander Tiersa Grommand, leader of the Embers of Korina, hugged him.

She'd strode across the room with her long legs, reached down with her long arms, and plucked Sevi off the floor until his feet no longer touched the wood, only to squeeze him in an embrace far, *far* tighter and longer than he would have *ever* wanted from her.

Choked, strangled sobs fell freely from her once stony mouth. Her ever-present stoical armor had shattered completely, and it. Was. *Uncomfortable.*

Sevi couldn't understand anything anymore. His mind flew out of his ears and abandoned his body, hovering in the space somewhere above them, looking down detachedly at what was going on. Even his discomfort deserted him, replaced only by a hollow, unfeeling nothingness.

"Isevidel," the commander said again, holding the back of his head and cradling him like a precious doll. "My little Sevi."

Sevi blinked. *Where am I? What did she just say? Her what?*

"Do you really not remember me?" she whispered to him. "Did the greenbloods rob you of that, too? From both of us?"

Sevi shook his head insensately. "Please let me go," he rasped.

Her hold loosened, but she didn't do as he asked. She pulled back, staring at him with her brow furrowed, searching his face for something. Reluctantly, she lowered him back to the floor, but kept her hands on his shoulders as though suddenly afraid he would disappear. "You really don't know."

Sevi clutched at his shirt, avoiding her gaze. What was he supposed to say?

"My dear boy," she said softly, her voice shaking. She curled a lock of his hair back, staring forlornly down at him. "Don't you remember your Aunty Tisa?"

Sevi wanted to say *of course not,* but something came over him at that name. His brain buzzed, as if a door somewhere deep inside of him had opened, and a wealth of emotion came pouring out. Undirected, uninhibited, unfocused. That name meant *something.* He could feel it. "Aunty Tisa?" he said slowly.

She smiled, wiping her face dry. "You used to have trouble saying 'Tiersa,' and when your front teeth fell out it only made it worse. So, you always called me Tisa."

Sevi reached up to hold his head. It felt like the fire was back, and that only by holding the two halves of his skull together could he avoid it from splitting open. But the fire wasn't here. This was different. "What is going on?" he said softly, more to himself than her.

Commander Tiersa laughed, wiping her eyes again. "I don't know. But by the grace of Tembra you've returned from the Waylands. They have seen fit to give you back to me." She lifted her hand, grazing her fingertips along Sevi's cheek with disbelief sprawled across every line in her face.

Sevi pulled away from her touch, reaching for the bed to steady himself. His legs shook fiercely, knocking his knees together, feeling that at any moment he could topple over and smash against the floor into a thousand pieces. "Can I sit down, please?"

Her hand dropped to take his, wrapping around his wrist and drawing him away from the bed. It wasn't painful this time. "Of course. Come."

Unfortunately, she led him to the sofa in front of the fireplace. The fireplace now missing its back. Its threshold yawned at him, much like the entrance to the mine at the Cut had. Just as sinister. Just as inevitable.

He leaned against the sofa back with a heavy sigh, staring at it bitterly. *Another doorway to toss my life into chaos.* He looked at Commander Tiersa—*I suppose, 'Aunty Tisa' now*, he corrected. She still stared at him with wide, incredulous eyes, but she made no move to take a seat with him. She stood straight with her hands on her swords, adjusting and readjusting her grip. Neither of them spoke.

His chest tightened as realization washed over him. This was someone who knew him. Someone who knew his life before the Cut. *Family.* His lips moved, and a question he'd asked himself for years fell timidly from his mouth. The most important question of his life. "Do you know who I am?" he asked quietly.

Commander Tiersa's face twisted with a wounded expression. "Of course, I do," she said lowly, shaking her head. "You're Isevidel Astraeda. Born son of Queen Korina and King Consort Marovhan. Surviving heir to the throne of Elkra."

Sevi's hand went to his chest, curling his fingers around his star, clutching it tighter the more she talked. "No... that... you're wrong."

She shook her head. "I'm not."

"You are. You have to be."

"I'm not," she said again. "Only one of royal blood can open the royal study."

Sevi glanced at the fireplace, silently cursing its existence again. Just when he had been adjusting to the Outside, this came along and tossed what little stability he'd retained over a cliff. In the face of this, a part of him wondered if leaving the castle was as frightening as he had made it out to be. A prince? What kind of joke was that? Lily would have laughed.

Gods. What would she think?

*She'll probably laugh.*

"Isevidel..." the commander said again.

*Stop calling me that.*

"This has been... quite a bit to process," she said gently. "I'm sure that you have much that you'd like to ask me. I have plenty that I would very much like to ask too, and it's all I can do to stop myself from overwhelming you."

*Too late for that.*

"But... Please. I have just one question. And then I'll leave you for the night, and we can continue this tomorrow."

Sevi stared at her, feeling his brain grind tumultuously in his head. But he nodded. Anything to be left alone. Anything for this to end.

She nodded gratefully. "Did anyone else survive?"

"What do you mean?"

"The night of the rebellion. The night they took you from us." Her stony armor came rushing back, and her face closed in memory. She gripped at her sword hilts until her knuckles were white. "Your father. Your brother and sister. Your... mother. Did they survive with you?" Her eyebrows lifted a modicum up her forehead as a thought came to her. "That girl that River mentioned. Was that Nahlra?"

Sevi shook his head bewilderedly. His family? He had a mother and a father? Siblings, too? "Who is that?" he asked hollowly.

The commander seemed to deflate. Turning her head, she looked away from him and glared into the darkness of the royal study, as if she, too, suddenly found it deplorable. "Wait here," she ordered.

She moved away from him. Sevi watched as, without any hesitation, she stepped into the hearth and entered the fireplace, quickly disappearing into the gloom beyond. A light came on from inside, brighter than all the sconces, giving him a better glimpse of what lay within. The room went on for a short distance with bookcases running along either side, but the commander stopped halfway in, blocking his view of the rest of the room with her body.

She didn't remain inside for long. No sooner had she entered did she turn around, lifted her hand, and waved it around. The light shut off, and she stepped from the reemergent darkness, looking grim. "Don't move, Isevidel," she said. A layer of steel had returned to her voice.

Striding to the double doors of the antechamber, she pulled both of them violently open, startling the men inside. "Captain River, Lieutenant Asgaillin, come with me at once."

"And me, ma'am?" Reynam asked.

"Corporal Enstrova... Captain River, how inclined is your corporal to keep quiet regarding sensitive issues?"

Digby let out a surprised chuckle. Captain River's mouth rose in a smirk. "Corporal Reynam Enstrova speaks often, but if you order him to, the most he will do is make jokes about how he knows something that others do not."

Reynam piped up, "Permission to speak freely, sir?"

"Denied," Digby said.

"Then, Corporal, let me make myself so incandescently clear on this matter that you can see my meaning with your eyes closed," Commander Tiersa said directorially. "I know what Captain River's word is worth, he's proven it to me time and again. I also know that Lieutenant Asgaillin, as he has just so recently demonstrated, would sooner throw himself at the mercy of the Fae, undergo torture, and crawl half-dead through a mountain, than betray this army. What I know of you and your reputation, however, does not fill me with confidence. So, if you so much as hint at what you are about to see to anyone at all, I will know. And I will know who it came from. Do you understand me?"

Reynam paused. "Yes, ma'am."

"After hearing that, do you still wish to enter?" Commander Tiersa said.

"Yes, ma'am."

"Then Captain River, Lieutenant Asgaillin, and Corporal Enstrova, attend to me, and do not speak a word about it from this moment forward."

She led the three men toward the fireplace. Each of them gave Sevi a different look. Tiersa avoided Sevi's gaze entirely. Captain River looked worriedly at him as he walked by. Digby's was similar but held a silent offer of assistance in the strain around his eyes, reminding Sevi of his promise.

Reynam, meanwhile, swiveled his head around the whole room, running his gaze over everything in sight. When he saw Sevi, he lifted his chin in a casual greeting and opened his mouth to say something but stopped and glanced at Commander Tiersa. Ostensibly thinking better of it, he substituted whatever he was about to say with a wave.

One by one, they all disappeared into the fireplace. The strange light came back on. No one spoke, at least nothing that Sevi could hear. Eventually a grim-faced Digby returned, frowning and avoiding Sevi's eyes as he walked up to the bed and threw its heavy bedding off. He tugged and grabbed at the thinner white sheets beneath it, bunching it all up into his arms, then hobbled back into the fireplace, leaving Sevi alone with a curious expression.

When they all returned, they carried a horrible, putrid smell with them. The Commander came out first with a large leather book under one arm, making for the double doors and opening them both. Then she moved into the smaller room and did the same to the far doors, surprising Promina, who stood just outside. Not far behind the commander, Captain River carried what looked to be the feet of a limp body swathed in a white bedsheet, while Reynam carried the upper torso. Digby limped slowly from behind, holding what, at a glance, could have been many different pieces of bark from the same tree.

They all walked wordlessly past Sevi, following Tiersa to the doors. None but Reynam looked at him as they walked by. "Lost again," Reynam muttered.

When Digby made it to Tiersa, she reached into the pile in his arms and pulled something out of it. She wiped the dust off it with a callous expression, studying it in great detail. From the way the light filtered in through the gaps in its form, it looked like the remains of a mask.

Shaking her head, she reached for the handle of one door and closed it. "I must attend to him, Isevidel," she said, reaching for the other door. "You have my word that I'll be back the moment I am able."

Sevi lurched. "Wait!"

She froze, looking at him with gentle, sad eyes.

"What's happening? Wh-where are you all going?"

Commander Tiersa took a deep, weary breath, and tried to smile. "Later. This evening has been much too eventful... for better, and worse. Allow me to provide what little peace I can for now, to make up for all these years we've been apart. At least until you're ready."

"Ready for what?"

She shook her head. "Later."

"What do I do now?" Sevi asked.

"Rest. If you can."

"H-here?"

Her smile tightened at the edges, straining her face as she glanced around the room. "Yes, Your Luminance. They're your bedchambers, now. Don't worry, I'll come back for you. I promise."

She closed the door gently behind her as she left, leaving Sevi completely alone.

# Chapter 34

*A road begins at the end of the stream, holding naught but a dark fall. Upon bargain struck, a crown found the mouse, ordained by a hidden fate's scrawl.*

At first, Sevi didn't move. He stared woodenly at the doors, expecting someone to whirl back in, ready to tell him what he should do and where he should go next. But they didn't.

He sat on the sofa for a while, staring at the open mouth of the hearth's hidden room. When the sight of it began to anger him, he walked to it and placed his hand on the stone that had opened it. Nothing happened. He tried again, placing his hand exactly as Commander Tiersa had put it, but to no effect. In a fit of rage, he punched it, bruising his knuckles. Perhaps the fire needed to be lit again. But Tembra take him, he wouldn't try it. He'd had enough of godsdamned *fire*.

Retreating glumly to the other side of the room as far away from the fireplace as possible, he curled himself up at the footboard of the bed with his arms around his legs. *So, this is why they saved me*, he thought morosely. *To prop me up and laugh at me. 'Look at the sad little orphan boy who's lost his memory, he'll make a fine joke, won't he? Something for the soldiers to laugh at? Let's give him a crown for a night and see what he does!'*

But no matter how long he sat there, the punchline never came.

*Perhaps they're listening in.* He stood and walked to the double doors, opening them both at once. There was no one in the parlor. No one snickering to themselves or each other about what fun they were having.

Furrowing his brow, he walked to the antechamber's exit, tentatively opening a single door and peeking outside.

Promina stood there, alone and at attention, facing forward. At the sound of the door opening, she turned around and looked warily down at Sevi. They stared at each other for several awkward breaths. "Is everything alright?" she asked at last.

Sevi gawked at her, then closed the door without a word. It finally dawned on him that Commander Tiersa may have been serious. She had given him her room.

That frightened him. His breathing picked up. No. *No.* He couldn't be a prince.

*But the way the commander cried over you.*

No.

*She knows you.*

NO.

*Prince Isevidel Astraeda.*

He clutched at his head. The pain had returned, bringing a dizziness with it. The walls seemed to narrow, closing in around him tighter than even the confines of his tunnels, threatening to squish him into clay. His body felt thinner, less corporeal, like his brain had detached itself again.

Sevi pounded at his skull, trying to reel it back in. The Cut. He needed his tunnels.

He frantically rushed back into the bedroom and crossed to the far wall. The Cut always ran around the outer wall of every outer room, which would place the loose stone...

*There.*

He pushed aside a small table and scrabbled at the stone, digging his nails into the mortar and desperately pushing at the brick, until finally one gave way, falling backward into the tunnels. He pushed his hand into the hole, tugging and hammering at the surrounding stones, wildly trying to widen the gap.

They resisted him, refusing to budge. Sevi grabbed hold of an upper brick with both his hands and placed his feet against the wall, then heaved his body back, putting his weight into it, until the stone finally broke off and sent him flying backward.

Sevi landed with a painful *thump*, clutching the stone to his chest. His world rocked, spinning around him. He went limp, staring up at the revolving ceiling until it decided to settle.

*If you disappear now*, Lily's voice whispered, *the whole castle will come looking for you, and they'll find me and Alyda, too.*

He regarded the stone in his hands before angrily tossing it to the side with resentful resignation. It was no use. Lily's phantom was just as painfully correct as the real thing. There was no going back. Not anymore.

He closed his eyes and lay his arms across the floor. *What do I do now?*

The air shifted. It wasn't much, but it was enough to make him open his eyes again. Shy stood over him, staring down with their floating orbs in a formless black mass, looking darker than ever. Sevi lifted his head up in instinctive delight, only to lose it immediately. "What do you want?"

Shy didn't answer, just like they normally did. That angered Sevi. "*Talk to me*," he spat, breaking all the promises he'd made to the shadow. "Why don't you ever *talk to me*? You can '*hmm*' and '*hum*' and watch with those two godsdamned white eyes, so why can't you talk! What are you even *doing* here if you're only going to show up when you feel like it! Why don't you just *disappear* again!"

Silence. Sevi found enough energy to retrieve the brick just so he could hurl it at the creature. It fell harmlessly through, and Shy only blinked at its passing.

Staring incredulously, a disbelieving laugh bubbled up at Sevi's lips, much like when he'd found that a disembodied hand had not actually been a hand. His body rocked with his insanity, sending him prone again across the floorboards, clutching at his head as tears rolled down his cheeks. And all Shy did was stand there, watching him.

He subsided when a knock came at the door. Promina's voice, muffled through the wood, called out, "Boy, you're being awfully loud. Is everything alright in there?"

Sevi wiped his nose and quickly dried his cheeks, getting into a sitting position and glancing back at Shy. Shy, in turn, pulled their shadowy mass in until they had formed a figure much like Sevi's, shifting their orbs into an inky head and cocking it to the side. The gesture made them look confused.

"I'm... I'm fine," Sevi called, then a little louder, "please go away!"

"Do you—"

"Would you *please* leave me be!"

There was silence from the other side of the door, until Sevi heard her footsteps retreat, and the sound of the far doors closing. Shy cocked their head to the other side, then back again, as if having a neck was a delightfully novel circumstance.

"Why are you like this?" Sevi demanded. "You disappear for years, and when you come back you only appear when I'm in danger. Why can't you stay formed above the ground like you used to? Then maybe *one* of my friends might be there for me!"

Shy did nothing. Sevi kept talking, bitterly looking at his hands. "I'm a prince now. I don't even know what that's supposed to mean. Am I supposed to be a hero in some story? Am I now meant to ride into the sky on a horse made of moonlight like Prince Badim and save the world?"

Sevi shook his head and clenched his fists. "Princes are meant to rule," he said softly. "They're handsome. Powerful. Cunning. They're leaders. But me?" He reached up and pulled the hair from his eyes, baring his grisly scar to the shadow. "I'm ugly. I'm weak. I'm not even smart enough to think on my own without some phantom telling me how, and I've spent the last four years of my life following the *real* Lily around like a whipped geisthound. Everything, every single thing I've ever tried, I've failed at. I'm a tunnel rat. I'm not a prince. I'm *me*." He stared pleadingly at Shy. "What... what am I going to *do*? I can't... I'm not..."

Sevi's neck muscles strained as fear and agitation welled up inside of him. His fingers curled in his hair, gathering bunches of his locks up and gripping them tightly, trying to keep his skull together again.

A third, colder hand joined them.

He flicked his head up. Shy had soundlessly moved next to him and had sprouted a limb with a facsimile of a hand at the end. They ran it weightlessly over his head, petting him. Sevi wondered briefly if the shadow meant to engulf him again, when to his surprise, Shy sprouted another limb, reached down, and actually took Sevi's hand.

"Shy?"

The shadow blinked slowly at Sevi, one eye at a time. Sevi felt a pressure around his wrist, and found the shadow pulling at his arm, but after several breaths of effort, its intangible limb crumbled, wisping up into the air. That seemed to irritate the shadow, and they whipped their remaining arm like a child throwing a fit.

The reaction surprised Sevi so much that he chuckled, momentarily forgetting his anguish. "Do you want me to stand up?"

The shadow tried grabbing hold of Sevi's wrist again. Sevi lifted his arm, giving it no resistance. "Fine. No need to pull." Shy kept pulling. Sevi shook his head as he stood, exhausted. "I'm too tired for this. Just hurry up."

He didn't have to go far. The shadow took him to the desk with the mirror and stopped. They looked down at the chair in front of it, then back up to Sevi, blinking their eyes.

*At least there's a seat.* Sevi settled on it with a sigh, shooting an impatient look at the creature. "Fine. Now what?"

Shy leapt into the mirror.

If Sevi had blinked, he would have missed it. As soon as he had turned his head to look, Shy jumped forward onto the desk and sunk into the glass as easily as slipping into water. Sevi jolted in his seat, jerking his head from where Shy had just been to the mirror, clutching at the edges of his chair.

"Sh-Shy?" Sevi probed. He leaned slowly over the desk. His red-eyed, scared-looking reflection did the same. Scanning every corner, he looked for any trace of the shadow. Shy, when it had been attached to him, had only ever risen from the ground, or hidden him in darkness. It had never done something like *this*. But there weren't any mirrors in the Cut. "Wh-what are you doing?"

His reflection smiled.

Sevi swung his head back, staring wide-eyed at himself. His reflection stayed where it was, grinning at him like a dear friend. Sevi panicked. "What is this?"

Shy-Sevi giggled, noiseless through the glass. Then he began to change. Before Sevi's very eyes, his hair shrunk and brightened. His skin softened. His scar faded away. His nose receded, and he shrunk in his seat. In a matter of breaths, mirror-Sevi had de-aged to how Sevi had looked from his earliest memory—the day he'd woken up in darkness, surrounded by stone—but without the scar.

Lifting his hand to his face to make sure the fault was still there, Sevi whispered softly, "How did you learn to do this?" He couldn't stop staring at his younger face. He'd never known himself without the mark. It had been a permanent part of him, and the idea that it hadn't at one point had never crossed his mind.

Shy-Sevi kept smiling, and from the edges of the mirror, two figures emerged. A boy taller than the other and a younger girl, both with brown-blonde hair, hazel eyes, and beaming smiles. The children from the courtyard. The girl still held Lily's helmet to her chest.

He snapped his head around, instinctively looking for them in the real world. But they weren't there. When he brought his gaze back, the children were no longer alone. The knight Sevi had seen standing guard outside of the officer's party had joined them, still grimly performing their duty with sword in hand, standing a distance behind the children. A bearded, handsome man dressed in finery, whom Sevi recognized from the infirmary, sat regally off to the side on one of the armchairs, staring pensively at him over steepled fingers.

The faceless lady, dressed in black, sat up from behind the sofa in the exact spot he had just been sitting, staring eyelessly at him through the glass. Sevi's blood ran cold. He jerked his head around again.

She wasn't stuck in the mirror.

"No," he breathed.

She got up from her seat and moved through the couch toward him, ignoring anything solid in her path to Sevi. He stood up from the chair and leaned back onto the desk, trying to get as far away from her as he could. "St-stay back. Stay BACK!"

She moved faster. And when she finally stood before him, she leaned over him, tilting her head like a predator cornering its prey, savoring the moment before the kill. She raised one ivory hand up from her side and reached out to him, and with an icy touch, pressed her fingers into his forehead and pushed him backward into the mirror.

He fell into the glass as easily as Shy. The moment his head passed through, the children took hold of him and pulled him the rest of the way. The room in the mirror disappeared, replaced by a pervasive darkness that rushed in to surround them. He tried to fight them off, but the moment he was through the children willingly dropped him, stepping away as one to vanish into shadow.

He didn't fall. Instead, he floated softly down, moving from horizontal to vertical until he stood right-side-up. Ground formed beneath his feet, as steady as any rock, and a soft, diffused light centered around him from some unknown source, pushing the darkness back.

"Shy," Sevi whispered. His voice, as quiet as it was, echoed all around him. "Stop. I'm scared."

*"I'm scared,"* his echo replied.

From the shadows came shapes. Then objects. Then people. Forming out of nothing into something, one by one. That same richly dressed man from the armchair, now with a crown on his head, held a grimy, crying boy in a blanket, gently cleaning his face with a cloth. Both sat on a lavishly decorated, cushioned bench, with two windowed, wooden carriage walls on either side.

"Don't be," the man said. "We'll get you fed and properly dressed."

"Am... am I in trouble?" the young boy asked. He was much younger than the two mirror boys, but he had the same brown-blond hair.

"No, of course not. But I must plead with you to watch where you walk from now on. The blasted horses nearly trampled you. I simply want to make—"

"—sure that you are well," Sevi whispered, finishing for the man. He couldn't stop the words. They had appeared in his mind and fell from his mouth faster than he could comprehend.

Both the man and the boy turned to look at him, each smiling. Their bodies frayed around the edges, then collapsed, dissolving into a fine mist that quickly joined the surrounding darkness.

"Is production on schedule?"

Sevi turned to the left. The faceless woman sat in one of the castle's two thrones, rifling through several papers in her hands and lap. She wore a crown on her head, as elegant as the man's, and was draped in an elaborate blue dress. From her right stepped a tall, familiar-looking woman, wearing two deadly looking swords on her hips, and dressed in a white and gold coat as brilliant as Promina's.

"Yes, Your Luminance," said Commander Tiersa. Except, she wasn't Commander Tiersa. She was—

"Aunty Tisa," said a young Sevi, forming from the darkness. The taller boy formed after him, standing a distance away with arms crossed. "Can we play yet?"

"Not now, child," Aunty Tisa said. "Your mother and I are busy."

"But you promised," Young Sevi whined.

"I know, and I will keep it. But do you remember what we talked about?"

Young Sevi nodded. Present Sevi opened his mouth. "The realm comes first," they each said in unison.

Aunty Tisa nodded her approval, turning her gaze from his younger self to his present self. "Very good," she said with a smile, before they all faded away together.

"Come on! He's going to catch us!"

"I can't... run... that fast! Why did you give me *everything* to carry!"

"Because you're supposed to!"

Sevi swept his head around again. The two little boys were running down a stony corridor. The larger boy stood a distance down the hallway from the kitchens, watching as Sevi's younger self hurried towards him carrying an armful of bread.

The kitchen door burst open, and a large, angry-looking man with a beard yelled after them, "Get *back* here!"

The taller boy waved frantically. "Hurry up! *Hurry up!*"

"I can't do this!" His younger self panicked.

"Then I will *leave* you here," present-Sevi said in unison again. And just as before, the phantoms smiled before they, too, disappeared.

Sevi held his head. There was an itching coming from behind his skull fiercer than any he'd ever felt. "Shy..."

All three children ran past him with the tall boy in the lead, the smaller one behind, and the little girl trailing at the back with a determined look on her face. "Wait for me!" she called in a high, sweet voice.

The itching in Sevi's head turned to pain and he gasped loudly, digging his nails into his scalp. The tall boy had run ahead to a tree that sprouted from the darkness, making short work of the climb up. The smaller one had stopped at the base, staring fearfully up into its branches, while the girl wandered around the trunk to admire the flowers sprouting up between its roots.

"Come on up you coward!" the tall boy called down.

"I can't, Al! It's too high!" the smaller one replied.

"What? I bet even Nahlra could do it!"

At that, the little girl hopped up from the flowers and spread her arms above her head, reaching for the sky. "Let me up! I wanna go up!"

"No, Nahlra—"

"It's n-not safe," present-Sevi finished, stumbling over his words as the pain in his head doubled.

"What's that one?"

A mound of grass faded into existence from the floor, on which was an old lady and that same young boy from the carriage again, swaddled in blankets against the cold, night wind. A spyglass twice as big as the one Sevi used to carry stood on a stand, pointed at the sky.

"That one's Regielo, The Scholar. See his long beard, there?" the old woman said.

A rumbling filled Sevi's ears, drowning out the boy's response, and his world abruptly exploded with a flood of streaking visions, appearing from the dark mist one by one and howling over each other in a fierce competition for his attention, driving him to his knees with his hands to his ears.

But no matter how hard he pressed against his skull, he could hear them. No matter how tightly he squeezed his eyes shut, he could see them. All running together, until sight and sound blurred completely into one.

*Lying beneath the great tree with the mirror children.*

*Watching an army walk away down a wide street corridor, lined with beautiful, glittering buildings, holding the hands of the crowned man and the faceless lady.*

*The man in the crown and the faceless lady turning their backs on him and walking into a tunnel cut into the mountain.*

*The small boy from the carriage hiding outside of a door, while a man and woman yelled at each other inside.*

*Elegantly decorated figures floating in midair on wings as delicate as Alyda's.*

*Well-dressed nobles dancing in a circle to the happiest music Sevi had ever heard.*

*Eating dinner with the boy, the girl, the crowned man, the faceless lady, and Aunty Tisa.*

*A smiling knight, teaching Sevi how to ride a horse while the other children looked on.*

*And a young girl in a knight's helmet with a torch, bringing him out of the dark.*

"Stop. Stop it, Shy, *stop!*" Sevi yelled.

At his command, the visions finally faded away. No more took their place, leaving him alone in the void.

Sevi fell to his knees with tears running down his cheeks. So many memories. So many things he did and didn't remember, all warring inside of his head, demanding to get out. But not all of them could. The most they could do was yell at him from a distance, insisting they be heard, and in the fighting for his attention all he could hear was a screeching cacophony.

But from that noise, a single drumbeat appeared.

*Bump... Bump... Bump...*

Sevi stared into the distance. Out of the dark, a figure clad in wooden armor manifested, tall and formidable. Twisting branches reached up from the crown of a mouthless mask in an array of sinister points. Wings stretched out behind it, then slowly folded against its back. In its hand it wielded a fiery sword, snapping and cracking with flame as red as blood, and it stared at him with eyes red enough to match.

Sevi scrambled to his feet, falling over in his haste. He... He *knew* that figure.

*Bump... Bump... Bump...*

Two more figures emerged behind the first, carrying the same fiery swords.

*Bump... Bump... Bump... Bump... Bump...*

From behind them, an army emerged. People of every shape, skin, and size, from every walk of life, in every garb imaginable. The first wooden figure raised its arm, bringing its sword in a blazing arc through the darkness above its head.

*Bump... Bump... Bump... Bump... Bump... BUMPBUMPBUMP.*

The sword swung down. A spark flew from it like steel striking flint as the creature swept it across the ground. That spark grew into a towering blaze that set the entire horizon alight. In its sinister glow, the true number of silhouettes surrounding Sevi was revealed.

Hundreds. Hundreds of people, all staring hungrily at him.

The leader of the wooden knights pointed its sword at Sevi's chest. The army yelled a murderous, bloodthirsty howl, and charged forward as one, running fluidly around the trio of wooden creatures as they dashed madly toward him, shoving each other out of the way in a bloodlusted fervor to be the first to sink their weapon into his flesh.

*Blow this whistle, and I'll come find you,* Lily's phantom voice whispered.

Sevi deliriously poured through his pockets. When the first person reached him, their sickle raised high, Sevi brought Lily's whistle to his lips and blew.

And the darkness took everything away.

# Chapter 35

*In shadows that withheld his mind from his body, shadows that sheltered his soul. From shadows he came with a piece of himself; a remnant of spirits once whole.*

---

T*ap.*
    *Tap.*

*Tap.*

Sevi slowly cracked his eyes open.

*Tap.*

Something struck him in the nose. His eyelids fluttered. It was dark, and the light was dim, but the ceiling he now stared at was different than he'd remembered. Not the stone of his tunnels nor that of the infirmary, but made of an intricately woven cloth, spun into a pleasing, elaborate pattern. He was in the Big Bedroom. Mother and Father's room.

His room, now.

*Tap.* Something struck his face again, bouncing off his cheek.

He sluggishly turned his head to the side just in time for another pebble to hit his forehead, making him flinch. The room was swathed in moonbeams filtering in through the wall's expansive window. A figure sat before it, lounging on the bench, stark against the glass. "Hello, boy," it said.

The dull, scratched, ratty helm of a knight shone brightly in the blue light. Attached to it was the head of a small girl with sharp, green eyes, made greener by the light of the fairy sitting on her one propped-up knee. The ghost of a smile graced Lily's mouth as she regarded him.

Sevi said nothing and received another pebble to the face for it. Lily sighed. "Darn. I was hoping that would land in your mouth." She looked soberly down at the pebbles in her hand, and as if losing interest in them, opened her fingers and let them clatter to the floor in a gentle rain. She carefully moved her feet until both of her knees were pointing up and turned from him, making sure not to jostle Alyda, and looked distantly out the window.

Alyda, however, continued to stare at him with open concern scrawled across her face. She tried to stand, but her legs gave out, and she slipped back down to Lily's knee. She fluttered her wings sheepishly as she pulled her own knees to her chest, ostensibly deciding to remain there.

An oppressive silence followed. Lily made no comment. No witticisms, nor pointed remarks. Whatever existed outside the window seemed to hold far more of her interest than anything the room could provide.

Sevi bored holes in the back of her head with his stare, desperate to hear her say something. To laugh at him. To voice surprise. *Anything.* But she didn't. "I'm a prince," he said softly. Lily's breath fogged up the window as she huffed out a chuckle. He knew she'd laugh. "And you knew. Didn't you?"

She didn't laugh at that.

Sevi pushed himself up from under the covers, slowly bringing his legs to hang off the edge of the bed. "Are you even real?"

She turned her head back to him at that. Her face was impassive, and her eyes flashed curiously in Alyda's light. Sevi stood, straightening his back. "My visions have gotten worse," he said. "I see things wherever I go now. Things that aren't there. People I've never known. Except... I have, haven't I?"

He took a step toward them. "I've even been hearing your voice, Lily, whenever I need you. Have I dreamed you up all this time? Or did the real Lily and Alyda die when the Embers invaded?"

Another step. Still, Lily said nothing. "Captain River said that they never found your body, and the only one who has seen either of you is me. How do I know you both didn't burn to death just like my parents? Like my brother and sister?"

He stopped in front of them. Lily looked up at him. Devoid of emotion. Devoid of life. "And you've come to help me again," he said softly, reaching out for her. She mirrored his action, reaching out to him in turn, and they both twined their fingers together, squeezing each other tightly. She didn't *feel* like an illusion. She felt real.

She flashed a smile, took the skin of his hand, and twisted.

"Ow!" Sevi gasped, ripping his hand free of her grip.

Lily swept her hand across her face to keep herself from barking out the laughter she so clearly wanted to. Alyda grimaced at her and put her chin in her hand. "*That was uncalled for.*"

Lily dropped her hand. "Heh... Want more proof?" she managed between snorts. "I'm happy to oblige."

Sevi gaped at her.

"Of course, even that could've all been part of your crazy mind, couldn't it?" she said, stretching her arms. "The truth is much more boring. Alyda and I are real. And we heard you." She picked up something from the seat and tossed it to him. He fumbled with it for a moment, and when it settled, he held it out into the moonlight. The carved flower of her bone whistle shone back at him.

"How did you get in?" Sevi asked.

She pointed her thumb over toward the wall—the same wall Sevi had tried prying open. The hole was much, much bigger now. "Bad news is we're going to have to hide it," Lily said. "I think the dresser will do nicely."

Sevi closed his fingers over the whistle and turned his attention back to her. She met his eyes. Not with shame, nor with aversion, but with open expectation. She opened her hand, inviting him to speak. "Well?"

"You *knew*," Sevi said, more accusingly than before.

She had the audacity to roll her eyes. "Of course, I knew, Sevi."

An anger unlike any he'd ever felt boiled up inside of him, and before he could stop himself, he'd wound his hand back and hurled her whistle at her. She flinched and raised her hands to block, her face warping with indignation. "YOU KNE—"

"*Shut up, you idiot,*" she hissed through her teeth, bolting from her seat. Alyda tumbled to the cushion. Lily strode right up to Sevi and shoved her helmet in his face, jutting her chin. "There are probably guards just outside this room!"

"Why shouldn't I *call* them on you!" Sevi growled, leaning into her just as aggressively until he'd shoved her back. "You said I was a *servant!*"

Lily looked skeptically at him. "You won't. And no, I didn't. I implied. You did the rest." With a searing surge of fury, Sevi drew in a breath to call the guards, but Lily cut him off. "You're not going to call anyone on me, Sevi."

"I *will!*"

"No, you won't. Know why?"

He scoffed. "Why?"

"Because I'm your friend, and I deserve a chance to explain."

Sevi snapped his jaw shut, glaring at her deadpan mien. He furiously crossed his arms and puffed out his chest, watching her from under a heavy brow.

Lily shook her head. "Before you start throwing your fists at me, would you *please* hear me out?"

He dragged in a hot, angry breath, as dangerously close to physicality as she suggested. "What. Could you. *Possibly*. Say to me. That would make up for four *years* of lies?"

"Well, if you'd let me speak, you'd hear it," she countered, crossing her own arms. Her logic only made him angrier.

Moments passed. Neither of them spoke. Lily broke the stand-off first. "Well?"

Sevi pursed his lips and closed his eyes, shutting out the sight of her. All he felt was rage, and betrayal, and *hurt* that his best friend could *ever* lie to him like this... but...

*But she's always looked after me.*

He couldn't just forget that. She may have been the reason why he'd never left the tunnels, she may have been the liar who'd kept the truth of his identity from him, but she was, even now, his best friend. He was mad—madder than mad. He was positively seeing red. But in all his anger, all his pain, he could not mistake one thing: he wanted, *needed*, a reason not to hate her.

She was right. After everything they'd gone through together, she deserved a chance.

Sevi breathed out through his teeth, fighting to get his temper under control. Mustering every scrap of willpower he could manage, he gave her the barest of nods.

Lily let out a breath. "Thank you, Sevi."

"Get on with it."

Lily tilted her head, regarding him from under her helmet. "Four years ago, near the night we met, the Fae had just invaded the castle, killed everything inside, and set it alight. Do you know how they did it?"

"They had an army."

"Yes. But do you know who made up that army?" Sevi looked at her blankly. "Humans," she said. "Not Fae. Not monsters. People. People who lived at the base of this very mountain. Do you know how they got them to do it?"

Sevi was about to shake his head when he was struck by a horrible epiphany. "Blood," he whispered.

Lily nodded. "Blood. The Fae are cunning, more so than any human I've ever known. It's in their nature. Many of the elders have lived countless years in this world. They've seen it all. Done it all. *Lived* it all. How can anyone possibly outsmart something like that? And worst of all, not all them have wings or bark for skin. Some of them would look just like a human if not for the pointy ears."

Her face scrunched up bitterly at that, getting a far-off look in her eyes before she angrily shook it away. "So how do immortal creatures, with way too much time on their hands, create an army within a foreign country's own borders? They wait. Patiently. Eternally. They send their most human-like soldiers into it and worm their way into its crevices until they've dug themselves in like ticks. Like bakers. Or fishermen. Or barkeeps. Or winemakers. Do you see where I'm going with this?"

Sevi's stomach dropped. "They drugged the entire town."

Lily nodded. "Do you know what it's like to live in a place where everyone has become a mindless thrall, Sevi? Where you don't know who's a Fae, who's possessed, and who's still human? Or when in the middle of the night they all sharpen their pitchforks, light their torches, and leave to murder everyone in the nearby castle?"

Sevi glowered. "*Yes.*"

Lily smirked. "You know all about that last part, or some of it at least. I'm not sure how much you remember, but you have no idea what it's like when you don't know who you can trust. How alone that makes you."

"How did you even know the Fae had anything to do with it? That they enslaved an entire town of all things?"

"Everyone knows the Fae and those held by them for too long burn at the touch of iron. It was by chance that I happened to watch a man's hand blister while he reshoed a horse in the street. He never even noticed when his skin began to peel. Until that point, I had convinced myself it was just my imagination that people were acting funny, or the heat, or something. As I said, not everyone was enslaved. Just many of them."

"And how did you escape becoming like them?"

She crossed her arms tightly to her chest and wrung her fingers in her shirt. "I didn't. I mean... I couldn't. It's..."

Lily abruptly turned her back on him and walked a short distance away. Sevi studied her in surprise. She looked small, all a sudden, as if each step she took stole a head of her height. "What do you mean?"

She said nothing. He heard her take a shaky breath, then tilt her head back to look up at the ceiling. "Don't be scared, Sevi. Alright? Promise me you won't be scared."

Sevi took a step forward. "Why—" He broke off as Lily reached up and took ahold of her helmet. Her hands paused in their purpose, clutching at the metal in a white-knuckled grip. Alyda chimed in alarm from her seat, making him look between the two. "Lily?"

Lily straightened her back and swept her helmet off her head in one motion, silencing him completely. Her scalp was completely bald, glowing pallidly in the diffused moonlight. Angry red scars crossed over each other in a horrific pattern of ugly splotches, dominating the crown of her skull and tapering off the lower they traveled. But they were so great and numerous that they ran all the way down to her ears.

Her sharp, pointed ears.

Sevi could only stare. She was one of his visions. She had to be. But her specter wouldn't disappear, solidifying into something he could not deny.

He still tried to. In his mind the helmet was still on Lily's head, and the girl who stood before him was the lie, brought about by a trick of the moonlight or his own weariness. A vision. Her helmet was as a part of her as her head itself. She would never... She couldn't be...

"This is why I knew it would be safer to live in the Cut, Sevi," Lily whispered, loud enough for him to hear. "Under the noses of the people who would harm you. Away from the monsters that look like me and the thralls that look like you, in a mountain made of poisonous quicksilver."

"You. You're not—"

"No. I'm not." Lily turned back to face him. Her face was flat, but her eyes were strained at the edges.

Sevi took a step forward, lifting one hand to touch her ear, distantly trying to ensure that she was really flesh and blood. She batted his hand away with a frown. They regarded each other for a long time before he said anything. "Why?" he asked softly, putting all his questions into one word.

She lifted her chin. "As I've always said, Sevi. To protect you."

"Why, Lily?" Sevi asked again, tightening his face. "Why do that for me? Why... you... you wore *iron*." He glanced in horror between the helmet in her hand and the scars across her head. "What have you done? Who... who *are* you?"

Lily clenched her jaw and fixed him with a long look before lifting her helmet back over her head. She didn't even wince at its touch. "Whoever I need to be. But always your friend. Always."

Sevi didn't know what to do with his hands. He wiped his eyes clear and fidgeted with his shirt, fighting to order his feelings into something manageable. "Answer me. Why did you do this? Who were you before you came here?"

She looked pained. "I was a gutter rat."

"Lies," Sevi muttered.

"I'm not one of *them*," she said, crossing her arms. "I left the woods of the Lynnweald long ago and hid among you humans. Nobody would ever suspect a Silvakin to wear iron, but there are a few, like me, who can weather its burn without dying. Though we have to get pretty damn close to find that out."

"Silvakin?"

"It's what we call ourselves. Silvakaen, or Silvakin. Not quite Fae. Not entirely."

"And why did you leave them? Why did you come here?"

"I don't get along with them, and that's all I'll say. As for why I came here, you already know. After the mob had finished their business, I searched the castle for something to steal, thinking my people had left." She shrugged. "But I was wrong. They hadn't left, they were just moving in, and it's thanks to this helmet" –she tapped its crown– "that I'm even here today. But here comes the part about you.

"In my hurry to escape, I found these tunnels. I'm small, and getting into tight places isn't exactly difficult. So, I hid, and in here... I found you. A half-dead boy, dressed in rags, huddled up in a corner like an animal. Scared me to death when I first came across you; I actually thought you were going to carve me up with that pointy necklace of yours."

Lily gave him a grim smile. "I could've left you. I could've gone on my way and left you to die. You were sputtering madness and seemed likely to kill me in my sleep."

"Then why didn't you?"

"Because... because you were alone. Like me." Her eyes softened, getting watery at the corners. "A gutter rat Silvakin surrounded by humans and an orphaned prince surrounded by fairies, each without a home. I couldn't just leave you there. If they found you, they would have killed you. So, I fed you a lie, and I watched over you. But you've found your home again."

She seemed to crumple under her words. What was left of Sevi's anger faded, stolen by her resignation. The extent of her sacrifice, her pain, her isolation; all emotions he had felt for four long years. Emotions he'd never expected her to have.

She was strong. She was smart. She was confident. She showed her affection sparingly, and he'd privately thought she'd always seen him as a nuisance. She was someone to mother him, to clean up after all the messes he made. Meanwhile, she had commanded all his awe and respect, running the Cut as surely as any general.

And she had done it all for them. For *him*. Keeping him safe from her own kin. How was he to sustain any anger against such a thing? Yet, one question remained. "Why did you never tell me about you? Alyda and I are friends. I never would've hated you for this."

"You needed a human," Lily said. "Someone to make you feel less alone. And I needed to keep the iron on, or the others would have felt me. It's something our kind can do."

Sevi closed his eyes as a fresh wave of remorse washed through him. *More sacrifices.* "And keeping me in the Cut?"

"You had no memory, which made tending to you difficult while you recovered. Escape was impossible, and I had no idea that any of your army had survived. But to the Silvakaen you were dead, and I knew that they would do anything to keep from entering a mountain full of quicksilver. Keeping you here was the best thing I could think of."

"Lily." He shook his head at her. "You should have told me everything. I could have handled it. I probably would have even *agreed* with you. Would you have kept the act up forever? Until I was a man?"

She tightened her arms across her chest. "I don't expect forgiveness. I did what I thought was right. And it worked, didn't it? You survived. We all did."

He said nothing, averting his eyes.

"Are you scared of me now?"

It took him a moment to collect himself, but Sevi shook his head. "You'd never hurt me."

She breathed out a sigh. "Still friends then?"

Sevi nodded, wiping away fresh tears. "I'm angry, Lily... but yes. Still friends. Now and forever, right?"

She cracked a wry smirk, wiping her own eyes.

A chiming sound tolled out behind her. Alyda, having remained on the window seat, sat crying, coughing, and wiping at her cheeks. She stood on wobbly legs and reached out to them both, fluttering her wings weakly with every step.

Sevi leaned toward her, setting his palm down for her to step into, and brought her up between them. Alyda waved a hand, demanding to be raised higher, and leaned in to kiss Sevi on the cheek, before chiming at Lily to come closer for the same treatment. Lily shared a small smile with Sevi before leaning in, taking the kiss on the nose where her iron helmet didn't reach. When she had finished, Alyda walked onto Sevi's shoulder and buried her face into his neck, muffling her tiny sniffles against him.

"So. Alyda," Sevi said. "You knew about her, didn't you?" She chimed bashfully in response, hiding her face. Sevi smiled softly, unable to summon any anger, but it faded with a worrisome thought. He turned back to Lily. "Was Alyda with the Silvakaen invasion?"

"No. She's... I made her," Lily said awkwardly.

Sevi balked. "Excuse me?"

"I needed help in our first year while you recovered, so I made her to help with growing food. I'm magic, remember? Used to be, anyway."

"Used to be?"

"I'm wearing iron, dummy."

"Oh. But... is she your daughter or something?"

"Can we not get into it right now?" she grumbled.

He let it drop, trying to glance at Alyda. He remembered how he'd first found her. She'd appeared out of thin air one day, sickly, without a voice, and shivering violently over a seed clutched in her arms. A seed that would later become the first sowed plant in their garden. He'd named her after a loving forest spirit from one of Lily's stories, and developed signs with her so that she could communicate. She, in turn, had taught him how to make things grow.

In a way, she was a piece of Lily's kindness, too. Quiet, but there when he'd needed her. Sevi sighed, trying to stifle his emotions before they welled up again. "So how do we tell everyone?"

Lily tilted her head. "Tell everyone?"

"About you and Alyda."

"We don't. Now we leave."

Sevi darted his gaze back to her. She looked serious. Fear reached its icy hand into his chest, clutching his heart. "L-leave? You're still trying to leave?"

"We can't stay here," Lily said, setting her jaw. "They'll kill me and Alyda. She and I need to leave before that happens."

"But you can't!" Sevi panicked. She couldn't leave. She couldn't! "I'm back to being a prince now. A prince's soldiers do whatever he says, right? I'll tell them not to harm either of you. None of us will have to live in the tunnels anymore. We can make the castle a proper home for all of us!"

She frowned. "Sevi, I'm happy that you're back where you belong. But this place... I can't live in these walls. I mean, not *in* in them. Every day would be spent looking over my shoulder. And think about it, if I were to join you in court, could you really see me wearing a dress?"

"You don't have to wear one!"

"That's not the point," she said, putting a hand on his arm. "Aside from the threat to my well-being, living a royal life sounds absolutely horrid, full of rules and stupid etiquette. And remember when I said how awful it is not knowing who to trust? Who's a friend and who's faking? Being a royal is just like that."

She shook her head, staring meaningfully at him. "And if you stay, things are only going to get harder for you. The moment news spreads that the royal line survived, you will be swarmed with people clamoring for your favor. To *use* you. You'll end up more alone out here than you ever were in the Cut."

Sevi opened and closed his mouth, taken aback by the cold, casual certainty in her voice. "Wh-what? No, that's not how it works!" *That's not how the stories go at all!* But Lily didn't budge. "How do you know?"

"Because I do," she said softly. "I've seen it." She looked around the room, then leaned in with a conspiratorial glint in her eye. "You don't have to go back to it, though. If you don't want to. We can go off again, just you, me, and Alyda."

"I... but... how would we even get out of here? I'm a prince now! They're going to be watching everything I do!"

"Why do you think I've been looking for a way to escape?" She gave him a coy smile that he was intimately familiar with—a smile that meant mischief. "How far along are they in repairing the airship?"

Part 3:

# Breath

# Chapter 36

*Sunbeams and shades with their grasp on his path; holding no end insofar. With flower, and Fae, and the lost to be found, they chased after the light of a star.*

---

"From the light of the father Sorvathos, sovereign of the celestial plane on high, protector of the World Gate, defender against Niurna the Watcher, came the spark of man, in all its resplendence and effervescence. From the arms of the mother Avinaea, protected in her eternal hold, led by her patient wisdom and generous bounty, were we nurtured, and led to prosperity. And in our deference, in our humility, and in our love, we give back that which was given."

Sevi, dressed in his loose-fitting uniform, sat at the head of the congregation, listening to Promina's impassioned speech, enhanced by the glittering embossments of her coat in the day's early light. Flanking him was Commander Tiersa, the man from the officer's party dressed in Empyrean leathers, and a solemn guard of silent soldiers with rifles nestled against their shoulders.

The courtyard before them must have been filled to the brim with every other person in the castle, save for the ones that manned the walls, peering across the valley for any signs of enemy Fae. Clouds of taloned raptors flew high above, circling the procession. And in front of Sevi, shrouded in cloth atop a pile of kindling on a cold stone slab, lay what remained of his father.

"Marovhan Cassangia, King of Elkra and all its peoples, husband to Queen Korina and father of Isevidel, Nahlra, and Alramar, defended his family to his last breath, and through his efforts, saved the life of one of his children, and the royal line itself. As protector of both his kin and his peoples, we honor him with this pyre, to free the noble spark of his spirit, so that it may return to the Sun Father and grant Him nourishment in His vigil. May the Mother accept the ashes of his flesh into her bosom, from which She may nurture two lives anew. And may Tembra, in Their fairness and Their honor, judge his soul well, and guide him through Their twilight lands in his final journey to Rebirth."

A row of soldiers carrying heavy war drums broke into a grave, steady beat, tapping out the march of a torchbearer who appeared at the back of the crowd. An order was called out, and as one, the army stood at attention and split in half down the middle. Two lines of officers dressed in blue divided the rest of the charcoal soldiers, leading the break in formation, then turned inward to face each other across the formed gap as the torchbearer entered their ranks.

Mirroring their counterpart across the path, each officer touched their far shoulder, put one foot forward, and bowed deeply at the passing of the burning light. The torchbearer's path ended at Promina, who accepted the light with a penitent bow of her head. With a crisp turn on her heels, she faced Sevi and took three very precise, very practiced steps forward, then bowed at the waist, offering the torch to him.

Sevi stared at the flames, making no move to take it from her. What little knowledge of the ceremony he'd been given from Tiersa drained from his open mouth before he could catch it and put it back.

"Your Luminance," Promina softly said.

*Stop calling me that.* Sevi slowly curled his hand around the handle, feeling the flame's warmth through the wood. Promina moved her hand away, forcing him to take its unwieldy weight with both hands, distantly aware of the hundreds of eyes on him.

He shifted his focus from the torchlight to the pyre. A surrealistic mood washed over him, convincing him he was in one of his visions, full of faces he both knew and didn't know, with a fire that would never stop chasing him. Any moment those soldiers would pick up their weapons and aim at him.

Another hand folded around the torch. When he looked up, he met the gaze of Commander Tiersa, standing as collected as ever. She put one foot forward, pulling him softly, forcing him to mirror her, lest he lose his balance. Then she did it again. On the third step he found his rhythm, just in time to reach the slab containing his father.

She leveled the torch for him, and when the first spark hit the oiled twigs, it called forth a great inferno that raced around its edges, quickly wreathing the shrouded body in its warm, hungry glow. It ate away at the fabric, leisurely and gluttonous, revealing the smiling teeth of the dead man's skull beneath, until it built, and raged so hotly that those were eaten away as well. And still the drums beat on, indifferent to its feast.

Sevi watched the flames with an expression devoid of emotion, glad of the gaps in his memory for once. He had spent the first two years after waking in the Cut wondering if he had any family, dreaming often of who and where they could be. But the repetition of living in the tunnels day in and day out had stolen such thoughts from him, as the hopelessness of ever learning the truth grated him down bit by bit.

Yet he'd only just remembered how it felt to be wrapped in a blanket by a father, telling him that all would be alright, and somehow that one memory stung more than years of loneliness. *Because I had it once*, he thought. *And now I never will again.*

If such a small memory was enough to create such pain, then he was glad not to know the rest while standing before the very blaze that reduced his old hopes to ash. It seemed as if the fire was destined to chase him, no matter what he did or where he went, be it the flames of a firedrake or that of a pyre.

*And even if the fire never catches me, it will still have me when I die.*

Commander Tiersa placed her hand on his shoulder, pulling him from his thoughts, and raised her voice so that all might hear it. "Today, we finally lay our liege, King Marovhan, first of his name, to rest. In his footsteps we welcome the last surviving child of the Astraeda line, Prince Isevidel. Brothers and sisters, make no mistake in your deliberations, this is exactly who I claim. Hiding from our enemy under their very noses since the Night of Treachery, in the very castle they stole from us. In taking back this castle we have not only reclaimed our territory, we have not only reclaimed our honor... we have taken back our *culture*.

"I say to you now, to each and every one of you, from the bottom of my heart, thank you. Thank you for following me here, to this shining, glorious moment, from the darkest, most forlorn pits of Torment. Here, right now, I hold your oaths fulfilled. But now I charge you with a new one. Leave, and no man or woman will ever dare to claim you a coward. But stay, and I will personally lift you to glory seen only by the errants of old."

She lifted her fist in the air. "Stay, and defend your culture. Stay, and defend the blood of your royalty. Stay, rebuild the Astral Guard with me, and I *swear* to you, your names will live on *forever!*"

Commander Tiersa drew her longest saber and lifted it high into the air with a flourish. "Long live the king!" she cried.

Rifles shot off in salute. The army lifted their fists and cheered in a fervor, "Long live the king!"

Sevi closed his eyes and lowered his head. "Long live the king," he whispered.

"You did well, Isevidel. As well as could be hoped," Tiersa said. "Given your memory loss and the last four years it's only to be expected," Promina added critically.

Tiersa shot a withering glare at Promina.

"Commander," Promina apologized.

Sevi sighed, walking behind the two ladies toward the main hall, and more importantly, the dining room. He was hungry enough to devour a whole turkey by himself. "You didn't tell me there would be people," Sevi mumbled, staring at his feet.

Tiersa and Sevi had spoken frequently after their dramatic reunion. She had come in the day after with a crew of three officers, all carrying brooms and wash buckets, and set to work on cleaning the royal study. While there, she discussed the identity of the body she had retrieved from the study and brought to the crypt, though Sevi had pieced it together by then.

He had sat quietly while she explained the ceremony for the fallen king the morning after that, listening as intently as he could. She had failed, however, to mention the crowd.

"I thought it was implied. I apologize," Tiersa said.

"Are there going to be more of these?" Sevi asked.

"Funerals? I would hope not." She gave a small, sad smile.

"I mean, how often do I need to be standing there like that? I don't like having that many people stare at me."

Promina shot a blank look at Tiersa. The commander ignored it, focusing on Sevi instead. She placed a hand on his shoulder and gave it a supportive squeeze. "You will get used to it in time. Eventually, whether you like it or not, the role slips over you like a shoe. If you step into it yourself, you may control how you walk. Otherwise, it may be forced on, and unbalance you."

She smiled at him, but it didn't escape his notice that she had failed to answer his question. He looked back down at his feet, huffing air from his nose. "Let's go see about lunch," Tiersa said, leading them on.

The dining room was blessedly empty when they arrived. Sevi went for a chair but looked up to find that he was the only one. Promina and Tiersa lingered by the door, speaking together in hushed tones. When Tiersa caught him staring, she said, "We're going to see the cooks about the food. We'll be back shortly."

They stepped back into the hallway, which was odd. Why didn't they just walk through the dining room to the kitchen? Sensing something amiss, Sevi got up from the table and moved silently to the door, crouching down low in order to put his ear to the gap between wood and stone.

"It's not going to work," Promina said. "It's been four years. The nobles have their teeth locked and their minds set. They're not going to believe it."

"Then I'll drag them to the study and show them myself," Tiersa rebutted.

"No, Tiersa, they *won't* believe it, and they're going to put up every obstacle they can think of to keep it that way. You'll have the support of House Kaymoor, probably, and the factions on the council still loyal to the crown. But you know what his presence means, don't you?"

Teirsa didn't respond.

"Now that he is known, the nobles will see him as a plot to keep the lot of them from controlling what remains of the realm. They will begin planning his deposal immediately."

"Silence."

"It will be a war. The moment the last greenblood is dusted or across the border, they will turn on him."

"I said *silence*."

"No. I'm sorry, my lady. When you granted me this role it was to be your hand and your voice, just as you were to *your* queen. I will not silence my counsel because you don't wish to hear it, and I am telling you right now that they will come for him. Your dislike for the nobles is well known, and even if he *is* the real Isevidel back from the dead, they will never see him as their king."

A hush fell in the hallway. Sevi strained his ear against the door.

"Then gather them," Tiersa said at last.

"My lady?"

"Gather them all. Friend and foe. I want them all in one place," Tiersa continued, her voice rising with conviction. "I want them to feel the pressure of the hallowed grounds they'd dare squabble over. I want them to know the danger of crossing the woman who won them this war, and of the army whose loyalty she earned through blood and tears, waiting on her beck and call."

"A fraction of our soldiers, and many of our officers, come from noble houses," Promina said.

"Who was on the front lines with them, Rinenne? Lord Jaska? Lady Rea? Or Lady Tiersa Grommand of House Astraeda?"

There was another long pause. Sevi held his breath.

"What do you propose?" Promina said.

"An Iron Masquerade. Let them come swear their allegiance to Elkra and the eradication of the greenbloods. Let us see who bows to Isevidel and the women at his shoulder, and who shies away. Let them hide their faces, let the drink loosen their tongues, and when they're comfortable enough to speak their true ambitions, we'll be there to listen. Both to the ones who speak too much and the ones who speak too little."

"And the ones who know just what to say?"

"We can't catch them all. This, at least, is a start."

Sevi felt a chill run down his spine. *What are they planning?*

"Hm. It is indeed a start." Promina trailed off. "It could work. I'll tell Vykka and Mirinki to start spreading propaganda announcing the prince's return. The soldiers will do it themselves after that speech of yours, but maybe the birds can speed up the process. It may be enough to get the general public on his side, so that any moves made will remain in the dark. It could stall them."

"See it done. And Rinenne?" Tiersa said.

"Yes, my lady?"

"Please see the cooks about our lunch before you go."

Promina grumbled. "Yes, my lady."

Sevi was so engrossed in their conversation that he almost didn't hear Tiersa's footsteps approaching. Scrambling away from the door a little less quietly than he would've liked, he landed in his chair the moment it opened.

"Sorry, Isevidel. Food will be here shortly," Tiersa said, walking around the table and sitting down across from him. "I sent Rinenne on an errand. While we wait, would you mind if we spoke?"

Sevi gulped. "A-about what?"

"That's the question." Commander Tiersa sighed, leaning back in her chair. One of her long fingers raised and fell in a steady beat against the wood, working through some private thought. "Where to begin? How do we reconcile four years, Isevidel? Or a life, even, considering your... condition."

Sevi shifted awkwardly in his chair and looked down at the tabletop. So that was it. "I have a lot I'd like to ask myself," he said quietly.

"Mm. I'm sure... Why don't we trade? Question for question."

Sevi raised his head back up, eying Tiersa. She sounded like Captain River, and while Lily had given her blessing to answer such questions, he couldn't repress the hurt he felt at being maneuvered by the man. He didn't want it to happen again, even by someone who called herself family.

Tiersa, however, no longer wore that desolate armor he'd seen on her at the officer's party. Her face was open and expectant, and more importantly, unsmiling. She offered no threats, like from Digby. No innocent-looking gibes, like from River. No conniving lies, like from Reynam. Just the deal as it stood. He nodded carefully. "Alright."

"May I start?" she asked.

"Sure," Sevi said.

"What do you remember? The night the castle was invaded, and before? What's the earliest thing you can recall?"

Sevi shook his head and spoke as the thoughts came to him. "It's just... scattered, now. Before it was nothing, but I've been getting flashes lately. Memories and visions. Of my mother, father, and my siblings. And you. Ever since Shy went into the mirror and started—"

"Shy?" Tiersa interrupted.

"My shadow."

Tiersa stared blankly at him. "Your shadow." Sevi nodded. "Lieutenant Asgaillin did say something about a missing shadow. I'll confess that I thought that was a product of his delirium. Do you mean to tell me that he was being serious?"

"He was."

"And you claim that it's somehow alive?"

"It is!"

She shook her head. "People don't have living shadows, Isevidel. And you certainly didn't four years ago."

Sevi shrugged helplessly. "They're here right now though," he said, gesturing to the floor. "They've always been with me, ever since Lily found me. Except for when I lost them in the Cut for a few years. But they found me again after I left the tunnels and started showing me my past."

Tiersa arched her eyebrow and slid her chair out from the table, peering critically beneath it to eye his shadow. "And... how does your, 'shadow friend,' do that, exactly?"

"They—" Sevi frowned, debating whether he should describe *all* his visions to her. He didn't want her to overreact. "They don't do much, mostly. They just say 'hmm' sometimes. But the other night, when we opened the fireplace, they started showing me things in the mirror. Old memories, like fire, and being attacked by many people. They felt... right, somehow. Real."

"Mm-hm." Tiersa expressionlessly righted herself. She tapped her finger again. "Is it possible for me to speak with this shadow friend of yours?"

"Oh. Um. I can try bringing them out, but I call them Shy for a reason." Tiersa raised her eyebrow and nodded slowly. "Alright." Sevi pushed his chair back, turning toward where his shadow, faint in the indoor light, outlined the stone. "Hey, Shy? Can you come out?"

His shadow didn't move.

Sevi tried again. "Shy? My, um, aunt, the one you showed me, wants to see you."

Again, nothing.

Sevi pursed his lips and shrugged, turning back to face Tiersa. "Sorry. They only come out for me."

Tiersa nodded slowly again. "Has anyone else seen Shy?"

"Lily did, back when she first found me. But they stopped showing themselves shortly after."

"Ah. Right. The elusive Lily. Tell me about her," Tiersa said, leaning against the table with her hands in a stately position.

"She's... wait, don't I get to ask something now?"

"Ah. Indeed. I got ahead of myself. Please." She waved.

"Alright." Sevi had rolled it around in his brain, struggling over which question to ask first, but there was really only one he could start with. "Who was I? Before?"

Tiersa smiled. "Prince Isevidel Astraeda. First Pureblood son to Queen Korina Astraeda and King Consort Marovhan Cassangia. Younger brother to Alramar Astraeda, of Found Blood, and older to little Nahlra Astraeda. May they all find peace in Tembra's Interregnum."

"What?" Sevi blinked dumbly at her list, moving too fast for him. "I—well, I want to know about my family, too. A lot. But I mean, who *was* I? What did I like? What was *I* like?"

"You were, and still are, Prince Isevidel," Tiersa said. "In the first few years of your life you came down with a sickness that wouldn't leave you. It broke everyone's heart to see. But you survived and grew into a healthy little boy. You loved running around after your big brother, no matter how much he teased you and Nahlra. You were curious like any little boy, pestered your parents like any little boy, got into trouble like any little boy, and picked on your sister like an older brother does. But you always loved her, and Alramar, too."

She got a far-off look. "I remember when Alramar stole a batch of jammed bread from the kitchen and stuffed it into your bed. You still said you were the one who did it. Alramar had probably gotten to you first, honestly."

Sevi's eyes got misty without warning. He reached up and scrubbed them with the back of his arm, forced to confront all the buried feelings that clearly weren't done with him, now rising with a vengeance. Tiersa was describing a *family*. The good parts. The bad parts. Everything. From the way she made it sound, he had been just like any other child. Weak, apparently, which was nothing new to him, but he had been *normal*, with a life full of people who loved him and a home that welcomed him. Everything he'd ever wanted.

How could that have changed? How could he have become this scarred, scared, manic boy, fearfully hiding for his life away in the dark?

"Isevidel?" Tiersa said.

"You go," he said, waving her off. He didn't trust himself to speak.

She gave him a pitying look and allowed him time to gather himself before continuing. "Tell me about your life here. How did you meet Lily? How did you manage for so long?"

Sevi let out a shaky breath. "Lily saved me... She came here the day after the attack. I think. She found me in the Cut, and she's looked after me ever since."

"She took care of you."

Sevi sighed. "Yeah."

"And where do you think she is now?"

Sevi's heart leapt into his throat. Tiersa stared at him expectantly. She had stopped tapping her finger. "I don't know," Sevi said, trying to look like he meant it.

A familiar touch of fear trailed itself down between his shoulder blades the same way it had whenever he'd tried lying to Lily. Tiersa had this aura about her that made it feel as if she could see right through him—as if she knew him just as intimately as Lily did. Perhaps she did. How much of his old self persisted through his amnesia?

"You must miss her," Tiersa said.

Sevi gulped. "Yes. A lot."

"Mm. Well, we'll find her." Tiersa leaned back in her chair. "I have to thank her for all she's done for you."

Sevi nodded, staying silent. The less he said, the better.

"And how did you both survive for so long? By staying in the tunnels? The Cut, as you call it?"

Again, Sevi nodded. "We rarely left, except to steal scraps from the kitchen. Lily had gathered a lot for us before the Fab... the Fae, had truly moved into the castle. There were fewer in the beginning, which made it easier to steal, but that changed pretty quickly. She was very strict about us keeping our heads down after that."

"Mm. Thank the gods for that," Tiersa said, closing her eyes. "I never would have thought those tunnels would ever prove to be anything other than a security hazard."

Hearing that, Sevi had a funny question pop into his head. "Why are they there?"

"The tunnels? Your grandmother, Queen Vicina, had some... irrational, ideas later in life, or so your mother and father told me. When this castle was being built under her and King Nevan, she demanded that an outer layer around the structure be built and filled with a combination of quicksilver and iron in order to repel the greenbloods if needed. This, however, was before we had realized what quicksilver could do to a person. When it became known, her madness had already begun to consume her, and the tunnels could not be dismantled without risking the integrity of the structure.

"So, they were completed, but never filled, and existed as an eternal thorn in my side during my tenure as Promina to your mother. The potential entry points for assassins and spies alone, to this day, continues to plague me. You and your siblings had found your way into them on more than one occasion, actually."

She had called Promina by a different name before. "Promina is a title, isn't it?"

"Indeed. Traditionally, the right-hand of the monarchy—their most trusted advisor. Your mother and father had me undergo training for years before taking the mantle myself. Rinenne, my Promina, joined us under unconventional circumstances. But she has a sharp mind and helps me to navigate more irritating roads. I'd trust her with my life." She smiled at him. "Maybe, Gods willing, I'll get to be yours one day."

Sevi nodded uncertainly, still unable to conceive that he could be in charge of a nation.

"I believe it's my turn." Tiersa leaned forward on her forearms and straightened her back. "And I'm afraid this one is rather important, so please do your best to remember any detail you can, understand?"

A bead of sweat dripped down the nape of Sevi's neck at her sudden change in demeanor. "Al-alright."

"In your time here, did you ever see the greenbloods doing anything strange? Particularly to the mountain?"

Frowning, Sevi closed his eyes and thought back. It was an odd question. The Fae hadn't ever done anything except perform drills and march around, until Redwood had come flying in with Digby on his airship. And as Lily had explained, they had done all that they could to avoid the mountain's deadly quicksilver. Except...

"A long time ago, there was a tunnel in the mountain from the gardens, but the Fae collapsed it a year or so after Lily found me." He opened his eyes. "Is that what everyone is digging for?"

Tiersa leaned forward again. Her knuckles had gone white. "Isevidel, listen to me carefully. Did they take anything out of there?"

"I... I don't know. I just remember the mountain shaking, and when we went to look for what had caused it, the tunnel was gone. Why? What's in there?"

Tiersa breathed out a long, steady sigh, and stared down at her hands. "It's not for you to worry about."

Sevi thought back upon one of the memories that Shy had shown him, of his parents walking into a tunnel and disappearing into the dark. "It's something to do with my parents. Isn't it?"

The commander's gaze flicked up and focused on him, as if from a great distance away. She started tapping her finger again. "Do you still have your necklace?"

Sevi raised his eyebrows, but nodded, tapping his chest where the pendant lay beneath his shirt.

"Good. May I hold onto it?"

Sevi tightened his fingers and firmly shook his head. Now that he knew that it came from his parents—parents that he'd just started to remember—he was even more resolved to never part from it. Tiersa nodded after a moment. "Then I want you to promise me one thing. Promise that you will never take it off, nor ever lose track of it. *Always* keep it with you. Protect it, as I will protect you. Can you do that for me?"

"Is it important?"

Commander Tiersa crossed her arms. "It might be."

Sevi didn't know what to make of that, but it wasn't like he was about to lose his necklace again anytime soon. "I will," he said. He took another breath. "May I ask one more thing? Could you tell me about my family?"

The kitchen door opened at the other end of the room, and a cook stepped in carrying two plates of food, drawing Sevi's attention. The smell was enticing as usual, but a flash of annoyance ran through him at the intrusion. *He couldn't have waited a little longer?*

When he turned his gaze back to Tiersa, he stopped. Her armor had regrown itself in the short span of time he'd looked away, but a deep sadness crept through in the way her shoulders slumped, as if something had been drained from her. She met his stare. "Your father and mother loved you," she said softly.

Sevi completely ignored the cook as he set their plates in front of them, focusing solely on the commander. She did the same to him and waved the cook away without so much as a glance. When he was gone, she continued.

"There's so much for me to say, Isevidel. But I'll start with this. King Marovhan would take every opportunity to be with you and your siblings. He loved doting on you all, especially his youngest. I remember how jealous you were when Nahlra came along. You would huff and try to demand more from the king—I think you thought you had been replaced. But of course, that wasn't the case. Your father loved you all equally, it was only that the youngest needed more help, having only just arrived in the world.

"Your mother. Korina..." She broke off, closing her eyes and dragging in a long, tired breath. "Your mother was beautiful. Noble. Full of conviction. I watched her sacrifice so much for the sake of you and the land she governed, including the time she could have spent being your mother. She even... I suppose you wouldn't remember this. Amnesia aside, you were too young, but she 'adopted' me into your family, and in so doing, saved me from a very harsh fate. I owed that woman my entire life." Her voice softened. "And I would've given it, too, had she only asked."

In a matter of moments, the great, tall, fierce woman he both barely remembered and knew intimately, whom he had feared within the first few breaths of seeing, had somehow shrunk two sizes in her chair before his very eyes. He moved his arm before he realized what he was doing.

Tiersa looked down at his outstretched hand in surprise, stilling her body the moment it came into view. She followed it up to meet his eyes. When he gazed into hers, he imagined taking her armor and breaking it apart to see what lay behind it, but what he found was nothing—a chasm, made from loss and loneliness. As though a skin of metal was all that was keeping her together.

It could have been his imagination—in fact, it most definitely was. But he knew what it felt to be incomplete better than anyone. If he were to give her a name, it would've been "Lady Night." But he didn't want to call her that. That was a lonely, awful name to have.

When she still hadn't taken his palm, he stretched out his fingers and insistently shook his hand, demanding it from her no matter how critically she stared. A glint returned to her eyes, and her sadness broke. She chuckled out a strained laugh. With a subtle shake of her head, she reached and finally took his hand in hers, squeezing it gently. "Thank you, little Sevi."

Sevi smiled, trying not to cry. She had given him too many emotions to feel all at once.

"Oh." She sighed, retracting her hand. "I wish they were here with us. I miss them deeply."

Sevi wiped his face. "What about... What about my brother and sister?"

Tiersa nodded. "Alramar was... he was a bit of a bully to you and Nahlra, honestly." She grimaced. "He was... complicated, shall we say? He came into the family a couple years older than you, having been adopted—much like me—and had already had a rough life for someone so young. He'd frequently get you all into trouble, or tease you a little too much, or... well. You understand. But I never believed that it was ever out of malice. Whenever anyone other than him picked on you, he made sure to let his displeasure be known." She chuckled. "He had a hard time showing his affection, but everyone knew where his heart was."

Sevi sniffed, feeling his eyes mist over again. "And my sister?"

"Nahlra... Nahlra was so young. She was still learning of the world, chasing after you and Alramar wherever you went, full of joy and wonder. She especially loved the gardens, and all its flowers and bugs. When I held her in my arms, it was like I was seeing the world afresh through her, in all its discovery."

Sevi sat back in his chair and stared down at his plate. What she said aligned with what he had seen in his visions, and he found himself grasping for what faded feelings he remembered as hard as he could. "I wish I could remember more."

"You will, Isevidel. Haven't some of your memories already returned? That's very encouraging, if you were to ask me. I have no doubt that the rest will come in time. Although, may I ask you for one more favor?"

"Sure."

"Please don't mention your amnesia to anyone else," Tiersa said seriously. "It will throw into question whether or not you are the true heir to the Elkran throne, and we must move carefully going forward."

"Why?"

"There are forces at work in Elkra other than the greenbloods who would use such knowledge to harm you. My oath to defend the Astraeda line from all who would seek to harm it, once made to your mother, now lives through you. And upon my word, I will not squander this second chance I've been given."

Staring meaningfully at him for several breaths, she broke the tension by picking up her fork and laying a napkin across her lap. "Now. Why don't we eat? I'm sure it's gotten cold, but I believe it will do us both some good."

They didn't say a word, leaving the silence to be filled by the clanking of silverware and gnashing of food instead. But when it was time to leave, and she wrapped her long arms around him in a hug, he hugged her back.

# Chapter 37

*The moon fell away and the morning returned, a fire in the sky and beneath. One to shine on a land bereft of its warmth, one as a grave marker's wreath.*

---◈---

The door to the royal chambers closed quietly behind Sevi as he stepped into the bedroom—the big, spacious bedroom for people bigger than him. And when Commander Tiersa had removed what belongings she had, it had gotten even bigger, until his footsteps echoed when he walked. It hadn't become any more comfortable in the few days since he'd moved in, either. On his second night he had taken the cover and pillow off the bed and used them to sleep on the floor—it was just too soft.

He slumped wearily onto the couch in front of the royal study, staring at the half-burnt logs in the hearth's grate. It was getting colder, and the stone castle did little to keep its warmth without a fire in every room. He eyed the flint starter next to the wood reserve and uselessly waved his hand like a Fabling, as if he could make them light on their own.

Then his gaze drifted, as it always did, to the dark threshold at the back of the fireplace. He still hadn't gone in. Tiersa had pulled out the dead body of his father from its mouth. What other frightening things could be in there, waiting to turn his world upside-down for a third time?

But his parents had used that study. It had been theirs.

He swung his legs back to the floor. Closing the distance, he stopped at the fireplace and took a deep breath before walking in, allowing the darkness to swallow him up completely.

None of the light from the bedroom had crossed with him, and the strange light Tiersa had summoned didn't appear. Maybe it was her height? Sevi tried jumping up and down. When that didn't work, he waved his hand about in the way Tiersa had.

Light snapped into existence immediately. Sevi threw his arm up to shield his eyes. It emanated from a large, glass orb set into the ceiling as big as his head, filled with a swirling vortex of silver, smoky, shifting particles that churned in its glossy depths. When his eyes adjusted, he dropped his arm and took another step forward, turning his head from side to side, studying the small room in detail.

Bookcases lined the left and right walls. The shelves to the left took up the entire length, running all the way to the end, and ending at an expansive window. A large writing desk had been turned over and smashed, and lay in an orderly pile, waiting for someone to gather it. Gouges haphazardly crisscrossed the floorboards as though a great battle had once taken place there, accentuated with burn marks that Tiersa's cleaners had been unable to remove. Some of the bookcases nearest the desk were in just as much disrepair, with their shelves having broken and all their books lying at their bases. Sevi could detect the distinct smell of soap still lingering in the air, as though the whole room had been given a bath.

The cases to the right went halfway into the room before stopping a distance away from yet another sofa and fireplace, before continuing on again to the far wall. A large, dusty painting, many handspans wide and high, hung above the mantle. On it was the king from his visions—his father. He was draped in deep blue finery and stared pensively at Sevi with a pair of hazel eyes. A long, dark, well-groomed beard sprouted from his chin and crawled up his cheeks to merge into an equally magnificent mane of hair, wreathed by a golden crown. And to his left stood the faceless woman, having found her face.

She had the same shimmering blond hair, the same well-cut, subdued dress, and the same jewelry, but a sharp nose and a pair of sapphire eyes and ruby lips had grown out of her featureless face. Austere and knowing, her mouth was turned down, a breath away from being a full frown. He froze in place as some part of him instinctively said to look away or hide, unwilling to risk her ire.

*My mother.* She had been his mother, all this time. He clutched at his shirt, fully expecting her to step out of her painting just as she had stepped out of his dreams. "Why didn't you show all of her to me, Shy?" Sevi whispered. "She wasn't trying to hurt me, was she? She was trying to show me myself, just like you've been." But his shadow hadn't formed since the night they had pulled him into the mirror world, and they stayed at his feet, giving no response.

Queen Korina's arm traveled down the painting to rest upon the shoulder of a young boy, wearing finery that matched the king and queen's, with brown-blond hair and hazel eyes like his. But the artist had painted him with a faint scowl, as though he was preparing to kick something over.

*That's Alramar, isn't it?*

Two blank white spaces marked the canvas to the left and right of Sevi's older brother, forming the empty silhouettes of two smaller children. The artist had ostensibly never gotten the chance to fill them in. The smallest sat at the feet of King Marovhan, while the taller one stood next to Alramar.

*My place,* Sevi thought. He approached the painting, reaching one hand up and tentatively placing his fingers against the space where he was meant to be. The space his body should have filled. The space he always should have known. "Why couldn't I remember everything?" he mumbled, gazing at his family. "I think I loved you. I saw it. I *felt* it. And I think you loved me, too. So why? Why couldn't you show me everything, Shy?" His heart grew heavy again. "I'd rather know nothing than only these pieces."

A sharp whistle jarred him out of his reverie. "Yoo hoo," came Lily's voice from outside the study. "Does this castle have any silly princes around, or is this room just for show?"

Sevi tightened his fist across his chest. He spared one last look at the painting, then turned angrily on his heel and marched toward the study's entrance, adopting his best impression of Tiersa as he waved his hand in the air and shut off the light. Lily lounged on the sofa in her careless, unbothered way, finding comfort wherever she sat. The visor of her helm had slipped over her eyes, making it look like she was dozing.

"For someone who loves telling me to be quiet all the time, you really have no problem shouting when it suits you," Sevi said. "How long have you been here?"

"When you do it, it's wrong. When I do it, it's right. I thought you knew that by now," Lily muttered. She tipped the visor back up her head, looking lazily out at him from beneath its shadow. "How was the funeral?"

Sevi walked past her, heading for one of the room's small tables where someone had considerately laid out a pitcher of water for him. "It was fine," he said, pouring a glass for himself. "Where's Alyda?"

"She hasn't been feeling well. I let her rest. Pour me one, too, while you're over there."

He rolled his eyes and poured another cup, carrying both with him to the couch. He sat at the edge farthest away from her and handed her glass without looking over.

"Thanks," she said brightly, sitting up and taking it from him. She took a long gulp from it, not stopping until the whole glass was drained. "Much better than waiting for hours to steal from the kitchen pail. I can't wait to get out of here and have our own little cave again."

"Mm," Sevi mumbled, staring at the glass in his hands.

Lily gently kicked his side. "Why so down?"

"I was just at my father's funeral, Lily," Sevi said, equal parts offended and incredulous.

Lily shrugged. "You didn't know him."

Sevi glared at her. "I would've liked to. I would've liked to know them *all*."

Lily let out a slow breath of air through her nose. "I thought we'd made up on this."

"We have... but I'm still angry." Sevi leaned back against the sofa, finally taking a drink. "All this time, and the answers were right here."

There was a lull. Lily carefully said, "There's answers out there, too, Sev. Not just in this castle."

Sevi shook his head. "Are there, Lily? Nobody knows about what happened that night better than the people here now."

"What are you suggesting?" Lily leaned forward on her knees, staring at him in disbelief. "Are you saying you want to *stay?*"

"Lily—"

"With the people who are going to *use* you?"

Sevi paused as Tiersa's heated conversation with Promina in the hallway came rushing back. They had been scheming about something that involved him, and Tiersa had purposely neglected to mention it during their conversation.

At his silence, Lily shifted next to him, moving her face near to his. "Listen. We are so *close* to getting out of here." She held up her index finger and thumb. "*This* close. Alyda and I have kept an eye on the supply trains, and we think we have it all figured out. We can get out of here as soon as *tomorrow*." She grabbed his hand, holding it tightly in hers. "But I don't want to do this without you."

His head couldn't swivel to face her faster. *Did she really just say that?*

She stared meaningfully at him. Her mask had broken, and the face she now wore seemed to signal some deeper, unspoken plea. He reeled under the intensity of her gaze, unused to this newfound raw emotion after years of her sarcasm and irony. "You can't know for certain that anything you said is going to happen, Lily."

"How often am I wrong?" she said archly. "Corporal Asshole tried to cheat you out of your necklace, and that was before you were a prince. Now that you are, people will be coming to you for knighthoods. Land. Power. Things you don't know the slightest bit about. Do you really think you'll be able to handle that?"

No, he didn't think he could. He slumped his shoulders and stared back down at his cup, peering at his faint reflection in its contents. To go off on an adventure with his best friend now that the Fablings were being driven out of Elkra? To live a story like the ones Lily had filled his head with, with Alyda on his shoulder and Shy at his feet? Maybe it wouldn't be so bad.

"I need you, Sevi," Lily said softly. "I don't want to go back out there alone. Not again."

A lump formed in his throat. He squeezed her hand. "I'm with you, Lily," he said softly. "Now and forever."

Lily sniffed. "Good." She reached into her pocket and drew something out. "Then you can have this back. You might need it. And don't throw it again. I'm not going to carve another one." She placed her signal whistle in his palm. He ran his thumb along its side, nodding, and put it away.

"Anyway," she continued. "I've always wanted to try a water closet, so I'm going to use yours. Then let's talk more about getting the dusk out of here."

She patted his arm and got up from the sofa, walking toward the little door in the stone that held the chamber pot. Sevi watched her go with a faint look of distaste and raised his glass to drain what remained of his water. When the door closed, he stood and walked to refill, but stopped halfway, looking at the mirror across the room. Then he looked down at his feet, where the faint outline of Shy clung to his soles.

The shadow had lost much of its dark after showing him his memories, but it hadn't run away. How many mirrors were there outside of the castle, though? He might not get this chance again soon. Sevi abandoned his glass by the pitcher and walked to the chair in front of the mirror. Sitting down, he stared hard at the polished glass, meeting his reflection with his chin up. "Shy? are you there?"

The reflection acted as all reflections did: by copying him, and nothing else. Nor did Shy rise from the ground.

"Shy," he tried again. "I'm... I'm leaving the castle. I don't know when I'll see another mirror again. Please... Can you show me something? Anything?" He reached out and touched the glass, sliding his fingers across its face. It didn't give. "Did it hurt when you showed me? Is that why you've gone quiet? Why are you so content to sleep at my feet now?"

He tried again, and again, calling out a little more desperately each time, each to no effect. Dejected, Sevi stood back up and turned for the sofa, only to stop.

He was no longer alone.

"What's that one?" his younger self asked an older lady, wrapped in a shawl. He was swathed in a blanket and was far younger than most of the other memories Shy had shown him. About as young as he had been in the carriage ride vision, back when his features were as nondescript as most children that age.

"That one's Regielo, The Scholar. See his long beard, there?" the old woman said, pointing out through the window into the light of day.

Sevi recognized this scene. It had shown itself just before his memories had all come crashing down around him. The old lady—whoever she was—and his younger self sat on the floorboards just as easily as sitting on a grassy mound, taking turns to stare up at the sky through their giant spyglass. As he watched, and the memory drifted from the fringes of his mind bit by bit, he realized that they were playing his favorite game. They were naming things.

*No. Not names. She's telling me their stories.*

"How did he get up there," he quoted along with his younger self, remembering the words as the vision said them.

"Well. He was so focused on wanting to know everything there is to know, that he learned how to build a rope out of moonbeams, so he could climb up, up, up into the sky and see what was there," the lady said.

"Why did he do that?"

"Well, you can't hear the stars or the moon from down here, can you? They're too far away."

"Oh..." Young Sevi said. It had made perfect sense at the time. "Did he see everything?"

"Oh, yes. You can see all there is to see from up there."

"Then why is he still there?"

The old woman smiled sagely. "Ah, well, you see, little one, that's the one thing he's been unable to learn." She sweetly wrapped her arms around him and hugged him gently, lending his small body her warmth against the night's chill. "Moonbeams disappear in the daytime after all, so when the sun rose, his rope vanished in his hands. He figured out how to go up, but the poor man was so eager to see the heavens that he forgot to learn how to come back down!"

Young Sevi looked up at the lady with wide eyes. "He's stuck up there?"

"Ooh, I'm afraid so!"

"Why doesn't he make a new rope?"

"He's afraid he won't make it down before the sun comes up," she explained. "You see, it took half of an entire night to weave the rope, and the other half to climb it. And every night, the sky gets a little bit further away. By the time he had spoken to all the stars and eaten sweets with the moon, the sky was twice as far from the ground! So, he has to take even more time each night to make his rope. But every time he does, he gets a little better."

She squeezed him again. "And it's said that once he gets it just right, he'll come down from the sky and share all that he's learned with us."

They sat in silence, each staring up at the constellation seen only by them. Sevi had never known a silence like this, wrapped up protectively by someone he loved, feeling as if the world and all its troubles could never touch him so long as she was there. Then his younger self pointed again to a pair of lights a distance away from the rest, seen clearly by his present self in the flashes of his memory. Lights that would be picked out years later on a cliffside by his best friend. "What are those?" Younger-him asked.

"Those are the Dancers," the old lady said. "A long time ago, when the moon was three, she and her siblings would hold these magnificent parties for all the world to see. There were so many stars gathered in one place that everyone here in Ilondia all swore it was daytime! And in that tangled mess of movement and life, somehow, those two found each other."

"Were they looking for each other?"

"No one knows. Some say they're Iviri and her husband Auros themselves, who made their way through all the roads of the Waylands only to be given new life by the Sun Father himself, together again as stars in the sky after thousands of years apart. Some say that they were stars born from opposite ends of the world, always blinded and separated by the rise of the sun, yet always destined to find each other no matter how many times it rises. And still some say that they are merely two partners right for each other, found by coincidence, and remaining with each other through the light they forged together."

Young Sevi huffed. "Which one is it?"

The woman shrugged. "I don't know. Which would you like it to be?"

Instead of answering the question, Young Sevi frowned and asked another. "Why do they dance?"

The woman chuckled and fondly tussled his hair. "So many questions." Young Sevi grumbled and shielded his head with his arms. She tutted. "They can't help themselves."

"How come?"

"It all started the moment their eyes met. Spellbound, they each gripped the other and started to dance, laughing with such happiness that it made all the thousands of stars in the sky weep for joy. But they swung each other so fast that they just couldn't stop! And yet, even if they could, they wouldn't. The very thought of letting go of the other was too much for either one to bear, even for a moment. So, they drew in close and continued their dance, long after the music of that heavenly affair had faded, each catching the other whenever they strayed too far or fell. And there they remain in the sky to this day, unable to part and unwilling to try."

She squeezed him tightly and got up from the ground, taking him with her. "Just like this." She suddenly swung him around and around, making him squeal with delight as the world spun by in a rush of streaking colors. He laughed and laughed, and when she tired, they both collapsed back onto the ground in a fit of giggles, each holding onto the other. She poked him in the sides, making him squeal even louder. "Stop! Stop it, Mimi!"

"Alright, alright, you're the little boss." She smiled, tussling his hair again.

"Oooh," he moaned, holding onto his head. "They must be really dizzy."

"Indeed they are," Mimi said. "But they're dizzy together, and that makes it easier."

"This doesn't feel easy," Young-Sevi said, making the old lady chuckle. He looked back up at the sky once the world stopped spinning. "Do they have names, too?"

"Hm. You know, I can't remember. How about we give them some?" Mimi leaned down and pointed to the star on the left. "What should we call that one?"

"Ah, that felt nice!" Lily exclaimed, opening the water closet door and wiping her wet hands on her clothes. "I still can't believe you have one right in your room, with a washbowl and everything! I'm going to use this until—" She stopped, staring at him. "Are you alright?"

Sevi hid his face with his hand. No. He wasn't.

# Chapter 38

*How is it to wander, no sense of oneself? To know that you're there, but
you're not? The more that the mouse had to learn of himself, the more of
himself that he sought.*

The next morning, after Sevi had regathered his resolve and finished
his planning with Lily, he stepped into the hallway outside the
royal chambers, seeking someone who could point him to Lieutenant
Digby. Instead, to his surprise, someone found him. Two someones.

"Good afternoon, Your Brilliance."

"Hey, kid!"

Cassik and Loma said it at the same, and in vastly different tones.
Where Cassik bowed, Loma moved forward and clapped him on the
back. Cassik scowled. "Loma! He's our king!"

"Says who?" Loma scoffed.

"Says Commander Grommand!"

"Well, I don't see a crown on his head. He looks like the kid from the
infirmary to me."

Cassik glared at her, and she pretended to ignore him, giving Sevi
a friendly nudge with her elbow. They were both wearing their dress
uniforms and carrying their rifles. The hallway was otherwise empty.
"Um... hi Loma. Hi Cassik," Sevi said lamely, looking between them.
"What are you two doing here?"

"Your personal guard, reporting for duty, sir!" Loma said, snapping a
lazy salute to her shoulder

"Personal guard? Why do I need—" He stopped. Of *course.*

"Lady Tiersa felt that you should not have free roam around the castle from this point on," Cassik said formally. "For your safety."

"And since we got so close in the infirmary, Captain River thought we'd be the perfect fit for you!" Loma said cheerfully. "Suits me just fine. Why march around in the cold when I could stand here for hours where it's warm?"

Sevi groaned inwardly. "Great," he mumbled. Just *great*.

"Mm-hm. Been settling in alright?" Loma asked. "Which is a silly question, because your bed must be twice as big as mine."

"We saw you at your father's funeral," Cassik added. "Though it is late to say it, I am sorry for your loss, Your Brilliance. King Marovhan and Queen Korina were great leaders, and they will be remembered with pride."

"Thank you." Sevi kept his face neutral, as though he hadn't just learned of his family's demise himself.

"Your Brilliance, if I may," Cassik continued. "Please accept my apology for my behavior in the infirmary, I had no idea you were one of the lost princes. If I had known, I wouldn't have been so informal."

Sevi shuffled his feet. "Um... that's alright. I didn't know—" He broke off. *I didn't know myself,* he almost said, remembering Tiersa's warning at the last moment. He said instead, "I didn't know if I could trust you all yet." Which was also true.

"I understand entirely, sir."

"*Anyway,*" Loma butted in. "What can we do for you today, little princeling? Hungry for breakfast?"

"I'm sure we can have someone bring something up for you," Cassik offered.

"No, I'm fine. I was actually going to go looking for Digby," Sevi said.

Cassik smiled. "Lieutenant Asgaillin? I can bring him to you."

Sevi stared at the man, taken aback by his eagerness. Loma joined him. "Mother save us, Cassik. What the dusk has crawled up your—"

"*Loma,*" Cassik warned.

"Foot," Loma grumbled, grimacing. But she'd voiced what Sevi was thinking. Cassik's change in demeanor was a stark reminder of how everyone now expected him to be in charge. He suddenly felt the cold stare of hundreds of phantom eyes on him, watching from the walls, as though all the attendees from his father's funeral had moved into the Cut and were now silently judging how much of a prince he actually was.

"This is my first promotion," Cassik said proudly, standing straight and puffing out his chest. "And he's our prince, back from the dead! Commander Tiersa and Captain River have both trusted us with the life of His Brilliance, and it would be a great stain upon my honor if I didn't give him the respect he deserves. So, *I'm* not going to squander that trust, even if *you* seem *perfectly* comfortable doing so."

"Yeah yeah, alright, might want to loosen up there, mister, I think you're turning to *stone* again." Loma smirked.

Cassik shook his head. "You don't deserve to be Astral Guard with that attitude."

Loma thought for a moment. "You're right. On second thought, the cold doesn't sound so bad compared to being stuck here with your bootlicking. No one deserves this kind of living Torment."

Cassik leveled a hard glare at her and opened his mouth to respond but was interrupted when Sevi broke out into a loud laugh. He clapped his hand over his mouth and turned away. Here he was, fretting over Cassik's formality, yet Cassik and Loma had started bickering in front of him not a moment after the worry had gone through his head. And to his relief, when he turned back, they both smiled along with him. It was like they were back in the clinic again.

*Gods. Why do those moments feel so distant, now?* Sevi thought.

Loma chuckled. "Alright, princeling. What do you want? Want us to fetch the lieutenant?"

Sevi looked down the hall. "No... I think I'd like to go for a walk."

Loma snapped her ankles together and straightened, as did Cassik, though he was more serious about it. She grinned. "After you, *sir.*"

They found Digby at the airship overseeing its repairs—the ship itself was looking more and more like the brilliant creature of Sevi's memory by the day. The holes in its hull had been patched up and sealed, and there were increasingly more soldiers on its deck, running through whatever checklists and repairs they had left. The one thing that was noticeably still missing was its balloon. Sevi wondered just how they'd fix it—hadn't it kept the whole thing in the air? How were they supposed to replace *that* of all things?

When Sevi approached and voiced his request to the lieutenant, Digby's reaction was not encouraging. "Ya want ta say that again?" Digby frowned.

Sevi shuffled. "I... I want to go into town."

The old soldier set down the bags he carried and lifted his little finger to his ear, working it around inside. "I must have cotton in me ears."

Sevi stepped back as airship workmen went by, all carrying tools and materials of one kind or another. "What do you mean?"

"Lad—er, Yer Majesty?"

"Don't call me that," Sevi said impulsively. It still sounded weird, even if it was true, but it sounded especially weird coming from Digby.

"Lad, if ya had asked me before all the fanfare the last couple o' days, I may have taken ya in with me. You were underground fer years, and it shows. Bein' around folk will do ya some good. But yer an Astraeda. The *last* Astraeda. Lady Tiersa would have me whipped bloody if she learned that I took ya out unguarded."

"But I'm not unguarded," Sevi said, pointing to where Loma and Cassik stood a short ways off. "And how many people outside of this castle know me?"

"More, after yesterday," Digby said, looking at Sevi's new guards. "An' if there are any soldiers in town on leave—which there are—then they'll point ya out. Sorry, lad, I won't do it. 'Sides, me leg is still in rough shape after the little accident with the door."

"But well enough for you to help fix an airship," Sevi mumbled.

"Eh?"

"Nothing." Sevi sighed. Digby had been his first choice, and he really didn't want to speak with his second choice if he could avoid him. But it seemed like there were no other options. "What if someone else comes along? Someone that Commander Tiersa approves of?"

"Like who?"

"I think this is a wonderful idea, Your Brilliance Isevidel Astraeda," Captain River said with a smile. "See? You have more than one name now! Your introductions will only get better from here!"

Sevi bit his tongue. This was the first time he'd seen the captain after he had formally presented Sevi to Tiersa. After all his games sussing out who Sevi was without ever mentioning a word to him, Sevi found that he was in no mood to humor Captain River's airiness. And in a few more hours, it was possible that he'd never have to deal with him ever again.

"You do?" Digby said incredulously, having followed Sevi.

"Of course! We can bring a few extra men if we need to. Maybe even an Empyrean. Our *risho* has spent too long inside these walls, and if he is to grow into a king, he must see his kingdom, yes?"

"Sir. I don' think it's a good idea," Digby said. "There's jus' not enough of us to secure the town fer 'im properly, what with much of our forces still engaged or en route. An' Lady Tiersa won't like divertin' our work at the castle fer a daytrip—not to mention how quickly word will spread after all the commotion she stirred up with that speech o' hers."

"And yet, what if this is his only opportunity to experience the city without any attention at all?" Captain River said. "His face is not yet widely known but that will change by the day. And Ilondia is secure enough—there has not been sighting of a Fae in weeks. If we dress him like a stable hand and surround him with a modest number of soldiers, perhaps in one of our supply trains, he will most likely be fine. We do not require an excuse to protect our stores, and consequently, Sevi."

"Most likely?" Digby grimaced.

"Would you like to join us?" Captain River asked. "If at any moment something causes you to fear for the boy's safety, tell me, and we will return to the castle immediately."

Digby looked at Sevi with worry. "This isn't a good idea, lad. Are ya certain you want to do this?"

Sevi forced a smile. "Of course."

"Of course," Captain River said, beaming. "A good break from the excitement. Something we can all use. This will be lovely!"

The spotted gray horse once again tossed its head and let out a braying whinny, stamping its feet impatiently. Its partner, a chestnut brown, tried to move away but was quickly calmed by Digby. An answering call came from a far distance, and the gray's ears swiveled toward the sound. Whoever the stranger horse was, the cloudy one was clearly eager to get out of its harness to go to them.

Its unease was infectious, and Sevi didn't need the help. He shuffled from foot to foot, trying to slow his breath, and backed away from the mare, nearly tripping over his loaner pants. He cursed under his breath. Was there nobody in this whole blazing army in his size?

A hand settled on his shoulder, steadying him. From behind, Captain River looked on with uncharacteristic worry, wearing a sword at his hip and a pistol in his belt. "I share your fear," he said. "I do not like these creatures either."

Sevi shrugged River's hand off. It wasn't that he didn't like horses. He just didn't like being this *close* to one. They were beautiful creatures, but they were better observed from far away.

He turned his gaze up to the airship looming over them. With this part of the wall having crumbled, the army had turned the area into a checkpoint. It was much easier to check a train of wagons at an open hole than it was to bother with opening and closing the gates, especially given the frequency of the trains, according to Lily.

"Do not worry. She will fly again. Soon," Captain River said, catching his gaze and smiling.

"I don't care," Sevi grumbled. "So can I go?"

Captain River blinked. "Commander Tiersa has agreed to let you into town—"

"Great, then let's—"

"—if I am with you at all times."

Sevi froze. "*Great*," he forced out.

"Yes. So, we will face the beasts together," Captain River said, smiling again.

Sevi glared down at his shoes and turned away, marching rigidly up to the cart without another word. Digby sat on the passenger-side, while Cassik and Loma sat in the back with a cluster of empty barrels and boxes, having eschewed their dress uniforms for simpler garb. Altogether, a train of ten wagons would be going into town. Sevi studied the assortment of containers, trying to pick out any that were Lily-sized as he hoisted himself up into the back with the others.

Cassik offered him his hand and helped him the rest of the way. "There you are, Your Luminance."

"Don't call him that, Cassik. He's a stable boy, remember?" Loma chided.

"Oh. Good point," Cassik said, directing a surprised look at Loma. "What should we call him then?"

"Same thing we called him in the infirmary. His *name*."

"Won't everyone know who I am then?" Sevi interjected.

Loma shook her head. "Not likely."

"There were a lot of babies named in honor of the royal family after the attack," Cassik said. "There's plenty of young Isevidels and Alramars and Korinas running around now. But it *would* be odd to call someone so old by that name."

"Well, then it's a good thing Sevi is so much easier to say than Isevidel," Loma said. "Sevi could stand for any number of things. He could be... uh... Seviron. Sevipo? Sevimoor!"

Cassik laughed. "Those sound incredibly bad."

"Oh yeah? What's your grand contribution then?"

"Sevinim."

Loma grimaced. Cassik smirked. She rolled her eyes. "*Fine,* damn you. That's pretty good."

Sevi couldn't get into their banter, too busy stewing over his escape plan. He tried his best to look relaxed, but he just couldn't remove his hand from his chest, nervously gripping at his necklace through his shirt. He flicked his gaze along the train from cart to cart, from barrel to barrel, from person to person. Did they know? Had Lily successfully stowed away? Or had she been found?

*Don't be silly,* Lily's phantom voice whispered. *If I had been found, you'd be the first to hear about it.*

*Go away,* he silently demanded. *The real Lily is alive. I don't need you anymore.*

The mighty, uproarious yell of dozens of people abruptly swept over the supply train, making Sevi jump in his seat and whip his head around, fully expecting to see soldiers pulling his friend out of one of the wagons.

"What's going on?" Digby yelled as soldiers abandoned their carts. He turned up to the airship. "OI, UP THERE! ARE WE UNDER ATTACK?"

"NO, SIR!" A worker atop the airship called down. "IT'S THE MINERS, SIR! THEY'VE DONE IT!"

"EH?" Digby exclaimed. But the worker disappeared atop the ship, running off to join everyone else. "Damn this," he grumbled. He slid himself awkwardly off the driver seat, taking his cane with him. "We're on a schedule, and we are goin' ta *keep* that schedule if I have ta club every last one o' them. *You all stay put!*" He swept his glare imperiously over the remaining soldiers, cowing them back to their posts, and hobbled off to mete out his wrath to those who had dared leave.

"Great, a delay," Loma said with a smile on her face. She slumped back and crossed her arms, setting her rifle to the side. Cassik shook his head disapprovingly at her.

Sevi's eyes trailed down Cassik's body to his feet. "Um... how's your leg?"

"Oh. It's alright," Cassik said, stretching the limb out and shaking his foot. "It's a little stiff sometimes. The doctors say it might act up when I march, or if I stand for too long. But I guess I'm just happy it can still move."

"My arm's all healed up, too, thanks for asking," Loma mumbled. "A bit of a scar though."

"You shouldn't have picked at it," Cassik said. Loma deflected him with a shrug. "And you, Your Majesty? Has everything healed by now?"

Sevi shrugged, laying one hand on his chest. "I'm alright... though I still feel the bullet sometimes."

Cassik grimaced. "I'm sorry."

Sevi shook his head. "You weren't the one who shot me." He turned to stare off across the courtyard, studying every face that passed, as though the man who had would walk by at the mere mention of him. Only when he looked back did he realize that the cart had settled into an uncomfortable silence. Cassik cleared his throat, averting his gaze to something other than Sevi.

*Maybe I shouldn't have said anything.*

Loma sighed loudly, breaking the tension. "Good riddance to him at least."

"What?" Sevi said.

"Solen. The man who shot you."

Sevi stared at her, wide-eyed. "Did you...?"

"What? No, we didn't kill him." Loma frowned, cracking an eye open at him. "When word got to Lieutenant Digby that one of his guardian children had been shot by our own, he sent a request to the captains to put the man on latrine duty permanently. Then to top it off, Lady Grommand came out yesterday, huffing and puffing about how that same kid is our long-lost prince? HA!" She chuckled. "He ran away the second the funeral was over. Can't say I blame him; I would've done the same."

Casski nodded at Sevi. "If he's smart, Your Brilliance, you'll never see him again."

Sevi closed his arms around his legs and held them tightly to his chest. Solen had appeared dozens of times in his nightmares, always with his rifle pointed at Sevi's chest, always forcing him to wake up the moment he went plunging over the cliff. He had feared for months that he'd see him again when he stepped outside like this, surrounded by people, all with rifles and the same charcoal uniforms. But he hadn't. And now he might never, just like that.

A wave of relief washed over him. Laughter bubbled up from deep in his belly, and a tension in his shoulders that he'd been carrying for months disappeared as easily as smoke wisping into the sky. He was gone. He was *gone!*

*But what if he's in town?* Sevi stopped laughing. Cassik and Loma stared at him. "What?" he asked. Both soldiers shook their heads and looked away, but not before sharing a knowing look with each other.

Eventually, Digby herded the straggling soldiers back to the carts, waving his cane about in a threatening manner. When all had rejoined, and the luggage had been properly stowed, he called out to Captain River, "All ready, sir!"

"Very good!" Captain River called back. "We are waiting for three more to join, then we will get underway."

It wasn't long after he'd made the proclamation that the three in question showed themselves. "Thanks for waiting, Caldwin," Captain Lorr said, walking up with Innavin Targa and River's aide, Tahno. He greeted his husband with a kiss on the cheek. Like River, he also had an officer's pistol and a sword strapped to his hip. Innavin and Tahno looked unarmed.

Captain River returned the kiss. "You're late."

"Had to make sure that Rya was prepared to take over without me," Lorr said. "This was pretty sudden, Cal. And the requested funds for something as frivolous as this? We're going to have to shift our budget around. I can understand why the commander would approve it, but—"

"It will be fine, Lorr. It is not such an expensive thing, is it?" River said.

"Are you kidding me? We're pinching every coppen that we can. The nobles have started pulling their funds now that we've taken Ilondia to shore up their own houses. They consider the war all but won."

"We will make due. We always have." River patted Lorr's arm.

"We also stopped to get our bags," Innavin said, holding up two canvas knapsacks. "It's been a while since we got some proper-"

"Not in present company, please," Captain River said, cutting him off.

Lorr and Innavin paused, then swiveled their heads to Sevi's cart, catching sight of him. Lorr broke into a smile. "Sevi!" He approached the side of the wagon. "How are you holding up, little guy? Haven't seen you since... well, yesterday, I suppose."

"Fine, I guess," Sevi said.

"Idiot, you forgot to say, 'Your Brilliance,'" Innavin chastised, walking around to place the bags in the back. "Not just any mere child anymore, but a shining star set to rise! Would you please lend me your hand, Your Brilliance?" Innavin asked Sevi, holding his hand out to him.

Sevi took it uncertainly in both of his and pulled back with all the weight his slight figure could provide, but it was enough. Innavin slumped into the cart next to him, immediately throwing his arms out over the wagon's rim, closing his eyes, and lackadaisically leaning his head back to the sky. He still wore his decorative black clothing, in stark contrast to his blond hair. "Ah, a fine day for a trip into town. One of the last before the cold sets in no doubt," Innavin breathed. "I haven't been able to visit Ilondia since before the war. An opportunity like this is most welcome. Do you suppose there will be time for the theater?"

"Move over, Vin, it looks cramped enough," Captain Lorr said. Innavin pulled his legs in, and Lorr hoisted himself in with everyone, moving to sit next to Cassik, opposite Sevi. Cassik and Loma visibly stiffened at his presence, straightening their postures. "If you go to the theater, you'll be going alone. We're not on leave."

"That suits me just fine. There is no greater intimacy in the world than that of two lovers, years apart, meeting again under a bright sky and cool breeze. And I have been gone from the Golden Spool for so very long."

"Just don't make love to the stage."

Sevi turned his head back to Captain River and found him talking with Tahno. Getting a closer look at the latter, Sevi noticed that he had to be a little older than he himself and stood a head taller. His left forearm, however, extended halfway past the elbow before vanishing, and his sleeve had been rolled up in order to keep it from dangling. He didn't move to join them in the cart and spent some time speaking to the captain in a language Sevi had only heard from River.

"Three glara says that Tahno joins us this time," Innavin said softly without opening his eyes.

Lorr snorted. "I'll take that bet."

Captain River stepped to the side and gestured to the wagons, looking expectantly at his aide. Tahno, however, shifted on his feet with a frown, then shook his head, taking a step back from the captain and sweeping his hand out from his chest in the same parting gesture that River had given Sevi at the officers' party. Captain River's shoulders drooped, and he gave Tahno the same sign before the younger man turned and walked away.

"You're out three glara," Lorr said.

Innavin hummed mournfully. "That's a pity."

"Why didn't he just order him to come?" Sevi asked. "Doesn't he work for River?"

"It's not necessary that he join us," Lorr said. "Caldwin had hoped that he'd want to come himself."

"Why's that?"

"It's complicated. And, as my husband would say, not my story to tell."

River slid next to Digby at the front of the wagon with a dissatisfied air. Turning, he shouted, "All ready!"

Nine answering voices called back from down the line, and with a nod, Digby cracked the reins and urged the horses forward. The wagon lurched, and one by one, the carts rolled out. Soldiers waved at them as they passed, and for the first time in Sevi's meager memory, he left the castle grounds.

Sevi turned to stare back at the place he'd called his home, perhaps for the last time ever as it all slowly pulled away. Its tall, pointed towers gave no words of parting nor wishes of luck, too steadfast in their duty to pay attention to someone like him. A knot formed in his stomach, one he tried untangling by repeating Lily's words of encouragement in his mind again and again, but it only tightened.

"Hey. I just realized something. Now I can continue my story of how I met my wife!" Innavin said to Sevi, breaking into a smile.

Lorr groaned. But as Innavin launched into his tale, something caught Sevi's attention: a noise from the far end of the line. The popping of firesnaps, and of soldiers crying out in confusion.

# Chapter 39

*"It's not safe," said the flower, "keep your feet on the ground, let us run through this stony abode! We have each other to hold and this world we can tread. Why try a celestial road?"*

⸺⊰∾⊱⸺

The further the carts pulled away from the castle, the more frequently Sevi looked back. His bastion of safety, with its grim prison tower and all its guardian sentinel spires, his only shelter from the world, and all that he'd ever known. As the supply train curled lazily around the mountain wall, it wasn't long before all he could see were the highest tips of its rooftops poking up from behind the cliff. Then eventually those were swallowed up as well.

Sevi slumped back against the cart's rough wooden wall and settled his chin against his chest, thinking of Commander Tiersa. He wasn't just leaving everything he'd ever known. He was leaving everything he used to know and everything he could've rediscovered.

He hugged his knees. Lily was leaving the castle with Alyda whether he liked it or not, and she had sounded so sure that it was the right decision for him, too. But uncertainty still gnawed relentlessly at him. "I can do this," he mumbled to himself, hoping once again that, if he said it enough times, he'd eventually believe it.

"Your Brilliance. Look." Innavin shook Sevi's shoulder. Sevi looked up at him, stiff and unfocused. He absently registered a smile on the man's face, but in his haze, he was more drawn to the shine of his golden hair. It was very slick and shone brightly in the sunlight. Innavin flourished with his hand, prompting Sevi to refocus. "Your domain's most wondrous city, patiently awaiting the return of its long-lost prince!"

Sevi swept his hollow gaze over the cliffside. He saw the familiar smattering of red rooftops poking out of the trees in sparse clusters first, growing more tightly packed the further to the right he looked. But without the cliff wall to cut them off, they just kept going, multiplying, growing taller and more decorated the further into the city they went.

Eventually, those very red rooftops sprouted white buildings beneath them as the trees thinned and finally disappeared, relinquishing their hold on man's work. And each building grew taller, and taller, reaching for the sky, until they had formed a staircase to the clouds that could bring The Scholar down from his heavenly prison.

Four tall spires, taller than even the castle's, pointed up like embellished fingers from the city, bone-white with blue mosaics swirling around their bases and up their stems in shining tendrils, sparkling in the sunshine. The red, clay rooftops of the fringe houses grew less and less abundant toward the inner city, replaced by slate-gray or blue roofs on the more impressive buildings. But the structure in the middle of the city put all the rest to shame.

A great, golden dome with an oculus on its roof towered atop a massive cathedral, with huge stained-glass windows that sparkled just as brilliantly as the city's four cardinal towers. A smattering of smaller golden roofs surrounded it at the edges of a wide, circular plaza, as though the cathedral had given birth to dozens of little children.

The river wound around the city in the background of these magnificent buildings, matching their shimmer with every wave rippling in the wind—a reminder from Mother Avinaea herself that, despite man's greatest attempts, nothing could match the natural beauty of her creations. It widened into a harbor, around which a long wooden dock had been built to host all manner of rivercraft as they came and went.

And just outside of the cathedral, carved into the plaza with a different color of stone, was a symbol. The angle of his perspective skewed its design, but the star was so big that Sevi could see it from the trail. A star just like the one that hung around his neck.

His star. His *family's* star. Waiting for him along with his people all this time, just beyond where his sight could reach.

His chest tightened as a familiar tugging of split emotions pulled him apart from within. If only he'd gone a little further, had braved a little danger—perhaps he would have found himself sooner. If only he hadn't followed Lily's every word. If only he hadn't lost his memory in the first place. If only.

"Gods." He choked, clutching at his pendant. "Why... What..."

Innavin raised his eyebrows in surprise. "I was merely enhancing the drama. Don't tell me that you've never seen your own capital before, Your Eminence. I thought that the royal family visited frequently prior to the invasion?"

Lorr kicked Innavin's leg.

"Ow! What was that for?"

Lorr shook his head, fixing the man with a hard stare until he quieted.

Sevi rocked with the motion of the wagon, boneless, and focused solely on the star, even after the road leveled out and the buildings rose to swallow it. He could still see it through the stone, burned into his pupils, silently beckoning to him.

When his thoughts quieted enough for him to refocus, an impressive stone wall had risen from the ground, ringed around the nearest buildings and spanning out to hug along the city's borders. A massive archway with a portcullis was set into it, attended to by a dozen Ember soldiers and a pair of stonemasons, carving away at the inner stone. Otherwise, the entrance into the city was largely unpopulated.

Captain River raised his hand and turned around, making a few quick gestures to the cart behind them, which was then passed on to the end of the train. The drivers pulled on their reins, and the horses slowed, putting the caravan into a steady walk as they approached the checkpoint.

The first guard saluted Captain River. "Afternoon, sir."

"Good afternoon," Captain River replied. He reached into his jacket and pulled out a bundle of papers, handing them to the man. "Another supply run for the troops at base, as scheduled."

"Aye. We'll take a peek, but don't expect ta wait too long," the man said, stepping away with the papers. He never even noticed Sevi, nor did any of the guards. His disguise, it seemed, was working.

Captain River turned around to face everyone in the wagon. "How are things here?"

"All fine, sir," Cassik said readily.

"Butt's a little sore, but I'm fine, sir." Loma waved.

"All good, Cal," Captain Lorr said.

"Eager to meet my mistress," Innavin said.

"You will see her soon. And how is our stableboy? Is he ready to see the city?" River inquired.

Sevi looked woodenly up at the captain. "Yes."

Captain River stared at Sevi with something like concern. Sevi looked away, choosing instead to watch the stonemasons above them. One was assisting the other, holding up a shallow crate full of tools for the latter to sift through as needed. The one doing the carving was much older than the assistant, completely swathed from neck to toe in a deep burgundy red, and he spoke in soft tones that echoed dissonantly in the archway.

Squinting, Sevi realized there was no mortar, nor building materials that one might expect a stonemason to have. Their work instead consisted entirely of carving what looked to be a series of runes into the stone at odd intervals, as though sculpting the archway into a work of art. Sevi stared, focusing on the hypnotic *tink, tink, tink* of their tools clinking away.

Innavin said, "I see the Runics are out of hiding. That's a good sign. I've missed seeing those cloaks of theirs."

"What are they carving, sir?" Cassik asked Captain Lorr.

"I'm afraid the specifics aren't for you to know, Private," Lorr replied. "It'll help the war effort. That's all that needs saying."

"I thought we were winning," Loma said, moving her gaze around the gate.

"'Winning.' Not, 'won,'" Lorr said. "And I'd recommend that we all keep that in mind."

"Runics?" Sevi asked softly, coming out of his stupor. "The... magic carvers?"

"The very same." Loma flashed a knowing smile, then lifted her chin and called, "OY! ENCHANTERS! HAVE ROOM FOR ANOTHER PUPIL?"

The man holding the crate full of tools turned, but the one in burgundy never so much as flinched, focused entirely on his task at hand. Neither answered. Loma shrugged. "We can ask them again on the way back."

"Looking to learn the craft, Your Luminance?" Innavin asked. When Sevi flushed, Innavin smiled broadly. "What a wonderful thought! Imagine if you had the gift. You'd be the first Astraeda in generations!"

*"Innavin,"* Lorr hissed, looking carefully around at the soldiers outside the wagon. He lowered his voice. "Stop speaking to him like that."

"How else are we supposed to address him?"

"We're calling him, 'Sevinim,'" Cassik supplied.

"Seh-vee-nim? That's not bad." Innavin nodded. Loma pointedly ignored Cassik's smug look.

The guard reappeared with Captain River's papers and marched up to the side. "All clear, sir. Welcome back to Ilondia."

"Many thanks," Captain River said. Standing in his seat, he turned back to face the train and gave another series of hand gestures, then lifted his hand to his mouth and yelled, "All forward! Slow! Our destination is the docks! If you get separated, head for the Runan Line at berth eighteen!"

Digby cracked the reins, and the wagons moved out once more. The shadow of the stone archway fell away, and the main thoroughfare of the city of Ilondia opened wide before them, stretching into the distance along a series of paved, rolling hills all the way to the river.

And it was beautiful.

Every house, every building, every structure and sculpture seemed to have been made under some grand, cohesive design. Every color, form, and shape flowed with each other, creating a living, breathing world that could live on its own even without the teeming citizenry bustling about its body. Buildings molded together, touching one another without even a finger span of space in most cases, and moved with the rocky, mountainous terrain in a dance of brick and stone, building around giant boulders in a way that drew the eye.

Atop the buildings lay a series of pathways and low-lying walls, allowing the citizenry to walk above the city on a more direct route on either side of the thoroughfare for as long as the buildings touched. There was some evidence of fighting, with bullet holes in walls and pieces of collapsed structures, marring the city's beauty, but it altogether seemed to be in alarmingly good condition. It was all so breathtaking that Sevi forgot to be scared of the crowd, idly walking through the plaza just beyond the gate.

A large fountain spewed water into the air in the middle of the square, catching the light as it fell in a froth. Children laughed and splashed in its waters while their parents gossiped nearby. Flanking the road to either side lay a never-ending line of stalls where merchants harked their wares, calling out to any who dared walk too close. But the greatest show of the city's wealth was along the main promenade itself.

Tall columns made of shimmering blue crystal, topped and lined with white alabaster and delicately carved with a sequence of reliefs that climbed up every monument, sprouted up from the road in rows, lining the path like silent, glimmering guardians. And in the center of each, dancing and sparking like glowbugs in a bottle, were glittering motes of silver dust, twirling around and around in their translucent prisons.

Sevi watched each one as they passed. The faintest vision of an army marching down these cobbled streets appeared for a moment over his waking eyes, gleaming in polished armor with banners whipping about in the breeze. In it, his parents stood with him, holding a small, crying baby. A strong sense of awe accompanied the memory, joining the wonder he felt at seeing everything for the first time as a different person.

In the face of such majesty, such prominence, such *life*, any despair Sevi felt quickly faded to a dull shadow. Until recently, his waking memory was full only of Fae, and stone, and plants, and fire, and bullets. But now, he realized, it could have this once more.

The road led straight through the center of the city, bringing them across the massive plaza outside of the cathedral. Its golden dome was almost blinding up close, with all the scintillant buildings that surrounded it shining just as brightly in the sun. Another large fountain stood at the plaza's center, resting just beneath the southern point of the plaza's star. The crowd thinned here, and the supply train sped up ever so slightly with a nicker from the horses.

Averting his gaze from the buildings' shine, Sevi looked down to watch the star as it slid past. It had been defaced and was missing many of its stones. His short-lived reprieve ended as raw remorse flooded through him. So close. It had been so *close*. Would he have made the connection if he'd seen this years ago? Could he have been bolder, if he'd only known? Or would he have hidden away again, too fearful to try?

"Things will get a little rougher, so stay in the wagon, Sevi," Captain Lorr said. "We're getting close to Caldwin's namesake."

"That is not your story to tell, *isi'kaa*. Not yet," Captain River called.

Lorr raised his hands. "My mistake!" he called back. "You'll have to ask him for the details yourself, but the name of the river ahead is Caldwin River. I think it was originally 'cold wind river,' or something, but it got shortened over time."

Sevi stared at the back of Captain River's head, trying, and failing, not to be curious. But he kept his questions to himself and looked down at his shadow instead, making sure that Shy was still there. The closer they got to the river, the more anxious he became. It was almost time.

The buildings to either side fell away abruptly, replaced with an open market. If the thoroughfare had been loud with the sound of merchants, then this place was deafening. Hundreds of people moved about in a densely packed mess, wearing dozens of different styles of garb and speaking a half a dozen languages. Guards stood at alert for pickpockets and thieves, and stalls carried foods and trinkets that Sevi had only ever seen in his daydreams.

Some of the traders and civilians looked fabulously wealthy, while others looked as though they hadn't eaten in days. A cluster of tattooed men standing off to the side gave Sevi's wagon an evil-looking stare as it passed, catching his gaze the moment he went by as if they'd rehearsed it. Each one carried a weapon. Sevi shrunk away, huddling into the cart.

A long wooden boardwalk hugged the rim of the river, beyond which a mixture of rivercraft bobbed about with sails tucked in. Digby turned the horses to the right once they reached the planks, leading them around a stall to travel parallel to the water, and revealing a fleet of magnificent, golden ships of various sizes and makes. Some were very close to being nothing more than sloops, but all had been painted a rich shade of golden-yellow, and accented with deep, ebony railing and trim.

Their forms were more streamlined and less blocky than the ships of any other berth, and each of their prows went out and curled downward at the tip, mimicking a cresting wave. Flags bearing a golden sea serpent on a black background whipped about high in the breeze, noble and proud. If the surrounding boats were the peasantry, then these were undoubtedly their royalty, glowing in the sun whilst all others looked on with envy.

As they approached the armada, Captain River stood once more and gave his hand signals, and Digby pulled firmly on the reins, bringing their cart to a slow and steady stop.

Lorr kicked Innavin's leg. "Wake up, we're here."

"Already?" Innavin yawned, stretching.

"Mm. Let's go, we can't keep Kylari waiting."

Innavin's eyes flew open. "No, we can't!" he exclaimed. He righted himself with a grunt and grabbed their bags, sliding himself out of the wagon first. "Let's go, slowbones!"

Lorr stood up far more slowly. "His energy never fails to impress," he said to Sevi. "Alright, lad, we're off on business. But you're in good hands. Stay close to the wagons, listen to Caldwin, and enjoy your time in town, understood?"

Sevi nodded slowly. "Thank you, Lorr... I will."

Captain Lorr smiled and stepped off the wagon, following in Innavin's wake, who was already several paces ahead and hopping about impatiently. Lorr waved to River before disappearing into the crowd, swept up by the city's flow.

Captain River came around to the back of the cart along with Digby, giving everyone a broad, beaming smile. "Welcome to my home."

"Your home?" Sevi asked.

"Yes! Please, allow me to welcome you to one of my family's many homes!" He swept his hand out toward the golden flotilla and proudly announced, "the Ta'Runa of Ilondia!"

Sevi followed his gesture. Working down the berth, dressed in loose, comfortable looking linens and silks, was a slew of sailors and traders that looked just like River, calling out to one another as they loaded or unloaded an assortment of goods. River's arrival hadn't gone unnoticed either, and several of the men and women waved at him with wide-armed gestures, happily calling out to him. Their smiles were wide enough to see even at a distance.

River called something back to them in his language and made the same hand motion back. He said to Sevi, "I must discuss business first, but with time, I will bring them over so that you and they may make introductions. Then I will escort you around the city. Private Tammavin, Private Novar, please keep an eye on our stableboy."

"Yes, sir," Cassik said.

"Can do, sir," Loma said.

"Good. Let us go, Lieutenant," Captain River said, marching ahead of Digby with an eager step.

"Hrm." Digby grumbled, lingering at the cart. "I hate this part. They're too... grabby." He reluctantly followed in the captain's footsteps, leaning on his cane more than usual.

Sevi tensed and cast his gaze down the supply line, assessing every cart again. This was it. The best opportunity he'd get to escape from the Embers, the castle, and the crown. He could feel it. There was so much noise, so much activity, and everyone was focused on something other than himself. No one expected him to just run off into the city of his own volition.

He could do it. He could escape and go back to living the way he used to, with nobody calling him a prince, or shooting bullets at him, or throwing him in a cell forever if he ever got caught.

So why did he hesitate?

Lily's phantom voice hissed at him. *Run. Now!*

He didn't. Instead, he watched the Embers as they steadily emptied out the carts. When they had finished, he turned to watch the Ta'Runa dock workers, distantly making out River and Digby as they each embraced a group of prominent-looking sailors.

Other Elkrans were on the dock with them, coming and going from the various ships with armfuls of exotic looking goods. He sat watching the world around him for so long that he had slipped into naming people in his mind as they walked by. And still he didn't move, nor did he see any sign of Lily.

*Do it, you coward! Are you going to abandon me?* Lily's phantom screamed.

"Um... may I get out of the wagon?" he asked Cassik and Loma. "T-to stretch my legs?"

"I wouldn't go too far, Your... Sevinim," Cassik said.

"Let the lad get a breather. In fact..." Loma stood and took a long, satisfying stretch. "I could use a little time out of this crate myself. After you, *Sevinim*."

"I guess I'll get out too then," Cassik said grudgingly, standing unsteadily and rubbing at his bad leg.

Sevi gulped, hesitantly sliding out of the cart. Loma followed shortly after, took another stretch, then walked around the side to lean against the wagon, looking out across the docks. "Best stay comfortable. Captain River is going to take his sweet time," she said.

"How do you know that?" Cassik asked.

Loma shrugged, staring wistfully at the Ta'Runa. "It's what I would do."

Cassik leaned against the inside wall of the wagon, adopting the same pensive look. Sevi shifted his gaze between them and the Runans, struck by the rare moment where they didn't bicker.

Sevi wondered when they had last seen their families. From their stories, it had sounded as though they hadn't since the war first started. All the Embers of Korina shared a common pride among them, both in their homeland and their culture, but it was a pride he couldn't share—not when all his memories consisted of the castle. Sevi wondered, *What pride could lead them to leave the ones they loved?*

"Why did you two fight in the war?" Sevi asked before he could stop himself.

Loma turned. "Didn't we tell you that?"

Sevi shook his head. "You said your father made you, and Cassik said he didn't want to move his family. But why? Why would you leave them and risk dying? Why not run away together?"

*And why are you asking them these stupid questions? RUN!* the phantom in his head bellowed.

"I'm sorry, that's... an odd thing for you to ask, Your—Sevi. If you don't mind me saying so," Cassik said, confused. "This is our home. Is it not obvious?"

"Couldn't you make a new home elsewhere?" Sevi insisted.

Loma and Cassik looked at each other. Loma shook her head with a smile creeping slowly up her face, which Cassik mirrored. She shrugged, and they both turned to look at him. "Some things you can't run away from, kid," Loma said. "Some things are that important."

"I agree. My family was safe in Tiburas through the war," Cassik said. "I could be with them now, and we would find a way to be happy together. But I was raised on the stories my father told me of his crossing from Salakir as a child. He spent many nights in fear, surrounded by strangers in a land whose language and ways he didn't know. He, my grandmother, and my grandfather used their entire lives to build up what we have now, and nobody is going to take that from us so long as I can do something about it. I'll not force such a life on my children. No more running. Not again."

"But why didn't you leave when Tiersa said you could?" Sevi asked. "Isn't the war over?"

"Money." Cassik shrugged. "Our house was destroyed in the fighting. My wife needs the funds to help rebuild, and being a soldier in peacetime is far easier than being one at war. This time, our family will not start from nothing."

"In my case, me da is all I have, and he can't move," Loma said. "We barely have half a coppen to our name, and the road is not kind to old folk. If I didn't fight back, the greenbloods would've killed us all, or taken what little we have, thus killing us anyway. And when you have nothin' to lose but yourself, then what's the use of sitting on your hands, waiting for the ax to fall? We all have to go sometime. Might as well make a spectacle of it." She shrugged. "And like Cassik said, the pay here is good. I send something back home every now and again."

"But your father could lose *you*," Sevi protested.

"And I told him that!" Loma laughed. "But *you* try reasoning with that old man and tell me how that goes. 'The old 'er meant to die, Loma, an' the young 'er meant ta keep what we made an' make it better. Sometimes that means a scrap or two. So, get out there an' keep it.' Stubborn fool, how exactly am I supposed to keep something after taking a blast of magic lightning to the chest?"

Sevi raised a hand to touch the star beneath his shirt. *Fighting for the home they made. Fighting to make something out of nothing.*

"What brought you to ask, kid?" Loma said. Sevi slowly shook his head, unable to bring himself to speak.

Cassik exited the wagon, stepping carefully onto the dock to stand a respectful distance away from Sevi, still taking his role as personal guard seriously, even when the whole point of the trip was to be inconspicuous. "Well. How does it feel to be back, Your—Sevi?"

Sevi looked around, trying to come to that same conclusion himself. "I'm not sure," he mumbled, looking across the market. Hundreds of people moving about as one, living their lives together. Open space. Fresh air. Different languages and cultures. It was scary. It was different. But at the same time, it felt *right*.

Cassik screamed. Sevi leapt back. The soldier clapped a hand against his injured leg and hopped about, red in the face with pain.

Loma grabbed her rifle. "What? What is it?"

"Something *bit* me!"

Loma paused. A lazy smirk crossed her face, and she let go of her gun. "Been in the castle too long, Novar? Did you forget the river has bu—OUCH!"

Loma started hopping about just like Cassik. But that wasn't what caught Sevi's attention. There had been a popping sound just before her scream.

"Not so funny, *is it?*" Cassik growled, setting his foot back down, but just as he did, a whole cluster of popping sounds battered his shins, singeing the fabric of his pants, and he tumbled over in a surprised cry of pain.

"What's go—OW!" Loma cried, falling against the side of the wagon, hopping from one stung leg to the other.

"*Pssst!*"

Sevi whipped his head around and down. Underneath the wagon behind his, holding a handful of firesnaps, lay Lily. She waved hurriedly at him, motioning for him to run.

Soldiers from the other wagons rushed up with rifles at the ready, alerted by Loma and Cassik's cries of pain. Sevi backed away from the ensuing bedlam purely out of instinct.

"*Run!*" Lily hissed.

Something snapped inside of Sevi at the sight of the real Lily urging him on. His legs started moving on their own, slowly, as if through mud. Then faster. He picked a direction, the first thing that came to mind, and ran. A hundred thoughts and emotions tangled up inside of him, clamoring for space. He focused instead on every breath until his lungs drowned them all out. In, out. In, out. Run away. Run away. Don't stay. *Run.*

He moved through the crowd faster than he thought possible, strengthened by his months of steady food and bedrest. He didn't look anywhere other than forward, pumping his arms with his shoulders set, running up the main road toward the golden cathedral and its prominent star.

Nobody called out to him. Nobody tried to stop him. Nobody fired a rifle at him.

He didn't stop until he made it to the plaza's fountain, collapsing against the ledge and heaving in breaths. Any moment the soldiers would realize he was missing, if they hadn't already. And every moment he spent against the fountain was one he should've spent looking for a hiding spot. But he didn't move.

He stared at his reflection in the water. The reflection stared back. No mirror children appeared, nor faceless mothers, nor old ladies with stories of every star in the sky. But it was still different.

It wasn't the reflection of Sevi, scared child of the Cut, tunnel mouse of Ilondia's castle. Not entirely. His back was too straight, and the edges of his eyes had more resolve than *that* Sevi ever had. The fear was still there, and the confusion—but someone else had moved in behind his gaze when he hadn't been looking.

"Shy?" he called softly. "Are you with me?"

Another body crashed into the fountain next to him, wrapping an arm fiercely around his middle and squeezing tightly. The motion made him jerk, and the pendant of his necklace fell out from the collar of his shirt, catching the light of day.

"We did it!" Lily exclaimed, laughing exuberantly. "We *did* it! We got *out!*"

They certainly had, and it had all unfolded as Lily had predicted. Their biggest obstacle had been convincing the officers to allow the trip, thus gaining support before approaching Tiersa herself. Captain River had luckily proven oddly amenable—and clearly possessed a good deal of the commander's respect, no doubt heighted by bringing Sevi to her—making for an excellent unwitting ally. If he had declined Sevi would have had to solicit Tiersa alone, which surely would have failed.

In the event that Tiersa declined, Sevi had suggested using Shy to escape during the night himself while Lily stowed away in a wagon. But Shy had proven too fickle to rely on, and Lily had argued that Sevi was too well watched to leave the castle without being readily noticed. Horsemen and Empyrean raptors would have flooded the land the moment he was discovered missing.

Going through the mines—for very obvious reasons—was also not an option, and scaling the mountain was both dangerous and too at risk for exposure. Running into a riverport crowd with a disguise, however, offered great possibilities, and seemed the only viable solution. Now all they had to do was disappear.

But Sevi didn't move. He stared at the necklace, swaying gently above his reflection. He grabbed it, squeezing its metal points until it hurt. "We did it," he said quietly.

*Isevidel Astraeda*, Tiersa's phantom whispered.

Lily pulled her knapsack into her lap and opened it, peering in. "You alright, Alyda?" A tiny fistful of dust erupted from the bag, making her squeeze her eyes shut and cough. She wiped her sleeve across her nose. "I may have jostled her a little too much during all this. Sorry, Alyda. Anyway, get on your feet, we have to get out of the open." She patted Sevi and stood, slinging her bag onto her back.

Sevi remained where he was. His hand holding the necklace trembled, and his eyes stayed fixed on his reflection.

"Sevi? Come on, we need to move," she said again, nudging him with his foot.

He didn't react.

"Sevi! *Move!*"

"I'm not going," he said quietly.

Lily froze. "Excuse me?"

"I said I'm not going," he said louder, not looking at her. He couldn't do it. He couldn't run from this place. He couldn't go back to the way he'd been before. But he also couldn't see the look of betrayal that was surely on his best friend's face. "I'm... I'm staying here. I'm going to find out who I am, Lily." He turned to her then, keeping his gaze level with her shoes. "And I... I really want you to stay with me."

An eternity passed. She slid her knapsack off her shoulder. She didn't speak, so he kept talking. "I know how dangerous it will be for you and Alyda. And I know why you have to leave. I understand... I... I want you both to be safe. But the Embers know who I am. *Tiersa* knows who I am. And I'm a prince, of all things."

He squeezed his necklace. "But I really don't think I'll be a good one. I think you're right. I think people will hurt me. Use me. I think that whatever I do, I will mess it all up... but I also think that, if you're here with me, and we look out for each other as we always have... then maybe we'll be alright."

He braved her expression. Her mask had reappeared to swallow her emotions, as if every sound he'd made had built it back up, piece by piece, until nothing else remained of her.

Then she started to laugh.

It began as an incredulous giggle, appearing so suddenly from the void of her face that it made Sevi's skin crawl. Then it built, and built, until she doubled over, gripping one hand on the crown of her helmet and the other on her belly, as if her insides were in danger of spilling out. She laughed, and laughed, and *laughed* until tears streamed down her face.

Sevi knew that kind of laughter all too well, and his eyes widened in fear.

"You." She wiped her face, turning her manic grin on him. "You... ungrateful, selfish, *stupid* BOY!" Her expression morphed into one of unbridled rage in the span it took to blink, wiping her smile away. "Get up. We're leaving."

"No! Lily—"

"*Shut up!*" she yelled. "After all I've done for you. After all I've... I've *sacrificed* for you. After all I did to get us out of there, you have the nerve to turn around and stab me in the godsdamned back? *NO.*"

She sprung forward and shoved him so hard he fell back onto the stone, bumping his head. He scrambled onto his hands, crawling back from her fury, but she just kept coming.

"After all our years together you would just throw me away and join up with *them?* People you don't even *know?*" She stalked toward him and grabbed him by the collar. "*I* was the one who protected you. *I* was the one who taught you how to survive. *I* was the one who *saved your godsdamned life*, and you would... you..."

Tears sprung freely to her eyes. She let go of his collar, standing up to furiously wipe them with the back of her sleeve before turning and walking away.

Sevi scrambled up from the ground, suddenly fearful that this is how she would leave. "Lily! *Lily!*"

She stopped with her back to him.

"I don't want to leave you!" he said, putting all his emotion into it. "I would never *want* to leave you! But you..." He shook his head. "You lied to me for *years,* and I—"

"So I *deserve* it?" Lily snarled, turning back to face him.

"No! I mean... Listen to me. Please," he said, softening his voice. "I understand why you did it, and I don't hate you for it. But I *need* to know. I need to know who I am!"

"Then use your shadow creature!"

"I can't! They haven't come out again. I think they're hurt somehow." Sevi looked at his feet. "And I thought you didn't like them?"

Lily squared her shoulders. "I'll live with it."

"It doesn't matter, Lily, it's not the same either way. Tiersa is family. I can't just *leave* her now."

"I thought I was your family."

That hit him like a slap across the face. She glared at him. "Don't I matter, too? Doesn't Alyda?"

"Of course, you do. You both do!"

"Then *come with us,*" she said, staring imploringly at him. "You don't *have* to be a prince to be who you are. You can leave. We can be whoever we want to be out here."

He shook his head and tightened his fists. "You don't get it. You've always known who you are. *Always.* There's *nothing* missing in you. You've never known what it's like to wake up as someone else, alone in the dark, with nothing and nobody to help you. You've never spent a *single* moment wondering where your parents are or thrown your whole fate into someone else's hands because you're so blazingly useless. But I have. That's every day of my *life.*"

"Sevi—"

"No. Listen to me talk. I spent the last four years of my life following you around while you risked your own to protect my useless hide from your own kin. Well now I have the chance to do the same for you." He grabbed her hand in both of his, holding it up between them. "If I can be anyone I want to be out here, then I choose to be the person who can protect *you* for a change. I can be someone worthwhile. I can be a *prince,* with you and Alyda by my side. So *let* me."

Lily pulled her hand back. "We can't."

"Yes, we can. Don't make me say the words."

"*No*, we *can't*."

"Why *not?*"

She was interrupted when a flock of black birds launched themselves from the plaza, streaking over their heads into the sky. Lily paled and flinched, staring wide-eyed as they settled a distance away on the nearby rooftops.

Sevi furrowed his brow. "Lily?"

She said nothing, fixing her stare instead on the fountain where a single raven perched, regarding her with one deep, dark eye.

"Lily," Sevi said again, taking a step toward her. "Please. I would give anything, *anything* you ask of me, to keep you by my side." She closed her eyes and pursed her lips, tightening her face as she struggled to decide. "Please," he pressed. His voice broke at the sight of her. "*Please* don't leave me."

She opened her eyes and fixed him with a distraught, watery stare.

"Sevi? SEVI!"

They both blinked and turned toward the new voice. Cassik, Loma, and three of the soldiers from the caravan sprinted toward them. Cassik lagged behind, clutching at his hurt leg, but seemed no less determined than the others.

Sevi looked back at Lily. An unspoken understanding passed between them. If she was going to leave, in the precious few breaths before the soldiers arrived, now would be the time. But she would be leaving without him. He shook his head at her and whispered, "Please..."

Something inside of her broke, and all her resistance abruptly drained from her shoulders. She slumped, looking miserably at the ground just as the first soldier came running up, drawing attention from across the plaza. If this didn't outright reveal Sevi, it would start the gossip at the very least.

"Kid, *why* in the ever-loving *dusk* did you go running off like that!" Loma huffed as she came up, looking irritated. Cassik followed shortly after, red in the face and clutching his leg in pain.

Before Sevi could answer, Lily threw her arms around him. The soldiers started forward in surprise. Yet no one was as shocked as Sevi. "Introduce me. Happily," Lily muttered in his ear.

"Sevi? Who is this?" Loma asked.

Sevi floundered, looking from Lily to the soldiers. "Um. This... This is Lily. My best friend," he added with an uncertain smile.

Loma's eyebrows shot up. "The girl you kept asking Lea about?"

"Yeah," Sevi said, wrapping his arms around Lily for good measure. "I-I did mention that she wore a helmet."

Loma, Cassik, and all the soldiers shared a look. The second child from Digby's story had been found, alive and well. "Well... let's..." Cassik grunted, hunching over. "Let's get back to the wagons. Lieutenant Asgaillin will be glad to see you."

"And *don't* run off again!" Loma scowled. "*Please.* It's not just your own skin that's in danger if you disappear around here." She turned and grumpily walked back the way she came. Cassik nodded to Sevi and spared one last quizzical glance at Lily before he turned to follow her. The rest of the soldiers did the same, but not too far.

Sevi dropped his arms from Lily, but Lily held on, squeezing him far tighter than was comfortable. Moving her mouth up the side of his head, she whispered very softly and inconspicuously into his ear. "I swear by every god there is, I'm going to kill you for this."

# Chapter 40

*The mouse had a viper guarding his ear with a tongue that knew all that he craved. A flower may only distract for so long; curse the night that conceals in the day!*

———— ◦~◦ ————

Predictably, there was drama when they got back to the wagons with Lily in tow. Captain River and Lieutenant Digby were noticeably angry, but the moment that Digby caught sight of Lily's helmet he immediately broke into a laugh. "Lass! You're alright!" he exclaimed, spreading his arms wide and moving forward as if to embrace her.

"Don't touch me, Blumpkin." Lily swatted his arm away, stepping out of his reach. "I've had a *really* bad day."

"Aye, it's you alright." He grinned. "Can't be so bad though! You an' the lad found each other again!"

"Oh, yes, and how wonderful that is, truly," Lily said flatly, darting a glance sharp enough to cut Sevi to the bone. He averted his gaze.

"So, this is the famous friend?" Captain River said, stepping next to Digby. "It is a pleasure to meet you, friend of Sevi. I am Captain Caldwin River Ta'runa, previously known as Sandro Adhal Ta'Runa, and Alai Royash Ta'Runa before that, and Orro Tawme Ta'Runa before that. You may call me Captain Caldwin River, or Captain River."

"That's nice," Lily said.

"I think so, too." Captain River smiled. "I know your name, but please, introduce yourself. Who are you?"

"Whoever I want to be." She shouldered her way past them without as much as a backward glance and climbed into Sevi's cart. She settled against the wood with her knapsack on her lap, tipped her visor forward, and crossed her arms around the bag, ending any further attempts at conversation.

"A very interesting introduction," River said with a nod. "Did you pay attention, *risho?*"

Sevi stared incredulously at the man but didn't rise to the bait—at least not out loud. On the inside, irritation grated. *Which part of that was a good introduction?*

"Am I to understand that you saw her and went running after her?" Captain River continued. Sevi said nothing. "I know why you did this, but never do it again, do you understand? The Dockside of Ilondia is very dangerous, and it is my job to protect you. I take that very seriously."

Sevi drew a long, tired breath. "I'm *sorry*. How much longer are we here for?"

"We will be here for some time. My people love to haggle, and I find that I still enjoy it myself. But I trust Lieutenant Asgaillin to handle it without me. He is very big, and now he has a cane to wave around." Captain River chuckled. "You and I will be going elsewhere while he finishes."

"To show me the city?"

"Yes and no. As we speak, Captain Lorr and Innavin Targa should have finished arranging something for you, at the behest of Commander Tiersa. We will go to them now. Introducing you to my family can wait until after."

Sevi looked fearfully back at Lily in the wagon. He didn't want to leave her alone, and she didn't look willing to move. Captain River followed his gaze. Pursing his lips in a strange way, he let out a shrill whistle that grabbed the attention of several caravan soldiers. "Privates Novar, Tammavin, Shoni, Cillio, Thorgoode. I am taking our stableboy with me for an hour, maybe two. While I am away, you are to let nothing, absolutely nothing, harm his famous friend. Am I understood?"

A chorus of agreement answered. Cassik, the lone dissenter, raised his hand. "Should I and Loma not come with you, sir?"

"Your leg is not well, Private Novar. And once I meet with Captain Lorr and Innavin, we will be well prepared to defend ourselves. Though I thank you for your concern."

Cassik nodded uncertainly but dropped the issue. Captain River turned his smile back on Sevi. "Let us go. We should not leave Kylari waiting."

Sevi looked once more at Lily. *Perhaps some distance would be good for us both.* "Tell everyone not to touch her helmet. She hates that," he said to Digby, before turning and following Captain River through the crowd.

He'd hoped to pass the walk in silence, but it didn't take long for the captain to strike up a conversation. "Did your friend speak of where she has been?"

Sevi took a moment to respond. "In town. She thought I was dead. She ran."

Captain River nodded. "Very sensible, unfortunately. I am happy to see you both reunited so—hm, the word is like 'fortunately,' but not—fortuitously! That is the one. What a strange sounding word."

"Mm."

"You did not say she had a star on her helmet," he said, looking sidelong at Sevi.

"You never asked."

River grimaced, looking askance. "You are odd, today."

Sevi blinked. "Excuse me?"

"Yes. Odd." The corner of River's mouth turned down in a puzzled frown. "You speak to me differently than usual. Very short words. And you do not seem happy after finding your friend. Why is that? Are you well?"

Alone with the man and charged with lingering emotion, Sevi lost all restraint and spat out, "Maybe it's because you tricked me. Maybe it's because you brought me to Commander Tiersa without a word to me about my identity. Maybe, for all I know, Corporal Reynam's job was to report to you on what he found out about me, which is why he asked me so many questions about my damn necklace every damn day."

Captain River paused mid-stride and turned to him with his mouth open. Sevi continued, "And now I'm following you somewhere else with barely a word from you. Maybe I really am a stupid boy and should have stayed back in the wagon with Lily."

"*Risho—*"

"*Stop calling me that.*" Sevi sneered. "What does that even *mean?* My name is not *risho.* Blackest night, it's barely Isevidel. My. Name. Is. *Sevi.*"

He stared hard at the captain, daring him to say something stupid about names and introductions. Yet despite his outburst, the captain didn't look angry—only concerned and confused, as if he couldn't quite understand what Sevi was saying.

People flowed around them, forming a circle, separating them from the rest of the world. The silence that fell between he and River was quickly filled by the babbling of the crowd, with dozens of shifting voices and tones that tangled together as energetically as Sevi's ire.

River covered his mouth, staring at Sevi from above his hand. Shockingly enough, his expression gradually smoothened, the sight of which only irritated Sevi further. How dare he not be affronted? How dare he not try to defend himself with some silly excuse? At last, Captain River said, "Sit down with me, Sevi."

"I'd rather stand."

Captain River sighed. "Very well. But I choose to sit." He turned and strode toward the side of the road where an empty stone bench waited, leaving Sevi in the middle of the crowd. Sevi begrudgingly left its current and stepped into the basin of empty space that the roadside provided. Captain River watched him with a dark, impassive gaze.

Sevi stepped before him, crossed his arms, and waited. "Well?"

River shook his head and leaned back against the wall, closing his eyes. "Not yet."

A long silence ensued. Sevi shifted from foot to foot. Captain River didn't move. Eventually, Sevi's anger broke into irritation. "Weren't we supposed to not keep Kylari waiting?"

"This is more important," Captain River said softly.

Sevi rolled his eyes and took position next to the bench, leaning against the wall. He kept his arms crossed and observed the traffic that went by. People carried jugs of water from the river, or crates of supplies, or any number of things needed for their lives. No two citizens seemed to be dressed the same. Above them, people strode along the rooftop walkways at a more leisurely pace, chatting with one another and laughing beneath an open sky.

Drawing in a long breath, Sevi watched them go about their business. Unhurried. Unbothered. Living lives that were far simpler than his. He wondered what it was like to be whole like them, with their memories unbroken from start to present. Was it better? Was it worse? Were they as anxious as he was all the time? They didn't look like they were.

He imagined what it would be like to swap places with someone in the crowd. Would life be as simple as he thought it to be, without the expectation of a royal dynasty suddenly pushed back onto his shoulders? He may have lived in a cave, but it was a cave he'd learned to adapt to. Out here most of what he knew was useless.

His gaze drifted back to River, studying him covertly. His upper body was straight and controlled, but his leg shook, bouncing up and down as though possessed by the need to run, rebelling against the stillness of his body. *What of him? How did he come to be a captain in a foreign war? Why did he take such interest in my life?*

Captain River's eyes sprung open. "There it is." A small smile had returned to his face

Sevi regarded him. "What?"

"The Long Breath," River replied, not looking at him. "My people say often that when the breath becomes short, it is the long one that replenishes. Though I think that sounds better in my language."

Sevi sighed. "Then we can leave now?"

"No. Now we talk."

Sevi shook his head. *Great. More talk.*

"First, you must know me, and my home," Captain River said. "The Ta'Runa are in every land, in every port. Everywhere the water touches. I had assumed that you knew us already. But you are missing your memory, of course you do not know us. That is my first mistake."

He folded his hands into his lap and looked up at the sky. "We believe in Earuna, mother of all, and guide of the Great Tide. She controls the flow of life, and it is through her signs that we divine our fate. Sometimes that fate is to become a merchant. Sometimes that fate is to become a mother. But when the sign is so great, so powerful, our fate leads us to become someone else entirely. This is why I urge you to not shy away from your introduction. Your name tells the world all that you are."

The captain looked over at him then. Shadows from the people above, coupled with a flock of passing crows danced across his face, playing with the light as much as any stream of water. "I have had three such signs in my life. The first two were for me, and me alone, and I will speak of them to no one. But the last one has led me to you."

"Me?" Sevi said.

River nodded. "There are many lands. Many people. Many different ways. But it is water that connects us all. The Ta'Runa follow the water—trading, learning, gathering stories from one land to share with another so that we may be even more connected. And it is on this journey, this *asha'keena*, that we find our fate. At the end of my third pilgrimage, I chose to follow a cluster of stars, to wherever it would lead me. So, I pointed my ship and my crew to this land, and offered my fate to the Great Mother.

"As we approached land, a terrible storm rose and dashed us against the rocks, at the very base of where this very river empties into the sea. Some of my crew lost their lives. Others lost other things. All were badly hurt. My legs were almost shattered, such was the sea's fury, and in the face of the Mother's might with all power robbed of me, I could only pray for mercy. Yet when I awoke, do you know what I found?"

Sevi said nothing. Captain River smiled. "Stars. I found stars. The Embers of Korina. And it was Captain Lorr Ferdino Gallan who pulled me from the rocks." He closed his eyes once more, smiling to himself at the private memory. "I thought he was my star, and that I was his. My purpose for my journey.

"He and the others healed me. They taught me more of their tongue than I had known. They taught me to use their weapons, and I taught them mine. And for the third time in my life, I fell in love. With a man this time. It was then that I knew, wherever these stars that walked as men went, I was to follow. Some of my crew joined me. Some have taken other roads. Yet I stayed and took the name of the river where I was born again, and it is that same river that has led me here. To yet another star. *Ik Earuna kah'eshaa.*"

He sighed. "The river ends here, at the mountains. And against such a fearful people as the Fae, I thought that my fate could only be to die where it was born. 'The end of a River where it begins.' When we took the castle, it was... difficult. Ferocious? Yes, that is a good word. Ferocious. I climbed the rock walls with my men and women, we stood atop the mountain with our chutes and the world beneath us. I offered myself up to Earuna once more, and we jumped. I thought it was to my death. But then the flying ship came by, just as I was. I grabbed it. I held on. I fought the Fae on its deck, and I crashed it into the ground... and here I am. Still alive. Still not at the end of my river."

He stopped, leveling a serious stare. "And then I found you. The little one that fell from the sky. A *risho*. Saved by a star of your own. I took it as a sign that my journey had more to it; that I was meant to find you. But I forget, time and time again, that this land does not see *asha'keena* as the Ta'Runa do. That is my second mistake. All here are happy to let it guide them silently, unseen, pretending that their lives are governed only by themselves. It is wrong to me. But it is the way of this place, and who am I to frown at it?

"So, I am sorry, *risho*. Very sorry. I ignored your *asha'keena* and focused only on my own. Perhaps it would have led you to this place without my help. Perhaps not. Perhaps I should have observed and not acted. But I have never been a watcher. I am here for a purpose; this, I still believe. And I know, now just as then, that it will show itself in time."

River quieted, turning away to look up at the sky again. Sevi stared at him. "Tiersa was going to throw me from my home if I wasn't who you thought I was," he said. "Why? Why didn't you *talk* to me about it before offering me up like that?"

"The truth is a simple thing, *risho*. It wants to be seen. Lies are messy and make a web to hide the truth, but it always breaks free. Always. I was very eager to pursue my tide, I admit that. But if I had told you of my thoughts, and the truth of your surprise did not show on your face when Commander Tiersa saw you, she would have seen a web that was not there."

Sevi paused. "She would have thought that we were tricking her somehow."

Captain River nodded. "Yes. And you passed her test. Just as I knew you would."

Sevi stared at the ground, at a total loss for words. His anger, in the face of such a story, had shriveled to a husk. But it hadn't changed his feelings. "I still don't appreciate what you did."

River sighed. "Understandable. Regrettable, but understandable."

"And you mean to say that you did all this because you had a *hunch?*"

"I watched. I waited. Then I made a choice. We may all do nothing, and Fate will still move us despite our stillness, no matter how stubborn a stillness it is. My people know this better than anyone. It is only by the choices we make that we grant ourselves any control in its flow, lest we do nothing and fall upon the rocks."

His expression turned sly, and a gleam appeared in his eye. "What choices will you make, I wonder? Will you be Sevi, the tunnel mouse? Or Isevidel, the prince? I am most eager to see. And Goddess willing, I will return to my islands one day with a new name, and another story to tell."

Sevi said nothing. He and River regarded each other for some time. Eventually, River stood. "Thank you, *risho*, for talking. Let us move, shall we? We still must go to Kylari. They have waited long enough." He gestured for Sevi to begin walking.

Sevi sluggishly turned to face the same direction, allowing the captain to lead him on again, too lost in his thoughts to bring his body fully back under his own power. After a while, he slowly said, "Captain River?"

"Mm?"

"What... What was the name of the constellation you followed? The stars that led you here?"

"Ah, *Okonnen* and *Nishira*, The Twins Tied by Fate. Though, in this land, I understand that you call them the Dancers."

# Chapter 41

*He leapt from her leaves and grabbed the star's light, no fear of the ground underneath. How quickly the pain of his fall was forgot when a river ran soft at his feet.*

— ⚬❧⚬ —

"What do you think? Shoulder pads? No shoulder pads?" Innavin asked.

"Shoulder pads. And with a tapered waist. He's so slight that he needs all the help he can get," Lorr said.

"What about the pantaloons? If we get a nice pair of light linen and match it with some black boots? Along with the midnight blue and gold coat? Very regal. Very Astraedan."

Lorr looked skeptically at Innavin. "You're not just saying that because you have a thing for those billowy-hip, pillow pants, are you?"

"Sun and stars he's the long-lost prince, Lorr! How is he supposed to return to the throne if not extravagantly!"

Lorr snorted. "How about something that makes it look like he won't use his pants as a mattress?"

Sevi, once again, held his arms out to allow Innavin to pull yet another shirt onto him. This one had a frilly collar that stood up like a funnel around his neck, preventing him from turning his head in any direction.

As it happened, Kylari wasn't a person. It was an entire shop. And Innavin had spent the hour prior to his arrival boisterously announcing the return of Isevidel Astraeda, the long-lost prince, entirely disregarding any pretense of secrecy. It had been enough to earn River's earnest annoyance. Now a "closed" sign hung on the door, and all the clothiers were scurrying about, bowing and scraping to everything that Innavin demanded of them, while Sevi stood on a little podium in a curtained-off room, miserably looking at his reflection in a mirror. *Maybe it's not too late to run away with Lily*, he thought.

"What in Nightfall is wrong with you, Vin? Look at him, he looks like a scarecrow!" Lorr said.

Innavin looked at Sevi as if noticing him for the first time. Sevi could barely meet his gaze over the collar frills. "Ah. Well, he's the prince! He'll practically be inventing the fashion once he's been crowned! Who's to say this won't be the latest trend?"

"Stop, just stop. Give the kid some air. Sevi, take that off at once. I know what he needs." Lorr disappeared behind the curtain that led to the front of the store. When he came back, he carried a plain, red tailcoat with a gray vest. "Here. This looks like it will suit him much better."

Innavin scoffed. "Lorr?"

"What?"

"That's a butler's uniform."

Lorr studied the clothes in his hand with a frown. "Oh. It's on sale, though."

"Royalty, Lorr. *Royalty*."

"Well, my point holds. Don't just throw every piece of fabric in the store on the boy!"

Innavin sighed. "I suppose, a step back to re-examine our options wouldn't be out of the question. What say you, Your Luminance?"

Sevi waddled stiffly around to face Innavin and Lorr. "I think that if I have to get anything, I would like something that I can walk in."

Innavin's face lit up. "Ah, casual wear! Yes, we can always get something plain and embroider it if necessary! My wife can do things with a needle that would make you *weep*. Miravena? Miravena! Show me your latest winter stock!"

Sevi pulled the offensive shirt over his head and tossed it to the ground with a huff as Innavin hurried off with the shopkeepers. Captain Lorr chuckled. "It's alright, lad. He gets like that with everyone. I'll go to the front and make sure he doesn't get too carried away, alright?"

Sevi nodded with a grimace. Lorr gave him a pat on the arm and disappeared behind the curtain after Innavin. Sevi looked at himself in the mirror, unable to summon even an ounce of enthusiasm. He had willingly chosen the life of a prince, so he couldn't be too upset. But Gods above and below, he *hated* dressing up in all these clothes! Why couldn't everyone just wear one kind for every season and stick to it? What was the point of *fashion?*

He bent with a sigh, gathering up a pile of discarded garments, and threw them off to the side. "I only wanted a shirt and pants that fit me," he muttered, reaching for a leather jerkin.

An oily hand shot up from the ground and grabbed his wrist.

He yelled and fell backward, but the hand refused to let go. It merely broke at the forearm, keeping its grip.

"Sevi? Is everything alright back there?" someone yelled from the front.

Sevi gaped at the hand's oily fingers twitching against his arm, close to screaming. They loosened slowly, then the whole thing dissipated into smoke before his eyes. Sevi soundlessly turned his gaze back to the floor. Two pale white lights bobbed about in his shadow, staring back at him. "Hmm," Shy hummed.

"Sh—Shy?" Sevi whispered.

Captain River called, "Sevi? Do you need help?"

"Ah, n-no, I just slipped!" Sevi called back. Shy's eyes bobbed about, watching him. He lowered his voice. "You're back!"

The creature wobbled at the fringes. Fragments of Shy's body tried to form a physical shape, straining upward from Sevi's shadow. But they couldn't do it. Every attempt to manifest themselves further failed, and they collapsed inward in a swirl of black smoke.

"Shy, *stop*, you're losing your dark again!" Sevi said with alarm.

But Shy didn't listen. Their eyes strained upward, as if trying to stand, but they only fell once more, bobbing up and down in a small puddle.

"You're hurting yourself! What is it? What do you want?"

Their eyes turned and swam to the edge of the shadow closest to the mirror, blinking in its direction. The little lights flickered sporadically, emphasizing Shy's intent.

"The mirror? No! Not if it will hurt you! How did this happen? Why did you go quiet?" Shy blinked up at him, flickering one light after the other, and made no sound. "Just... just go back to sleep, or into hiding, or whatever it is you do until you're better. I'll—"

The dressing room's curtain was thrown back. Sevi jumped. Captain River stood staring in with his hand on his pistol, looking down at Sevi with concern. "Are you alright?"

Sevi opened and closed his mouth. He darted his gaze back to Shy. Their lights had disappeared back into his shadow, reverting to a normal silhouette. He shook his head. Commander Tiersa had looked at him like he was crazy when he'd talked about the creature—and, as far as Sevi was concerned, he was. Non-crazy people didn't see visions, hear voices, and get shoved into mirrors. But he didn't need her or River *treating* him like one.

"I-I'm fine. I just slipped. There's a lot of clothes in here," Sevi said.

Captain River scrutinized the room before releasing his grip on his weapon. "I am sorry to disturb you." He nodded in apology before withdrawing, closing the curtain behind him.

Sevi remained on the floor for a while, watching his shadow. "Please be alright," he whispered, patting the darkness with his hand.

When he left the back, he'd donned a simple pair of black pants and a white long-sleeve shirt, much to Innavin's obvious disappointment. When he tried to convince Sevi further of buying more, Lorr was quick to shut him down. "One or two more pairs of clothing, and that's it. The commander didn't authorize buying the whole store."

The sun had moved a fair bit in the sky by the time they left. The city bells rang out three chimes past midday. Innavin's demeanor brightened at the sound. "It's still so early! If we leave now, we could all—"

Lorr cut him off. "No."

"I—"

"No."

"You don't even—"

"Know what you're going to say?" Lorr finished for him. "I told you that you'd be going alone. We came to gather supplies for one of our own. We have. I'm not about to waste military funds on watching, '*The Cobbler's Curse,*' for the twelfth time."

"I find that play quite charming myself," River said. "Who would have thought your language could make so many jokes about feet?"

"Please don't encourage him, Cal." Lorr sighed.

"What about our own funds?" Innavin persisted. "I still have... let me see." He fished out some coins from his pocket. "One glara, five chroma, and six coppens. Plenty to get us all in."

Lorr shook his head, flicking his gaze to Sevi. "I don't like the idea of prolonging our trip, given our current company. You all saw who we passed by the docks, didn't you?"

Some unspoken understanding passed between the men. Captain River looked troubled. "Who did we pass?" Sevi asked.

River shook his head. "Thugs. They are not so bold to challenge two Ember captains, especially with my family in port."

"We shouldn't risk it with the lad here," Lorr said, nodding to Sevi.

Captain River turned to Sevi, raising an eyebrow in speculation. "I promised to show our *risho* the city, dear, and I will not allow their fragile storm to steer me from my course. I do not think any harm will come to him from them of all people—not with Ilondia under our control."

"How about we ask His Luminance then?" Innavin suggested. "What do you say, Your Brilliance? Would you like to see a play at the best theater in the city? It's not a far walk from here by any comparison. I wouldn't mind going on my own if I must, but I would adore the chance to introduce my love to you all."

All three men looked at Sevi. He shifted. He'd only ever seen plays through his spyglass, when the Fablings brought them into the courtyard for special events. He, Lily, and Alyda had made it their own occasion, substituting the actors' dialogue with their own as they watched, while Alyda acted out her own responses.

The chance to see one up close proved to be too enticing to ignore, but he wanted to see it with his friends. It felt wrong, otherwise. "I want to see," he said. "But not without Lily."

Innavin smiled knowingly. "Ah. Caldwin mentioned your reunion. Not to worry! We can gladly bring her with us the next time we're in town!"

"The boy gave his answer, Vin. Let's go back to the wagons," Lorr said, adjusting his pack on his shoulder.

"If we head back now, we'll miss the matinee and there will be no point. Are you sure, lad?" Innavin pressed Sevi. "Is that what you want?"

Sevi looked down the street that led back to the docks. "I..."

"Your friend looked very tired when we found her," Captain River said. "Surely, we should let her sleep?"

"Cal." Lorr huffed.

Sevi sighed. True, if he woke Lily so soon after their argument, only to make her run through the city to catch a play, she would've laughed, turned on her side, and gone back to sleep, or joined with a sour mood. It wasn't as though Alyda could see out of Lily's bag, either. And Innavin had made another good point: now that Sevi had chosen to remain, he and his friends would have all the time in the world to see a play whenever they wanted.

*I'm a prince now. I need to start doing things on my own, right?*

Sevi straightened. "I'll go."

Innavin pumped his fist in celebration. Captain River smiled, and Lorr groaned. Innavin said extravagantly, "Let's hurry then! For fortune and glory!"

Captain River rested his hand on Lorr's back. "It will be fine. We will handle all that comes."

Lorr shook his head. "It wouldn't hurt to slow down, Caldwin. We could come back with a greater guard."

"We are guard enough, are we not?"

"Are we?" Lorr leveled a serious look. "Do you think we're enough to protect him?"

"So long as we keep our heads down, we will be fine."

"Tell that to *him*," Lorr said, hooking a finger at Innavin.

Innavin straightened his back. "I'll admit that I got carried away at Kylari, but I won't say a word more about our Sevinim, Lorr. I promise."

Lorr eyed Innavin for several moments, then drew in a long breath. "Fine. But, let it be known that I was the lone dissenter here. It will be your heads under the commander's blade, not mine."

"Agreed," Innavin said. "Now let's hurry!"

Innavin led the way, moving far faster than anyone else, forcing them to call for him on multiple occasions before they lost sight of him. Their path eventually led them to a broader street near the main one, as indicated by the cathedral's golden dome poking above the rooftops a short distance away. Unlike many of the other more monotonous alleyways they'd passed, this one held nothing but colorful buildings, each advertising a playful name such as, "*The Drippy Draught*," or, "*The Full Body*."

Innavin made a beeline for one in particular. It was unlike any of the buildings around it, boasting a large, closed dome that sat low and wide to the ground like a tortoiseshell. Above it was a long sign with a spool of thread at its end, writing out, "*The Golden Spool*." He stopped in front of two grand, crimson doors inlaid in an intricately carved stone threshold with his hands on his hips, staring at a sign hanging over one of the knobs.

Sevi squinted at it. *Closed for Rehearsal.* Lorr opened his mouth, but Innavin drew his fist back and pounded hard on the wood before he could utter a sound. When there was no response, he drew his leg back and kicked the wood hard. The doors shuddered violently under the blow.

"*Vin!*" Lorr gasped.

An angry voice yelled from within, "What in the name of Vikellin? Who's out there!"

Someone stomped heavily enough to the entrance that Sevi felt vibrations through the stone. The doors unlocked, and each pulled back to reveal a woman large enough to match Digby for size. She had deep, red hair and gray eyes as hard as iron, which she fixed on them from a stern countenance.

Innavin was completely unphased. "Jan, would you be so kind as to explain what fresh Torment this is? The Golden Spool does not close its doors for Innavin Targa, lest it face ruin and destruction."

Jan paused, flicking her gaze down to Innavin. Her hands looked big enough to wrap entirely around the smaller man's golden skull. Her demeanor, however, shifted completely, and she let go of the doors to cross her arms. She regarded him, and him alone, for a long while before she spoke. "Ain't ya supposed to be dead?"

Innavin looked affronted. "Excuse me?"

"Ya hadn't been here in four, maybe five years, Pip. And not a single letter. So ya were either dead, or yer lady finally got wise ta you an' me."

"*Madam.*" Innavin puffed out his chest. "How dare you insult my honor like this. As if Ryaliss wouldn't gladly be here herself."

"I don' see her though, do I?"

"That's because she wears a uniform now. She's at the castle, working her hands to the bone."

"What, one like them?" Jan nodded to River and Lorr. "Ya brought those uniforms, but not hers? I don' much mind watchers, Pip, but I'm surprised. You of all people."

"Sometimes, dearest, my passion moves me in such a way that even I cannot resist the allure of taboo. Such as the poor mistreatment of your precious door while you were otherwise occupied."

She and Innavin stared at each other for several breaths. A smirk slowly crept up the side of her face, and Innavin's shoulders trembled. Sevi looked between the two with growing confusion. "Get in here, Pip," Jan finally said, stepping aside. Innavin strode forward but turned and wrapped his arms tightly around her waist before he passed her. She returned the embrace with a deep, resonant chuckle. "It's good ta see you, too."

"I do apologize for the door," Innavin said, stepping back.

"Ya couldn't snap a twig let alone those doors." Jan smiled. "An' who're yer friends?"

"Ah. Yes. Please, allow me to make introductions. Captains Lorr Gallan and Caldwin River of the Embers of Korina, please meet my dear friend Eidijan Kinny. Owner and director of the Golden Spool."

"Pleasure." Jan nodded to the two men. "And who's the lad? Yer kid? He's a wee bit old, isn't he?"

"No, my dear lady, he's—" Innavin broke off at Lorr's glare, quickly recovering with, "He's Sevi. He's also a friend."

She looked Sevi over. Sevi found with some surprise that he didn't instinctively shrink from her gaze, having become familiar with that same look of appraisal on so many people after leaving the Cut. Jan clicked her tongue softly. "Not a soldier. That's good. Yer too young ta be playin' war." She put her hands on her hips. "Well come in, all o' ya. But keep yer lips shut, please. Ya interrupted our work."

Sevi and Lorr shared a look of discomfort, but Innavin and River entered with the air of two men returning home. They stepped into a small antechamber lined with colorful paintings. A doorless archway with luxurious cloth curtains stood before them, along with an unattended booth off to the side.

Innavin waited for them just before the arch along with Jan, and when they approached, he smiled and swept a single curtain back with a flourish. "Welcome, dear friends, to the finest theater in all Elkra. No! The finest theater known to mankind!"

Jan took the other curtain. "Yer stealin' me lines."

Sevi, River, and Lorr walked through. A massive room opened wide before them, split by an aisle that ran down a slope to end at a cylindrical stage. The platform connected to another by a catwalk, where a handful of impatient-looking actors waited, watching them all with critical stares. Rows of seats stretched to either side, traveling up a dozen steps before ending at the back wall, where box seats jutted out from higher levels. The one in the very middle was embossed with the golden crest of Astraeda.

The most interesting aspect of the room, however, was its ceiling. Every inch of its concave dome had been carved with a web of spiraling runes, each big enough to be distinguishable from the others. Glowing orbs, much like the orbs in the royal study, had been spaced evenly apart from each other, emitting a soft golden light.

"What's the meaning of this, Eidijan? This was supposed to be a closed rehearsal," a lady in a sheer white gossamer dress demanded. Two other ladies in the same outfit stood behind her with varying levels of annoyance.

"Sorry everyone!" Jan said. "We have an unexpected guest. An' he brought his friends."

Innavin waved at everyone. "Hellloooo, golden players! Your most prodigious patron returns to bask in your distinguished presence once more!"

"Is that Targa?" one actor said.

"You mean he's not dead?" another said, then louder, "Ain't you supposed to be dead?"

"So I've been told!" Innavin laughed. He squeezed his way through everyone to get to the front but was dragged roughly back by Lorr.

"Remember your promise, Innavin," Lorr said quietly. "Not a word."

Innavin tried to wave him off, but Lorr wouldn't let him. Innavin sighed and nodded. "I promise, oh Scowling Guardian, that not a word of Sevi's heritage shall pass mine lips, lest the storm goddess finish what she started all those years ago and strike me down. Satisfied?"

From the frown on his face Lorr looked anything but. "Say hello to your friends, and then let's leave. Don't take long." He relinquished his grip.

Innavin strode to the small stage, raising one hand above his head. "Help me up, Lock! Or are those muscles just for show?" He climbed up to embrace each of the actors one by one like long lost family, banishing the irritation from the face of every person he hugged. Sevi marveled at the infectiousness of the man's enthusiasm. It was as though he carried around a tiny sun inside of him that shone out from the locks of his hair, warming all it touched. "How long has it been since he was here?" Sevi asked.

"Not since the revolt four years ago," Lorr answered. "Maybe longer. He's been eager to return."

"I did not realize that he knew the actors personally," River said.

Jan chuckled from behind. "Aye. Came ta every show, helped with every costume, and spent every spare coppen he an' his wife had ta support us whenever we were short. I'm happy ta see the little man hasn't lost his smile after all this time. Did he do any fightin'?"

"No, but his wife has made an excellent lieutenant," Lorr said.

"Makes sense. Pip isn't much of a knight. His wife, on the other hand." Jan shrugged. "She's got iron in her enough ta forge a sword."

The actors on stage, once done with their reunion, began talking among themselves. Innavin gestured back at the two captains and Sevi, leading some actors to cast curious looks their way. Then Innavin lowered his voice and *all* of them turned to stare.

"I'm going to crack that fool's head open," Lorr grumbled.

"He enjoys being the center of attention far too much," River agreed, looking similarly vexed. Sevi's earlier confidence withered. He took a step back, hiding himself behind the two taller men.

Innavin made a remark that caused everyone on stage to laugh, then separated from them and turned to face the room. "My wonderful friends have agreed to put on a small show for us!" he announced. "Would that be alright with you, Jan?"

"We're in the middle of rehearsal!" Jan protested.

"Precisely! They're going to demonstrate the scene you all have been rehearsing! Would you allow me to help you work the dome?"

"Not happenin', Pip. Too much trouble. Ya can watch us workshop if you'd like."

"But my friends deserve the best, my dear lady! They've never seen true runic dreamlights at work!"

Jan put her hands on her hips with a frown. "Then ya can all come back on openin' night."

Innavin paused, then smiled wide. "What a wonderful idea. And what if I brought all my friends in the Embers with me? I might even be able to lure Promina Rinenne Kaymoor herself. I've mentioned the Spool to her before, and she seemed fairly impressed."

Jan stopped at that. Though her face was impassive, her eyes were wide.

"And..." Innavin continued, glancing over at Sevi and company.

"Here it comes," Lor muttered.

"I might even bring some other royal friends with me."

"*Royal* friends?" Jan said. "*What* royal friends?"

"Do this for me, and you'll find out," Innavin said, still smiling.

Jan tapped her finger on her hip, staring hard at Innavin. "Rinenne Kaymoor?"

"The very same."

"I have yer word?"

"Upon my honor, you have my word." Innavin put a fist to his heart.

Jan shook her head. "You little... *Fine*. I trust ya haven't fergotten how ta work the stones?"

Innavin hopped down from the stage. "As though I'd ever."

"Alright. Well. Places, everyone." Jan waved at the actors.

There was a smattering of laughter and chatter among them as they all did as instructed, with some leaving the stage altogether until only a few remained. Innavin walked back down the aisle, purposefully ignoring Lorr to wink at Sevi before joining Jan.

"I suppose we must now take our seats." Captain River shook his head, picking a suitable spot near the stage and sitting down. Sevi tentatively did the same, sitting next to him.

Lorr stood in the aisle with a grim look of resignation before finally sitting on the other side of River. "There's no helping fools."

"Sometimes it is best to join them," River said. "But I agree. Innavin is acting much like... one of those small furry creatures, from that saying."

"A weasel," Lorr supplied.

"Yes. A weasel." River looked at Sevi. "I am sorry for his behavior, *risho*."

Sevi shrugged, keeping his head away from the actors' view. "They'll all know about me eventually, I guess."

"Nobody knowing now was the whole point. We never should have brought him," Lorr muttered.

River patted his hand. "We will head right back afterward."

They settled into silence and waited for something to happen. Finally, the lights in the ceiling dimmed on their own, bringing the light level in the room down until it was completely dark. Sevi gripped at his chair and cast a nervous look around, for all the good it did him.

"Ladies and gentlemen," a soft, feminine voice called from the darkness. "Thank you for attending. Tonight, we give you, *The First Light*."

A rune lit up on the ceiling, throwing out a sharp beam of light that cut through the darkness to illuminate two figures on the stage: a lady, swathed in hues of green, and a man wearing orange.

"Far beyond the mind of man," the bodiless voice announced. "In ages long ago. In a time only the Timeless Lord, Eonin, truly knows..."

The man and lady stepped forward and faced one another, then slowly began to pace in a circle with gazes locked.

"When the Father and the Mother, under love's command. Birthed a world that each could touch, though not their lover's hand."

Sorvathos and Avinaea moved toward each other, lifting their hands to each other as close as they could get without actually touching. From their palms a light began to glow, beginning as a tiny speck that grew before their very eyes. They stepped apart from one another in time with its growth, giving it space, until it had become the size of a large pumpkin. And still they circled it, around and around.

"When the sky lay unbound, and Caela's realm lay free. When people walked through the air with naught but their feet. Where one domain spread 'cross every sea and ground, there, dearest friends, is where our story may be found."

The two gods flicked their arms out, and the entire ceiling burst into color, flashing with runes that dazzled for several breaths before extinguishing and plunging the room back into darkness. From the left of the stage, a trio of villagers appeared, each holding a lantern.

"The nights were darkest in those days, no single star to guide..."

The trio stopped, as before them, dust began to swirl about from the floor, climbing upward on top of itself, assembling into a shape. A monster with terrible horns and claws manifested from the dust, looming threateningly above the group. Sevi gripped at his shirt, staring wide-eyed at the creature. What strange vision was this?

"Shadows preyed with strength that made the brightest fires hide."

The villagers flung their arms up in fear, cowering before the vision, and each turned and fled the way they came. The monster crumbled to dust, disintegrating to the floor in a heap as a hazy, bluish light appeared to dimly illuminate the stage.

A new shape emerged from the dust of the monster's broken body: pointed towers and rooftops that rose proudly from the ground, accompanied by buildings of every size behind a vast wall, until an entire city had formed.

"Cities strong in Father's day and made of Mother's stone, would fall when night crept over land. Silent. Still. Alone."

A cracking sound violently rang out, and a deep fissure appeared across the face of the miniature city, crumbling it back to dust. Sevi clutched at Captain River's sleeve. "Is this real?" he whispered.

"From the darkest of these nights, when all were gripped with fear, the shadows broke, and from the sky, the smallest lights appeared."

Three tiny beams of light shot out from the back of the room, lancing toward the stage one after the other, forming three small circles against the back wall.

"One, two, three little shimmers, each no bigger than a pin. But grew with every passing night, 'til night itself gave in."

The lights widened into three massive circles that stood equidistant from each other. A trio of runelights lit up along the dome, and above the stage, the three ladies wrapped in flowing white cloth descended, entering the light of the beams as gracefully as falling snowflakes, floating through the air with nothing to support them.

Sevi tightened his grip on River's sleeve. They were *flying*.

Sorvathos and Avinaea appeared from the left and right of the stage, approaching one another as they had before, lifting their hands to recreate the glowing orb that was Iaela before resuming their dance around it. But this time, the three ladies joined them, stepping in between them to walk in their steps.

"When sun had set, where shadows laid, now only light would rest. Soothing blues and restful silver swathing every crest. Upon this gift, upon their word, they vigiled in the sky, and knew no sleep 'til shadows deep knew nothing but to die."

Monsters formed to the left and right of the dancers for but a moment, each crumbling to dust as quickly as they appeared. The scared villagers from before reappeared on stage, and the hazy blue light brightened to white, illuminating their happy, frolicking faces as they jumped about with joy.

"And with their light, a second gift, that we might rule our fate. On every eve they filled the air with magic's potent weight."

The villagers reached out their hands, and from the stage, lights shot up into the sky. From each light, a translucent plant sprung into being, climbing high into the air.

"All Creation at our touch would bow to but a thought... but every night these sisters grew, an omen of their plot."

The three ladies broke from their dance and moved closer to the world between the gods, each reaching out a hand with clawed fingers, as if to rake their nails across it. The plants that the villagers celebrated around suddenly shook, and broke, falling to the ground in piles, and their joy abruptly turned to horror.

"The aether turned to poison, every harvest turned to ash. Monsters born from dying night returned to kill and crash."

The monsters returned where the plants had withered, and the villagers flung themselves back in silent fright. Sorvathos flicked his arm away, and the light between he and Avinaea disappeared as he flung himself before her, blocking her from the three ladies who stalked after them across the stage.

"To save his love, the Father cast a great heavenly shield..."

Sorvathos lifted his hand toward the assailants, and they slowed.

"But poison still crept through its cracks to make our Mother yield."

Avinaea reached for the ceiling and fell to her knees, heaving and shuddering in obvious pain. Sorvathos turned to look back at her in anguish, reaching his free hand out to her. But she didn't move. Two of the sisters broke off and approached him, circling around him with coy, curling smiles.

"Twice these sisters tried to guile. Twice they were repelled..."

Sorvathos flung his arm up, and two beams of light flashed across the stage in rapid succession, silhouetting all its occupants in the brief moments of its existence. The two sisters rejoined the third, and each looked upon the god with fury.

"Before a third blow could be struck, our Parents sought them felled."

From the middle of the trio of villagers, a fourth rose from the floor. A woman dressed no differently than them, with her chin raised and her arms crossed, staring ahead as though the monsters assaulting the villagers were beneath her notice.

She raised one gloved hand above her head, and a light brighter than any other descended to encase her. She closed her fingers. The light retreated. And from her fist a magnificent shining bow made of silver dust appeared.

"A champion from the soil, on a sunlit bow lay claim..."

She strode forward, lifting her bow before her. With a snarl, she pulled back its ghostly string and struck at the attacking monsters, freeing the villagers from their onslaught, and continued forward down the stage's narrow walkway to the smaller stage reaching into the audience. She lifted her bow above her head. A rune on the ceiling glowed, and that same light crashed to the ground to envelop her once more.

"The Foremost Star. Mankind's First Light. Iviri, was her name!"

When the light dimmed, she was no longer wearing peasant's clothes. Now her entire body was armored in glowing, ghostly silver plates, as resplendent as any champion of old. She turned to face the main stage. The villagers and the gods departed, leaving only Iviri and the three sisters.

Each of the sisters spread out their arms. More lights along the ceiling lit up, and as one, Iviri and the three rose into the air, staring viciously at one another. Iviri pressed off with one foot as if to jump forward. Each of the three did the same. And then the theater went black.

Sevi's breath caught. A light flashed, briefly illuminating each of the actors in a new state of attack. Then it flashed again, and again, until the room strobed with it. The dome's runelights flickered on and off in a mesmerizing pattern as the battle unfolded. The sisters clawed and flung orbs of light at Iviri, while she would return a deadly hail of arrows from the sky, shooting them off as fast as the three in a breath-catching stalemate.

But then one of the sisters screamed. A silver arrow sprouted from her chest. The remaining sisters looked on in horror, and in their distraction, Iviri claimed the life of another. But the third sister would not be felled, and with a scream more terrible than the first two's dying howls, she unleashed a devastating burst of light on Iviri that caught her full in the chest. The last thing Sevi saw before the theater went black again was the hero falling limply from the sky. His heart hammered against his ribcage, the only sound in the theater, save for his quick breaths.

"For thirteen days, she fought these foes, her arrows striking true. Breaking two of foulest three for all Iaela's view."

The dome glowed. From the darkness, a pinprick of light appeared, and gently split into two. Then four. Then... many. The entire room became swathed in a vast field of silver, glowing stars, as though they had climbed a rope of light to walk among the night sky as gods themselves. Lucent motes floated by Sevi's face, no mere beams of light, but actual stars that shone on their own.

"Their pieces turned to silver lights, to birth a field of stars..."

Sevi reached out tentatively to one, wrapping his palms around it as delicately as holding water, as though any gap between his fingers would cause its light to drain from his hands. "A dream," he whispered, passing his fingers through the star.

"Our champion worn, her body spent. The third could not be scarred."

Another light lanced across the theater. There, a single sister remained, hanging suspended in the air alone with her head down in mourning.

"In a flash of light, the great Iviri fell to world below. Her body swathed in flower soft, her spirit set aglow."

That same hazy blue light appeared to illuminate more of the stage. The villagers had gathered around Iviri, resting her body on a bed of flowers, no longer shining. One of them carried a lantern, which they morosely touched to the flowers. An orange light slowly rose from beneath the plants.

"No longer did we feel the sting of ethereal bane. But nor did such a thing disperse... for one sister remains."

The remaining sister curled inward on herself with her arms around her legs, turning parallel to the stage. From the shadow behind her a grisly form manifested, full of spikes and thrashing tendrils, as if it had taken a monstrous life of its own.

"But do not fret, my dearest ones. Do not shrink nor cry. Don't look upon this specter with fear in any eye."

Sorvathos and Avinaea reappeared on the stage, standing just behind the weeping villagers.

"By Father's hand her spirit flew for endless vigil's chill..."

The glow surrounding Iviri's body intensified, and ever so gently, she lifted off the ground. The villagers looked up, gasping with amazement, as Iviri ascended. Midway up to the ceiling, she slowed, and stopped, turning gradually until she stood upright. Sorvathos and Avinaea strode across the stage, and they too ascended, rising in the air to join her.

"To guard her children every night..." the voice said softly.

Iviri's eyes sprung open, and she crossed her arms with a smirk.

"And to this day, she watches still."

# Chapter 42

*High where the voices were listless and free, where stories were born and retold. Was my song to your liking? Will you carry my words? May I share in a piece of your soul?*

———— ❧ ————

"That was *incredible*," Sevi exclaimed outside the theater. Innavin and the captains, despite Lorr's objections, had spent an hour conversing with the actors after the show, while Sevi listened with rapt attention. The play had borne a startling resemblance to the story Lily had told him about the three sisters, but it differed wildly in tone. He'd tried voicing his confusion to everyone, only to be met with equal perplexity from the actors. "That's how *The First Light* goes," Jan had said. "Haven't ya heard it before? It's a classic."

It was only when Lorr had cited the time that they ended their conversation and said their goodbyes. And just as he had promised, the moment they had left the theater, Lorr pounded Innavin on the head hard enough to make him totter.

The sun hung low in the sky as they made their way through the streets, casting the alleys into shadow. Innavin beamed at Sevi. "I knew you would like it, Your Luminance."

"How did they do all that? How did they *fly?*" Sevi asked.

"Runic magic! Once upon a time, when your family regularly visited, the Golden Spool had enough money to hire their very own Runic to enchant all manner of things. It was such a delight to see the spellwork hasn't faded yet, though the effects were considerably less impressive this time, I'm sorry to say."

"*That* was unimpressive?" Sevi said incredulously.

"Fair enough!" Innavin laughed. "There aren't many theaters who can match that alone!" He stretched his arms. "Ah, what a lovely day. Two of my favorite establishments, still around after the war. What else could I ask for? And Rya will love what I picked out for her, I'm certain."

"Why not just buy Kylari already?" Lorr said.

"I've considered it, actually. If Rya is ready to settle down, and if we have enough between us, then maybe I'll make an offer. The Golden Spool could use a dedicated clothier."

"They do not already have one?" River asked.

"I stand amended—a *good* dedicated clothier."

The corner of Lorr's mouth turned down. "It's all the same to me."

"That's why Caldwin comes to me for advice and not you." Innavin smirked.

"Caldwin?" Lorr raised an eyebrow at River.

Captain River shrugged. "He is very... em... knowledgeable? He knows much about this country's clothes."

"Well, it's not too late for our little prince at least," Lorr aimed at Sevi. "You can still run if you want."

Sevi looked at Lorr with alarm. "I'm not running."

"Ha! That's two, Lorr!" Innavin said.

"Well, *this* is one you'll never sink your nails into," Lorr retorted, hooking his thumb at himself.

Innavin laughed. "Oh, ye of little foresight. Tis but a matter of time."

Sevi sighed. The play had restored some energy, but the day's excitement had left him feeling drained. "Where are the wagons?"

"Close," River replied. "Have you enjoyed your trip into the city?"

For such a harmless question, it was difficult to answer. "It was... nice," Sevi said.

"And there will be plenty of trips just like it once you wear the crown, Your Brilliance!" Innavin announced.

"*Innavin*," Lorr snapped.

"Ah. Your stableboyness."

Their path took them around a corner and deposited them beneath a large bridge above the street. Beyond it lay the river and the vibrant bustle of the market. The sun cast a golden hue across the gentle, sparkling waves of the harbor, enhancing the prows of the Ta'Runan riverboats bobbing up and down. At a glance, the crowd was no different than the water; shifting, breathing, babbling, and dancing in the light and shadows of the fading day.

Relief washed through Sevi at the sight. But as they moved underneath the bridge, a figure stepped out to block their path. A short, burly, bearded man, covered in tattoos. He gave them an unfriendly smile. "Evening, boys."

The four of them drew to a halt. Captain River grabbed hold of Sevi and pulled him in as at least a dozen similarly tattooed men appeared from the alleys behind them, blocking any retreat. Knives, swords, and all other manner of dangerous metal glinted menacingly among them.

The leader's grin widened as two more men joined him at his sides. One carried a large cudgel. The other carried a rifle. Sevi clutched at his chest, seeing visions of the man who'd shot him in the stranger's bearded face.

Any people walking by hurried away until the street had emptied completely. Captain Lorr was the first to recover. He dropped his bag and stepped forward, putting himself between the leader and Sevi. "Lads, you are attempting to keep two officers of the Embers of Korina from their duties. Surely there is easier prey about?"

The leader's smile never wavered. A long, dangerous looking rapier swung at his side as he approached Lorr, stopping a careful distance away. "Aye. There's plenty of pickings. *Plenty* of pickings," he said slowly, drawing a laugh from the surrounding men. "But"—he brought one finger up to Lorr's face— "I see only one officer here, friend."

Captain River's hand clenched at Sevi's shoulder.

Lorr arched his eyebrow. "Maybe I need to get my uniform cleaned."

"Oh no no no, you're the spitting image of a knight!" the leader said, turning casually to the man with the rifle. "Innit he, Karsh?"

"Aye, he's got a look of Sier Valdor about 'im, Torv," Karsh said.

"That he does. That he certainly does," Torv continued smoothly, facing Lorr once more. "And far be it from me to scrape up a mug like that. The Father would throw me out to the Watcher the moment I smoked."

"Gentlemen, nobody knows theater better than I," Innavin said, stepping forward to join Lorr, "and I daresay this show is, I'm sorry to say, a drag. What is your intent?"

Torv scowled. "Wasn't talking to you, frills. I'm talking to Sier Valdor."

Captain Lorr's face remained impassive. "Torv, was it? I'm afraid I must echo my friend here. What are you getting at? If you attempt to hurt us, you will answer to the Embers, and all the strength we have to bear."

"Maybe. Maybe not," Torv said, looking unbothered. "There's no need for this to get messy. We're chums, you and us. Your lot did such a good job cleaning up the goblins; we're just cleaning the spots you've missed. So, I'll cut you a deal, Valdor. You, and the lad, and the ponce can walk free. But the river-shit stays."

Lorr's fists tightened at that, and his posture noticeably changed. Sevi looked up at Captain River. His face, normally so carefree, had hardened into solid stone.

"That man," Lorr said through a clenched jaw, "is an officer of the Embers."

"He's a tick pretending to be the dog whose blood it's sucking," Torv said. "And if you don't hand him to me, right now... well. Think of the kid, Valdor. I always hate beating a man to death in front of a kid. Don't you, Karsh?"

"Not really." Karsh shrugged with a wicked smile.

"Not really, he says," Torv laughed. "So be glad that I'm the one you're dealing with." He held out his hand to Lorr, staring pointedly into the captain's eyes. "Well?"

Captain Lorr blew a breath out of his nose in what could have been a laugh. "You know something? I think—"

"That's a *marvelous* idea!" Innavin finished loudly for him.

Both Captain Lorr and Torv swiveled to Innavin. He was positively *beaming.* "Quite right, quite magnificent, you big, beautiful, generous man!" Innavin sidled up in front of Lorr. "I always did like generosity in a man you know." He reached out a flirtatious hand to touch Torv's bicep, drawing a look of disgust from the man. Innavin looked up at Captain Lorr. "I'm sorry, Lorr, darling, I really am, but you know how my skin bruises, don't you? I can't do violence, I really can't, and it's a fair deal he's offering, isn't it?"

Lorr started. "What? What—"

"But of course, we will get out of here *right* away!" Innavin continued exuberantly, raising his voice above Lorr's. "What's one dead Runan, right Lorr? He's hardly worth it... however"— Innavin moved his hand from Torv's bicep, sneaking it around his back conspiratorially— "I must say, you really don't know the company you're addressing, do you, dear?"

Torv shoved Innavin's hand off him. "What are you getting at, frills?"

Innavin put his arm right back. Torv looked ready to draw his sword. "Oh, come now, surely you've heard the rumors, haven't you? We live just up the road at the castle, where His Luminance, crown prince Isevidel Astraeda, has been found *alive.*"

Torv froze. His band of brigands muttered among themselves. "Start talking sense, frills," he said darkly to Innavin, "or you get to stay with the river rat."

"Well, you see, sir, our prince, bright be his name, bedazzling be his house, is standing right before you!" Innavin waved at Sevi dramatically. Sevi's heart plummeted into his stomach. *What the dusk is he doing!*

Torv was silent. Karsh was silent. All the thugs around them were silent.

Then Torv threw his head back and laughed.

Each of his followers did the same, pointing and jeering at Sevi and Innavin. Torv's face went completely red as he choked on his own breath, thumping one fist against his chest. "That... that's good... that's a *good* one, you lacey little bender!" the man roared.

"Oh, ye of disbelief!" Innavin called, raising his voice above their laughter. "Disbelievers! Heathens, I say! Can you not see the truth before thine very eyes? How doth his hair not match that of our dearly departed monarchy? How doth his eyes not shine as King Marovhan's had?"

Innavin left Torv's side and trotted imperiously over to Sevi, grabbing hold of his wrist and pulling him from River's grasp. A look passed silently between him and River before he turned away. He brought Sevi over to stand before Torv and pulled at Sevi's necklace, tugging the star out of his shirt. "And see you, nonbelievers! He doth wear their mark!"

Torv quieted at the sight of the silver star. On cue, his band did the same. Innavin now commanded everyone's undivided attention. "So you see, darling," Innavin said, taking Sevi's hand and strolling casually between Torv and Karsh, marching Sevi along in front of him. "Unless you allow the prince to pass, you will not merely feel the weight of the Embers! NAY! Ye shall feel the weight of Iviri's wrath herself!"

"Hey!" Torv barked, moving toward them, "*Stop walk—*"

Someone shouted above them, interrupting whatever Torv was going to say. Torv jerked his head up, and as if waiting for that very moment, Innavin hurled his knapsack at Karsh and yanked Torv's rapier from its sheath. Then he reeled his leg back and kicked him hard in his belly, sending him careening backward.

Right into Lorr's waiting arms.

Captain River spun to face the brigands behind him, pressing his back to Lorr's. His gun appeared in his hands, leveled dangerously at the crowd. Lorr, meanwhile, had drawn his own, placing it snugly against Torv's temple.

"Go!" Innavin shouted, pointing his newly acquired rapier at Karsh's throat. But the man with the cudgel was free to move, and he was coming right at Sevi. Swatting the rifle out of Karsh's hands, Innavin tugged the man forward and pushed him into the other.

Sevi backed away in shock.

"SEVI! *GO!* GET THE OTHERS!" Innavin yelled.

More violence. More bloodshed. More fear. It had all happened so quickly that it had frozen Sevi's legs to the stone. But at Innavin's order, he moved.

Lowering his head, Sevi bolted out of the alleyway and into the light, running pell-mell toward the Ta'Runa's ships. He didn't stop. He didn't look back. He let his fear drive him forward, ducking and weaving through the crowd, taking every opening between people faster than they could close, and making one when he couldn't.

But there were so many of them. Too many. They pressed in on him at all sides with all the noise of a hundred conversations, threatening to box him in entirely, ready to crush him and any hope of saving his friends with impunity. A loud noise sounded out behind him. He didn't turn. The ships grew bigger as he got closer, calling to him with the promise of sanctuary. So close, yet just beyond reach.

He almost didn't recognize Digby's face when it appeared from the small crowd of charcoal Ember uniforms and golden Ta'Runan silks, mingling together with a batch of crates and barrels between them. "Sevi?" Digby said in alarm as Sevi came crashing into the huddle.

"River... Help... *Help.*" Sevi panted, pleading with his eyes and gripping the big soldier's arm, unable to get it all out.

Diby shook him. "Lad! What is it? What's wrong? Where are the others?"

Sevi screamed in his head, *stop standing here! Go help them!* But the words couldn't get out. He took a breath, forcing himself to calm. "They're... they're under *attack!*" Sevi pointed back the way he came, begging him to move.

Digby blinked and looked the way Sevi pointed just as a gunshot sounded.

Every conversation along the dock died, plunging the market into unnatural silence. Looking back the way he'd come, Sevi saw a large plume of smoke dispersing in the sky above the rooftops. As he watched, another cloud appeared from nothing, popping into a red mist, accompanied by the sound of a blaring horn. It had a noticeable effect on the Ta'Runa, who shouted with sudden urgency and leapt into motion.

Lieutenant Digby didn't hesitate either. He pulled a silver whistle from his coat and brought it to his lips, blowing out a loud, shrill noise that caught every soldier's attention. "ARMS!" Digby cried.

As one, the Embers dropped whatever they carried, gathered their guns, and closed ranks. Digby turned to the remaining Runans and said something in their language. The person he addressed, a short, muscled man with a sash around his middle, nodded to him with a serious expression, shouting out to several of his people who went sprinting past, all carrying deadly looking crossbows.

More gunshots rang out.

A call was taken up by every Runan on the dock. From the decks of the nearest ships, sailors appeared with swords, spears, crossbows, and rifles, throwing them down to those below, who in turn passed them all the way up to the front of the berth. When the closest sailors had rifles in their hands the leader nodded to Digby once more.

Digby took a deep breath and shouted, pointing across the market. "Novar, Tammavin! Stay with the Ta'Runa and protect our cargo! All else to the captains!"

The Embers rushed forward in loose formation, guns across their chests with barrels pointed up. The crowd parted before them as they went sprinting through. More of the armed Runans followed, mingling gold with charcoal and looking no less deadly.

Digby and the Runan leader quickly saluted each other before Digby turned to follow his troops, slowed by his bad leg. The Runan leader stayed, taking cover behind the wagons with some of his crew and peering across the crowd with a fearsome look, as though they had suddenly become his enemies.

Sevi tried to follow the Embers, but Digby flung an arm across his chest, blocking him. "Get in the wagon," Digby ordered.

Sevi tried to protest. "But—"

"*Get,*" Digby growled. Sevi jolted, shrinking at the lieutenant's guttural tone. The soldier's eyes softened at the edges. "Ya did good gettin' here, lad. I have it now." He jerked his head toward the cart, offering no further argument. The metal on his jacket caught the sun when he turned away, and for the briefest of moments, a knight's full plate manifested around him, only disappearing when Sevi blinked.

Reluctantly, Sevi climbed up into the wagon to join Cassik and Lily, the latter of which was yawning drowsily, only just waking up. "What's going on?" she mumbled, pushing her visor up.

"Where's your spyglass?" Sevi demanded.

"What?" she muttered, rubbing her eyes.

"Do you have your spyglass with you?"

She fixed him with an annoyed look. Without a word, she opened her knapsack and reached carefully inside, rooting around for a few breaths before pulling out her brass spyglass. "Sorry Alyda," Lily whispered softly into her bag's opening before closing it again.

Sevi hurriedly took the glass and joined Cassik at the side of the wagon facing the commotion. Loma stood with her rifle ready on the dock, stamping impatiently from foot to foot. Sevi brought the spyglass to his face and stood up as tall as he could, looking over the sea of people to the alley with anticipation.

Lorr and River stood back-to-back among a ring of thugs. When one moved, so did the other, matching each other's actions in a deadly performance of precision, as though they'd rehearsed it countless times. They pressed against each other, constantly at attention, ready to fend off the next attack from any direction.

Lorr had lost his gun and had drawn his sword, parrying and deflecting any metal that came within his reach. River carried both his sword and a knife, standing in a strange stance with arms held loosely before him. When an enemy ran their blade at him, he moved to the side, stepped in, swatted their arm with his sword and stabbed his dagger into the meat of their limb. When a thug came at him with a cudgel he swept to the side. Lorr mirrored his motion, maneuvering around to bring his sword up to deflect, fighting him off with the superior speed and reach of the steel.

They moved in perfect harmony. Like dancers in a ballroom. Like waves in the sea. But it wasn't flawless. They were outnumbered six to one, and the thugs didn't stand back to run at them one at a time. Multiple tears and cuts covered the two captains' arms and legs. Lorr had a nasty red gash along his ribs, visible even through Sevi's spyglass. And at every breath that passed, their odds of survival dwindled.

The only thing saving the captains was the disarray of their enemy; each brigand looked too afraid to step within striking distance of the two battle-hardened soldiers, and the six bodies at their feet served as a stark warning. But it wouldn't last forever.

Sevi squinted harder through the spyglass, clenching at its brass. One of those bodies had brilliant golden hair. Innavin, lying with his head in a puddle of blood. "No," Sevi choked. He hadn't been quick enough.

He shifted his focus back to the captains, suddenly terrified. They were tiring. He could see it. What had felt long to Sevi in his mad dash through the market had been an eternity for them. Their movements were slowing while the thugs had bodies to spare.

Lorr stumbled. A brigand moved forward with a sword. River shoved Lorr over, standing firmly in his place, ready to take the sword himself.

Just as a crossbow bolt struck the brigand in the chest.

Two more followed, fired from the hands of the Ta'Runa. The swordsman wobbled back, staring at the arrows sticking out of him in shock.

And then the Embers opened fire.

The line of thugs behind Lorr and River fell as a hail of bullets ran through them, filling the world with their horrible crackling and dropping them to the cobblestone. River ducked instinctively at the first shot, throwing his body on top of Lorr's.

Sevi watched as the rest of the brigands, a hair's breadth away from felling the captains, dropped their weapons in fear and ran back up the alley, melting into the shadows of the corridor with the Embers in dogged pursuit. The Runans stayed behind, forming a loose, protective circle around River, Lorr, and Innavin's body.

The last thing Sevi saw before the spyglass fell from his boneless fingers were the two captains hugging each other. His legs gave out from under him, and he sank to his knees. "Thank the gods," he whispered.

"What happened?" Lily said, still groggy. She ambled over sluggishly, picking up her fallen spyglass. "Careful with this, I only have one." She lifted it to her eye, peering toward the bridge.

"W-we were attacked," Sevi stuttered, staring at his hands.

"What?" Lily's tone sharpened.

"Inna... Innavin is dead."

"Who the dusk is Innavin?"

"He..." Sevi closed his eyes. "He..."

"Is he the tall one or the short one?" she asked.

Sevi looked up at her. "W-what?"

"He's not the one with all the fancy names, and I'll bet he's none of the shirtless ones in gold, so is he the tall one or is he the short one?"

"Th-the short one."

"Well, he's standing up."

Sevi gaped. "What!?"

"Look." Lily handed him the spyglass.

Sevi jumped to his feet, lifting the scope back up. Lorr, River, *and* Innavin were all standing! Lorr was held by River, supporting his wounded side, while Innavin stood under his own power, holding the side of his bloody head. His other hand was on a Runan's shoulder, and he wobbled unsteadily on his feet. Perhaps sensing he had an audience, Innavin widened his arms out to the officers and the Runans as if he could embrace them all at once. He lifted his pallid, smiling face up to the sky and took a sweeping bow, like an actor on his stage thanking all in attendance from the bottom of his heart.

# Chapter 43

*A dream in place of a memory to be. War where she could not be found. So quickly he grew to be wind in her grasp for the sake of a dangling crown.*

The return trip to the castle was an expedient one. Every Ember had been mustered after the attack, and the city placed under curfew. The Embers and the Ta'Runa hastily closed their deal, and the guard presence around the Runan berth was increased.

Innavin was able to hobble back to the wagons, but he had a nasty gash across the side of his face, and a piece of his ear had been ripped clean off. When he saw Sevi, he managed a large, senseless grin, and garbled, "Yer Lumer-ince! Howass my performince?" Then he laid down in the wagon, and after his head had been bandaged, went to sleep without a sound. Captain River joined Lorr in the back, each tiredly resting against the other while clutching their wounds.

Sevi explained to Lily what had happened and tried asking about the assailants, but Captain River had shaken his head, only saying, "You recall how people love how I look? Those ones love me too much." The cart then fell into a state of torpor that lasted throughout the ride back.

The sun had set by the time they returned. The castle lanterns had been lit, and Commander Tiersa, Promina, and an entire host of soldiers were standing at attention in the courtyard when they came rolling through the wall. Sevi spotted Corporal Reynam among them toward the front, but he turned away from Sevi's gaze.

"I was about to lay waste to that entire godsdamned city if you had taken even half an hour longer," Tiersa said to Digby with a thunderous expression, clenching the hilts of her swords.

"Sorry, Commander," Digby said, tiredly letting go of the reins once the horses had come to a stop.

"Was it the greenbloods?" Promina asked.

Digby shook his head. "No. Some gutter dogs from the Dawn cornered the captains when they were out with the lad."

Commander Tiersa loosened her grip on her weapons, stoically walking around to the back of the cart to face its battered occupants. "A simple, quiet trip into town to buy Isevidel new clothes?" she said pointedly to Captain River.

Captain River removed his arm from around Lorr and offered the commander a weary salute. "Not as quiet or simple as I had hoped."

Tiersa lowered her chin. "If anything had happened to Isevidel, River, I would have killed you myself."

"I understand."

"You're lucky nobody was killed at all."

Lorr arched his eyebrows. "Well—"

"Nobody I care about, Captain Gallan," Commander Tiersa cut him off crisply. "And I intend to have you all explain yourselves the second you're out of the infirmary. Come here, Isevidel, we must get you cleaned up at once." She reached out to Sevi.

Sevi arduously pushed himself up and carefully navigated around Innavin, who shifted where he lay, moaning softly. He nudged Lily with his foot as he passed. She had fallen asleep yet again. One of her many talents.

"Wha-are we there yet?" Lily yawned, uncurling her arms from around her knapsack and stretching all her limbs. She lifted her visor and looked around, jolting at the number of people staring into the cart. "Something on my face?" she challenged, hugging her knapsack back to her chest.

Tiersa noticed Lily for the first time, fixing her with a surprised stare. "Who is this?" she asked as Sevi put his hand in hers, jumping from the wagon.

Sevi turned to help Lily down, but she swatted him away irritably and got out herself. "This is Lily," he said. "My friend. The one who saved me after the invasion."

"Lily?" Commander Tiersa repeated. "Where did you find her?"

"She's been in town. She thought I was dead and ran when you all attacked."

Tiersa continued to stare at her. "Where did you get that helmet?"

Lily wrinkled her brow and placed her hand on her helmet's crown, staring distrustfully at the commander. "What? The last guy wasn't using it. It's mine now."

"Are you aware that it's the helm of the former Astral Guard?"

"Lady, it could've been worn by the king for all I care. It's mine now."

Sevi hurriedly interjected. "*Lily*, this is Commander Tiersa. *Leader of the army*. And my... aunt?"

"More or less. Has she been tested?" Tiersa said tersely.

Sevi froze. "Can't that wait until tomorrow?"

"All must be tested upon entering the army, Isevidel. We mustn't allow any of the enemy into our ranks, especially now that you've returned to us."

"Enemy? Lily has been with me for four years, and she's never taken off that helmet. She's not a Fae!"

"She's been missing for several months, hasn't she?" Tiersa beckoned at Promina. "Anything might have happened in that time. She must be tested. After which, I will personally welcome her with open arms, as anyone who rescued you should be."

Promina stepped up to the commander and proffered a vial of quicksilver. Tiersa reached into her hair and pulled out the same pin she had used on Sevi. "Step forward, Miss Lily," she ordered.

"Sevi?" Lily said softly.

Sevi turned to look at her. Her eyes were wide and afraid. He panicked. *No. No, no, no.* He *couldn't* fail her so soon. He needed more *time!* "S-stop! I'm telling you, she's not Fae!"

Tiersa raised her eyebrow. "It's just a drop of blood."

"I..." Sevi desperately grasped for an excuse. "There's too many people. Sh-she's afraid of needles." Commander Tiersa frowned.

Promina looked skeptically at Sevi from behind her, along with everyone else. "It's true! We should get Doctor Lea to do it, she could—"

Shaking her head, Tiersa grabbed Lily's hand and brought it up, plucking her finger with the tip of the needle. Lily gasped and reflexively tried to pull away, but Tiersa's grip held firm. With a casual turn of Lily's hand, she emptied her drop of blood into the vial of quicksilver.

Nothing happened.

There was no flash of light, as what *should* have happened when quicksilver met faeblood. Tiersa shook the bottle and held it up to the light, watching its contents swirl around with a critical eye. It stayed silver.

Sighing, Commander Tiersa returned the vial to Promina and fixed Lily with a small smile. "Forgive me. I had to be sure."

Lily said nothing. She brought her finger to her mouth, sucking on the wound with a distant expression while clutching her bag tightly to her chest.

"Please," Commander Tiersa continued, stepping sideways with her arm open. "Come eat with us. You must be hungry."

Lily took several breaths to answer, distantly saying, "Famished."

Tiersa nodded once to Promina. "Keep the Empyreans up. I don't care if this was caused by the scum from the Dawn, I'll not allow the greenbloods to hit us while our attention is divided. Every bird stays in the skies tonight."

Promina stepped up in her place to address the soldiers. "You assist the injured. You squads help unload. Every Empyrean stays. The rest are dismissed."

Loma tried to join them while Cassik sought out a doctor for his leg, but Tiersa waved her off, dismissing her for the evening. Sevi spared a backward glance at the cart one last time as the soldiers gingerly put Innavin on a stretcher. One of them, a woman wearing an officer's uniform, stood by his head with a dark expression, staring rigidly at the unconscious man. Then the rest of the assigned groups crowded around, blocking Sevi's sight, and he turned away.

The commander led Sevi and Lily to the dining room and ordered the cooks to gather what remained of dinner for the two of them. She asked them questions while they ate, which Sevi answered to the best of his ability. Lily remained silent, picking at her plate with a scowl. At the end of it, Tiersa crossed her arms and slipped back into her stone-faced armor. "The New Dawn," she grumbled. "More like a fresh eclipse. Now I must deal with those mongrels in Ilondia as well?"

"Who are they?" Sevi asked.

"Pretenders, hounding the light of my success with their shadow, with equal parts anger and ambition," she said. "Until now they've been content to let me carry the weight of the resistance, whilst picking at whatever lowly straggling Fae crosses their path. But to attack two of my officers in the light of day? They must be—"

She broke off, darting a look at Sevi. "Ignore me. This is for me to handle. I... am very glad you are well, Isevidel. They could have hurt you. I should have gone with my instinct and ordered a larger guard; River and his subtlety be damned."

Sevi shook his head. "He couldn't have known."

"No. But he should have assumed the worst. Instead, he believed that everything would transpire exactly as he'd thought."

Sevi shrugged. "Well, it might not have been exactly as he thought, but I think he'd say that things did work out in the end if he were here."

Tiersa barked out a surprised laugh, startling Sevi at the sound. It was the first bit of earnest humor he'd heard from her. "Gods, that would be just like him, wouldn't it?" she said.

Recovering, Sevi chuckled. "Yeah."

"*Ack!*"

Lily thumped her chest, rolling something in the back of her throat with an off-putting hacking sound and swallowing loudly. When Tiersa and Sevi looked at her, she shrugged. "That chunk of lamb was a little too big. Please, don't let me interrupt you."

The commander arched an eyebrow at her. "I have been neglecting you, Miss Lily, I apologize. As someone who has also looked after Isevidel, surely you can share my joy that he was unharmed?"

Lily shrugged, glancing at Sevi. "Sevi is a coward. But maybe he can look after himself now. He did a decent job of it for four years."

"With you there to guide him," Tiersa said. "From the way he talks about you, it's obvious that he holds you and your abilities in high regard."

"We protected each other," Lily said flatly.

"But the fact that you were there to save him at all, and for four years no less, means more to me than you can know, young lady." Tiersa leaned forward against the table. "If there is anything that you want, anything at all in my power to give you, then you need only name it."

"Anything?" Lily tilted her head and crossed her arms, adopting a thoughtful expression. "I'll have to think about it."

"Please do," Commander Tiersa said, leaning back. "It would please me to no end if I could repay Isevidel's savior with compassion in kind. I'll have a word with the quartermaster and see if we might be able to reserve a room in the castle entirely for you."

Lily waved her off. "Nah. I'll sleep in Sevi's room."

Commander Tiersa froze. "It would be highly improper to have the unwed prince share a room with anyone."

"Well, you can write it up as part of that favor then. If he's the prince, I'll bet he has his own chamber pot."

Commander Tiersa eventually relented and allowed Lily to share Sevi's room at Sevi's prompting. When dinner ended, she bid them both a good night, ordering two soldiers to escort them back to the royal chambers while she went off on other business. Much to Sevi's delight, she also promised to send someone in the morning with hot water for a bath, provided that a screen be put up to maintain a level of decency.

Sevi immediately headed for his bundle of blankets on the floor once they'd gotten to the bedroom, only to find that someone had removed them and placed new ones on the bed. Grumbling, he yanked the cover off the mattress and threw it back into his corner before collapsing into it with a weary sigh, heavy with exhaustion. "Thank Gods," he breathed, elated to be someplace quiet again.

Lily moved across the room, saying nothing.

"Hey. Why didn't the quicksilver work?" he asked, muffled through the sheets. "Thank the gods it didn't."

"No clue. Who cares?"

A scraping sound filled the air as something heavy moved across the floor. Sevi opened his eyes and watched as Lily pushed the dresser away from the Cut. "What are you doing?"

"Getting out of here," she said, not looking back.

Sevi's tiredness disappeared in a flash. He bolted upright. "What?"

"I need to cool my head." Lily loosened the top of her bag and reached in. She carefully withdrew Alyda's small green form, shining dimly in the low light of the room. "And Alyda has had a rough day in my bag. I'm going to bring her somewhere she can stretch her wings." Alyda sluggishly flicked her wings and chimed a long, tired note in agreement.

Sevi started to stand. "I'll come with you."

"I have a better idea. Don't." Lily glared at him. "I'll be back before dawn. Or not. So don't wait up for me, princeling."

"Wait!" Sevi called. "Lily! I'm sorry! I'm sorry about the quicksilver! I didn't think Tiersa would be there!"

She turned her back on him, ducked low, and entered the Cut, disappearing into its waiting darkness without another word. Sevi watched until Alyda's light disappeared. Turning back to his pile, he curled himself up in the blankets and stared at the wall. Sleep came slowly, impeded by his guilty thoughts, and when it arrived at last his dreams were tumultuous. Visions of Iviri shining in the night sky, ready to do battle with the Three Sisters, warred with those of the persistent fires that had become so familiar, swallowing Lily and Alyda as they turned their backs on him and vanished into the Cut forever.

When day broke, Lily had not returned. Sevi sat up against the wall, watching the Cut from across the room for an hour, hoping to catch a glimmer of Alyda. But they never showed. He made the decision to slide the dresser back over its entrance rather than risk exposing it to a visitor. It might not have been necessary, but it gave him comfort knowing that some small piece of the Cut's secret remained with him and his friends, should they ever need it. He then returned to staring at the wall.

The soldier that delivered breakfast looked oddly at him before leaving. Though once Sevi would have avoided his gaze, now he stared right back from under a stormy brow. Didn't he have more important things to do than deliver food? Or how about just putting the food in the waiting room outside? Wasn't that what the parlor was for—waiting on the royalty? He almost ignored the platter out of spite, but his stomach, conditioned from years of hunger, rebelled audibly at the smell.

Eating helped somewhat. Every bite ate away at his irritation until only melancholy remained, latching onto him like a gripvine plant. He took his food over to the sofa, facing away from the Cut, and chewed on his bread without emotion. He thought back to his fight with Lily, raking his mind for anything he could have done differently. But try as he might, there was nothing he could think of. Eventually he sighed and pushed his plate away. "I can't get anything right, can I?" he said softly to himself.

"Those are the Dancers."

Sevi flicked his head around. The vision of the old lady was back, looking out the big window just as before. He groaned. "Shy, for all Gods' sake, I'm not in the mood for this today."

"A long time ago, when the moon was three, she and her siblings would hold these magnificent parties for all the world to see," the old lady continued. Because of course she couldn't hear him. She wasn't real.

He rubbed at his temples and closed his eyes, leaning forward with his elbows on his knees, listening to her drone on and on about the two stars in the sky dancing around each other. Every syllable was a knife twisting against his ear, pushing into his brain. Closing his hands over them did nothing to stop her voice. How could it? She was in his head.

"Do they have names, too?" Young Sevi asked.

Sevi angrily pushed himself off the couch and hurried across the room. *Maybe I can drown this out with enough noise.*

"Hm. You know, I can't remember. How about we give them some?" the old lady replied.

Moving to the doors, he flung them open into the waiting room beyond, then strode across to the others and flung those open as well. The guards outside jumped. There were four of them now, absent Loma and Cassik. "Take me to the infirmary," he demanded.

"Oh, I don't know, it's not so bad," Innavin said, touching the side of his head with the damaged ear.

His wife, Lieutenant Ryaliss Targa, sat beside him. "The entire side of your head is caved in, goldenheart," she said, cradling his other hand in hers. She was slightly taller and had straight, black, jaw-length hair. She fidgeted as she spoke, tapping her foot nervously against the floor as though in distress.

"It's just another scar, my loveblossom. Perhaps it will make me the luckiest man in Elkra and sway you into falling for me a second time."

"Oh, my dear, the moment we can get some privacy—"

"Would you both *please* shut up?" Captain Lorr demanded from the bed next to them. "Tembra take me, why did they have to put me next to you? Sevi, could you please order the doctors to move me somewhere else?"

Innavin and Ryaliss shared a mischievous glance. Innavin said, "I'd only follow you, Lorr. Try as you might, we are bound, and you shan't ever escape my beautiful face."

Sevi watched the group with a small smile. "I'm happy that you're both alright," he said. A knot he'd carried in his belly since he saw Innavin's bloody head loosened.

"Of course, we are!" Innavin declared. "Those criminals couldn't kill a blade of grass, running across a field, with snow cleats, let alone the mighty duo of Captains Gallan and River!"

"And when we find them," Lieutenant Ryaliss said darkly, glaring distantly at something only she could see, "I'll be sure to give them a lesson in it."

Innavin quieted, bringing his wife's hand to his mouth and kissing it softly. "So vengeful. Like Sier Margo in *The Knight and the Raven*." He cleared his throat, stretched his neck, and said in a deep voice, "Let those cowards find the farthest stone in the deepest cave of all the Mother's creation and hide under it. I shall find them, lest I turn the world over."

Ryaliss brightened a bit. "I shall aid thee, Lady Knight, from wings of dark and eye as godly as the Father's; I say to thee, nor will the heavens go unturned in thy conquest."

Lorr groaned and turned to face away from the pair. "Please. Both of you. I am *begging* you. Stop."

Again, Ryaliss and Innavin shared a private smile. Sevi looked between them, then at Lorr's back. "Are you alright, Captain Lorr?"

Ryaliss' and Innavin's smiles vanished. They turned to Sevi with a look of warning. Lorr tiredly said, "I'm fine, lad. Just fine."

Innavin hooked a discreet finger at Sevi and beckoned him to lean in closer. "Don't worry," he whispered, "but don't press him. We'll draw him out of his mood as surely as Lieutenant Digby draws a note from a fiddle."

Sevi looked once more at the captain. "Where's Captain River?"

"Getting chewed out by the commander, as she promised," Ryaliss said.

"I know you're talking about me, Targas," Lorr said loudly.

"You told us to keep it down! We're merely obliging!" Innavin called back without missing a breath.

Lieutenant Ryaliss touched her hand to her shoulder and bowed in her chair to Sevi. "Thank you for visiting us, Your Brilliance. It saddens me to think that you were put in harm's way on your first trip back into your city."

Sevi's expression flattened, unable to enjoy the sentiment. Some part of him felt that, if he had fled with Lily after all, that Innavin and the captains wouldn't have been put in harm's way. But he said, "Me too. I'm glad everyone got to you in time."

"All thanks to you, Your Luminance!" Innavin said proudly, doing his best to mimic Ryaliss' bow. "You were surely blessed with the speed and grace of a divine zephyr."

Sevi shook his head. "I was only able to get away because of you. All of you were so brave. But all I could do was run away." *As always,* he didn't say.

"Mm, it's said in many a production that the stoutest of hearts can be measured by the length of their sword," Innavin said wistfully. Sevi looked mournfully down at his feet, feeling his heart sink at someone else voicing his inadequacy. "Personally," Innavin continued, "I think that if someone wants to brag about the length of their sword, they should take it to a blacksmith or a brothel."

Sevi looked back up in surprise. Innavin smirked scandalously at him. Ryaliss covered her mouth and laughed into her hand. Innavin said, "Your Luminance, I was shaking. Absolutely shaking. That was, by far, the most dangerous play I've been in in my *life*. And if I may be so candid, I'm not actually that good of an actor. I just love the magic of the show, that rush of commanding the eyes of all who watch, and of slipping into someone else's skin for a bit. In reality, I haven't been on stage in *years*.

"But when the villains had assembled, cocky and certain of their victory, I knew the runelight was ready for a hero who could out-guile them, for I am even worse at fighting than I am on the stage. So, I acted, the only way I could. Just as River and Lorr acted. Just as *you* acted, Your Brilliance. And you were spectacular. Absolutely spectacular."

Sevi said nothing, fighting unexpected emotion. Ryaliss leaned towards Innavin. "Should you really be speaking to the crown prince so informally, dear?"

"Aaah, I suppose not. Please forgive me, Your Radiance," Innavin said, giving a slightly more flourishing bow while Sevi wiped his eyes.

"Thank you," Sevi choked out.

"Of course, Your Shining Lustrousness."

Sevi glanced around the clinic, unable to look either of them in the face. Cassik, he noticed, was not among the beds. "Do... do either of you know where Digby is?"

Ryaliss hummed. "I believe that Lieutenant Asgaillin is helping with repairs to the airship today. It's getting close to completion, and it's no secret how badly Captain River wants to see it done. Almost as badly as the commander."

"Are you off to see him, Your Brilliance?" Innavin asked. "Please give him my regards. And if I may be so bold to suggest, perhaps you'd care to join him? A task to complete, no matter how small, is just the thing one needs to lighten a heavy mind."

Ryaliss tutted. "Innavin, darling, again: he's a prince."

"Of course, of course. I apologize again for all the liberties I'm taking, Your Effulgence, but do think it over. A hammer must be felt by a king as much as a mason."

"*A Man Among Kings,*' Act IV, Scene twelve?" Lieutenant Ryaliss asked.

Innavin beamed. "Gods, I love you, Rya."

"I know."

---

"Ho, lad!" Digby called down from the airship's deck, waving at Sevi and his entourage. "Lookin' fer another view of the ship? 'Fraid it's a wee busy up here at the moment. Lots o' parts lyin' about."

"Can I come up anyway? Maybe I can help!" Sevi called back.

"Eh, not sure if that's a good idea! Don't want anythin' fallin on ya!"

Sevi tried not to let his disappointment show. Innavin had been right. What he really needed was a distraction. "Well, when can I come up?"

"Few days, give or take! We're puttin' the balloon up!"

Sevi balled his hands in excitement. He shouted, "You mean it's going to fly again?"

"Aye!" Digby called.

"Can I join!?"

Digby boomed a powerful laugh. "Aye, Yer Brilliance! Maybe not her maiden voyage though! Don't want ya on board if she falls from the sky!"

Sevi paled a little at the thought. Experiencing one fall over the mountain had been enough. But still, if repairs went well, then the chance to fly might no longer be just a dream! "Alright! Three days!" Grinning from ear to ear, he waved to Digby and practically danced away from the airship, momentarily forgetting his troubles.

He headed back toward the castle but stopped at the sight of the mountain wall across the yard. A large, gaping hole had been opened in the cliff face where the miners had spent months digging. The miners, however, were gone. He regarded it curiously, mildly surprised to see the tunnel back in place after so long. "Hey," he said, turning to one of his guards.

The soldier stood at attention. "Sir?"

Sevi grimaced. Hearing anyone address him as 'sir' continued to sound odd. "Why was everyone digging into the mountain?"

"Commander Tiersa's orders, sir. She wanted something found, and they found it."

"What was it?"

"A door."

Sevi blinked. "A door? What?"

"Aye, sir. Commander Tiersa was very pleased. Gave everyone who worked on it three extra days of leave."

Sevi nodded absently, continuing to stare at the tunnel, when a gunshot broke him from his musings. He flinched and turned toward the sound. A group of soldiers stood in a loose circle around the practice range, watching a man shoot cans into the air with pinpoint accuracy.

Reynam.

Sevi watched one of the ruined targets fall into the grass, then looked at the man who had shot it. The corporal hadn't shown himself after the night Sevi had become a prince. Perhaps, now that he was royalty, the soldier was done trying to gain possession of his necklace.

Feeling an improbable sense of mischief, Sevi marched toward the gathered crowd. *Let's see how he enjoys being bothered for a change.*

Some of the soldiers bowed and made room for him as he approached, some just shifted out of the way, but all looked at him oddly. The notion that one of Digby's tunnel mice had been elevated from pet to prince was still a novel one, and not everyone had readily accepted it. He tried to ignore their glances, placing his hands behind his back in what he hoped was a regal posture, and watched Reynam with a critical eye, waiting for a chance to interfere.

Reynam hadn't noticed his arrival, to busy focusing on the scope at his eye. He stood completely still, all concentration dedicated to the scourge of targets down the range. Then he pulled the trigger and sent a can sailing into the air with a *pop*.

He followed it with the barrel of his gun, cranked the lever to eject the spent shell, and pulled the trigger again. The can flew higher, spinning around and around with great momentum. On the third shot it split completely in two, and Reynam moved his rifle away with a smile.

There was a round of applause with a smattering of groans mixed in. Reynam cranked the third spent shell with satisfaction before setting his rifle down and bringing out a pipe much grander than his last one. He took a celebratory puff and gestured triumphantly to his audience, breathing smoke through the gaps in his grin. "Thank you, thank you, ladies and gentlemen. And thank you who bet against me most of all."

He grabbed a hat from where it lay on the ground and took it around the circle. Some men and women only smiled. Others grumbled and grudgingly put coins in, but not many. When he came to Sevi's side his smile faltered, and he moved past him without a word.

That caught Sevi's attention. "Hey, Reynam," Sevi called. Reynam didn't react. "Reynam!"

The corporal sighed and turned to face him. "Hey, ki-Your Brilliance. Just let me collect my things before I go."

Sevi blinked. "Excuse me?"

"It's happening a little quicker than I expected, honestly, but I see you've already put together my farewell party." Reynam grimaced at Sevi's four guards.

Again, Sevi said, "Excuse me? What?"

"Can't say I blame you, really. I'd say it was fun while it lasted, but..." He shrugged. "Well. It had its moments."

Sevi shook his head and walked up to him, crossing his arms. "Start talking sense."

Reynam paused and looked down at him. Confusion replaced his resignation. "You're kicking me out."

Sevi fixed him with a skeptical stare. "Says who?"

"Says..." He looked at Sevi's guards again.

"They're here to protect me. Why do you think I'm throwing you out?"

"Kid-uh, Your Majesty, are you seriously suggesting that you're *not,* after... everything, I guess?"

"I can't—" Sevi stopped, glancing around at the ring of soldiers. They were still staring at him funny. *Right. I'm missing a crown, but I'm their prince now, aren't I?* He could throw Reynam out if he wanted to, and the man had certainly earned it after all his duplicity. But he had been trying to get the necklace over something about his father. Sevi moved his gaze to where Reynam's rifle lay in the grass. Now, he realized, was the perfect chance for mischief. "I'm not throwing you out, Reynam," Sevi said, slowly smiling as a joke came to mind that would have made Lily proud. "Every prince needs his jester."

Reynam's eyebrows shot up. A few loose chuckles rose from those standing closest. The corporal darted a glance at them but kept his attention on Sevi. "You're not?"

Sevi tried to look nonchalant. "Not if you tell me why you wanted my necklace so badly."

The soldier's eyes hardened. He took a long drag from his pipe, breathing the smoke out through his nose. "Playing games with me, kid?"

"Mm-hm. You like games, don't you?"

"I think I'd rather go pack my things, *Your Luminance*," he said with a glare, taking another drag from his pipe.

Sevi frowned. "You also like bets though, don't you?" He walked to where the corporal had left his gun, swallowing his instinctive fear as he picked it up.

Reynam furrowed his brow, but the ghost of a smile played on his lips. "What's on your mind?"

"I bet that I can hit those cans with this gun on my first try," Sevi said. "If I do, then you have to tell me why you care so much about my necklace."

Reynam smirked. "Are you serious?"

"Oh, yes."

"And what do I get if you don't?"

Sevi shrugged. "I'll knight you."

Reynam barked out a laugh, along with several nearby soldiers. "You know what? Deal. Step up to the range, Your Brilliance." He bowed deferentially to Sevi.

There was another round of applause. The demeanor of the soldiers changed from curiosity to amusement, quieting with rapt attention as Sevi approached the line with Reynam's gun. The corporal followed, standing a respectful distance behind Sevi's shoulder. "Far be it from me not to assist a greenhorn," Reynam said, taking the rifle from Sevi and reloading it with fresh bullets. "Put the butt of the rifle into your shoulder. It'll kick, and you don't want to fall over."

Sevi took the rifle from Reynam once he had finished. "Alright."

"Look through the sight and line up the dash with your target."

"Alright."

"Breathe out when you pull the trigger."

"Alright."

"Good. Yeah, you look ready to kill greenbloods. Or at least a stiff breeze, as I imagine that will be all you hit." He chuckled at his own joke. "All set, princeling? I'm looking forward to that knighthood. Sier Enstrova has a charm to it."

"I'm ready."

"Then have at it." Reynam took a step back with a confident grin.

Sevi lowered the rifle and ejected every bullet, cranking the lever back and forth rapidly until they fell like rain. Reynam's smile froze on his face, morphing with perplexity.

Sevi calmly stepped off the line, and the corporal's expression crumbled with horrified realization. Walking down the range, Sevi lifted the rifle up by the barrel, brought it around as far as he could turn, and swung the butt of it like a club across the entire line of cans, knocking them off their perch with a clatter of metal.

Turning his smile on his audience, he waved as ostentatiously as an actor from the Golden Spool. "Hey! I hit them all with the gun on my first try! Does that mean I win?"

There was a beat of silence. Sevi's smile faltered. Did this count as cheating? Had he overstepped?

The crowd burst into a roar of laughter so loud that all passersby stopped to watch. Sevi breathed out in relief, returning to the line with his chest out and proudly handing the rifle back to a doubled-over Corporal Reynam.

"My father made the necklace, as I said," Reynam said from the corner of his mouth, taking another puff of his pipe while leaning against the courtyard wall.

Sevi wondered where the corporal got the replacement; it looked much better than the other one, with freshly polished wood embellished with little carvings. His guards stood a respectful distance away, giving them both a little privacy. Reynam continued, "Along with my three brothers. Best jewelers in the Eastern Hills, called upon by lords, ladies, and the monarchy itself."

He blew out a cloud, taking a long breath before resuming. "They all died in a very sudden, very efficiently made fire when the Fae invaded. Burnt the whole manor to the ground with them inside." He turned and offered the pipe to Sevi. "You're old enough to handle a little smoke."

Sevi looked at it critically. He still hated the smell. "No thanks."

"Suit yourself." Reynam shrugged, putting the stem back in his mouth.

"That's why you wanted my necklace?"

"More or less," Reynam said, closing his eyes. "There was nothing left of the house but charcoal. It's something to remember them by. But it's fair to say that I might have been a bit aggressive about it."

"Mm." Sevi ran his gaze over the corporal, thinking. "You asked me about something called an Argennium."

"That I did."

"Does my necklace have anything to do with it?"

Reynam smiled. "I do believe I've sufficiently held up my end of our bet, Your Luminance."

"This still involves why you might want my necklace though," Sevi countered.

Reynam's smile widened, and he blew another quick puff of smoke. "My father had mentioned an important project for the king and queen before I left. That star around your neck was the last thing I saw on his desk before he shut the door on me. He mentioned the project in his letters, referring to his work as 'Argennium,' and made some cryptic reference to 'all the pieces being nearly assembled.' He made it sound like it was his finest work ever and had me swear not to reveal it to anyone. I even burnt the letters. Guess that was just another broken promise, though."

Reynam paused, shaking his head. "The way I see it, that necklace is a piece of it. I was hoping that since you, a tunnel mouse, living in the very castle he died in, had taken possession of it, that you might have stumbled across something big, shiny, and silver. But surprise, you're the amnesiac prince of the very king and queen he worked for, making you the heir to his final project. Our goddess of luck, Namini, clearly isn't without a sense of humor."

Sevi narrowed his eyes. "Did you want this Argennium so you could sell it or something?"

"Ah-ah-ah. My intentions for either the necklace or the Argennium were not part of our bet. I've already told you why I wanted them, but what I intend to do with them is something else entirely."

They felt rather connected, actually, but Sevi didn't feel the need to press the issue. "Well... Thank you for finally telling me. I'm sorry about your family."

"Mm," Reynam hummed, staring blankly at the sky.

"And I promise that I'm not going to throw you out... although you do deserve it," Sevi added. "You could have just told me all this from the beginning."

"Would you have given me the necklace if I had?"

"No."

"Then what would have been the point?"

Sevi shrugged. "Maybe we could have been friends."

Reynam eyed Sevi thoughtfully. "You'd better take good care of it... Your Luminance."

Sevi regarded him for a few breaths before giving an awkward nod and turning to leave. It felt appropriate. He had only gone a few steps when Reynam called out, "Hey. Kid." He turned back around. Reynam held up his pipe. "If you see Lea, tell her I like the pipe. And that her new hat is on the way."

# Chapter 44

*Though danger presided he knew not her fear; she was caught between both night and day. Losing all hope to protect what she loved, and their light, once bright, faded gray.*

———————

"Sevi! SEVI!"

Sevi paused mid-step on the threshold of the throne room, nearly colliding with the guards behind him. He turned to face the voice, catching Lily just as she barreled through a group of Embers and stumbled to a halt in front of him. "Come! Right now!" she said hurriedly, grabbing his wrist.

Sevi tried to get his brain to work faster. "Lily? What?"

"*Just come with me!*" Lily tugged at his wrist again. "To the room! Now!"

Too taken aback to do anything else, he took off with her, doing his best not to outpace her with his longer stride. The thunder of Sevi's guards' footsteps followed them, clapping their heavy boots against the stone as they ran through the castle to the royal chambers.

Lily went through first, flinging the doors open one after the other. Sevi instructed the soldiers to stay outside unless he called for them before following her. When he entered the bedroom, he saw that Lily had run over to the Cut's entrance and had dropped to her knees, looking down at something in front of her while pulling on her helmet in anguish.

"What's going on, Lily?" Sevi asked, joining her, only to stop. Alyda lay on a bundle of leaves, curled up in a fragile ball and completely devoid of light. Her wings, normally so shiny and gossamer, had dulled until they were nearly completely opaque. Their tips had curled at the edges like dead leaves, and a tiny stain of bile sat next to her face from where she'd been sick.

"She's dying," Lily choked out.

"Alyda," Sevi breathed, falling to his knees. He reached out with his fingers, tentatively grazing their tips against her diminutive form. She stirred at his touch, turning her large, bleary eyes up to look at him, and started coughing her sickening, horrible cough. It had gotten so much worse.

His stomach dropped with guilt. He had been so preoccupied with his own issues that he hadn't noticed. "I'm s-sorry," he whispered. "How could I not have seen?"

"She needs amber!" Lily said, wiping her eyes.

"What?"

"We drink it. It rejuvenates us. Makes us more Fae." She grabbed her bag and fumbled around inside it. When she brought her hand out she held a cracked, empty vial. "I thought I had enough, but it must've broken during our escape yesterday."

Sevi stared hard at the vial. "Where can we get more?"

"The Fablings kept their stores in the cellar, but they're *gone*. I can't find them anywhere!"

A sickening coughing fit wracked the little fairy's whole body, shaking her with the deathly sounds of rattling glass. Sevi's heart stopped. Her condition was worsening with every breath. "H-how much time does she have? Are there any plants that could help her?"

Lily shook her head. "I... I don't know!"

Sevi cursed and placed a finger on Alyda's cheek. "Aly. Alyda! What can we do to help you?" She didn't stir. His throat went dry. "We need help."

Lily laughed bitterly. "I don't know any Silvakin doctors, Sevi!"

"No... but we can get the next best thing."

She looked at him with horror. "They'll snap her neck like a twig!"

"And if we don't do something she'll die anyway!" Sevi countered, already rising.

Lily grabbed his pant leg, balling it in her fist, and pointed an accusatory finger at him. "I would rather watch her die like this than see her tortured by these people for their amusement. If you do what I think you're doing, and *anything* happens to her, I will *never* forgive you for it."

"She might know where the amber went!"

She clenched her jaw and stared down at Alyda. The little fairy coughed again, and her wings shriveled even more, curling to the point of almost falling from her body. Lily let go of him. "Fine. *Fine.* Go!"

Sevi ran from the room, flinging open the parlor door to face the guards outside. He lifted his chin and deepened his voice, addressing them with as much authority as he could muster. "Get me Doctor Lea. *Now.*"

octor Lea arrived after what felt like a lifetime, breathing heavily with a tinge of red in her cheeks and a bag slung over her shoulder. "What is the meaning of this, Sevi?" she said, very pointedly closing the doors on the nosy guards behind her.

"Doctor Lea," Sevi said, "before I explain, I need you to promise me something."

She furrowed her brow, unslinging her bag. "Promise what?"

"You have to promise that you'll stay calm, and that whatever you do, you won't talk about this to anyone. Ever."

The doctor shook her head. "Sevi, I never discuss my patients with others unless I'm forced to. Whatever is wrong with you, you can rest assured that it will stay with me."

"You don't understand. This is big. Very big. It could get us into trouble."

"I'm certain that whatever it is, it's nothing that I haven't seen before."

The dome of Lily's helmet caught the light as she stood up from behind the furniture. Doctor Lea's gaze flicked over to her, arching her eyebrows in mild surprise, until she saw Alyda's trembling body in her hands and stiffened completely. Lily carefully brought Alyda over and laid her down atop the table beside the couch. Her face was hard, and the look she gave the doctor was steely and distrustful. "Help her," Lily ordered.

"*Please*," Sevi added, putting as much emotion into the single word as he could. "She needs something called amber, or she'll die. The Fae used to keep it in the cellar. Did the Embers take it somewhere?"

Doctor Lea stared hard at Alyda. "Where did you get her?" she said slowly.

"She's been mine and Lily's friend for years. She helped us grow food when we lived in the tunnels," Sevi said, desperately trying to refrain from tugging Lea froward with impatience. He took a pleading step towards the doctor. "Please. *Please* help her, Lea."

"Lily?" Her gaze shifted to her. "The girl you've been looking for?"

"That's right."

Doctor Lea slowly shook her head, looking between them. "Years, you say?"

"Please!" Sevi begged again, close to shouting. "Can you help her?"

Drawing a deep breath and letting it go, Doctor Lea nodded, taking her bag over to the table and placing it next to Alyda. She turned the fairy slowly onto her back, careful not to press too hard, and rested her finger on Alyda's little chest, before closing her eyes in concentration. After a dozen breaths passed, she took out a tiny wooden toothpick and gingerly poked Alyda's arm, pressing down hard enough to break skin.

"What are you doing?" Sevi exclaimed, moving forward.

"Hush," Doctor Lea said absently, staring at the fairy. Grimacing, Doctor Lea leaned back and wiped her hand across her face. "Dry," she muttered, dropping her hand into her coat pocket.

Sevi looked between the doctor and his friend. "W-what does it mean?"

"As you said. She needs amber."

"Do you have any? Do you know where it is?"

Lea sighed. "Oh yes." She reached into the inner pocket of her coat. When she withdrew her hand, she held a vial much like the quicksilver bottles the Embers carried. Except this one had a syrupy orange liquid in it that gleamed warmly in the light. She looked down at it with an unreadable expression, turning it around in her fingers. "I have it right here."

Sevi stared at the remedy in disbelief, dumbstruck that she would pull a miracle out of thin air. "Then give it to her!" he nearly screamed.

Lea looked at him as though coming out of a trance, then back down to the vial. "Yes... that would be best," she said with building resolve. "One of you, please tilt her head back for me."

"Hold still, Alyda," Lily said, getting to her first. She placed the pad of her index finger on the fairy's forehead and another beneath her chin, carefully positioning her skull. "Open wide, you can do it."

Alyda blinked rapidly, hacking up another grating cough. But she did as Lily asked, opening her mouth as wide as she could. Doctor Lea took the vial, dipped her toothpick in it, and started feeding the tincture into Alyda's mouth bit by bit.

Sevi crowded the table next to Lily and the doctor, clutching at his shirt with worry. Nothing happened at first, and he feared that the medicine wouldn't take. But the more Lea gave her, the quieter the fairy's coughs became. Then her wings uncurled, her body loosened, and she unwound herself from the stiff ball she had rolled herself into.

When the bottle was half-empty, Alyda's shine burst into being like a newly born star. Her eyes sprung open, and she bolted upright, shaking her head akin to how a hound shook water from its pelt. She stared up at everyone around her with confusion, letting out a puzzled chime as she got to her feet with a flutter of wings.

"Alyda," Sevi breathed, covering his mouth with his hand.

Lily punched the air. "YES!" She picked up the fairy and brought her into an embrace made for someone ten sizes bigger.

"Don't crush her!" Sevi laughed with relief, squeezing Lily with one arm while placing his free hand on top of Alyda.

Alyda chimed with surprise, wriggling as the hug got too tight, before finally pulling herself free from their hands with an indignant flurry of notes. Sevi and Lily watched her hover, laughing and wiping their eyes with relief. "*Thank you*, Lea," Sevi said, turning to the doctor. "You saved her. Gods above and below, I won't ever forget this. I promise."

"Mm," Doctor Lea mumbled, gathering her bag. "May I talk to you, Sevi? Privately?"

Sevi's smile faltered. "Um... sure." He stepped closer, but she turned and walked out of the room completely, moving into the parlor. He traded an uncertain glance with Lily and Alyda. "Don't worry. If anything happens, take Alyda and run. I won't let anything happen to her."

Lily raised her chin and nodded. Straightening his shirt, Sevi turned and followed after the doctor. She waited for him in the middle of the room with her bag on the table, standing with her hand on her hip and a ruminative expression on her face. "You said you've been with that Fae for years?"

"Yes. Why?"

"Because your friend Alyda is a Vexi. They need a constant supply of amber or they shrivel and fade, just as she was doing now. It makes sense that she was getting her supply from the Fae that were garrisoned here; we did find several boxes of vials. But with the Fae gone, I'm afraid your friend won't be able to survive much longer."

Sevi's anxiety returned in an instant, hitting him in the gut like a physical blow. He reached for his pendant. "What...?"

"I'm sorry, Sevi," Lea said, watching him sadly.

"H-how long does she have?"

She shook her head. "A month. Maybe two."

"Two months?" Sevi uttered in horrified disbelief. "But what about the other vials? You can get her another one, can't you?"

"Including the vial I used just now, I can get you possibly three at most. They are kept under tight guard, and I may only requisition them with direct approval from the commander."

Sevi closed his eyes. No. *No.*

"I'm sorry, Sevi," Lea said again, softer. "I can see she means a lot to you."

He sniffed, swallowing his emotion. "Y-you won't tell Tiersa, will you?"

Doctor Lea pursed her lips.

"Lea? You promised."

"I—"

The door to the bedroom opened with a creak. Sevi turned around. Lily stood there, leaning against the doorframe with her arms crossed, staring hard at the doctor. Lea regarded her with her own arms crossed, unimpressed by the girl's glare. "Is there a problem, miss?"

"That depends on you," Lily said.

Doctor Lea turned from Lily to her bag. "I won't tell," she said flatly, opening the bag and reaching in. "As strange as it is to find one alone, a Vexi is hardly a threat. But before I go, I do have something for you, Sevi." When she withdrew her hand, she held a small black box.

"Oh!" Sevi exclaimed, stepping forward and taking the Faen seedbox from her.

"You left it in the infirmary. Understandable, given all the excitement."

"Thank you!" Sevi said, managing a smile.

Lea nodded, restringing her bag shut and slinging it over her shoulder. "I have to see to my other patients. I'd advise that you both be careful going forward."

"Same to *you*, Doctor," Lily sneered.

"*Lily*," Sevi warned.

Doctor Lea rolled her eyes. "I said don't worry, Miss Lily... It was *Lily*, wasn't it?"

"I always worry," Lily said, maintaining her glare. "You saved our friend, sworn enemy to you and your people, for nothing, and give us only your word and the promise that it's good enough? You just *happen* to know what Alyda is and how to fix her? You just *happen* to keep a bottle of amber on you? And in your *pocket*? Your bag I could understand, but your pocket?"

Sevi froze, turning to Lea with surprise. Lily had raised some shockingly good points. Lea's expression, however, looked more exasperated than defensive.

"You're one of *them*," Lily said, leveling a finger. "You're not human. You're—"

"A Fae?" Doctor Lea finished, sweeping her long hair back to reveal an ear with an unmistakable point to it.

Sevi's jaw dropped. Even Lily paused, blinking in surprise.

"Forgive me for stealing your dramatic reveal, but I felt it best that we skip to the end." Lea let her hair fall back with a pointed flick of her hand. "Yes. I am Fae. Or at least I was, until I gave it up."

Lily snorted derisively. "Nobody just gives up being what they are."

"Is that right?" Lea smiled faintly. "I'll admit to your point that amber is highly addicting, but not impossible to quit. The less I drank, the less I continued to drink, and the more human I became."

"Why?" Sevi shook his head in disbelief. "What are you doing here?"

"The lifestyle of my countrymen stopped agreeing with me. So, I left, changed my name, and now I help heal those they would hurt. It's really that simple."

"But... the iron you wear? How have you not been found out?"

"Yes, that does chafe quite a bit, but after so long without amber I've learned to ignore it. And my ears have rounded enough to be labeled an unfortunate birth defect, which suits most around here fine. I've been with them from the very start. It's fooling the quicksilver that's the tricky part. But one can do wonders with a false finger and berry juice, and I find it much easier to fool when I'm the one giving the tests." She closed her eyes, shaking her head. "I will confess, though, that being near that dreadful substance still makes me shudder. Luckily, I've had it successfully banned from my clinic."

Lily tapped her finger on her arm with an unreadable expression. "You're telling the truth, aren't you?"

Lea nodded. "I am."

"Why? You could have said your ears were born weird and left it at that."

"No, I couldn't have. I haven't known you but half an hour, and it's clear as crystal that you do not nor will not trust me. You would've taken it upon yourself to find the truth. And as you're friends with the prince, your suspicion would have revealed me to anyone watching closely enough, whether you meant to or not. Besides, I'm a doctor. I deal in truths, not lies."

Lily snorted again. "Says the Fae pretending to be human?"

Lea sighed. "You asked for proof of what my word is worth, and I've given it to you. A secret for a secret, so that we all may begin to trust one another. I won't reveal yours, and you won't reveal mine. I trust that's sufficient?"

"Lily—" Sevi began.

Lily darted a sharp look at Sevi, silencing him. "Tell us where the amber is being kept."

Lea shook her head. "Not only will you get caught, you might arouse suspicion of me."

Lily ground her teeth. "Tell. Me."

"No."

Lily stamped her foot and turned her back to them, crossing her arms across her chest.

"We won't tell anyone about you," Sevi said. "I promise."

"I believe you." Doctor Lea smiled softly. "If there's nothing else, I'd like to see my other patients."

"Please." Sevi nodded. "And thanks, Lea. For everything."

Lea nodded back. "Very well. It was a pleasure meeting you, Miss Lily. Take care, all of you. And good luck."

Lily made a long, annoyed sound with her nose after the doctor's exit. "Let's get out of here," she said. "I could use some fresh air."

# Chapter 45

*Flower and mouse begged a stranger for help, "rekindle this life at its thinning!" The stranger, familiar, both callous and kind, took death, and kept end from beginning.*

—❧—

T he Cut remained the same as always, even in the face of so much change. Same walls, same creatures, same isolation. Here, Sevi wouldn't be called sir, or princeling, or Isevidel, or Your Brilliance. He wouldn't be attacked by street thugs, or questioned by persistent soldiers, or watched at all times. When he couldn't leave, it had been repressive. Now stepping through its tunnels felt like reuniting with an old friend, as dear to him as Lily and Alyda. It felt like coming home. "Why didn't you tell her?" he said to Lily.

"I don't trust her," Lily said, keeping her back to him.

"She's the same as you."

"No, she isn't. She's an Ember. Embers kill Silvakaen."

"She saved Alyda's *life*," Sevi insisted.

"And she kept the location of the amber to herself," Lily countered. "She didn't actually save Alyda's life. She just extended her death."

Sevi scoffed. "And that's not good enough for the moment? She bought us time to find a solution and she obviously can't do anything more!"

"Yes, she can. There is *always* a way." Lily rolled her shoulders. "I'll find where it's hidden myself if I have to, just you watch. We're *not* going to lose her."

Alyda stayed quiet while they argued. Sevi watched her flutter through the air, illuminating their path, and readjusted the black box underneath his arm. Each of them could have navigated the Cut in total darkness, but Sevi found that he never wanted to be without Alyda's glow ever again.

Yet someday soon, he would have to.

He tried to shove the thought from his mind, but his gaze always drifted back to the fairy. She noticed of course, and the more he looked, the more her expression soured from polite, deliberate avoidance to open exasperation. She flew over and smacked his forehead with her hand, rapidly flittering her wings to bob in the air. *"Stop staring at me, I'm fine!"*

*But you're not,* he thought. *How can you be so relaxed about it?*

Alyda let out a noise that sounded like a snort and flitted ahead to fly next to Lily. Seeing her light suddenly appear in front of her, Lily glanced back over her shoulder and called, "You alright back there, princeling?"

"Don't call me that," Sevi muttered. "Not now."

Lily quirked her eyebrow and turned to face forward. "What's in the box?"

Sevi looked down at the container. "A seed."

"A seed of what?"

"I'm not sure. Something the Silvakaen left behind."

"The Silvakaen?" She swung back around. "Where did you find it?"

"On the airship. It was locked behind a door."

She frowned. "And I'm guessing you want to plant it? What if it's dangerous?"

"And what if it's beautiful?" Sevi said, staring at Alyda again. Lily raised her eyebrows but made no response.

When they got to the cliffside, Alyda flew into Lily's sleeve, hiding herself from any guards who may have been patrolling the exterior section of the Cut. But they got lucky. Soldiers manned the wall, but not the cliff, and the rope that led up was still there.

They crept up as quietly as they could, avoiding the attention of the sentries, and hurried into the mountain cave, now missing all its beautiful glowing plants. Alyda reappeared out of Lily's shirt but kept between them in case an Ember patrol still guarded these pathways, ready to hide again the moment any materialized.

The rest of the journey to the garden went by without issue. At first, Sevi was overjoyed to see his old plants again, still alive and drinking their fill of sunlight under their window to the sky. But when he looked closer, he stiffened.

Months of neglect had not been kind to their carefully curated plants. Some had withered and shriveled, some had overgrown and invaded the space of other plants, choking them to death, and fruit lay rotten and stinking where it had gone ungathered. It hurt for him to see. Gone for so little time, yet it had been enough for order to turn to chaos.

He shook his head in sorrow as Alyda flew over the garden, echoing his sentiment with annoyed chimes. *Look at the state of this mess!* He couldn't agree more. At least there would be plenty of room for the Silvakaen seed.

"Yeesh," Lily said.

Sevi sighed. "Yeah. Could you help me move some things around?"

She grunted. "I guess I can help a little. Just don't expect me to stick my hands in the dirt."

He nodded. "Alyda? Could you uproot a few things for me?"

Locating his old trowel, Sevi placed his box down and got to work with his friends. Some plants had to be relocated, others trimmed. Some had become invasive and needed to be culled or removed altogether, which Alyda did with great zeal, chiming at each like a disapproving mother. He also made sure to harvest a little effizine while he was at it.

When they were done, a large space in the center of the garden had been cleared. Sevi returned to the box. At this, Lily perked up. She joined him with Alyda, both looking over his shoulder to see just what lay inside. When he opened it, Lily raised her eyebrows and looked blankly at the ordinary pit, but Alyda practically flipped in the air, chittering excitedly.

"What is it?" Sevi asked her.

Alyda moved both of her hands in against her chest and exploded them up over her head and outward, repeating the gesture a couple times as if that explained everything. At Sevi's confused expression, she huffed and landed on his hand, picked up the pit with both arms, and took off with a furious buzzing of wings, hobbling in the air under the pit's unwieldy weight.

Sevi glanced at Lily questioningly. She shrugged, and both turned to watch. Alyda landed on the ground and stamped at the soil, pointing down with great zeal. Sevi took the trowel and dug a hole at an appropriate width and depth, then leaned back, letting Alyda roll the seed into the ground. He refilled it without her prompting, and when the top of it had been covered entirely, Alyda took off into the air and urgently shooed at him to get clear.

Confused, Sevi straightened and stepped back, taking position next to Lily. "What's going on, Alyda?"

The ground tremored.

Alyda chimed excitedly as a bud shot out of the dirt, growing before their eyes. A stem followed it, then two leaves, then four. It grew larger and larger, widening, stretching up toward the sun, its bulb growing so big that the stem bent under its weight. Then it bloomed.

A vibrant, golden flower with a set of glorious petals spread out, stretching wide to drink in the sun. Each petal pulsed with streaks of glowing veins just beneath the membrane, as though it contained a heartbeat, pumping the plant with dim, yellow nectar. When it grew to a decent size its upward momentum halted on its own, as though the flower had found the height satisfactory, and chose to stop.

But then the ground shook again, and two more flowers arose from the dirt to join it. Then four. Then six, and so on, until the entirety of the garden's empty space had been filled by them, quickly turning a barren patch of soil into a field of glittering gold.

Lily breathed out. "Lightblossoms."

Sevi turned to her. "You've seen them before?"

"Once," she said, walking over to the edge of the patch. "Watch this." She smacked a group of the lightblossoms and a bright, shining ripple ran through them, washing across their surface like a wave of energy from the point of impact.

Sevi squinted. He had seen that before.

"You were right, Sevi," Lily announced. "We both were. Beautiful. But also dangerous."

Alyda nodded her head vigorously, but readily dove into the flower patch. She squealed with laughter as she danced across the petals like a dragonfly, readily braving whatever danger Lily warned of as though she hadn't just narrowly avoided death an hour ago. "Alyda doesn't seem to mind them," Sevi said.

"Because she knows how to handle them."

"By dancing on them?"

Lily laughed. "You could dance on them all you'd like so long as you don't break their bulbs."

"Why? What happens?"

She bent down low and very carefully scooped the nearest lightblossom out of the dirt. It continued pulsing with golden energy even when uprooted. She carried it over to the far side of the cave. When it passed into shadow its striations continued to glow for several breaths before disappearing, fading into a dun ochre. Placing it on the ground, Lily pulled her knife out of her sleeve. "Stay back," she called. She cut the flower's bulb with one swift motion, turned on her heel, and bolted back the way she came, taking Sevi's arm and pulling him further away.

First, nothing happened. Then the flower sparked with little streaks of lightning, dancing among its petals with a light crackle. It swelled, growing rounder at the ovary, glowing from inside as if lightning danced within it, too, and was trying to get out. It grew and grew, and just when it looked like it had stretched as much as it could, it *exploded* with golden light far more intense than it had any right to be, filling the cave with a harsh, thunderous *boom*.

Sevi threw up his arms and shielded his head, his ears ringing. "Oh, my Gods," he breathed, staring at the soot-stained rock where the plant used to be.

"Yeah," Lily said. "Still want to dance on them?"

"I think I'll pass."

"That's what I thought."

They both stood together at the edge of the lightblossom patch, transfixed by its beauty despite the danger it posed. Alyda skipped and pirouetted across the blossoms as light as a breeze, merrily availing herself of her garden's newfound majesty as though Sevi and Lily no longer existed. Sevi glanced at Lily, running his gaze over the dome of her helmet and down to her face. "I'm sorry," he said.

Lily turned to him with a look of mild surprise. Alyda paused mid-flight with a similar expression. Sevi clenched at the hem of his shirt. "I'm sorry for making you both stay here. I... I want you to know how grateful I am that you're still with me. I don't think I could go out and be a prince if I didn't know you were here to help me do it. And I'm sorry for the quicksilver, Lily; I had no idea we would have so little time. So, thank you. Thank you both so much. I'll do better from here on out, you have my word."

The ghost of a smile graced Lily's lips. She closed her eyes and sighed, turning back to face the flowers. Alyda darted for his face, giving it a quick squeeze with a big, beaming smile before flying off into the lightblossoms again. Sevi eyed Lily, growing anxious at her silence. He silently lowered his gaze to his boots, praying for her to say something. Anything.

"Thanks, Sev," she said.

His spirits soared. He looked back at her, ready to give her his full attention. When she didn't speak, he turned to face the garden with her once more, side by side, watching their friend dance in her personal field of golden light.

# Part 4:
# Light

# Chapter 46

*A field of gold in the mouse's old nest, a dance for the brightest of lights. A smile, a plea, a hand for amends, to warm on this coldest of nights*

————— ❧ —————

Tiersa gave Sevi an encouraging look from across the table. A fire crackled in the parlor's hearth, filling the room with a comfortable heat. It reminded Sevi to ask her how to close the royal study. He had been shivering pretty violently when he awoke that morning, and he wouldn't have the proximity of the kitchen this winter.

"A what?" he asked her, pretending he hadn't heard the term before.

"An Iron Masquerade," she repeated. She picked up several official-looking documents from the stack in front of her and scanned them. "It is one of the longest running traditions of our queendom, meant to honor the hero knights of old. In the past it was customary to outfit yourself in an iron helmet, coupled with a face guard and chest piece, but it has evolved in practicality over the years. We've kept the masks but now we make them from wood and paint. One can only dance in armor for so long after all."

She smiled faintly. "I sent out letters of invitation to every lady and lord still living, and I'm certain that the Regent Council—those still left of your mother and father's inner circle—would be more than eager to preside over the ceremony for the child of their former leaders."

Sevi tapped his finger on the table in a close imitation of Tiersa's tic, thinking back to the conversation he'd overheard between her and Promina. "Why, though? Is this when I get a crown?"

"This isn't a coronation. Think of it as more of a memorial ball, commemorating the noble deeds the knights of old and new have done in service to our country. Now that we have beaten the goblins, and found you, it seems fitting to celebrate where it all began. Word has already traveled, far and fast, of your return, and this celebration gives us an opportunity to formally introduce you. It's an important step in being recognized as our prince and eventual king."

A ball full of important strangers. Sevi took a deep breath, trying not to visibly shake. *This is what I stayed for*, he reminded himself. "When will it happen?"

"I requisitioned supplies from Ilondia and the neighboring towns several days ago. I expect the responses from the nearest individuals within a week, and the furthest by the week after. That will give us between three weeks to a month to prepare both the grounds and yourself for the event. We have a lot to do, and not long to do it." She dropped the papers with a sigh.

Sevi crossed his arms and leaned back in his chair. "It sounds like you decided this would happen before speaking to me."

Tiersa nodded. "Yes, and I do apologize for that, but there are forces at work beyond your perception, Isevidel. People who would seek any reason to deny you your rightful place on the throne. I had to move fast to retain our momentum, or someone would have taken it from us."

"And a *party* allows you to do that?" Sevi asked, unable to keep his tension from contaminating his tone.

"Very much so," Tiersa said with a reassuring expression. "Parties, as frivolous as they are, are how the Embers raise funds. Everyone in high society will be under tremendous social pressure to attend, if not for support of renewing our homeland to its former glory, then to see you. To not attend could be construed as an insult to the Elkran legion, me, and potentially the royal heir. It would be seen as open hostility, and that, Isevidel, would be very, very unwise." She lowered her eyes meaningfully at him.

Sevi felt a blossom of confidence sprout in his chest at her self-assuredness. "Will I need to dance?"

Tiersa laughed. "Yes, and a bit more. Given your... your memory." She looked down at the papers in front of her, shuffling through them. "I'll have to reteach you all the ceremony's nuance, as well as the proper formalities and forms of address. Then there's Elkran history, the names of all the noble families and their vassals, the lands they rule, table etiquette... thank the Mother and Father your ability to read was unharmed."

Sevi frowned at her. *Table* etiquette? "Fine. Where do we start?"

"I've instructed Rinenne to teach you about Elkran high society when she can be spared from her duties. Captain River will touch upon our geopolitics and trade with our surrounding lands, and I will teach you our history. If we spend about eight hours a day on your tutelage, perhaps ten, then we should have you prepared enough for the ball."

"*Ten hours!*"

"Perhaps more, depending on your progress."

Sevi sunk deeper into his chair, gritting his teeth in frustration. "I was going to fly on the airship in a couple days."

Tiersa frowned. "I'm not sure who told you that, but they're misinformed. You're certainly not setting foot on that contraption until it has been thoroughly tested."

His fingers curled into fists. First the news about Alyda, and now this. *Blazes.* "Is there anything *else* you need from me?"

"Yes, I need to measure your face for your masks. Are you still fond of horses or do you have a new favorite animal?"

"Each house bears a constellation," Promina said. "Lady Tiersa will explain during her lesson. House Kaymoor, my house, bears the sigil of the Soldran constellation, or the Rising Sun. It currently holds the largest faction among the nobles and has supported Commander Tiersa in her resistance from the beginning through a series of shadow businesses fronting as laborers. In actuality, these businesses are used to funnel funds from neighboring countries that the Fae had otherwise tried to embargo, thus securing Noble business interests and opening supply lines for the Embers.

"They have a high level of influence with Tiburas and the Ta'Runa, possess many members in the clergy, and economically are more successful than any other house, having also kept vigil over what remains of the monarchy's fortune since their demise. When you speak to any representative of Kaymoor, it is important to bow deeper than the others out of respect for their efforts, but not too deep, as your station is still higher than theirs if not yet formally recognized. Never bow lower than the waist to anyone but bow close to the waist for Kaymoor.

"Their affiliated houses are Umara, Lumin, Arvenhill, Waelstonne, Vakenni, Remorannd, and Torsold. Their constellations are the Silver Eel, the Three Wolves, the Hunted Hart, the Ancient Wave, the All Seeing Falcon, and the Stone Giant.

"Second to Kaymoor is Engrom, which bears the Orrin constellation, or the Watchful Bear. They helped secure much of the Ember armaments through daring raids against Fae supply depots, thus securing our access, experimentation, and production of firearms, though it is suspected that they already had access to such weaponry prior to the Fae invasion, which would explain the speed in which we were supplied.

"They have not revealed their methods and you should not ask or mention this, as they are rather secretive of it. Full body armor was discarded shortly after this acquisition in order to place a greater emphasis on speed of movement for our troops, and also due to the damage that a bullet causes the wearer when it ricochets inside. Breastplates, though, are occasionally used in prolonged battles to negate the enemy's magic. Iron-wear is also still being used in our fashion and ceremonies, so expect to compliment the guests on their metalwork, especially those from Engrom. A bow at the chest to them will do.

"Their affiliated houses are Margov, Likinnsey, Derringen, Rexfeld, and Oppingham. Their constellations are the Blooming Flower, the Lone Rider, the High Tower, the Coiling Serpent, and the Enduring Shield.

"Then there is the faction of the lower houses—socially speaking they are not lower than any other house, but they possess less power than either Kaymoor, Engrom, or the houses affiliated with them. They often band together if they wish to oppose any action of the larger factions and possess enough stopping power to do so if they come close to a majority agreement among themselves. They are made up of Inglay, Nevlish, Yorung, Eddletine, Jirandich, Parolovinn, Hevok, Karkim, Revolar, Greylev, Morlan, Cyradin, Ha—"

Sevi coughed.

Promina broke off. "Your Luminance? Are you well?"

"Um... yes."

"As I was saying. Havaal, Gorgumm, Thistlegem, and Borgium. Their constellations are—"

Sevi sighed.

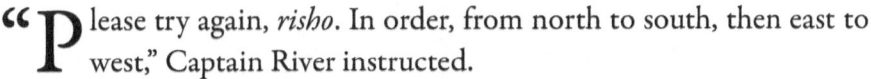

"**P**lease try again, *risho*. In order, from north to south, then east to west," Captain River instructed.

Sevi kneaded his temples. "May I please take a break?"

"You may take one after this. Please, once more, from the start."

Sevi groaned, trying his best to remember the names of each realm as he'd heard them, and trying not to confuse any with all the names that Promina had given him. "The Lynnweald, or Misty Kingdom, is the northern kingdom, known for its reclusive Fae denizens who hide behind a wall of giant trees, and have access to both magic as well as advanced technology. Elkra has had tense relations with them for years, until they infiltrated and launched a successful invasion... starting with the deaths of my family. We've been at war ever since."

"Good. To the east?"

"The kingdom of Tiburas, or the Long Kingdom. Known for its vibrant culture and jewelry exports, they are separated from Elkra by the Dordren mountains. It is a largely flat land with a strong naval force and economy. We have had close ties with them for generations. My...great grandfather? No, my great *great* grandfather is from there, marrying into the family from House... Vidoras."

Captain River nodded approvingly. "Promina is teaching you well. I knew she would, she taught me much when I first landed here. Now, to the west please."

"To the west is the kingdom of Áilé, separated from Elkra by the Spirithorn River," Sevi added, recalling his discussions with Loma.

"Very good. And what is it commonly referred to as?"

"The Green Kingdom, for its bright green rolling foothills. Known for its animal husbandry, tall citizenry, and most of all, the origin of magical stonework. Many of Elkra's best horses—"

"Be more specific. What is the name of this stonework?"

"Runic," Sevi said readily. Out of all subjects, that one hadn't failed to hold his attention.

"Very good."

"I think I could say 'magic bricklaying' and people would still understand what I mean."

"Runic is one of several studies of magic. You must be specific."

Sevi perked up. "There's more?"

River shook his head. "Later. How does Runicism work?"

Sevi sighed. "Fine. Runic. The name of the process for capturing aether using specific symbols to perform specific tasks, as well as the people who carry out this process. How the runes capture aether is a secret known only by the Runic Order, and all attempts to replicate them by non-Runics have been met with failure. Satisfied?"

"Very. Continue."

"Where?"

"With Áilé."

"Where did I stop?"

"Many of Elkra's best horses."

"Many of Elkra's best horses come from Áilé, as well as the best Runic rune stones. But the latter are rare, because the Runic Order accepts only a handful of people into its ranks every year. It is suspected that the ability to enchant is very uncommon."

"Good. Now to the south."

"To the south is just water," Sevi said innocently. "Are we done now?"

Captain River raised an eyebrow. "Are you trying to insult me?"

*Blazes.* "Are the Ta'Runa considered a kingdom? They live in every port, like you said."

"My islands are small compared to the continent, and we make our living in other lands. But we are very much a people, binding all nations in sea trade, and very much important to Elkra and the Embers. When the Fae invaded, the Resistance was pushed south to the sea, where they and my people met and became partners in trade. Without us, Elkra may not have survived. Now please, explain. You want a break, do you not?"

Sevi sighed. "The... Iza'kaima islands?"

"Correct. Though your pronunciation could use work. Continue."

"Does it have a moniker like the others?"

River stroked his chin. "I have heard it called, 'The Convoy Kingdom' before, though it is not quite a 'kingdom.'"

"Alright. The Convoy Kingdom. Homeland of the Ta'Runa. Known for their shipbuilding, powerful navy, and long economic reach, they can be found in every major coastal and river-port town on Iaela. Whoever their monarchy is also leads the country in its religion. The Iza'kaima islands also serve as a waypoint between our continent, Imithin, and the southern continent of Lovithin. The Ta'Runa also, according to you, make the best storytellers."

River smirked. "And according to many others."

"Will anyone from the Ta'Runa or any of the surrounding countries even be at the ball?"

"Other than those among our rank from these realms, it will be a decidedly Elkran affair, as I understand it. The commander has made it clear that it will be very political, and my people would rather not involve themselves in internal matters unless business is to be discussed. But do not worry. I am certain you will meet them all in time." Captain River smiled. "And while we are on the subject, tell me about Elkra. This, above all, will be most important."

"Elkra..." Sevi trailed off. The country he would be expected to rule one day. "The Crossroads Kingdom. Or Queendom, rather, until..." He awkwardly cleared his throat. "Known also as the corridor to the east, its geography has allowed for ample sea, river, and caravan trade from as far as the northern kingdoms and the southern continent. Frequently in competition with Tiburas over jewelry and ore exports from the Dordren mountains, it is mostly known for its export of... some kind of rock that holds aether."

"Solinite."

Sevi recalled the crystal pillars along the main boulevard of Ilondia, full of dancing silver dust. "What exactly is aether, Captain River?"

"What exactly is air?" River shrugged. "It exists and it is everywhere. I leave its study to the scholars and magicians. What else can you tell me about Elkra?"

Sevi tapped his finger on the desk, unsatisfied, but continued. "It's the birthplace of Ivirism. The veneration of my ancestor, Iviri, for answering the Parents' call to protect Iaela, and losing her life in the process. What confuses me is whether or not we worship her as a god, too. Especially after seeing that play at the Golden Spool."

"She is a... *kinna*, what is the word?" Captain River pursed his lips in thought. "The commander will tell you about it. If you wanted to know of Earuna I could speak of Her the whole afternoon. But your Iviri remains confusing to me, years after learning of her. I am meant only to discuss trade with you, which you have listened to rather well."

"So, are we done?" Sevi asked hopefully.

"No, you have only learned of the nations closest." Captain River stood and stretched. "You must learn the remaining five lands as well."

"I need to know *all* of them?"

"We will continue after our break!" River said, walking toward the door.

"Isevidel, please wake up," Commander Tiersa prodded.

Sevi snorted. "I'm awake. I'm awake."

Tiersa waited until he met her gaze, staring severely at him. "Please try to take this seriously, Isevidel. I understand that it's not as thrilling as an airship, but it *is* important."

"I am! I am taking it seriously," Sevi objected. It wasn't his fault that he'd fallen asleep. After getting so much information crammed into his head all at once, and on his first day of lessons, he had no energy left to spare.

"Well then please do a better job of paying attention."

Sevi sighed. "I'm listening. Please go on."

"What's the last thing you remember before you dozed off?"

"You were talking about the Ardent Star."

She grimaced. "I'll have to start over."

"Sorry..."

Tiersa cleared her throat. "The Ardent Star symbolizes two things. The first is our origin—the star that birthed us. When this origin star and its partner sacrificed their lives in the pursuit of making something new, our plane of existence, and by extension, our own existence, came into being.

"From them rose the high gods Caela and Eonin, lady and lord of creation and time. Through them came their court: Sorvathos, the Father, sentinel of the sun. Avinaea, the Mother, keeper of the world. And Tembra, The Faceless, shepherd of Abeya—or the Waylands, where the dead cross. Together, Sorvathos and Avinaea breathed life into us—one to give us our divine spark of life, the other to mold our shapes. They taught us the ways of the world, nurtured us, and raised us to civilization. And when it is our time to leave for Tembra's domain, the Faceless Shepherd guides us to either Torment or Rebirth."

Sevi grimaced at the talk of the Faceless Shepherd, uncomfortable at how similar their description was to his own faceless mother, leading him through his dreams. "The second thing the star symbolizes is Iviri Astraeda," Tiersa continued. "The first star of the sky."

"I thought the Origin Star was the first star?" Sevi asked.

"Yes, but before the collision of the origin star and her partner, Nothing, there was no sky to be a star in."

Sevi frowned. "That doesn't make any sense. Why is the Origin Star called a star, then?"

Tiersa smiled wryly. "I believe the clergy thought it sounded poetic, if I'm being honest. Think of it this way. The Origin Star was everything, and Nothing was nothing. Everything and Nothing collided, and what resulted made something in between."

"That makes even less sense," Sevi muttered.

Tiersa shrugged. "It's what the clergy speaks of. Let's return to Iviri. Before her, as the stories go, the night was completely dark, save for the sparse fires of humankind. Until, from the very depths of this darkness, three creatures came to us, cloaking themselves in a guise of false light stolen from Sorvathos in an effort to destroy us. We call the strongest of them, the one that remains to this day, Niurna the Watcher. And on most nights, you can see it in the sky, waiting for an opportunity to slip past our parents in order to finish what it started."

Sevi's gaze sharpened on her. *Back when the moon was three.* "You mean the moon, don't you?"

Tiersa waved her hand. "Such as the legend goes. In the story it was Iviri Astraeda, noblest and most powerful of humans, who was blessed by the Parents to do battle with the Watcher and its siblings before they could break the land and sky into pieces. She managed to slay two of them before the Watcher struck her down, and the pieces she broke from them scattered across the sky to become the stars we see today.

"Without its siblings, Niurna did not have the power to break past the World Gate—the great wall that Sorvathos built and maintains to protect his love, Avinaea, and their children. In recognition of her sacrifice, the Parents raised the house of Astraeda to prominence as rulers of the land. The noble houses then each chose a constellation as their banner in honor of her battle. Elkra has since split into many lands, but Iviri's sacrifice is remembered to this day. It is also said that, so long as Astraeda's blood still flows, Elkra will never fall to man, beast, nor demon."

She looked fondly at Sevi, watching him for several breaths. "Or greenblood," she said softly.

Sevi shifted in his chair, looking down at his notes. "Why do I need to know this for a ball?"

"Much of the ball's traditions revolve around this story. But it's important that you know of the divine right placed upon you. The Mother and Father chose you to lead us, so do not think that you're not worth the weight of the crown. You're a prince for a reason, Isevidel."

Sevi didn't look up. "If I'm being honest, when you said that these lessons would be about history, I was hoping that it would have more to do with my own mother and father."

Commander Tiersa stilled, and a beat of silence rushed in between them. She let out a soft, lengthy sigh. "I... suppose that would be prudent to know." She leaned back in her chair and started idly tapping her finger on the table. "The Astraeda line is matriarchal, beginning with Iviri. King Marovhan Cassangia married into the family from the kingdom of Ivindris, though there have been cases of men ruling when a female heir is unable to be produced. If you hadn't reappeared then it was likely that one of your distant family members from the other houses would have ruled at the war's end, with favor going to the eldest. If the Night of Treachery hadn't happened, then the crown would have fallen to your sister Nahlra."

"But it did happen," Sevi muttered, growing distant.

Tiersa nodded. "When our own turned against us. Through Fae trickery and infiltration, they spread propaganda through the lowest of our citizenry, railing against the supposed crimes of your parents. At the time, taxes were high, a famine was ravaging the wheatlands, and some of the pettier nobles were squabbling among themselves at their borderlands. Morale in the country was incredibly low. However, after much investigation and study, I have come to believe that all of it was due to sabotage carried out from damned Fae meddling.

"Tariffs arose wherever Elkra conducted business, thus raising taxes. Our wheat fields had been set alight on multiple occasions, and the nobles? It doesn't take much to get them to bicker, children that they are. Then, on a night of celebration, when our guard was at its lowest, the Great Treachery took place, and our citizens revolted."

Sevi tilted his head. "I thought that the Night of Treachery happened because of faeblood?"

"Faeblood? I'm certain that had a hand in it but dosing an entire country's population would require a lot of it. No Isevidel, the truth is much more terrible. Some of our citizens were enthralled, but most of them were simply angry. Angry, downtrodden, and looking for a reason to be violent. All it took were the right agents in the right places to light the match that burnt our country down. But the invasion gave me the perfect opportunity to bring us together against a common enemy.

"You see, we call ourselves the Embers of Korina not just to honor your mother, but also to remind ourselves of the sin we committed. It is a brand of shame. In lashing out against ourselves we paved the road for our greenblood occupiers. It is only now that we have retaken our capital that we may cool our burns in the Caldwin River's waters, at the place where it all began."

Sevi's tiredness had vanished entirely. He regarded Tiersa with newfound respect, only now realizing the full extent of what she had lived through. She and her army had not only successfully liberated their entire country against a vastly superior foe, but had also brought a divided people together to do so. "How did... How did you escape, while my family died?"

He immediately regretted his question from the way she closed her face. But she answered. "The tunnels," she said softly. "That thorn in my side had become my salvation. It was through the quicksilver mines that I escaped and regrouped with what forces remained. And from there, a long, long road back."

She stopped tapping her finger as she stared off with a hollow expression. But she shook her head, refocusing on him, and attempted a smile. "It was worth it in the end. We found you. No greater gift could ever be given, and I thank the Mother every day."

Sevi shook his head. There it was again—some deeper emotion beneath the surface that was greater than joy in seeing her prince alive. "Commander, what are we to each other? I know I'm the last prince, I know I'm important, I know you're supposed to be my aunt, but there's more to it, isn't there? Why do you care about me so much?"

Tiersa pursed her lips, growing still again. Pain radiated through her facade. "I owe much to your mother, Isevidel. She and your father had very big hearts. Both, at different points in their rule, claimed the Right of Found Blood: the right of the monarchy to adopt. All under the law are given titles, and treated as royals, but are not allowed to hold the throne as heirs.

"The king saved Alramar from the streets and took him as their adoptive son when he was only four, maybe five winters old. Then your mother saved me, when I was a younger woman, working under the harsh lady of House Morlan. I'd rather not disgust you with those details. The scars from that time still haven't faded."

She coughed, pausing to swallow her emotion. "She was like Iviri to me, there to save me from the darkness. She took me in as her daughter, and although children of Found Blood may never take the throne, I swore on the day she made me her Promina that I would serve and protect her, her family, and the throne to my final breath. For years I thought that I had failed on all accounts. But upon making it here, and finding you…"

Her face tightened with an ambiguous expression, as if she couldn't decide which emotion to feel. "I never believed in second chances until now. And all I can hope is that when Tembra finally takes me, I'll get to see your parents, and they'll forgive me for failing them. But until then, I am here, ready to protect you and the throne one more time."

Sevi's eyes misted over. *Now* he understood. She wasn't just an old servant of the crown. She wasn't just a close friend to his family. She wasn't an aunt, like he used to call her. She was like a sister. She *was* his family. There had been a piece of him holding back, refusing to believe it could be true, but now…

When he looked down, taking deep breaths to get himself under control, she reached out a hand to him across the table with her palm facing up. She smiled at him with eyes just as watery as his. He laughed a short, remorseful chuckle and placed his hand in hers, squeezing her palm just as she did to him. "Can… can I take a break, Tisa?"

"Take the night, Little Sevi. Why don't we have dinner? Maybe Lily would like to join us."

Sevi sniffed, nodding. "I'd like that."

# Chapter 47

*The moment the walls of our home had been breached, I knew how our story would end. The way that you looked in that circlet of gold. The way that I tried to pretend.*

---

**D**ays came and went. Sevi attended his studies as dutifully as he could, with an eventual voracity that surprised him. Along with his desire to relearn what he'd forgotten, he felt a need to prove himself—that he *was* the prince, that he *could* perform the duties of one, and that he was someone Commander Tiersa could be proud of.

When Promina spoke for hours about how important it was to eat the furthest fork at the table first and work inward, he listened. When Captain River spoke about all the important rocks from another country and what they meant in trade, he listened. When Commander Tiersa spoke about the long, storied history of Elkra, and the many traditions that arose around its errant knights, he listened, perhaps a little more closely than to the other two.

The importance of the masquerade hung over him and his teachers' heads like an ominous cloud, and the nearer it got, the less tolerant they were of failure. Promina was the harshest of the three, frequently having him redo entire recitations whenever his diction didn't suit her. Then there were the joint lessons where both she and Tiersa would take turns questioning him as nobles would, over subjects he had only ever heard in passing. Some days, it was all he could do not to hide in his bed in fear, as if his blankets could cushion the weight of the mantle he'd taken upon himself. But he always rose, and he always tried.

Lily, meanwhile, had not sat idly by in their room while he was occupied. Every morning after breakfast she left with the guard Tiersa had assigned her to explore the castle as freely as she was able, taking great pleasure in her ability to slip away from her escort in the process. She always returned each evening with a cocky grin on her face, claiming that she *had* to be getting nearer to where the amber was being kept. For Alyda's sake, Sevi hoped she was right.

One day he fell into an unexpected gap between lessons. His teachers were still officers of an army, and as no official declaration of peacetime had yet to be announced, they still had military duties to perform. At about midday, during a lesson with Promina regarding the Iron Masquerade's "Dark Hour," she was surreptitiously called away on the urgent orders of Commander Tiersa.

When asked about it, she had reluctantly said, "the Empyreans have given word to the commander that there are flying Fae in the area. But do not worry, Your Brilliance. Please, go to the library and read up on the masquerade's ceremonies. They should have a copy of *The Songs of Elkra* by Corrin Raquel. That should have some information for you."

Even at the mention of Fae, Sevi felt a gentle thrill. He had never seen the library proper before, and he had not had the time to visit it since his emergence. The prospect of finally being able to read whichever books he wanted, *whenever* he wanted, was enough to send his spirits soaring.

Striding through the castle with an eager step, flanked by Cassik, Loma, and the rest of his guards, he approached the royal library's double doors and pulled one open without preamble. Leaving his escorts outside, he stepped inside with a smile on his face, ready to be met with glistening shelves filled to the brim with voluminous tomes of every kind.

What he got, instead, made him pause. The room itself was fairly big, with a second level and a ceiling that could rival that in the throne room. But many of the shelves it housed lay barren, missing, and even burned. A few soldiers and non-uniformed people milled idly around what remained, or had claimed a chair at what few tables had been provided. Swallowing his disappointment, Sevi took a tentative step further into the room, wondering where he should start.

"Can I help you?"

He turned. A familiar man with a gold serpent earring sat at a desk beside the door between two piles of books. He stared at Sevi blankly, reclined in his chair with a book in his lap, balancing it with one handless arm beneath its spine. When Sevi said nothing, Tahno said, "What is it that you are here for?"

Sevi blinked. "Um... I'm here for a book. Promina sent me."

"Which one?" he asked flatly.

"*The Songs of Elkra* by... Corvin—"

"Corrin Raquel," Tahno finished for him, closing the book in his lap with a snap. "Follow me. And please be silent." He stepped out of his chair and strode away without looking back, forcing Sevi to scurry to catch up.

The soldier said nothing as he led him through the stacks, peering at the shelves with a critical eye, as if a hard enough stare could command the book to magically appear. He finally stopped at one shelf in particular, crossing his arms in front of his chest while sweeping his gaze over row after row.

Standing uncomfortably off to the side, Sevi glanced from the shelves, to Tahno, and back. "Um... you're Tahno, right?" The soldier didn't react. Feeling it polite to introduce himself in the Runan way, he continued with, "I'm Sevi. Or rather, Isevidel Astraeda. Son of Queen Korina and King—"

"There is no need for that... Your Majesty," Tahno said, adding the 'your majesty' as an afterthought. "Yes, my name is Tahno."

"Oh." Sevi shifted again in confusion. "I'm sorry. Did I do that right?"

"Yes." Tahno reached into the shelves and pulled out a book bound in red leather. He turned and offered it to Sevi. "Be careful with this book, and bring it back in a week. Will there be anything else?"

"Oh. No." Sevi took the book from him. "Thank you."

Nodding, the man offered a fleeting touch to his shoulder in the quickest bow imaginable before brushing past Sevi, marching back the way he came and disappearing around the corner.

Sevi watched him leave with confusion, wondering if he had somehow insulted him. After several breaths, he looked down at the book, turning it about in his hands. *The Songs of Elkra by Corrin Raquel* shown back at him in faded golden letters. He briefly considered taking another book or two for his own recreation, but wondered if such a thing would risk Tahno's irritation and decided against it. *There won't be time to read anything until after the masquerade, anyway,* he thought.

With the book in hand, and with nowhere else to go, he stepped back through the shelves to the middle of the room. He briefly considered sitting down at one of the tables, but his presence had not gone unnoticed, and some of the library's occupants were beginning to stare. He decided to leave the library altogether, walking past Tahno, who had resumed reading behind his desk. He didn't glance up as Sevi passed.

Rejoining his guard, Sevi thought, *I guess I can just go back to my room.* Except, he had an entire castle that he could now freely move about, and he had seen an awful lot of the royal chambers already. Perhaps it was time to join Lily in her exploration.

"Do you happen to know where Lily is?" he asked Cassik.

Cassik shook his head. "I'm afraid not, sir."

"I doubt anyone does," Loma said.

One of Sevi's new guards, Marin, stepped up. "I saw Weskin on our way here," she said, mentioning the name of the soldier assigned to Lily. "I didn't see Miss Lily though, sir."

Loma chuckled. "Shocking."

"Where was he?" Sevi asked.

"Standing outside the stairwell to the west tower."

*The Sunset Tower.* "Let's speak with him," Sevi said.

Retracing their steps back the way they'd come, they found Weskin standing outside the stairwell to the tower with his back against the wall and his rifle at his side. He stood at attention at their approach, offering a quick nod and touching his shoulder. "Your Brilliance," he said.

"Hey, Wes," Loma said companionably. "I see you lost someone again."

Weskin smiled grimly. He had a fearsome scar across his lip, marring his expression, but his demeanor seemed good-humored. "I'll gladly swap with you, Tammavin, if you'd like a try at watching her yourself."

"Where did you last see Lily?" Sevi asked.

"Up the tower, sir," Weskin said with a nod of his head. "She's lost me up there several times now. But the only way down is through this archway, so I'll often wait for her here."

*That's what you think.* "I'll see if I can find her," Sevi said. "Thank you for your help."

"Good luck, sir." Weskin waved as they left.

Marching up the steps with his guards in tow, Sevi searched each floor for signs of his friend, knocking on every door and checking every room. The Sunset Tower had always had the nicest furniture and decorations compared to most of the other rooms in the castle, so he was surprised to find it completely deserted.

"Why is no one here? What do we use this tower for?" Sevi asked his guards.

"Whatever you'd like, Your Brilliance," Loma said.

Cassik ran his hands along the glistening wood of a dresser. "Some friends of mine in another company were ordered to clean these rooms recently. The furniture looks grand enough to be a noble's quarters."

"Maybe this is where the commander will stuff all the shiny-shoes, then," Loma said. "I still need to get my mask for the ball. You think they'll let us have any of the wine?"

Moving upward, Sevi reached the last room on the highest floor—a room so big that it almost took up the entire level, and found it empty, too. Crossing his arms, he gazed out the nearest window, turning over the possibilities in his head. "Would you all please wait for me outside?"

"Sir?" Cassik said.

Sevi turned to him. "We can't find Lily, and I still need to read this book. Here is as good a place as any. And if she's still in the tower, then who knows. Maybe she'll find me."

His guards shared a fleeting look, but they shrugged. "Let us know if you need anything," Cassik said, saluting briefly before turning and walking out with the rest of his detail.

When the door had closed, Sevi looked down at his shadow. "She's in the Cut, isn't she, Shy?" He placed his book on the nearest table and approached the wall, pressing in on every stone at floor-height that he could find. When he touched the stone closest to the bed, it gave. "That's what I thought," he muttered, leaning his weight into it until he had opened the way.

He put the stone back before moving deeper into the tunnel. Bringing out Lily's whistle, he chirped two notes before calling out, "Lily?"

A flutter of wings echoed gently off the walls in answer, but not at the rapid pace of Alyda's wingbeats. These sounded much bigger, and full of feathers. Walking around the curve of the inner tower, the light level of the tunnel increased dramatically, and he stopped as he met the source of the sound.

Lily sat with her back against the wall and a trio of ravens at her feet. The brick to the outer wall had been removed, and a stark beam of sunlight poured through, illuminating her and the birds like one of the Golden Spool's runelights. She watched him approach with an eyebrow raised, and at his appearance, the birds cocked their heads and cawed in surprise, flapping their wings and hopping back from him.

"They let you out of the dungeon early, eh?" she said, tossing a handful of crumbs to her feet. The ravens immediately scrambled for the food, pecking and fighting over the biggest scraps.

"Promina got called away. I came looking to see if you'd show me what you've found in the castle." Sevi eyed the birds from a distance. "What are you doing?"

"Feeding some new friends," she said, watching the birds eat. "Though the big one is a bastard."

As if hearing the sleight, the largest of the ravens cocked its head at her, twitching it from side to side, before going back to eating, pushing one of the smaller ones away from its morsels.

Sevi approached carefully, unwilling to startle them, and slumped against the wall next to her. "What are you doing in here, though?"

She inhaled a deep breath and let it out slowly. "It gets a little noisy in the castle sometimes. You know?"

Sevi nodded. He understood completely. They had each become familiar with every kind of silence that the Cut had to offer, but outside of it there were very few to come by, and each one felt new. She continued, "But I don't want to be in our room all day. And I can't always disappear into the Cut now that I'm being watched. So sometimes I come here."

He nodded again, turning as two of the smaller ravens squabbled with each other, cawing gratingly in a cloud of feathers. "It's amazing that they're still around given all the Empyrean falcons," Sevi remarked. "They have astounding control over their animals. Why do you think that is?"

"Maybe they're just good trainers."

"Certainly, but how do you think they do it?"

Lily thought for a moment. "Signal whistles, probably. Like how the Fablings controlled their geisthounds. I haven't exactly looked into it." She grimaced as the fight among the birds got out of hand. She kicked her foot, breaking them up. "Alright, get out of here, all of you."

The birds took off, each darting toward the opening in the wall. The biggest one went last, pausing to snatch one more piece of bread before following, leaving Sevi and Lily alone.

Lily stretched. "So. How are lessons, your princeliness? Is it everything you expected? Are you feeling royal, yet?"

"Not really. The warm food is nice, but the lessons are... a lot. Tiersa is cramming my head full of names of distant relatives, River is going through economics using math I can't possibly follow, and Promina has me dancing. Dancing, of all things." He stared off into the near distance. "I find myself wondering how much of what I'm learning now are things that I've already learned... before."

Lily nodded, saying nothing.

"How's Alyda doing? I'm upset that I haven't been able to see her lately."

"She's fine. Her cough has returned, though. I've been considering giving her the rest of the amber that the doctor left us, but Aly wants to wait until she gets worse."

Sevi nodded. It was the best they could do. "Bring her down sometime, if you can. I'm sure she'd love to hear about what's been happening."

Lily gave an exaggerated salute. "You got it, princeling."

The two of them lapsed into silence and stared out through the hole in the wall, leaving the wind whistling through to be the only spoken voice. The soft, distant sounds of people in the yard carried on the breeze, no more than vague murmurs, reminiscent of all the other times that he and Lily had sat in this very spot, telling stories while the sun set over a courtyard of drilling soldiers. For a moment, it felt as if Eonin had turned back his wheel, and they were Lily and Sevi of the Fabling Castle once more.

"How are the visions?" Lily asked.

"They've lessened. Quite a bit," Sevi said. "Maybe... Maybe with every day that I learn a bit more about my family, and who I used to be, the less my visions feel the need to throw themselves at me. I am still having nightmares though, sometimes."

"I know. I've heard you sleep-talking. And you've lost your shadow again, I see."

Sevi blinked and stared down at his feet. Shy had disappeared. He groaned. "Mother and Father below and above, what is it with them and the Cut?"

Lily chuckled. "If any of the other times are any indication, it'll come back. Unfortunately."

Sevi frowned at her. "Why don't you like them? It's never done anything to hurt me."

"For all we know it's a parasite, Sevi, feeding on your memories. Maybe it ate your real shadow."

"Shy would never," Sevi said, lifting his chin.

Lily snorted. "Just watch it for me, alright? And call for me with the whistle if it tries anything."

"Fine. I suppose. If only to show you there's nothing wrong with them." Sevi sighed. "I guess I should probably leave. They'll need time to return, and I might scare the soldiers if I come back without them. Then there's this book I have to read for Promina."

"And we mustn't upset the Golden Prude." Lily smirked.

Sevi cracked a grin along with her despite how mean the name sounded. Promina had been incredibly displeased with Lily's mannerisms, and had said as much, so naturally Lily had doubled her crudity around her at every opportunity. He got up from the floor and dusted himself off. "Want to come with me? I do still want to see the rest of the castle. Maybe I can help you find the amber."

Lily shook her head. "I'm too tired to get up to much right now. I think I'm going to stay here for a bit. Maybe get a nap in or three."

"You could always sleep in the bed outside."

She waved the thought away. "Nah. These beds are too soft."

"Alright, but I'll be there for a while. If I don't see you anytime soon, see you at dinner?"

"See you at dinner." She tipped her visor down to shield her eyes and was snoring before Sevi had even reached the entrystone.

Weeks into his lessons, classes with Captain River, specifically, considerably improved. He had been assisting Digby in overseeing the final repairs on the airship and had been on deck when the ship first lifted from the ground. It hadn't shot into the sky as Sevi had expected, thought, much to his disappointment. They had anchored it tightly to the plateau and allowed it to rise by several headspans, in case anything went wrong experimenting with its controls.

"Sensible, if not exciting," Captain River said, eager to discuss it at every opportunity. "The canvas balloon held nicely, and the cloud kegs had enough gas to lift the hull. I was surprised, I had never thought this gas could be used for anything other than to burn. Is it not a horrifying thing, to have fire push a flying ship, held by a cloud that burns?" He sighed. "We have learned that the steering works quite well. Also that it has cloth flaps that shimmer like the old balloon, which extend from the hull's sides when we pull a certain lever. We think they stabilize the ship. But we do not know what makes the fires roar, and there is no hearth on the ship."

"Aren't they made through sunlight?" Sevi asked.

Captain River cocked his head. "Sunlight?"

"Yes." Sevi paused as realization washed over him. There had been a lightblossom seed onboard, whose plants shimmered just as the cloth of the balloon had. *Gathered from the sun itself,* Lily had said. "Were those flaps open the entire time you tried the controls?"

River searched Sevi's face. "No. We put them back before doing anything else."

"Try keeping them open next time," Sevi said, smiling.

Sure enough, when River came back the next day, he was exuberant. "It was spectacular, *risho!* We nearly burned an entire squad of troops, but the fires live again!"

Sevi had heard the airship come to life from clear across the castle, just like everybody, but he couldn't help feeling excited all over again. "I know! I heard! It sounded *amazing!* Is it going to fly soon?"

"It might, once we learn how to control its height! How did you know of the cloth?"

Sevi left out any mention of Lily, but told him of the lightblossom seed he and Digby had found, and of the flowers that had bloomed from it. River laughed with delight. "What beautiful magic!" He beamed. "It is very good that we have not destroyed what was left of the first balloon, now we will have cloth to spare! I will have to talk to Lieutenant Asgaillin. He should not have given you anything from that ship, and you should not be wandering into the mountain alone anymore, but it appears that it was for the better! *Ik Earuna kah'eshaa!*" He tossed his head and laughed. "We must tend to these lightblossoms!"

Sevi stopped smiling. Even now he didn't like the idea of anyone going into his garden, and he told River as much. The captain took it in stride. "As His Brilliance wills! Tell me when you next intend to visit your garden, and I will send guards with you. Bring us a seed when they may be harvested, but until then, you have become the most important gardener in the land!"

Which, of course, gave Sevi another thing to worry about, if not a small sense of pride.

Within another week, the Embers had learned enough about the airship's mechanisms to control the level of fire to the point where the vessel was at danger of breaking its bonds. River mentioned that it could only get to half-power and suspected that the missing original balloon had something to do with it. Repairing the fabric would be top priority once the lightblossoms could be harvested and spun into cloth.

They next discovered the method of controlling the amount of cloud in the balloon, and thus its altitude. But doing so required pumping and venting the gas, which required more cloud kegs, which required coin, so Commander Tiersa ordered that the ship was not to fly to greater heights without her explicit approval.

Bound by his lessons, Sevi could relate with the contraption. It was eating into what time he had left with Alyda, and he had decided that every night, even when he could barely stay awake, he would make the trip up to their garden to accompany her alone, ignoring Captain River's misgivings. He would tell her stories of everything he'd learned, and she would walk him through the garden to show him all the changes she had made.

In the fifth week of his lessons, the first guests of the masquerade arrived.

Sevi and Lily were out by the airship in the recently replanted castle gardens on one of the few breaks that Commander Tiersa allowed him. The air had chilled considerably with winter's approach, and they huddled close while watching Captain River and Digby experiment with the airship's helm. Sometimes Lily called for them to pull at certain levers, normally ending with hilarious results whenever they listened to her.

The officers were unfurling and folding the 'fire flaps,' as they called them, in further attempts to see how that would affect the ship's propulsion and stability. Sevi was trying to come up with a better name for them and was arguing with Lily over calling them "Lightwings" versus her name of "Suncatchers," when a blaring of trumpets interrupted their debate.

The large gates of the castle wall started to open, and the portcullis raised, which seemed silly to Sevi, considering the still unrepaired, gaping hole in the wall. Curious, he and Lily rushed up the ramparts with a group of Embers, looking for the source.

A caravan of carriages rolled sluggishly up the incline, decorated ostentatiously in vibrant red and gold livery. A host of foot soldiers and bannermen dressed in half-plate armor guarded them, stamping along in time with the horses. While the foot soldiers carried halberds and glaives, the men and women riding next to the horse-drivers carried the more deadly rifles with their barrels pointed up, continuously swiveling their heads from side to side in an unending sweep for danger. Their shields and chests bore the rising sun constellation of House Kaymoor.

Promina appeared from the depths of the castle, out of breath and red in the face with her hair out of place. She adjusted her clothing and smoothed out her coat, approaching the opening gates with her hands behind her back in a stately posture. She didn't move, staring ahead intently while the first of the carriages leveled out on the plateau and entered the courtyard, leading the rest on an ambling path.

The horses were larger than the ones the Embers used in their supply trains, and they had silky blond manes and glossy brown coats. They made no sound of annoyance, nor did they buck or stamp as they came to a halt, standing as noble and disciplined as the soldiers that surrounded them.

The Kaymoor soldiers approached the doors of each carriage and opened them with a bow of deference to those inside, offering their hands out to assist the occupants down. Lords and ladies stepped genteelly out of each, dressed in all manner of red and gold coats and dresses, managing to look graceful and composed even when they stretched.

Promina approached an older couple leading several younger children and a young lady, bowing to them. They received the gesture with similar bows of their own. Sevi recognized the flourishes from Promina's teachings as bows made to those of a family, conveying respect from juniors to elders and vice versa. But when the formalities finished, they embraced all too readily, with Promina taking time to give each of the younger kids a kiss, much to their obvious and unhidden irritation. She looked happier than Sevi had ever seen her.

"Oh, how lovely," Lily said with a smirk. "More fodder for the Name Game."

The sea of red and gold flowed through the gates of the main hall with Promina and her family at the head, disappearing within. Mere moments after the last of them vanished, a second blaring of trumpets sounded from down the castle path, deeper, stuttering, and more resonant than those of Kaymoor's. A second caravan came rolling up from around the cliffside, as slow and unconcerned as the first, but with far fewer carriages. A squad of thunderous, stamping soldiers filled the gaps between the sparse train of vehicles to make up the difference, wearing gleaming plate armor that shone like tiny suns.

Bannermen at each corner of every company carried the flags of the Watchful Bear—the mark of House Engrom. Every single other soldier carried a rifle, held across their chests at an angle as though ready for battle at a moment's notice.

A captain approached the gates this time wearing the leathers of an Empyrean. Sevi recognized him as the man who'd stood off by himself at the officers' party, and beside him during his father's funeral.

The caravan circled into the courtyard just as the first had. The carriages had a darker wood, and the horses had grey coats with black manes but were just as large as the previous ones. The soldiers stamped in place in perfect time until the last of the vehicles came to a halt, pulling up next to the red-and-gold line of Kaymoor, before standing at attention with a final stomp. A call went out, and as one, they set their rifles up against their shoulders and turned on their heels to face the castle, placing their free hands down against their legs.

The carriage doors opened without assistance. Nobles dressed in green and brown stepped out this time, looking grim and rigid. No soldier offered to help them down, even when a lady got the hem of her dress stuck on the wood. She tore at it in annoyance, disregarding any harm to the fabric, and walked off with the other woman that accompanied her.

The Empyrean captain approached the lord that led them; a stout, grizzled man with a shock of white hair that traveled down his face to end in a beard. There were no formal bows or gestures of respect. Instead, the two openly hugged outright, laughing with each other. This repeated several more times, until all the lords and ladies stood about, talking far longer than the Kaymoors had.

Eventually, the white-haired man extracted himself from the group and blew several sharp trills into a signal whistle. All the knights at attention relaxed and took off their helmets. Then they set their rifles down on the ground to face parallel with the castle, placing their helmets behind them to form orderly rows of steel. When the last had finished, the white-haired man blew the whistle again, and the soldiers immediately formed into two columns behind the lords and ladies, following them in a dutiful march into the great hall.

"Did I say fodder? I meant *feast*." Lily chuckled. "Get ready, princeling. The lords and ladies are finally here to poke at you."

Sevi nodded as the last of the Engroms disappeared. It had been about a month, just as Tiersa had said. "Right on time."

Lily looked warily at him. "What do you mean?"

"Did nobody tell you?"

"Tell me what?"

"Why did you think I was having so many lessons?"

"Tell me *what?*" she repeated.

"We're going to have a ball."

"A *ball?*" she exclaimed. "*What ball?*"

# Chapter 48

*Oh mouse, how you hoped, how you gathered your light, weaving a heavenly band. Shining as bright as the moon in her veil, as one with the star in your hand.*

———— ✦ ————

"Remember when I said I was going to kill you? That hasn't changed, but now I'm going to enjoy it."

Sevi sighed. Lily hadn't stopped complaining since she'd learned about the party, and had only gotten more vocal when the tailors arrived to lay out their clothing. He examined his options with an uncertain eye, unsure of what to pick, while Lily contented herself with throwing the dresses left for her across the room. "How could you forget to tell me there was a ball?" she continued. "It's bad enough that I'm here, but now I have to be here and be at a *ball!*"

"You don't have to come," Sevi said, holding up a flowery blouse to his chest and looking in the mirror. He grimaced at the colors.

"And what, stay up here listening to all the noise? Not being at a ball, but being forced to listen to one, is *just* as bad as being at one!"

"Why do you hate it so much?"

"*Because it's a ball, Sevi!*" She spread her arms out as if that explained everything. "And what has you in such a good mood? I thought you hated being around people."

He held up another shirt and tossing that one aside as well. "I do. But I'll be wearing a mask, and I don't know... that kind of feels like it will help."

"A mask—oh. This is a *masquerade*." She huffed, shaking her head at him. "Sevi, is there anything else I should know? Will there be flying purple wrasks and nemikin butlers to shine our shoes for us?"

"What's a nemikin?"

"Don't change the subject."

Sevi rolled his eyes and turned to her. "I'm sorry that I forgot to tell you, alright? It's been a busy month for me in case you don't remember."

"Too busy to mention these things to your best friend, apparently."

"Again, for the one hundredth time, I'm sorry." Sevi spread his hands in deference. "Will you please come though? I can have someone bring you a mask."

She looked at him for several breaths, then reached up to her helmet and flipped her visor down. "There. That works, doesn't it?"

Caught off guard, Sevi laughed. "Better than you know! Apparently, everyone used to wear iron helmets to these things."

"Oh, Gods, where am I going to find an iron helmet at this time of day?" She smirked, lifting her visor back up. He chuckled and lifted another vest up to the mirror.

A knock came at the door, accompanied by a familiar voice. "Hark! Your Shining Effulgence! Your champions have arrived bearing gifts fit for a king!"

Sevi furrowed his brow at Lily. Discarding the vest, he crossed the room and opened the door into the parlor, only to come face to face with the smiles of Innavin Targa and Captain Lorr Gallan. Each of them held a long, paper box in their hands.

"Ah, Your Luminance! Please pardon our interruption, but we have a matter most pressing for you that must be addressed at once," Innavin said.

"And if I had held him back any longer, he might have died from apoplexy," Lorr said.

"Innavin? Lorr? Hi!" Sevi smiled at the two, but his humor immediately vanished under a wave of guilt. "I'm so sorry I haven't been to the infirmary; I've been so caught up with my studies! How are you? I'm happy to see you both well!"

Lorr waved him off. "Not an issue, lad, we understand. Gods help anyone who shirks a schedule set by Promina Rinenne Kaymoor. And I'm fine. Still have bandages around my ribs, but at least I can walk."

"And I'm doing far better than well, Your Brilliance," Innavin said. "Remember when I mentioned how everyone loves a scar? Well Rya has—"

Lorr groaned. "Vin, I swear, if you say one more word—"

"Fine, fine, I apologize. There I go, forgetting myself again." Innavin laughed off Lorr's annoyance. "Best not to tarry regardless. We have gifts for you and your knight!"

Sevi balked. "My *what?*"

"Come, come," Innavin said, lying his box on the table and waving him over. Lorr followed suit. "Lady Knight! Are you in there, too?"

Lily poked her head out from around the corner, clearly having eavesdropped. "What?"

"We have a gift for you!"

Lily warily stepped into the room. "Is it tasty?"

"Only figuratively." Innavin smirked.

Lily joined Sevi at his side, staring at the boxes with him. Her face scrunched into a distasteful scowl. "I'll tell Sevi to have a gallows built if there's a dress in there."

Innavin feigned offense. "My lady. I would hardly insult you that way. Everyone knows that knights do not wear dresses."

"Enough of the theater. Let's get on with it," Lorr said.

"Allow me this last flourish, Lorr. Here you are, both of you—from the best that Kylari has to offer. Behold," he announced, lifting the lids of each box at once.

The box in front of Sevi held a long, midnight blue tailcoat with gold trim and buttons, a pair of white linen pants, a matching waistcoat, and a shirt that gleamed up at him with golden, floral lining. Beneath the clothing at the base of the box were two black boots and matching gloves, shining with freshly oiled leather. But completing the ensemble, nestled just atop the clothing, was a golden circlet inset with the star of Astraeda. Sevi picked it up, studying it fixedly. It looked just like the one his father had worn.

"Not too extravagant, not too plain. Just right," Innavin said proudly. "The original crowns, I'm afraid, were lost in the Treachery. This was the best we could do."

Sevi shook his head. "Innavin. Lorr. This is—"

"*Awesome!*" Lily blurted.

Sevi turned his gaze to her box. Inside of it, settled just as neatly, lay a charcoal half-coat and a matching shirt, an equally dark pair of pants, a slightly lighter waistcoat, and two black boots. But whereas his outfit was bright and regal, hers had metal plates sewn into her jacket and pants in imitation of a knight's armor.

"Credit where credit is due, this one was Lorr's idea," Innavin said.

Lorr shrugged. "I've seen you running around the castle, stuck inside that old helmet from the Astral Guard, and I thought every prince must have a knight. His champion, right?"

Lily barked a laugh and punched Lorr in the leg. "I like you."

"Ouch." He grimaced. "That's still tender."

"Now that I'm seeing you myself, perhaps we could have your helmet shined? It looks rather... used," Innavin remarked.

Lily snorted. "Not going to happen."

"Hm..." Innavin tutted. "Well. Unfortunately, since we couldn't size you, we had it made a little baggier than it should be. But there will be plenty more balls to come, and I'm sure you'll grow into it. Or maybe we can get it adjusted before the dance?"

"No, leave it, it's *perfect.*" Lily took the half-jacket out and put it on immediately. It sagged on her, as Innavin predicted, but she didn't seem to mind. "And it's so light! This isn't iron at all, is it?"

"Good eye. It's aluminum! Notoriously tricky to get a hold of, but the Ta'Runa had a fresh batch of ships in port last week and we were able to grab a little while picking up His Brilliance's clothing."

"I never, ever thought I'd be excited over clothes." Lily laughed, taking the box and jogging back into the bedroom. "Sevi, shut the door, I'm going to change! Hey, can I wear a sword with this?"

Lorr chuckled and closed the bedroom door. "I like her. You chose your champion well."

"Thank you," Sevi said, running his fingers over the circlet. "Both of you. I don't know what to say."

"Say that you'll wear it to the masquerade," Innavin said, beaming.

"Absolutely!"

"Then that's all the thanks we need."

"We look forward to seeing you at the ball, Your Luminance," Lorr said, patting Sevi on the back before moving toward the parlor's exit. "Unfortunately, we must be going now. I have to look through the party's expenses one more time, and Innavin has his own outfit to assemble."

"Until we meet again, Your Majesty!" Innavin gave a flourishing bow. Sevi returned the bow in accordance with Promina's etiquette lessons, much to Innavin's delight. "My goodness. You're looking more and more like a prince by the day." He winked before turning and leaving with Lorr.

Gathering the box in his arms, Sevi nudged the door to the bedroom open, and found Lily standing there in her outfit, her visor down, and a big grin on her face. "My wonderful, brilliant, bedazzling *lord*," she said, clinking all the different metal parts of her clothing together as she bowed deeply at the waist. "Your champion awaits!"

Sevi smiled at her. "How does it fit?"

She pulled up her trousers. "That blond one was right—maybe I should get it tailored. Or maybe I'll just wear a belt? Yeah, that seems easiest. I'm sure there's one somewhere in this mess."

Sevi set the box down and walked over to the mirror, looking at himself in the glass with the circlet still in his hands. He was struck by how different he looked. His skin had smoothed. His cheeks were fuller. His hair was no longer the rat's nest it used to be and now hung straight on his back and shoulders. But the scars remained, trailing down his eye and poking out from beneath his shirt, impervious to change. Did they make him seem less princely? When it came time to bear his face, would the Kaymoors, Engroms, and all the other houses look at him with disgust?

Lily clapped her hand on his back, joining him at the mirror with a black belt tied tightly around her waist. "Maybe this thing won't be so bad after all! Ready to dance, your princeliness?"

Sevi placed the circlet on his head. "No. But I'm ready to try."

# THE DANCE BETWEEN

The night of the masquerade arrived. Promina had visited Sevi and Lily to brief them one last time before the party, but she could have spoken for an hour, and Sevi still wouldn't have been able to keep his knees from knocking.

He and Lily left the royal chambers dressed in their outfits. Lilting music trilled distantly down the hallway. Cassik, Loma, and his other two guards were waiting for them, all dressed in their formal military attire, with swords on their belts and shiny, painted half-masks hanging around their necks.

Some had adorned themselves with additional ornaments such as iron neck bands in the likeness of Tiersa's, or cuffs around their wrists. Loma had put on two metal earrings that dangled from her earlobes like teardrops. Her eyebrows rose when she laid eyes on Sevi in his outfit. "Is that you, kid?"

Sevi shifted uncomfortably. He and Lily had waved away the people that had tried to dress them, having both felt very uncomfortable in allowing someone else to do it for them. He suddenly wasn't sure if that had been a good idea. "Do I look silly?"

"No sillier than us." Loma lifted her mask and placed it on her eyes. "How about me, how do I look?"

"Remarkably improved," Cassik noted.

"Thank the gods for paint," Loma continued. "I don't think I could wear iron around my face all night without a helmet to catch its weight. The wristbands are heavy enough."

"Where are your masks, Your Luminance?" Cassik asked.

"Tiersa said she'd give them to me at the stairwell," Sevi said.

"I see your friend is all ready to go. I love the jacket, little sister." Loma nodded to Lily. Lily, with her visor down, returned a half-smile but didn't reply. Loma turned back to Sevi. "Are you both ready?"

Sevi looked at Lily, who rolled her shoulders at him. "I guess so."

"Alright then." Loma tied her mask on. The rest of the soldiers did the same, then laid their rifles up against their shoulders and stood at attention. "After you, Your Luminance."

Swallowing, Sevi glanced at Lily. He couldn't see her eyes through the visor, but she smiled at him in her usual way, as if nothing about this could bother her. He took strength from it. Straightening, he smoothed out his waistcoat and jacket, then raised his chin and looked ahead. The hour had come to be Prince Isevidel, whether he was ready or not.

He led the group down the hallway toward the stairwell. The music grew louder, floating through the air with a peaceful tenor meant to calm the spirit. It had the opposite effect on Sevi, causing his heart to beat and his legs to shake. His knuckles turned white as he gripped the banister leading down. There were more guards on the stairwell, all wearing their masks, all staring at him as he passed.

Tiersa and Promina were waiting for them at the bottom. Tiersa wore the guise of a silver snake with large almond eye-shapes and filigreed scales etched into the wood. The top ridge of the mask followed the curve of her forehead, keeping her hair neatly in place, acting in stark contrast to its sable tones. At each cheekbone a small, delicate-looking fang protruded, following the shape of her face. They went well with the swords at her hips, which were joined by the grip of an officer's gun poking out from behind her belt.

Promina's mask was far more intricate, with a shining sun rising from the middle of her forehead inset with gemstones. Leaf motifs sprouted from its edges and ran backward along her scalp, and whereas Tiersa wore her formal military uniform, she wore a white, form-fitting dress that sparkled as much as the gems in her mask. In her hands she carried a lidless box, and another rested at her feet.

The commander smiled when she saw him. "You look wonderful, Isevidel," she said, stepping forward and placing her hands on his arms. "I was right to trust Innavin Targa with this; he did an admirable job."

"Th-thanks. Lorr helped, too," Sevi said.

"I'll give my thanks to them both. And hello, Miss Lily, you're looking rather formidable yourself."

"Ah-thank you, Your Commandership," Lily said with a bow. "I look forward to slaying every evil creature here."

Tiersa chuckled. "Do your best to limit your bouts, noble Sier, lest we have more enemies by the end of the night than we did going in."

"Eh. Alright. I'll just fight the grossest ones."

Tiersa returned her gaze to Sevi. Her face softened the longer she looked at him, until she reached up to tuck a stray lock of hair behind his ear, leaving her hand to cup the side of his face. "Your parents would be so proud of you," she said softly. "Remember. The nobles will push you. Not everyone so readily believes you to be the prince. It's up to you to prove them wrong."

Sevi placed his hand on hers, pursing his lips and trying not to lose his composure. She slowly slid her hand out from his touch and stepped aside, waving with her other hand to Promina. "Please. Come see."

Promina looked seriously him as he stepped up and peered in. "I hope you're ready, Your Brilliance," she said.

On a bed of straw lay two masks; one for the ceremonial introductions, and one for the event afterward. A dark blue hood intended to cover his whole head was attached to the former, extravagantly engraved with the Argent Star, streaks of light, and curling wisps of wind along its forehead. Vines and floral plants framed the mask's chin and jaw, signifying Sorvathos, Avinaea, and Iviri in equal measures between the soil and the sky.

The second mask, childish by comparison, was a half mask with the upper face of a frog, much like the bubble toads of the Cut. It had round cheeks, a small, pointed beak for a nose, and two large round eyes with ridges that extended past the top of the face. Swirling engravings flowed around its rim, doing their best to elevate its countenance.

"I had hoped that you would pick a more dignified creature, but it will certainly draw attention away from your status during the Dark Hour," Tiersa said.

Sevi shook his head, smiling at it. "I love it."

Promina motioned with the box. "Your Luminance, if you would, may I please have your circlet? I'll return it once it's time for the first dance."

When Sevi had swapped his circlet for the ceremonial mask, covering his face and forehead entirely, Promina placed the box on the ground and reached into the other, drawing out a shimmering, flowing blue cloak that matched the hood. She clasped it around his neck, then draped the rest around his shoulders until the entirety of his body was shrouded in it. When she was satisfied with how it lay, she stepped back and bowed.

Sevi peered out at everyone from the confines of his new face, rattling his deep breaths through the nose holes. Promina regarded him with a critical eye, but the corner of her mouth curled up in what could've been approval. Commander Tiersa looked at him with fondness, and his guards all had polite smiles on their faces, though Lily's was considerably broader. He didn't need to guess what she was thinking.

Tiersa stepped forward and lowered her voice. "Do you remember what we discussed about your memory?"

He let out a shaky breath, dipping his head in a jerky nod. "I w-won't say a word."

"Very good. I know you'll do brilliantly, Isevidel." She gave him a gentle, encouraging pat. "I hope you'll pardon the pun, but as your father used say, it's time to shine."

Sevi turned reluctantly to face the stairwell's threshold, thankful for the cloak. Nobody could see his trembling as he strode into the throne room. He had just enough time to hear Commander Tiersa say, "Have you been drinking, Private Tammavin," before he was hit with the full force of a bardic orchestra.

The great hall had undergone a massive transformation. Where once there were bare walls, Ember flags, charts, maps, and arguing Embers, now there were tapestries, food and wine, decorated Ember guards standing at attention, and a band of magnificently dressed people carrying an entire array of different instruments, playing a song joyous enough to lighten the heaviest of hearts.

Filling the room around the circle of musicians, wearing every kind of color and cloth imaginable, was an entire pageant of masked lords and ladies, laughing and fraternizing so freely that the sounds of their collective conversations fought the music for attention. Candlelight from the sconces and chandeliers bounced off the metal in their outfits, playing with shadow in a dance of its own.

Both music and conversation died upon his entrance, gradually at first, then all at once. He had been expecting it, but it still made his heart beat wildly. He kept his back straight, staring ahead at the two thrones as he made his way up their steps, forcing himself to take his time. Promina had said that a prince did not need to hurry himself with anything. Everyone else must hurry for the prince.

When he arrived at the nearest throne, he turned to face his audience as the rest of his entourage stepped in with him. His four personal guards took their positions, with Cassik and Loma flanking the thrones. The other two stepped down the stairs toward the dance floor, joined by another four guards at the base of the steps. Commander Tiersa moved to his right, standing straight with her hands settled against the hilts of her swords, while Promina took position at his left with her hands behind her back.

He glanced left and right. Where was Lily?

Someone squeezed his arm from behind. Lily stepped between him and Tiersa, flashing a quick, reassuring smile. A bit of the tension in his chest loosened, and he faced the crowd once again, ignoring the shortness in his breath as he scanned the sea of faces.

In another life, when he was still Sevi the tunnel mouse, he had watched a terrifying Silvakin captain take this very spot at the head of a massive gathering and imagined what it was like to be him with a castle at his command. Pulling from the memory, Sevi put his hands behind his back and turned his nose up as Captain Redwood had—a gesture that was lost beneath his mask and cloak but helped steady his nerves, nonetheless.

"My lords. My ladies. My Siers and officers. Thank you for joining me," Commander Tiersa called out, stepping forward. Her voice was magnified by the hall's arching walls, lending extra power to her words with every fading echo. "I know that some of you have traveled a far distance to be here, and your dedication to the crown has not gone unnoticed. Today, we celebrate not only the recapture of our capital city and the possible ending of a war with a formidable enemy, but also the return of our royalty and our culture, kept safely hidden for us all these years and brought from the darkness at long last. The rising of a new star, Prince Isevidel Astraeda."

Sevi stepped forward and lifted his chin higher. There was a round of polite applause from the nobles, coupled with a smattering of whispers.

"It is at this time that the Embers of Korina formally recognize the person who rescued him from the clutches of the Fae, and saw fit, in her selflessness, to care for and protect His Brilliance all these years, until he could be reunited with his family and his throne once more. As such, she is to be treated with as much respect as anyone present today. Please allow me to introduce to you Squire Lily, Favored of the Crown."

Tiersa beckoned at Lily, who stepped forward, frowning. No one had mentioned she would be introduced along with Sevi. She covertly reached for Sevi and held onto his cloak, bunching up a small amount in her fingers. He touched her hand through the cloth, silently staring down the audience together as they applauded and whispered once more.

"As the night is short and the ride to town long, His Brilliance will permit those in attendance to make their introductions now as they see fit, until the tolling of the Dark Hour rings out. Please, everyone, enjoy yourselves." She ended with a humble bow before stepping back and placing her hands once more on her sword hilts.

Sevi bowed his head to the assembly, taking his time with it, then turned and stalked toward the throne like he owned it. *Which I do*, he supposed. Turning once more with a swish of his cloak, he slowly sat himself down and rested his head against the backing, placing his arms along each rest with his gloves poking out. *This is my chair. This is my chair,* he thought over and over again. *I'm meant to be here. I can do this.*

The band struck up another melody, and with it, the conversation built until it was eventually at the same level as when they had walked in. Surveying the room, Sevi had to fight to keep his head on his shoulders, feeling the telltale signs of detachment as his mind threatened to run away from what was actually happening.

His mentors had described the masquerade in detail for weeks, and here it was, happening exactly as they'd said. Yet it felt unnatural to sit on a throne he'd only ever viewed from a distance. Lily made to hop onto the other throne, but Promina swiftly intercepted her as though sensing her intentions, turning her from her course and marching her to stand to the right of Sevi. "I told you *no,* young lady," she said sternly.

"Didn't the commander say I was 'favored?' Come to think of it, she still owes me a *favor*, too," Lily countered. "And what was that about, anyway? You didn't tell me she'd be saying that."

"Favored yes, queen no, and favors only go so far," Promina hissed. "What she did was in itself a favor to you, and you'd best be grateful for it." She returned to her position facing the crowd, placing her hands behind her back and smiling as though nothing were the matter.

"Another reason why I hate stuff like this. Too many stiffs." Lily made a rude noise at Promina's back. "So. Now we stand here and look pretty? Oh, I'm sorry, *I* stand here and look pretty?"

Sevi shrugged, only half-present. "More or less."

"Then I'm getting some food. You want anything?"

Before he was aware of his mouth moving, he said, "Wow. You actually do scavenge for food."

She let out a surprised laugh. "Wow. And you can actually crack jokes. Just for that, you get nothing."

Sevi blinked, finally turning from the party to refocus on her. She was smiling at him with her back completely turned to the room, as if it wasn't there. He smiled back, though she couldn't see it. "It's... probably for the best. I'm not supposed to eat anything until after introductions are made."

"That's weird, I thought you were a prince or something. Who told you that?"

"Promina."

"Of course, she did." Lily shook her head. "Just a reminder: you chose this. Just think, we could have been eating roasted tunnel rat right now."

She turned and left him, swaggering down the steps toward one of the numerous banquet tables that lined the walls. Regarding her with interest, some of the nearest nobles tried speaking with her. But all who approached were waved away no matter what, completely outmatched by the food she so ravenously set upon.

It heartened Sevi to watch her. Not even a room full of fairy killers had shaken Lily the Silvakin.

"Your Brilliance," Promina said urgently.

He faced forward just as a trio of nobles approached. He recognized them as Promina's family, composed of an older lady and lord, and a girl near his age. He froze in his chair at the sight of the latter the moment he saw her, as his half-connected head came crashing back to his body.

She wore a flowing red and gold dress, just like her parents. Like Promina, she had lustrous blond hair with braids tied at precise intervals, forming an intricate weaving pattern accented with silver and golden beads. A golden necklace hung around her neck with a red ruby inset in the middle of a full sun. Deep, caramel eyes stared out at him from behind her golden half mask, painted with streaks of white and red that chased after a phoenix as it flew across her eyes, leaving ruby and topaz gems behind as sparks.

The heavy fire motif made Sevi feel vaguely uncomfortable, but it was almost nothing compared to the awe he felt at her beauty. Looking at her imbued him with a sense of dizziness he couldn't describe, heating his face and making him extra thankful for his mask

Commander Tiersa eyed the newcomers silently while Promina approached them, giving a neutral, formal bow reserved for ceremonies. They exchanged a quick word before Promina turned to Sevi. "I present Lady Meldine Kaymoor, her husband Lord Velis Kaymoor, and their daughter, the young Dela Kaymoor."

The Kaymoor family bowed to Sevi as one, bending deeply at the waist or gathering their dresses and curtsying with their heads down. When they had finished, Sevi wrenched his eyes away from Dela and stood from his throne, bowing at the stomach with an awkward jerk as Promina had instructed.

"Your Brilliance." Lady Meldine stepped forward, but kept a respectful distance, never getting so close as to actually pass Promina. Her mask was similar to Promina's, with sun beams radiating out from the ridges along her cheeks. "It pleases us greatly to find you alive and well. We were truly overjoyed to find that the royal line had weathered the Fae incursion, and not just for its survival, but in knowing that a piece of Korina's legacy remained."

Sevi needed to take a breath before speaking, letting it out slowly through his teeth. *I am Prince Isevidel Astraeda. I am Prince Isevidel*

*Astraeda.* "It... p-pleases me to meet the house of Kaymoor... once more, Lady Meldine," Sevi said, sickened by his stutter. Hours spent practicing in front of the mirror seemed to mean nothing in the face of the real thing.

Lady Meldine's face didn't change, but her husband's mouth curled higher at the corners. Sevi gulped and took another breath. "It... is my understanding, after discussing with the c-commander, that the war would not have succeeded as well as it had without the efforts of your house... So. Thank you."

*Gods help me, that sounded terrible.* He thanked the gods he couldn't see Tiersa or Promina's faces just then.

"It was our honor, Your Luminance," Lady Meldine said, dipping in a shallow curtsey. "This is our country. In the face of such adversity, our people expected House Kaymoor to lead, and so we did. We are merely pleased that it was enough."

Sevi nodded his head silently, hoping that the action looked more dignified than he felt.

"Would you please allow me to inquire about your own experience through the war, Your Brilliance? It must have been difficult for one so young."

Tiersa had made it abundantly clear how often he would get this question as the night went on and had spent many lessons coaching him on how to respond. "When the castle was invaded, and my family killed, I was able to escape and make my way to the tunnels that wind through this castle," he recited. "My friend Lily, a serving girl at the time, also escaped. With her help, I made it to the quicksilver mines, taking refuge where the Fae's magic or their thralls could not find us. And there we stayed, waiting all these years until it was safe to leave again."

"Incredible." Lady Meldine smiled. "To think those tunnels would not only aid in the rescue of our capital, but also yourself. You are surely blessed with the very protection of Iviri herself, Your Brilliance. How could it be anything else?"

Sevi lifted his chin. Her posture gave nothing away, but there was an odd tone to her voice, as if she found his story amusing. His anger flared greater than his fear for the briefest of breaths. "I owe no small part of my survival to Lily... my lady," he said earnestly, remembering his manners at the last moment. "Perhaps Iviri had one hand in my rescue, but Lily had two."

"Of course, Your Brilliance. May we all be thankful for her intervention. My thanks for indulging me." Lady Meldine bowed her head. "And if I may say so, you must surely be glad to be free from those tunnels. Living like that for four years is a powerful feat, Your Brilliance, especially for a child. After such bravery, I imagine that ruling the queendom must seem trivial in comparison. You must be so eager to return, ready to take the mantle."

There was that tone again—as if she couldn't believe some part of his story. Sevi crossed his arms under his cloak and shrugged his shoulders. "The food is certainly better."

Lady Meldine tilted her head and laughed. Her husband and daughter joined in as though he'd made the funniest joke under the sky. "Quite right, Your Luminance. I imagine that we'll all be eating much better now that the war has reached its end."

"Speaking of, if I may," Lord Velis said, stepping up behind his wife with their daughter in tow. His mask swirled in the likeness of a roaring blaze. "May I pose an inquiry of my own to His Brilliance regarding his post-war reconstruction plans? There is much to repair, and it will take great effort to rebuild what we had. Would I be overstepping if I volunteered the hands of House Kaymoor for such a task, Your Brilliance?"

Both Tiersa and Promina had readied him for this request. Another recurring point of the night would be the number of nobles looking for his favor, seeking opportunity in the rebuilding of their land. "We... Our concerns still lie in driving the Fae from our borders and preventing their return. However, you are correct. Reconstruction should be in all our thoughts. Naturally we would not presume to ignore House Kaymoor's voice."

Lord Velis bowed. "It would be an honor to lend our assistance once more, Your Luminance."

"I would also look forward to seeing my family's wealth returned," Sevi added. Tiersa had stressed how important that was. "I understand that House Kaymoor has kept a careful watch over it. Yes?"

"Certainly, Your Luminance," Lord Velis said, a little more stiffly.

"Good. Very good." Sevi took a deep, anxious breath. *That sounded good.*

"If I may be so bold, Your Luminance," Lady Meldine said, stepping in, "I believe I speak for everyone in attendance when I say that the late king and queen would be very proud of you. House Kaymoor was very close to the monarchy once—you may not remember, but I was a personal friend to Her Radiance when she wore the crown. It is my hope, and the hope of my house, that we may serve the house of Astraeda just as diligently once more."

Sevi grit his teeth. This was the trickiest part. Tiersa had warned him that if any of the nobles caught wind of his missing memory that they would not hesitate to use it to their advantage. It wasn't like he could will the rest of his memories back as he pleased, and Shy continued to be elusive, having remained inside his shadow.

His teachers had done their best, but there was only so much he could learn in under a month. He needed to find a way to move the conversation away from points of familiarity. *You may not remember.* He turned those words around in his head. If Promina already knew about his missing memory, then didn't that mean that her family knew, too?

"It... has been a long time," Sevi said, deciding to err on the side of caution. He took another few breaths to puzzle out his strategy. "While I have... been so focused on preserving my line, I have forgotten the lines of my houses. If I may return your same question, how is it that House Kaymoor survived?"

"Much the way your servants in the Embers have, Your Brilliance. By always moving, and with a touch of cleverness, if I may say so."

"Did the Fae not attack your house as they did mine?"

"They did, Your Majesty, and House Kaymoor suffered for it. Our ancestral estate was besieged by its own citizens in a manner similar to this castle. But House Kaymoor is a house of business, and you can find us at any point within one hundred leagues of each other, if not into our neighboring countries outright, chasing down one opportunity or another. To end our house is, I'm happy to say, almost a logistical impossibility."

Sevi nodded as if he understood that entirely. "Interesting... It pleases me to see such success for your family."

"Thank you, Your Brilliance." She dipped her head.

Unable to summon any further points of conversation, Sevi took a step back and inclined his chin as he'd been told to do whenever he felt it was appropriate. "I hope that you will enjoy the festivities."

"Your Majesty." Lady Meldine gave one final curtsey and turned to move away, but paused. "If I may, I have one last rather selfish request. You would honor my house if you graced my daughter Dela with a dance after the Dark Hour passes."

Sevi almost choked. He recovered his composure at the last moment. Dela watched him with her hands placed demurely in front of her. "I... I will consider this," he managed, hoping that none of them would notice the tremor in his voice. Lady Meldine nodded before walking down the steps holding her husband's arm. Was it his imagination, or did Dela glance back at him?

Promina moved in when they were out of earshot. "You're still stuttering, Your Brilliance. You must get yourself under control."

"I'm trying," he said through gritted teeth. "What was it that you told them?"

"Told them?"

"They're your family." He looked at her. "What did you tell them? What do they know about me?"

Promina looked vaguely affronted. "Nothing. I am Lady Tiersa's Promina. I cut ties with my family's politics when I took this position."

Sevi clutched at his necklace, turning to watch the retreating Kaymoors. "They didn't seem to take me seriously."

"We warned you of that, Your Brilliance."

"I know. I know." Sevi huffed, letting go of the pendant. "Is this what you have to deal with? All the time?"

"Isevidel, I'm sorry to say that was nothing," Tiersa said. "Steady your nerves. You can only do better with practice."

"And some here have had more practice than most," Promina added wryly.

Sevi regarded her. She had taken on an oddly distant look, staring off into the party. She straightened. "Your Brilliance."

He followed her gaze. Another group of three wearing green, brown, and white had detached itself from the mass to approach the throne. Their leader wore a dark bear half-mask that stood out against his long white beard, and had a helmet and an iron chest piece in the masquerade's traditional style. The lady and man to his left and right also bore bear masks, but the man wore the leathers of an Empyrean, stained brown—the mysterious captain of the fairy killers.

This time Promina stepped back, and Commander Tiersa moved forward. The man with white hair sharpened his posture, standing at attention before Commander Tiersa like one of her soldiers. She did the same, but she lifted her hand to her far shoulder and bowed, much as any Ember would for her. Sevi stared in shock.

"Still alive then, little viper?" the bearded man said flatly.

"More than you, you old bear," Commander Tiersa replied, straightening.

They stared at each other for several heartbeats, then the old man broke into a wide, craggly smile and dipped his chest, returning the bow to her. He moved forward, tossing out all propriety, and hugged Commander Tiersa in... well, a bear hug. And to Sevi's surprise, she hugged him back, lifting the smaller man up to his toes much to his obvious delight.

"Good, good, you still have your strength." He chuckled. When she let go, he looked at her and sighed, reaching out to hold her by the arm. "Tiersa... you did it."

"We did it," Tiersa corrected.

The man grunted, beaming a proud smile. Then his gaze flicked over to Sevi, and his smile dropped. There was a calculating look in his eyes, one that he wore openly and without constraint. One that demanded to be impressed. "Is this the boy?"

Commander Tiersa grimaced. "The *prince*. Be polite, Yorga. I'm not above throwing you out."

The man grunted again, not looking away from Sevi. It was as though that gaze could see right through his mask, able to discern everything that Sevi was, had been, and could be. A boy, too immature to lead. A weakling he could snap in half with his massive hands. A fraud, who didn't belong.

Under such a look, Sevi felt himself shrivel as some part of him tried to disconnect once more, but he tightened his fists. He was meant to be here, just as Captain River believed. He wouldn't run from this. Maybe it was his fate, or maybe it was from the choices he'd made, but he was here, he was Prince Isevidel, and he would not allow any further embarrassment from people he didn't even know.

"Your Luminance," Tiersa said, formally addressing Sevi. "May I introduce the head warrior of the Engrom clan, and my old mentor, Lord Yorga. With him is his wife, house leader Lady Kellyn, and their son Captain Vykka, leader of my Empyreans."

Both Lady Kellyn and Captain Vykka bowed formally to Sevi, but Lord Yorga merely gave a shallow nod—a great insult to one of Sevi's station. Sevi's body stiffened, instinctively feeling the need to run away from who he could tell was a dangerous man. But he turned the flinch into a roll of his shoulders, squaring off against the lord as though he felt no fear.

No, he couldn't just be unafraid, he had to be *angry* at the lord for *daring* to sleight his prince. He could do that. He had watched the upper Fablings lord themselves over their subordinates plenty of times.

Sevi took a step forward, craning his head up to the taller, broader man, and stared daggers at him, doing his best to radiate displeasure through his mask. He wanted the man to know that he could have him removed the second he raised his hand. He wanted him to know that he belonged here, on his throne, while the lord was meant to serve. He wanted him to know that he. Would. Not. Be. Bullied.

Instead of cowing, Lord Yorga only smiled. "Heh. He'll do."

"Yorga—" Tiersa started.

"Bow," Sevi hissed.

Lord Yorga's eyebrows lifted behind his mask.

"H-has the mask muffled me?" Sevi continued. "I said *bow*."

Still, Lord Engrom did nothing. *He's testing my resolve,* Sevi thought with shock. This was about respect, and he, prince or not, had to earn it. He found himself in the strangest silence he'd ever experienced, surrounded by noise save for the pocket of quiet between the lord and him. As if nothing else mattered in the world but their standoff.

"H-has all respect for tradition disappeared in my family's absence?" Sevi finally said. "Shocking, considering the armor you wear." He stepped forward again, raising his voice, filling it with the strength he'd seen in Innavin when he'd faced down the thugs. Standing with the pride Digby had shown when facing down a room of angry Silvakin. "Have my houses forgotten basic etiquette to those they serve? The vows they took? Is it now *normal* for my lords to stand before me and stare at their prince like a hound stares at a rabbit?"

Sevi got right up to the lord the same way Doctor Lea did to Reynam, as though a difference in height didn't matter compared to what he could do. "Bow," he said, low enough for only Lord Engrom to hear. "I won't tell you again."

There was a pregnant pause. He and the lord regarded each other for many breaths, staring into each other's eyes as each waited for the other to stand down.

And to Sevi's surprise, Lord Yorga did.

His face crinkled into a smile, and he threw his head back and laughed, bellowing out a cackle that made Sevi draw back in surprise. "Yes! Good! He'll do just fine! Our prince has returned with a little mettle!" Lord Yorga reached under his mask to wipe his eyes. He took a step back from Sevi and bowed low, at the waist, as a lord properly should to their prince. "Apologies, Your Luminance."

Sevi took a deep, relieved breath before returning the bow at the chest. "I accept."

Lord Yorga straightened, still smiling, and took another step backward as Lady Kellyn stepped forward. "Please excuse my husband, Your Majesty," she said, curtseying deeply. "He is old, and the war has been hard on our house."

"Old? Preposterous," Lord Yorga muttered to Vykka.

"Th-think of it no more," Sevi said, glancing at Tiersa. She raised the corner of her mouth in a small smirk, and motioned with her hand in a downward gesture, as if to say, *ease up a little.* He searched for a topic to speak about. There was no point in asking how they'd weathered the invasion. Given their guns and, frankly, Lord Yorga's attitude, he had a pretty good idea. He examined their clothes instead, falling back on Promina's advice. "I r-really must commend you on the metal you wear, Lady Kellyn. I don't believe I've seen anything so finely engraved before."

And it was true. The bracers on the lady's arms and the lord's helmet had been detailed with such precision that it was hard to believe it was done by human hands. Lady Kellyn smiled. "You have a good eye, Your Majesty. Our metal was engraved by the finest Tiburan jewelers, and then blessed by an Áilén Runic. It's said that the marks will protect us from danger, though thankfully we have not needed to test it."

"Hm. Runes. Unreliable, feckless scribbles. Who's to say she merely claimed to be a Runic? Give me a good sword or rifle any day," Lord Yorga grumbled.

"Runes." Staring at Lady Kellen's garb, then Vykka's leathers, Sevi made a strange connection. "Captain Vykka, I have a question for you."

One of Captain Vykka's eyebrows rose, but the rest of his face remained neutral. "Your Prominence?"

"I confess, I have never asked anyone how you control your birds. My friend Lily believes you control them with light and sound. But now I believe you control them with runes. Is that so?"

A ghost of a smile passed across the captain's face. "In a sense you're both right, but I would give the edge to you, Your Majesty. We place a hood with glass eyes around our birds, bearing runes of sight engraved in the leather. Then we hang a small bracelet around their leg containing a rune of sound. We track their movements through the rune of sight's sister mark, and when we see the bird's target, we cause a whistle to emit from the rune of sound, directing the bird to its prey."

Sevi let out a breath. "Incredible... I imagine those runes aren't easy to replace."

"You would be correct, Your Majesty. Which is why I ensure that those I command are the best fairy killers ever trained. You won't see so much as a wing with my hunters around."

*Oh, if only you knew,* Sevi thought. Thankfully Alyda had kept her daytime excursions to an absolute minimum. "Very... very impressive, Captain. Commander Tiersa is lucky to have you and the iron of House Engrom in her ranks."

"Much obliged, Your Prominence." Vykka bowed.

"Yes... it is my understanding that House Engrom is to thank for much of the Embers' armaments. And watching your convoy approach the castle, I can easily believe your house to be full of fierce fighters. I won't forget your efforts."

"The gratitude is all ours, Your Majesty," Lady Kellyn said.

Sevi stepped back and bowed his head. "I hope that you enjoy the festivities. You have earned a respite."

Lady Kellyn curtseyed. Lord Yorga bowed, adding a small flourish for good measure before grinning and walking away with his wife. Captain Vykka lingered, throwing a knowing smile at Commander Tiersa, then a sly look at Sevi, before also bowing and leaving. Commander Tiersa stepped beside Sevi after they'd gone. "'Like a hound stares at a rabbit?'"

Sevi shifted sheepishly. "Was that too much?"

"Mm. Maybe a little."

"Your Brilliance," Promina interrupted. "The next guests would like to introduce themselves. Members of the Regent Council."

"Blazes," Sevi muttered, still shaky from his stand-off with Lord Engrom. Taking a deep breath, he straightened his back. "Fine. Let's greet them."

# Chapter 49

*Did you laugh when you watched? Was my face so surprised? At all, did my mien make you pause? Were you blinded by the glitter of hundreds of shimmers, or did you see me as I was?*

---

Every house and knight stepped up to introduce themselves to Sevi, one after another, normally requesting some favor while hinting at how fond they were of his parents. The parents he could barely remember. It was equal parts flustering, amusing, and exhausting. By the time the last Sier something-or-other had mingled back into the crowd he couldn't feel his feet, so he sat on his throne while greeting the lower houses. Promina urged him not to, but not vehemently, which hinted that he could probably get away with it.

At some point during the introductions, Lily snuck back up with a plate full of food, which she ate noisily beside him with gusto, letting out an unladylike belch when she finished. It was loud enough to make Promina fix her with a distasteful stare, which Lily pointedly ignored. "So. Enjoying your night, your princeliness?" she asked him.

"No." Sevi groaned. "I'm so hungry that my stomach is eating itself."

"Mm. Just remember—"

"I asked for this," Sevi finished with her. "I know. Next time, I'll eat beforehand."

"Better grow stronger legs, too. Don't want Miss Fancy-Hair over there yelling at you for sitting down again."

"You saw that?"

"It's a little hard to miss when you're several steps higher than everybody else in the room."

He sighed, reminded once more of how heavily scrutinized he was. And it would only get worse once he left the sanctuary of his disguise. "Well... What do you think so far?"

Lily surveyed the room from behind her visor. "I think you should be tired of me being right by now."

"Oh, I am. But do you suppose we're in any danger?"

"Of course. You don't get to sit in that big chair with the comfort of anonymity, Sevi. These people are making moves, both for and against you, even if you can't see it. And if you *can* see it, they're either very clever or very dumb."

"Or maybe I'm just perceptive."

Lily tapped the side of her helmet, right over her ear. "Are you sure about that?"

Sevi drummed his fingers on the arm of the throne. "What have you heard out there?"

"Not much. The commander brought a lot of attention to me with her big announcement. Whenever I got close to any whisperers, they'd shut up like I'd grabbed them by the lips. But many of them can't decide if you're actually the prince or some street rat that Tiersa has been grooming. They're waiting to see how similar you look to your parents. They're all scheming though, make no mistake."

"And my memory isn't helping my claim," Sevi said, echoing Tiersa's concerns.

"Not one bit."

Sevi watched a group of nobles twirl by in time to the music, a myriad of colors flashing in a blur, and wondered why it mattered to cover one's face when they all had masks growing under their skin. "I'm glad you're here, Lil."

She sighed. "I wish I could say the same, Sev. But I'm with you. Partners, and all that junk."

He nodded, stifling a fresh pang of guilt. It was the best response he'd get from her. "I wish Alyda could see this. Do you think she can hear the music from the garden?"

"It's certainly loud enough."

A bell chimed, echoing throughout the great hall. It rang until the conversation and music died down. Commander Tiersa stepped forward as the last note faded away. "The Dark Hour is upon us. It is here that we honor the brave Iviri Astraeda, who fought valiantly in the name of the gods and our ancestors all those generations ago. Who led us through the night where the false light of the Watcher and her siblings menaced the sky, seeking our destruction. It is at this time that His Brilliance will join the celebration as one of you, symbolizing Iviri's humble beginnings, before performing the first dance, in honor of her sacrifice.

"As a reminder it is politely requested, should you discover His Brilliance's identity, that you keep the knowledge to yourself. And please keep aware, my lords and ladies... you are not allowed to touch the prince during this time."

Her voice lowered toward the end, and her grip shifted on her swords. Sevi was grateful for the threat. He'd gotten used to being surrounded by Ember soldiers, but he didn't think he could enter a crowd like this without knowing someone was watching over him.

Tiersa raised her hand, and soldiers went to work dimming the lights along the walls, allowing only the chandeliers above to shine down upon the guests. The light level dropped considerably within moments. Satisfied, Tiersa turned to Sevi and nodded.

Sighing, he lifted himself off the throne and turned toward the stairwell, drowsily descending the steps with his guard. Commander Tiersa caught him before he reached the threshold and gingerly steered him in the direction of the kitchens instead.

Lily followed them to the dining room, where they left the guards outside. Sevi all too happily shed his cloak and mask, sitting down to tear into a waiting plate of chicken and vegetables, forgetting not to make a mess of his clothing in his haste. He reined himself in, but not without difficulty.

"This still seems silly to me," Lily said, crossing her arms. "Sevi shouldn't be walking around alone and unprotected."

"Every guest was tested for faeblood upon arrival and searched for weapons," Tiersa said. "I have men and women stationed around the room with rifles at the ready, as well as people I trust within the party itself. Not to mention an entire castle full of soldiers at my command and a sky full of Empyrean scar owls. An attempt to harm Isevidel is extremely unlikely."

"But not impossible," Lily rebutted. "A human can hurt him just as easily as a Fae. How thoroughly did you search the nobles? I doubt any of those creeps were happy about a pat-down."

"No, they weren't, but this is my castle, my army, and Isevidel is my charge. My orders are law here, and my soldiers were told to turn anyone away who disregarded them, without exception. Every guest out there was willing to suffer a little indignity for the chance to see the prince. The potential rewards were too great."

"Well. Glad to know you have it all figured out."

Commander Tiersa let out a long, tired sigh. "Miss Lily, I share your concerns. Do you think I'm any happier than you to let Isevidel out from under my direct supervision, especially after what happened in the market? We've taken every measure we possibly can to ensure his safety. Now we must project our confidence in those measures."

Lily grumbled. "Don't you have another outfit for me? I could stay with him."

"Putting aside how noticeable your heights and ages are, especially together, do you mean to say that you'll take off your helmet?"

"Gods of stone and root, this tradition is so *dumb*." Lily scowled.

Sevi took his time finishing his meal, drawing out his break for as long as possible. But his excuses vanished with the last scrap on his plate. He cast a look of longing around the room as he stood. *I could run off into the Cut until the night is over.* "I'm ready," he said instead. "Please have Promina bring me my mask."

He and Commander Tiersa fussed over his clothing until Promina arrived, while Lily blessedly kept her remarks to herself. "I've informed the guests that we have a special surprise waiting for them in the gardens," Promina said. "It'll be enough to keep them occupied while His Luminance joins them."

"What's the surprise?" Sevi asked, placing the frog mask over his face.

"It's as much a surprise for His Majesty as it is for his houses." She left them on that cryptic note with a smile.

"I will go ensure there aren't any lurkers around the hallway," Commander Tiersa said. "Do you have your alias ready?"

"Selkev of House Gorgumm."

"And to House Gorgumm?"

"Selkev of House Borgium."

"Good. People will assume they misheard you." She nodded in approval, looking him over. "How are you faring?"

Sevi took a deep breath. "I'm alright... I think."

"You've done well so far, Isevidel. I'm very impressed. Pray continue." She smiled before exiting out the door after Promina.

Lily lifted her visor, fixing her eyes on his. "Now that it's just the two of us, how are you actually feeling?"

He rolled his shoulders. "Not great, honestly. I feel like a cloud trying to fight the wind just to keep its spot in the sky."

"A pretty metaphor. Except you don't have to go back out if you don't want to."

Sevi shook his head. "Unfortunately, I think I do. I chose this, remember?"

A twinkle came to Lily's eye, and the corner of her mouth lifted in a gentle smirk. "My my. Look at you now." She stepped up in front of him and clapped him on the shoulder, looking at him with all seriousness. "You know something? I have to agree with your new ma. You haven't done half-bad tonight."

"Thank you, Lily," Sevi said, "but it doesn't feel that way."

"Look and feel are two different things, silly boy. Anyway. Can't keep the frog from the flies. I'll head out ahead of you. And don't worry, I'll be watching." She lifted a hand and dropped her visor, cracking one last grin before leaving him by himself.

He watched her go. When the door closed, he counted one hundred breaths, taking what strength he could from Lily and Tiersa's words before opening the door. Loma and Cassik stood flanking it while the other guards had spread out down the hallway. They both looked at Sevi as he emerged with amusement, though Cassik had the decency to try to hide it.

"You're... Looking g-great, Your Majesty," Cassik said through heavy chortles.

"Have a nice meal of slugs, kid?" Loma snorted.

Sevi blushed. "You know I can have you both executed, right?"

Cassik sobered immediately. "I apologize, Your Luminance."

Sevi turned to him. "Cassik?"

"Yes, Your Luminance?"

"That was a joke."

Loma laughed louder. Cassik breathed a sigh of relief, shifting awkwardly. "Are you rejoining the party, Your Brilliance?"

"Yes, But I need to go alone. Having guards would give me away."

"I... understand," Cassik said, though he clearly didn't like it.

"Hop along, kid. We'll see you after the dance." Loma smirked.

He gave them a curt nod before leaving down the hallway with stiff limbs. This was it. No one to guide him or watch over him, and just over a couple hundred strangers looking for him at once. He wished the hallway would never end.

But it did. And when he reached the end, he was surprised to find that Commander Tiersa had made good on her promise. Not a single guest remained near the corridor's entrance, nor the entire throne room, save for the Ember guards along its walls. Even the band had left.

His curiosity won out against his anxiety, and he found himself hurrying toward the gates, only slowing down when he heard the voices of the crowd outside. Everyone had their heads craned up to the sky, pointing and speaking to one another in excited tones. When he walked out from beneath the overhang and joined them fully in the cold night air, he saw why.

A dark shape moved through the night sky, separate from the clouds, blocking out the stars as it swept past on a lazy, lingering path. A pointed nose turned into a thick, sleek hull, strung up by a balloon lighter than air, until its full shape was silhouetted starkly against the silver light of the nearly full moon. Its lightwings unfurled from its sides, catching moonbeams and flaring brightly with a pulsing silver-blue, making everyone in the crowd gasp.

The airship, so diligently restored to its former glory, hung in the sky like a star of its own. The fires at its back brightened to life in a gentle burn, keeping the ship in place against the mountain's headwinds. Ever so slowly, the ship turned to point its prow at the castle, and with another flare of its fires, pushed closer to the grounds.

Sevi beamed. It may have been missing its Faen balloon, but the airship flew once more!

Promina's voice called out from the front of the crowd. "My lords, my ladies, my Siers, Regents, and soldiers, tonight, we are happy to present to you this marvel of creation. Captured from the Fae upon retaking our capital, and repaired with great effort over many months, we present to you now, the *Aethercrest*, Elkra's very first airship!"

An enthusiastic round of applause manifested, lingering for many breaths. After it died down, Promina continued. "Flown by the man who captured it, our very own Captain Caldwin River Ta'Runa, and his first lieutenant, Digby Asgaillin. They will be assisted on the ground by Corporal Reynam Enstrova—a name some of you may be familiar with, as the son of the late Lord Matigo Enstrova—but also known as the finest shot in the Embers of Korina!"

Another round of applause, and the crowd moved forward with an eager step. Sevi raced over to the side where he could see, hopping over the walkway's fence to peer out from under the overhead. Across the lawn, surrounded by freshly placed autumn plants, was Reynam, just coming up from a bow. With a practiced motion, he brought his rifle up to attention and swung around to face the other direction.

"Corporal! Are you ready?" Promina shouted.

Reynam set his rifle to his shoulder and pointed it at the airship.

"On our signal!"

A hush fell over the crowd. A soldier stepped out from among them with a lit torch and waved it around energetically, paused, then repeated the pattern again.

The lightwings on the airship pulsed, and the fires on its stern grew brighter. Slowly, the ship picked up speed. Two doors on its underbelly fell open, illuminated by the light from the courtyard below.

"Fire when ready!" Promina commanded.

A small object fell from the hatch attached to a blanket, whipping about in the air. When it had reached a decent distance away the sheet flung open, billowing out as the wind filled it like a sail, arresting its fall to the plateau.

The ship pulled away from its floating package. An expectant silence fell as the crowd anxiously waited for something to happen. Reynam lined up his shot and fired.

The object erupted with a burst of green sparks that spiraled out, climbing up into the sky and erupting into even tinier sparks with every curling branch. The flames ate away at the sheet until it was a brilliant conflagration in the night, burning green for a heartbeat before disappearing entirely, leaving nothing but a wisp of smoke behind.

The crowd *oooed* and applauded, but Reynam and the airship weren't done yet. Three more chutes fell from the ship, and three more shots rang out from Reynam's rifle, turning each one into a blaze of blue, white, and green. Then five fell out all at once. Reynam tracked each of them with expert skill, shooting all in rapid succession until the sky was painted with their sparkling colors.

The airship's fires brightened, and it picked up speed, circling around the gardens. More and more chutes fell from its underbelly at an increasing pace. Reynam quickly reloaded his nine shots, snapped his rifle up to his shoulder, and fired as rapidly as he could, bursting each balloon as fast as the airship could launch them until the night sky was alight with color in every direction.

Then the airship stopped, right where it had started, hanging in place for a dozen long beats. A chute fell out, then another, then another. When one unfurled, the others wobbled, as if tied together by a string. At least a dozen dropped, all moving with the same wind, all wobbling when one of their group shifted a little too suddenly. The airship moved off, rising into the sky.

Reynam shot the lowest one. It went up in a brilliant blue blaze. Then the next caught and erupted, burning a vibrant pink, then green, then white, all the way up the string in a spiral of beautifully streaking sparks. The entire group exploded with a loud *bang,* streaking a rainbow of color that framed the airship brilliantly against the moon, showering the grounds in a rain of delicate, glowing cinders.

When the last of the colors faded the entire assembly erupted with applause, shouting their approval to Corporal Reynam, who shouldered his rifle, turned to face them, and gave a bow so ostentatious that the Targas would have been put to shame. Sevi clapped and cheered along with everyone else, laughing in utter delight at such beauty.

With the show at an end, Sevi inserted himself into the crowd, turning back to watch over his shoulder as the airship swung around toward the far tower's dock, venting its cloud in a controlled descent. *Soon,* he thought. *Even if I must sneak my way on.*

The people around him chatted excitedly. No one even looked at him. He peered around in disbelief, expecting anyone at any time to pick him out in the crowd, but no one did. He shifted with the movement of the guests, flowing back into the warmth of the throne room to stand awkwardly near one of the columns at its perimeter.

Some gave him a passing glance on their way to refill their goblets, others a more studious one. A circle of nobles to the side spoke low among themselves, periodically looking over at him, until a man from their ranks detached himself and approached with a cup in his hands, smiling from beneath the bronze mask of a stone golem. He had crossed half the distance between them when a voice piped up from behind Sevi. "Wonderful coat, my lord. Where did you get it?"

Sevi turned and looked up to find Lorr, holding two goblets in his hands and smiling from beneath a silver mask. His chest swelled with joy to see another familiar face, but he dropped his rising smile and forced a blank look. "Thank you, sir... I know a very good tailor."

"Please pass along my regards," Lorr said with a smirk. "Here's your drink, my lord. Only the light stuff, I promise."

Biting down another smile, Sevi took it and raised it up in a toast. They clinked glasses and each took a swig. Lorr asked him, "Everything alright so far?"

"I'm... managing," Sevi replied.

"Mm. Sometimes that's enough. I'm off in search of my husband, but if you do need something just look for me. The others are all mingling about as well, I'm sure. Vin and Rya wouldn't miss the opportunity to gather new patrons for the Golden Spool. And I think Digby brought his fiddle."

"Thank you, Lo... Captain. I will."

"Think nothing of it. Enjoy the feast, my lord." Raising his glass in parting, the captain disappeared into the crowd.

Sevi took a deep breath and drank the rest of the goblet. *I can do this.* He tried to follow Lorr's lead, fearlessly diving into the gathering like he belonged, walking among the different noble circles and listening in on their conversations. Some disregarded him or laughed when they saw his mask. Some changed the topic when they caught him hovering nearby.

Others noticeably attempted to discern his identity, and he did his best to dissuade them, but the more perceptive ones would change their demeanor entirely if he fumbled for too long, oftentimes launching into a diatribe about their loyalty to the crown. The one blessing was that those people didn't follow him when he extracted himself, realizing that if they gave too much attention to Sevi then his identity would be revealed, and the game would end early.

As Lorr had said, there were familiar faces in the crowd. Captain River and Digby had returned from the airship and were the talk of the night, along with Reynam, who seemed to excel in the attention. It heartened Sevi to see them, and he would frequently look over just to reassure himself that they were still there. Even Reynam, oddly enough, now that he'd gotten some measure of where he stood with the man.

As the hour passed, and the questions of his background blurred together without much variation, he got better at answering them. More composed. More ready with his responses. Eventually the only ones who could pick him out in the crowd were the ones he'd erred with at the start.

Then Dela found him.

"My lord?"

Sevi turned from the group of younger lords and ladies he had been attempting conversation with. Most of them spoke of their latest horse, or their plans to vacation in southern Ivindris during the winter, or who was interested in who. It was incredibly uninteresting. There was an airship outside, and magic runes that allowed people to see from the eyes of a hawk. How could no one talk of that? It was almost a blessing when she pulled him away. Almost.

He froze at the sight of her, forcing himself not to stare. She smiled politely at him and gave a shallow, neutral curtsey. "Forgive me for distracting you, but where did you get such a distinguished mask?"

It took Sevi awhile to remember how to talk. He gulped and hurriedly bowed in courtesy, perhaps a little too low. "I... I'm afraid I couldn't tell you, my lady. My servants purchased it for me."

"Mm. It's quite adorable."

"Thank you, my lady. Though most seem to be laughing at it tonight."

"Perish the thought. You have a lovely face," she said, tilting her head and running her gaze over him.

"The... the mask?"

"Of course."

Sevi gulped again. "Right. Thank you, Lady Kaymoor."

She raised her eyebrows. "My. You knew me on the first try. Am I so obvious?"

"The red and gold are rather prominent," Sevi said, thinking quickly.

She laughed lightly. "And yet... Who are you, my lord?" She tilted her head to the other side and stepped forward, pacing around him in a slow, appraising circle. "I daresay I haven't seen you before. Are you from one of the outer houses? If I didn't know any better, I'd say that you bear colors similar to House Astraeda."

Sevi closed his mouth and silently cursed Innavin and Lorr. Had neither of them thought of something so simple? He cursed himself, too, while he was at it. "Are... Are the colors of House Astraeda not the colors of our country?"

"Mm. Very true, I suppose," she said, coming back around him. "Then what house do you hale from? Clearly one of the water-faring ones. Perhaps Umara? Or maybe Gorgumm?"

"Borgium," Sevi said. The hairs on the back of his neck prickled, feeling the familiar instinct to bolt. Something wasn't right.

"Borgium," she repeated, staring at him. "I don't recall seeing House Borgium approach His Brilliance tonight."

Blazes. *Blazes.* Had they not? He couldn't remember. He stared hard at her, studying her face and posture for any trace of a lie, but found nothing but coyness.

*She knows.* Why did that fluster him so much? "Our interests don't lie with His Brilliance tonight," he said, gambling that she told the truth.

"And what interests would those be?"

He gritted his teeth, willing his body back under control. He couldn't allow her to continue steering the conversation. "W-while we're on the topic of interest, why all the interest in the son of a lord from an undistinguished township, Lady Kaymoor? It isn't as though my house has anything to offer yours."

"I wouldn't say that. Sometimes interesting things come from the most unexpected places." Her painted lips curled even higher.

*She's* enjoying *this*, Sevi realized. But he had had enough. Pushing his awkwardness aside, he straightened and looked her in the eye. "I'm n-not sure what's more unexpected. The time you've spent drawing this out or the time I've spent listening to it. Goodnight, Lady Dela." Sevi nodded, turning away.

"Your Luminance," she called.

Sevi whipped back around at the sound of his title, staring at her in disbelief. She met his shock with open amusement. He glanced to the side to find others looking their way, whispering. He stiffened, ready to hurry around a column where he could lose himself in the crowd, when Dela strode right past him. "Your Luminance! Is that you?"

The boy she'd picked out bore a mask with a flock of birds crossing from cheek to cheek. He blinked in surprise. "No, Dela. It's me, Reg."

"Oh, Regimeer! So sorry, you have such a similar cut to you as the prince! Forgive me, so silly of me." She dipped in a quick curtsey before stepping away, waiting for enough eyes to leave her before stepping back up to Sevi.

Sevi stood where he was, dumbfounded. "What is it you want, Lady Dela?"

"That should be rather obvious, shouldn't it? I would like to dance with Prince Isevidel."

"You have a funny way of asking."

"But effective, I'd say. I'm certain to find him if I have to speak with every lordling here. Tell me, have you found the prince yet? And would you happen to know if anyone here has caught his eye? Anyone at all? Marquel of House Derringen strikes a very soldierly figure if His Majesty prefers a lad. Or perhaps Iria of Arvenhill? She's a dear friend and quite lovely."

"I already have a partner," Sevi blurted, trying to shift her from this line of discussion.

"Why of course *you* do, lordling of House Borgium. But we're discussing the *prince*. If you see him, would you mind passing along my interest? I've always wanted to dance with a prince at an Iron Masquerade, ever since I was a little girl."

She stepped closer to him. "All the stories say that those who dance together here tonight will be bound forever, even in death. It's incredibly romantic, if you ask me. I'd even settle for dancing second, if it came to that."

Again, Sevi stared, astounded by her brazenness. He floundered for some kind of response but was spared by the ringing of a bell. Heads turned to face the thrones, where Promina called out from the top of the steps. "The Dark Hour ends, and the light of Astraeda rises. Come forth, noble light, and lead us from the dark."

Breathing a deep sigh of relief, Sevi shook his head and tried not to smile. "Please excuse me," he said, turning away from her. He took several steps toward the thrones but turned at the sound of footsteps following close behind.

Dela met his gaze and shrugged. "I'm curious to see His Brilliance and his partner. Whoever they might be."

# Chapter 50

*As the hour grew dark, you drove it away, as you'd done for me so many times. Did I ever say? Did I fear the words? Shall it add to the list of my crimes?*

Sevi waited at the edge of the line of nobles, listening to Promina sermonize while clutching gently at his chest. Dela watched him with amusement on his left, which only flustered him further. He tried to ignore her, focusing only on the speech.

"And upon vanquishing the Watcher's sisters, Iviri returned to Iaela, clad in a silver burial shroud with a wreath of fire around her head—"

"Ooh a wreath of *fire.*"

He turned to the right. Lily smirked at him from under her helm. "How was mingling with your subjects, your shininess?"

Sevi nodded to her. "I made it somehow. Many of them saw through me immediately. But I'm unhurt, which is something, I guess."

"And you found a pet along the way."

"She prefers to be called Lady Dela Kaymoor, thank you," Dela said with a touch of irritation.

"Named her already, have you?" Lily asked dispassionately. "That's nice. Pups that lick their masters' feet for scraps always have the fanciest names."

Sevi balked at her. He turned to look at Dela, afraid of what he might see on her face. Her mouth hung open in shock. But instead of hurling back indignation she tightened her lips into a tense smile. "If I have done something to offend the noble Squire Lily, I would apologize."

"Offend? No, of course not. You're far too smart for that. You'd do me a great favor by taking your wagging tail elsewhere though."

"That's thrice you've likened me to a dog, *Squire* Lily. One would expect a knight in training to have better manners."

"Want me to go for a fourth? Then stop hounding my friend for attention in your little play for power." Lily put a hand to her mouth. "Oops."

Dela gasped. "You presume too much!"

"Oh, I'm sorry, what was it then? Love at first sight?" Lily gibed.

"And what of you, Squire Lily?" Dela asked, squaring her shoulders and crossing her arms. "If there were ever a mongrel among us, you would certainly put it to shame. I think the howl of my own hound is a gentler voice than yours, and she possesses far better manners, even after eating shit."

Lily laughed. "A Kaymoor princess said the 'S' word. I guess we're being serious now! Then let me make myself clear." She pulled Sevi by the arm away from Dela and strode up to the other girl, looking up at her through her visor. "You and your family will not use Sevi for your politics. Not while I'm around."

Dela raised a single unimpressed eyebrow. "Who's to say it's all about politics, Miss Lily? Who's to say I don't have a legitimate interest in the prince?"

"Because Kaymoors only care about money and power."

"Except my family already has his family's money," Dela pointed out. "And power? Really? Life has gone on after the deaths of Queen Korina and King Marovhan, and the wheels of power have turned without them just fine. If anything, our prince needs me *far* more than I need him."

Lily smirked. "Is that what your mother told you?"

Dela paused. Lily's smirk deepened. Then Dela smiled, and Lily's expression froze. "I suppose the point is moot," Dela said airily. "He's already agreed to dance with me."

Lily's head swung around to Sevi. "You what?"

Sevi's eyes grew as wide as his mask's as he flicked his gaze between the two girls. "I... I said I had a partner."

"Mm. Sadly I've been relegated to second choice." Dela sighed, leaning in toward Lily. "But I will get that dance, *Squire* Lily."

"Partner?" Lily repeated, keeping her stare fixed on Sevi. "*What* partner?"

"Prince Isevidel! Please step forward!"

Sevi turned at the sound of Promina calling his name. She had her arm out to him across the floor, beckoning him forward. From the side, Commander Tiersa stepped out with the box containing Sevi's circlet, striding across the floor to stand beside Promina.

Every head in attendance turned to face his direction. Gulping, he spared one last apologetic look at Lily before stepping out from the crowd, raising his head high and trying not to clutch at his necklace. A wave of whispers rippled behind him. He did his best to block it out, trying to remember the steps of the dance with every stride he took.

"Are you ready, Your Brilliance?" Promina asked when he got close enough. "Do you remember what I taught you?"

"K-kind of," Sevi stuttered, betraying his nervousness.

"You'll do fine, Isevidel," Commander Tiersa said, holding the box out to him. "It's an easy waltz. No need for flourishes."

"More importantly, have you found a partner?" Promina asked, leveling a serious gaze at him.

Sevi studied Promina with renewed suspicion. Did she know about Dela's advances? Had she planned them with her? "I have."

"Very good." Stepping forward, Promina placed her hands gently on Sevi's mask and lifted it from his face. His heart sank as its weight left him, already missing the protection it afforded. She placed the mask into the box, and from it she withdrew his circlet, raising her voice. "The children of our hero Iviri, favored by the gods, continued to lead their people with kindness and honor until the end of their days. And now, after four long years, we honor her sacrifice again through the blood of her child, Isevidel. May his line continue to be a beacon of light for us all."

The guests clapped as she placed the circlet upon Sevi's head. He looked up at Promina, trying to be strong. Without his disguise, and his face now bare to the world, it was all starting to hit him. His status, the life he chose, the reputation of his family. All of it. What had he been thinking? He couldn't do this. He couldn't lead a blazing *country*. He couldn't be a blazing *prince*.

Promina opened her mouth to speak again, but Commander Tiersa stepped in. She placed one hand on Sevi's shoulder and the other on his chin, forcing his gaze up to hers with a gentle touch of her finger. He swallowed, breathing quickly with anxiety. Her hand dipped down to his neck, and he felt the chain of his necklace slide across his skin. Blinking, he looked down as the Astraeda star was pulled from beneath his shirt, shining softly in the dim light of the chandeliers above, with the bullet that almost killed him still lodged in its center.

"Show yourself, Isevidel," Tiersa told him. "Scars and all. You're an Astraeda. You're stronger than you know. And should you fall, I'll be here."

She touched her hand to the center of the pendant and pressed it against his chest in a silent offering of luck, keeping it there for several heartbeats before pulling away. With a nod to Promina, she took a step back.

"His Luminance Prince Isevidel will now select a partner for the first dance and the end of the Dark Hour," Promina announced.

Promina and Commander Tiersa both bowed and retreated to the base of the thrones, standing with their arms politely behind them. Sevi watched them until they had turned back to him, drawing what support he could from the looks they gave him before facing the crowd.

Everyone watched him expectantly, eager to see who he'd choose. Scanning from left to right, he could just make out the faces of all the friends he'd made in his time outside the Cut. Captains Lorr and River stood shoulder to shoulder with their arms around each other and Digby beside them, absent his cane and looming a head above the crowd. Innavin and Lieutenant Ryaliss stood further down the line, with Innavin's golden hair looking extra oiled for the evening. Even Reynam had shown himself, with his arm around a well-dressed woman he was surprised to recognize as Doctor Lea, out of her coat and in a beautiful black dress.

But there was only one face he was looking for. Setting his eyes on her from across the room, he stepped back the way he came until he stopped in front of Lily.

Her mouth fell open, and he gave her a small smile as the nobles around them murmured. She had one of those expressions he never got to see on her. He'd seen angry-surpise, taken-aback-surprise, even disgusted-surprise. But never pure, unadulterated surprise-surprise. He held his hand out and bowed, silently beckoning her to join him on the floor. She gathered herself and hissed, "*Something important you forget to tell me?*"

Sevi dipped his head lower and whispered, "You might have said no."

"I *would* have!"

"Which is why I didn't tell you!"

"Sevi." She darted her head around at all the people watching. "I can't dance!"

He raised his eyebrows at the admission, but didn't let it sway him. "Neither can I," he said, staring meaningfully at her. "Let's not-dance together."

Her gloved fists tightened and loosened at her sides. Dela, who had remained where she was, watched her with open amusement. Lily noticed, and her frown deepened.

"Please, Lily," Sevi continued to whisper. "I've asked so much of you already, I know. But there's no one else I'd rather have out here." Her fingers unfurled. He could feel her eyes boring into him from behind her visor. "We look out for each other. Partners and all that junk, right?" he pressed, stepping closer. "You watch my feet, and I'll watch yours."

"Sevi." She shook her head. "No. I can't."

"You *can*, Lily," he persisted. "I'll be there with you the entire way, even when we trip and fall. *Especially* when we trip and fall. Just as you've always done for me. Always."

There was a tense beat of silence. He searched her face, trying to see through her helmet, guessing at the expression she wore. When she didn't answer, he whispered, "Don't you trust me?"

She averted her gaze. "Of course, I do."

"Then what do you say? It could be fun, you know? Upping all our guests, when neither of us can dance?"

Another pause. Still, she said nothing.

"Please," Sevi implored.

Her shoulders sagged, and her head followed suit, drooping to her chest. Resignedly, she reached up to her visor and lifted it from her face, fixing him with a grave look. "If you step on my feet, I'm kicking your shins."

He beamed at her. "I would expect nothing less!"

Lily straightened her back, then smacked her hand into his, clasping it tightly, and allowing him to lead her from the crowd. The people around them broke into an encouraging cheer, having heard most every word they'd said. Even Dela clapped, regarding them both with a smirk. "Stupid boy. This is why I hate parties," Lily grumbled, blushing a scarlet red.

Sevi led her to the base of the thrones, where they turned to face each other, parallel to their audience. He lifted his arms. "I-I've only ever done this with Promina," Sevi breathed, trying to calm his nerves as he placed his hand on her hip. "I'll try to lead, but I don't know how well I'll do. She's... taller—"

"And I'm so short?" Lily finished for him, mirroring his gesture and folding her hand into his, taking his opposite hip in the other. "Just... just don't run me over."

"I'll do my best."

"No. I mean it. *Don't* run me over. I'll do more than kick your shins."

"Like throw me off a mountain?"

"*Yes.*"

The band struck a note, and they both froze. They each turned uncertainly toward the orchestra, then back at each other. "Are you ready?" Sevi asked.

"No," Lily breathed. "Not at all."

The music grew louder, assembling itself into a song. Sevi bounced lightly on the balls of his feet, timing the beat. Lily did the same, copying him. Then, very carefully, Sevi took a step.

She followed. He took another, sweeping his leg out in the corner of a box, and she stumbled, swearing as she rushed to catch up. He stepped again, flowing back the way they'd come to complete the box, and her cursing grew louder. He said, "It's alright, Lil, it's alright. Look. One, two, three. One, two, three. Just like this."

"I know, I know, just... Stop talking," she muttered, watching his feet. "One, two, three. One, two, three."

"Good. Now we turn."

"What?"

Sevi turned them. She breathed sharply in alarm, stumbling as she was forced to follow. "*More warning next time!*" she hissed, righting herself quickly.

"I'm sorry, you're right. But, look, you're already so much better."

She blinked and looked down at her feet, watching with surprise as she followed him instinctively, step for step, having fallen immediately into rhythm with him. "I guess I am," she said softly. She looked back up at him, meeting his eyes with her brows furrowed in worry. But there was a smile on her face.

And from there, everything flowed.

The music picked up, and so did their steps. One, two, three, one, two, three. Lily's stare never wavered, nor did he look away, allowing the music to carry them across the floor from end to end, gripping at each other when one lost their balance and helping them back into the rhythm once more.

One, two, three, one, two, three.

When they spun, Lily followed with her head held high. She caught him as he overextended, pulling him back toward her with a coy smile. An idea visibly flashed behind her eyes. He had just enough time to open his mouth before she spun him herself, stealing the lead away from him with a mischievous laugh.

He tried to recover his footing, but she wouldn't let him go, continuing the spin until they revolved around each other several more times, laughing all the while at the trick. An answering laugh bubbled out of his throat.

He wrestled the lead back from her, took her by the hand, and stepped away, pulling her hand up over her head as he did. She answered in kind, instinctively rising on her toes and allowing him to twirl her, spreading her arm out at the end with a flourish and reaching away, then pulling back and spinning into his arms.

He took her and spun her once more, falling back into the box step and turning to face a new direction, letting the world and all its faces and wonders fall away, whirling past them in a streak of light, color, and sound.

Maybe they were on rhythm. Maybe they weren't. But all he saw was her, and all she saw was him. And they were having fun.

They let go of one another, leaving each other's orbit, moving across the floor with a flurry of hops and bounds. Lily had her arms out to the ceiling while she spun. Sevi had his closed, spinning faster, until he exited the step with a sweep of his hands.

Their gazes caught across the floor.

One.

They stilled.

Two.

They tensed.

*Three.*

They sprung, twirling their crazy pirouettes and laughing louder than the music, deaf to all but each other as they rapidly closed the distance.

"*Those are the Dancers,*" the old lady said.

Her voice rang clearly in Sevi's head as he caught Lily by the arm. She flashed a roguish grin, took him by the hand, and spun him around again.

"*In that tangled mess of movement and life, somehow, those two found each other.*"

Sevi swung his free arm in a flourish as exuberant as hers, reaching out into the distance, grasping at the wind to bring it into their dance. But it slipped through his fingers, and Lily pulled him back in, demanding their dance remain for two, and two alone. He tightened his body and twirled inward, stepping into her arms with a laugh.

*"Spellbound, they each gripped the other and started to dance, laughing with such happiness..."*

He tripped over his feet. She stretched out her arms. Their bodies collided with a release of breathless laughter, flush with excitement. But they did not fall.

She closed around him. He closed around her. And the world, left abandoned and forgotten somewhere beyond their observance, finally crashed over them with the end of a song and a wave of applause. He pulled back, the joy on his face matched only by that in hers.

*"And there they remain in the sky to this day,"* the old lady whispered, trailing off in a soft, distant echo. *"Unable to part, and unwilling to try."*

Sevi and Lily squeezed each other tightly, catching their breath before stepping apart. He dipped into a low bow to her, grinning ear to ear. She made more of a show out of it than him, crossing her legs and waving her hands about in elegant circles. When they stood back up, they turned as one to face the crowd and bowed to them as well, accepting their ovation.

Promina and Commander Tiersa approached them from behind, clapping along with the crowd. "That was... unorthodox," Promina said, a slight frown on her lips. "But it had a certain charm to it, I'll grant it that."

"Charming is a good way to put it. We'll have to work on your posture, Isevidel," Commander Tiersa said, but the corners of her mouth betrayed a smile.

Lily nudged him. "Yeah, Isevidel, your posture was absolutely awful."

Sevi laughed. "So now what? Do I just dance some more?"

"The ceremonies are complete," Promina said. "Now the guests may continue to dance if desired. His Luminance may certainly join them if he wishes, but it's almost mid-bell. It would be entirely acceptable to return to the throne at this time."

"I'd love to rest, if possible," Sevi admitted.

"Don't you and your betrothed still have a dance to do?" Lily said.

Sevi turned to where he'd last seen Dela. She was in the arms of a man, twirling about as the music picked up again. But she seemed to peek over at him whenever she turned. Commander Tiersa's sharp eyes easily noticed his stare. "Ah. Your younger sister moves quickly, Rinenne."

"You mean our mother does." Promina grimaced, shaking her head. "I won't get in the way of any affections you might have for her, Your Brilliance, but do be careful. Sometimes a smile is more than a smile."

"That's what I said," Lily said, then did a double-take. "Wait. Sister? That explains so *much*."

Sevi glanced once more at Dela. He had been warned, time and again, to be on his guard for any who would try to ingratiate themselves to him. It was his first public appearance since the invasion, his first attempt at politics *ever*, and he knew that everyone knew it.

*But surely one dance wouldn't hurt. Would it?*

"I'll think it over," Sevi said.

Commander Tiersa nodded. "Always a wise choice."

Sevi took a step toward the throne, then paused, looking back at Promina. If she and Dela had planned anything together, why would she trouble herself with warning him about her? "Promina?"

"Yes, Your Brilliance?"

"You don't have to call me, 'Your Brilliance' or anything all the time. You can call me Sevi if you want."

Promina raised her eyebrows. "That would be highly improper."

Sevi shrugged. "I thought I'd offer." He started up the stairs to the thrones, but he hadn't gone more than a few steps when a hand clamped his shoulder and pulled him back. Turning around in confusion, he stared up into the suddenly grim face of Commander Tiersa. Suddenly on edge, he asked, "What? What is it?"

"Your guards," she growled. Sevi slowly turned to face the thrones again. There was nothing wrong with his guards. They just weren't there. "Stay with me," Tiersa ordered. She waved at several of the nearest soldiers along the room's perimeter, beckoning them closer. "Promina, go to the kitchens. Check if they've abandoned their duties and punish them severely if they have."

"Yes, My Lady." Promina bowed before hurrying away.

Four Embers approached from the walls and stood before the commander. "Be on your guard. Something may be wrong," she told them, loosening the straps on her swords. "Stay with me and protect the prince."

The soldiers saluted and took positions at four points around them, facing all directions. Sevi and Lily looked at each other in confusion. "Are we alright?" Sevi asked.

Tiersa didn't answer, scanning the sea of moving faces and twitching her fingers. Sevi and Lily watched with her, standing shoulder to shoulder. Some of the guests closest to them picked up the shift in mood and started glancing around the hall themselves. Sevi spotted a familiar figure as she came stumbling out of the rim of nobles, clutching at her head, with the stock of her rifle dragging along the floor. "Tiersa," Sevi called, pointing at Loma.

Tiersa followed his finger, frowning when he saw her. "I knew that fool had been drinking. Private Vorlo, bring Private Tammavin over to me at once."

The soldier to Sevi's left nodded and marched across the dance floor, bobbing out of the way of shifting dancers on his way to Loma. When he reached her, he exchanged a quick word before taking her by the wrist and dragging her back with him. "She's speaking nonsense, ma'am," Private Vorlo said, presenting Loma to the commander.

"Private Tammavin. Would you care to explain why you're not at your post?" Tiersa demanded. Loma shook her head slowly back and forth, still clutching it and muttering. "*Private Tammavin.*"

Loma looked up sluggishly with glassy eyes. "Have to save him..."

"What?" Tiersa stepped forward with a growing frown. "What are you muttering about? Save who?"

Loma didn't reply. Tiersa opened her mouth again, but caught sight of something over Loma's shoulder and clamped her jaw shut. She straightened, snapping the guards of her scabbards off entirely. Sevi looked in the same direction. Promina had returned with Digby at her side. He held a person, carrying them across the floor with one arm slung around his shoulder and their feet dragging limply behind.

Cassik. And he was bleeding.

"STOP THE MUSIC!" Tiersa yelled.

The music died with a whimper. The nobles stopped dancing, turning to her in confusion. A new sound rushed to fill the silence, shrieking from outside.

The sound of guns firing and piercing metal whistles.

And then the world exploded.

Every window in the room blew inward, raining deadly shards of broken glass down upon the revelry. People screamed, and from the night, clad in wooden armor from head to toe, flew six monsters with mouthless faces and glowing red eyes, brandishing vicious swords of burning metal. Monsters Sevi recognized all too well from nightmares he had almost every night.

They had returned for him.

The creatures bellowed and raised their flaming swords high, ready to end the hunt they began four years ago.

# Chapter 51

*If I have but a wish, please remember that moment. Dream it at every chance. May your heart fill your body with a love that renews you...*

———

"OPEN FIRE!" Tiersa screamed, pulling out her pistol and unloading all six bullets into the nearest hovering Fae in one fluid motion. Its armor withered and blackened wherever she hit, crumbling around the wounds. The creature whipped its mouthless face towards her, flicking its blazing sword out in challenge.

Sevi panicked, clutching at Lily's arm. "Can you see this? *Is this real?*"

"FORM ON ME! PROTECT THE PRINCE!" Tiersa screamed again, dropping her empty pistol and smacking the sides of her scabbards. Something audibly cracked inside.

"SEVI!" Lily yelled, tugging at his arm. Dumbly, he turned, staring blankly at her finger pointing toward the Lonely Stairwell.

The nearest creature dove toward them. Soundless. Fast. Faster than he could see. Reaching out for him with one deadly claw, pointing its sword and ready to strike.

Someone pushed him to the ground.

The Silvakin's hand brushed past his hair just as two swords streaked through the air, meeting fire with steel and bursting in an aura of blinding light. Metal struck metal with a vicious ring, showering sparks across Sevi's face. Commander Tiersa had stopped the Silvakin dead in its flight, catching its blade between both of hers. A shimmering shield of magical incandescence separated her from the creature.

Her back strained through her coat, and her arms rippled with muscle as she leaned forward into the strike with an angry, feral snarl. Each of her swords dripped with shimmering silver oil, and the handle of each blade glowed red beneath her palms from a tight scrawl of glowing runes. "Not again," she spat. "Do you hear me? *Never again, you son of a BITCH!*"

She curled the long blade beneath the Silvakin's guard. The wall of light vanished just as she yanked her short sword back and plunged it through the monster's wooden armor, skewering its heart.

The Silvakin shrieked within its wood, abruptly cut off as a radiant blaze of silver fire sprung from the creature's wound. It ate at its body, tearing into armor and flesh alike without discretion until white flames poured from the eyes of its mask. The sword dropped from its hands, extinguishing the moment it hit the floor, and the rest of the creature crumbled into ash, leaving a broken heap of armor behind.

Tiersa flicked her blades clear, splattering the floor with silver and blood. She stood with arms spread wide in open challenge, her head down and hair undone, baring her teeth in a snarl that would make any mother wolf cower in fear.

Sevi shrunk away. Lady Night had returned.

"EMBERS!" she screamed. "I SAID *OPEN FIRE!*"

The Embers filled the room with a deafening cacophony of sound, firing their weapons as fast as they could. Nobles and guests, stunned by the violence, erupted with activity, screaming and scrambling over each other in a mad dash to escape. The creatures, open targets for the Embers, tucked in their wings and dropped to the floor in a deadly storm, bringing their blades down on soldiers and guests in indiscriminate slaughter.

Two of the five remaining Silvakaen ignored the gathering, marching toward the thrones with eyes blazing as bright as their swords. "No," Sevi uttered in horror, falling inward on himself. "*No!*"

"Get up! *Get up, lad!*"

Someone pulled at him. He didn't resist, letting Digby and Lily yank him off the ground. He dimly registered that the lieutenant had picked up the fallen creature's weapon, brandishing it toward the approaching

Silvakaen. Promina was there, too, carrying Cassik as best as she could, with Loma beside her, absent her rifle and looking dazed.

One of the three soldiers fell beneath the sword of a Silvakin, screaming as his body burned black in the sudden flame that erupted from his torso. Sevi found his feet just as another soldier fell, having spent all her bullets and clicking the useless trigger of her gun with wide, terrified eyes. She died without a sound.

Commander Tiersa stood firm with enchanted swords at the ready. Her back was the last thing Sevi saw before Digby scooped him up into his arms and sprinted toward the stairwell. The others followed, crossing into the room just as a flock of raptors poured in through the gaping windows, screeching as they dove at the Silvakaen with talons bared.

Soldiers flowed past them, forming a line of deadly barrels pointing the way they came. *They won't be enough,* Sevi thought numbly. They had just made it to the base of the steps when Cassik suddenly pushed away from Promina and sprung in front of Digby's back.

A cold blast of wind hammered them. Digby grunted and stumbled, catching himself on the banister before he could fall on top of Sevi. He turned around. Cassik lay on the ground in a heap, right where Digby would have been, staring wildly ahead in terror. A white substance formed at his feet and branched into tendrils, slowly creeping up his legs, hardening his body wherever it touched.

Turning him to stone.

"Get... away... from... he—" He gasped, reaching out to them. Then the white covered his face and slipped into his mouth, eating away at his insides as eagerly as his outsides. His hand froze in the air, reaching for someone to save him.

"Move!" Digby barked. He dashed up the stairwell with Sevi in his arms, faster than his age or his bad leg should have allowed, quickly outstripping Lily, Promina, and Loma. Promina stopped to rip the hem of her dress before chasing after him, with Lily and Loma at the rear.

Lily snarled in annoyance. "Godsdamnit, *wait! You're the only one with a gun, Digby!*"

Digby slowed at the top of the steps until the others caught up. Sounds of the fight echoed from below, bouncing off the confines of the hallway in a horrible melody. "Orders?" Digby asked, walking hurriedly beside Promina.

"Get the prince to his chambers and barricade the door, then seal ourselves into the royal study and wait for help to arrive," Promina said, staring ahead determinedly. Her hair had come undone, and she had lost her mask, but she looked as unshakable as ever.

Digby grunted. "As good a plan as any."

A gust of wind blew at them from behind.

They stopped. Turning back, they watched as a Silvakin warrior touched down at the top of the steps, its wings large enough to touch each side of the corridor at once. It regarded them with its flat red eyes from within a sea of murky black. Malevolent. Lifeless. Ruthless.

Digby slowly set Sevi on his feet. "Get to the room."

"W-what?" Sevi stuttered. Visions flashed before his eyes of a blood-splattered knight facing down an enemy he knew he couldn't beat, and he clutched desperately at Digby's sleeve. "No, you're coming with me! *This can't happen again!*"

"Private Tammavin, take the revolver and cover Lieutenant Asgaillin," Promina ordered.

"Get to the room, Sevi," Digby said again, keeping his eyes on the Silvakin. He turned his body to face it, pulling his revolver from its holster in his left hand and readying his sword with the right. "I'll see ya there. Ya have me word."

Sevi clenched at Digby's coat. "No! *Digby!*"

"Let's go, Sevi," Lily said through gritted teeth, wrenching him away from the lieutenant. "Digby, if you die, I swear to every god that I'm spitting on your grave every godsdamned day."

Digby chuckled. "Aye, lass... Take care of the lad for me."

"Private Tammavin!" Promina barked.

"DIGBY!" Sevi yelled.

Promina shouted, "Godsdamnit, just *move!*"

They had to pull Sevi away from him, and he fought them every step, never taking his eyes off the old soldier. Digby raised his left hand and stared down at something on his wrist. Something that made him smile.

With a sigh, he turned his body sideways and pointed his gun at the creature. "Alright, ya big, wooden bastard, come taste Áiléan steel."

A crackle of energy formed around the Silvakin, gathering into a whirlwind that spiraled violently down the hall. Digby fired, emptying his bullets into the creature's chestpiece and blackening its wooden carapace. The wind dissipated in an instant, and the energy around the Silvakin dispersed, banished at the iron's touch. The monster hissed loudly and readied its sword, swinging it to the side. Digby dropped his empty gun and leveled his own.

The creature jumped, beating its wings in a powerful leap across the hallway, bringing its fiery weapon down in a blazing arc at Digby's head.

Digby swung his sword up and stepped to the side, deflecting the strike in an expert use of momentum. He stepped back, balled his free hand in a fist and slammed the full weight of his entire body into the face of the creature with all the force at his command.

A loud *crack* echoed through the hall. Digby slammed the pommel of his sword into the other side of the Silvakin's face, jerking its head back the way it came. Using that same motion, he pointed his faeblade at the creature and drove it forward.

The Silvakin swept its sword up in a parry, beating its wings in a swift step backward, putting distance between itself and Digby. Its wooden mask now bore two cracks on either side. It jerked its head about, shaking the dizziness out of its skull with another hiss. The left side of its mask flew off, revealing a smooth, green face with a pointed ear, black hair, and a large, angry red eye that fixed itself maliciously on Digby.

"*That's for Ann!*" Digby yelled, red in the cheeks. "Come on! Come on! Let's go see her *together!*"

Then Lily tugged Sevi around the corner, and he could see no more.

He cried as he stumbled away. Promina ushered him and Lily into the parlor, waiting with a furious expression as Loma straggled in along with them. The moment the doors shut, Promina stepped up to Loma and slapped her across the face. "*What is wrong with you?*" she shouted, losing all composure. "Get the *fuck* back out there!"

"Have to protect him..." Loma said without emotion.

"Promina," Lily said.

"YOU should be the one out there fighting that *thing*, not *him!*" Promina continued to yell.

"*Promina!*" Lily shouted.

"WHAT?"

"Her *ears!*"

Sevi looked at Loma's ears. Burns sprouting from around her metal earrings marred her skin.

Iron.

"L-Loma?" Sevi whispered.

Loma swiveled to face him, slowly pulling her mouth up in an eerie smile. "There you are." Her sword appeared in her hands. She lunged at him, baring her teeth in a manic grin as she brought it down. She stopped mid-fall, jerking back abruptly as something caught her from behind. The blade swept a breadth away from Sevi's nose, kissing his face with the breeze of its swing.

"*Go! Get to the study!*" Promina yelled, digging her hands into Loma's clothes. Loma flailed her sword and snarled, turning to attack her.

Lily tugged at Sevi before he could protest, throwing him into the bedroom, then slamming and locking both doors behind them. "Get to the Cut," she ordered.

Sevi didn't move. Any threads he had stitched between his body and his head over the course of the night had been severed completely. "The study..."

"We know the Cut! The mountain is full of quicksilver; they won't find us there!" Lily said, already hauling the dresser aside.

"Alright, Lily," Sevi mumbled hollowly. "You know best."

Lily ran back over and took him by the wrist, pulling him with her to the open hole in the wall. Their faces had only graced the edge of the tunnels when something inside hissed as angrily as a firedrake. From the darkness a fire appeared, flaring up along the deadly line of a sword, accompanied by two flashing, red eyes.

"No," Lily gasped in horror. "Get out. Get *out!*" They scrambled out of the tunnel. Lily threw her weight against the dresser as hard as she could, blocking the hole before backing away. "The tunnels. He used the godsdamned *tunnels.*"

A pounding came at the bedroom doors, like a body throwing itself against it. A horrible *crack* resounded as the frame buckled.

They were surrounded.

"The study!" Lily yelled.

They bounded into the secret room. Sevi had never bothered to close it. He waved his hand and the light inside came on, casting an eerie glow. Lily said frantically, "Shut it! Quick!"

"A stone in the wall," Sevi muttered. Aunty Tisa had told him how.

"Press it!"

Sevi pressed the marked stone. At first nothing happened. Then the wall began to shift, melting slowly into existence from the top of the room, called by the magic of the runes.

The dresser in the bedroom erupted with fire, and a wooden soldier burst out of its wreckage, rolling into a crouch and snapping its head up directly at Sevi.

Sevi took a step backward.

The creature's entire body crackled with energy, and it flung out a hand. An invisible grip tightened around Sevi's body, yanking him through the air and out of the study. "*Sevi!*" Lily screamed, running to him just as the wall solidified between them.

The grip around him released. Sevi fell to the floor, immediately scrambling to his feet and pushing his back up against the newly formed hearth.

He and the creature stared at each other, silent, save for the pounding of the doors. It didn't seem to notice, keeping its eyes on Sevi and tilting its head to the side in a curious gesture, as if listening to something.

Then it waited.

And waited.

Sevi's heartbeat thumped in his throat, waiting for it to attack. It eventually brought its fiery sword up and flicked it, extinguishing the flames along its metal at the motion. It then raised its free hand and undid a clasp on its forearm before whipping its arm down. The gauntlet flew off, revealing a bare, green hand underneath. It sliced its sword across its palm, dripping black, oily blood onto the floor. Somewhere in the depths of his dissociation, Sevi put together what was happening. It meant to feed him its blood.

"Shy. Help me. Hide me," Sevi whispered.

The shadow didn't appear.

"*Shy!*"

The Silvakin clenched and unclenched its hand, as though the wound were a curious thing. Sevi whipped his head around the room. Iron. He needed *iron*.

*Iron in your belly,* Digby's voice whispered.

A glint of metal on his chest caught his eye. He looked down. His family's star shimmered up at him. As well as the bullet lodged in its middle.

*With luck like that, why not carry it around?* Reynam's voice said.

He yanked the necklace over his head and slammed the pendant back against the wall. The creature hissed and stepped forward. Sevi brought the necklace down again, and again, hammering metal against stone, summoning sparks with every strike, before finally digging his fingers into it in a desperate bid to yank the bullet free.

The monster was upon him, reaching out with one bloody hand, ready to enthrall him.

The bullet came loose.

Crying out, Sevi brought the iron to his mouth and swallowed it whole.

The creature gripped his face tightly, smearing its blood across his cheeks and forcing its palm into his mouth. Its blood tasted sickly sweet—not like blood at all—and sent a shock through him strong enough to make him gag. He tried to wrench his head away, but the Silvakin merely tightened its grip, effortlessly keeping him pinned to the wall and watching him with its lifeless red eyes.

Then the creature jerked its hand back and let out a loud, aggravated hiss. It darted forward and closed its fingers around Sevi's neck, squeezing hard enough to choke, before lifting him from the floor and furiously hurling him across the room.

Sevi flung his arms out, sailing weightlessly through the air before crashing into the bed frame, gasping as all the breath was driven from his lungs. He hit the ground and saw stars, shining as bright as his pendant, spinning and twirling like dancers in the sky.

The fire along the monster's sword blazed back into existence. It strode forward, weapon at the ready, hissing a vindictive dirge at having its quarry dare outdo it. Sevi stared at the fiery tendrils, unable to move.

Exhaustion overcame him. He was so tired. So tired of being afraid. So tired of running. So tired of *trying*. His vision blackened at the edges, promising a peaceful, dreamless sleep that would save him before he could feel the fire's burn through his chest.

The creature raised its sword above its head with the point toward him.

*Everyone... I'm sorry you had to die for a stupid boy like me.*

The Silvakin hissed. The weapon came down.

"*Hey!*"

A glass vial caught the sword's light just before crashing against the creature's helmet, shattering into pieces. It let out a snarl of alarm as its body abruptly locked up, freezing mid-thrust not a handspan away from Sevi's face. Sevi blinked, focused on the weapon, sweating beneath the sword's heat radiating across his body. The Silvakin slowly turned its head to the side, jerking and twitching with every movement as it tried to look behind. Sevi slowly followed its gaze.

Lily stood outlined in the light of the open study, pointing her arms at the creature with clenched fingers. She had taken off her helmet. A patchy crop of dull, red hair had sprouted from her scalp, and her eyes were aglow with amber light. "No... you... *don't*," she snarled.

The creature screeched, thrashing its head from side to side and flapping its wings with desperate beats. Its weapon began to turn, shaking in its hand. It clutched at its wrist and tugged, trying to budge its arm in any other direction as the point of the sword turned away from Sevi's chest and toward its own.

Lily tightened her hands and forced her palms closer to each other. The Silvakin screeched as the tip of its sword pressed into its breastplate. Lily bellowed a scream to match and slammed her hands close. The sword plunged through the Silvakin and out its back with a sickening sound, setting its armor alight.

The creature shook and wailed, burbling black blood from behind its mask until its body finally went limp and slumped backward, falling to the floor with the wet splatter of viscera and the crackle of fire.

Lily gasped and collapsed to her knees, her chest raggedly heaving up and down, struggling to breathe. Her cheeks were wet with tears.

"Lil... ly," Sevi breathed.

Her face tightened in agony, and she fell to the floor. She didn't get up.

The pounding on the bedroom doors grew louder. The last thing Sevi saw before the darkness took him was Tiersa, bursting into the bedroom with her silver swords ablaze in scorching light, leading a seething mass of Embers in to chase the monsters away.

# Chapter 52

*May you always remember our dance.*

<hr/>

S evi awoke from a dreamless sleep with a gasp. It made sense. His nightmares had broken free from his mind to become real. Why would they linger?

Gone were the dancing nobles. Gone were his bedchambers. Gone was the monster with its flaming sword. In their place was the infirmary, filled with beds of injured, dying people.

He settled back into the mattress, unafraid. Why should he be? He'd been here before.

His body felt heavy, like something was pressing him down. Stiffly creaking his head to the side, he found someone lying against his legs. Someone with dark hair and formerly well-kept braids.

Tiersa stirred when he did, groaning lowly with a jerk of her body before pulling back and rubbing at her eyes. Sevi glanced around the room. It was full of no less than two dozen Ember soldiers on guard, watching over the many wounded nobles and Siers. But he knew they weren't here for them.

"Isevidel," Tiersa said slowly, then her eyes sprung open. "Isevidel!"

She grabbed him in a hug too tight and squeezed him like he'd disappear at any moment. "I'm sorry. I'm sorry. I'm *sorry*," she repeated over and over. "I never should have left you. I never should have left. Thank the Mother and the Father. Thank the gods. Thank you, thank you."

Sevi looked dazedly up at the ceiling, half-listening to her, and only vaguely aware of the pain along his body. His spirit was somewhere outside of him again, looking down at them both, as if he hadn't woken up at all. But then his heart hammered, and his mind was sucked back inside of his head with a jarring jolt.

It all came back to him. It had all happened. By the gods it had *happened*.

The party. The dancing. The masks. The monsters. Cassik. Digby. Promina. Loma.

He squeezed his eyes shut as tears welled, closing his arms tightly around Tiersa and burying his face into her shoulder. They hugged each other for so long that he became aware of her own heart pounding against his chest, beating as powerfully as his. He balled his fingers in her shirt. "Tiersa... What happened?"

Tiersa leaned back and wiped her eyes, keeping one hand on his arm. She fixed him with an exhausted, desolate expression. "We were attacked. Some of the supplies were drugged, and some of my soldiers turned. We're still testing everyone in the castle."

Sevi reached up to his chest. His hand brushed against flat muscle, and his fingers closed uselessly over where his necklace should have been. "Digby?" he whispered. Tiersa's lips tightened and she looked away. Fresh tears slid down his cheeks. "No..."

"He was a mighty man," Tiersa said softly, "to fell that creature on his own. Those monsters were Fae of the Silent Grove—elite soldiers of the Lynnweald who know no fear. I had my blades enchanted, and their steel coated in quicksilver. But him?" She shook her head, closing her eyes. "His name will be remembered."

Sevi's grip tightened on his shirt, and he stared wretchedly down at his legs. Lieutenant Digby Asgaillan. Smiling, kind, loyal Lieutenant Digby Asgaillan. Wiped from the world forever. Had he ever told him how he'd come to appreciate him? That his oath was no longer needed? That he was a good man? "And Promina?"

"Unconscious, but alive, thank the gods."

"Cassik? Loma?"

"No."

Sevi hung his head. His friends had died because of him, and just because he was a prince. Why? What was so special about that? Why was that so important that people had to kill him? To fight and die for him?

After all his lessons, all the reassurances, he couldn't understand. He'd give it all up in a heartbeat to see them again. To laugh with them. To hold them and tell them the things he'd always loved about them. And now he never could. "Lily...?" he asked softly.

Tiersa went silent.

Sevi looked up. "Lily?"

"We'll talk more about her after you've rested."

"Blackest night, we'll talk right godsdamned *now*." Sevi darted his hand out and gripped her wrist. Tiersa's armor snapped into existence as she regarded his hand. She moved her gaze up to meet his eyes. He didn't flinch away, staring hard at her. "Did you kill her?"

Again, Tiersa said nothing. Sevi angrily shook her wrist and shouted, "*Did you kill her!*"

"No."

Sevi blinked. Tiersa gingerly extracted her hand from his fingers. "I wanted to," she said. "Gods, how I wanted to the moment I saw those ears. But I'm not a fool." She leaned back in her chair and closed her hands in her lap. "The creature that attacked you drove its own blade through its chest. Why was that?"

He shook his head, still processing the rush of relief he felt in knowing that Lily was still alive. "I don't know. She did something to it."

"Which begs the question, why?" Commander Tiersa said with a scowl. "Why has a Fae saved your life, not only once but twice, and against her own kin? Why does she not burn in her iron helmet? And why didn't the quicksilver work on her?" She shook her head. "She's refused to answer any questions. I'm keeping her in the tower until she cooperates."

"I want to see her," Sevi said immediately.

"No, Isevidel." Tiersa frowned. "You're not to go near her until we understand what she's been trying to achieve."

"Achieve? She's my *friend!*"

"She's a *Fae*," Tiersa spat, her eyes welling up with that same familiar, haunting darkness. "A Fae that locked you away from the world inside a *cave*. A Fae that was probably part of the very force that invaded our home and killed our family. A Fae that schemes, and tortures, and betrays. You don't know them, Isevidel! I've seen what they do—it's been my life for *four years*. She's been *using* you for some convoluted plot, and I swore an oath to you upon my honor to protect you from greenblood monsters like her. She—*it*—is *not* your friend, and you will *not* see it again under *any* circumstances."

Sevi's own anger grew. How dare she. How *dare* she make such accusations about Lily. He didn't know them? He had lived in an entire *castle* with them! Who cared if she was a Fae? He *loved* her, *and* Alyda. "You have no authority to speak that way to your *prince*," he growled back. "Or were those all lies you told me to keep power from the nobles and in your own hands?"

Tiersa's jaw dropped. She twisted her lips into a sneer and stood, placing her hands on her swords. "You don't have a crown yet. Until then, I have the only authority," she said with dispassionate finality. "You are confined to your quarters until further notice." She turned her back on him and walked away without so much as a backward glance.

The anger inside Sevi refused to fade. It ballooned, expanded, and boiled over. He took his pillow and hurled it across the room, screaming his rage at the ceiling until his vision went dark.

The royal chambers were a mess. Soldiers went about with brooms and dustpans, doing their best to clean up the wreckage. Sevi sat on the sofa with a blanket around him, staring at the gaping royal study for what felt like the hundredth time. Unmoving. Unfeeling. He didn't look up when a mason came in to seal the hole leading into the Cut, nor when the parlor doors were fixed. He didn't budge when a platter of food came in for him. He didn't look up when someone called his name. Eventually the sun set, they all left, and he was finally, blessedly, alone.

He got up from the sofa and walked woodenly toward the bed. The canopy had been removed, having snapped under the weight of his impact. The wall, now completely repaired, was missing the dresser that had covered it, and an ominous stain darkened a patch of the floor where the Silent Grove monster had died.

He closed his eyes and fell across the bed, hitting the mattress with a solemn *thump*, letting its unusual softness close around him in an attempt to swallow him whole. If it could have, he'd have let it. He rolled onto his back, then each of his sides, trying vainly to fall asleep, but despite his weariness and sorrow, his thoughts just wouldn't let him.

He pounded the bedsheets, pushing himself up to sit on the edge of his mattress. What was the use of all this fluff if he couldn't get any godsdamned *sleep!*

*I failed her. Just like I always do.*

Sevi the failure. Sevi the weakling. A crown hadn't changed that about him.

He pulled Lily's whistle from his pocket, holding it in his palm and gazing at the carved lily flower running down its side. *Blow this whistle, and I'll come find you.* "Can you hear this, Lily? Wherever you are?" he mumbled, bringing the whistle to his lips and blowing. A soft, two-tone note fluttered through the air, surprisingly melodic for such a crude instrument

A shadow sprung up at his feet.

He flinched, jerking his head down in surprise as Shy rose from the floorboards. The creature struggled to form. Their body wriggled and fuzzed at the edges, and their two white eyes bobbed listlessly in their dark pool of a body.

"Hrrrmmm," Shy sighed weakly.

"Shy?" Sevi muttered, staring at the pathetic creature as they struggled to find shape. He clenched Lily's whistle. "Why," he muttered. "Why are you showing yourself *now! I could have used your help! You could have saved us!*"

The shadow shrunk at the sound of his voice, quivering in fear or pain. He opened his mouth to yell at them again but stopped, overcome by a sudden thought. He stared back down at the whistle. *Shy appeared*

*I blew this*, he realized. Bringing it to his lips, he took a breath and blew another note.

Shy cringed inward on themselves even more violently, and their two eyes huddled together, growing dimmer at the sound. Their body suddenly lengthened, tugging away from Sevi's feet until it had severed itself completely and slid away across the floorboards.

It suddenly clicked. Shy and the mirror world had disappeared after he'd blown the whistle. They had *always* disappeared after he'd blown the whistle!

*It's a parasite,* Lily's phantom voice whispered. *It's probably eaten your memories.*

Lily was the maker of the signal whistles. Lily, who had never hidden her distaste for the shadow. Lily, the Silvakin.

"She *did* this!" he exclaimed. "*She* drove you away!"

The shadow gave no response, already halfway across the room. Sevi picked himself off the bed and hurried over to the mirror. He placed the whistle on the desk in front of him, then reached down and picked up his boot.

How many times had he blown such a whistle over the years? How many times had he unknowingly hurt his friend?

"No more," Sevi said, raising the shoe above his head. "I'm fixing this. For both of us." He slammed the boot down. The whistle broke beneath the blow with a *crack*. A bubble of energy flared around the instrument and dispersed with a flash of light, and Shy burst out of the ground, full of dark and eyes aglow, growing limbs as it formed an almost corporeal, androgenous body made entirely of shadow.

When they finished forming, they stood staring down at their hands, wriggling their fingers in impossible directions as if in disbelief. They blinked each eye, one after the other, and then flung their arms out wide and jumped in obvious glee, making no noise when they landed. They bounced onto and off of the bed, landing with a roll and twirling up with a spin, circuiting the room in a silent dance of pure joy.

Sevi couldn't bring himself to join in their fun. "Shy," he called gently.

Shy stopped. Their head swiveled around completely to face back at him, then their body, and with frightening speed they threw themselves at Sevi and wrapped their small arms around his torso, like a child running to its mother. Sevi started in surprise, feeling no weight to the creature as they pressed themselves in. He placed one hand on top of the shadow's head and found that there was some substance to it, allowing him to run his palm down their head comfortingly. "Shy," Sevi said again, "Why did Lily chase you away? Did you eat my memories?"

The shadow looked up at him and blinked.

"Can you give them back to me?" Sevi whispered. "Can you show me... Can you show me what happened that night?"

Shy trembled at their edges.

"Please," Sevi implored. "Show me who I am."

After a long while, the shadow slowly nodded and wrapped Sevi's hand in their own before leading him over to the mirror. Sevi followed without protest, taking a steadying breath as they dove into it together.

The bedroom fell away, replaced with the cloudy murk of the mirror world. Shy's grip left him as Sevi turned vertical, gradually descending to the black floor. The diffused light from before faded into existence, revealing the scene around him.

It was like he was back at the Iron Masquerade. Sevi found himself in the throne room standing at the base of the thrones' steps. Nobles flowed about wearing an unfamiliar assortment of clothing and masks, dancing across the floor to a majestic beat, while his father, mother, and Tiersa looked on.

Tiersa still had her viper mask. His father's appeared to be made of pure silver, with a ring of stars on his forehead that ended at his cheekbones. His mother's, however, was completely blank, save for the eyes. Beside them, the maskless faces of Sevi's brother, his sister, and his younger self manifested from the shadows, followed by the rest of their bodies. He looked up at them with longing, which only increased the more he stared.

Knights in full plate flanked the stairs leading up to the thrones, carrying polearms and wearing helmets just like Lily's. Sevi had taken the first step up toward his family when a noble detached himself from the crowd, ascending alongside him without a glance. He had tan skin and black locks, kept in line by a magenta mask inlaid with gold, and wore an outfit far different than the other Elkran nobles. In his hands he held a rosewood box, which he presented to the king and queen with a bow.

Tiersa stepped forward, wearing her white Promina uniform, and took the box from his hands. She opened it and looked inside, running her gaze over its contents, before turning it toward his parents. Both the king and queen nodded in approval, though the queen looked more enthusiastic, taking her mask off entirely to reveal a smile. "Very fine work, Lord Enstrova," Queen Korina said, running her hand over what lay inside.

Sevi stepped closer and peered in. Two very familiar silver necklaces bearing the star of Astraeda rested on a bed of cloth, twinkling in the dim light. His younger self and his older brother leaned in to get a look at them, while Nahlra, too little to see, jumped up and down with a huff of annoyance until Tiersa shushed her.

"Thank you, Your Luminance," Lord Enstrova said with a bow.

"And the runes?"

"Engraved within a hollow chamber and encased within the silver. I've been assured that so long as the necklaces remain intact the magic will continue to work as expected. Each necklace has been given a rune of durability for added protection against any future damage."

"Astounding," Queen Korina said. "How can aether reach within solid silver and iron?"

"That is an answer known only to the Runics, Your Luminance."

"Mm." Korina nodded. "As I've said. Very fine work. You and your sons should be very proud. Would you care to join us for the latest test?"

"*Korina*," King Marovhan warned softly. Queen Korina ignored him, keeping her eyes trained on the lord.

"I... am humbled to be offered such an honor, Your Luminance," Lord Enstrova said, "but I am but a jeweler at heart. I'm afraid that I do not have the stomach for these things."

"Yet you are the mind behind its inception," Queen Korina persisted, tilting her head. "Are you not the least bit curious about the Argennium's capabilities?"

"Certainly curious, Your Luminance. Every crafter hopes to see their work live up to its greatest potential. And your cause is just, that I still believe. But I do not believe I can stomach the sight of the destruction the test will entail."

"But creating the instrument of such destruction is something that you *can* stomach." The queen arched her brow.

"A blacksmith is not responsible for the deaths at the point of the sword he forges, Your Luminance. He merely plies his trade and hopes that his creations are wielded with wisdom."

"Yet he does not sell his blades to artisans."

"A blacksmith also forges shields, Your Luminance."

"A sword makes for a poor shield," Korina countered.

"But an apt deterrent, Your Luminance, to those with only a sword. Thus, it may serve as one adequately enough."

The queen's smile turned into a frown. "Do you doubt our intentions, Lord Enstrova?"

"No, Your Luminance. But who's to know the intentions of your grandchildren?"

"Or the conditions in which they take the throne," Queen Korina said.

Lord Enstrova bowed. "Just so, Your Luminance."

Queen Korina sighed, tapping her finger on the arm of her throne. "Very well. Wash your hands of this business, Lord Enstrova. You will be paid in full."

"Thank you, Your Luminance." Lord Enstrova gave her and the king another deep bow, holding it for several breaths before righting himself and turning away, rejoining the party below.

King Marovhan frowned. "Was that really necessary?"

"I had to ensure that his loyalties hadn't changed," Queen Korina said.

Marovhan regarded her. "Were you honestly considering it?"

"I was." Queen Korina took the box from Tiersa.

"You would risk open war with Tiburas?"

"Better war with an enemy we know than one we don't," Queen Korina said, lifting a necklace from the box. She admired it in the light before slipping it over her head.

The scene changed. The guests and the room whirled about in a gust of wind and shadow, disappearing for but a moment before reappearing in different positions. The dancers and musicians on the floor, previously so happy and carefree, now huddled on the far side of the room closest to the thrones, staring in horror at the gates to the great hall.

A great pounding could be heard outside, filling the room with an ominous thudding. The flickering of firelight poured in through the windows. Many of the knights that stood guard now surrounded the doors, with some pressing their backs up against them in a desperate attempt to keep whatever was outside from getting in.

Sevi looked out through one of the windows. The night was burning, and in its crackling flames, a horde of silhouetted fighters clashed with a song of steel meeting steel.

"You need to go with your father, my loves," Queen Korina said.

He turned. His family stood away from the thrones near the entrance to the Lonely Stairwell, having discarded their masks, with five knights around them in a ring. Korina was on her knees with her arms spread wide open, holding both his younger self and his little sister in a tender hug that seemed to ignore the tension of the moment. Only his older brother, Alramar, stood apart, clenching his fists and staring at the queen with anger and disbelief. "You should be coming with us," he said, trembling.

"I can't, my dear," Korina said gently. "Look at everyone around us. Even our knights are terrified, hoping for someone to save them. To lead them. I can't leave them."

"Yes, you can." Alramar wiped his face. "They'd do the same to you."

"Alramar, do you remember what we talked about?"

Alramar looked away.

"Do you remember who a ruler serves? Who comes first?"

"What about *us*," Alramar cried. "You're leaving *us*. You're my... you're our..."

"My dear, dear boy," Korina whispered, holding out her arm for him. The pounding on the doors outside intensified, and a slash of fire appeared across its wood, making all the guests in the room gasp. "Come here, Alramar."

Alramar stayed where he was.

"Please," Queen Korina said, her voice tightening. "Don't say goodbye to me like this."

Alramar now cried openly. He took a step forward and stopped, balling his fists. Another fiery slash blazed across the hall's doors, as though the flames outside were trying to scratch their way in.

"We have to leave, your majesties," a knight said, pulling Young Sevi and Nahlra away from Queen Korina.

"No!" Alramar shouted, finally leaping into Queen Korina's embrace. "I don't want to go! Don't make me leave!"

"Alramar," Queen Korina choked, closing her arms around him.

Another slash. The doors began to buckle.

"Now!" the knight yelled.

Marovhan pulled Alramar away from the queen and moved in himself, spending several precious breaths in an embrace with her. "Keep it safe. Keep *them* safe," the queen said.

"I will, my love. My beautiful Korina," Marovhan said mournfully. "I swear by it. By every star in the sky."

They extracted themselves. Korina raised a hand and placed something in the king's, who clutched it and put it over his head—the second necklace. With one final anguished look of parting, the king took their children and left the queen, surrounded by their loyal knights.

Tiersa remained by his mother, looking just as anguished as Alramar. The queen turned to her. "I have a job for you, Tiersa," she said, lifting her own necklace over her head. That was the last Sevi could hear from her before the scene forced him to follow his younger self, dashing with his siblings up the stairwell with the knights clanking around them, feeling a sense of terror, and confusion, and anger.

They had gotten halfway up the steps when the sound of the doors breaking reached them, and the loud yells of a hundred bloodthirsty people filled the hall. "Faster!" King Marovhan ordered.

They passed a window. Outside, a fire raged across the grounds below, and people carrying weapons and torches ran about in a frenzy. Three silhouettes hung suspended in the air above the melee, clad in the wooden armor of the Silent Grove. The soles of their boots were aglow in the light of the flames beneath them, with the rest of their bodies silhouetted by the full moon.

Nahlra lagged behind, crying. Young Sevi pulled at her, trying to make her go faster while trying not to cry, too, until a knight finally scooped her up and carried her along in his arms. "It's alright, little princess," he said. "Sssh. Don't fret. We need to be quiet, understand? Can you do that for me? Can you be brave?"

Nahlra quieted for a moment before wailing again with renewed vigor, howling her pitiful cries shrilly down the hall. "M-Mommy!"

"Ssh ssh ssh. Here, here," the knight said, lifting his visor to reveal a wrinkled, kindly face. He undid the strap of his helm and took it off entirely, showing a head of dark hair that was graying at the edges. "Here, put this on. There, you see! You're a knight now! Sier Nahlra! The king and queen need brave knights, you know. Can you be brave for me, Sier Nahlra?" He placed the helm over the little girl's head. She reached up with both hands and pulled it down tightly, muffling her small, hopeless sounds.

Young Sevi clutched at his father's robes, trying to keep pace with the king while Alramar flanked the other side, angry and tear-stricken. They passed by another window, granting another look outside.

One of the three Silvakin was missing.

A horrible crash echoed behind them. They turned and watched in horror as a wooden soldier of the Silent Grove barreled into the hallway from the window, sending glass shards flying as it untucked itself from a roll and flared its wings. It brought its sword out in one smooth motion as it stood up, readying it at them.

The king didn't waste a breath. "Argold! Galvor! Vanathier!"

Three of the knights left the ring, discarding their polearms in favor of their swords within the tight confines of the hallway.

Another window crashed. A second Silvakin appeared ahead of them just as the first, cutting off their route to the royal chambers. Both warriors lifted their swords in perfect unison, setting them aflame with a flick of their wrists.

"Blazes!" King Marovhan spat, picking up a polearm without hesitation.

The knight carrying Nahlra set her down next to Alramar. "Look after your brother and sister, my prince," he said, facing the second enemy and drawing his sword.

They all turned their backs to the children, creating a ring of protection around them. Marovhan readied the polearm at the second Silvakin. "My knights, tonight, I hold you to your vows. Defend my family and *see your own again!*"

The Silvakin hissed and leapt forward, swinging their fiery swords down into the knights. The knights yelled and fearlessly met their blades, hacking and thrusting without hesitation, fighting with all the strength and desperation of cornered men. Alramar put himself in front of Young Sevi and Nahlra, backing them against the wall with a scared but determined expression.

The first Silvakin moved like a demon, swinging, thrusting, and slicing its blade fast enough to keep up with the three knights, beating its wings to crop up a distracting wind and gain distance whenever it felt pressed. But whenever one of the knights' swords glanced off its armor, the wood withered, blackening at the touch of the deadly steel. One even scored a hit across the Silvakin's mask, cracking it like porcelain and eliciting a hiss from within, drawing the creature's ire.

The Silvakin swung its blade with startling speed, slashing a fiery streak through the air and catching the audacious knight before he could block. Where the iron should have succeeded in dispelling the fiery hex of the blade, the faeblade inexplicably sliced through his armor like butter, slitting his belly open and sending him screaming to the floor.

King Marovhan and the helmless knight's fight went evenly at first, with the king and the knight trying to trap the Silent Grove warrior between them, but there wasn't enough room to maneuver. The Silvakin slashed its sword at the knight before battering the king's face with a vicious backhand, cutting open his cheek and flinging his crown from his head.

The knight stepped in front, taking the blows from the Silvakin while Marovhan retreated, blood spilling down his throat. But he didn't waver. He stayed behind the knight and timed his thrusts with the polearm, stabbing at the creature with practiced movements born from years of the finest training. The knight, in turn, followed the Silvakin whenever it retreated, unbothered by its beating wings and pressing the advantage in a deadly display of intuition, slowly gaining ground toward the Royal Chambers.

"KIDS! WITH ME!" King Marovhan yelled.

Alramar tugged Sevi and Nahlra after their father, keeping a distance away from the king while he fought, but close enough not to be left behind. The king held the weapon before him with eyes focused on the Silvakin, taking a step back to give the knight more room, letting the creature focus on him.

The knight swept his sword in an arc from the side, parrying the blade, then brought his foot back and delivered a savage kick, breaking the creature's guard.

Marovhan struck, driving the polearm straight into the Silvakin's chest, but failed to pierce its carapace. The Silvakin grabbed the weapon's shaft, trying to free itself before its armor crumbled, and lifted its sword to cleave the pike's head from the staff.

The knight was ready for it. He caught the blade with his own, grabbed the Silvakin, and swept it off its feet. Marovhan followed through, stepping forward and running his iron spike deeper into its body, gritting his teeth and letting out a fierce, howling yell as the Silvakin crashed to the ground.

The Silvakin's armor disintegrated. The iron ran through, and the creature let out a pitiful, wailing shriek, dropping its sword and clutching at the shaft as a fountain of blood spurted from its belly. King Marovhan twisted the weapon and the creature wailed louder, until the knight swept his blade and lopped the Silvakin's head off completely, silencing it forever.

"RUN!"

Marovhan, the knight, and all three kids whipped their heads around as one. Another knight had been cut down by the first wooden warrior, and the one remaining was desperately trying to hold it off, rapidly losing ground and slipping in the pools of blood spreading from his fallen comrades.

"*Move!*" the helmless knight shouted, sheathing his sword before scooping up both Nahlra and Sevi. They bolted around the corner of the hall, sprinting toward the waiting doors of the parlor, reaching its handle just as a horrified scream echoed down the corridor before cutting off abruptly.

The knight settled Nahlra and Sevi back on the floor, then stood up and took the polearm from Marovhan. "Get to the study. I'll keep it at bay."

The king hesitated, flicking his gaze down the hall then back to the knight. "My children and I owe you our lives."

"Thank me by surviving," the knight said, turning away. "*Go.* Now." He tried to step forward, but stopped short, looking down in surprise.

Nahlra had grabbed his leg. She still had his helmet on. She stared up at him with wide, watery eyes on a tight-lipped face. With small, trembling hands, she lifted the helmet off her head and held it up to him in silent offering.

The knight blinked, then gave her a small, sad smile. "Hold onto it for me, Sier Nahlra. Your family still needs a knight to protect them."

The little girl's face broke, and she started to cry even harder, pulling the helm to her chest.

A fire appeared down the hallway. The remaining Silent Grove soldier turned the corner with its blade at its side, leaving bloody footprints in its wake.

"*Go!*" the knight barked.

"Thank you," the king said, pulling the children into the parlor and slamming the door behind him. The last thing Sevi saw was the Silvakin raising its sword while the knight stepped forward to meet it.

The man had never said his name.

King Marovhan threw open the doors into the bedroom and got his children inside before shutting and locking them. He ran over to the fireplace, wiping the blood from his face before taking scraps of tinder and hay from the pile and throwing it into the hearth.

The sound of striking metal echoed from outside. The king didn't pause for a moment, taking the firestarter and striking flint against steel in desperate scrapes, over and over again, until at last the hay caught. He dropped to his knees and began to blow, coaxing the flames higher and higher, until a small fire crackled in the logs.

The sounds of battle outside grew louder. Sevi could hear the knight's shouts through the doors. The king threw himself at the secret mark, pressing his hand into it and holding his palm in place for a torturous ten breaths. The fire turned black and blazed up, eating away at the wall to reveal the study. "Get in!" Marovhan yelled.

The kids rushed to obey. Marovhan entered last and resealed the door. When the royal chambers disappeared, silencing the horrible sounds outside, his shoulders finally sagged, and he let out a long, weary breath, turning to his group of terrified children. He beckoned softly, approaching them with arms wide and dropping to his knees. "My loves."

They all huddled in, clutching at each other in a tangle of trembling limbs. Tears were running down their father's cheeks, mixing with the blood from his wound. Sevi had never seen him cry before. "We're alright," Marovhan said softly to them. "We're alright."

Alramar was the first to back away, furiously wiping his face with the back of his hand. He turned and stalked into a corner, sitting with his back to the room. Marovhan sighed and turned to Nahlra, asking, "How about a treat? Would you like that?" Nahlra sniffed and bobbed her head, still clutching the helmet to her chest. Their father led her by the hand toward the back of the room.

Sevi remained where he was, staring at Alramar's back and wiping his eyes free of tears. "Al?" His brother didn't respond. "Alramar?"

"Go away," Alramar muttered.

"Al... please." Sevi stepped closer.

Alramar whipped around and shoved Sevi over. "*I said leave!*" Alramar yelled. Sevi stared up at his brother in shock, pulling himself backward along the floor. Alramar stood and balled his hands into fists, full of rage.

"Stop that this instant!" King Marovhan demanded from across the room.

"Why are we *here?*" Alramar shook his head, tense with emotion. "Why isn't Mother with us? *Why are we being attacked?*" Nahlra began to cry again. "Shut up, Nahlra."

"Alramar, *stop it*," the king ordered. "You're scaring your brother and sister."

"*I'm* scaring them?" Alramar scoffed. "Why are we hiding? Why aren't we *doing* something about this? You're supposed to be the king!" He pointed his finger at Father. "YOU should be the one out there facing whatever those things are, *not Mother!*"

"ALRAMAR."

Their father's voice rose to encompass the whole room. Deep, powerful, and angry. He only used that voice when they had been especially bad. Marovhan dropped Nahlra's hand and approached Alramar with a stony expression, but it didn't hold. Sadness ingrained itself in every facet of his face with such intensity that even his beard couldn't hide it. Alramar reflexively shrunk away, but the king didn't move to punish him. He simply closed his hands on Alramar's shoulders and stared deeply into his eyes. "I worry for her, too," the king said softly.

Alramar's rage crumbled completely. He dove for the king's legs, clutching his father's pants and sobbing furiously against him. The king held him silently, closing his eyes, and said nothing more.

Nahlra barreled into the king's other leg, doing the same as Alramar. Squeezing his shirt, Sevi stood up from the floor and moved to join them when a wind blew behind him. Alramar stopped crying. The king looked up. Sevi stopped mid-stride and turned slowly around.

The doorway was opening again.

"NO!" the king yelled in sudden panic, leaping away from his children and diving toward the marker stone. His fingers had only just grazed it, setting it to close, when something leapt over the threshold and rolled with the creak of heavy wooden armor and the flap of massive wings.

The Silvakin's armor had cracked all across its carapace, and its mask had crumbled at the mouth. A pair of ruby lips pulled up to bare a set of glistening white teeth as the creature snarled ferally at them. In one hand it held its burning sword. The other dripped with blood.

Marovhan's eyes widened. He lifted his hand to the cut at his cheek just as the Silvakin leapt.

Their father threw up his arms, stumbling back.

The monster's burning sword plunged into the king's chest and out his back. He gasped with shock, blood burbling at his lips, and slumped his head toward the terrified faces of his children. His clothing caught, setting him ablaze. "No," he breathed. Then the light left his eyes, and he saw no more.

The Silvakin dipped its sword, letting the king's body slide off it with contempt. It turned its evil gaze on the children. They each stood frozen, clutching each other in fear.

The study's door finished closing. The creature approached them, unhurried and inevitable. There was nowhere left to run, and nowhere left to hide. All that remained was death. It reached for Sevi, the closest, spreading its fingers to close around his neck. Sevi opened his mouth to scream, but he had forgotten how.

Something moved beside him. The Silvakin yanked its hand back with a hiss. Sevi looked down. Nahlra stood beside him, holding her helmet out with shaking arms, putting herself between him and the monster. Trying to defend her brother. Her eyes were hollow and red with tears, and her small body trembled so violently that she couldn't walk straight.

The Silvakin swung its sword.

Alramar shoved his sister from its path.

The sword struck Alramar across the face. He fell. But the Silvakin didn't stop. It stepped forward, winding its hand back and swinging it in a terrible backhand, cracking its knuckles across Nahlra's cheek with a sickening *snap*. The little girl went flying, crashing into the furniture and landing in a heap of twisted limbs. She didn't move.

The creature got to Sevi and closed its hand around his neck, effortlessly lifting him off the floor and slamming him into the wall, driving the air from his lungs. It leaned in, hissing through its terrible teeth.

"Help," Sevi gasped. "Help me! *Alramar!*"

With a jerk of its arm, the Silvakin pulled its sword back and drove it through Sevi's belly.

Sevi flinched. Blinking, he turned his head down, just as his father had, to stare at the sword sticking into him. It didn't hurt. It didn't burn.

It felt cold. So very, very cold. The monster curled its mouth up in a sneer and met his gaze, boring its red, hateful eyes into Sevi's soul as it stole his life from him.

Then Alramar jumped onto its back and slammed Nahlra's helmet over its head. "GET AWAY FROM MY FAMILY!" Alramar screeched.

The Silvakin screamed and pulled its sword from Sevi, dropping him to the floor. Alramar clung on to the creature's back as if possessed, wrapping his legs around its hips and holding the iron helmet down with all his strength, determinedly not letting go no matter how the Silvakin flailed.

The creature whirled with a flap of wings, flinging its arms out and dropping its sword. It grasped at the helmet, desperately trying to get it off, even jumping backward and slamming Alramar into the bookshelves. His brother didn't let go.

The creature wailed again. The iron ate at its gauntlets, crumbling them into dust, and soon it couldn't touch the helmet without burning its hands, making it wail even more. It rammed its back into the bookshelves again, and Alramar grunted, loosening his grip as his head struck the wood. Sensing an opening, the Silvakin stepped forward and rammed its back again.

Alramar slumped, but only tightened his grip.

The Silvakin rolled, tumbling across the floor. More and more of its protective mask fell away. It got onto its knees and threw its head back, bashing the iron into Alramar's face, and the boy, at long last, fell off its back, gushing blood from his nose.

The upper half of the creature's mask fell away. Its face was blistered and burned, its skin was green, and its eyes were bloodshot and red, but the real Sevi would recognize the face of his best friend anywhere.

Lily screamed, curling her fingers into claws as her body snapped taut with pain. She screamed and screamed and screamed, trying over and over to get the helmet off to no avail, sobbing as it flayed the flesh of her palms and skull.

Her wings drooped and crumbled away. Her green skin turned white. Her eyes dimmed, losing the terrible red that filled her pupils and turning them back into the familiar emerald he knew. After a final scream of pain, her jaw went slack and her body listed. She fell to the stone with a heavy, lifeless *thud*, blistering and burning wherever the iron touched. Silent, and still.

Alramar coughed, pulling himself shakily to his feet. He held his head in his hands, trying to staunch the blood that fell freely from his nose. He stumbled back to Sevi, who had watched the fight without a word, clutching his open belly with blood bubbling from his lips.

"Sev... Sevi," Alramar muttered, falling to his hands and knees.

Sevi coughed, reaching out with a trembling hand.

"Y-you're al-alright," Alramar stuttered, grabbing at Sevi's hand. A wound, grisly and burned at the edges, swept down his face from the top of his forehead and across his cheek. "We're alright. We're alright."

"Nahlra." Sevi choked. He flung a weak hand to where the little girl had landed. She still hadn't moved.

"We're alright. We're alright," Alramar said again, holding Sevi's hand in both of his.

Sevi looked at his brother. His wonderful, smart, strong older brother. The one who had gotten them into so much trouble. The one who had never stopped bullying him and Nahlra. The one who would snap, and lose his temper, and hide away in his secret tunnels so that no one would see him cry.

The one who would sacrifice himself to fight a monster, just to save his family.

Oh, how he loved him.

Sevi's eyes rolled back, and his hand fell from Alramar's grip. Alramar watched it go, choking out a gasp, scrabbling at his younger brother's arm in desperation.

The room grew silent, save for the crackling of their father, burning on the floor.

Moments passed. Alaramar didn't move from his brother's body. Eventually, the fires on King Marovhan's clothes went out on their own, leaving the room in the ghastly glow of the ceiling's runelight with an overwhelming smell of burnt flesh.

Only then did Alramar stand up and slowly face the room. A chuckle bubbled out of his throat. Then a laugh. Then a hysterical cackle.

"They're all gone." He chortled, bursting with insane giggles between words. "They left me. They *left* me!"

He strode over to his father's corpse, reached down, and yanked the necklace off him, putting it over his head. He didn't flinch as the hot metal seared into his chest. "Long live the *king!*" he cried, bowing to the tomb before him.

His body gave out. Gravity took hold of him, bringing him to his knees, then tugging him down entirely. He stayed on the floor, curled himself into a ball with his arms over his eyes, and let darkness take the world away.

The scene faded. When it returned, it was in flashes of half-lucid memories of all that transpired after the death of his family. Fleeing the royal study and all its corpses through a magical, disappearing door. Shoving aside an entrystone and throwing himself into the safety of the Cut, where no one could find him. Scrambling through the pitch black and babbling to himself, living off tunnel moss and cave rats whenever he got hungry.

His world became darkness. Darkness was where he couldn't be found. Darkness was where he was safe. Darkness was where he could survive. He would take the darkness, fill up his head with it, and never live in pain again. And it worked.

Then the fire found him again.

Alramar threw himself back against the wall, shielding his eyes from the blinding light that banished his precious dark. He whimpered, crying out in fear and pain as it seared into his brain.

"Hello, boy."

He stilled, slowly lowering his arms and squinting through the haze of his blindness. A voice. When had he last heard a voice? Had he ever heard a voice?

A form materialized from the fog, and Lily, with an intimately familiar helmet on her head, emerged, now absent her Silent Grove amor and shrunk to her normal size. She held a torch before her, peering at Alramar from beyond the flames. Alramar stared in fear at the fire, pressing his back into the stone. "It's alright," Lily said softly, approaching him with her free hand extended. "I won't hurt you."

More voice. More sounds. Ripping away his quiet darkness. No. Bad. Pain.

Lily unslung a bag from her shoulder and dropped it to the floor. "You have a lovely shadow, you know," she said just as softly, bringing out a glass jar. Inside of it lay a swirling void of night, with two small, little stars glinting out from its depths. She got to her knees and set the torch down, then undid the cork. "Would you mind sharing it with your brother and sister?"

She placed the rim of the jar against the ground, and the night inside of it spilled out, slithering across the floor. Alramar scrabbled at the stone, trying to dig away from it before it touched him, but no matter how hard he pressed his bloody fingers into the wall, it wouldn't give. The sliver of night found his feet, binding itself to the flickering shadow already there and matching its form, until the two were indistinguishable. The two little stars within faded away.

Lily breathed with relief, offering him a small smile. "There. That wasn't so bad, was it?"

No. Bad. Pain. Such feelings drove out all memory of the magic that had only just occurred. Intruder. Danger. Run. Alramar bunched up a handful of rocks and flung them at Lily with a screech.

She merely stared at him. Soft. Pitying. Guilty. He found himself stilling, ensnared by her gaze. So green. So colorful. When had he last seen color? Had he ever seen color?

"What's your name?" the girl asked softly.

It came to him from a great distance, piercing his fog for but a moment. A name he used to love. "S...Sevi," he said softly.

"Sevi," Lily repeated, lifting her chin. "I'm going to take care of you, Sevi. I'll make you better. You and I are going to be partners. Now and forever. I promise."

The mirror world dissolved, dropping the real Sevi unceremoniously back into the bedroom. Sitting at the mirror, he stared wide-eyed at himself and raised a hand to his cheek, touching the scar on his face.

Isevidel? No.

Alramar.

# Chapter 53

...

———— ⚬∽⚬ ————

The boy traveled through the tunnels of his home. Soundless. Formless. Nameless.

The shadows were his only company. Some with eyes, some without. Those feelings that had clamored inside of him for so long, fighting for control of his will, had fallen still. But now they each had grown a face and a name, following the boy through the dark.

Nahlra. Isevidel. Alramar.

Opening the way had been a trivial matter. A lock of the doors with a table beneath the handles. A chair as a ram on a wall of drying mortar. They had tried to stop him. They had pounded on the doors, crying out a name that wasn't his. Lady Night should have left a pair of her eyes in the room to watch over him. She was foolish. She was blinded by the darkness inside of her. But not him. Not anymore.

He came around a corner. There were strangers in the tunnels with him. He took back what he thought about Lady Night. She was thorough. She was searching for the monsters that lurked in the dark with burning blades, and green skin, and red eyes.

The strangers looked afraid. They shouldn't be. Darkness wasn't just fear. Darkness was whatever one made it to be. So, the boy called upon the newly replenished darkness that followed him and made it into a cloak that shielded him from the strangers' light, and they passed him by without a word.

He went on. He didn't need light. He didn't need to see. He knew his home, and most importantly, he knew how to find the place where stone met sky. Where the castle's largest tower imprisoned those it deemed unsightly.

Up, up, up he climbed. Away from the ground. Away from the world. Away from the light.

The light was pain. It showed the world for what it really was. It made him feel things he never wanted to feel again. And yet, he was drawn to it. A piece of that light resided in him, begging for its other half. He had to make it whole once more, or the pain would flutter forever in his chest as a broken thing, stabbing at him from the inside and adding new misery to the old.

He had to find the rest. And he knew where to look.

The boy searched through every crack in the walls just as he had for so many years, peering into every nook and cranny, searching high and low for the light, until he stumbled across a strange sound. A sad sound. Sad, and beautiful.

It sang through the walls. It made the stone weep. It filled him with such misery and longing that the darkness within him receded a fraction, and the darkness that followed him faded to mist, blinking its two little lights before disappearing entirely. It was scared of that voice. But it would be back when he called for it. It wouldn't leave him again.

He touched his forehead to the wall, letting the song wash over him.

*The moment the walls of our home had been breached,*
*I knew how our story would end.*
*The way that you looked in that circlet of gold.*
*The way that I tried to pretend.*
*Oh mouse, how you hoped, how you gathered your light,*
*weaving a heavenly band.*
*Shining as bright as the moon in her veil,*
*as one with the star in your hand.*
*Did you laugh when you saw? Was my face so surprised?*
*At all, did my mien make you pause?*
*Were you blinded by the glitter of hundreds of shimmers,*
*or did you see me as I was?*

# THE DANCE BETWEEN

*As the hour grew dark, you drove it away,*
*as you'd done for me so many times.*
*Did I ever say? Did I fear the words?*
*Shall it add to the list of my crimes?*
*If I have but a wish, please remember that moment.*
*Dream it at every chance.*
*May your heart fill your body with a love that renews you...*
*May you always remember our dance.*

The singing stopped. The boy angrily wiped his face as fragments of light inside of him threatened to spill out. But he took them and stuffed them into his belly, smothering them with darkness before they could take hold. He placed one hand on the wall and pushed a stone forward. It fell into the room beyond, revealing a window he would sometimes look through, back when he had a name—a false name for a false person.

Inside was a girl, wreathed in moonlight that glittered on every piece of patchwork metal in her clothing. She had a scarred head that had somehow managed to grow a ratty patch of short, red hair. Sharp ears ran along her skull, and she sat with her back up against a wall, gazing out of her barred window with an expression of total peace. She didn't look at him, but she knew he was there. She always knew everything. And sure enough, she spoke.

"Hello, boy," she said. "Did you like my song?"

The boy didn't answer. The wind whistled through the bars of her cell, shaking the tower gently. "It's a Lament," she explained, reaching her hand out as if to grab one of the moonbeams. "It's tradition to sing one on nights like this, when the moon is full and watching."

Still, the boy did not answer.

"I told you one, not long ago. Though it was meant to be sung. I could sing it for you, if you'd like."

"They're all lies," the boy said at last.

The girl didn't speak for a while. "Sometimes we need to lie," she said at last. "Sometimes the truth is too much to bear."

"Your lies ruined my life."

The girl fell silent.

"I was becoming someone," the boy mourned. "I was finding who I was. Who I was meant to be. But the who that I thought I was is a lie. Nothing but a lie. More truths you kept from me."

She turned her head away from him.

"Now I'll never know. I'm not Isevidel, yet I wear his face. I'm not Alramar, yet I have his scar. Am I Nahlra, too?" He looked down at his hands. "I haven't even aged as I should. How much of me is them? How much of me is what you've turned me into? How much was left after you murdered everything I had?"

"You've remembered," the girl said, barely loud enough for him to hear.

"Tell me why you killed them," the boy demanded. "And tell me the truth."

The girl stayed silent, looking as carved from stone as the brick in the walls. But when she turned to face him, there was no mask on her face. No attempt to hide her emotions—there were no emotions to hide. Only emptiness.

The boy slammed his hands against the wall. "*Tell me!*"

"Do you think I'm a monster, Sevi?" she asked, using his stolen name.

The boy clenched his fists. "I do."

"Then I'll tell you the story of a monster." The girl pushed off the wall and stood up, shimmering with every motion until she fell into shadow. She moved across the room slowly, dragging an iron chain attached to her ankle behind her, to eventually sit down before his window, staring into his darkness as though she could see through it. "This is the story of a monster named Lily," she began.

"I don't *care!*" the boy spat.

She continued as if she hadn't heard him. "Once upon a time, Lily lived in a far away land, in a cottage in the woods with her many brothers and sisters. Not Fae, but half, with some of the power of their mother, and the mortal spirit of their father.

"In this forest was a tree. A giant tree with branches that reached up to the sky. She and her family would drink from this tree and grow strong. Wings would grow from their backs. Fire would form in their hands. Rain would fall at a whisper. It was a very, very special tree.

"Lily lived there for many years. Or maybe not. She can't remember some of them, and she never bothered to count. Perhaps it was five. Perhaps it was ten. Perhaps it was fifteen. But she was never unhappy. Whenever she felt even the slightest bit sad, she would merely think a thought, and all her brothers and sister's voices would come spilling into her head to remind her that she wasn't alone.

"But not all of her siblings were nice. Some of them were very, very mean. Some of them bullied her and made her do things she didn't want to do. Sometimes they would make her play games she didn't want to play. They were so very old you see, and so knowledgeable on how to move their younger siblings as they wanted. But after living for so very, very long, and after discovering so many things, and playing many games, they grew bored.

"They went looking for something different. They had heard, in a nearby land, that a new toy had been created—one that could really hurt them. So, they decided that they would take that toy for themselves, or break it, if they couldn't have it.

"They went in with wings and toys and magic to impress the people of this land, to draw all eyes to the things they could do, so that they knew that they were strong but kind. Then they sent Lily and their other younger brothers and sisters in with faces that looked just like the people of this land, to watch and to learn.

"She spied on the Kaymoors, who held such strong command that all would bow to their whims. She spied on the Engroms, who fought with such honor that even death could not break them. She spied on so many, many people... And Lily found that she loved them. Even as she worked against them, spreading lies and feeding them blood. She couldn't hear their thoughts, but the only people who bullied her were the ones she allowed.

"But when her elder siblings had seen enough and learned enough, they poured so much of the tree's amber down Lily's throat that her arms and legs grew, her skin turned green, and her eyes turned red. Then they put her in armor and sent her out to kill the very people she'd fallen in love with. And she did. Very, very well, until not an inch of her skin was left untouched by blood... And then..."

The girl stopped. Her voice tightened, and her eyes turned glassy as she looked off at a distant memory, buried in the darkness of her own being. "And then she was *saved*," she whispered. "By a young boy. A prince, whose family she had only just slain, locked her in a metal box. The box hurt. The box was heavy. In that box was a fire birthed by iron that ate her skin and drank all the magic she held dear. It should have killed her... but it didn't. As fate would have it, she was one of the very few Silvakin who could withstand its touch without dying. But more than that, she couldn't hear her brothers and sisters anymore. She had become herself again. Drained... but herself. And when she awoke, she tried so desperately to fix all that she had ruined.

"First, she went to the prince's father, who she had set ablaze. He was beyond her help. Then she went to his brother and sister, who she had crushed, but who's breaths still blew—if only faintly. She pressed her hands to each of them, begging them to come back to life. But the best she could do was give them half. For magic needs two things to be: tinder, and a spark. She was almost too weak to light the flame, and too much of their lives had seeped away. All she could manage was... was tying them to one who had enough. Thus, the prince gained a second shadow."

Again, the girl wiped her face. "The prince had lost his mind, having seen all that he loved destroyed before him, and with no one left to care for him. At first, wrought with guilt, the girl thought to leave him. But there were other monsters like her outside, and she had become very, very small. She waited with the boy, alone in their tunnels, and tried to call him back, but he couldn't hear her voice. And his new shadow, she found, had retained a mind of its own. It whispered to him, changed him, body and mind, giving him the face of his brother and the gentleness of the sister he loved. Just as he was lending his life to it, it was giving pieces of itself in return.

"This scared Lily. She had no idea what more her spell would do—perhaps the shadows of the brother and sister would steal too much. And it appeared to feed the prince memories as more of its strength returned. So, she fashioned two instruments—one for each soul—to bind the shadow. To keep it at bay... And to keep the prince from remembering her.

"But now, she realizes, far too late, that she shouldn't have. The shadow still had the spirit of the brother and sister. Their souls. The souls of *children*. Children afraid of the monster that had killed them and forced them to live alone in the dark; both unable to die, and now unable to be with their elder brother. How could she ever do something so horrific? How could she think that they would ever hurt someone they loved?"

The girl's face tightened and she closed her eyes. "Eventually, the rest of the monsters outside left, and Lily, small, weak Lily, had nowhere to go, and no one to help her. But the prince? The prince had his castle. And it had so many, many tunnels. Enough to get lost in and hide away forever. He just needed someone to help him, and if he couldn't remember Lily, then maybe... maybe she could have a second chance. To help him. To be with someone who wouldn't use her, nor see her as the monster she saw in herself. To save him, like he'd saved her.

"So, she poured what little of her magic remained into a flower, breathing life into her and only drawing from her when she needed. She let the prince name her as his third companion, then disappeared into the castle's deepest, darkest, most hidden places with him, where the monsters outside couldn't reach. And when those monsters returned, preventing them from leaving, she devoted all of herself to protecting him, secretly praying that he would never remember who she used to be.

"And there she remains in the dark, too afraid to brave the outside alone and hoping that the world she fell in love with will one day invite her to stay... The end."

The light from inside the boy, finally whole, leaked from his eyes and ran down his face. With it came the name he had stolen, latching onto him and refusing to be thrown away again. Not Isevidel, but Sevi; the identity he'd built for himself over four years. He couldn't be the former anymore, nor Alramar—he had to be someone new.

But what did that mean? Sevi the tunnel rat. Isevidel the sickly prince. Alramar the adopted. Nahlra the gentle. And now the entire country believed him to be Isevidel the Reborn.

Was he any of them, all of them, or none of them?

Sevi wiped his face and sniffed, staring cheerlessly through the wall at Lily. The cause of his pain, and his salvation. The person he'd saved. The person who'd saved him. The girl he hated and loved with all that he was. "You should have told me," he whispered.

"I know," Lily said, spilling silver from her emerald eyes. "I love you, Sevi. I love you so, so much. And I'm sorry. So very, very sorry. With all my heart." She looked down. "Please... find the amber. I can feel Alyda slipping away again."

She picked up the brick and pushed it back into the wall, sealing them both away inside their prisons of stone.

# Chapter 54

...

━━━━━━━━━━━━━━━━━━━━━━━━━

Sevi let the soldiers in the Cut take him when they found him. He dutifully followed them back to his room, with its new guards and freshly broken-in doors, and sat on the sofa with a plate of cold food, staring at the study. Its threshold had taken on an entirely new meaning to him. He finished his plate by the time Lady Night appeared, angry and formidable.

"You went to see her," Tiersa said.

Sevi looked at her. "What's the Argennium?"

She froze. Her hands drifted to the hilts of her swords. "Did she speak of it to you?"

"It's what this is all about, isn't it?" Sevi went on. "It's why the Fae came here in the first place. It's why you fought so hard to get here. The fact that it's the place where our family died was just a convenient excuse."

Tiersa jerked her head at the guards in the room. "Leave us."

Sevi kept his eyes trained on Tiersa as the soldiers left. "Tell me."

Tiersa adjusted and readjusted her grip on her sword hilts. "I didn't want to involve you," she said at last. "It could be dangerous. And you've seen so much blood already."

"But I'll bet you need me for it," Sevi said. "I've been thinking. If this is a weapon, why didn't the Fae take it? Why did they collapse the mountain instead? It's because they couldn't get to it. The mountain is full of quicksilver, and if one needs royal blood to enter a private study of all things, then I'll bet there's more to whatever it is that guards the weapon. So, the best that the Fae could do was seal it up and pray that it was never found again.

"Also," he continued, "my necklace is missing. You took it, didn't you?" He leveled a hard stare at her. She didn't look away. Slowly, she took her hand off one sword, dipped it into her coat, and pulled out his scratched up, damaged necklace, now missing its bullet. He flicked his gaze down to it then back up at her. "You tried using them for something, didn't you? You couldn't just use your own."

"Yes," Tiersa said plainly.

"And it didn't work." She gave no response. He stood. "Take me to it."

"No, Isevidel—"

"Tiersa, I'm tired," he said, crossing his arms. "Tired of people dancing around me with their little lies, their plans, and treating me based on things I don't remember or never knew. My memory is healing, but even if it never does completely, it won't matter. I'm someone else now, and that someone is telling you, in no uncertain terms, to take me to the *godsdamned weapon* so that I can finally understand what the *fuck* is going on."

Tiersa's expression cracked as she stared at Sevi in open surprise. He didn't back down. He waited, watching her expectantly. "I promised to protect you, Isevidel," she finally said. "You're demanding that I put you in danger."

Sevi lifted his chin. "I was attacked, in this very castle, surrounded by hundreds of your soldiers. I'm going to be in danger for the rest of my life—there's no escaping it. And if this Argennium is truly meant for me, then something tells me that it, out of everything else, won't hurt me."

Commander Tiersa tapped at the hilt of one sword, letting silence fall between them. Finally, she stepped forward and held his necklace out to him. He took it. "Follow me," she said.

—— ◈ ——

# THE DANCE BETWEEN

"Your mother didn't tell me everything," Tiersa explained, walking through the castle. She sent orders ahead of her to gather several captains, and to meet her with their companies in the gardens. "I know that work on the Argennium began one or two generations before your parents, and under them, finally completed. I know that it was meant to be a deterrent, or a weapon, for the sake of defense against the Fae. And I know from the documents that I've gathered from the royal study that it's been tested, but there were complications. That is the extent of what I've learned."

Sevi raised an eyebrow. "Is it?"

"Do not test me Isevidel," Tiersa said, flashing a disapproving glare at him. "It is as you said. We've found the door, but even with the keys, we've been unable to enter. The only possible reason left to us is that it's enchanted."

"Then I guess we'll soon find out."

They didn't say anything further until they reached the gardens. Most of the nobles' carriages were gone. Two squads of soldiers and one squad of Empyreans had been mustered, sluggishly assembling in the courtyard, facing toward the castle. Three captains arrived and stood at the front of each company: Captain Vykka, Captain River, and a third captain that Sevi didn't recognize.

But there were others as well. A person stood next to Captain Vykka with a bag over their head, wearing a dirty but familiar green uniform that marked them as a Silvakin soldier. Sevi was also surprised to see Corporal Reynam standing behind River, now wearing a blue lieutenant's uniform. Reynam caught his stare and rolled his shoulders, as if to say, *I'm just as surprised as you are.*

"Captain Vykka, I want every owl you have up in the sky, all night," Tiersa commanded when the last soldier had assembled. "Captain Ornavel, man the walls and grounds. Stop anyone who crosses them and send them back to the castle. Captain River, you and I will be going into the mountain. Bring half of your men in and leave the other half to guard the entrance. Get to it, everyone."

The Empyreans and foot soldiers split to accomplish their assigned tasks, with River's company falling into line behind Sevi and Tiersa.

Tiersa took the hooded figure from Captain Vykka and pushed them over to Reynam. Captain River and Reynam each cast curious looks at Sevi. "Are the Fae returned?" River asked Tiersa, stepping beside her with his hands behind his back.

"No," she replied. "And with any luck after tonight, they never will again."

Captain River raised his eyebrows but didn't comment. He slowed his steps to join Sevi. "I am happy to see you well, *risho*."

"I'm alive, if that's what you mean," Sevi said stiffly.

"I have heard of what has happened. I am very sorry about your friend. And... I share your sorrow at the loss of my lieutenant," he said softly. Sevi pursed his lips and swallowed his grief, focusing only on the path ahead.

Two guards stood at the tunnel leading into the mountain. Commander Tiersa paused beside them and gathered a bundle of torches, handing one to River and Sevi each before proceeding. Sevi lingered at the threshold, staring at the rock as visions of his mother and father played across his mind, but he gritted his teeth and entered with a determined shake of his head.

The tunnel was deep enough for its end to be obscured. The air was filled with the sound of marching boots and mutterings as River's soldiers squeezed in single file, following the light. Captain River passed his torch back along the line, letting one of his soldiers take it to brighten the path for the others.

After a short while of walking, the tunnel opened into a small cavern. A beam of moonlight from a hole cut into the ceiling illuminated the room, where at its far end, set into the surrounding rock, lay two big iron-plated doors. Flat, and entirely featureless, save for two insignias in the shape of the Astraeda star, burnt into the metal where handles should be.

The floor was completely covered in dust and debris. Strangely, a pile of discarded Silvakaen uniforms, singed along the edges, had been piled up in a corner. Tiersa approached the doors while River's soldiers funneled in, spreading out around the perimeter. Captain River followed after a moment of inspection, waving for Reynam and his charge.

# THE DANCE BETWEEN

"Come here, Isevidel," Tiersa called. Sevi trudged forward, nervous now that the moment had arrived. He clutched at his necklace as he stood before the doors, running his gaze over their dull sheen, flickering orange in the torchlight. Tiersa took her necklace off and placed it in his hands. "You must be the one to do it. Everyone else, close your eyes, and do not open until I command it. When I was here last a great beam of silver washed over me and nearly blinded me. A trap set for a greenblood, no doubt."

She took Sevi's torch from him then stepped away, taking position next to River. Sevi stared at the pair of stars in his hands. One damaged, one whole. He ran his thumbs over the face of each, lingering at the now empty dent in the middle of his own. Taking the necklaces in one hand, he approached the left door and touched its insignia, whispering, "In that tangled mess of movement and life..."

After several breaths, the insignia rippled beneath his touch as though alive. Then the metal melted, retreating into the door to reveal a star-shaped slot within an encompassing circle. He lifted Tiersa's pendant, slotting it into the iron with barely any effort. "Somehow, they found each other," he said, repeating the process with the other door. His star, bent and damaged, needed to be pushed, but it clicked into place.

The moonlight filtering in from above dimmed as something moved in front of it, then vanished altogether. Sevi took a timid step backward, waiting for something to happen.

Something hissed. A series of runes appeared from the bottom of the doors, glowing red as though burning their way out of the steel. They scratched a path all the way to the ceiling in a hundred different shapes, organically flowing and shifting off each other, but never touching. When both doors had been completely covered, the star insets shook, dispelling dust gathered from years of neglect, and began to spin.

Around and around they went in their metal rings, turning in half a dozen revolutions. A heavy humming reverberated from somewhere within the walls, shaking the doors gently. The cylinders trembled, and then popped partway out of the walls with a synchronous *thunk*, expelling the pendants from their slots.

The humming stopped. The doors opened a sliver, and a gust of wind blew out from within strong enough to extinguish the nearest torches. Sevi let out a long breath as it washed over him. "And there they remain," he whispered.

"Open your eyes," Tiersa ordered. There was a tremor of excitement in her voice.

Sevi took hold of one door while Tiersa took the other. Captain River waved for the soldiers to pass forward the remaining torch, relighting the other two while they pulled. The doors swung open on ungreased hinges, creaking and groaning in protest until there was space enough to enter. Gathering the necklaces, Sevi stepped forward, but Tiersa held him back, taking the lead instead.

The room was pitch black, and much, much bigger than the cavern they had just left. The walls to the left and right were made entirely of iron, as was the floor beneath them, though it was just as covered in dust as the room outside. To the right of the doors sat two levers, each set into the ground on their own half-wheel of some kind.

River held a torch aloft when he entered, lighting the room as much as he could, but the light would not reach across. Frowning, Tiersa approached the first lever and reached for it, but pulled jerked her hand back. "Isevidel? Would you please?"

Sevi approached with caution, taking the lever in his hand with a wary look and giving it an uncertain yank. It didn't budge. He tried with both hands, putting his whole weight into it, but it only gave the barest of amounts. Commander Tiersa joined him, grabbing it with both hands and pulling it down with their combined weight. It landed in place with a *click*.

Runes appeared on the walls and floor at once, burning their molten orange glow and lighting up one after the other in a ring around the room. Sevi tracked their path, his breath catching in his throat as he waited for both trails to run into each other, but they never did. When they approached the center of the room they stopped, as though disappearing behind something enormous

A terrible screeching filled the air as a massive object began to move, making Sevi jump. Captain River, Reynam, and every soldier went for their guns while Commander Tiersa grabbed hold of her swords, darting glances around the room.

A silver light in the shape of a crescent formed on the left side of the floor. Looking up, Sevi found an immense slab pulling itself away in the ceiling, revealing the night sky and the full moon above, until the entire cavern was flooded in moonlight.

Sevi felt overcome by the strangest understanding of what it was like to be a bug, having its rock peeled away by a curious giant. His gaze wandered, mesmerized by the patterns of dust particles in the moonbeams, until he landed on the mechanism in the middle of the room.

It was as though someone had taken his old spyglass and enlarged it, then given it big, metal arms to hold a series of lenses in increasing sizes. A small, tiered podium rested beneath them with a grate on its top, shielded on the left and right by two curved walls that ran part-way around it, leaving a gap to its front and back. All the runes around the walls and floor seemed to run toward the device in a spiral, ending just around the edges of the podium. And surrounding the mechanism itself, shimmering with all their captured silver dust, stood eight large columns like the ones Sevi had seen on the streets of Ilondia.

"Earuna," Captain River breathed. "What is this place?"

Commander Tiersa eyed the walls where large, vertically-cut slots had been carved into the iron. "Are all of your troops inside the room, River?"

"I believe so, my lady."

Nodding, she experimentally threw the second lever herself. The whole room shook, causing the soldiers to ready their guns again. Tiersa, however, didn't flinch, not even when the floor began to rise.

Runes flashed in rings along the walls as the platform lifted, pushed by some unseen force, ascending higher and higher up the iron shaft. Creaks and groans of metal against metal sounded around them, coupled with a steady humming under their feet, as if something large moved about beneath. The floor jittered, shaking the sand and dust on it like a hundred hissing snakes, pulsing its runes and those along the walls in a rhythmic heartbeat, until the walls fell away and were replaced by open air.

The platform came to a grinding halt. Sevi looked around in amazement. They had gone up the mountain and now stood in a vast sky with nothing but stars above and the world at their feet. The iron beneath them continued to hum, and the runes across the floor flashed in a dazzling display.

The soldiers renewed their whispering and looked around with wonder. Commander Tiersa stepped forward. She didn't need to beckon to get Sevi to follow, struck by the device as he was. She dipped behind one of the columns, picking out another pair of levers in the floor, each marked with a number. The second lever had a column behind it just like the ones that ran around the device, but much smaller. A slab of iron with star-shaped insets stood to the side of the row.

Tiersa looked to Sevi and nodded, stepping aside to the first of the levers. Sevi gulped, feeling his conviction fade beneath the mechanism's alien aspect. But he shook himself and straightened. "No more lies," he said, pushing each star into their slots.

The iron slab lit up with runes. Retreating, he nodded to Tiersa. But before she could do anything, Reynam, his prisoner, and Captain River approached them. "Alright, what's going on?" Reynam demanded. "I've kept my mouth shut at everything from getting rolled out of bed to the big scary doors, but I draw the line at magic rooms. Is *this* what my father had been working on?"

"I agree with my cor—my lieutenant," Captain River said. "My lady, I must demand an explanation."

"All will be revealed, Caldwin," Tiersa said, a smile on her face. "You've put your faith in me thus far. All I ask is for a little bit more. Lieutenant Reynam?"

"Ma'am?"

"Place our guest on the podium beneath the device."

"Yes ma'am," Reynam said, looking askance at the prisoner before marching them forward.

Commander Tiersa followed him closely. As Reynam walked the Silvakin up the steps, the commander bent at the waist and pulled what looked like iron chains from the grate, also etched with runes. "Have it kneel," Tiersa ordered.

Reynam did as he was commanded, pushing the Silvakin to their knees. Commander Tiersa took the chains and bound the cuffs around their wrists, pulling them tightly to the grate until the prisoner groaned and shifted in discomfort. Only when she was certain that they couldn't move did Tiersa grab their hood and yank it away.

A lady with black hair and scaly skin looked up at her. Tiersa gazed down with a smile and said something soft that only she and the prisoner could hear. The woman spat on Tiersa's boots. Unbothered, the commander turned her back and retreated to the controls, still wearing her smile as she took the first lever and flicked it.

The columns full of silver dust bubbled, and the liquid inside of them dropped a level. The humming increased. A light appeared beneath the Silvakin woman, and she looked down into the grate beneath her with confusion.

The small column behind the second lever began to fill with the same liquid as the larger columns. A rune appeared at its top when it was full. Tiersa motioned for Sevi to come closer. Taking his hand, she placed it on the final lever. "The honor should be yours," she whispered.

Sevi looked from the mechanism to the chained woman struggling with her bonds. He didn't need to think hard over what this lever would do. "I d-don't want to," he stuttered, withdrawing his hand.

Tiersa frowned. "Pull it, Your Luminance."

He paused, but shook his head. "No."

"The Argennium was made to end the war, Isevidel, and that thing is an enemy that tried to kill you. Just like all who killed our family, and our countrymen in their invasion. But this will give us peace. This will ensure that none of them ever hurt you, or anyone again. Now pull. You can do this." Tiersa placed her hand on his shoulder.

Sevi touched his chest. "T-tell me what it will do."

"As I said," Tiersa said softly. "It will end the war. Forever."

Sevi didn't move. A paralyzing fear took hold of him. He looked to Captain River for support, but all the captain did was shake his head, just as lost as Sevi. With no other option, Sevi did all that he could think to do. He closed his eyes, inhaled, and took a Long Breath.

He thought of all the Fablings in the castle he'd spent his days watching, and the lives they used to have, all ended the day the Embers had invaded. But how many had been killed on the Night of Treachery? How painful was it to lose one's country and fight for its return?

He thought of the Silent Grove soldiers that had twice overran his home to kill his family and friends. One of them had killed an old warrior who had stood by his side, fighting and dying so that Sevi might survive. Another wore his best friend's face, trapped in a prison of her own body. The Silvakaen had done that to her... but *she* had come from them.

He thought of being attacked in a dark alleyway by tattooed men he didn't know, who sought to inflict pain on one he did. River wasn't a Silvakin, yet he had been different enough to warrant violence in their eyes. Would that continue once the war was over?

He thought of Solen's face for the first time in a month, firing his gun out of fear without knowing who or what Sevi was. Saved only by a necklace, taken from someone he once loved.

He thought of Tiersa, the pain she must have felt at being forced to leave her family behind and her four years of struggle to undo what had been done. Just like Lily, desperately trying to save him and his siblings, protecting them with all that she could give.

He thought of the Cut, and its many twisting corridors. It had been made years ago out of fear and madness by a woman he never knew, and since filled with joy and laughter by two that he did.

He thought of his garden, and Alyda, and all the flowers and plants she had taught him how to care for. He thought of Lily, showing him the airship, just so she could see him smile.

The airship... The Silvakaen could command magic without the use of any runes, yet they also had technology that let them fly without wings. Lily, in her story, had suggested that they'd come for the Argennium itself. Was the Argennium made to end the war, or did the war begin because it was made?

Sevi reopened his eyes to stare at the lever. If Tiersa had asked him to pull it after Shy had shown him the night his family died, he would have. In a *heartbeat*. But after speaking with Lily, he no found that he longer had the will.

Not all the Silvakaen were his enemies. How many of them were like Lily, forced to be a soldier? How many were like Alyda, who only wanted to see things grow, and cursed with a predestined fate? How many were like himself, beholden to a world that had been breathing longer than he'd been alive, living by rules he didn't understand?

How many were searching for the rest of themselves?

He had ascended the mountain in search of truth. He'd found it, but that didn't mean he had to become an executioner for it. It wasn't in him. It wasn't who he *was*.

"No," Sevi said at last. "I won't do this. You said it yourself, we have our country back. Why should I strike at a retreating army? Why should I kill someone on her knees when we've won the war? They're gone, Tiersa. Let's use this weapon against them if they ever return."

Tiersa stepped closer and placed both hands on his shoulders. "Isevidel. They *just* tried to kill you again. The Argennium can end the war *permanently*. They'll never even get the chance to return because they'll be *gone*. You will *never* be hunted by them ever again. You will *never* have to hide in the dark out of fear for your life. We can live on without their threat hanging over our heads. Do you not want that?"

Sevi took a deep breath, staring up into his aunt's eyes. She had heavy bags beneath them, and seemed strained around the edges, like she was desperately holding herself together by the barest of threads. Her armor was there, but it was cracking. "Tisa, what won't you tell me?" he asked softly. "Please. How will it end the war? What does the Argennium do?"

She clenched her jaw, and Sevi flinched as something inside of her snapped before his very eyes. She grabbed his wrist. "Fine. *I'll help you.*"

She pushed his hand to the lever before he could react. A beam of blinding silver light shot from the Aregnnium's grate, enveloping the Silvakin woman and pouring through the device's many lenses until it had magnified to a great width, shooting up into the night sky in a massive pillar.

The prisoner let out an ear-splitting scream, outlined for not more than a breath before the light began to eat away at her body. It wormed its way into her skin, shining through like the tendrils of Innavin's scar and bursting out of her in rippling cracks, breaking her body apart like pottery. She exploded into a cloud of dust and tattered clothing, and her scream abruptly ceased.

The light disappeared the moment she died. The night rushed back in. The humming of the platform stopped, the runes dimmed, and the only sound among them was that of Commander Tiersa laughing softly to herself.

# Chapter 55

...

———— ⟋∾⟍ ————

Sevi stared in disbelief at where the woman had been, then down at his feet and all the dust around him. Realization washed through him, along with fresh horror. He yanked his hand back from the lever and clutched it to his chest, suddenly unable to breathe.

"What did you *do?*" Captain River gasped, looking as aghast as Sevi felt.

"I used our weapon to execute an enemy combatant," Commander Tiersa replied, pulling the second lever back into its upright position.

The awful smell of burnt flesh blew over them, making Sevi's stomach churn violently. He ran to the edge of the platform and retched, unable to quell the image of the Silvakin in her final moments. He had never killed anyone before.

"So, what was all that about ending the war, ma'am?" Reynam asked. "Because as interesting as that light was, somehow, I feel like the war is still on."

Sevi's eyes drifted to a strange shape in the mountainside, listening to the conversation behind him with half an ear. Tiersa laughed bitterly. "How astute of you, Lieutenant. Yes, the war is still on. But not for much longer."

"How's that, ma'am?"

"Not all of this is your father's work, Enstrova, though some of the more important parts of it are—like the heart, made to direct the weapon's energy through that grate. This mastery of engineering, ladies and gentlemen, is called the Argennium, and it has been many years in the making. It will end the war by combining the magic of the Fae with human Runic, taint it with quicksilver, and direct it into the very center of the Lynnweald to kill every greenblood in existence."

She spoke with such detachment that it stunned everyone into silence. "Did... did it not do this now?" Captain River asked at last.

"No."

"Why?"

"Queen Korina and King Marovhan left coded notes in their study before they passed—I've spent the past month deciphering what I could. According to them, the light should have 'stretched to the moon.'"

"Why did it not?"

"I wasn't sure, until I saw this demonstration. I see now what complications our king and queen had to deal with: their subjects were too *fragile*. They had kept remarking that the Argennium's heart was *too* powerfully built—truly your family's crowning achievement, Enstrova. Be proud. I assume they would have added a way to temper its effects or replaced the heart entirely. But then the Night of Treachery occurred, and most of the project's overseers perished or disappeared."

She broke off, letting them process her words before continuing. "But why use a dampener, soldiers, when we can simply use a stronger creature?"

Sevi turned at that. Commander Tiersa had spread her arms wide and wore an eager. "I have just recently come into possession of a greenblood who can withstand the touch of quicksilver. One who has tempered its hide with iron, all while living within a mountain made of quicksilver for the past four years."

A spike of terror rammed itself through Sevi's gut. He pushed off the ground and scrambled back to Tiersa, drawing up in front of her. "You said you wouldn't kill her!"

"I said I would discover its purpose and why it could withstand the quicksilver," Tiersa said flatly, not looking at him. "But now it doesn't matter. Not in the face of what we have just discovered. With this, I may finally fulfill my oath to you and the Astraeda line. I can *protect* you, and together, we will have retribution! I understand why you might have some affection for your greenblood captor, Isevidel, but I beg of you, cast it aside. It is *entirely* misplaced."

Sevi's mouth dropped. "Tisa... you... you're talking about *genocide*."

"I'm speaking of *peace*!" Tiersa exclaimed. "Do you still not see it? Do you not see why your *friend* has kept you around? You're the only one who could get to the *one* weapon in Iaela that could decimate the greenbloods. Who's to say they didn't keep you here as a contingency if they failed to bury it?" She shook her head, lifting her chin. "But their little scheme backfired, and tonight I will ensure their mistake is a fatal one. Tonight, we take back full control of both our country and our *lives*."

"Contingency? They never knew I was here! They only attacked us *because* my family built this thing!" Sevi cried.

"Who's to say?" Tiersa said indifferently. "They're greenbloods. They're evil. They don't think like us. Who's to say they wouldn't have invaded us anyway simply because they were bored? Your family built this weapon in order to defend their people, and it's about time that we use it."

"But—"

"*Silence!*" Tiersa yelled. "There will be no further argument on the matter. This war ends *tonight*. There is nothing you will do to stop it. And in time, when our crops have regrown and our people prosper once more, you will come to thank me."

Sevi clenched his teeth and balled his fists. "What's the point of a crown if you're going to ignore it whenever it suits you?"

"I said there will be no argument on the matter," Tiersa said, drumming her fingers on the hilts of her swords. "But I will allow you to say your goodbyes. My debt paid to the girl, as thanks for her delivery of you back to me. And take solace, Isevidel—if four years here didn't kill her, then maybe this won't either, and we can keep her under guard just as she did to you. Like a pet."

Sevi stared her down. She turned from him dismissively, striding to the slab that held their pendants. "Shy," he said.

Commander Tiersa paused, turning to look back at him with a stern expression. "One more word—"

"Hide me."

Shy leapt from the ground to full height. Their darkness sliced through the moonglow as they stretched and swallowed him from head to toe, vanishing him from the world before the eyes of all the Embers.

"Oh, my *Gods*," Reynam breathed, jumping back.

"Earuna!" River gasped.

"*Isevidel!*" Tiersa yelled, running toward his last known location. She whipped her head from side to side in a frenzy.

Sevi held his breath in Shy's miasma and sprinted past Tiersa toward the two necklaces. The commander spun, feeling the gust of wind he left in his wake. "Isevi—NO!"

He slipped his hand into the loop of his necklace and pulled with all his might. It came free after several tugs, and he went stumbling in the dust, leaving a visible trail for all to see.

"His footsteps! *After him!*" Tiersa bellowed.

Sevi bolted, putting the necklace around his neck and running right for the edge of the platform. He jumped over it without hesitation and hit the rocky slope with a painful scrape, sliding down the mountain toward the shape he'd spotted earlier, carved into its stone.

His window to the sky.

Sevi waved his hand in a frantic gesture. Shy felt his intention and unwrapped themselves from him, allowing him to take a breath just as he hit the edge of the gap and dropped into his garden.

He hit the ground at an angle and rolled, just narrowly missing the lightblossoms, and came to a stop in the dirt, coughing and painfully sucking in lungfuls of air. The soldiers that followed would be in for a nasty surprise if they weren't careful.

"Alyda! *Alyda!*" he yelled, getting painfully to his feet.

A small, weak chime cropped up from the flowerbed. He hobbled towards it, spotting Alyda's green light amid all the glowing yellow. She had her legs curled to her chest, looking much as she had when she first lay dying. "Don't worry, Aly, I've got you now," he said, scooping his friend into his hands as gingerly as he could. Shouts echoed from above, hastening his movements. "Let's save you and Lily, and then let's leave... and take some flowers with us while we're at it."

# Chapter 56

...

Sevi scrambled through the Cut faster than he'd ever run, holding Alyda to his chest as securely as he could, and using Shy to hide from the Embers whenever possible. He had to remind himself over and over to be careful—he carried dangerous plants in his jacket.

By the time he'd reached the shaft leading up the tower he was well out of breath, but he steeled himself and made the climb. He had to pause as he got to Lily's level, feeling the vigor in his blood gradually ebbing away, leaving nothing but aches and pains. But still he moved, fearful for Lily and what would happen if he failed to save her. Alyda coughed, rattling out her tiny, grating chimes into his palm, and he moved all the quicker. He would *not* lose any more family.

He got to the wall separating the Cut from Lily's cell and searched for the spyhole, almost pushing his entire arm through it in the process. "Lily!" he hissed furiously, tugging at another stone.

Lily's voice drifted in faintly from the other side. "Sevi? What are you doing?"

"I'm getting you out of here!" He slammed his fist in frustration. "Blazes! Where were those stones that moved the whole godsdamned wall!"

"Sevi! *Sevi!* Keep it down! *Stop!*" Lily rushed over. "Tell me what's going on!"

"They're going to burn you *alive!*"

"What? Sevi, *look at me.*"

Sevi paused in his frantic search and lowered his face to the window, meeting her eyes. "Tell me what's happening," she demanded.

He quickly recounted everything that had occurred since he'd left her, skipping to the important bits. Her eyes widened in disbelief. "It can kill *all* the Silvakaen?"

"Yes! Tiersa has gone *mad!* She's going to use you to destroy your whole *country!*" Lily gave him a look that felt very at odds with the moment, taking him aback. "What is it?"

"Maybe I'll let them take me," Lily murmured, closing her eyes.

"*What?*"

"Sevi," Lily said, shaking her head, "my people are beautiful—more than you know. But there's a sickness in them. Cruelty, too. Now more than ever, I feel like humans and Fae were not meant to mix."

"What are you talking about? Lily, we have to get you *out* of here! I need you! *Alyda* needs you!" He raised the fairy up for her to see.

At her light, Lily opened her eyes and gazed at Alyda, cradled in Sevi's palms. "My lovely little flower," Lily said softly. "I put you through a lot of pain, didn't I?" Alyda weakly turned her head to look at Lily, chiming out a small, sad note. Lily pursed her lips. "And I hurt you too, Sevi—even when I was myself. Maybe... maybe it would be better if I just disappeared. If we all just disappeared."

"*What's wrong with you?*" Sevi snapped. "Letting them take you? So they can kill *thousands?* This is *not* the girl I know!" He hammered his fist against the wall. "The girl I know is *strong* and *brave!* The girl I know has a plan for *everything!* The girl I know would *never leave me!*"

"Sevi—"

"Don't 'Sevi' me, I'm getting you out of here! Can a lightblossom make a big enough hole in the wall?"

"That's enough—"

"No!"

A sound in the cell caused them both to quiet. Lily whirled around and put her back up against the wall.

"Hello, creature," Tiersa's low voice said, dripping with disdain.

Lily cried out in pain as she was suddenly yanked away from the wall. "Lily!" Sevi yelled. There was a pause. Clapping his hand over his mouth, Sevi threw himself to the side and put his back up against the stone.

"Ah," Tiersa sighed. "If only I had gone with my intuition and sealed these tunnels. A thorn in the side only digs deeper the longer you leave it, doesn't it, Isevidel?"

Sevi squeezed his eyes shut. *No.*

"But without them, I suppose we never would have reunited. No matter. There will be plenty of time once I've reduced the greenbloods to ash and we're finally free of their threat."

He clenched his hands against Alyda, causing her to chime softly in discomfort.

"Let me make myself perfectly clear, Isevidel," Tiersa said softly through the wall. "I don't need your friend. I'll find another greenblood who can withstand the touch of iron, and there are plenty more of them still in these cells. All I need to do is lock one into helmet and wait for them to change. And who's to say I need to wait four years? Perhaps merely a month will do.

"But I will make a deal with you. Bring me that necklace before the moon sets, and I will still allow you to say goodbye to your friend. Refuse, and I will repay my debt with a bullet to her skull. A swift, painless death. I will wait at the Argennium until sunrise. The choice is yours."

Her steps echoed across the cell as she stepped away. The door closed with a final *clang*.

Sevi buried his face into his arm.

No. No. *No.*

Alyda coughed in his hand, and he closed his fingers protectively around her. His plan hadn't changed. Save Alyda. Save Lily. Then leave and never return, just like Lily wanted.

He tried to ignore the hopelessness crushing his chest.

Sevi stepped quietly through the castle grounds with Shy wrapped around him. He had never asked so much from his shadow before, and he hoped that they could withstand the constant strain. But their guise held all the way to the barracks door, and Shy dispelled themselves so that Sevi could breathe.

He decided that he wouldn't call upon them again and risk tiring them—who knew how many times he'd need them tonight? He'd just have to rely on the natural darkness around him as best as he could and summon his brother and sister in an emergency.

He cupped Alyda with both hands, blocking her light from the rest of the room full of wounded Embers and nobles. They all appeared to be asleep, but he remembered very clearly the fitful nights he'd endured during his time here. He doubted that each was sleeping soundly, and there were bound to be doctors or assistants periodically checking on them.

Taking several torturous moments to allow his eyes to adjust to the room, Sevi tiptoed over to Doctor Lea's desk and got to his knees. He drew the first drawer out carefully, trying not to make a sound. "Sorry, Alyda, I need your light," he said softly to the fairy, lifting her up in his hand and allowing streaks of her dim, green glow to leak through his fingers. A part of him had hoped to find Doctor Lea there, toiling away on notes into the late hours of the night as she had the tendency to do. She, more than anyone in the castle, would be the one to help Alyda. But if he couldn't find her, then maybe he could find the amber.

He rummaged around, all the while turning over what he could possibly do to rescue Lily on his own. Could Alyda cause a distraction while Sevi ran in to free her? Could Shy wrap around them both, and they could make their escape? *Would* they? He was so engaged in his thoughts that he forgot that Shy no longer shielded him, and didn't see the lantern appear until it was too late.

"What are you doing?" Doctor Lea said sternly, manifesting from the dark with a disapproving glare.

Sevi fell backward in alarm. "Lea!"

"Wha—you brought her *here?*" she exclaimed, quickly dimming the light.

"Lea, I can explain, but there isn't any time. Alyda needs amber, and she needs it now."

Doctor Lea took a deep breath. "Would this have anything to do with all the commotion outside tonight?"

"Yes," Sevi answered without hesitation. "And I told you, I'll explain, but right now I need to save my friend."

Doctor Lea's face was unreadable in the dark.

"Will you *please* help us?"

Sighing, Lea reached into her coat and pulled something out. "Here," she whispered, placing a vial of amber in his hand. "Feed her while you explain. But be quiet."

Sevi recounted the night's events in quick, hushed whispers. The more he spoke, the more shocked Doctor Lea looked. When he'd finished, Alyda had returned to her usual self, and buried herself under his shirt to hide her light.

Doctor Lea crossed her arms and looked into the near distance. She didn't speak for a long while. "That was like something from a play... So?"

"So what?"

"What do you plan to do?"

Sevi blinked. "You believe me?"

"You've given me no reason not to."

"And you're not going to call the guards on me?"

She shook her head. "I'm a doctor, Sevi. I swore an oath to mend, not to kill. Death is indifferent to us, but life? Everyone deserves a second chance at life. And while I may not have the best opinion of my family, killing my people robs them of that chance. Fighting a war to reclaim independence is one thing, but what Tiersa plans to do is completely unconscionable. So no, I don't plan on raising the alarm."

Sevi breathed out a breath he'd been holding. This was exactly what he had hoped for—an ally. Someone, anyone, who would be willing to help them. "What do you think I should do?"

Doctor Lea sighed. "I'm not sure, Sevi. What can we do?"

"We?"

"Oh yes. I'm not—"

The door to the barracks started to open, silencing whatever Lea might have said. Lea swiveled her head, and she gestured at Sevi to duck. He threw himself beneath the desk, scrunching himself in tight. Lea brought the lantern's light up and held it before her. "Caldwin?" she said in surprise.

"Forgive me for the late visit, Doctor Lea," the captain said softly, stepping into the room and closing the door behind him. No other footsteps joined his.

"What are you doing here?"

Captain River sighed. "I... I have come here in search of clarity."

"Surely Lorr would be better for that?"

"This is not meant for my husband. This is meant for me."

"What is it? Should we step outside?"

"No, I... no. I am in search of Sevi. Have you seen him tonight?"

"Not at all," Doctor Lea lied easily. "Is he hurt?"

"No."

"Then why come here?"

There was a pause. "This is where it began," River said softly. "I followed two stars to this land. From there I found one who led me to the end of the river, only to find the other where river met sky, waiting for me. Now... Now the stars have split, and my way is lost. One calls for death, while the other calls for life. And there may even be a third. Is one of them false? Which am I to follow? Where is the wind to take me?"

"You're not making any sense, Caldwin. Where's Lorr? You should go be with him."

"I am sorry, Doctor Lea. Please allow me to stay for longer. I am hoping for a sign."

Doctor Lea sighed. "A sign of what? Why do you need a sign?"

"I must find my bearings. Without one, I am lost."

Lea clicked her tongue. "This isn't like you. Captain Caldwin River Ta'Runa does not let fear get the better of him. Haven't you always done what you've felt is best?"

Another silence. "Many possible innocents could die. I do not want that," River said. "They have done things. Horrible things. Their soldiers have killed my friends, yet have I not done the same? Is that not the nature of war? Is destruction not its name? I fight and I kill to protect what I love... but I do not want to fight because I fear. I do not want to kill when I have won. I do not want to hate because of what they are and what I am."

Lea chuckled softly. "Caldwin, shouldn't a thought like that be as good a sign as any?"

River didn't respond, but Sevi had heard enough. Steeling himself, he stood up from under the desk and met Captain River's shocked gaze. "If you want a sign, River, then here," Sevi said, lifting his chin. "My name is Sevi Astraeda, known before as Alramar, Nahlra, and Isevidel Astraeda. I was born a commoner, then made a prince, then a tunnel mouse, then a prince again. I have been friends with Fae and humans alike and have been hurt by, and loved by, both more than I ever could have imagined. I lost my memory. I lost myself. But I think I'm finding it again, and who I am is not who Tiersa wants me to be."

"*Ik Earuna kah'eshaa,*" River whispered.

Lea's brow furrowed. "Alramar? Nahlra?"

"Come out, Alyda," Sevi said, staring unflinchingly into Captain River's eyes. The fairy hesitantly pulled herself out of the collar of his shirt, looking uncertainly up at Sevi before joining him in gazing at River, fixing him with her crystalline stare. The captain's jaw gently fell. "Will you join me?" Sevi implored.

There was a beat of tense silence where both Sevi and Lea regarded River, waiting for him to react. His gaze stayed fixed on Alyda, unreadable and frozen.

Then the captain threw back his head and laughed.

Alyda disappeared back into Sevi's shirt with a fearful sound. Doctor Lea dimmed the lantern and shushed River. He covered his mouth, rocking his body and shoulders with his guffaws. Wiping his eyes, he flashed a wide grin. "Sevi Astraeda," Captain River said softly, moving forward and wrapping Sevi in an embrace. "That the best introduction I have heard since I left the sea. Well done, *risho*. Well done."

"Will you help me?" Sevi asked again.

"Aye," Captain River said. "I think I will."

"I'm coming, too."

Both Sevi and River turned their heads to Doctor Lea. She stared back defiantly, daring them to argue with her. "Lea," Sevi said. "It's going to be very dangerous." *Especially for you*, he didn't say, hoping that she would understand. They were going into a mountain full of quicksilver, toward a weapon that specialized in killing the Silvakaen. She would be at the greatest risk.

"Yes. It will. That's why I'm coming. In case anyone gets hurt," she said, sticking her hands into her coat pocket and giving him a knowing smile. "And for tonight, Sevi, you may call me Azalea."

His heart swelled at her bravery. He turned down to whisper at his collar, "And you, Alyda? Will you join me? It will be just as dangerous for you. You don't have to come."

Alyda took a handful of his skin and twisted, making him wince. "*What a silly question.*"

Captain River cleared his throat. "You are not a soldier, Doctor Lea. I share Sevi's worry."

"It's my choice, Caldwin. Or will you try to rob me of that?" Lea rebutted.

Captain River tried to further dissuade her, but it was useless. She would not be argued with. With a resigned smile, he said, "I suppose we could use as many friends as we can. I am sure that my husband will help, but I doubt our soldiers will turn from the commander. Nor will Lieutenant Enstrova."

"What about Tahno?" Lea asked.

River slowly shook his head. "No. If I am to die at the river's end after all, then I would have him take my story back to our people. He will know what happened here and where my heart was placed. In truth, I do not know how we will stop this."

Lea opened her mouth to speak but stopped and turned to face the room. Its occupants were beginning to mutter. "Maybe we can discuss this somewhere else?"

"I... I think I have an idea," Sevi said softly. While they had been talking, he had been turning his mind over and over again, mulling over everything they had at their disposal. Everything and anything that could tip the balance in their favor.

"What is it?" Captain River asked.

Sevi took a deep breath. *Think like Lily.* "River. Can you get to the airship?"

# Chapter 57

...

The moon had traveled far across the sky by the time Sevi left the infirmary, holding the hem of his shirt in a white-knuckled grip and escorted by Doctor Lea. They said nothing as they crossed the courtyard. An owl swooped silently overhead, fixing its eyes down at them through its Empyrean hood before fading back into the night.

Soldiers across the grounds quickly took notice, falling in behind them as they approached the tunnel leading to the Argennium, where Commander Tiersa waited with her hands on her swords. She gave Sevi a flat, expressionless look, hiding once more behind her alabaster armor. Behind her stood Reynam, guarding Lily with a rifle in his hands. Her wrists were bound in front of her with iron chains. She looked at Sevi with a tear-stricken face.

"I was growing impatient," Tiersa said, turning her gaze on Lea. "What happened?"

"He came to me," Lea said with an easy shrug. "He was hysterical, saying that you were going to kill his friend. I didn't believe it, but seeing that she's tied up... are those *Fae* ears?"

Tiersa flicked her hand. "Give him to me."

"Certainly, but listen to what he has to say first. I promised him you'd listen."

"He has already spoken, and I have already listened. There will be no further argument."

Lea raised a critical eyebrow. "Are you about to make a liar out of me, Tiersa?"

"You shouldn't have made a promise that you couldn't keep."

Doctor Lea rolled her eyes. "Then at least allow me to accompany him. He's distraught, and I don't want him getting hurt."

Tiersa tightened her grip on her swords. "He *won't*."

"Can you say that for sure?"

Commander Tiersa quieted, drumming her fingers on her hilts.

"What's going on in that mountain, Tiersa? Is it dangerous? Please, at least allow me to come, in the event that something does happen."

Tiersa breathed out a tired sigh. "Fine. I'll allow it."

"Thank you." Lea patted Sevi on the shoulder. "Don't worry, I'll be here with you, no matter what."

Tiersa's face stiffened before she turned away, striding into the tunnel. "Please don't do this, Tisa!" Sevi yelled after her. She didn't turn around.

"Move," Reynam ordered, nudging Lily. "Sorry about this, kid," he muttered to Sevi, turning and following the commander.

Sevi and Lily locked eyes before Reynam's body blocked her. He followed them closely, with Lea trailing behind. The path into the mountain felt longer than before, stretching before Sevi like a walk to his execution.

The iron doors waited for them, wide and inviting. Reynam pushed Lily into the room. Sevi maneuvered himself next to her as the rest of the soldiers filed in behind Doctor Lea. Commander Tiersa shoved the lever to lift them the moment the last person entered.

"Can I... May I have some privacy with her?" Sevi tentatively asked Reynam.

Reynam looked down at him, then at Tiersa. She stood with her back to them, facing the mechanism in the middle of the platform.

"Rey," Lea said. "If what Sevi told me is true, then they deserve time together." Still, Reynam hesitated. She walked in front of him. "How about we play for it?"

Reynam brought his head back in surprise. She reached her fingers into his breast pocket and plucked out a coin, holding it up. "I call Crowns."

A faint smile crossed Reynam's face. "That's not fair."

"Is that right?" Doctor Lea flicked the coin with her thumb. It sailed into the air and landed with a sharp, metallic ring as it struck the iron floor, rolling to a stop at their feet. "Oh look. Crowns," she said, not even glancing down. "You lose, Lieutenant."

Reynam chuckled softly. "Fine. You win." He shot one last fleeting look at Lily and Sevi before joining Lea at her side and moving away from them.

Watching his retreating back, Sevi felt the sudden urge to call after him. "Reynam!"

The soldier stopped.

"Why are you helping her? What do you have to gain?"

Reynam's shoulders slumped, and he put his hand in his pocket, looking down at his feet. He turned back to Sevi. "This is all that's left of him, kid. Him and my brothers... thanks to her and her people." He nodded at Lily. "The least I can do is protect what they left behind. To see it used. Otherwise, what was the point?"

"And we should use it to kill an entire culture?"

"It's what they deserve."

"Oh, you *stupid* man, have you *seen* their airships?" Sevi flung his hands up. "They've got boats that can *fly*. They've got *magic*. They've got blood that can *turn us into slaves*. Who knows what else they have! If they wanted to wipe us out, they godsdamned well *could* have! *So why didn't they?*"

Reynam closed his mouth. A beat of silence passed before he breathed out a surprised laugh. "You're a smart kid. I'll tell you what. Care to make one last wager? If you can stop this, then I promise you, I'll lay my rifle down. You have my word... For whatever that's worth."

He didn't wait for Sevi's answer. He turned on his heel and walked across the platform with Doctor Lea, leaving Sevi and Lily alone together.

"You stupid boy," Lily whispered to him. "Why did you come?"

"I came to save you," Sevi said, holding her by the biceps. "We look out for each other, now and forever. Your words, not mine."

She laughed bitterly. "Forever? I killed your whole family, you dumb prince! That was a lie to keep you in *line!*"

Sevi raised his eyebrows. "You've told me a lot of lies, Lily, but that has to be your worst one yet."

"It's the *truth!*"

He snorted. "It isn't. Know why?"

"Why?" she scoffed.

"Because you're my friend."

She quieted. The humming of the Argennium rushed in to fill the silence between them. "I don't want you here," she said lowly. "I didn't... I don't want you to see me. To watch when I..." Her voice cracked, and she angrily wiped her tears away. "Just *leave*. Let her shoot me! You'll save my people and I'll get what I deserve!"

"Hey." Sevi gently touched one of her cheeks and dried the other with his sleeve. She froze, watching him fearfully. "Don't worry. I'm going to take care of you, I promise. Do you know what this is?" He reached into his pocket and pulled out a vial.

Lily looked down in shock. "Is that *amber?*" she whispered.

"Maybe."

"You stole it!"

"Maybe."

"And Doctor Lea—" She jerked her head over to Lea, who looked back at them with a coy smile.

Sevi patted her. "Mischief, silly girl. Just wait for my signal." He looked up, watching the sky growing nearer. Standing in the light of the full moon, he closed his eyes and mustered every ounce of courage he had. Whatever happened next, he could not fail. Not again.

"Sevi?" Lily said softly. He turned back to her. She stared at him, hands bound, shoulders hunched, and helmetless—a mere shadow of the fearless girl she used to be. "I'm sorry."

Sevi sighed. "I know," he murmured.

"If I don't make it—"

"You *will*."

"*If* I don't," Lily repeated, voice wavering, "I'm glad I had a friend like you."

The iron walls of the shaft disappeared, opening once again to the sky. The platform came to a juddering halt, shaking the dust of countless dead Silvakin across its floor. "Isevidel! Come here!" Tiersa demanded.

"Trust me," Sevi said. He leaned forward and kissed Lily on her forehead, before turning soberly to face Tiersa. He didn't approach her. Instead, he walked toward the edge of the platform.

"Please don't think about running again," Commander Tiersa said wearily.

Sevi took the necklace from around his head and held it out by the chain, swinging it over the rim of the mountain, before turning to face Tiersa with a determined glare.

She tilted her head and regarded him with an arched eyebrow. "Let me guess," she said, pointing at him. "I must let your friend go, or else you'll drop the key?"

Sevi shrugged. "Something like that." *Come on, River, where are you?*

Tiersa smiled humorlessly. They regarded each other. Then a shadow detached itself from the sky and streaked toward Sevi on silent wings, tearing the necklace out of his hands before he could react. He stumbled, slipping on the dust and pinwheeling his arms. A soldier darted in to steady him, pulling him back from the edge. He brought his head up just in time to see an owl deposit his necklace in Tiersa's gloved hand before flying off. She raised it to her face, regarding it, and said, "Are we done here?"

Sevi slumped his shoulders, as if the fight had gone out of him. "Please, Tisa. I'm begging you. *Please* don't kill her."

"It's almost sunrise, Isevidel. I hope you've said your goodbyes." She spread her arm out, beckoning him forward. "Now come here, or I will order Lieutenant Enstrova to shoot her. It's your choice."

Sevi clenched his fists, moving his legs as if they had turned to iron. Reynam took hold of Lily's shoulder and marched her after him. When he got to the controls, Tiersa took his hand and dropped the necklace into it. "Do it," she ordered.

"Please, Tisa," he said again, clutching the familiar star to his chest.

"*Now.*"

Sevi stared up at her. Something moved behind her, so great against the sky it blocked the stars. He smiled. "No."

The *Aethercrest's* lightwings flared as it rose over the lip of the mountain, fully extended and shining in all their glory. Captain River manned the helm, turning the wheel and pulling the levers with a practiced hand. Lorr stood on the deck with his rifle pointed at the people below. A gleaming scope reflected on its barrel. "Don't move, Commander!" Lorr yelled.

Tiersa whipped around. "What...? What is the meaning of this! You... You *traitors!* TRAITORS! I *trusted* you, Caldwin! I trusted you *both!*"

"I am sorry, Commander Tiersa, but the signs are clear! I will not be a hand in this destruction!" River called, pulling a lever and arresting the ship's momentum.

"Stop this *immediately!*" she screamed. "Enstrova!"

Sevi moved next to Lily and took her hand. "Hold your breath," he said with a smile. "Shy. Hide us."

But Shy didn't come.

Sevi looked down and tried again. "Shy! *Now!*"

Nothing. As he had feared, his brother and sister were still frightened of Lily. A warning shot rang out from Lorr's rifle, ricocheting off the ground and scattering soldiers. He'd have to try something else, and fast.

Reaching into a pocket in his coat, he pulled out a handful of firesnap seeds and slammed them into the floor. They sounded as loud as gunshots off the metal, making the remaining soldiers around him jump away in alarm. He tugged Lily by her bonds before they could recover and pulled her after him toward the airship, sprinting away together as fast as they could run.

Lorr fired his rifle again, and more of the Embers scattered. Reynam dipped behind a column while Tiersa took another, angrily shouting orders.

Sevi panted, looking at nothing but the airship. Close. They were so *close.*

A flash of light sprung to life from the side. A powerful gust of wind whipped up, and a wall of incandescence slammed into him and Lily from behind, sending them crashing into the ground end over end.

Sevi's ears rang. The world spun violently around him. He pushed off from the floor, calling out Lily's name, but he couldn't hear his own voice. When the night finally righted itself and his senses returned, it was with the sound of a gunshot, and Lorr crying out in pain.

He turned to face the airship just in time to see Captain River abandoning the controls, shouting in despair. "That was a warning shot, Captain!" Reynam called. "The next one goes between your eyes!"

"*Enough of this!*" Tiersa yelled, striding over to Sevi and Lily and angrily sheathing one of her enchanted swords. She reached for Sevi and yanked him by the wrist. He tried to pull back, futilely tugging at her steely grip, but it was no use.

"Shy! *Please!* She's not a monster! *She's not a monster!*" Sevi yelled, fighting Tiersa with every step.

Reynam walked over to Lily and pulled her up, keeping his rifle in the crook of his arm in case he needed to fire it again.

No. No. *No! "Let go of her!"* Sevi yelled. He was so distracted by the sight of his friend being marched to her death that he didn't notice Tiersa push his hand against the slab, shoving the star into place.

The runes on its iron face burned. The machine began to whirr.

She pushed Sevi away before he could lunge for the necklace, blocking it with her body. She waved another soldier over. "Take him and hold onto him. *Tightly.* No more vanishing acts, or I'll have you hanged," she growled. Then she grabbed Lily by her bound wrists and tugged her forward, ignoring the way her legs dragged.

"Sevi! *Sevi!*" Lily cried.

"*Lily!*" Sevi shouted.

No. No. NO!

*All your fault. All your fault. You should have seen. You should have known.*

He watched in horror as Lily was shoved to her knees. She tried to rise, but Tiersa delivered a vicious blow to her face, and her legs folded beneath her. "NO!" Sevi screamed. The iron cuffs around Lily's wrists were undone, replaced by the enchanted chains right where the first Silvakin had been.

Sevi couldn't let this happen. "TIERSA!"

The commander paused, turning her head to Sevi just as he dropped to the ground and rolled, shedding his coat and pushing away from the soldier's grip. The soldier yelped in alarm, flailing for him, but failed to grab him in time. When Sevi came up and got a good distance away from the soldiers, he held the vial of amber in his hand. "Do you know what this is!" he yelled.

Tiersa straightened with stunned recognition.

"If you don't let us go, I'll drink it! I'll become just like her, and you'll have to *kill me, too!*" The commander's hands stiffened on her blades, and she took an alarmed step forward. He held his breath. This was it. His last resort.

Tiersa's face contorted into a snarl, and in one terrifying motion, she drew her gun, pointed, and fired a single shot. All went still as it echoed against the mountainside, fading into silence.

Lea gasped.

Sevi jerked his head to the side. Doctor Lea clutched at her ribs. A blossom of red had sprouted through her coat, redder than any rose.

"Lea?" Reynam said in confusion, lowering his rifle. Then she collapsed to the ground, and he threw it away completely. "LEA!"

"Is everyone around me a *traitor!*" Tiersa yelled. "You. Would. DARE give him amber, Lea? How long have you been plotting against me? How long have you *all* been planning to stab me in the *back?*" She kicked Lily where she lay on the grate, eliciting a moan from her, then marched to the controls. "Drink it, Isevidel! I'll find the cure! But know that *you were the one who chose this!*"

She grabbed the second lever and pulled.

The Argennium hummed, the runes around them pulsed, and the night was ripped away for a second time by a blinding beam of devastating light.

Lily let out a bloodcurdling scream. Sevi shielded his eyes from the beam erupting from the Argennium's depths. The night hadn't just been ripped away. All the world had been robbed of its color, stolen by the magic of the machine. And in its glow, his best friend burned.

Lily screamed again, shrieking louder than the device. Her body was black within its light. Tendrils of silver snaked up her arms, more slowly and less apparent than the light's last victim. And all the while the Argennium's beacon stretched higher and higher into the heavens, like a rope that could climb all the way to the moon.

And it did.

The beam pierced the sky, thinning until it could barely be seen, and hammered into the moon's surface. A ripple burst from where it struck, filling all Iaela with a menacing moan as the blue halo around the moon glowed brighter, and brighter, until it shone almost as brightly as the sun.

The beam rebounded, streaking away from the moon and into the distance, racing across the world in a thin, white line before falling and exploding far off on the horizon. Sevi saw a face form on the Watcher's surface, laughing in delight.

Lily's screams began to break under the strain of her suffering. Sevi snapped his gaze back to her. The fissures in her arms and face had deepened.

He looked to the soldiers around him. Reynam had taken Lea and was cradling her in his arms, pressing his coat into her side. The others just stood, staring at the Argennium and the dying girl within.

But not Lady Night. She was coming for him, with black eyes shining white.

"Shy," he breathed.

Closer. Closer.

"Nahlra. Isevidel."

Step. Step.

"She hurt us. She lied to us. She killed us all in some way."

One. Two. Three.

"But she saved us. She saved you. She saved me. She *tried to help us.* She's tried so *hard* for *four years* to make up for something she *never wanted to do!* She *loves* us!"

So close now, her shadow stretching before her like a specter of vengeance, clouding his face and filling his vision with her dark.

"Now we have to save *her*. We don't have to be afraid! I'm right here, with you. We can do this. *You* can do this! You can forgive her! You can give her a second chance! And if you're scared, always remember your brother is here. I'll *always* be here, like you're here for me. Nahlra. Isevidel. Please. *Please*."

A hand reached out.

*"Help me!"*

Tiersa closed her grip on his collar, and as she did, Shy sprang from the ground.

His brother and sister leapt as one from his shadow in the forms of their old bodies, each with a single ball of light inside their chests, and hurled themselves at Tiersa. Their arms spread out to impossible lengths, winding around her leg and arm and firmly latching on.

Tiersa gasped, stumbling back. Her eyes widened in shock, then realization. "No. It's a trick! It can't *be!*"

Sevi didn't wait for her to recover. He dove past her in a mad sprint to the beam. His shadows jumped to follow, leaving Lady Night to scream after them.

He leapt. His shadows leapt. And the light that had so callously ripped the dark from the night was parted as the night stole a piece of itself back.

His brother and sister melded back into Shy, then flung themselves out in a film so wide that it wrapped around Sevi *and* Lily, forming a bubble of air in the center and blocking the terrible light.

The beam abruptly cut off. Lily fell to the ground, charred along her body with glowing silver snakes running just under her skin. What hair she had regrown was gone, and every visible part of her now matched the scars along her head. But she was breathing.

Sevi shook her shoulders. "Lily! *Lily!*" Her eyes remained shut. He looked hopelessly around for help, but there was nothing outside of their bubble of dark. Merely blinding, painful light. And Shy was beginning to crumble, losing their dark in the intensity of the beam. "No. We're alright. Y-you're *alright*. I can fix this. I c-can fix this," Sevi stuttered, pulling out the vial of amber.

Lily's hand shot up and grabbed his wrist, making him freeze. She cracked one eye open at him. "Burns... amber," she rasped. "Are you trying... to kill me?"

"Lily!" Sevi pulled her into a hug.

She groaned in pain. Something wriggled between them. Alyda appeared from Sevi's shirt, chiming indignantly, but stopped abruptly at the sight around her. "Hey, Alyda," Lily mumbled, rolling her eyes deliriously. "Is that... a new dress?"

"Don't worry, I'll get you out of here," Sevi said, putting the vial back in his pocket and setting her down. He tugged at the clasp around her wrist, yanking it open. "Nahlra! Isevidel! Just a little longer!"

"Why?" Lily mumbled. "Why... did you... come back?"

"Because I love you, too, you stupid girl." Sevi grunted, tugging the second clasp free.

"Heh... softy."

Sevi scooped his arms under her. Shy was losing more and more dark by the moment, letting streaks of light in. He had to act fast. "We need to get you out of here. Shy! We're leaving! Take a deep breath, you two."

The bubble closed, turning into a cloak that wrapped around them all. Lily closed her eyes and leaned her head against Sevi's chest. "Thank you," she mumbled just as Shy cut off their air.

Sevi struggled under her weight, stumbling forward and tumbling down the steps on the far side of the platform. The beam cut off the moment Lily left it.

"Hmm," Shy whispered softly, loosening their hold. Their cloak dissolved and slid away, making Sevi gasp as the crisp night air came rushing back. A murky, half-lit figure appeared from the gloom, giving his eyes something to focus on.

Tiersa pointed her sword and glared murderously down at them. "Put. It. *Back*."

Sevi turned his head to look at Lily. She rolled her head groggily, the tendrils in her skin slowly fading now that the beam's light no longer fed them. But she was badly burned, and wisps of smoke still rose from her skin. He couldn't count on her to run. He lowered his gaze down to his shadow, searching for options. Shy had lost a lot of dark and had lightened considerably.

*We have nowhere to flee, and nowhere to hide,* he realized.

A green light appeared in the corner of his vision as Alyda zipped out from his collar, flying at breakneck speed around the platform and away. Tiersa's attention flicked toward her only for a moment before resettling on Sevi. *At least one of us will make it,* he thought, watching her go.

"No," Sevi said, staring Tiersa down. "And if you put her back, then you can put me there, too." Tiersa snarled and shoved him aside, grabbing Lily by the back of her shirt. Sevi dove for Tiersa's leg. She wound her hand back and smacked him across the face.

The world spun. He let go and fell on his side. She moved up the steps, dragging his best friend with her once more. All he could do was lay helplessly as his body failed him, watching as they both got further and further away.

"No." He reached out a hand in a desperate attempt to haul himself limply after them. *"Please.* Don't take her from me."

Tiersa's boots stopped.

Sevi drew his brow together in confusion, watching Tiersa's back. Something floated up into the air over her shoulder—a green light carrying a golden orb. Alyda, holding a bundle of lightblossoms.

"Aly?" Sevi mumbled.

She raised one hand to her mouth, kissed her palm, and held it out to him. As if to say...

*"Goodbye."*

"Alyda!"

Tiersa took a step forward with one hand out. Alyda didn't hesitate. She ripped her hand across the lightblossoms, tearing her nails into their bulbs, then curled her wings in and dropped like a stone, disappearing through the Argennium's grate in a rain of petals just as Tiersa drew her sword.

*"NO!"* Sevi screamed.

His anguish ripped across the platform, echoing loudly off the mountain. He scrabbled wildly at the steps. He could still save Lily. He could still save Alyda. He could still save *everyone.* But he had barely made it up a single step when the stairs rippled beneath his hands with a sudden vitality, growling like a waking giant.

And then the world exploded.

Golden light streamed out of the Argennium's heart, streaking up into the sky, magnified by every ocular until the entire mountain was awash with it. The platform shook. The runes across its surface flickered wildly. A terrible groaning resonated from deep within the machine just before the floor bucked, throwing everyone off their feet.

The soldiers scrambled for their only place of safety: the airship, throwing themselves onto it in terror while River and Lorr caught and heaved them aboard. Reynam went hobbling last with one of Lea's arms slung over his shoulder, leaving his rifle behind. Then the floor buckled and a massive blast of air burst from its center, tearing through steel as it erupted into the air in a blinding flash of brilliance, sending Tiersa, Lily, and Sevi flying.

Tiersa and Lily hit the platform a distance away, tangling together in a heap. But Sevi flew backward alone, slamming into the metal and racing toward the edge, carried swiftly by its layer of dust—the retribution of the many Silvakin killed by his family.

He scrabbled at the world for anything and anyone to help him, reeling from the furious bombardment of light and sound. But there was no one to save him. Not this time.

He fell into open sky.

The wind rushed up to meet him. He spun, throwing his hands out in a desperate attempt to right himself as the world went streaking by. He flattened his body against the wind and slowed the barest of amounts. But he was still falling.

And Alyda... Alyda was gone. She had stopped Tiersa, who might have died with Lily in the explosion, and he was falling.

He closed his eyes as they filled with tears, wrenched heartlessly away by the draft. He had tried. He had tried so *hard*. And now the ground was racing up to bring all his pathetic attempts to an end. A miserable end for a miserable life.

What had it mattered? What had been the point of any of it? His friends and family were dead or dying, and he would soon join them, having failed in every conceivable way. He wasn't a prince. He wasn't even a mouse. He was nothing.

Lily. Tiersa. Alyda. Everyone. Dead because of him. Simply because he lived.

*I'm sorry. I'm so, so sorry.*

No more trying. No more running.

He hoped death wouldn't hurt. He hoped that Nahlra and Isevidel would be there when he awoke, and together they could walk the Waylands to where Mother and Father waited for them. They'd be together again, at long last, ready to—

Something rammed him.

He gasped. Wiry limbs latched onto him, forcing the breath from his lungs. He opened his eyes, squinting through the wind, and came nose to nose with Lily's burned face. She screamed at him. He couldn't hear her over the rushing air, but he read her lips just fine.

*"No you fucking don't!"*

He gazed into her eyes, always so determined, always so safe, dimly aware of her reaching into his pocket. Somewhere, from the farthest reaches of his memory, the kindly voice of an old woman he once loved whispered to him.

*"Somehow, those two found each other."*

Lily pulled something into her hand. Something made of glass.

*"Spellbound, they each gripped the other and started to dance..."*

She tipped her head and poured every last drop of amber into her mouth, bound by iron and quicksilver no longer.

*"And there they remain in the sky to this day. Unable to part..."*

Lily gasped. The wind snatched the empty bottle from her fingers, sending it spinning away.

*"... and unwilling to try."*

Streaks of newborn light burst across the world as day broke, filling the sky with color and banishing every star. All save for the brightest two, who stayed behind to watch Lily and Sevi dance.

Lily dug her fingers into Sevi's shirt as her whole body rippled, growing to fill the tattered remains of her knightly clothing. Her burns smoothed and her scars faded, dispelled by a light glowing from within her very being, and from her scalp burst a long, fiery flame of red hair, whipping behind her in a trail as brilliant as the dawn.

The back of her shirt split open. Two massive wings of lace came ripping free of the fabric, spreading wide enough to embrace the entire sky, and shining like crystal in the sun's glow. Lily screamed in pain as they filled with wind, but their fall, so certain, so inevitable, stopped.

Sevi jolted and gasped as his arms wrenched violently in their sockets, but Lily's hold on him never faltered. She only clutched him tighter, stealing him from gravity's deadly grip in a claim of her own, leaving the unforgiving ground far below to soar off into the sky together.

A fierce laugh tore from Sevi's throat. The world lay before him in all its glory, rushing by beneath them as they joined the clouds, yet all he could look at was the wondrous girl above him in all her grandeur, shining brighter than any star could ever hope. She hadn't let him go.

Of course she hadn't. She was Lily, his champion. And a champion never lets go of her prince.

# Epilogue

...

———— ⟨∾⟩ ————

S evi took a deep breath, letting the cool mountain air fill his lungs, at odds with the heat from the rising sun. From his vantage point at the bow of the airship, hovering beside the smoking wreckage of the Argennium, it appeared as though he could reach the edge of the world by merely walking forward, crossing over villages and rivers in a single stride. He had experienced this view so many times from the Overlook, yet today it seemed different. It felt brand new.

Birds circled about above their heads—many of them Empyrean raptors. Their humans would have watched the night's events through their eyes with undoubtedly great confusion. There would be much explaining to do upon returning to the castle, but none of that mattered. Not now.

"Hey."

Sevi turned as Lily stepped beside him while scratching her head. It was odd to see such a vibrant tangle of red falling from her scalp, grown long enough to rest below her shoulders. At his look she said, "I forgot how itchy hair was. What's the point of having any if it's only going to be on your head?"

He didn't know why she complained; it looked beautiful. She had even arranged it so that her ears would show, flaunting them as proudly as her wings. Odder than her hair or her wings, however, was her height. "Gods you're tall now," Sevi muttered, looking her up and down.

"I know, isn't it nice? And now I can do this." She gently beat her wings, lifting herself off the ground to gain a head of height above him.

He smiled up at her. "You look great."

"I always look great."

He laughed, and she settled back onto the deck. Soldiers meandered about behind them, still looking shocked or at a loss. Sevi half-wondered if—once they had gathered their wits—they would attack Lily, but quickly dismissed it. She had survived the full blast of the Argennium before their very eyes only to emerge stronger than ever. Even if the soldiers could somehow work up the morale after witnessing *that*, he doubted a couple of bullets would be enough to kill his friend, now.

"How's Lea?" Lily asked.

"Awake and at work, surprisingly."

"And the other one?"

"Do you care, or are you being polite?"

"She did try to kill me and all of my people. Painfully, I might add."

At his firm insistence, Lily had managed to fly them back to the Argennium in time to rescue the unconscious Commander Tiersa before she fell over its collapsing edge. Now she rested belowdecks being tended to by the very doctor she had shot, and the man that doctor loved.

Sevi turned his attention back to the bow. So much had happened in only two nights, and he was finding it hard to sort out his thoughts. How would he face Tiersa when she awoke? What would he say when they reached the castle? Would the Embers throw him in the tower for what he did?

He put it all aside for later, resolving to handle such events as they came. Whatever happened, he knew there would always be at least one person there for him. He turned to face his friend with a meaningful expression, putting all of his gratitude into the look he gave her. There was so much to say—too much, and he found himself unable to conjure any words capable of conveying every emotion. So all he said was, "Thank you for saving my life, Lily."

Lily smirked and opened her mouth, looking ready with a witty retort, but something changed in her as she met his eyes, and her demeanor softened at once. "Thank you for saving mine," she said.

Sevi reached for her hand. She let him take it, tangling his with hers and squeezing. She lifted their joined fingers, putting them in the space between their chests, and regarded them with a tilt of her head. Then she pulled her free hand back and punched him in the other shoulder with a snort. "Softy."

He chuckled. "I know." He kept his hand in hers, fully expecting the hand of another to join theirs in their moment of joy. But she didn't. His mood soured, and he tightened his grip.

Lily raised her brow at him. "What is it?"

"Alyda."

She withdrew her hand, holding it to her breast. "Oh."

"Is she really...?"

"She's gone." Lily shook her head. "No one can claim another's soul, Sevi. She's gone, and no magic in the world will bring her back." She closed her eyes. "But the moment she died, her spark returned to me—her knowledge, her love, her spirit. It gave me the strength to stand and leap after you. I can feel her now, right in my chest. So she'll always be with us, won't she? Always."

Sevi turned away from her, leaning his face into the wind with his hand at his collar, clutching for a necklace that was no longer there. Tears dominated his vision as the reality of the fairy's fate finally sunk in. "Always. Now and forever," he whispered. Lily stood quietly, looking at the horizon with him. He glanced at her. "Just like you and I."

She nodded slowly. "Yeah."

"Hey!"

Sevi wiped his eyes and turned. Captain Lorr approached with a bandage on his ear. "Caldwin says that everyone is aboard and accounted for. We're ready to cast off. Move away from the railing—she's a little bumpy on the turns, or so I'm told."

Sevi waved a hand in acknowledgement. "You know that Innavin is going to say something about that ear, don't you? And how it's the opposite one from his?"

"Don't remind me," Lorr grumbled. "I'm looking forward to all the flowery, 'it's fate!' talk I'm bound to hear from both him and Caldwin. Though I *am* looking forward to the friendly chat I'll have with our newly appointed Lieutenant Enstrova once we land." He turned and walked away.

Sevi didn't immediately retreat from the side of the ship, choosing instead to stare once again at all of the world's majesty stretching into eternity. His gaze wandered to the ship's balloon, then along the railing to where the *Aethercrest's* lightwings extended. They looked so much like Lily's, glowing with a spiritual light that only sparkled brighter in the sun. "We both have a pair of wings," he said softly. "We can go anywhere, now."

"Mine are prettier," Lily said.

"Mm... I'm not sure about that." Sevi smiled. "I like mine quite a bit."

She raised an eyebrow at him in clear disagreement, gently extending her wings as if to show off how brilliant they looked with the sunlight filtering through their crystal membrane. Then the deck rocked as River activated the engines, and Sevi went stumbling towards the rail. It drew a smile from Lily, who had merely swayed with the motion, perfectly balanced. "Careful. Don't make me catch you again."

Memory of the fall returned readily, and with it the fierce exuberance that came after she'd grabbed him. Even now, so shortly after their ordeal, she looked as proud as ever. Ready to take on the world. Ready to throw herself off a mountain after him the moment he slipped. She was a true hero. A monster-slayer. A knight.

His friend.

Sevi backed away from the railing with an embarrassed smile, clearing his throat. "Right. I'll um... I think I'll go check on Tisa and Lea again."

Lily's smirk vanished, replaced by a faint scowl. "Be sure to give her ladyship a hug or a kiss for me."

Profound emotion swept through Sevi, straining his chest. "Not without giving you one, too."

"What?"

He stepped forward and fiercely wrapped his arms around her body—wings and all—and buried his face into her shoulder. She went rigid with surprise at first, but gradually relaxed and returned his embrace, slipping her arms around his back with her chin nestled on him.

It felt good to be like this with her—to finally be on equal footing with the person he admired most. To know she loved him as much as he loved her. "Lily?" he whispered.

"What?" she asked just as softly.

"Do you think... do you think Digby would have been proud of what we did to the Argennium? Or my parents?"

"What do you mean? Of course they would. Why do you ask?"

"It's just... My parents built it. Tiersa was so certain it was the only way to keep us safe, and Digby..." Sevi paused to clear his throat. "The war caused so much pain. I don't regret saving you, and I don't regret destroying the weapon. At *all*. But without it, who's to say your people don't come back? What if Tiersa was right? What if, without it, we'll be destroyed?"

"Sevi, I love you, and I understand where you're coming from, but that's the wrong way to think about this."

He drew his head back, looking at her with confusion.

"Who's to say they do return?" Lily said. "What if Tiersa was wrong? What if everyone goes on to live happy lives and never have to worry about another pointy-eared Fae ever again?"

Sevi let his mouth hang open before arranging it into a smile. "I think I'll always have at least one to deal with, actually."

She laughed and gripped his shoulder. "That's right. You're stuck with me. But the rest? Well." She shrugged. "Who's to say? They've left, haven't they? Prepare for them as much as you want, it's not a dumb thing to think about. But if it ever happens again... I think you'll know what to do."

Something broke inside of him and he renewed their hug, letting his tears flow freely. Something inside Lily must have broken too, because she hugged him back just as tightly, pressing her wet face into his own. They stayed like that for some time, silhouetted by the dawn's golden light, letting the warmth of the sun and each other's bodies banish the cold of the night. "Love you, Lil," Sevi murmured.

She squeezed him. "Love you, Sev."

Sevi dropped his arms and tried to extract himself, but she didn't let go. He furrowed his brow. "Lily?"

"Sevi," Lily whispered. "Did you mean what you said? That I'm your friend? That you don't regret saving me?"

He tried turning to look at her, but she didn't let him. "Of course I do."

"Will you never regret it?"

"Never. How could I?"

She took a deep, shuttering breath and rattled it out next to his ear. "I can't do this anymore."

Sevi furrowed his brow. "What?"

"You know my lies were meant to protect you, right? That I would rather die than hurt you?"

He paused. He said slowly, "What's wrong, Lily?"

She shook her head. "Do you remember the day the airship appeared? The day Redwood nearly discovered you in the throne room?"

"I wish I could forget it, honestly."

"Sevi. He did."

Sevi froze.

Her arms tightened around him. "I had to do something that day. I had to keep him away from you. I had to make a deal."

Sevi's heart dropped into his stomach. No. *No.* "What did you do?"

"What I had to do to save your life."

He forced himself away from her, fixing her with his hardest stare. "*What did you do?*"

Lily bowed her head. "You deserve the truth. No more lies. No more games. And if you tell me to leave at the end of it all, I will." She took a step towards him, meeting his eyes with a sudden intensity. "But you need to know that I did it for *you.* I had no other choice; he would have killed you and taken your blood to get to the Argennium if I hadn't done something! So banish or kill me if you have to, but know that no matter where I go, I will never stop fighting for you—not even if you send me back to the Lynnweald itself."

Sevi retreated from her, balling his hands into fists. *She's lied to me* again. *After everything we went through together, what was waiting for me at the end of it? More* lies. "Enough! Explain yourself. Right *now.*"

She opened her mouth, then turned sharply towards the prow, staring at the birds flying by with a suddenly taut back. Sevi followed her gaze but saw nothing to warrant alarm. "Go below," she said suddenly. "I have to deal with something."

"*Excuse* me? No! You're going to tell me what you mean right *now!*"

"I swear to you upon every god in existence that I will, but not now." She darted her hand forward and grabbed his. "If I never ask you for anything ever again, then let this be my last request. Go below, and trust me. *Please*. I'll give you a full explanation tonight when we're alone."

Sevi shook his head and pulled his hand back, clenching his jaw. "You swear to me—on Alyda's *soul*—that you will tell me everything?"

She lifted her chin. "Better than that. I'll show you."

Monster-slayer. Knight. Friend.

Liar.

Sevi stepped up to her, putting his face a mere fingerspan away from hers. ""Let me make something clear, Lily. Not only will you tell me all there is to know about whatever it is you've lied to me about *this* time, but if our friendship really means as much to you as you say then you will *never* do this to me again. *Do you understand me?*"

She flinched, but met his eyes with enough resolve to make him pause. "I do. I promise."

He glared at her for several breaths. Then he turned on his heel and walked towards the stern, almost making it to the steps before looking back. A raven had joined Lily at the bow, settling next to her on the railing as companionably as Sevi had. Cawing once, it flapped its wings before dropping over the edge and flying off. Eagles rushed to pursue it, yet none proved capable of closing the distance as it streaked away, running as dark as ink against the sky.

The rest of the day passed in a blur. Soldiers demanded answers, nobles demanded both answers and compensation for the attack at the masquerade, everyone demanded to see Commander Tiersa (who still hadn't awoken), and whispers abounded over what had happened on top of the mountain last night.

Sevi hadn't been able to summon the energy to care about a single shred of it. He'd tried his best, but he was still new at being a prince—not to mention suffering under immense fatigue. And with Lily's words preying heavily on his mind his focus had been utterly nonexistent.

Lily, meanwhile, had taken off before the airship had docked, using her newfound flight to disappear among the castle's turrets. It had been a bitter sight that hadn't helped his mood.

After an hour of explanations and assurances, Sevi had finally charged River and Lorr with managing in his stead before retreating to the royal chambers, seeking the comfort of its bed and quickly falling asleep. His dreams were no more peaceful than usual.

"Sevi."

He awoke to someone shaking his arm. The sun had set, and the room was bathed in moonlight. The only noise came from the wind beating gently against the windowpanes, clattering them in their frames. When he looked up, groggy and annoyed, he found Lily standing over him wearing a grave expression. She held a sword in one hand that glittered strangely, as though she had dipped it in quicksilver.

"What—" Sevi began, trying to sit up.

She pushed him back down and placed a finger to his lips. "You're asleep. You've taken your medicine." She reached into her pocket and pulled out a leaf. "Chew this, but spit it out and hide it under your pillow."

Sevi took the leaf uncertainly. "What are you doing?"

Lily let out a breath and rolled her shoulders. "Giving you all the answers. Now do as I say, and remember: you're asleep. Don't open your eyes for *any* reason." She stepped away from him and took position at the foot of his bed, facing away to stare across the room with the tip of her sword pointed at the floor.

Sevi watched her back for several breaths, debating whether or not to follow her orders—as far as he was concerned, she had no right to tell him to do anything anymore. But there was a strangeness to Lily's demeanor; a rigid awareness, like a soldier facing down an enemy.

*I'll play along for now.*

He chewed the familiar effizinum and spat it out before it could take effect. Then he arranged himself in the bed as though he had fallen into a deep slumber, and waited.

And waited. And waited.

So much time passed that he nearly fell asleep again. But then a cold breeze rushed over him, causing the hair along his body to stand on end and bringing him to attention with a jolt. It carried a voice with it. "My lovely little flower," it murmured, as soft as velvet. "I put you through a lot of pain, didn't I?"

Sevi tensed. He knew that voice.

"Such a touching scene," Captain Redwood said. "I have to say, that was some of the best entertainment I've had in centuries."

"Leave," Lily said briskly.

There was a creak of wood as someone strode across the floor. Sevi risked cracking one eyelid open the barest of amounts to peer through his lashes. Captain Redwood's eyes pierced darkness and moonbeams alike from across the room, alight with their ominous amber glow. He wore a cordial smile, standing with his arms placed politely behind his back while regarding Lily. "So cruel," he said. "I thought every actor craved a round of applause."

Lily brandished her sword, sparkling with poison. "I said *leave.*"

"Not without you, Lily Flower." Redwood curled the corners of his mouth further. "Pride of the Lynnweald. Sword of the Silvakaen. Monster of the Silent Grove. Step up! Take a bow! I held up my end of the bargain, and now you've held up yours! Rather splendidly to be sure—not just in opening the path but destroying the weapon as well! Although..." He broke off with a frown. "There was that... episode, where you tried to flee. And the weapon *did* fire."

"Held up *yours*? You tried to have him *turned!*"

"Well, you never said I couldn't! It was hardly an issue; it would have worn off eventually," Redwood bared teeth that shone almost as brightly as his eyes. "You clearly needed a push. And it wasn't *me* or *my* forces who attacked him, it was those of the Silent Grove. Come now, you know how these things work, my dear."

Lily stepped forward threateningly. "Leave, or I will run you through."

Redwood stepped back, disappearing into a shadowy mist. Lily whipped around. Sevi nearly turned his head to follow her gaze when a hand touched his head from behind, running its fingers tenderly through his hair. He squeezed his eyes shut, nearly biting through his tongue in terror. "What a sweet boy," Redwood crooned, his voice so near that his mouth may as well have been kissing Sevi's ear. "Did you ever tell him? Of how you sent your voice to me, begging me to spare his life the day he revealed himself? It was quite moving."

"Get away from him!"

"You allowed the weapon to fire, Lily Flower. We lost the towns of Argulvold, Nillengully, and half of Tormolstad. Maybe I should even the score a little? Just a finger or two. One for each town, now turned to dust."

Wood creaked, wings beat, and Redwood's hand disappeared from Sevi's head as something whipped through the air above him. Something wet landed on his cheek, and he had to fight the urge to wipe it away.

Redwood's humored voice came from a distance away. "I jest, of course. He's the other shining star in this play! Our second star in the sky, if you'd prefer."

"*Leave!*" Lily bellowed.

"You know that I can subjugate you now that you're missing your helmet, don't you? Make you lower that toothpick as I please? Though I'm certain your swings are as weak as your kicks—that wasn't very nice, by the way. Or maybe I'll have you run it through your own chest! A rather impressive sight, I'll admit. I hadn't expected you to still have it in you."

"You can *try*."

"My dear, calm yourself. If I had intended any sort of harm, both you and your prince would be dead."

"*Then why are you here?*"

"I *told* you, to *congratulate* you, you stupid girl!" Redwood paused. "But also to warn you."

"Yeah? Warn me about what?"

"As I've said, their weapon fired."

"Get to the point!"

"It pierced the World Gate."

Lily fell quiet. A sudden silence filled the room, heavy with expectation. Sevi's heart hammered against his ribs.

"Our grandmother is waking," Redwood murmured. "Something may have come through already."

More silence. Then Lily muttered, "Oh, Gods." Sevi's breath caught at her voice—there was true fear in it.

"'Gods?' You've been among humans too long." Redwood chuckled. "But at least you understand, and now you know why I'll keep my word. Who cares about this filthy little backwater in the face of *her* ire?"

Lily said nothing.

"You really must come back with me, you know," he continued suggestively. "If you truly wish to protect your little pet, you'll do more good for him where you can keep an eye on me. Who knows what I'll get up to away from your careful, loving gaze? Especially now that we know the quicksilver can be conquered. I may just go looking for subjects to test. Maybe your little prince would like to volunteer?"

"Get out," Lily said sharply. "Now."

Redwood sighed. "Fine. I suppose I can give you that. I've delivered my warning out of respect for your efforts, though I must voice my confusion. Why stay with these humans who meddle with magic in ways they've only just begun to understand? Their little experiment has harmed more than just the Lynnweald. I will feel no pity for them when they destroy themselves, and neither should you."

"That will be for them to decide, *not* you. Now for the very last time before I call the guards, *leave!*"

"As you command, Sier Lily!" Redwood mocked. "Ah. What a lovely night. We destroyed a terrible weapon and got one of our own: the gift of protection against our darkest, most horrible bane. And don't worry, my dear," the Silvakin captain added with a clear smile in his voice. "I know we'll meet again."

There was a rush of wind strong enough to billow the bed's sheets. Sevi shifted, ready to jump to attention, but Lily stopped him. "Stay down," she whispered. She muttered something, and the bed rocked back and forth like it had developed a will of its own. A tense moment passed until Lily finally said, "Alright. He's gone."

Sevi threw off the covers and wiped his cheek, coming away with a palm full of silver. He hurriedly cleaned it on the sheets and planted his feet on the floor, only to draw back in surprise. The entire bed had been surrounded by a small field of vibrant flowers, finding purchase in the boards and stone as confidently as a patch of soil.

"Don't be afraid," Lily said, making him look up. She had settled against the foot of the bed with her sword beside her, staring at him wearily. "It's a barrier of sorts. It will protect you."

Sevi said nothing. She attempted a smile and held up her hands. They were shaking. "Look at this. Can you believe this?"

He didn't respond. Her smile fell apart. She shook her head and turned away, letting out a ragged breath. Sevi tentatively stepped around the bed to stand before her, staring down at her with a mouth that had forgotten how to work. "Tiersa was right," he said at last. "You *used* me. Redwood *knew*. He knew all this time. You were working for him!"

Lily nodded. "Ever since your visit to the throne room."

Sevi looked at the floorboards, shaking his head in shock.

"I bargained your life for the Argennium," Lily said softly. "If I hadn't then Redwood would have killed you and stolen your blood to open the way himself. And it wouldn't have even worked."

"What do you mean it wouldn't have worked?"

"As fate would have it, you're adopted," Lily said, smiling humorlessly. "But your brother and sister aren't. Some of the magic in their blood must still live on through Shy, allowing you to open the royal study and the Argennium's gate when they're with you. If you had died, then Shy would have disappeared, fled, or died with you, and the weapon would have remained out of the Silvakaen's reach forever. It's what kept Redwood from hurting you."

"Is that why he sent those Silent Grove soldiers? To turn me?"

She shook her head. "No. That was a warning for me. The doors to the weapon were rigged with a trap meant to kill any with amber in their blood. No Silvakin could have forced you to open them, at least not like that." She shrugged. "He might've tried taking me hostage and threatening you if he'd had Tiersa's medallion, which probably would've worked. We're lucky he didn't know where it was."

Sevi had to take a long while before speaking again, and when he did it was with barely restrained anger. "Why? Why would you *dare* keep this from me?"

She averted her gaze. "I was trying to get out of the deal. The only chance I had was luring you away from the castle, and I failed." She let out a bitter laugh. "No, that's wrong, I never had a chance. He was watching us the entire *time*. If I told you, he would've taken you and... I don't know *what* he would've done. But I had to protect you. So, I told him everything."

"But not me? You couldn't find a way to tell *me*?"

Lily drew a tired breath. "No. I couldn't. He has a wide network of spies that take on the forms of all kinds of animals, and Redwood himself is able to hide so completely in shadows that he becomes almost invisible. I never knew when he or any of his underlings were watching, and I couldn't open my mind to sense them without taking off my helmet, which would've exposed me to his control. Even with it on I could still hear his voice sometimes, whispering to me in my head, letting me know he was always there. He's... he's so strong, Sevi. If it wasn't for that iron he would have had me."

She gave him an odd smile. "But I don't need it anymore."

"And why's that?"

She regarded her hand, turning it over. "The Argennium did something to me. I'm different now. Changed. There's amber in my blood, but also quicksilver, somehow. It lets me block his voice whenever I want." She looked out the window, gazing at the moon. "You know, when I was in the beam, I prayed that—if nothing else—maybe it would kill Redwood, too. But pests have a way of surviving, don't they?"

Sevi suddenly felt the immediate need to sit. He dropped slowly to the bed, sitting perpendicular to her. They lapsed into a long, heavy silence, each staring at nothing. "Is this all my fault?" Sevi said at last. "Did I cause all of this?"

"*No,*" Lily said forcefully, turning sharply towards him. "You didn't—"

"Lily! *I caused this!*" Sevi shouted. "If I had just stayed at the Overlook that day then none of this would have happened! You never would have been forced to work for Redwood, the Argennium would have remained hidden, and Alyda would still be *alive!*"

"And the Embers would be dead, we would still be living as rats inside the Cut, and the entire country would still be under the Silvakaen's rule," Lily countered. "Don't think for a moment that Redwood didn't know the Embers were coming. Redwood took his troops away and *let* them come under the pretense of chasing down Digby, all so he could make a play for the Argennium. Because of that, Elkra's genocidal weapon is destroyed, the Silvakaen have left, and you're back to being a prince."

"*But I killed Alyda, Lily!*"

"*No,* you *didn't!*" she snapped. "It's not your fault, Sevi! None of it is! And you know damn well Alyda would say the same thing!"

Sevi placed his face in his hands, unable to staunch the guilt. "You paint a lovely picture, but I'm not about to believe that things are somehow better because of my mistakes. Not when Alyda is dead."

"Sevi, that's *life,*" Lily insisted. "Making a mistake is just as likely to improve a life as making no mistakes is to ruin one! There are too many moving pieces, too many people, and too much *chance*. Sometimes you can manage to steer your fate, but you can't control every little thing that happens! Just look at Alyda! From the moment she was born she was meant to die, and she spent every moment of her life depending on me giving her enough amber to last another month. She never had a choice of her own—not until the very end when she grabbed her fate by its godsdamned neck, saved *my* life, and went out on *her* terms! Until then she'd been completely at the mercy of fate's stupid plan for *years*! And she never gave up!"

"And what does fate have planned for me now, Lily?" Sevi tilted his head expectantly at her. "I've never really been given a choice myself, have I? My entire life has been controlled by someone else—getting adopted, being forced into the Cut, then maneuvered to the Argennium. *You're more the weaver of my life than I ever was.*"

A slow smile formed on Lily's lips. "Exactly my point, dummy."

Sevi drew his head back as Lily stood up from the bed. She dropped to one knee in front of him and fixed him with a weighty stare. "Sevi. I've lived with the voices of my family's Elders in my head my entire life. They drove me to such insanity that they turned me into a mindless monster. I never controlled my life—*they* did. Until I met you."

He gave her a blank look. She smirked. "Don't forget, silly boy, it was you who saved me first. You broke me from the amber. You *never* stopped caring for me, no matter how bitter I was from being trapped in an iron helmet and feeling its burn every damn day. You made me feel like I had real worth, and you were willing to risk all you had regained outside the Cut to save me, even while knowing what I had done to you. So if I'm more the weaver of your fate than you, then you're more the weaver of my fate than *me*.

She placed her hand on her chest. "I know that I've betrayed your trust a dozen times over, and there may be no fixing what I've broken. But now I offer you something I've only ever had stolen from me: my fate. All of it. Send me back to the Lynnweald and I'll chase its monsters back into its woods where they belong. Keep me by your side and I'll stand with you no matter what comes. Take my sword and kill me now for all that I've done to you. In this moment my life is yours to do with as you will, but know this: of all the lies I've ever told you, loving you was never one of them."

Sevi shifted where he sat, studying her. She didn't turn away. "You may be the best liar on Iaela, Lily. How do I know this isn't another trick, and that maybe you're still working for Redwood? That you're simply trying to get back into my good graces?"

"If that were the case then why did I save you after the Argennium was destroyed? That was all my people were here for. If I really wanted to hurt this country then it would've been far better for me to let the last Astraeda die with the weapon, wouldn't it?"

"And yet, Redwood seemed awfully eager to take you with him. Something about your grandmother waking up?"

She made an annoyed noise with her nose. "Give me my sword."

Perplexed, Sevi grabbed the sword and held it out to her. Instead of taking it she placed her hand on its blade and sliced her finger open.

"Lily!" he exclaimed.

"Look." She held her bleeding finger beneath the sword and allowed quicksilver to drip onto the wound. Expecting her arm to crack just as it had in the Argennium's beam, Sevi moved forward with alarm. But nothing happened.

"He wanted me back because a Silvakin has survived the touch of quicksilver for the first time in our history." She shook her finger free of the liquid before placing it in her mouth, then spat on the floor. "Just as with iron, it can't kill me anymore. And as I said, I can't hear Redwood's voice in my head even with my helmet off. That means I can't hear the other Elders either, and Redwood knows it. Someone like me would be immensely valuable to him in the Lynnweald, so he tried to sway me into going where he could keep using me for his own benefit. But what else is new?"

"Then why did he let you go?" Sevi asked.

"He had to honor our deal whether he liked it or not. The more of a Fae you are, the more you have to follow their rules. An Elder will always do as they say—provided the contract isn't broken by the other party—but only to the letter, and with some pretty loose interpretations. A pureblood would move land and sea to fulfill a pact's word and spirit, both. As our grandmother willed, there are no lies among her children.

"But I barely had to follow any of it. I'm far more human than Fae after wearing iron for so long. Though maybe not anymore—now I don't know what I am. And the contract wasn't broken in the end, was it?" Lily curled her lips in an ironic smirk.

Sevi closed his eyes. *For his own benefit.* That may have been the true difference between Lily and Redwood. One lied for personal gain, the other lied to protect what she loved. Even Tiersa—Sevi's own family—had lied to him in order to get what *she* had wanted in the end.

But not Lily. She had proven time and again that all she ever wanted was to protect her friends, even if she had to lie to do it. She had stolen control of his life from him, but someone had stolen hers away, first. Now with Redwood gone, and her fate in her hands, she would offer it to him freely? The mighty Lily? "And all that about your grandmother?" Sevi asked carefully. "What did Redwood mean? You were terrified when he brought her up."

Lily stilled. "Do you remember the story of the three sisters?" Sevi nodded. "Fae—true, pureblood Fae—don't come from Iaela, Sevi. They come from somewhere else. And their mother—my grandmother—lived for many years in solitude and grief beyond the World Gate before falling asleep. If the Argennium really did manage to strike her hard enough to wake her then she won't be very happy when she does. She might come looking for what hit her." She closed her eyes. "I hope that was a lie if nothing else."

Sevi searched her face for a long while, but no matter how hard he looked he couldn't find any trace of her usual mask. "You really mean it this time, don't you? You're telling the truth."

"I meant what I said. No more lies. No more running. I'm going to face whatever comes. Like you."

Sevi blinked. "Like *me?*"

"You," she repeated. "My fate, my life—whatever happens next is your choice to make. I owe you that much." She lifted one finger with the suggestion of a smile. "And this is the only time you'll ever hear me say that."

Sevi's mouth twitched reflexively. He lifted her sword to peer down its length. *She's been running all this time,* he realized with lingering shock. Angling the weapon, he stared at his reflection in the blade. *We both have.* "Your life," he murmured.

"You don't have to decide now. I'm not going anywhere," she said, moving to get up.

"Stay down."

Lily froze mid-motion. He stared coolly at her, pointedly nodding his head at the floor. Slowly, she brought herself back to a kneeling position.

He cleaned the blade of its quicksilver on the bedsheets and lifted its tip towards the ceiling before standing up. "I've made up my mind."

Sevi gently touched the weapon to Lily's shoulder, letting its edge kiss her neck. She didn't flinch. "Upon pain of death," he began, "do you, Lily, swear to never lie to me again? To trust me with all your knowledge, and to let me stand beside you as your equal?"

Lily furrowed her brow.

"Answer me."

"I do," she said slowly.

Sevi nodded, moving the blade to rest on her other shoulder. "Do you swear to fight for me—as penance for all the crimes you've committed against my family and I—until I release you from my service, or death take you?"

Understanding crept across Lily's face. She nodded quietly, looking stunned.

Sevi returned the blade to her first shoulder. "Do you swear to always be my friend?" he asked softly. "To never betray me? To care for me as I'll always care for you? To govern my fate as I'll govern yours? To save each other when we've lost ourselves in the dark, now and forever?"

Lily's eyes filled with tears. "Now and forever," she echoed hoarsely.

"Then get up, Sier Lily." Sevi pointed the sword at the floor, offering her the hilt. "By my understanding, you haven't yet fulfilled the first deal we ever made. You have much to do, and much to make up for."

Lily wiped her eyes, sniffing loudly as she stood. She placed her hands over his on the hilt with trembling fingers, but she didn't take it from him. Sevi tilted his head at her in silent question.

"It's a full moon," she said. She kept her head down, speaking to the floorboards. "When I was in that cell thinking that my life was about to end, I made a Lament in the hope that someone—like my grandmother—was listening. That she would hear it and remember me, and all the time you and I spent together wouldn't be forgotten. That it would be remembered as *I* remember it. I'll have more to sing now, I think. The lyrics will have to change. But no matter how much of our story is left, Sevi, I think I know its final verse."

Lily met his stare, gazing at him for a long, long while with their hands joined on the sword. And then she started to sing.

*"A star in the sky is surrounded by darkness,*
*beyond it lies millions of kin.*
*Lost within moonglow that shadows their shimmer,*
*seeing all but the light from within.*
*Its siblings live blithely, resplendent and clear,*
*and die with a fiery streak.*
*Extinguished before ever touching the ground,*
*and in death, command all eyes to see.*
*But how this star glistened, and still, it goes burning,*
*its death not the heavens to claim.*
*Though he could not see, though he could not know,*
*though he gave himself all to his name,*
*that his family were lost in a dark like his own,*
*a mortar as much as a fetter.*
*In his prominent glow, they went hand in hand,*
*and outshined the moon, all together.*
*But a star does not see light within its own self,*
*in this, 'twas his lot to be blind.*
*But they know, and I know, and to my last breath I swear—"*

She pushed the sword down, slamming its tip against the floorboards. As she did a small lily flower uncurled from beneath their hands, spreading its petals in a breath to drink its fill of moonbeams. "I'll remember how brightly you shined," Lily murmured.

Sevi looked between her and the flower. "What are you doing? What spell is this?"

"I'm giving you another vow, Your Princeliness, since I'm so generous." She smiled, holding the flower out to him. "Abeya take Redwood, the Silvakaen, Grandmother, and any prissy little noble who comes looking for a fight. If they want one, we'll make sure they get one. Together. As always, and forever."

The End

# Name Pronunciation

<u>People</u>

**Sevi**: Seh - vee

**Lily**: Lil - ee

**Alyda**: Ah - lee - duh

**Digby Asgaillin**: Dig - bee - Az - gay - lin

**Reynam Enstrova**: Ray - num - En - stro - vuh

**Lea**: Lee - uh

**Cassik Novar**: Kass - seek - No - var

**Loma Tammavin**: Lo - ma - Tam - uh - vin

**Caldwin River**: Call - d - win - Ri-ver

**Tiersa Grommand**: Teer - sa - Grohm - mend

**Promina Rinenne Kaymoor**: Prah - mi - nuh - Rin - een - Kay - mor

**Tahno**: T - ah - no

**Lorr Ferdino Gallan**: Lor - Fer - dee - no - Guh - lan

**Innavin Targa**: In - uh - vin - Tar - guh

**Ryaliss Targa**: Rai - al - liss - Tar - guh

**Korina Astraeda**: Kor - ee - nuh - As - stray - duh

**Marovhan Cassangia**: Mar - o - von - Kass - an - jee - uh

**Alramar**: Al - rah - mar

**Nahlra**: Nahl - ruh

**Meldine Kaymoor**: Mel - deen - Kay - mor

**Velis Kaymoor**: Vell - liss - Kay - mor

**Dela Kaymoor**: Dell - uh - Kay - mor

**Yorga Engrom**: Yor - guh - Kay - mor

**Kellyn Engrom**: Kell - in - Ang - grom

**Vykka Engrom**: Vik - kuh - Ang - grom

**Iviri**: Iv - veer - ee

**Badim**: Bah – deem
**Eidijan Kinny**: Ai – di – jan - Kin – nee
**Ta'Runa**: Ta - Roo - na
**Silvakaen**: Sil - vuh - kayn
**Silvakin**: Sil - vuh - kin

---

# Places with Orientation

**Áilé** (Ai - lay): Country west of Elkra, above Ivindris, and below Skorrvold.

**Arathean Empire** (Air - rath - thee - uhn): Country south of Salakir, west of the Lynnweald, above Skorrvold.

**Elkra** (El - kra): Country the story takes place. South of the Lynnweald, west of Tiburas, east of Áilé, north of the Iza'Kaima islands.

**Iaela** (Ee - ay - luh): The world the story takes place in.

**Illondia** (il - lon - dee - uh): A city in Elkra.

**Imithin** (Im - mith - in): North continent, on which the story takes place.

**Ivindris** (Iv - vin - dris): The southwestern peninsula country below Áilé.

**Iza'Kaima** (Ee - zuh - Ky - muh): Southern island-chain country, south of Elkra.

**Lovithin** (Lo - vith - in): Southern continent of Iaela.

**The Lynnweald** (Lin - weeld): Home of the Fae/Silvakaen. Middle of the continent, above Elkra and Tiburas, below Salakir, and east of the Arathean Empire.

**Rykkad** (Rik -kahd): Isolated northern peninsular country to the northeast of Salakir.

**Salakir** (Sal - la - keer): Country above the Arathean Empire, southwest of Rykkad.

**Skorrvold** (Ss - kor - vold): An eastern country north of Áilé, below the Arathean Empire.

**Tiburas** (Tee - bur - ahs): Southeastern country, east of Elkra.

# About the Author

An avid reader from an early age, Christopher is a self-taught writer with a deep, abounding love for storytelling across all media. The greatest inspirations of his childhood and adolescence came from the stories written by Cornelia Funke, Eoin Colfer, and Rick Riordan, though he has since developed an appreciation for the works of Mark Lawrence, Naomi Novik, and Brandon Sanderson. Greatly influenced by his past love for poetry, Christopher endeavors to instill a sense of poetic narration in his style, believing it to be the greatest vehicle for wonder and beauty in the literary arts. When not writing or reading, his favorite activities include singing with his ukulele, playing tabletops, learning how to swing dance, and dreaming about finally getting that dog he's always wanted

Read more at https://thedancebetween.my.canva.site/.

www.ingramcontent.com/pod-product-compliance
Lightning Source LLC
Chambersburg PA
CBHW030739030726
47497CB00001B/46